Praise for Harry Turtledove

Ruled Britannia

"Bestseller Turtledove buckles a handsome Elizabethan swash with his latest fascinating what-if. . . . Superbly realized historical figures. . . . An intricate and thoroughly engrossing portrait of an era, a theatrical tradition, a heroic band of English brothers and their sneering overlords."
—*Publishers Weekly* (starred review)

"An amalgam of Elizabethan stagecraft and spy craft: at once elegant and engrossing." —*Home News Tribune* (East Brunswick, NJ)

"Turtledove's language and wit must be praised . . . characterization is superb. . . . Shakespeare's life, as engineered by Turtledove, is even grander than the original's." —Science Fiction Weekly

"One of his finest achievements . . . full of scenes that provoke tears, as well as of Turtledove's hallmark good humor. A thoroughly magisterial work of alternate history." —*Booklist* (starred review)

"[A] tale of personal heroism and the power of language. Turtledove's command of facts and his understanding of the period allow him to portray his characters with believability, while his prose, liberally salted with Shakespeare's own words, stands as a tribute to both the man and his work." —*Library Journal*

"Whether you read this story just as an interesting tale, or as an alternate history with many historical parallels, I would recommend *Ruled Britannia*. . . . A welcome addition to his booklist." —SFRevu

"Fascinating. . . . Using Shakespeare as the hero and reluctant catalyst to signal the beginning of the revolution is an inspired plot device, one that guarantees reader interest for more than just Mr. Turtledove's legion of fans." —*Midwest Book Review*

"This tale alternates readily between thriller and history, with a dash of romance and a double heaping of detail thrown in. Turtledove masterfully captures the pomp and circumstances of occupied England as he equally masters the mode and idiom of Elizabethan dialect."
—*Talebones*

continued . . .

Days of Infamy

"The [premise] is worked out with rigor and an astonishing mastery of the period . . . Harry Turtledove has shown us what might have happened if America hadn't had another of its astonishing strokes of luck."

—S. M. Stirling

"Harry Turtledove is a historian by training and a masterful teller of tales. This is a fun read. *You'll love it.*" —SciFi Dimensions

"[Turtledove] provides brain candy for history buffs. . . . [*Days of Infamy*] is a gripping book that makes it clear just how lucky the United States was to have things go its way in 1941; it's a read worthy of an all-nighter." —*Sacramento News & Review*

"Starkly realistic. . . . This exciting, well-researched alternate history will please history buffs and SF fans alike." —*Publishers Weekly*

"Factions come alive, from the Japanese warriors to the Americans who make Hawaii their home to the natives who find their loyalties torn. Turtledove excels at showing the big picture through the eyes of the individual men and women whose daily lives reflect the urgency and desperation of their times." —*Library Journal*

"Turtledove captures the feel of the 1940s as he shows the Japanese running roughshod over the unprepared Americans. . . . While characterization of people and Hawaii is really what drives this novel, Turtledove's descriptions of the military tactics and strategies of the Japanese are never far from the foreground and are enough to please fans of military science fiction."

—SF Site

"Demanding, irresistible, and magisterial—to say the very least."

—*Booklist*

RULED BRITANNIA

Harry Turtledove

A ROC BOOK

ROC
Published by New American Library, a division of
Penguin Group (USA) Inc., 375 Hudson Street,
New York, New York 10014, USA
Penguin Group (Canada), 90 Eglinton Avenue East, Suite 700, Toronto
Ontario M4P 2Y3, Canada (a division of Pearson Penguin Canada Inc.)
Penguin Books Ltd., 80 Strand, London WC2R 0RL, England
Penguin Ireland, 25 St. Stephen's Green, Dublin 2,
Ireland (a division of Penguin Books Ltd.)
Penguin Group (Australia), 250 Camberwell Road, Camberwell, Victoria 3124,
Australia (a division of Pearson Australia Group Pty. Ltd.)
Penguin Books India Pvt. Ltd., 11 Community Centre, Panchsheel Park,
New Delhi - 110 017, India
Penguin Group (NZ), cnr Airborne and Rosedale Roads, Albany,
Auckland 1310, New Zealand (a division of Pearson New Zealand Ltd.)
Penguin Books (South Africa) (Pty.) Ltd., 24 Sturdee Avenue,
Rosebank, Johannesburg 2196, South Africa

Penguin Books Ltd., Registered Offices:
80 Strand, London WC2R 0RL, England

Published by Roc, a division of Penguin Group (USA) Inc.
Previously published in New American Library hardcover and Roc mass market editions.

First Roc Trade Paperback Printing, May 2006
1 3 5 7 9 10 8 6 4 2

Roc Trade Paperback ISBN: 0-451-46084-7

The Library of Congress has cataloged the hardcover edition of this title as follows:
Turtledove, Harry.
Ruled Britannia / Harry Turtledove.
p. cm.
1. Shakespeare; William, 1564–1616—Fiction. 2. Spaniards—Great Britain—Fiction.
3. Dramatists—Fiction. I. Title
PS3570.U76 R84 2002
813'.54—dc21 2002025464

Set in Minion
Designed by Alice Sorenson

Printed in the United States of America

I

TWO SPANISH SOLDIERS SWAGGERED UP TOWER STREET TOWARDS William Shakespeare. Their boots squelched in the mud. One wore a rusty corselet with his high-crowned morion, the other a similar helmet with a jacket of quilted cotton. Rapiers swung at their hips. The fellow with the corselet carried a pike longer than he was tall; the other shouldered an arquebus. Their lean, swarthy faces wore what looked like permanent sneers.

People scrambled out of their way: apprentices without ruffs and in plain wool caps; a pipe smoking sailor wearing white trousers with spiral stripes of blue; a merchant's wife in a red wool doublet spotted with white—almost a man's style—who lifted her long black skirt to keep it out of puddles; a ragged farmer in from the countryside with a donkey weighted down with sacks of beans.

Shakespeare flattened himself against the rough, weather-faded timbers of a shop along with everybody else. The Spaniards had held London—held it down for Queen Isabella, daughter of Philip of Spain, and her husband, Albert of Austria—for more than nine years now. Everyone knew what happened to men rash enough to show them disrespect to their faces.

A cold, nasty autumn drizzle began sifting down from the gray sky. Shakespeare tugged his hat down lower on his forehead to keep the rain out of his eyes—and to keep the world from seeing how thin his hair was getting in front, though he was only thirty-three. He scratched at the little chin beard he wore. Where was the justice in that?

On went the Spaniards. One of them kicked at a skinny, ginger-colored dog gnawing a dead rat. The dog skittered away. The soldier almost measured himself full length in the sloppy street. His friend grabbed his arm to steady him.

Behind them, the Englishmen and -women got back to their business. A pockmarked tavern tout took Shakespeare's hand. "Try the Red Bear, friend," the fellow said, breathing beer fumes and the stink of rotting teeth into his face. "The drink is good, the wenches friendly—"

"Away with you." Shakespeare twisted free. The man's dirty hand, he noted with annoyance, had smudged the sleeve of his lime-green doublet.

"Away with me? Away with me?" the tout squeaked. "Am I a black-beetle, for you to squash?"

"Black-beetle or no, I'll spurn you with my foot if you trouble me more," Shakespeare said. He was a tall man, on the lean side but solidly made and well fed. The tout's skin stretched drumhead tight over cheekbones and jaw. He slunk off to earn his pennies—his farthings, more likely—somewhere else.

A few doors down stood the tailor's shop to which Shakespeare had been going. The man working inside peered at him through spectacles that magnified his red-tracked eyes. "Good morrow to you, Master Will," he said. "By God, I am glad to see you in health."

"And I you, Master Jenkins," Shakespeare replied. "Your good wife is well, I hope, and your son?"

"Very well, the both of them," the tailor said. "I thank you for asking. Peter would be here to greet you as well, but he is taking to the head of the fishmongers a cloak I but now finished: to their hall in Thames Street, in Bridge Ward."

"May the fishmongers' chief have joy in it," Shakespeare said. "And have you also finished the kingly robe you promised for the players?"

Behind those thick lenses, Jenkins' eyes grew bigger and wider yet. "Was that to be done today?"

Shakespeare clapped a hand to his forehead, almost knocking off his hat. As he grabbed for it, he said, " 'Sblood, Master Jenkins, how many times did I tell you it was wanted on All Saints' Day, and is that not today?"

"It is. It is. And I can only cry your pardon," Jenkins said mournfully.

"That doth me no good, nor my fellow players," Shakespeare said. "Shall Burbage swagger forth in his shirt tomorrow? He'll kill me when he hears this, and I you afterwards." He shook his head at that—fury outrunning sense.

To the tailor, fury counted for more. "It's near done," he said. "If you'll but bide, I *can* finish it within an hour, or may my head answer for it." He made a placating gesture and, even more to the point, shoved aside the doublet on which he'd been sewing.

"An hour?" Shakespeare sighed heavily, while Jenkins gave an eager nod. Drumming his fingers on his arm, Shakespeare nodded, too. "Let it be as you say, then. Were it not that the royal robe in our tiring room looks more like a vagabond's rags and tatters, I'd show you less patience."

"Truly, Master Will, you are a great gentleman," Jenkins quavered as he took the robe of scarlet velvet from under the counter.

"I trust you'll note this unseemly delay in your price," Shakespeare said. By the tailor's expression, he found that not in the least gentlemanly. While Shakespeare kept on drumming his fingers, Jenkins sewed in the last gaudy bits of golden thread and hemmed the robe.

"You could wear it in the street, Master Will, and have the commonality bow and scrape before you as if in sooth you were a great lord," he said, chuckling.

"I could wear it in the street and be seized and flung in the Counter for dressing above my station," Shakespeare retorted. " 'Tis a thing forbidden actors, save when on the stage." Jenkins only chuckled again; he knew that perfectly well.

He was finished almost as soon as he'd promised, and held up the robe to Shakespeare as if he were the tireman about to dress him in it. "You did but jest as to the scot, I am sure," he said.

" 'Steeth, Master Jenkins, I did not. Is mine own time a worthless thing, that I should spend it freely for the sake of your broken promise?"

"Broken it was not, for I promised the robe today, and here it is."

"And had I come at eventide, and not of the morning? You had been forsworn then. You may have mended your promise, but that means not it was unbroken."

They argued a while longer, more or less good-naturedly. At last, the tailor took five shillings off the price he'd set before. "More than you deserve, but for the sake of your future custom I shall do't," he told Shakespeare. "Which still leaves you owing fourteen pounds, five shillings, sixpence."

"The stuffs you use are dear indeed," Shakespeare grumbled as he gave Jenkins the money. Some of the silver and copper coins he set on the counter bore the images of Isabella and Albert, others—the older, more worn, ones—that of the deposed Elizabeth, who still languished in the Tower of London, only a furlong or so from where Shakespeare stood. He looked outside. It was still drizzling. "Can you give me somewhat wherewith to cover this robe, Master Jenkins? I am not fain to have the weeping heavens smirch it."

"I believe I may. Let me see." Jenkins rummaged under the counter and came up with a piece of coarse canvas that had seen better days. "Here, will this serve?" At Shakespeare's brusque nod, the tailor wrapped the cloth around the robe and tied it with some twine. He bobbed his head to Shakespeare as he passed him the bundle. "Here you are, Master Will, and I am sorry for the inconvenience I put you to."

Shakespeare sighed. "No help for it. Now I needs must—" Horns blared and drums thudded out in the street. He jumped. "What's that?"

"Did you not recall?" The tailor's face twisted. "By decree of the Spaniards, 'tis the day of the great auto de fe."

"Oh, a pox! You are right, and it had gone out of my head altogether." Shakespeare looked out into the street as horn calls and drums came again. In response to that music, people swarmed from all directions to gape at the spectacle.

"A lucky man, who can forget the inquisitors," Jenkins said. "A month gone by, as is their custom, they came down Tower Street making proclamation that this . . . ceremony would be held." He might have been about to offer some comment on the auto de fe, but he didn't. Shakespeare couldn't blame him for watching his tongue. In London these days, a word that reached the wrong ears could mean disaster for a man.

He felt disaster of a different, smaller, sort brushing against him. "In this swarm of mankind, I shall be an age making my way back to my lodgings."

"Why not go with the parade to Tower Hill and see what's to be seen?" Jenkins said. "After all, when in Rome . . . and we are all Romans now, is't not so?" He chuckled once more.

So did Shakespeare, sourly. "How could it be otherwise?" he returned. In Elizabeth's day, Catholic recusants had had to pay a fine for refusing to attend Protestant services. Now, with their Catholic Majesties ruling England, with the Inquisition and the Jesuits zealously bringing the country back under the dominion of the Pope, not going to Mass could and often did mean worse than fines. Like most people, Shakespeare conformed, as he'd conformed under Elizabeth. Some folk went to church simply because it was the safe thing to do; some, after nine years and more of Catholic rule, because they'd come to believe. But almost everyone did go.

"Why not what?" Jenkins repeated. "Think what you will of the dons and the monks, but they do make a brave show. Mayhap you'll spy some bit of business you can filch for one of your dramas."

Shakespeare had thought nothing could make him want to watch an auto de fe. Now he discovered he was wrong. He nodded to the tailor. "I thank you, Master Jenkins. I had not thought of that. Perhaps I shall." He tucked the robe under his arm, settled his hat more firmly on his head, and went out into Tower Street.

Spanish soldiers—and some blond-bearded Englishmen loyal to Isabella and Albert—in helmets and corselets held pikes horizontally in front of their bodies to keep back the crowd and let the procession move toward Tower Hill. They looked as if they would use those spears, and the swords hanging from their belts, at the slightest excuse. Perhaps because of that, no one gave them any such excuse.

Two or three rows of people stood in front of Shakespeare, but he had no trouble seeing over any of them save one woman whose steeple-crowned hat came up to the level of his eyes. He looked east, toward the church of St. Margaret in Pattens' Lane, from which the procession was coming. At its head strode the trumpeters and drummers, who blasted out another fanfare even as he turned to look at them.

More grim-faced soldiers marched at their heels: again, Spaniards and Englishmen mixed. Some bore pikes. Others carried arquebuses or longer, heavier muskets. Tiny wisps of smoke rose from the lengths of slow match the men with firearms bore to discharge their pieces. The drizzle had almost stopped while Shakespeare waited for the tailor to finish the robe. In wetter weather, the matchlocks would have been useless as anything but clubs. As they marched, they talked with one another in an argot that had grown up since the Armada's men came ashore, with Spanish lisps and trills mingling with the slow sonorities of English.

Behind the soldiers tramped a hundred woodmongers in the gaudy livery of their company. *One of those robes would do as well to play the king in as that which I have here,* Shakespeare thought. But the woodmongers, whose goods would feed the fires that burned heretics today, seemed to be playing soldiers themselves: like the armored men ahead of them, they too marched with arquebuses and pikes.

From a second-story window across the street from Shakespeare, a woman shouted, "Shame on you, Jack Scrope!" One of the woodmongers carrying a pike whipped his head around to see who had cried out, but no faces showed at that window. A dull flush stained the fellow's cheeks as he strode on.

Next came a party of black-robed Dominican friars—mostly Spaniards, by their looks—before whom a white cross was carried. They chanted psalms in Latin as they paraded up Tower Street.

After them marched Charles Neville, the Earl of Westmorland, the Protector of the English Inquisition. The northerner's face was hard and closed and proud. He had risen against Elizabeth a generation before, spent years in exile in the Netherlands, and surely relished every chance he got for revenge against the Protestants. The old man carried the standard of the Inquisition, and held it high.

For a moment, Shakespeare's gaze swung to the left, to the gray bulk of the Tower, though the church of Allhallows Barking hid part of the fortress from view. He wondered if, from one of those towers, Elizabeth were watching the auto de fe. What would the imprisoned Queen be thinking if she were? Did she thank King Philip for sparing her life after the Duke of Parma's professional soldiers swept aside her English levies? "Though she herself slew a queen, I shall not stoop to do likewise," Philip had said. Was that generosity? Or did Elizabeth, with all she'd labored so long to build torn to pieces around her, reckon her confinement more like hell on earth?

'Twould make a splendid tragedy, Shakespeare thought, *were setting so little as a single line of't to paper not worth my life—and a hard, cruel death I'd have, too.* Written or not, though, those scenes began to shape themselves in his mind. He shook his head like a fly-bedeviled horse, trying to clear it.

More than a little to his relief, a murmur in the crowd brought his attention back to the parade. Behind the Protector of the Inquisition stalked Robert Parsons, the Archbishop of Canterbury. His cold, thin features made Neville's look genial. He'd spent a generation in exile, struggling from afar against English Protestantism.

After the prelate marched another company of guardsmen. These were wild Irishmen, brought over to help the Spaniards hold England down. Most spoke only Irish; the few who used some English had brogues so thick, it was hard to tell from the other tongue.

The crowd stirred and buzzed. A couple of men pointed. A woman exclaimed. *After the sallet comes the main course*, Shakespeare thought. A couple of dozen men exhibited life-sized pasteboard images of those convicted by the Inquisition who had either died in gaol or had escaped its clutches and were being outlawed. More servitors carried trunks that bore the bones of the former. The sides and tops of the trunks were painted with hellfire's flames.

Then came the prisoners themselves. First was a group of about a dozen men and women with conical pasteboard caps fully a yard high on their heads. Most of the caps had HERETIC written on them in large letters in English and Latin. One said ALCHEMIST, another SODOMITE. In the first years after the triumph of the Duke of Parma's men, Shakespeare remembered, the words had been written in Spanish as well. These days, though, the English Inquisition operated on its own, with little help from its former teachers. Each of the condemned had a rope around his neck and carried a torch in his right hand.

More prisoners, also carrying torches, followed the first lot. They wore sanbenitos—coarse yellow penitential tunics without sleeves—with the cross of St. Andrew painted on the back in red. Some of them, after their condemnation at the ceremony, would return to imprisonment. Others would be released, but sentenced to wear the sanbenito forever as a mark of their crimes. "More ignoble and more humiliating than death itself," a fat man near Shakespeare said. Two familiars of the Inquisition accompanied each of them.

And after them tramped the dozen or so who had been condemned to the flames. They wore not only sanbenitos but also pasteboard caps, all of which were painted with flames and devils. Along with the familiars of the Inquisition, four or five monks accompanied them to prepare their souls for death.

One prisoner, a big, burly man, shook off all attempts at consolation. "I go gladly to my death," he declared, "knowing I shall soon see God face to face and rejoice in His glory for ever and ever."

"You are wrong, Philip Stubbes," a monk said urgently. "If you confess your sins, you may yet win free of hell to Purgatory."

"Purgatory's a dream, a lie, one of the myriad lies the Pope farts forth from his mouth," the Puritan said.

The monk crossed himself. "You will also win an easier death for yourself, for the executioner will throttle you ere the flames bite."

Stubbes shook his head. "Elizabeth cut off my brother's hand for speaking the truth. Torment me as you will, as the Romans tormented the martyrs of old. The flames will have me for but a little while, but you and all your villainous kind for an eternity."

Another man, a red-bearded fellow with a clever, frightened face and cropped ears, spoke urgently to a somber monk: "I'll say anything you want. I'll do anything you want. Only spare me from the fire."

A vagrant drop of rain landed on the monk's tonsured pate. He wiped it away with his hand before answering, "Kelley, your confessions, your renunciations, are worthless, as you have proved time and again. You *will* return to your alchemy, as a dog returneth to its vomit. Did not the heretic Queen's men petition you for gold wherewith to oppose the cleansing Armada?"

"I gave them none," Kelley said quickly.

"And did you not die for this," the monk went on, inexorable as an avalanche, "you surely would for coining counterfeit money in base metal."

"I did no such thing," Kelley insisted.

"Each lie you tell but makes the flames of hell hotter. Compose your spirit now, and pray for mercy from a just God Whose judgments are true and righteous altogether."

And then, to Shakespeare's horror, Kelley's eyes—green as a cat's, and showing white all around the iris—found his in the crowd and locked on them. "Will! Will! For the love of God, Will, tell 'em I'm true and trusty!"

Shakespeare wondered if he turned white or red. He felt dipped in ice and dire, both together. He'd met Edward Kelley perhaps half a dozen times over as many years, enough to know he'd lost his ears for making and passing false coins. The alchemist moved in some of the same circles as Christopher Marlowe, and some of Marlowe's circles were also Shakespeare's. *Wheels within wheels, as in the epicycles of Master Ptolemy*. But for Kelley to point him out to the Inquisition . . .

Before he could speak, either to curse Kelley—which was what he wanted to do—or to praise him, the monk said, "Where your own words will not save you, why think you any other man's might? Go on, wretch, and die as well as you may."

But he looked in the same direction the alchemist had. And his eyes, too, met Shakespeare's. He nodded thoughtfully to himself. *He knows my face*, Shakespeare thought with something not far from despair. Other people saw as much, too, and moved away from him, so that he stood on a little island of open space in the ocean of the crowd. He'd come down with a disease as deadly as smallpox or the black plague: suspicion. *Devils roast you black, Kelley, and use your guts for garters.*

On went the procession. Other voices drowned out Edward Kelley's whining claims of innocence. Behind the condemned prisoners rode the Grand Inquisitor, somber in a purple habit, and several members of the House of Commons, their faces smug and fat and self-satisfied. Another company of soldiers—Spaniards and Englishmen mixed again—and the parade was done.

As it went past, the pikemen who'd been holding back the crowd shouldered their weapons. Some folk went on about their business. More streamed after the procession to Tower Hill, to watch the burnings that would follow. Shakespeare stepped out into the muddy street. Along with the rest of the somber spectacle, he wanted to see Edward Kelley die.

"Say what you will about the Spaniards, but they've brought us a fine show," said a man at his elbow.

The fellow's friend nodded. "Better than a bear-baiting or a cockfight, and I never thought I'd say that of any sport."

Tower Hill, north and west of the Tower itself, had been an execution ground since the days of Edward IV, more than a hundred years before. Things were more elaborate now than they had been. Stakes with oil-soaked wood piled high around them waited for the condemned prisoners. Iron cages waited for them, too, in which they would listen to the charges that had brought them here. More iron cages, small ones, awaited the pasteboard effigies of the folk who had died in gaol or escaped the Inquisition's clutches.

At a safe distance from the stakes stood a wooden grandstand. Queen Isabella and King Albert sat on upholstered thrones, surrounded by grandees both English and Spanish on benches. The Archbishop of Canterbury, the Grand Inquisitor, and the other dignitaries from the procession joined them. The first group of soldiers fanned out to protect the grandstand along with the men already there. The rest kept back the crowd.

After Philip Stubbes was locked in his cage, he began singing hymns and shouting, "Vanity and lies! Beware of Popish vanity and lies!" A monk spoke to him. He defiantly shook his head and kept on shouting. The monk unlocked the cage. He and several of his fellows went in. They bound Stubbes' hands and gagged him to keep him from disrupting the last part of the ceremony.

That worked less well than they must have hoped. When the charge of heresy was read out against him, he made a leg like a courtier, as if it were praise. More than a few people in the crowd laughed and clapped their hands.

Shakespeare didn't. *No way to know whose eyes may be upon me, and all the more so after that Kelley—damnation take him!—called out my name.* He nervously fingered his little chin beard. *A hard business, living in a kingdom where the rulers sit uneasy on the throne and their minions course after foes as hounds course after stags.*

He plucked out a hair. The small, brief pain turned his thoughts to a new channel. *In a play, could I place a man of Stubbes' courage?* he wondered. *Or would the groundlings find him impossible to credit?*

One by one, the captives sentenced to more imprisonment or to wear the sanbenito were led away. Only those who would die remained. They were led out of their cages and chained to the stakes. As monks made the sign of the cross, executioners strangled a couple of them: men who had repented of their errors, whether sincerely or to gain an easier death.

Edward Kelley cried, "Me! Me! *In nomine Patris et Filii et Spiritus Sancti*, me!" But his Latin, his learning, did him no good at all.

The inquisitors looked toward the Queen. Isabella was in her early thirties, a couple of years younger than Shakespeare, and swarthy even for a Spaniard—to English eyes, she seemed not far from a Moor. The enormous, snowy-white ruff she wore only accented her dark skin. Swarthy or not, though, she was the Queen; Albert held the throne through his marriage to her. She raised her hand, then let it fall.

And, as it fell, the executioners hurled torches into the waiting fagots. They caught at once. The roar of the flames almost drowned out the screams from the burning men. The roar of the crowd came closer still. That baying had a heavy, almost lustful, undertone to it. Watching others die while one still lived . . .

Better him than me, Shakespeare thought as fire swallowed Edward Kelley. The mixture of shame and relief churning inside him made him want to spew. *Oh, dear God, better him than me.* He turned away from the stakes, from the reek of charred flesh, and hurried back into the city.

LOPE FÉLIX DE VEGA CARPIO HAD BEEN IN LONDON FOR MORE THAN nine years, and in all that time he didn't think he'd been warm outdoors even once. The English boasted of their springtime. It came two months later here than in Madrid, where it would have been reckoned a mild winter. As for summer . . . He rolled his eyes. As best he could tell, there was no such thing as an English summer.

Still and all, there were compensations. He snuggled down deeper under the feather-filled comforter and kissed the woman he kept company there. "Ah, Maude," he said, "I understand why you English women are so fair." He had a gift for language and languages; his English, though accented, was fluent.

"What's that, love?" Maude Fuller asked, lazy and sleepy after love. She was in her middle twenties, around ten years younger than he, and not merely a blonde—blondes were known in Spain—but with hair the color of fire and a skin paler than milk. Even her nipples held barely a tinge of color.

Idly, Lope teased one between his thumb and forefinger. "I know why thou art so fair," he repeated. "How couldst thou be otherwise, when the sun never touches thee?"

He let his hand stray lower, sliding along the smooth, soft skin of her belly toward the joining of her legs. The hair there was as astonishingly red as that on her head. Just thinking about it inflamed him. *Since the weather here will never warm me, as well the women do*, he thought. Of course, the women back in Spain had warmed him, too. Had he sailed off to America instead of joining the Armada and coming to England aboard the *San Juan*, no doubt he would have become enamored of one, or two, or six, of the copper-skinned, black-haired Indian women there. Loving women was in his blood.

"What, again, my sweet?" Maude said around a yawn. But his caresses heated her better than the embers in the hearth could. Before long, they began once more. He wondered if he would manage the second round so soon after the first, and knew no little pride when he did.

Ten years ago, I'd have taken it for granted, he thought as his thudding heart slowed. *Ten years from now . . .* He shook his head. He didn't care to think about that. *God and the Virgin, but time is cruel.*

To hold such thoughts at bay, he kissed the Englishwoman again. "Ah, *querida*—beloved, seest thou what thou dost to me?" he said. But lots of women did that to him. He had two other mistresses in London, though Maude, a recent conquest, knew about neither of them.

And she had secrets from him, as he discovered the worst way possible. Downstairs, a door opened, then slammed shut. "Oh, dear God!" she exclaimed, sitting bolt upright. "My husband!"

"Thine husband?" Despite his horror, de Vega had the sense to keep his voice to a whisper. "Lying minx, thou saidst thou wert a widow!"

"Well, I would be, if he were dead," she answered, her tone absurdly reasonable.

In a play, a line like that would have got a laugh. Lope de Vega mentally filed it away. He'd tried his hand at a few comedies, to entertain his fellows on occupation duty in London, and he went to the English theatres whenever he found the chance. But what was funny in a play could prove fatal in real life. He sprang from the bed and threw on his clothes by the dim light those embers gave.

Drawers. Upperstocks. Netherstocks. Shirt. Doublet with slops. He didn't bother fastening it—that could wait. Hat. Cloak. Boots. Too cursed many clothes, when he was in a hurry. Footsteps on the stairs. Heavy footsteps—these beefeating Englishmen were ridiculously large men. A quick kiss for Maude, not that she deserved it, not when she'd tried to get him killed.

Lope threw open the shutters. Cold, damp air streamed into the bedchamber. "*Adiós,*" he whispered. "*Hasta la vista.*" He scrambled out the window, hung by his hands from the sill for a moment, and then let go and dropped to the street below.

He landed lightly and didn't get hurt, but his left foot came down with a splash in a puddle of something that stank to high heaven. A rough male voice floated out the window he'd just vacated: "What the Devil was that? And why are these shutters open, Maude? Art mad? Thou'lt catch thy death."

Much as Lope would have liked to, he didn't stay to listen to Maude's excuses. He didn't fear fighting her husband, but an adulterer had no honor, win or lose. Instead of using the rapier at his hip, he hurried round a corner.

Behind him, the Englishman said, "What's that?" again, and then, " 'Swounds, woman, play you the strumpet with me?"

"Oh, no, Ned." Maude's voice dripped honey. *Oh, yes, Ned,* de Vega thought. He didn't hear whatever else she said, but he would have bet she talked her way out of it. By all the signs, she had practice.

Whatever Lope had landed in, it still clung to his boot. He wrinkled his nose. Had the Englishwoman's husband chosen to come after him, the man could have tracked him by scent, as if he were a polecat. When he stepped on a stone in the roadway, he scraped his heel and sole against it. That helped a little, but only a little.

He looked around. He'd gone only a couple of blocks from Maude's house, but in the fog and the darkness he'd got turned around. *How am I supposed to find my way back to the London barracks, let alone to Westminster, when I don't think I could find my way back to the bedroom I just left?* Madrid boasted far more torches of nights.

Lope shrugged and laughed softly. He had a long, bony face that seemed ill-suited to humor, but his sparkling eyes gave those bones the lie. *One way or another, I expect I'll manage.*

To make sure he *did* manage, he drew his rapier. London had a curfew, and he was out well after it. That wouldn't matter if he came across a squad of Spanish soldiers patrolling the streets. The only Englishmen likely to be out and about, though, were curbers and flicks and nips and high lawyers: thieves and robbers who might have a professional interest, as it were, in making his acquaintance. If they also made the acquaintance of his blade, they wouldn't bother him.

Down an alley, a dog growled and then started to bark. The rapier would also keep him safe against animals that went on four legs. But a chain clanked, and the dog yelped in frustration. Lope nodded to himself. He wouldn't have to worry about that, anyhow.

He picked his way westward, or hoped he did. If he was going in the right direction, he was heading toward the barracks, which lay not far from St. Swithin's church. Who St. Swithin was, he had no idea. He wondered if Rome did.

He heard footsteps from a side street. His right hand tightened on the leather-wrapped hilt of the rapier. Whoever was going along that street must have heard him, too, for those other footsteps stopped. Lope paused, listened, muttered, "The Devil take him, whoever he is," and went on. After a few strides, he paused to listen again. A woman's sigh of relief came to his ear. He smiled, tempted to go back and see who she was, and of what quality. After a moment, he shook his head. *Another time*, he thought.

A few blocks farther west—he thought it was west, anyhow—he heard noise he couldn't ignore. Half a dozen men, maybe more, came toward him without bothering in the least about stealth. He shrank back into a doorway. Maybe that was a patrol. On the other hand, maybe the men were English bandits, numerous and bold enough to take on a patrol if they ran into one.

They turned a corner. The fog couldn't hide their torches, though it tried. Lope tensed as those pale beams cast a shadow across his boot. Then he recognized the sweet, lisping sounds of Castilian.

"*¡Gracias a Dios!*" he exclaimed, and stepped out into the roadway.

The soldiers had had no notion he was there. They jerked in surprise and alarm. One of them swung an arquebus his way; another pointed a pistol at him. "Who are you, and what are you doing out after curfew?" their leader growled. "Advance and be recognized—slowly, if you know what's good for you."

Before advancing, before becoming plainly visible, de Vega slid the rapier back into its sheath. He didn't want anyone to start shooting or do anything else he might regret out of surprise or fear. When he drew near, he bowed low, as if the sergeant leading the patrol were a duke rather than—probably—a pigkeeper's son. "Good evening," he said. "I have the honor to be Senior Lieutenant Lope Félix de Vega Carpio."

"Christ on His cross," one of the troopers muttered. "Another stinking officer who thinks the rules don't matter for him."

Lope pretended not to hear that. He couldn't ignore the reproach in the sergeant's voice: "Sir, we might have taken you for an Englishman and blown your head off."

"I'm very glad you didn't," Lope de Vega replied.

"Yes, sir," the sergeant said. "You still haven't said, sir, what you're doing out so long after curfew. We have the authority to arrest officers, sir." He might have had it, but he didn't sound delighted at the prospect of using it. An officer with connections and a bad temper could make him sorry he'd been born, no matter how right he was. Lope didn't have such connections, but how could the sergeant know that?

"What was I doing out so late?" he echoed. "Well, she had red hair and blue eyes and—" His hands described what else Maude had. He went on, "While I was with her, I didn't care what time it was."

"You should have spent the night, sir," the sergeant said.

"I would have liked that. She would have liked that, too. Her husband . . . alas, no." Lope shook his head.

"Her husband, eh?" The sergeant's laugh showed a missing tooth. A couple of his men let out loud, bawdy guffaws. "An Englishman?" he asked, and answered his own question: "Yes, of course, a heretic dog of an Englishman. Well, good for you, by God."

"And so she was," de Vega said, which got him another laugh or two. With the easy charm that made women open their hearts—and their legs—to him, he went on, "And now, my friends, if you would be so kind as to point me back to the barracks, I would count myself forever in your debt."

"Certainly, sir." The sergeant gestured with his torch. "That way, not too far."

"*That* way?" Lope said in surprise. "I thought that way led south, down toward the Thames." The soldiers shook their heads as one man. He'd seen it done worse on stage. He gave them a melodramatic sigh. "Plainly, I am mistaken. I'm glad I ran into you men, then. I got lost in this fog."

"The Devil take English weather," the sergeant said, and his men nodded with as much unity as they'd shown before. "Yes, the Devil take the cold, and the rain, and the fog—and he's welcome to the Englishmen while he's at it. They're all heretics at heart, no matter how many of them we burn." The rest of the patrol nodded yet again.

"Amen," de Vega said. "Well, now that I know where I'm going, I'll be off. I thank you for your help." He bowed once more.

Returning the bow, the sergeant said, "Sir, I'm afraid you'll only get lost again, and the streets aren't safe for a lone gentleman. I wouldn't want anything to happen to you." *If anything does happen to you, I'll get blamed for it*—Lope knew how to translate what he said into what he meant. The underofficer turned to his men. "Rodrigo, Fernán, take the lieutenant back to the barracks."

"Yes, Sergeant," the troopers chorused. One of them made a splendid flourish with his torch. "You come along with us, sir. We'll get you where you're going."

"That's right," the other agreed. "We know this miserable, fleabitten town. We'd better—we've tramped all through it, night and day."

"I throw myself on your mercy, then," Lope said. They wouldn't be sorry to take him back, not when it got them out of the rest of the patrol. He didn't know how long that was; he'd lost track of time.

They proved as good as their word, too, guiding him back to the big wooden building by the London Stone. Some Englishmen swore the great stone with its iron bars was magical; some Spaniards believed them. Lope de Vega didn't care one way or the other. He was just glad to see it looming out of the mist.

A sentry called out a challenge. The soldiers answered it. "What are you bastards doing back here?" the sentry demanded. "You only went out an hour ago."

"We've got a lost gentleman, a lieutenant, with us," the trooper named Fernán replied. "Sergeant Diaz sent us back with him—couldn't very well leave him running around loose for some English *cabrón* to knock him over the head."

"I may be a lieutenant, but I am not a child," Lope said as he advanced. Fernán and Rodrigo and the sentry all found that very funny. *What sort of lieutenants have they dealt with?* he wondered. *Or am I better off not knowing?*

The sentry did salute him in proper fashion, and let him go in. A sergeant inside should have taken his name, but the fellow was dozing in front of a charcoal brazier. Lope slipped past him and into his room, where he pulled off his hat and boots and sword belt and went to bed. Diego, his servant, already lay there snoring. Diego, from everything Lope had seen, would sleep through the Last Judgment.

I might as well have no servant at all, de Vega thought, drifting toward sleep. *But a gentleman without a servant would be . . . Unimaginable* was the word that should have formed in his mind. What *did* occur to him was *better off.* He yawned, stretched, and stopped worrying about it.

When he woke, it was still dark outside. He felt rested enough, though. In fall and winter, English nights stretched ungodly long, and the hours of July sunshine never seemed enough to make up for them. Diego didn't seemed to have moved; his snores certainly hadn't changed rhythm. If he ever felt rested enough, he'd given no sign of it.

Leaving him in his dormouse-like hibernation, Lope put on what he'd taken off the night before, adjusting the bright pheasant plume in his braided-leather hatband to the proper jaunty angle. He resisted the temptation to slam the door as he went out to get breakfast. *My virtue surely piles up in heaven*, he thought.

He joined a line of soldiers who yawned and knuckled their red eyes. Breakfast was wine and a cruet of olive oil—both imported from Spain, as neither the grape nor the olive flourished in this northern clime—and half a loaf of brown bread. The bread was local, and at least as good as he would have had back in Madrid.

He was just finishing when his superior's servant came up to him. Captain Guzmán's Enrique was the opposite of his own Diego in every way: tall, thin, smarter than a servant had any business being, and alarmingly diligent. "Good day, Lieutenant," Enrique said. "My principal requests the honor of your company at your earliest convenience."

Gulping down the last of the wine, Lope got to his feet. "I am at his Excellency's service, of course." No matter how flowery a servant made an order, an order it remained.

No matter how much Lope hurried, Enrique got to Guzmán's office ahead of him. "Here's de Vega," he told Guzmán in dismissive tones. As a captain's man, he naturally looked down his nose at a creature so lowly as a lieutenant, even a senior lieutenant.

"*Buenos días*, your Excellency," Lope said as he walked in. He swept off his hat and bowed.

"Good day," Captain Baltasar Guzmán replied, nodding without rising from his seat. He was a dapper little man whose mustaches and chin beard remained wispy with youth: though Lope's superior, he was a good fifteen years younger. He had some sort of connection with the great noble house of Guzmán—the house of, among others, the Duke of Medina Sidonia, commander of the Armada—which explained his rank. He wasn't a bad officer, though, in spite of that. *Enrique wouldn't let him be a bad officer*, Lope thought.

"And how may I serve you today, your Excellency?" he asked.

Captain Guzmán wagged a forefinger at him. "I hear you were out late last night."

"She was very pretty," de Vega replied with dignity. "Very friendly, too."

"No doubt," Guzmán said dryly. "Our job, though, is to hunt down the English who are *not* friendly to King Philip, God bless him, not to seek out those who are."

"I wasn't on duty then." Lope tried to change the subject: "Is there any new word on his Majesty's health?"

"He's dying," Baltasar Guzmán said, and crossed himself. "The gout, the sores . . . Last I heard, those are getting worse. He may go before the Lord tomorrow, he may last a year, he may even last two. But dying he is."

Lope crossed himself, too. "Surely his son will prove as illustrious as he has himself."

"Surely," Guzmán said, and would not meet his eyes. Philip II was no great captain, no warrior whom men would follow into battle with a song on their lips and in their hearts. But such captains did his bidding. In his more than forty years of gray, competent rule, he had beaten back the Turks in the Mediterranean and brought England and Holland out of heresy and back into the embrace of the Catholic Church. More flamboyant men had accomplished far less.

His son, the prince who would be Philip III, also was not flamboyant. But, from everything Lope de Vega had heard—from everything everyone had heard—he was not particularly competent, either. Lope said, "God will protect us, as He has till now."

Guzmán crossed himself again. "May it be so." Now he did look de Vega full in the face. "And, of course, our duty is to help God as best we can. What are your plans for today, Lieutenant?—leaving Englishwomen out of the bargain, I mean."

"There is to be a play this afternoon at the Theatre," Lope replied. "I shall go there and stand among the groundlings, listen to them, see the play, and chat with the actors afterwards if I have the chance."

"A duty you hate, I'm sure," Captain Guzmán said. "I do wonder whether your attendance is for the benefit of Queen Isabella and King Albert, God bless them; for the benefit of King Philip, God bless him and keep him; or for the benefit of one Lope Félix de Vega Carpio."

"And may God bless me as well," de Vega said. Guzmán's nod looked grudging, but it was a nod. Lope went on, "When I stand among the ordinary English, I hear their grumbles. And when I mingle with the actors, I may hear more. Some of them are more than actors. Some of them have connections with the English nobles who are their patrons. Some of them, now and again, do their patrons' bidding."

"Some of them indeed have *connections* with their patrons." Guzmán gave the word an obscene twist. But then he sighed. "Still, I can't say you're wrong. Some of them *are* spies, and so . . . and so, Lieutenant, I know you are mixing pleasure with your business, but I cannot tell you not to do it. I want a full report, in writing, when you get back."

"Just as you say, your Excellency, so shall it be," Lope promised, doing his best to hide his relief. He turned to leave.

Baltasar Guzmán let him take one step toward the door, then raised a finger and stopped him in his tracks. "Oh—one other thing, de Vega."

"Your Excellency?"

"I want a report that deals with matters political. Literary criticism has its place. I do not argue with that. Its place, however, is not here. Understand me?"

"Yes, your Excellency." *You're a Philistine, your Excellency. It's God's own miracle you can read and write at all, your Excellency*. But Guzmán was the man with the rank. Guzmán was the man with the family.

Guzmán was also the man with the literate, intelligent, curious servant. As de Vega left the office, Enrique said, "Sir, your English is much better than mine. *I* would be glad to hear what these playwrights are doing, to compare them to our own."

Keeping Enrique sweet might help keep Captain Guzmán sweet. And Lope *was* passionate about the theatre. He wished his useless Diego were passionate about anything but slumber. "Of course, Enrique. When I get back."

The Theatre stood in Shoreditch, beyond the walls of London and, in fact, beyond the jurisdiction of the city. Before the Catholic restoration, the grim Protestants who called themselves Puritans had kept theatres out of London proper. Many of the same men still governed the capital of England. They had made a peace of sorts with the Church, but not with gaiety; there still were no theatres within the bounds of the city.

Lope's cloak and hat shielded him from the endless autumn drizzle as he made his way out through Bishopsgate and up Shoreditch High Street. Leaving the wall behind didn't mean leaving behind what still seemed like a city, even if it was no longer exactly London. Stinking tenements lined narrow streets and leaned toward one another above them. Here a man might be murdered without even the excuse of sleeping with another man's wife. Lope kept a hand on the hilt of his rapier and strode on with a determination that warned all and sundry he would be hard to bring down. Instead of troubling him, people scrambled out of his way. *Better to be bold*, he thought.

Stews flourished beyond the reach of the London city government, too. A skinny, dirty bare-breasted woman leaned out a window and called to de Vega: "How about it, handsome?"

What went through his mind was, *God grant I never grow so desperate*. He swept off his hat, bowed, and kept walking. "Cheap bugger!" she shouted after him. "*¡Maricón!*" Did she know him for a Spaniard, or was that just another insult, one new here since the coming of the Armada? He never found out.

Buildings ended. Fields, orchards, and garden plots began. Plenty of people were making their way toward the Theatre. Lope tremendously admired it and the other theatres on the outskirts of London. No such places in which to put on plays existed in Spain. There, actors performed in a square in front of a tavern, with the audience looking down from the buildings on the other three sides of that square. Real playhouses . . . Did the Englishmen know how lucky they were? He doubted it. From all he'd seen, they seldom did.

Though brightened with paint, the Theatre's timbers were themselves old and faded; the three-story polygonal building had been standing for more than twenty years. Gay banners on the roof helped draw a crowd. So did a big, colorful signboard above the entrance, advertising the day's show: IF YOU LIKE IT, A NEW COMEDY BY WILLIAM SHAKESPEARE. Dissolute-looking men were making pennies for drink by going—staggering—through the streets bawling out the name of the play.

Lope paid his penny at the door. "Groundling!" called the man who took the coin. Another man directed de Vega to the standing room around the brightly painted stage, where he jostled his way forward. Had he paid tuppence or threepence, he could have had a seat in one of the galleries looking down on the action. Here among the poorer folk, though, he would likely find more of interest.

Hawkers fought through the press, selling sausages and pasties and cider and beer. Lope bought a sausage and a cup of cider. He stood there chewing and sipping, guarding his place with his elbows as he listened to the men and women around him.

"Nasty way to die, burning," a white-bearded fellow remarked.

"You ever see anybody braver nor Parsons Stubbes the other day?" a woman said. "Couldn't be nobody braver. God's bound to love a man like that—only stands to reason. I expect he's up in heaven right now."

"How about them what burned him?" another man asked.

"Oh, I don't know anything about that," the woman answered quickly. She'd already said too much, and realized it, but she wouldn't say any more. Nine years of the Inquisition had taught these talkative people something, at least, of holding their tongues. And before that they'd had a generation of stern heresy under Elizabeth, and before *that* Catholicism under Mary and Philip, and before *that* more heresy under Henry VIII. They'd swung back and forth so many times, it was a marvel they hadn't looked toward the Turks and had a go at being Mahometans for a while.

Then such thoughts left him, for two actors appeared on stage, and the play began. Lope had to give all his attention to it. His English was good, but not so good that he could follow the language when quickly spoken without listening hard. And Shakespeare, as was his habit, had cooked up a more complicated plot than any Spanish playwright would have thought of using: squabbling noble brothers, the younger having usurped the elder's place as duke; the quarreling sons of a knight loyal to the exiled rightful duke, and the daughters of the rightful duke and his brother.

Those "daughters," Rosalind and Celia, almost took Lope out of the play for a moment. As was the English practice, they were played by beardless boys with unbroken voices. Women didn't act on stage here, as they'd begun to do in Spain. One of the boys playing the daughters was noticeably better at giving the impression of femininity than the other. Had the company had real actresses to work with, the problem wouldn't have arisen.

But Shakespeare, as de Vega had seen him do in other plays, used English conventions to advantage. Rosalind disguised herself as a boy to escape the court of her wicked uncle: a boy playing a girl playing a boy. And then a minor character playing a feminine role fell for "him": a boy playing a girl in love with a boy playing a girl playing a boy. Lope couldn't help howling laughter. He was tempted to count on his fingers to keep track of who was who, or of who was supposed to be who.

Spanish plays ran to three acts. Shakespeare, following English custom, had five acts—about two hours—in which to wrap up all the loose ends he'd introduced and all the hares he'd started. He did it, too, getting the daughters of the two noblemen married to the sons of the knight and having the usurping duke retire to a monastery so his older brother could reclaim the throne.

How would the Englishman have managed that if his kingdom were still Protestant? Lope wondered as the boy playing Rosalind, the better actor, delivered an epilogue asking the audience for applause. That struck Lope as almost as unnatural as not employing actresses. He'd used the last couple of lines in his plays to say farewell, but he never would have written in a whole speech.

But it didn't bother the people around him. They clapped their hands and stamped their feet and shouted till his ears rang. The actors came out to take their bows. Richard Burbage, who'd played the usurping duke, made a leg in a robe King Philip wouldn't have been ashamed to wear. His crown was surely polished brass, not gold, but it gleamed brightly. Shakespeare, who'd played his older brother, also had on a royal robe, but one that was much less splendid, as befit his forest exile—*a nice touch*, Lope thought. When Shakespeare doffed *his* brass crown, his own crown gleamed brightly, too. Lope, who had all his hair, noted that with smug amusement.

One further advantage of a stage—from the company's point of view—was that they could sell a few seats right up on the edge of it, and charge more for those than for any others in the house. The men and women who rose from those seats to applaud showed more velvet and lace and threadwork of gold and silver than all the groundlings put together. Pearls and precious stones glittered in the women's hair. Gold gleamed on the men's belts, and on their scabbards, and on the hilts of their rapiers.

Despite those visible signs of wealth and power, the groundlings behind the rich folk weren't shy about making their views known. "Sit you down!" they shouted, and "We came to see the players, not your arses!" and "God sees through you, but we can't!"

One of the grandees half turned and set a beringed hand on the fancy hilt of his sword. A flying chunk of sausage smirched his orange doublet with grease. Safe in the anonymity of the crowd, another groundling threw something else, which flew past the nobleman and bounced halfway across the stage. The poor folk in their frowzy wool raised a cheer.

Just as a Spanish noble would have done, the Englishman purpled with fury. But the woman beside him, whose neckline was even more striking than her pile of blond curls, set a hand on his sleeve and said something in a low voice. His reply was anything but low, and thoroughly sulfurous. She spoke again, as if to say, *What can you do? You can't kill them all.* Grudgingly, he turned away from the groundlings, though his back still radiated fury. They jeered louder than ever.

After the last bow, the players went back into the tiring room behind the stage to change into their everyday clothes once more. Most of the crowd filed out through the narrow doorways by which they'd entered. Friends and sweethearts of the company pressed forward to join the actors backstage. So did the stagestruck: would-be actors, would-be writers, would-be friends and sweethearts.

The tireman's assistants—a couple of big, burly men who kept cudgels close by—stood in front of the doors leading to the tiring room. Lope de Vega, though, had no trouble; he went backstage after every performance he attended. "God give you good day, Master Lope," one of the assistants said, doffing his cap and standing aside to let the Spaniard pass.

"And to you also, Edward," de Vega replied. "What thought you of the show today?"

"We had us a good house," Edward said—the first worry of any man in an acting company. Then he blinked. "Oh, d'you mean the play?"

"Indeed yes, the play," Lope said. "So much going on there, almost all at once."

"Master Will don't write 'em simple," the tireman's assistant agreed. "But he hath the knack of helping folk recall who's who, and meseems the crowd followed tolerably well." Nodding, de Vega passed by. Edward glowered at the Englishman behind him. "And who are *you*, friend?"

Chaos reigned in the tiring room. Some of the players were still in costume; some had already returned to the drabber wear normal to men and boys of their class; and some, between the one stage and the other, wore very little. They took near nudity in stride, as Spanish actors would have done. The room was close with the reek of sweat and perfume and torch smoke.

Lope moved through as best he could, shaking hands, bowing when he had the space, and congratulating the players. Someone—he didn't see who—handed him a leather drinking jack. Sipping, he found it full of sweet, strong Spanish wine. The English were even fonder of it than his own folk, perhaps because they had to import it and couldn't take it for granted.

He bumped into a woman—someone's wife, he couldn't remember whose. "So sorry, my lady," he said. "With your permission?" He bowed over her hand and kissed it. She smiled back in a manner that might have been encouraging.

"Watch out for Master Lope," round-faced Will Kemp said behind him. "Lope the *loup*, Lope the *lobo*." The company clown howled wolfishly. Raucous laughter rose. Lope joined it, the easiest way he knew to deflect suspicion. The woman turned to talk to an Englishman, so there was no suspicion to deflect, anyhow. *Así es la vida*, de Vega thought, and sighed.

He congratulated Burbage and the boy who'd played Rosalind. "I thank you kindly, sir," the youth replied. In his powder and paint, he still looked quite feminine—even tempting—but his natural voice, though not yet a man's, was deeper than the one he'd used on stage. He wouldn't be able to pretend to womanhood much longer.

At last, de Vega made his way to Shakespeare. The actor and playwright stood off in a corner, talking shop with darkly handsome Christopher Marlowe. Lope bowed in delight. "My two favorites of the English stage, here together!" he cried.

"Good day—or should I say good even, Master de Vega?" Shakespeare replied. "Have you met Master Marlowe here?" To Marlowe, he added, "Lieutenant de Vega writes plays in Spanish, and more than once hath trodden the boards with Lord Westmorland's Men as extra."

"Indeed?" Marlowe murmured. His cool, dark eyes measured Lope. "How . . . versatile of him." He nodded and bowed. "A pleasure to make your acquaintance, sir."

"We have met once or twice, sir, but how can I be surprised if you recall it not?" de Vega said. By the way Marlowe eyed him, though, he wondered if the Englishman ever forgot anything. Enrique, Captain Guzmán's servant, had that same too-clever-by-half look, and *he* never did.

But then Lope started talking shop with the English playwrights, and forgot everything else for a while. He didn't worry about spying. He didn't even worry about the pretty women in the room. What did any of that matter, next to the passion for the word, for the play, the three men shared?

A TORCH GUTTERED OUT, SENDING SHADOWS SWOOPING THROUGH the tiring room, filling a quarter of it with darkness, and adding the reek of hot fat to the crowded air. Christopher Marlowe clapped a hand to his forehead in one of the melodramatic gestures he used so naturally. " 'Struth!" he burst out. "Would the poxy Spaniard never leave?"

Shakespeare stood several inches taller. He set a hand on the other playwright's shoulder. "However long he lingered, he's gone now, Kit. He's harmless, or as harmless as a man of his kingdom can be. Mad for the stage, as you heard."

"Think you so?" Marlowe said, and Shakespeare nodded. Marlowe rolled his eyes. "And think you babes are hid 'neath cabbage leaves for their mothers to find?"

The tireman coughed. He wanted the room empty so he could lock up the precious costumes and go home. Only a few people were left now, still hashing over what they'd done, what they might have done, what they would do the next time they put on *If You Like It*. Even Will Kemp, a law unto himself, took the tireman seriously. With a mocking bow to those who remained, he swept out the door.

Irked, Shakespeare stayed where he was. He snapped, "I know whence babes come—I know better than you, by God." Even in the dim, uncertain light left in the tiring room, he saw Marlowe flush. The other poet chased boys as avidly as prickproud Lope went after other men's wives.

"All right, Will." Marlowe visibly held in his anger. "You're no blushing maid—be it so stipulated. But he loves us not for ourselves alone. Were we wenches, then yes, mayhap. Things being as they are . . ." He shook his head.

"What, you reckon Lope Stagestruck an intelligencer?" Shakespeare almost laughed in his face. "Where's the reason behind that?"

"*Imprimis*, he's a Spaniard. *Secundus*, he's a man. *Tertius*, an you suspect a man not, he'll ever prove the viper who ups and stings you."

He meant every word. Shakespeare saw as much. He let out a sigh as exasperated as the tireman's cough. "A pretty world wherein you must live, Kit, there within the fortress of your skull."

"I *do* live," Marlowe said, "and I purpose living some while longer, too. Were I so careless as you, I had died ten times over ere now. Quarrels are easy enough to frame: a swaggering bravo imagining an insult in the street, peradventure, or over the reckoning in a little room. You're a better man than I am. See to it your goodness harms you not."

"Gentlemen, *please*," the tireman said, something close to despair in his voice.

Shakespeare walked out of the Theatre, Marlowe in his wake. Autumn twilight came early, and was falling fast. Before long, the gray clouds overhead would turn black. With the play over, the streets around the Theatre were almost empty. As he started back toward London and his lodgings, Shakespeare said, "Well, the Spaniard's not about. What would you say to me you could not say within the spying rascal's hearing?"

"You make a mock of it," Marlowe said. "One day you'll be sorry—God grant it be not soon. What would I say? I've said already more than I *would* say."

"Then say no more, and have done." Shakespeare lengthened his stride; Marlowe had to half trot to try to keep up. Over his shoulder, Shakespeare added, "Enough real worries in the world—aye, enough and to spare—without the hobgoblins bubbling from the too fertile cauldron of your fears."

"Damn you, will you listen to me?" Marlowe shouted. A limping old woman carrying a pail of water stared at him.

"Listen? How, when you will not speak, save only in riddles?" But Shakespeare stopped.

Marlowe took a deep breath. Slowly, deliberately, he let it out. "Hear me plain, then," he said, and gave Shakespeare a mocking bow. "I should like you to meet a friend of mine."

"A friend?" Shakespeare said in surprise. As far as he knew—as far as anyone in London knew—Christopher Marlowe neither had nor particularly wanted friends. He did have a great many acquaintances of one degree of intimacy or another, that being defined by how useful they proved to him.

He was almost as aware of the lack as were other folk. He hesitated before nodding, and added, "A man with whom I've been yoked in harness some little while."

"Yoked in harness of what sort?" Shakespeare asked.

"Side by side, vile-minded lecher, not fore and aft," Marlowe said. " 'Tis a matter of business on which he's fain to make your acquaintance." His shoulders hunched. He glared down at the ground. He was furious, and not trying hard at all to hide it.

Shakespeare judged he would burst like the hellburner of Antwerp if not humored. Marlowe in a temper was nothing to take lightly, so Shakespeare said, "I'll meet him, and right gladly, too, whosoever he may be. Bring him to my ordinary while I dine or sup, an't please you."

"I'll do't," Marlowe said, though he sounded far from pleased. If anything, he seemed angrier than ever.

In God's name, what now? Shakespeare wondered. Now, instead of hastening on toward Bishopsgate, he stopped in his tracks. Marlowe was the one who kept striding on before also halting a few paces farther on. "I have said I will do as you would have me do, Kit," Shakespeare said. "Wherefore, then, wax you wroth with me still?"

"I do not." Marlowe flung the three words at him and started on again.

"What then?" Now Shakespeare had to hurry after him—either that or shout after him and make their talk a public matter for any who cared to hear it. He asked the only question that occurred to him: "If not for me, is your anger for your 'friend'?"

"It is." Two more words, bitten off short.

"Here's a tangled coil!" Shakespeare exclaimed. "Why such fury for him?"

"Because he's fain to see you in this business," Marlowe said sullenly.

By then, with the darkness coming on fast, with a few drops of drizzle falling cold on his hand, Shakespeare was beginning to lose his temper, too. "Enough of riddles, of puzzles, of conundrums," he said. "Do me the honor, do me the courtesy, of speaking plain."

"I could speak no plainer—because he's fain to see you in this business." But then, unwillingly, Marlowe made it a great deal plainer: "Because he's fain to see you, and not me. Damn you." He hurried off, leaning forward as if into a heavy wind.

"Oh, Kit!" Now Shakespeare knew exactly where the trouble lay. What he did not know was whether he could mend it. Marlowe had been a success in London before Shakespeare rose from performing in plays to trying to write them. Some of Shakespeare's early dramas bore Marlowe's stamp heavily upon them. *If a man imitate, let him imitate the best*, Shakespeare thought.

Marlowe remained popular even now. He made a living by his pen, as few could. But those who had given him first place now rated him second. For a proud man, as he surely was, that had to grate. If the "business" had to do with the theatre, if his "friend" wanted Shakespeare and not him . . . No wonder he was scowling.

"Wait!" Shakespeare called, and loped after him. "Shall I tell this cullion that, if he be your friend, the business should be yours?"

To his surprise, the other playwright shook his head. "Nay. He hath reason. For what he purposes, you were the better choice. I would 'twere otherwise, but the world is as it is, not as we would have it."

"You intrigue me mightily, and perplex me, too," Shakespeare said.

Marlowe's laugh held more bile than mirth. "And I might say the same of you, Will. Did you tender me this plum, I'd not offer it back again. You may be sure of that."

Shakespeare was. In a cutthroat business, Marlowe owned sharper knives than most. Unlike some, he seldom bothered pretending otherwise. After a moment's thought, Shakespeare said, "God be praised, I am not so hungry I needs must take bread from another man's mouth."

"Ah, dear Will. An there be a God, He might do worse than hear praises from such as you. You're a blockhead, but an honest blockhead." Marlowe stood up on tiptoe to kiss him on the cheek. "I'll bring the fellow to your ordinary at eventide tomorrow—I know the place you favor. Till then." He hurried toward Bishopsgate. This time, the set of his shoulders said Shakespeare would have been unwelcome had he tried to stay up with him.

With a sigh, Shakespeare trudged down Shoreditch High Street after him. Just when a man looked like understanding Marlowe, he would do something like that. He could not praise without putting a poison sting in amongst the honey, but the kiss had been, or at least had seemed, real.

"Hurry up, hurry up," guards at the gate called. "Get on in, the lot of you." They were a mixed lot, Englishmen and rawboned Irish mercenaries. The Irish soldiers looked achingly eager to kill someone, anyone. Rumor said they ate human flesh. Shakespeare didn't care to find out if rumor were true. Not meeting their fierce, falconlike gazes, he scuttled into the city.

His lodgings were in Bishopsgate Ward, not far from the wall, in a house owned by a widow who made her living by letting out most of the space. He had his own bed, but two others crowded the room where he slept. One of the men who shared the chamber, a glazier named Jack Street, had a snore that sounded like a lion's roar. The other, a lively little fellow called Peter Foster, called himself a tinker. Shakespeare suspected he was a sneakthief. He didn't foul his own nest, though; nothing had ever gone missing at the lodging house.

"You're late today, Master William," said Jane Kendall, Shakespeare's landlady. "By Our Lady, I hope all went well at the Theatre." She made the sign of the cross. From things she'd said over the couple of years he'd lived there, she'd been a Catholic even before the Armada restored England's allegiance to Rome.

"Well enough, I thank you," he replied. "Sometimes, when talking amongst ourselves after the play, we do lose track of time." With so many people living so close together, secrets were hard to keep. Telling a piece of the truth often proved the best way to keep all of it from coming out.

"And the house was full?" Widow Kendall persisted.

"Near enough." Shakespeare smiled and made a leg at her, as if she were a pretty young noblewoman, not a frowzy, gray-haired tallowchandler's widow. "Never fear. I'll have no trouble with the month's rent."

She giggled and simpered like a young girl, too. But when she said,

"That I'm glad to hear," her voice held nothing but truth. A lodger without his rent became in short order a former lodger out on the street. Still, he'd pleased her, for she went on, "There's new-brewed ale in the kitchen. Take a mug, if you care to."

"That I will, and right gladly." Shakespeare fitted action to word. The widow made good ale. Hopped beer, these days, was commoner than the older drink, for it soured much more slowly. He savored the mug, and, when his landlady continued to look benign, took another. Nicely warmed, he said, "Now I'm to the ordinary for supper."

She nodded. "Don't forget the hour and keep scribbling till past curfew," she warned.

"I shan't." *I hope I shan't*, Shakespeare thought. *Or do I?* The eatery made a better place to work than the lodging house. On nights when ideas seemed to flow straight from his mind onto the page, he could and sometimes did lose track of time. He'd ducked home past patrols more than once.

From the chest by his bed, he took his second-best spoon—pewter—a couple of quills, a knife to trim them, ink, and three sheets of paper. He sometimes wished he followed a less expensive calling; each sheet cost more than a loaf of bread. He locked the chest once more, then hurried off to the ordinary around the corner. He sat down at the table with the biggest, fattest candle on it: he wanted the best light he could find for writing.

A serving woman came up to him. "Good even, Master Will. What'll you have?"

"Hello, Kate. What's the threepenny tonight?"

"Kidney pie, and monstrous good," she said. He nodded. She brought it to him, with a mug of beer. He dug in with the spoon, eating quickly. When he was through, he spread out his papers and got to work. *Love's Labour's Won* wasn't going so well as he wished it would. He couldn't lose himself in it, and had no trouble recalling when curfew neared. After he went back to the lodging house, he got a candle of his own from his trunk—Jack Street was already snoring in the bed next to his—lit it at the hearth, and set it on a table. Then he started writing again, and kept at it till he could hold his eyes open no more. He had his story from Boccaccio, but this labor, won or lost, reminded him of the difference between a story and a finished play.

The next day, he performed again at the Theatre. He almost forgot he had a supper engagement that evening, and had to grab his best spoon—silver—and rush from his lodging house. To his relief, Christopher Marlowe and his mysterious friend hadn't got there yet. Shakespeare ordered a mug of beer and waited for them.

They came in perhaps a quarter of an hour later. The other man was no one Shakespeare had seen before: a skinny little fellow in his forties, with dark blond hair going gray and a lighter beard that didn't cover all his pockmarks. He wore spectacles, but still squinted nearsightedly. Marlowe introduced him as Thomas Phelippes. Shakespeare got up from his stool and bowed. "Your servant, sir."

"No, yours." Phelippes had a high, thin, fussily precise voice.

They all shared a roast capon and bread and butter. Phelippes had little small talk. He seemed content to listen to Shakespeare and Marlowe's theatre gossip. After a while, once no one sat close enough to overhear, Shakespeare spoke directly to him: "Kit says you may have somewhat of business for me. Of what sort is't?"

"Why, the business of England's salvation, of course," Thomas Phelippes told him.

II

"WELL, ENRIQUE, WHAT DOES CAPTAIN GUZMÁN WANT TO SEE me about today?" Lope de Vega asked.

"I think it has something to do with your report on *If You Like It*," Guzmán's servant answered. "Just what, though, I cannot tell you. *Lo siento mucho*." He spread his hands in apology, adding, "Myself, I thought the report very interesting. This Shakespeare is a remarkable man, is he not?"

"No." Lope spoke with a writer's precision. "As a *man*, he is anything but remarkable. He drinks beer, he makes foolish jokes, he looks at pretty girls—he has a wife out in the provinces somewhere, and children, but I do not think it troubles him much here in London. Ordinary, as I say. But put a pen in his hand, and all at once it is as though God and half the saints were whispering in his ear. As a *playwright*, 'remarkable' is too small a word for him."

Guzmán's door was open. Enrique went in first, to let him know de Vega had arrived. Lope waited in the hallway till Enrique called, "His Excellency will see you now, Lieutenant."

Lope strode into his superior's office. He and Baltasar Guzmán exchanged bows and pleasantries. His report on his latest trip to the Theatre lay on his superior's desk. He saw that Guzmán, in the style of King Philip, had written comments in the margins. He gave a small, silent sigh; he enjoyed being edited no more than most writers.

Presently, the captain nodded to Enrique and said, "You may go now. Shut the door on the way out, *por favor*."

"As you say, your Excellency." Guzmán's servant sounded reproachful, which, as usual, did him no good. Lope wondered if he would slam the door to show his annoyance, but Enrique had more subtlety than that. He shut it with exaggerated care, so it made no noise at all.

Captain Guzmán noticed that, too. Chuckling, he said, "He's got his nose out of joint again. Because he's clever, he thinks he ought to be important, too."

"Better a clever servant than a dolt like my Diego, who'd forget his own name if people didn't shout it at him all the time," de Vega said.

"Oh, no doubt, no doubt, but Enrique *will* make too much of himself." Tapping the report with his forefinger, Guzmán got down to business: "Overall, this is a good piece of work, Lieutenant. Still, I need to remind you again that you visit the Theatre as his Majesty's spy, *not* as his drama critic."

"I'm very sorry, your Excellency," Lope lied.

Guzmán laughed again. "A likely story. You're a lucky man, to be able to enjoy yourself so much at your work."

"I would enjoy myself even more if the benighted English let women take the stage," Lope said.

"Indeed. It frightens me, Lieutenant, to think how much you might enjoy yourself then." Baltasar Guzmán tapped the report again. His fingernails were elegantly manicured. He looked across the desk at de Vega. "I note that you met this Marlowe back in the tiring room after the presentation."

"Yes, your Excellency." Lope nodded. "He was talking shop with Shakespeare. A good bit of the time, he was telling him how he would have done things differently—and, in his opinion, better. This is, you understand, sir, something playwrights do."

"No doubt you would know better than I," Guzmán said. "But Christopher Marlowe is a dangerous character. He knows too many of the wrong people. Knowing so many rogues makes him likely a rogue himself. I am given to understand the Inquisition has taken several long, hard looks at him. They do not investigate a man merely for their amusement."

"While I was there, he and Shakespeare spoke of nothing but their craft."

Guzmán ticked off points on his fingers. "First, Lieutenant, you do not know this for a fact. They could have hidden any number of coded meanings in their talk, and you would have been none the wiser. Second, who knows what they said *after* you left the Theatre? They do, and God does, and no one else. You do not."

That he was right made his supercilious manner no less annoying: more so, if anything. Lope protested: "Say what you will of Marlowe, but Shakespeare has always stayed with the stage and fought shy of politics."

But his superior shook his head. "Not necessarily. At the recent auto de fe, one of the men relaxed to the Inquisition for punishment—a notorious sorcerer and counterfeiter—saw Shakespeare in the crowd and called out for him to testify to his good character. This fellow, a certain Kelley, was also an intimate of Christopher Marlowe's. So Shakespeare is not above suspicion. No man is above suspicion," he added, sounding as certain as if he were reciting the Athanasian Creed.

Though the news shook Lope, he did his best not to show it. He said, "A drowning man will clutch at any straw."

"True," Captain Guzmán agreed. "Or it may be true. But I find it interesting that this Kelley should reckon Shakespeare a straw worth clutching." Without giving de Vega a chance to answer, he rolled up the report, wrote something on the outside, and tied it with a green ribbon. Holding it out, he said, "I want you to take this to Westminster, to an Englishman there who has worked closely with us for a long time. He already knows of the business with the sorcerer, and he is well suited to judge just how important this meeting between Shakespeare and Marlowe may be."

"Very well, your Excellency." Lope took the report. "An Englishman, you say? Am I going to have to translate my work here? I would want a secretary's help with that. I speak English well enough, but I cannot say I write it."

Captain Guzmán shook his head. "No need for that. He's fluent in Spanish. As I say, he's been with us since Isabella became Queen."

"All right. Good. That makes things simpler. This is the fellow's name here?"

"That's right. Get a horse from the stables and take it over to him right away. *Vaya con Dios.*" The farewell was also a dismissal.

A wan English sun, amazingly low in the southern sky, dodged in and out from behind rolling clouds as Lope de Vega rode through London toward Westminster. When he went past St. Paul's cathedral, he scratched his head, wondering as he always did why the otherwise magnificent edifice should be spoiled by the strange, square, flat-topped steeple. *Not so much as a cross up there*, he thought, and clucked reproachfully at the folly of the English.

The horse, a bay gelding, was no more energetic than it had to be. It ambled up Ludgate Hill and out through the wall at Ludgate. London proper didn't stop at the wall; de Vega rode west along Fleet Street past St. Bridget's, St. Dunstan's in the West, and the New Temple, the church of the Knights Templars before the crusading order was suppressed. They all lay in the ward of Farringdon Without the Wall.

Lope couldn't tell exactly where that ward ended and the suburbs of the city began. He had thought Madrid a grand place, and so it was, but London dwarfed it. He wouldn't have been surprised if the English capital held a quarter of a million people. If that didn't make it the biggest city in the world, it surely came close.

Westminster, which lay at a bend in the Thames, was a separate, though much smaller, city in its own right, divided into twelve wards. The apparatus of government dominated it much more than London proper. Isabella and Albert dwelt in one of the several castles there. Parliament—Lope thought of it as the equivalent of the Cortes of Castile, though it was even fussier about its privileges than the Cortes of Navarre—met there. Westminster Abbey was an ecclesiastical center, though the senior archbishop of England, for no good reason de Vega could see, presided at Canterbury, fifty miles away. And the clerks and secretaries and scribes who served the higher functionaries also performed their offices in Westminster.

By the time he finally found the man he was looking for, Lope felt as if he'd navigated the labyrinth of the Minotaur. He'd spent most of an hour and most of his temper making his way through the maze before he knocked on the right door: one in the offices of the men who served Don Diego Flores de Valdés, the commandant of the Spanish soldiers stationed in England.

"Come in," a voice called in English.

Lope de Vega did. The fellow behind the desk was unprepossessing: small, thin, pale, pockmarked, bespectacled. As de Vega walked in, he flipped a paper over so the newcomer wouldn't be able to read it. Lope caught a brief glimpse of pothooks and hieroglyphs—some sort of cipher. Maybe the man made up in brains what he lacked in looks. Peering down at the report, Lope said, "You are Thomas . . . Phelippes?" He'd never seen the name spelled that way before—but then, the vagaries of English spelling could drive any Spaniard mad.

"I am," Phelippes said in English, and then switched to good Spanish: "You have the advantage of me, *señor*. Would you sooner use your own tongue or mine?"

"Either will do," Lope replied, speaking English himself. After giving his name, he went on, "My superior, Captain Baltasar Guzmán, ordered me to bring you my report on possible suspicious business at the Theatre the other day, and so I give it you." He held it out as if it were a baton.

Phelippes took it. "I thank you. I am acquainted with Captain Guzmán. A good man, sly as a serpent." Lope wouldn't have used that as praise, but the Englishman plainly intended it so. He also spoke of the Spanish nobleman as an equal or an inferior. *How important are you?* Lope knew he couldn't ask. Phelippes went on, "Is there anything he desires me to look for in especial?"

"Yes—he desires your opinion of the trustiness of the two poets, Marlowe and Shakespeare," de Vega said.

"I had liefer put my hand in the wolf his jaws than put my trust in Christopher Marlowe," Phelippes said at once. "He companies with all manner of cozeners and knaves, and revels in the doing of't. I fear me he'll come to a bad end, and never know why. Though boys throw stones at frogs in sport, the frogs die in earnest."

Lope smiled. "You are a man of learning, I see, to bring Plutarch forth at need. Now, what of Shakespeare?"

Feature for feature, Thomas Phelippes' face was in no way remarkable. Somehow, though, he managed a sneer any aristocrat might have envied. "Shakespeare? He knows no more than a puling babe of great affairs, and cares no more, either. All that matters to him is his company of players, and the plays he writes for 'em."

"This was also my thought." Lope did his best not to show his relief. "And I'd not have mentioned his name, save only that Captain Guzmán noted a certain Edward Kelley had called out to him on his way to the Inquisition's cleansing fire."

"Ah, Kelley. There was rubbish that wanted burning, in sooth," Phelippes said with another fine sneer. "But he was no intimate of

Shakespeare's: that I know for a fact. Only a wretch seeking succor with none to be had." The Englishman proved to own a nasty chuckle, too. "I misdoubt he affrighted Master Will like to stop his heart."

"I should say so!" De Vega wouldn't have wanted an inquisitor noting *his* connection to a man about to die. He inclined his head to Phelippes. "You do set my mind at ease, for which I thank you. I'll take your word back to Captain Guzmán."

"Your servant, sir." Phelippes tapped the report with a fingernail, much as Guzmán had done. "And I'll put this in brief for Don Diego. You know the tale, I'm sure: the greater the man, the less time hath he wherein to read."

"Not always," Lope said. "There is the King."

"What? Albert? I would not disagree with a new acquaintance, *señor*, but—"

"No, not Albert," de Vega said impatiently. "Philip. *The* King, God preserve him." He crossed himself.

So did Phelippes. The way he did it told Lope he hadn't been doing it all his life. "Amen," he said. "But what hear you of his health? The last news I had was not good."

"Nor mine," Lope admitted. "He hath now his threescore and ten. He is in God's hands." He made the sign of the cross again.

"He always was, and so are we all." Phelippes signed himself again, too, no more smoothly than he had before.

Lope nodded approval. He hadn't thought the Englishman so pious. "I'm for London, then," he said. "I hope to see you again, sir, and my thanks once more for setting my mind at rest."

"My pleasure, sir." Even before Lope was out the door, Phelippes returned to the ciphered message on which he'd been working.

When rehearsals went well, they were a joy. Shakespeare took more pleasure in few things than in watching what had been only pictures and words in his mind take shape on the stage before his eyes. When things went not so well, as they did this morning . . . He clapped a hand to his forehead. " 'Sdeath!" he shouted. "Mechanical salt-butter rogues! Boys, apes, braggarts, Jacks, milksops! You are not worth another word, else I'd call you knaves."

Richard Burbage looked down his long nose at Shakespeare. He was the only player in Lord Westmorland's Men tall enough to do it. "Now see here, Will, you've poor cause to blame us when you were the worst of the lot," he boomed, turning his big, sonorous voice on Shakespeare alone instead of an audience.

He was right, too, as Shakespeare knew only too well. The poet gave the best defense he could: "My part's but a small one—"

"Ha!" Will Kemp broke in. "I never thought to hear a man admit as much."

"Devils take you!" Shakespeare scowled at the clown. "Not recalling your own lines, you aim to step on mine." He gathered himself. "If we play as we rehearsed, they'll pelt us with cabbages and turnips enough to make soup for a year."

"We'll be better, come the afternoon. We always are." Burbage had a wealthy man's confidence; the Theatre and the ground on which it stood belonged to his family. Though several years younger than Shakespeare, he had a prosperous man's double chin—partly concealed by his pointed beard—and the beginnings of an imposing belly.

"Not always," Shakespeare said, remembering calamities he wished he could forget.

"Often enough," Burbage said placidly. "There's no better company than ours, and all London knows it." He eyes, deep-set under thick eyebrows, flashed. "But you, Will. You're the steadiest trouper we have, and you always know your lines." He chuckled. "And so you ought, you having writ so many of 'em. But today? Never have I seen you so unapt, as if the very words were strange. Out on it! What hobgoblins prey on your mind?"

Shakespeare looked around the Theatre. Along with the company, the tireman and his assistants, the prompter, and the stagehands, a couple of dozen friends and wives and lovers milled about where the groundlings would throng in a few hours. Musicians peered down from their place a story above the tiring room. He had to talk to Burbage, but not before so many people. All he could do now was sigh and say, "When troubles come, they come not single spies, but in battalions."

Burbage tossed his head like a horse troubled by flies. "Pretty. It tells naught, of course, but pretty nonetheless."

"Give over, if you please," Shakespeare said wearily. "I'm not bound to unburden myself before any but God, and you are not He."

Kemp's eyes widened in well-mimed astonishment. "He's not? Don't tell him that, for I warrant he did not know't."

A flush mounted to Burbage's cheeks and broad, high forehead. "Blaspheming toad."

"Your servant, sir." Kemp gave him a courtier's bow. Burbage snorted.

So did Shakespeare. The clown would mock anyone, and refused to let any insults stick to him. Shakespeare said, "Shall we try once more the scene that vexed us in especial, that in which Romeo comes between Mercutio and Tybalt fighting? We've given this tragedy often enough ere now, these past several years. We should do't better than we showed."

"Too many lines from too many plays, all spinning round in our heads," Kemp said. " 'Tis a wonder we can speak a word some scribbling wretch did not pen for us."

Shakespeare had rarely felt more wretched. As Mercutio, he crossed swords with Burbage's Tybalt. The other player had fought against the invading Spaniards, and actually used a blade; Shakespeare's swordplay belonged only to the stage. And Burbage fenced now as if out for blood; when the time came for him to run Mercutio through under Romeo's arm, he almost really did it.

"By God," Shakespeare said, arising after he'd crumpled, "my death scene there came near to being my death scene in sooth."

Burbage grinned a predatory grin. "Nothing less than you deserve, for havering at us before. Satisfies you now this scene?"

"It will serve," Shakespeare said. "Still, I have somewhat to say to you on the subject of your swordplay." *And on other things as well*, he thought. Those, though, would have to wait.

The other player chose to misunderstand him. Setting a hand on the hilt of his rapier, he said, "I am at your service."

If they fought with swords in earnest, Shakespeare knew he was a dead man. What had Marlowe said about fanning quarrels? *Surely not Burbage*, Shakespeare thought, *not when we've worked together so long.* That such a thing could even occur to him was the measure of how many new worries he carried. *I'll be like Kit soon, seeing danger in every face.*

"Let it go, Dick," Kemp said. "An you spit him like a chine of beef, what are you then? Why, naught but a ghost—a pretty ghost, I'll not deny, but nonetheless a ghost—left suddenly dumb for having slain the one who gave you words to speak."

"There are other scribblers," Burbage rumbled ominously. But then he must have decided he'd gone too far, for he added, "We, being the best of companies, do deserve that which we have: to wit, the best of poets." He turned toward Shakespeare and clapped his big, scarred hands.

When the afternoon came, the play went well. Thinking about it afterwards, Shakespeare shook his head. The *performance* had gone well, but there was more to it than that. A couple of the gentlemen sitting at the side of the stage smoked their pipes so furiously, the thick tobacco fumes spoiled the view for the groundlings behind them. The rowdies, having paid their pennies, were convinced they were men as good as any others, and pelted the offenders with nuts and pebbles—one of them, flying high, incidentally hitting the boy playing Juliet just as he was about to wonder where Romeo was. They didn't quite have a riot, but Shakespeare had trouble figuring out why not.

"Ofttimes strange, but never dull," he said in the tiring room. "Pass me that basin, Dick, if you'd be so kind."

"I'll do't," Burbage said. Shakespeare splashed water on his face and scrubbed hard with a towel to get rid of powder and rouge and paint. He looked in a mirror, then scrubbed some more. After the second try, he nodded. "There. Better. I have my own seeming once again."

"I shouldn't be so proud of it, were I you," Kemp said slyly.

"Were you I, you'd have a better seeming than you do," Shakespeare retorted. People laughed louder than the joke deserved. The biter bit was always funny; Shakespeare had used the device to good effect in more than one play. Will Kemp bared his teeth in what might have been a smile. He found the joke hard to see.

"Magnificent, Master Will!" There stood Lieutenant Lope de Vega, a broad smile on his face. "Truly magnificent! . . . Is something wrong?"

He'd seen Shakespeare start, then. "No, nothing really," Shakespeare answered, glad his actor's training gave his voice a property of easiness: for his was, without a doubt, a guilty start. "You did surprise me, coming up so sudden."

"I am sorry for it," the Spaniard said. "But this play—this play, sir, is splendid. This play is also closer to what someone—a man of genius, of course—might write in Spain than was *If You Like It* . . . though that too was most excellent, I haste to add."

"You praise me past my deserts," Shakespeare said modestly, though the compliments warmed him. He'd never known a writer who disliked having others tell him how good he was. Some had trouble going on without hearing kind words at frequent intervals. Marlowe, for instance, bloomed like honeysuckles ripened by the sun at praise, but the icy fang of winter seemed to pierce his heart when his work met a sour reception—or, worse still, when it was ignored. He fed on plaudits, even more than most players. Shakespeare knew he had the same disease himself, but a milder case.

And Lope shook his head. "Not at all, sir. You deserve more praises for this work than I have English to give you." He gave Shakespeare several sentences of impassioned Spanish. Hearing that language in the tiring room made several people turn and mutter—the last thing Shakespeare wanted.

"I say again, sir, you are too generous," he murmured. Lieutenant de Vega shook his head once more. He did, at least, return to English, though he kept talking about plays he'd seen in Madrid before the Armada sailed. *This work of mine likes him well, for its nearness to that which he knew before-time*, Shakespeare realized. That took some of the pleasure from the praise: what woman would want a man to say she was beautiful because she reminded him of his mother?

After some considerable time, de Vega said, "But I do go on, is't not so?"

"By no means," Shakespeare lied. He couldn't quite leave that alone, though. "Did you write with celerity to match your speech, Master Lope, you'd astound the world with the plays that poured from your pen: you'd make yourself a very prodigy of words."

"Were my duties less, my time to write were more," the Spaniard answered, and Shakespeare thought he'd got away with it. But then de Vega reminded him that he was in fact Senior Lieutenant de Vega: "In aid of my duties, sir, a question—what acquaintance had you with Edward Kelley, that he should call to you when on his way to the fire?"

I never saw him before in my life. That was what Shakespeare wanted to say. But a lie that at once declared itself a lie was worse than useless. *Marlowe was right, damn him. De Vega* is *a Spaniard first, a groundling and player and poet only second*. Picking his words with great care, the Englishman said, "I shared tavern talk with him a handful of times over a handful of years, no more." Though the tiring room was chilly, sweat trickled down his sides from under his arms.

But Lope de Vega only nodded. "So I would have guessed. Whom would Kelley have known better, think you?"

Marlowe, Shakespeare thought, and damned his fellow poet again. Aloud, though, he said only, "Not having known him well myself, I fear I cannot tell you." He spread his hands in carefully simulated regret.

"Yes, I see." Lope remained as polite as ever. Even so, he asked another question: "Well, in whose company were you with this rogue, then?"

"I pray your pardon, but I can't recall." Shakespeare used his player's training to hold his voice steady. "I had not seen him for more than a year, perhaps for two, before we chanced to spy each the other in Tower Street."

The Spaniard let it drop there. He went off to pay his respects to a pretty girl Shakespeare hadn't seen before, one who'd likely got past the tireman's assistants because she was so pretty. Whoever she was, de Vega's attentions made her giggle and simper and blush. Shakespeare could tell which actor she'd come to see—one of the hired men who played small parts, not a sharer—by the fellow's ever more unhappy expression. But the hired man had no weapon on his belt, while Lieutenant de Vega not only wore a rapier but, by the set of his body, knew what to do with it.

Not my concern, Shakespeare thought. He felt a moment's shame—surely the Levite who'd passed by on the other side of the road must have had some similar notion go through his mind—but strangled it in its cradle. Catching Burbage's eye, he asked, "Shall we away?"

"Let's," the other big man answered. With a theatrical swirl, Burbage wrapped his cloak around him: it had looked like rain all through the play, and, with day drawing to a close, the heavens were bound to start weeping soon.

A drunken groundling snored against the inner wall of the Theatre. "They'll need to drag him without ere closing for the night," Shakespeare said as the two players walked past him.

Richard Burbage shrugged. "He's past reeling ripe—belike he's pickled enough to sleep there till the morrow, and save himself his penny for the new day's play." But the idea of the man's getting off without paying that penny was enough to make him tell one of the gatekeepers outside the Theatre about the drunk. The man nodded and went off to deal with him.

Shakespeare skirted a puddle. Burbage, in stout boots, splashed through. It did begin to rain then, a hard, cold, nasty rain that made Shakespeare shiver. "This is the sort of weather that turns to sleet," he said.

"Early in the year," Burbage said, but then he shrugged again. "I shouldn't wonder if you have reason."

They walked on. As the rain came down harder, more puddles formed in the mud of Shoreditch High Street. A woman lost her footing and, flailing her arms, fell on her backside. She screeched curses as she struggled to her feet, dripping and filthy. "Would that Kemp had seen her there," Shakespeare said. "He'd filch her fall for his own turns."

"Clowns." Burbage packed a world of scorn into the word. "The lackwits who watch 'em do laugh, wherefore they reckon themselves grander than the play they're in."

Shakespeare nodded. Kemp in particular had a habit of extemporizing on stage. Sometimes his brand of wit drew more mirth than Shakespeare's. That was galling enough. But whether he got his laughs or not, his stepping away from the written part never failed to pull the play out of shape. Shakespeare said, "Whether he know it or no, he's not the Earth, with other players sun and moon and planets spinning round his weighty self."

"Or the Earth and all round the sun, as Copernicus doth assert," Burbage said.

"He, being dead, may assert what pleases him." Shakespeare looked around nervously to make sure no one had overheard. "His Holiness the Pope holding opinion contrary, we enjoy not the like privilege."

Burbage frowned. "If a thing be true, it is true with the Pope's assent or in his despite."

"Here is a true thing, Dick," Shakespeare said: "An you speak such words where the wrong ears hear, you'll explicate 'em to the Inquisition."

"This for the Inquisition." Burbage hawked and spat.

Easy for him to be brave, Shakespeare thought. *He lies under no suspicion . . . yet*. As Edward Kelley's frantic plea had, the questions from Lieutenant de Vega reminded him of the sovereign power of fear. The Spaniard still seemed friendly enough and to spare, but Shakespeare knew he would never think of him as silly and harmless again. *By the time this ends, I'll see foes and spies everywhere, as Marlowe does*. He'd had that thought before.

But Burbage's scorn let Shakespeare ask the question he knew he would have to ask sooner or later: "Would you, then, we lived still under Elizabeth?" A field lay by the left side of the street. When he turned his head that way, he could see the looming bulk of the Tower in the distance. What was Elizabeth doing there? What was she thinking? A pretty problem for a playwright.

Burbage walked on for several strides without answering, taking the chance to ponder it. At last, though, the player said, "A man will do what he needs must do, that he may live and prosper if prospering's in him.

So we know. Did we not, these past nine years had schooled us. But when you ask, what would I?—I'm an Englishman, Will. If you be otherwise, run tell your lithping friend." He mocked de Vega's Castilian accent.

He's no friend of mine. Shakespeare started to say it, but it wasn't true, or hadn't been true till de Vega asked questions about Kelley. The Spaniard was clever, amusing company; he knew everything there was to know about his own country's theatre, and had learned a great deal about England's. If he ever settled down to write instead of talking endlessly, he might make a name for himself.

"You were an idiot to speak your mind to me, did you reckon I'd turn traitor," Shakespeare replied after some small silence of his own.

" 'Treason doth never prosper: what's the reason? For if it prosper, none dare call it treason,' " Burbage quoted, and then cocked his head to one side. "I misremember—is that yours?"

Shakespeare shook his head. "Nay: some other man's. I thank you; I am answered."

"And had I cried hurrah! for Queen Isabella?"

"Many who cry so prosper," Shakespeare said.

"The dons are here, and here to stay, by all the signs," Burbage said. "A man must live, as I said just now, and, to live, live with 'em. So far will I go, so far and no further. A fellow who sniffs and tongues the Spaniards' bums, like some scabby whining cur-dog with a pack of mastiffs . . . This for him!" He spat again.

They separated not far inside the wall. Shakespeare went off to his lodgings. Burbage had a home of his own in a more prosperous part of town farther west. *I could go back to Stratford*, Shakespeare thought. *I have a home there, and my wife, and my children.* He cursed softly under his breath. His son Hamnet had died the year before of some childhood fever, and had gone into the ground before Shakespeare could make his way back to Warwickshire.

A terrier proudly trotted by, a dead rat clamped in its jaws. Shakespeare sighed and clicked his tongue between his teeth. When he'd gone back to Stratford, Anne had wanted him to stay there. Had he stayed, he wouldn't have had to worry about swaggering Spaniards. Hardly a one had ever been seen in the West Midlands.

But how could I stay? He asked himself now the same question he'd asked his wife then. He was making a far better living in London than he could have in Stratford: enough to send money off to Anne and their daughters, Susanna and Judith. And Anne wasn't always easy to get along with. He was happier and freer admiring her virtues from a distance than having them ever before his eyes.

When he walked into the house where he lodged, Jane Kendall greeted him with, "A man was asking after you today, Master Will."

"A man?" Shakespeare said in surprise and no small alarm. His landlady nodded. Fighting for calm, he found another question: "What sort of man? One of the dons?"

The tallowchandler's widow shook his head. Shakespeare hoped he didn't show how relieved he was. "He was about your own age," the widow said, "not a big man, not small. Ill-favored, I'll say he was, but with a look to him. . . . Did he ask me to play at dice with him, I'd not throw any he brought forth."

Shakespeare frowned and scratched his head. "Meseems that is no man I ken," he said slowly. "Gave he a name to stand beside this his ill-favored visage?"

Before his landlady could answer, Peter Foster laughed raucously. "Was't the name of his wife or his sweetheart or his daughter?"

"Go to!" Shakespeare said, his ears heating. He didn't live a monk's life in London, but he hadn't, or didn't think he had, given anyone cause to come after him for that kind of reason. Lieutenant de Vega boasted about the horns he put on husbands. Shakespeare, by contrast, reckoned discretion the better part of pleasure.

Again, Widow Kendall shook her head. "He said naught of any such thing. And he did leave a name, could I but recall it. . . . I'm more forgetful with each passing year, I am. It quite scares me." But then she suddenly grinned and snapped her fingers. "Skeres!" she exclaimed in delight.

"Your pardon?" Shakespeare said, thinking she'd repeated herself and wondering why.

"Skeres," she said once more. "Nick Skeres, he called himself."

"Oh." The poet smiled at having his confusion cleared away. Even so . . . "He may know me, or know of me, but I ken him not. Said he when he might again come hither?"

"Not a word of't," the widow replied. "I told him, seek Master Will at the Theatre of days, I said. He's surely a ninny, and a fond ninny at that, to know where you lodge but not where you earn your bread."

"My thanks for speaking so." Shakespeare wasn't at all sure he should thank her. He would have wondered at any time why a stranger was sniffing around him. Now . . . He exhaled through his nose, a silent sigh. No help for it.

Peter Foster sounded sly and clever and most experienced, saying, "Have a care, Master Will, do. This rogue could be a catchpole, come for to carry you off to the Clink or some other gaol."

"I've done naught contrarious to law," Shakespeare said. *Yet.*

Foster's smile pitied a man capable of such naïveté. "If so be he's paid, he'll care not a fig for that. A few shillings weigh more than a man's good name." Again, his tone was that of one who knew whereof he spoke. His eyes flicked to Shakespeare's belt. "You haven't even a sword."

" 'Twould do me but little good," Shakespeare said sadly. "Even for a player, a man of make-believe, I'm a cream-faced loon with blade in hand, and I give proof thereof whenever we practice our parts for a show with swordplay."

"You know that, and now I know that, but will this Nick What's-his-name know't? Give me leave to doubt." Foster winked. "An he see you with rapier on hip, what will he think? Belike, *Here's a hulking brute, could run me through*, or summat o' the sort. The porpentine need not cast his quills to make the other beasts afeard; he need only have 'em."

Again, the tinker—if that was what he was—made good sense. Shakespeare bowed. "Gramercy, Master Foster. I'll take your advice, me-thinks."

He got his writing tools from his trunk and went off to the ordinary to eat and work. The threepenny supper, the serving woman said, was, "A fine mess of eels, all stewed with leeks. Master Humphrey went down to Fish Wharf and fetched back a whole great tun of 'em."

"Eels?" Spit flooded into Shakespeare's mouth. "Bring 'em on, Kate, and a cup of sack to go with 'em."

"Beer comes with the threepenny supper—the wine's a ha'penny extra," Kate warned. Shakespeare nodded; he wanted it anyhow.

When the eels arrived, he dug in with gusto, savoring the rich, fatty flesh and pausing every now and then to spit fish bones onto the rush-strewn rammed-earth floor. Then he got out his paper and pens and ink and settled down to write. He made slow going of it: every time some-one came into the ordinary, he looked up to see if it were the fellow who'd asked Widow Kendall about him. But there were no ill-favored strangers, only people who, like him, supped here often. Some of them exchanged a word or two with him; most, seeing him at work, left him to it. He sometimes got testy—a couple of times, he'd got furious—when interrupted.

Tonight, though, his own misgivings were what kept interrupting him. It was not a night when he had to worry about forgetting curfew. That he got anything at all done on *Love's Labour's Won* struck him as a minor miracle.

THE TWO ACTORS—ACTUALLY, THE TWO SPANISH SOLDIERS—PLAYING Liseo and his servant, Turín, appeared at what was supposed to be an inn in the Spanish town of Illescas, which lay about twenty miles south of Madrid. The one playing Liseo hesitated, bit his lip, and looked blank. Lope de Vega hissed his line at him: "*¡Qué lindas posadas!*"

"What lovely inns," the soldier—his real name was Pablo—repeated obediently. He might have been a slightly—a very slightly—animated wooden statue, painted to look lifelike but wooden nonetheless.

"*¡Frescas!*" agreed the fellow playing his servant (*his* real name was Francisco). He knew he was supposed to say, "Fresh air," to suggest a hole in the imaginary roof, but sounded even deader doing it than Pablo did.

Before they could go on to complain about the likelihood of bedbugs and lice, Lope threw his hands in the air. "Stop!" he shouted. "God and all the saints, stop!"

"What's the matter, *Señor* Lieutenant?" the soldier playing Turín asked. "I remembered my line, and Pablo here, he looked like he was going to remember his next one, too."

"What's the matter? What's the matter?" Lope's volume rose with each repetition. "I'll tell you what's the matter. What's the name of this play of mine?"

"*La dama boba*," Francisco answered. "That's what's the matter, sir?"

"God give me strength," de Vega muttered. He turned back to the soldiers. "That's right. The lady Finea is supposed to be a boob. You two aren't supposed to be boobs. *So why are you acting like boobs?*" He started roaring again.

"We weren't," Pablo said in injured tones. "We were just giving our lines."

"If you give them like that, who'd want to take them?" Lope demanded. "You couldn't be any stiffer if you were embalmed. This is supposed to be a comedy, not a show of mourning for—" He started to say *for King Philip,* but broke off. The King of Spain wasn't dead yet. "For Julius Caesar," he finished.

"We're doing the best we can, sir," Francisco said.

That might have been true. It probably *was* true. But it wasn't excuse enough, especially not in Lope's present excited condition. "But you can't act!" he howled. "You ought to go to a play here and see how these Englishmen do it. They're actors, by God, not—not—so many tailor's dummies!"

"Devil take these Englishmen," Pablo said. "We came up to this miserable country to make sure the buggers behave themselves, not to make fools of ourselves in stage plays. If you don't like how we do it, we quit!"

"That's right," Francisco said.

"You can't do that!" Lope exclaimed. "You're supposed to start performing in a week."

"So what? I've had a bellyful, I have," Pablo said. "This isn't part of my duty. If you think the damned Englishmen make such good actors, *Señor* Lieutenant, get them to put on your play for you. *Hasta la vista*." He stomped away. The soldier playing his servant followed, slamming the door behind them.

Lope swore. He sprang to his feet and kicked the bench on which he'd been sitting, which toppled the bench and almost ruined one of his toes. As he hopped around, still cursing, he wondered how in God's name he was going to put on *La dama boba* without two of his leading characters. If he could have got men from Shakespeare's acting company to recite Spanish verse, he would have done it. Except when they swore, Englishmen didn't want to learn Spanish.

Cautiously, he put weight on the foot he'd hurt. It wasn't too bad; he didn't think he'd broken anything.

"I'd like to break their thick, stupid heads," he muttered. He was an officer. They were only soldiers. He could order them to perform. But he couldn't order them to be good, not and make it stick. For one thing, they weren't very good to begin with. For another, they were only too likely to be bad out of spite. Had he been a common soldier ordered to do something he didn't really want to do, he would have tried his best to pour grit in the gears. Oh, he understood the impulse, all right.

Suddenly, he snapped his fingers in delight. He hurried off to Captain Baltasar Guzmán's office. Guzmán was sanding something he'd just written to soak up the extra ink. "*Buenos días*, Lieutenant de Vega," he said in some surprise. "I didn't expect to see you this morning; I thought you'd be busy with your theatricals. Does this mean a brand new devotion to duty?"

"Your Excellency, I am always devoted to duty," Lope said. It wasn't strictly true, but it sounded good. He added, "And the powers that be have been kind enough to encourage my plays. They say they keep the men happy by giving them a taste of what they might have at home."

"Yes, so they say." Captain Guzmán seemed unconvinced. But he went on, "Since they say so, I can hardly disagree. What do you require, then?"

"Your servant, Enrique," Lope answered. Guzmán blinked. Lope explained how he'd just lost two actors, finishing, "God must have put the idea into my head, your Excellency. Enrique loves the theatre; he's bright; he would perform well—and, since he's a servant and not a soldier, he wouldn't get huffy, the way Pablo and Francisco did. If you can spare him long enough to let him learn Liseo's part, I'm sure he'd do you credit when he performs."

One of Captain Guzmán's expressive eyebrows rose. "Did he bribe you to suggest this to me?"

"No, sir. He did not. I only wish I would have thought of using him sooner."

"Very well, Senior Lieutenant. You may have him, and I will pray I ever get him back again," Guzmán said. "Now, whom did you have in mind for the other vacant part—Liseo's servant, is it not?"

"I was going to use my own man, Diego."

Guzmán's eyebrow rose again, this time to convey an altogether different expression. "Are you sure? Can you make him bestir himself?"

"If he doesn't do as I need, I can make his life a hell on earth, and I will," Lope said. "As a matter of fact, I rather look forward to getting some real work out of him. However much he tries to sleep through everything, he *is* my servant, after all. I may not own him so absolutely as I would a black from Guinea, but I'm entitled to more than he's ever given me."

"You're certainly entitled to it. Whether you can get it may prove a different question. Still, that's your worry and none of mine." Guzmán's chuckle sounded more as if he were laughing at Lope than with him. "I wish you good fortune. I also tell you I think you will need more than I can wish you."

"We'll see," de Vega said, though he feared his superior was right. "He's supposed to be blacking my boots right now. He hates that.

Maybe he'd rather act than do something he hates." He sighed. "Of course, what he wants to do most of all is nothing."

When he strode into his chamber in the Spanish barracks, Diego wasn't blacking his boots. That wasn't because he'd already finished the job, either; the boots stood by the side of the bed, scuffed and dirty. And Diego lay in the bed, blissfully unconscious and snoring.

Lope shook him. His eyes flew open. "Mother of God!" he exclaimed around a yawn. "What's going on?" Then intelligence—or as much as he had—returned to his face. "Oh. *Buenos días, señor*. I thought you were gone for the day."

"So you could spend the rest of it asleep, eh?" de Vega said. "No such luck. Congratulations, Diego. You are about to become a star of the stage."

"What? Me? An actor?" Diego shook his head. "I'd rather die." He made as if to disappear under the blankets.

The *wheep!* of Lope's blade sliding out of its scabbard arrested the motion before it was well begun. "Believe me, you lazy good-for-nothing, that can be arranged," he said. "If you think I am joking, you are welcome to try me."

He didn't know that he would run his servant through. But he didn't know that he wouldn't, either. Nor did Diego seem quite sure. Eyeing Lope with sleepy resentment, he said, "What do you want . . . *señor*?" His gaze kept flicking nervously to the rapier.

"Get up. Get dressed. You will—by God, Diego, you *will*—learn the role of Turín. He's a servant and a bit of a sneak, so it ought to suit you well."

Yawning again, Diego deigned to sit up. "And if I don't?" he asked.

Lope kept the rapier's point just in front of his servant's nose, so that Diego's eyes crossed as he watched it. "If you don't . . ." Lope said. "If you don't, the first thing that will happen is that you will be dismissed from my service."

"I see." Diego had no great guile; de Vega could read his face. *If I am dismissed, I will attach myself to some other Spaniard, and cling to him as a limpet clings to a rock. Whoever he is, he won't want me to act, either.*

Sadly, Lope shook his head. "I've already discussed this with Captain Guzmán. You know how short of men—good, strong, bold Spanish men—we are in England. Any servant dismissed by his master goes straight into the army as a pikeman, and off to the frontier with Scotland. The north of England is a nasty place. The weather is so bad, it makes London seem like Andalusia—like Morocco—by comparison. The Scots are big and fierce and swing two-handed swords they call, I think, claymores. They take heads. They do not eat human flesh, as the Irish are said to do, but they take heads. I think you would make a poor trophy myself, but who knows how fussy a Scotsman would be?"

He was lying, at least in part. Not about the north of England—it did have an evil reputation, and Scotland a worse one. But servants sacked by their masters didn't automatically become cannon fodder. Diego, of course, didn't know that. And Lope sounded convincing. He wasn't a Burbage or an Edward Alleyn, but he could act.

"Put that silly sword away, *señor,*" Diego said. "I am your man. If I have to be your actor, I will be your actor." As if to prove it, he got out of bed.

"Ah, many thanks, Diego," Lope said sweetly, and sheathed the rapier. "I knew you would see reason." The servant, still in his nightshirt, muttered something pungent under his breath. As anyone with a servant needed to do, Lope had learned when not to hear. This seemed one of those times.

WILLIAM SHAKESPEARE CAME OUT OF A POULTERER'S ON GRASS Street with a couple of fine new goose quills to shape into pens. "Come again, sir, any time," the poulterer called after him. "As often as not, the feathers go to waste, and I'm glad to make a couple of pennies for 'em. 'Tis not as it was in my great-grandsire's day, when the fletchers bought 'em for arrows by the bale."

"The pen's mightier than the sword, 'tis said," Shakespeare answered, "but I know not whether that be true for the arrow as well. Certes, the pen hath lasted longer."

Pleased with himself, he started back towards his Bishopsgate lodgings. He'd just turned a corner when a man coming his way stopped in the middle of the narrow, muddy street, pointed at him, and said, "Your pardon, sir, but are you not Master Shakespeare, the player and poet?"

He did get recognized away from the Theatre every so often. Usually, that pleased him. Today . . . Today, he wished he were wearing a rapier as Peter Foster had suggested, even if it were one made for the stage, without proper edge or temper. Instead of nodding, he asked, "Who seeks him?" as if he might be someone else.

"I'm Nicholas Skeres, sir." The other man made a leg. He lived up to—or down to—Widow Kendall's unflattering description of him, but spoke politely enough. And his next words riveted Shakespeare's attention to him: "Master Phelippes hath sent me forth for to find you."

"Indeed?" Shakespeare said. Skeres nodded. Shakespeare asked, "And what would you? What would he?"

"Why, only that you come to a certain house with me, and meet a certain man," Nick Skeres replied. "What could be easier? What could be safer?" His smile showed crooked teeth, one of them black. By the glint in his eye, he'd sold a lot of worthless horses for high prices in his day.

"Show me some token of Master Phelippes, that I may know you speak sooth," Shakespeare said.

"I'll not only show it, I'll give it you." Skeres took something from a pouch at his belt and handed it to Shakespeare. "Keep it, sir, in the hope that its like, new minted, may again be seen in the land."

It was a broad copper penny, with Elizabeth looking up from it at Shakespeare. Plenty of the old coins still circulated, so it was no sure token, but Skeres had also said the right things, and so. . . . Abruptly, Shakespeare nodded. "Lead on, sir. I'll follow."

"I am your servant," Skeres said, which Shakespeare doubted with all his heart: he seemed a man out for himself first, last, and always. He hurried away at a brisk pace, Shakespeare a step behind.

He'd expected to go up into the tenements north of the wall, or perhaps to Southwark on the far bank of the Thames: to some mean house, surely, there to meet a cozener or a ruffian, a man who dared not show his face in polite company. And Nicholas Skeres did lead him out of London, but to the west, all the way to Westminster. At the Somerset House and the church of St.-Mary-le-Strand, Skeres turned north, up into Drury Lane.

Grandees dwelt in these great homes, half of brick, half of timber. One of them could have housed a couple of tenements' worth of poor folk. Shakespeare felt certain Skeres would go on to, and past, St. Giles in the Field, which lay ahead. But he stopped and walked up to one of the houses. Nor did he go round to the servants' entrance, but boldly knocked at the front door.

"Lives your man *here?*" Shakespeare said in something close to disbelief.

Skeres shook his head. "Nay—that were too dangerous. But he dwells not far off. He—" He broke off, for the door opened. The man who stood there was plainly a servant, but better dressed than Shakespeare. Nick

Skeres said, "We are expected," and murmured something too low for the poet to catch.

Whatever it was, it served its purpose. The servant bowed and said, "Come with me, then. He waits. I'll lead ye to him."

Carpets were soft under Shakespeare's feet as he went up one corridor and down another. He was more used to the crunch of rushes underfoot indoors. The house was *very* large. He wondered if he could find his way out again without help. *Like Theseus of Athens in the Labyrinth, I should play out thread behind me.*

"Here we are, good sirs," the servant said at last, opening a door. "And now I'll leave ye to't. God keep ye." Smooth and silent as a snake, he withdrew.

"Come on," Nick Skeres said. As soon as Shakespeare entered the room, Skeres shut the door behind them. Then he bowed low to the old man sitting in an upholstered chair close by the hearth in the far wall; a book rested on the arm of the chair. "God give you good day, Lord Burghley. I present Master Shakespeare, the poet, whom I was bidden to bring hither to you."

Shakespeare made haste to bow, too. "Your—Your Grace," he stammered. Had Skeres told him he would meet Queen Elizabeth's longtime lord high treasurer, he would have called the man a liar to his face and gone about his business. But there, without a doubt, sat Sir William Cecil, first Baron Burghley. After the Duke of Parma's soldiers conquered England, most of Elizabeth's Privy Councilors had either fled to Protestant principalities on the Continent or met the headsman's axe. But Burghley, at King Philip's specific order, had been spared.

He had to be closer to fourscore than the Bible's threescore and ten. His beard was white as milk, whiter than his ruff, and growing thin and scanty. His flesh was pale, too, and looked softer and puffier than it should have—almost dropsical. Dark, sagging pouches lay under his eyes. But those blue eyes were still alert and clever, though a cataract had begun to cloud one of them. The Order of the Garter, with St. George slaying a dragon, hung from a massy gold chain around his shoulders.

"Well met, Master Shakespeare," he said, his voice a deep rumble without much force behind it. "I have for some while now thought well of your plays and poems."

"You are generous beyond my deserts, your Grace," Shakespeare said, still bemused. Surely he hadn't been summoned for pretty compliments alone. He shook his head, annoyed at himself for being so foolish as even to think such a thing. Thomas Phelippes' hand lay somewhere behind this. Phelippes, whatever else he was, was not one to waste time on inessentials.

"Sit. Sit." Lord Burghley waved Shakespeare and Nicholas Skeres to a pair of plain wooden stools in front of his chair. He coughed wetly a couple of times as they perched—Shakespeare nervously—then went on, "Now is the winter of our discontent." Shakespeare stirred. Burghley's smile showed several missing teeth, and another one broken. "Ay, I heard Burbage, as Richard, mouth your words. They hold here truer than they did for the Plantagenet. Know you that King Philip fails?"

"I've heard somewhat of't," Shakespeare answered cautiously, thinking Sir William Cecil himself did likewise.

No sooner had that crossed his mind than the nobleman let out a rheumy chuckle. "We race each other into the grave, he and I. But when the worms take us, mine the victory, for my son is greater than his sire, his far less. Belike you'll treat with Robert ere this business end—but, for now, with me."

"I am your servant, my lord," Shakespeare said, as Nick Skeres had before him. But Skeres had only been greasily polite. Shakespeare could not imagine disobeying Lord Burghley—and did not want to imagine what would happen to him if he did.

"My servant?" Sir William Cecil shook his head. The flesh of his cheeks wobbled like gelatin, as no healthy man's would have done. "Nay. You shall be my good right arm and the sword in the hand thereof, to strike a blow for England no other man might match."

Shakespeare thought of Christopher Marlowe, and of Kit's fury at being excluded from this plot. He also thought he would gladly have given Marlowe his role. But if it were to be done, the best man had to do it. Shakespeare and Marlowe both knew who that was. "By your leave, sir," Shakespeare said, "I tell you the chance of all going as we would desire. . . ." His voice trailed off. He could not make himself tell Burghley how bad he thought the odds were.

The gesture served well enough. Lord Burghley chuckled again—and then coughed again, and had trouble stopping. When at last he did, he said, "Think you not that, on hearing of Philip the tyrant's passing, our bold Englishmen will recall they are free, and brave? Think you not they will do't, if someone remind them of what they were, and of what they are, and of what they may be?"

Shakespeare bared his teeth in a grimace that was anything but a smile. "Am I Atlas, your Grace, to bear upon my shoulders the burthen of the whole world his weight?"

"I'll lighten somewhat the said burthen, an I may." Lord Burghley picked up the book. Even though he set a pair of spectacles on his nose, he still had to hold the volume at arm's length to read. He flipped through it rapidly, then more slowly, till at last he grunted in satisfaction. Then, to Shakespeare's surprise, he switched from English to Latin: "Know you the tongue of the Romans, Magister Guglielmus?"

Remembering Thomas Jenkins, the schoolmaster who'd made sure with a switch that his Latin lessons stuck in his mind, Shakespeare nodded. "Yes, sir, though it is some while since I used it aloud. You would do me a courtesy by speaking slowly."

Nicholas Skeres looked from one of them to the other. A slow flush rose in his cheeks. Sir William Cecil said, "He understands us not, having no Latin of his own."

"Are you certain?" Shakespeare asked. "He seems a man who shows less than he knows."

Burghley nodded heavily. "In that you are not deceived. Beware of him in a brawl, for he will always have a knife up a sleeve or in a boot. But you must believe me when I say Latin is not among the things he conceals."

"Very well, sir." It wasn't very well; Shakespeare trusted Nick Skeres not at all. But he'd taken his protest as far as he could. "What would you say to me that you will not say in his understanding?"

"If you were a scholar of Latin, you must surely have gone through the *Annals* of Tacitus?"

"So I did." Shakespeare nodded, too. "I made heavy going of it, I confess, for he is a difficult author."

"Recall you the passage beginning with the twenty-ninth chapter of the fourteenth book of the said work?"

"Your pardon, sir, but I recollect it not. Did you tell me to what it pertains, my memory might be stirred."

"I shall do better than that. Attend." Peering down at the book now on his lap, Burghley began to read the sonorous Latin text. After a couple of sentences, he glanced at Shakespeare over the tops of his spectacles. "Do you follow?"

"I take the meaning, yes, though I should not care to have to construe the text."

"Meaning suffices," Lord Burghley told him. "You are a scholar no longer, and I am not your master. I will not whip you if you mistake an ablative for a dative. Shall I continue?"

"If you please, sir."

Sir William Cecil read on to the end of the passage. To Shakespeare's relief, he went more slowly after the poet admitted having some trouble following the grammar. When he'd finished, he eyed Shakespeare once more. "See you the dramatic possibilities inhering to that section?"

"I do indeed." Shakespeare had to pause and go slowly and put his thoughts into Latin. The possibilities Burghley had mentioned boiled inside his head. He wanted to talk about them in the plain English in which he wrote. Even more than that, he wanted to flee this fancy house in Drury Lane, get paper and pen and ink, and sit down in his ordinary or some other tolerably quiet place and get to work.

Maybe Lord Burghley saw as much, for he smiled. "And see you how I would have the drama springing from this passage be shaped?"

"Yes." Shakespeare nodded. "You would have the audience construe the Romans here as . . . shall we say, some more recent folk speaking a tongue sprung from Latin. From this, it would follow—"

Burghley held up a hand. "You need say no more, Magister Gulielmus. I see you have nicely divined my purpose. Therefore, to my next question: can you do it?"

Shakespeare fell back into English, for he wanted to be sure he made himself clear: "My lord, I *can* do't; of that, there's no doubt. But *may* I do't? There lies the difficulty, for even the first scratch of pen on paper were treason, let alone any performance based thereon."

"You can say that in English, sure enough, for I already know it," Nick Skeres said.

William Cecil also returned to his native tongue, saying, "One performance is all I expect or hope for."

"By Jesu Christ, God His Son, I do hope so!" Shakespeare said. "For after the first, never would there be—never could there be—a second."

But Burghley shook his head. "Not so. If the first shape events as we hope, think you not that your works will endure not of an age, but for all time?"

"There's a weighty thought!" Nick Skeres' bright little eyes glittered. "I'd give a ballock to be famed forever, beshrew me if I wouldn't."

That such fame might be his had never crossed Shakespeare's mind. Any player who dreamt of such things had to be mad. By the nature of things, his turns on stage were written in the wind. The youngest boy who saw him would grow old and die, and then what was he? A ghost. Worse—a forgotten ghost. He dared hope his plays would last longer than memories of his performances, but hope was only hope. The one playwright he knew who *expected* to be famous was Marlowe, and Kit owned arrogance for an army, and to spare.

Lord Burghley had a point, though; no doubt about it. If he could bring this off, or help to bring it off . . . His own eyes must have gleamed, as Skeres' had a moment before, for Burghley said, "You'll do't, then? You'll bring it to the stage at the appointed time?"

"My lord"—Shakespeare spread his hands helplessly—"you will, I trust, be persuaded I bear you naught but good will. And, bearing you good will, I needs must tell you this presentation you so earnestly desire is less easy to bring to fruition in the proper season than your Grace supposes."

Sir William Cecil's frown put Shakespeare in mind of black clouds piling up before a storm. Here, plainly, was a man unused to hearing qualms or doubts. But, after a long exhalation, the nobleman's only words were, "Say on."

"Gramercy, my lord. Hear me, then." Shakespeare took a long breath of his own before continuing. "I can write the play. With what you have given me, I can shape it into the weapon you desire. I can put the groundlings to choler straight. Being once chafed, they shall not be reined again to temperance."

"Well, then?" Burghley folded his velvet-sleeved arms across his chest, covering the Order of the Garter he wore. "What more is wanted?"

Here a wise man shows himself a fool. Shakespeare reminded himself the theatre was not Burghley's trade. "Look you, my lord, you must bethink yourself: a play is more than words set down on paper. It's men and boys up on the stage, making the words and scenes seem true to those that see 'em."

"And so?" Burghley remained at sea.

But Nick Skeres stirred on his stool. "I know his meaning, my lord!" he exclaimed. "We can trust him—we think we can trust him, anyway." He spoke quickly, confidently; he was at ease in the world of plots and counterplots, as Shakespeare was while treading the boards of the Theatre. "But the play engrosses the whole company. Any one man, learning what's afoot, can discover it to the Spaniards, at which—" He drew his finger across his throat.

"Ah." Now William Cecil nodded. Swinging back toward Shakespeare, he asked, "Think you your troupe of players holds such proditors, as Eden held the serpent?"

"I know not. I would not—I could not—say ay nor nay or ever I sounded them . . . and, in the sounding, I might myself betray."

"A point," Baron Burghley admitted. "A distinct point." He seemed anything but happy, yet did not reject Shakespeare's words because they weren't what he wanted to hear. Shakespeare admired him for that. He asked, "What's to be done, then?"

"A moment, first, an't please you," Shakespeare said, "for I had not rehearsed all the troubles hereto pertaining." He waited for Burghley to nod again before continuing, "This secret, as Master Skeres hath said, must be held by the several men of the company. That alone were no easy matter."

"True enough." Another nod from Burghley. "What else?"

"Not only must they keep it close, sir, they must keep it close over some long stretch of time, wherein they learn their parts and learn to play 'em: all this, of course, in secret. And we shall have to contrive costumes for the Romans and the—"

"Wait." Lord Burghley held up a hand. "How much of this might you scant?"

"Why, as much as you like, my lord," Shakespeare answered. The nobleman looked pleased, till he went on, "If it suit you to have presented a clumsy, aborted botch of a show, we'll dispense with rehearsal altogether. But such a play, wherein we're hissed and pelted from the stage, meseems would serve your ends less well than you desire."

A wordless rumble came from deep within Lord Burghley's chest. "You show me a sea of troubles, Master Shakespeare. How arm we against them? Here you must be my guide: you, not I, are the votary of this mystery."

"I see no sure way," Shakespeare told him, wishing he could say something different. "What seems best is this: to sound the players one by one, in such wise that I give not the game away should a man prefer the Spaniards—or even simple quiet—to daring the slings and arrows of outrageous fortune."

"And if one of them be a cozener or an intelligencer?" Nick Skeres asked. Sure enough, he took conspiracy and betrayal for granted. "How shall you hinder him from sending the lot of you to the block or the gallows or such delightsome toys as only a Spaniard would think to devise?"

"Such is the risk inherent in the exercise," Lord Burghley remarked.

You can say that, Shakespeare thought resentfully. *You'll likely be dead ere we're well begun*. And the nobleman would die in his own time, having lived a long life. But if the players were found out . . . *Skeres had the right of it. Such delightsome toys* . . . He shuddered. He was not a particularly brave man. Counterfeiting courage on the stage, he'd seldom needed it in humdrum everyday life.

"Would you see England free again?" Burghley asked softly.

Ay, there's the rub, Shakespeare thought. Every hamlet in the land dreamt of England free again. He found himself nodding. He could do nothing else.

"Then we'll find ways and means, find them or make them." The baron sounded perfectly confident. Again, Shakespeare silently fumed. *But what can I do save go forward?* He'd already heard enough to make him a dead man if he didn't sing to the Spaniards—*and if things miscarry*, he reminded himself. *If all go well, they'll make of you a hero*.

He had trouble believing it.

Sir William Cecil briskly rubbed his hands together. "We are in accord, then—is't not so?" Shakespeare nodded, still rather less than happily. The nobleman smiled at him. "Commence as quickly as may be. The sooner the play is done, the sooner the players have their parts by heart, the better. Only God knows how long Philip—and Elizabeth—will live. We must be ready."

Shakespeare didn't scream, but he came close. "My lord," he said carefully, "I am now engaged upon preparing a new play for the company, and—"

"This hath greater weight behind it," Burghley said.

Again, screams bubbled just below the surface. "Your Grace, if I cease work upon a play half done, who will not wonder why? Were it not best that I draw no questions to myself?"

"You quibble," Burghley said ominously.

"By God, sir, I do not," Shakespeare answered. "And here's the rest of't: Lord Westmorland's Men will pay me for *Love's Labour's Won*, and pay me well. Who'll pay me for this Roman tragedy? A poet lives not upon sweet breezes and moonbeams; he needs must eat and drink like any man."

"Ah." Burghley nodded. Taking from his belt a small leather sack, he tossed it to Shakespeare, who caught it out of the air. It was heavier than he'd expected. When he undid the drawstring, gold glinted within. His eyes must have widened, for William Cecil let loose another of his wet chuckles. "There's fifty pound," he said carelessly. "An you require more, Nick Skeres will have't for you."

"G-Gramercy," Shakespeare choked out. He'd never made anywhere near so much for a play; most of his income came from his share of the Theatre's takings. He also eyed Skeres. Any sum of money that came through the sharp little man would probably be abridged before reaching its intended destination. Skeres stared back, bland as butter.

"Have we finished here?" Baron Burghley asked. Numbly, Shakespeare nodded. When he got to his feet, his legs, at first, didn't want to hold him up. Burghley said, "Get you gone, Master Shakespeare. I'll away anon. We should not be seen entering or leaving together, nor should you come to my house, though it be nigh. I am here on pretense of waiting on my nephews, Anthony and Francis Bacon."

"Do I meet them on repairing hither another time, know they of this our enterprise?" Shakespeare inquired.

Sir William Cecil looked through him as if he hadn't asked the question. Chuckling, Nick Skeres said, "Any cokes can see you're new to the game. What you know not, e'en the bastinado can't squeeze from you."

Shakespeare made a noise down deep in his throat, nothing close to a word: "Urrr." Skeres might call it a game, but games didn't kill. *Some do*, Shakespeare corrected himself: *baiting the bear or the bull*. He could almost feel fangs tearing into him.

Still shaking his head, he left the house in Drury Lane. He was halfway home before realizing no one had said anything about how Nick Skeres would return to London. He shrugged. Skeres, he was sure, would prove as slippery and evasive as a black-beetle or a rat. He wished he could say the same for himself.

III

Lope de Vega waved to a tall, scrawny Englishman in ragged clothes who stood, as hopefully as he could, by a rowboat. "You there, sirrah!" he said sharply. "How much to row us across to Southwark?" He pointed to the far bank of the Thames.

"Tuppence, sir," the fellow answered, making a clumsy botch of his bow. "A penny each for you and your lady."

"Here, then." Lope gave him two bronze coins. "Put us ashore as near to the bear-baiting garden as you may."

"To the old one, or the new?" the boatman asked.

"To the new," de Vega replied.

"Yes, sir. I'll do't." The Englishman smiled at his companion. "Mind your step as you get in, my lady."

"Have no fear, my dear, my sweet," Lope said grandly, and gave Nell Lumley his arm. She smiled as she took it. She was as tall as he, blond and buxom, and called herself a widow for politeness' sake, though de Vega doubted she'd ever wed. But she was fond of him, and he always enjoyed squiring a pretty woman around. He expected to enjoy lying with her afterwards, too. *Cold country, hot blood*, he thought; Englishwomen had pleasantly surprised him.

And he enjoyed the feeling of being half, or a little more than half, in love. It heated his own blood, as a cup of wine would. As often as not, he discarded one mistress and chose another for no more reason—*but also*, he told himself, *for no less reason*—than to have that sweet intoxication singing through his veins.

So now: he swept off his cloak, folded it a couple of times, and set it on the bench for Nell. She wagged a finger at him. "Ah, Lope, my sweetheart, thou needst not do that."

"I do't not for that I need to," he answered. "I do't for that I want to. Sit, sit, sit, sit." He clucked like a mother hen. Laughing, she sat.

The boatman pushed the rowboat into the Thames, then scrambled aboard himself, his boots dripping. He knew how to handle the oars, feathering them so next to no water dripped from the blades. They hadn't gone far when Nell Lumley wrinkled her short, pert nose. "By Jesu, the river stinks." A dead dog, all puffy and bloated, chose that moment to float past them, heading downstream.

"How can it help stinking?" Lope replied. "It is London's sewer. And London stinks. What city stinks not? The city of heaven, mayhap, proving angels dwell therein."

Of course, folk downstream drank the water into which folk farther upstream poured their shit and piss and offal. Lope knew that. He'd always known it. How could he, how could anyone, help knowing it? But it wasn't anything he usually thought about. He took it for granted, as anyone did. Now, bobbing *on* the stinking stream, he couldn't. He gulped.

" 'Steeth, lean over the side or ever you cast!" the boatman exclaimed.

And put more filth in the river, de Vega thought. He clamped his teeth together. In a little while, the sick spell passed. Nell said, "If passage over the Thames makes thee like to sick up thy dinner, what of coming here in the Invincible Armada?"

Remembering the passage from Lisbon to Dover almost did make him lose his last meal. He patted his mistress' hand and gave her the prettiest lie he could come up with: "The company I keep here makes me forget all that chanced before I set foot on England's shore."

Nell Lumley blushed and stammered. The boatman, sweat starting out under his arms despite the chilly weather, made a distinct retching noise. Lope shot him a hard look. He stared back, only effort on his face. Nell didn't seem to have noticed. Lope let it pass—for the moment. Englishmen were rude by nature.

The boat's keel grated on mud less than a furlong west of London Bridge. "Southwark, sir," the boatman said, as smoothly as if he hadn't been insolent a moment before. He pointed. "There's the new bear-baiting garden—you can see it past the roofs of the stews."

"Yes. Thank you." De Vega handed Nell out of the boat. He tipped the boatman only a farthing. True, the fellow had rowed well, but he didn't intend to forget the way the man had mocked his compliment.

Without a word, the boatman pocketed the small coin. Without a word, he shoved his boat into the Thames and started rowing back toward London. And then, out of range of Lope's rapier, he let fly: "Leather-jerkin, crystal-button, knot-pated, agate-ring, puke-stocking, caddis-garter, smooth-tongue Spanish pouch!"

No matter how useless it was, Lope's hand flew to the hilt of his sword. Nell giggled, which did nothing to improve his temper. She said, "Fret not. He's jealous, nothing more."

"And so he hath good reason to be," Lope answered, mollified, "for am I not the luckiest man alive in Christendom?"

"Ah," Nell said softly, and dropped her eyes.

They had to walk down a street of stews to get to the bear-baiting. Even though de Vega went arm in arm with his companion, the lewd women called out invitations that made his ears burn. Pretending he didn't hear, he kept walking.

"He wants you not," one of the women called to another, "for see you? He hath already a whore of his own."

Where Lope had been angry at the boatman, Nell was furious at the prostitute. "Stinking, poxy callet!" she yelled. "I bite the thumb at thee!" That was the *thee* of insult, not of intimacy.

The contents of a chamber pot came flying out of a third-story window and splashed in the street just in front of them. Fortunately, most of the splash went the other way; Lope and Nell weren't badly fouled.

Nell was still fuming. "Henry VIII closed the stews," she said, "nor did they open again until the coming of . . . Queen Isabella and King Albert."

In different company, she might have said something hot about the Spaniards, Lope thought. But he said only, "King Henry may have closed *these* stews, but surely, in a town the size of London, others flourished."

"That they dared cast whoredom in my face . . ." But Nell didn't directly answer Lope's comment, from which he concluded she couldn't very well disagree with him.

They hurried on toward the bear garden. A long queue of Englishmen and -women of all estates, leavened by a sprinkling of Spaniards, advanced toward the entry. The building was an oval that put de Vega in mind of a Roman amphitheater, though built of wood and not enduring stone. Inside, dogs were already barking and growling furiously.

At the entryway, Lope gave the fellow taking money a pair of pennies. The Englishman waved him forward. At the stairs farther on, most people went up. He handed fourpence to the man waiting there with another cash box. The man gave him a professionally courteous nod. "Want to be in at the death, eh?" he said. "Go on down, then, and find places for yourselves as close to the pit as ye may."

"There!" Nell pointed. A few spaces remained in the very lowest row of benches. "If we hurry—" Now she led Lope, not the other way round. She went so fast, she tripped on the hem of her skirt as she hurried down the stairs. She might have fallen had he not held her up. "Gramercy," she said, and kissed him on the cheek.

An Englishman and his wife and their young son were making for the same seats. They gave Lope and Nell sour looks when they found themselves edged out. The man, a big, burly fellow, muttered something into his beard. "Nay, hush," said his wife, whose pinched face bore what looked to be a perpetually worried expression. "Beshrew me if he be not a don."

"He's a thief, that's what he is," the man rumbled. "He'd steal an egg out of a cloister, he would, like all his breed." But he went off and found seats for himself and his family a good distance away from de Vega. Lope looked back over his shoulder and bared his teeth in what was as much a challenge as a smile. The Englishman would not meet his eye. Lope nodded to himself, proud as a fighting cock that hadn't had to use his spurs to beat a rival.

Down in the pit, the first bear was already chained to the stout iron stake in the center of the earthen floor. He was a good-sized beast, and didn't look too badly starved. His hot, rank odor filled Lope's nostrils. The mastiffs, still caged, smelled him, too. Their barking grew more frantic by the moment.

The Englishman sitting next to Lope nudged him and said, "Half a crown on old bruin there to slay before they kill him six dogs or more. If you like, a crown."

Lope eyed him. He wasn't all that well dressed; five shillings—even two and sixpence—would be a lot of money for him. And he looked a little too eager, a little too confident. Men who knew too much about bears and dogs were the bane of the garden, cheating those without inside information. "I thank you, but no," de Vega said. "I'm here for to watch the fight, no more." The Englishman looked disappointed, but Lope had declined too politely for him to make anything of it.

"A cozener?" Nell asked in a low voice.

"Without a doubt," Lope answered.

A wineseller moved through the crowd. Nell waved to him. Lope bought a cup for her and one for himself.

He looked around the arena. It was almost full now. Before long, they would . . . He couldn't even finish the thought before they did. One man with a lever could lift the movable sides of all the mastiffs' cages at once. Baying like the wolves their cousins, the great dogs swarmed into the baiting pit.

One died almost at once, his neck broken by a shrewd buffet from the bear's great paw. The rest of the mastiffs, more furious than ever, leaped at the bear, clamping their jaws to his leg, his haunch, his belly, his ear. Roaring almost like a lion, he rolled in the dirt, crushing another animal beneath him. A couple of other mastiffs sprang free before his weight fell on them. Muzzles already red with blood, they sprang back into the fight.

"Oh, bravely done!" Nell Lumley cried from behind Lope. She clapped her hands. Her eyes glistened. "Tear him to pieces!"

Nor was hers the only voice raised in the bear garden. Shouts of, "Kill him!" and, "Bite him!" rose from all three levels. So did yells of, "Rend the dogs!" and, "Rip 'em to rags!" Some of those surely came from folk who'd put money on the bear. But the English, seeing one animal chained and attacked by ten, were perversely likely to take him into their hearts, at least for a little while.

As if by accident, de Vega let his hand rest on Nell's thigh. She stared at him in surprise; she might have forgotten he was there. Her cheeks were flushed, her lips slightly swollen. She set her hand on his. He smiled and kissed her. The noise she made at the back of her throat was almost as fierce as the ones coming from the pit. Lope laughed a little when they finally broke apart. Bear- and bull-baitings always made her wanton.

Three dogs were dead now, and a couple of others badly hurt. But blood dripped and poured from the bear everywhere. He wobbled on his feet; a pink loop of gut protruded from his belly. His grunts and bellows came slower and weaker. "He'll not last," Lope said. Nell nodded without looking at him—she had eyes only for the pit.

As if directed by a single will, all the mastiffs left alive, even the injured ones, sprang at the bear. As their teeth pierced him, Nell groaned as if Lope were piercing her. The bear fought back for a moment, but then sank beneath the dogs. The din in the arena all but deafened de Vega.

The shabby Englishman sitting next to him nudged him again. "See you? You'd have won. He slew but four, unless that fifth be too much hurt to live."

Lope said, "Such is life," a remark that gave the other man no room to comment.

Dog handlers in thick leather jerkins and breeches came out to drive the mastiffs back into their cages. They needed the bludgeons they carried to get the big dogs off the bear's carcass. Once the dogs were out of the pit, an ass that rolled its eyes at the stink of blood dragged away the body. It would be butchered, and the meat sold.

"Hast thou eaten of bear's flesh?" Lope asked Nell.

She nodded. "Seldom, but yes. Mighty fine it was, too: sweet as pork, tender as lamb."

"I thought the same," Lope said. "I ate it once or twice in Spain. Were bears common as cattle, who would look at beef?"

More attendants raked the ground and spread sand and fresh dirt over the pools of blood. The first bear-baiting might never have happened. So Lope's senses said, at any rate. But when the handlers brought the next bear out to the stake, the lingering scent of blood in the air made him so wild, he almost broke free of them.

A fresh pack of mastiffs assailed the bear. He was smaller than the one that had fought before, but seemed wilier. He rolled again and again, and hunched himself so the dogs had trouble reaching his belly and privates. Mastiff after mastiff went down. Another one dragged itself out of the fight on stiff forelegs, its back broken. A handler smashed in its head with a club.

"He'll kill them all!" Nell was as happy to cheer for the bear as she had been to clap for the dogs in the first fight.

And the new bear *did* kill them all. As the last mastiff, its throat torn out, staggered off and fell down to die, Lope thought, *Most of the bettors want to hang themselves—that hardly ever happens. And the dog breeders, too, with so many expensive animals dead.* A whole new pack of mastiffs had to be loosed against the bear. Since it had taken so many wounds from the earlier pack, the baiting ended in a hurry.

That was as well. London's short day was drawing to a close. Lope rose and gave Nell Lumley his arm. "Shall we away to the city and find a place for the two of us?"

Her answering smile had nothing coy in it. "Yes, let's," she said. Sure enough, after a bear-baiting her own animal spirits were in the ascendant.

Lope and Nell had just left the bear-baiting garden when someone called his name from behind. It was a woman's voice. As if in the grip of nightmare, Lope slowly turned. Out of the arena came his other mistress, Martha Brock, walking with a man who looked enough like her to be her brother, and probably was.

He would be, Lope thought in helpless horror. *If she were betraying me, she couldn't get in much of a temper. But if she's not . . . Oh, by the Virgin, if she's not . . . !* Too late, he realized the Virgin was the wrong one to ask for intercession here.

"Who's that?" Martha Brock demanded, pointing at Nell.

"Who's *that*?" Nell Lumley demanded, pointing at Martha.

"Dear ladies, I can explain—" Lope began hopelessly.

He never got the chance. He hadn't thought he would. "You are no surer, no, than is the coal of fire upon the ice, or hailstone in the sun!" Nell cried. "And I loved you!"

"Impersevant thing!" Martha added. "A truant disposition!"

Lope tried again. "I can expl—"

Again, no good. They both screamed at him. They both slapped him. They didn't even quarrel with each other, which might have saved him. When they both burst into tears and cried on each others shoulders, Martha's brother said, "Sirrah, thou'rt a recreant blackguard. Get thee hence!" He didn't even touch his sword. With de Vega so plainly in the wrong, he didn't need it.

Jeered by the Englishmen who'd watched his discomfiture, Lope walked back toward the Thames all alone. When Pizarro's men conquered the Incas, one of them got as his share of the loot a great golden sun . . . and gambled it away before morning. He'd made himself a Spanish proverb, too. *But here I've outdone him,* Lope thought glumly. *I lost not one mistress, but two, and both in the wink of an eye.*

WILL KEMP LEERED AT SHAKESPEARE. THE CLOWN'S FEATURES WERE soft as clay, and could twist into any shape. What lay behind his mugging? Shakespeare couldn't tell. "The first thing we do," Kemp exclaimed, "let's kill all the Spaniards!"

He didn't even try to keep his voice down. They were alone in the tiring room, but the tireman or his assistants or the Theatre watchmen might overhear. "God mend your voice," Shakespeare hissed. "You but offend your lungs to speak so loud."

"Not my lungs alone," Kemp said innocently. "Are *you* not offended?"

"Offended? No." Shakespeare shook his head. "Afeard? Yes, I am afeard."

"And wherefore?" the clown asked. "Is't not the desired outcome of that which you broached to me just now?"

"Of course it is," Shakespeare answered. "But would the fountain of your mind were clear again, you prancing ninny, that I might water an ass at it. Do you broadcast it to the general before the day, our heads go up on London Bridge and cur-dogs fatten on our bodies."

"Ah, well. Ah, well." Maybe Kemp hadn't thought of that at all. Maybe, too, he'd done his best to give Shakespeare an apoplexy. His best was much too good. He went on, "An you write the play, I'll act in't. There." He beamed at Shakespeare. "Are you happy now, my pet?" He might have been soothing a fractious child.

"Why could you not have said that before?" Shakespeare did his best to hold his temper, but couldn't help adding another, "Why?"

"You want everything all in its place." Again, Will Kemp might have been—likely was—humoring him. "I can see how that might be so for you—after all, you'd want Act First done or ever you went on to Act Second, eh?"

"I should hope so," Shakespeare said between his teeth. What was the clown prattling about now?

Kemp deigned to explain: "But you're a poet, and so having all in order likes you well. But for a clown?" He shook his head. "As like as not, I've no notion what next I'll do on stage."

"I've noticed that. We've all of us noticed that," Shakespeare said.

"Good!" Kemp twisted what had been meant for a reproach into a compliment. "If I know not, nor can the groundlings guess. The more they're surprised, the harder they laugh."

"Regardless of how your twisted turn mars the fabric o' the play," Shakespeare said.

Kemp only shrugged. Shakespeare would have been angrier had he expected anything else. The clown said, "I know not what I'll do tomorrow, nor care. If I play, then I play. If I choose instead to morris-dance from London to Norwich, by God, I'll do that. I'll do well by it, too." He seemed to fancy the ridiculous idea. "Folk would pay to watch me on the way, and I might write a book afterwards. *Kemp's Nine Days Wonder*, I'd call it."

"No man could in nine days dance thither," Shakespeare said, interested in spite of himself.

"I've ten pound to say you're a liar." By the gleam in Kemp's eye, he was ready to strap bells on his legs and set off with a man to play the flute and drums. He'd meant what he told Shakespeare—he didn't know what he'd do next, on stage or anywhere else. "Come on, poet. Will you match me?"

The man's a weathervane, blowing now this way, now that, in the wind of his appetites, Shakespeare thought. He held up a placating hand. "I haven't the money to set against you," he lied. "Let it be even as you claim. Fly not to Norwich, nor to any other place." He realized he was pleading. "You perform this afternoon, you know, and on the morrow as well."

"There's no more valor in you than in a wild duck," Kemp said scornfully. "You are as valiant as the wrathful dove, or most magnanimous mouse."

He told the truth. Shakespeare knew too well how little courage he held. But he wagged a finger at Will Kemp and said, "If you'd bandy insults, think somewhat before you speak. You twice running used *valor*; it might better in the first instance have been *courage*."

"Woe upon you, and all such false professors!" Kemp retorted. "O judgement! Thou art fled to brutish beasts."

Shakespeare threw his hands in the air. "Enough!" And so, however maddening, it was. Kemp had, in his own way, said he'd do what needed doing. Shakespeare didn't think the clown would betray him to the Spaniards after that—not on purpose, anyhow. "Not a word now, on your life," he warned. *On my life, too, not that Kemp cares a farthing for't.*

"What, gone without a word?" the clown said. "Oh, very well, for your joy."

When Shakespeare came out of the tiring room, he felt he'd aged ten years. The tireman gave him a curious glance. "What's toward?" he asked.

"That Kemp is more stubborn-hard than hammered iron," Shakespeare said disdainfully, telling the truth and acting at the same time. "At last, meseems, he hath been brought towards reason."

"Towards doing what you'd have him do, you mean," the tireman said. His name was Jack Hungerford. His beard, which once had been red, was now white; that only made his eyes seem bluer. He'd had charge of costumes and props for decades before Marlowe's *Tamberlane* made blank verse the standard for plays, and he had all the shrewdness of his years.

Here, though, he played into Shakespeare's hands. "I'll not say you're mistaken," the poet replied, and Hungerford looked smug. But keeping the tireman happy wasn't enough. As much as the players, he would be a part of what followed. Shakespeare picked his words with care: "How now, Master Jack? You've seen more than is to most men given."

"And if I have?" Hungerford asked. His eyes were suddenly intent, while the rest of his face showed nothing whatever. Shakespeare had seen that blank vizard more times than he could count, these years since the Armada landed. Indeed, he'd worn that blank vizard more times than he could count. It was an Englishman's shield against discovery, against treachery, in a land no longer his own. Having it raised against him saddened Shakespeare, but he understood why Hungerford showed so little. The safest answer to the question *Whom to trust?* was *No one*.

He'll make me discover myself to him, Shakespeare thought unhappily. *Then the risk is mine, not his. Well, no help for't.* He said, "You well recall the days before Isabella and Albert took the throne."

" 'Twas not so long ago, Master Will," Hungerford replied, his tone studiously neutral. "You recall 'em yourself, though you've only half my years."

"Good days, I thought," Shakespeare said.

"Some were. Some not so good." The tireman revealed nothing, nothing at all. Behind Shakespeare's back, one of his hands folded into a fist. *I might have known it would be like this.* But then Hungerford went on, "Better days, I will allow, than some of those we live in. I say as much—I hope I say as much—not only for that a man's youth doth naturally seem sweeter in the years of his age."

"Think you those good days might come again?"

"I know not," Hungerford said, and Shakespeare wanted to hit him. "Would it were so, but I know not."

Was that enough encouragement to go on? Shakespeare didn't think so. *Damn you, Jack Hungerford*, he raged, but only to himself. He stalked away from the tireman as if Hungerford had offered him some deadly insult. Behind him, Hungerford called for one of his assistants. If he knew where Shakespeare had been heading, he gave no sign of it.

That day, Lord Westmorland's Men put on Marlowe's *The Cid*. Shakespeare had only a small part: one of the Moorish princes whom the Cid first befriended and then, in the name of Christianity, betrayed. He unwound his turban, shed his bright green robe, and left the Theatre early, hoping to take advantage of what little daylight was left in the sky.

Booksellers hawked their wares in the shadow of St. Paul's. Most of them sold pamphlets denouncing Protestantism and hair-raising accounts of witches out in the countryside. Some others offered the texts of plays—as often as not pirated editions, printed up from actors' memories of their lines. The volumes usually proved actors' memories less than they might have been.

Shakespeare ground his teeth as he walked past a stall full of such plays. He'd suffered from stolen and surreptitious publications himself. That he got nothing for them was bad enough. That they mangled his words was worse. What they'd done to his *Prince of Denmark* . . .

He'd added injury to insult by buying his own copy of that one, to see if it were as bad as everyone told him. It wasn't. It was worse. When he thought about the Prince's so-called soliloquy:

> To be, or not to be. Aye there's the point.
> To die, to sleep, is that all? Aye all:
> No, to sleep, to dream, aye marry there it goes.

He'd seen that, burned it into his memory, so he could quote it as readily as what he'd really written. He could—but he didn't have the stomach to get past the third line.

Splendid in his red robes, a bishop came out of St. Paul's and down the steps, surrounded by a retinue of more plainly dressed priests and laymen. The soldiers on guard at the bottom of the stairs stiffened to attention. One of them—by his fair hair, surely an Englishman—knelt to kiss the cleric's ring as he went past.

The Spaniards enslaved some of us, Shakespeare thought. *Others, though—others enslaved themselves*. No one had made that soldier bend the knee to the bishop. No one would have thought less of him had he not done it. But he had. By all appearances, he'd been proud to do it.

Even if I go on with this madcap scheme, will it have the issue Lord Burghley desires? Shakespeare shrugged. He'd come too far to back away now unless he inclined to treason. *That might save you. It might make you rich.* He shrugged again. Some things were bought too dear.

Motion up at the top of St. Paul's caught his eye. A man in artisan's plain hose and jerkin was walking about on the flat-roofed steeple, now and then stooping as if to measure. *We have a Catholic Queen and King once more. Will they order the spire finished at last?* Shakespeare shrugged one more time. *It would be yet another sign we are not what we were, what we once set out to be. But how many even care?* Gloom threatened to choke him.

Gloom also made him inattentive, so that he almost walked past the stall he sought. It wasn't the sight of the books that made him pause, but the sight of the bookseller. "Good den, Master Seymour," he said.

"Why, Master Shakespeare! God give you good den as well," Harry Seymour replied. He was a tall, lean man who would have been good-looking had he not had a large, hairy wen on the end of his nose. "Do you but pass the time of day, or can I find summat for you?"

"I'm always pleased to pass the time of day with you," Shakespeare answered, which was true: he'd never known Seymour to print or sell pirated plays. He went on, "But if you've the *Annals* of Tacitus done into English, I'd be pleased to buy it of you."

"As my head lives, Master Shakespeare, I do indeed. And I'll take oath I fetched hither some few of that title this morning." Seymour came around to the front of the stall. "Now where did I put 'em? . . . Ah! Here we are." He handed Shakespeare a copy. "Will you want it for a play?"

"I might. But my Latin doth stale with disuse, wherefore I'm fain to take the short road to reminding me what he treats of." Shakespeare admired the ornate first page, illustrated with a woodcut of swaggering, toga-clad Romans. "A handsome volume, I'll not deny."

" 'Twould be handsomer still, cased in buckram or fine morocco." Like any book dealer, Seymour sold his wares unbound; what boards they eventually wore depended on the customer's taste and purse.

"No doubt," Shakespeare said politely, by which he meant he didn't intend to bind the book at all. Not even Baron Burghley's gold could tempt him to such extravagance. As a player and a poet, he knew too well how money could rain down one day and dry up the next. He would cling to as many of those coins as he could. In aid of which . . . He held up the translation. "What's the scot?"

"Six shillings," Harry Seymour answered.

"My good fellow, you are a thief professed," Shakespeare exclaimed. "But your theft is too open. Your filching is like an unskilful singer; you keep not time."

"Say what you will, Will, but I'll have my price or you'll not have your book," Seymour said. "I give thanks to the holy Mother of God that I can stay at my trade at all. Times are hard, and grow no easier."

"I am not some wanderer, staggering half drunk past your stall. I do regularly give you my custom when I seek some work of scholarship—or so I have done, up till now." Shakespeare's indignation was part perfectly real, part feigned. If he gave in too easily, the bookseller might wonder why—and Seymour's oath had proved him a Catholic. *I must seem as I always was*, Shakespeare thought. The deeper into this exercise he got, the harder that would grow.

"You know not what I had to pay Master Daniels, the which rendered into our tongue the noble Roman's words," Seymour protested.

Sensing weakness, Shakespeare pressed him: "That you're a subtle knave, a villain with a smiling cheek, makes you no less a knave and a villain." He made as if to thrust the *Annals* back at Seymour.

The bookseller had grit. "Save your player's tricks for the stage," he said. "I gave you my price."

"And I give you my farewell, if you use me so." Shakespeare didn't want to have to search for a different translation elsewhere, not when he had this one in his hands, but he didn't want to pay six shillings, either. Nine days' wages for a soldier, on one book?

Harry Seymour made a rumbling, unhappy noise down deep in his throat. "Five and sixpence, then," he said, as if wounded unto death, "and for no other man alive would I lessen the price e'en a farthing."

His honor salved, Shakespeare paid at once, saying, "There, you see? I knew you for the gentleman you are, exceedingly well read and wondrous affable: stuffed, as they say, with honorable parts."

"You reckon him a gentleman who doth as you list," Seymour said sourly. "Go your way, Master Shakespeare; I am yet out of temper with you. May you have joy of the sixpence you prised from me."

His joy in that sixpence quite quenched, Shakespeare strode north and east, back towards his Bishopsgate lodgings. Light faded from the sky with every step he took. The winter solstice was coming soon, with Christmas hard on its heels. They were both coming sooner, indeed, than he reckoned right. After their coronation, Isabella and Albert had imposed on England Pope Gregory's newfangled calendar, cutting ten days out of June in 1589 to bring the kingdom into conformity with Spain and the rest of Catholic Europe. When Shakespeare looked at things logically, he understood those ten days weren't really stolen. When he didn't—which was, mankind being what it was, more often—he still felt as if he'd had his pocket picked of time.

Some stubborn souls still celebrated the feast of the Nativity on what Gregory's calendar insisted was January 4. They did so in secret. They had to do so in secret, for the English Inquisition prowled hardest at this season of the year, sniffing after those who showed affection for the old calendar and thus for the Protestant faith adhering to it.

Along with darkness, fog began filling the streets. Here and there, men lit cressets in front of their homes and shops, but the flickering flames did little to pierce the gloom. Shakespeare hurried up Cheapside to the Poultry, past the smaller churches of St. Peter and St. Mildred, and up onto Threadneedle Street, which boasted on the west side churches dedicated to St. Christopher-le Stock and St. Bartholomew. He let out a sigh of relief when Threadneedle Street opened on to Bishopsgate. A moment later, he let out a gasp, for a squad of Spaniards tramped toward him. But their leader only gave him a brusque jerk of the thumb, as if to tell him to hurry home.

"I thank our worship," he murmured, and touched his hand to the brim of his hat as he ducked down the side street that would take him to the Widow Kendall's. The Spaniard nodded in return and led his men south and west along Threadneedle. *A decent man doing well the task to which he was set*, Shakespeare thought. More than a few of the occupiers *were* decent men. Still, the task to which Philip had set them was the subjugation of England. And, on nine years' evidence, they did it well.

"Oh, Master Will, 'tis good to see you," Jane Kendall said when Shakespeare came into her house. As he went over to stand by the fire, she continued, "I was sore afeard them Spanish devils had took you."

"Not so. As you see, I'm here." Shakespeare looked around the parlor. "But where's Master Foster? Most days, he is before me, and, having somewhat to do betwixt close of Theatre and my coming hither, I know I am later than I might be."

"Later than you ought to be," the Widow Kendall said in reproving tones. "And as for Master Peter—"

Before she could go on, Jack Street broke in: "He's in the Hole. They nabbed him at last. I wouldn't guess what his law was, but outside *the* law, certes."

Shakespeare didn't know what his missing roommate's illegal specialty was, either, but wasn't surprised to learn those in authority thought Peter Foster had one. "Can we do aught for him?" he asked.

Jack Street gloomily shook his head. "Not unless we want them bastards asking after us next," the glazier said, which struck Shakespeare as altogether too likely.

"He's paid till the end of the month," Widow Kendall said. "An he bide yet in gaol then, I'll sell his goods for what they bring." She thought more of what she might do for herself than for her lodger.

After warming himself by the fire, Shakespeare went off to the ordinary around the corner for supper. A sizzling beefsteak and half a loaf to sop up the juices made him a happy man. He took out his quill and his bottle of ink and set to work on *Love's Labour's Won*. "By God, Master Will, what is it like, to have so many words in your head?" the serving woman asked.

"So that they come forth, Kate, all's well," he answered. "But if my thoughts be dammed, then I'm damned with them." He pounded his forehead with the heel of his hand to try to show her the feeling he got when the words would not move from his mind to the page in front of him.

She laughed and nodded and said, "Will another mug of beer loose the flow?"

"One other may," he said, and she poured his mug full from the pitcher she carried. He went on, "Ask me not again, I pray you, for with too much drink I've trouble knowing whether the words that come be worth the having."

"I'll leave you to't, then," Kate said, and she did.

But tonight the words, whether worth the having or not, did not want to come. Shakespeare stared into the candle flame and tried all the other tricks he knew to break the wall between his wit and his pen, but had little luck. While the upper part of his mind dutifully tried to get on with *Love's Labour's Won*, the deeper wellspring, the part from which inspiration sprang, dwelt with the woes of the ancient Iceni, not with his present characters. He smote his forehead again, this time in good earnest. The sudden pain did him no good, either.

He looked around in frustration. He had none but himself to blame for his troubles. The hour grew late; he was the only customer left in the place. With everything quiet and serene, he should have written as if fiends were after him. He muttered a curse. Fiends *were* after him, but not the sort that set his pen free.

When Kate came by again, he laid down the pen with a sigh. She gave him a sympathetic smile, saying, "I saw you troubled, but did not like to speak, for fear I might send flying the one word that'd free you."

"That word's nowhere to be found tonight, or else already flown," Shakespeare answered ruefully. "Were my pen a poniard, it would not stab."

"Say not so, for I know thy yard pierces," Kate said. Her smile, this time, was of a different kind.

"Ah. Sits the wind in *that* quarter, then?" Without waiting for an answer, Shakespeare got to his feet. Even at such a moment, he was careful to gather up his precious manuscript and pens and ink before heading for the stairway with the serving woman. "Thou'rt sweet, Kate, to give of thyself to a spring gone dry like me."

"Spring's a long way off, and it's cold outside," she said. "And I doubt me thou'rt dry in all thy humors. Else, after last we lay between the sheets, why found I a wet spot there?"

Laughing, he slipped an arm around her waist. "I own myself outargued," he said. She snuggled against him and sighed softly. He held up his papers. "Belike thou couldst outwrite me, too. Art fain to try?"

"Go to," she said. "Me that needs must make a mark to set down my name?"

They came to the top of the stairs. Her door stood just to the right. She opened it. They went inside. Kate closed the door. Shakespeare took her in his arms. "Kiss me," he said. She did.

When he left the ordinary, he'd come no further forward on *Love's Labour's Won*. His head was high and he had a spring in his step even so. He started to whistle a ballad, then fell silent and shrank into a dark doorway when he heard other footsteps coming down the dark street. If it wasn't curfew time, it was close. Running into a patrol now was the last thing he wanted. The men who walked by spoke in low voices, and in English. He would have bet they too didn't want to run into a patrol.

And he didn't want to run into them, either, and silently sighed with relief when they vanished into the fog.

He sat down at the table in the parlor once he got back to his lodgings, hoping he could set a few words down on paper before he got too sleepy to work. But he hadn't written above a line and a half before Peter Foster stuck his head into the room to see what was going on. "Oh. Master Will. God give you good even," he said.

"Give you good even," Shakespeare echoed automatically. Then he gaped. "They said you were in the Hole!"

"Why, so I was." Foster laid a finger by the side of his nose. "God gave me a good even, and a good set of gilks and a bit of charm besides." He held up the skeleton keys for Shakespeare to admire. He looked like a man used to picking locks, sure enough.

"Bravely done," the poet said. "But will they not come after you again?"

"Since when? Belike the turnkey knows not I'm gone," Peter Foster said with fine contempt. "Nay, Will, I'll couch a hogshead here tonight, then budge a beak come morning. I tell you true, I'll be glad to 'scape that sawmill who sleeps with us."

"As you reckon best," Shakespeare said with a shrug. "Me, I'd not care to sleep here in my own bed before fleeing the sheriffs."

"You fret more than I," Foster said, not unkindly; perhaps he was doing his best not to call Shakespeare a coward. "May I turn Turk if they're here or ever I'm gone. You've seen naught of me, mind."

"Think what you will of me, but I'm no delator," Shakespeare said. *And if they pull off my boots and give me the bastinado till I can bear no more?* He did his best not to think about that. He was glad when Peter Foster nodded, apparently satisfied, and went off to bed. But, by the way *Love's Labour's Won* foundered, it might have been aboard Sir Patrick Spens' ship on the luckless voyage to Norway. Shakespeare went to bed himself. Jack Street did indeed make the night hideous, but his snores were the least of what kept Shakespeare awake so long.

When he got up, Foster was gone. No one had come after the clever little man with the interesting tools. Shakespeare went off to the Theatre in a thoughtful mood. His roommate knew crime as he himself knew poesy, and might well have made a better living at his chosen trade.

"*BUENOS DÍAS*, YOUR EXCELLENCY," LOPE DE VEGA SAID, SWEEPING off his hat and bowing to Captain Baltasar Guzmán. "How may I serve you this morning?"

"*Buenos días*, Lieutenant," Guzmán replied. "First of all, let me compliment you on *La dama boba*. Your lady was a most delightful boob, and I thoroughly enjoyed watching her antics yesterday."

Lope bowed again, this time almost double. "I am your servant, sir!" he exclaimed in delight. His superior had never before paid him such a compliment for his theatrical work—or, indeed, for work of any other kind.

Captain Guzmán went on, "And my compliments especially for wringing such a fine performance from your Diego. I know that cannot have been easy."

"Had I known I would have to use him, I would have made the servant a sleepier man," de Vega said. "As things were—" He mimed cracking a whip over Diego's back.

"Even so." Guzmán nodded. Then he raised an elegant eyebrow and asked, "Tell me: after which of your mistresses was Lady Nisea modeled? Or should I say, which of your former mistresses? The story is, they had it in mind to throw you into the bear pit for the mastiffs' sport."

"Please believe me, your Excellency, it was not so bad as that." He asked Captain Guzmán to believe him. He didn't tell his superior that what he said was true.

Guzmán's eyebrows rose higher still. "No, eh? It certainly has been a mighty marvel hereabouts. I suppose I should admire your energy, if not your luck at the bear garden. Everyone who saw them says a man would be lucky to have one such woman, let one two."

How can I answer that? de Vega wondered. Deciding he couldn't, he didn't try. Instead, he repeated, "How may I serve you, sir?"

Rather than answering him directly, Baltasar Guzmán said, "Your timing could have been better, Lieutenant. In fact, it could hardly have been worse."

"Sir?"

"Have you forgotten you are to meet with Cardinal Parsons this morning?" Guzmán eyed him, then assumed a severe expression. "I see you have. What a pity. It could be that the Cardinal, being an Englishman and having just come from Canterbury, has not heard of your, ah, escapade. It could be. I hope it is. But I would not count on it. The man is devilishly well informed."

Lope sighed. "Yes, sir. I know he is," he said glumly. "I'll do the best I can."

"Splendid. I'm sure you said the same to both your lady friends."

Ears burning, Lope beat a hasty retreat from Captain Guzmán's office. As he'd feared, Enrique waylaid him in the hall. Guzmán's servant also bubbled with enthusiasm for *La dama boba*. "I especially admired Nisea's transformation from a boob to a woman with a mind—and a good mind—of her own," he said.

Since Lope had worked especially hard to bring off that transformation, Enrique's praise should have delighted him. And, in fact, it did leave him pleased, but he had no time for Enrique now. "You will excuse me, I hope," he said, "but I'm on my way to St. Paul's."

"Oh, yes, of course, for your meeting with the Archbishop of Canterbury." Enrique nodded wisely. *Everyone knows my business better than I do*, de Vega thought with a stab of resentment. Captain Guzmán's servant continued, "He is a very wise man, and a very holy man, too, no doubt."

"I know," Lope said, desperate to be gone. "If you will excuse me—" Retreating still, he hurried out of the Spanish barracks and west to the greatest cathedral in London. The booksellers near the steps tempted him to linger, but he resisted temptation and went up the stairs and into the great church. *If books came bound in skirts, though* . . . Annoyed at himself, he shook his head to try to dislodge the vagrant thought.

A deacon came up to him as he stepped into the cool, dim quiet. "And you would be, sir . . . ?" the fellow asked in English.

Lope proudly replied in his own Castilian tongue: "I have the honor to call myself Senior Lieutenant Lope Félix de Vega Carpio."

He was not surprised to find the deacon spoke Spanish, too. "Ah, yes. You will be here to meet the Archbishop of Canterbury. Come with me, *señor*."

Quiet evaporated as the deacon led de Vega through the cathedral. Masterless men dickered with merchants and artisans who might have work for them. Lawyers in rich robes traded gossip. Smiling bonarobas, fragrant with sweet perfume and showing as much soft flesh as they dared, lingered near the lawyers. One of the women smiled at Lope. He ignored her, which turned the smile to a scowl. He didn't care to buy a tart's favors, no matter how fancy and lovely she was: he preferred to fall in love, or at least to imagine he'd fallen in love. *And what's the difference?* he wondered. *Only how long the feeling lasts.*

"Do have a care," the deacon warned him. "Picking pockets, or slitting them, is a sport here."

"This too, I suppose, is Christian charity," Lope said. The deacon gave him an odd look.

Away from the vast public spaces of St. Paul's were the chambers the clergy used for their own. The deacon led de Vega to one of those. Then, like Enrique going in to see Captain Guzmán, he said, "Wait here for a moment, please," and ducked into the room by himself. When he returned, he beckoned. "His Eminence awaits you with pleasure."

"He is too kind," Lope murmured.

Even in the rich regalia of a cardinal, Robert Parsons looked like a monk. His face was long and thin and pale; his close-cropped, graying beard did nothing to hide the hollows under his cheekbones. He held out his ring for de Vega to kiss. "I am pleased to make your acquaintance, Senior Lieutenant," he said in Latin.

"Thank you, your Eminence," Lope replied in the same language. He switched to English: "I speak your tongue, sir, an you have no Spanish."

"I prefer Latin. It is more precise," Parsons said. By his appearance, he was nothing if not a precise man.

"As you wish, of course." Lope hoped his own Latin would meet the test. He read it well, but he was no clergyman, and so did not often speak it. "I am at your service in every way."

"Good." Cardinal Parsons looked down at some notes on his desk and nodded to himself. "I am told you are the Spanish officer most concerned with sniffing out treason in the English theatre."

"Yes, your Eminence, I believe that to be true," Lope answered, pleased he'd remembered to use the infinitive.

"This is because"—the Archbishop of Canterbury checked his notes again—"you are yourself an aspiring dramatist?"

"Yes, your Eminence," de Vega repeated, wondering if the English churchman would take him to task for it.

But Parsons only said, "I am glad to hear it, Lieutenant. For treason *is* afoot in that sphere, and you, being familiar with its devices, are less likely to let yourself be cozened than would someone uninitiated in its mysteries."

Lope had to think before he answered. The cardinal's Latin was so fluent, so confident, he might have been whisked by a sorcerer from the days of Julius Caesar to this modern age. He made no concessions to

Lope's weaker Latinity; Lope got the idea Parsons made few concessions to anyone, save possibly the Pope.

"Your Eminence, I go to the theatre more to watch the audience than to watch the actors," de Vega said. "Many of them I know well, and they have not shown themselves disloyal to Queen Isabella and King Albert."

Robert Parsons snorted like a horse. Lope needed a moment to realize that was intended for laughter. Parsons said, "And how likely is it that they would declare their treason before an officer of his Most Catholic Majesty of Spain?"

"You make me out to be a fool, a child," Lope said angrily.

"By no means, Lieutenant." The Archbishop of Canterbury's smile was cold as winter along the Scottish border. "With your own words, you make yourself out to be such."

Without his intending it, de Vega's hand moved a couple of inches toward the hilt of his rapier. He arrested the motion. Even if he was insulted, drawing sword on a prelate would certainly send him to gaol, and probably to hell. He gave the cardinal a stiff bow. "If you will excuse me, your Eminence—"

"I will not." Parsons' voice came sharp as a whipcrack. "I tell you there is treason amongst these men, and you will be God's instrument in flensing it out."

"But, your Eminence"—Lope spread his hands—"if they do not show it to me, how can I find it? There is no treason in plays that are performed. The Master of the Revels sees and approves them before a play reaches the stage. Sir Edmund Tilney is the one who will know if the poets plan sedition—indeed, he has arrested some for trying to say what must not be said."

Like Parsons' face, his fingers were long and thin and pale. When he drummed them on the desktop, they reminded de Vega of a spider's legs. "Again, you speak of overt treason," Parsons said. "The enemies of God and Spain, like Satan their patron, are more subtle than that. They skulk. They conspire. They—"

"With whom?" Lope broke in.

"I shall tell you with whom: with the English nobles who still dream of setting at liberty that murderous heretic jade, Elizabeth their former Queen." Parsons' eyes flashed. "King Philip was too merciful by half in not burning her when first she was seized, and again in not slaying more of the men who served her and upheld her while she ruled."

He had, Lope remembered, spent more than twenty years in exile from his native land. When he spoke of skulking and conspiring, he spoke of what he knew. Cautiously, de Vega asked, "Have you anyone in particular in mind?"

He expected the Archbishop of Canterbury to name Christopher Marlowe—everyone seemed to put Marlowe at the head of his list of troublemakers—or George Chapman or Robert Greene (though Greene, he'd heard, was ill unto death after eating of a bad dish of pickled herring). But Parsons, after an abrupt nod, replied, "Yes. A slanderous villain by the name of William Shakespeare."

"Shakespeare?" Lope said in surprise. "I pray your Eminence to forgive me, but you must be mistaken. I know Shakespeare well. He is a man of good temper—of better temper than most poets, I would say."

"What of the friends of poets?" Cardinal Parsons asked.

Lope needed a heartbeat to notice he'd put the feminine ending on *friends*. Well, Baltasar Guzmán had warned not much got past the cardinal, and he was right. "Your Eminence!" Lope said reproachfully.

"Let it go. Let it go. Forget I said it," Parsons told him. "But I warn you, Lieutenant, there is more to that man than meets the eye. He has been seen in homes where a man of his station has no fit occasion to call, and he keeps company no honest man would keep, or want to keep."

"He knows Marlowe well," Lope said. "Knowing Marlowe, he will also know Marlowe's acquaintances. Many of them, I fear, are men such as you describe."

"There is more to it than that," Cardinal Parsons insisted. "I do not know how much more. That, I charge you to uncover. But I tell you, Lieutenant, there is more to find." His nostrils quivered, like those of a hunting hound straining to take a scent.

Captain Guzmán had dark suspicions about Shakespeare, too. Lope had dismissed those: who ever thinks his immediate superior knows anything? But if Robert Parsons and Guzmán had the same idea, perhaps there was something to it. "I shall do everything I can to aid the cause of Spain, your Eminence," de Vega said.

Chill disapproval in his voice, Parsons answered, "It is not merely the cause of Spain. It is the cause of God." But then he softened: "I do take your point, Lieutenant. Work hard. And work quickly. My latest news is that his Most Catholic Majesty does not improve, but draws closer day by day to his eternal reward. With his crisis, very likely, will come the crisis of our holy Catholic faith here in England. No less than the inquisitors, you defend against heresy. Go forth, knowing God is with you."

"Yes, your Eminence. Thank you, your Eminence." Lope kissed Cardinal Parsons' ring once more. He left the cardinal's study, left St. Paul's, as fast as his legs would take him. No doubt Parsons had intended a compliment in comparing him to an inquisitor. But what he'd intended and what Lope felt were very different things.

The Inquisition was necessary. Of that de Vega had no doubt. But there was also a difference between what was necessary and what was to be admired. *Vultures and flies are necessary. Without them, the ground would be littered with dead beasts,* he thought. *No one invites them to dinner, though, and no one ever will.*

SHAKESPEARE KNELT IN THE CONFESSIONAL. "BLESS ME, FATHER, FOR I have sinned," he said. The priest in the other side of the booth murmured a question he hardly heard. He confessed his adultery with the serving woman at the ordinary, his rage at Will Kemp (though not all his reasons for it), his jealousy over Christopher Marlowe's latest tragedy, and such other sins as came to mind . . . and as could safely be told to a Catholic priest.

As Shakespeare had conformed to Protestant worship during Elizabeth's reign, so he conformed to Romish ritual now that Isabella and Albert sat on the English throne and Philip of Spain stood behind them. More often than not, conforming came easy. The Catholic Church's rituals had a grandeur, a glamour, missing from Protestantism. Had Shakespeare been able to choose faiths on his own, he might well have chosen Rome's. His father had quietly stayed Catholic all through Elizabeth's reign. But having invaders impose his creed on him galled Shakespeare, as it galled many Englishmen.

The priest gave him his penance, and then, with a low-voiced, "Go, and sin no more," sent him on his way. He went up toward the altar in the small parish church of St. Ethelberge the Virgin—the church closest to his lodgings—knelt in a pew, and began to say off the *Ave Maria*s and *Pater Noster*s the priest had assigned him. By the time he finished, he *did* feel cleansed of sin, although, being a man, he knew he would soon stumble into it again.

Nine years of conforming to Catholic ways was also long enough to leave him full of guilt about what he hadn't confessed. Despite the sanctity of the confessional, any mention of his meeting with Lord Burghley would have gone straight to the English Inquisition, and no doubt to the secular authorities as well. He was as sure of that as he was of his own name. Even so, he raised his eyes to the heavens as he finished his last *Ave Maria*. The priest wouldn't know what he kept to himself, but God would.

Crossing himself—another gesture that had grown close to automatic since the coming of the Armada—he got to his feet to leave St. Ethelberge's. As he walked down the aisle toward the door, Kate came out of the confessional and started up toward the altar. Dull embarrassment made Shakespeare look down at the stone floor. She'd probably confessed to the same passage of lovemaking as he had. For her, of course, it was only fornication, not adultery.

He forced himself to look her in the face. "God give you good day," he said, as if he knew her, but not in the Biblical sense.

"And you, Master Will," she answered quietly. "Shall we see you again at the ordinary this even?"

"Belike," he said. She walked on by him. Her small, secret smile said she might have confessed, but hadn't fully repented.

He started back to the Widow Kendall's. He wanted to get in what writing he could while some daylight lingered, and before most of the other lodgers came home and made the place too noisy for him to think in the rhythms of blank verse. He wished he were a rich man, like the Bacons in whose home he'd met Lord Burghley. Being able to sit down in a room without half a dozen other people chattering in his ear . . . *is beyond your means, so what point fretting yourself over it?*

He hadn't gone far before an apprentice—easy enough to recognize by his clothes, for he wore a plain, flat cap and only a small ruff at his throat—pointed to him and said, "There goes Master Shakespeare."

Being a man whose face many saw, Shakespeare had that happen fairly often. He almost made a leg to the 'prentice, to acknowledge he was who the young man thought he was. But something in the fellow's tone made him hold back. The apprentice hadn't just recognized him; by the way he sounded, others were looking for Shakespeare, too. He didn't care for that at all.

Sure enough, though, another man and a woman pointed him out to their friends on his way back to his lodgings. And, when he got there, Jane Kendall was in a swivet. "Oh, sweet Jesu!" she exclaimed. "First Master Foster, now you! Whatever shall I do?"

"What mean you, Madam?" he asked, thinking, *What will you do? Find more lodgers; what else? But if they pursue me as they pursue Peter Foster, whatever shall* I *do?* He doubted whether running to Stratford would help him. They'd track him down there. Could hc get over the border to Scotland? *Have they got theatres in Scotland? Might a player live there, or would he slowly starve?*

"Why, Master Shakespeare, the fellow asking after you, he looked a right catchpole, he did," his landlady answered. "Had a great gruff deep voice, too, enough to make anybody afeard. Oh, Master Shakespeare, what *have* you done?"

"Naught," Shakespeare answered. And that was true, or something close to true. He'd set down not a word on paper. The closest thing to evidence anyone might find among his possessions was the translation of Tacitus' *Annals*. But it wasn't the only work of history in his trunk, and he hadn't so much as dogeared the relevant page. As far as proof went, they'd be on thin ice.

But how much would that matter? The bastinado, the rack, thumbscrews, the water torture the English Inquisition favored . . . If they hauled him away and began tormenting him, how long could he hold out? He shuddered. Sweat sprang out on his forehead. He was no hero, and knew it too well. If they tortured him, he would tell all he knew, and quickly, too.

Doing his best not to think of such things, he went to the ordinary for supper and for work. All he knew about what he ate was that it cost threepence. He did notice Kate's smile, and absentmindedly gave it back. After she took away his wooden trencher, he got to work on *Love's Labour's Won*. Tonight, the writing went well: better than it had for a fortnight, at least. He dipped his quill in the bottle of ink again and again; it raced across the page.

Kate knew better than to talk to him when the words tumbled forth like the Thames at flood. When at last she came over to his table, it was only to warn him: "Curfew's nigh."

"Oh." He didn't want to stop, but he didn't want to be caught out, either, not if they were looking for him anyway. As he gathered up his pens and papers and ink, he came back to the real world. Now the smile he gave the serving woman was sheepish. "Another time, I fear me."

She nodded, not much put out. "When I saw you writing so, I knew that would be the way of't." Her voice softened. "God keep thee."

"And thee." Shakespeare pushed his stool back from the table. He couldn't have gone on much longer, anyhow; the candle was burnt almost to the end. With an awkward nod—almost the nod a youth might have given a pretty maid he was too shy to court—he hurried out of the ordinary.

He rose the next morning in darkness; in December, the sun stayed long abed. Porridge from the pot on the hearth and a mug of the Widow Kendall's ale broke his fast. And he wasn't the first lodger up; Jack Street went out the door while he was still eating.

When Shakespeare followed the glazier out of the lodging house, a big man stepped from the shadows and said, "You are Master William Shakespeare." He had to be the fellow who'd spoken to Jane Kendall; his voice came rumbling forth from deep in his chest.

"And if I be he?" Shakespeare asked. "Who are you, and what business have you with me?"

"You are to come with me to Westminster," the man replied. "Forthwith."

"But I'm wanted at the Theatre," Shakespeare said.

"You're wanted in Westminster, and thither shall you go," the big man said implacably. "The wind lies in the east. Come—let's to the river for a wherry. 'Twill be quicker thus." He made the sign of the cross. "God be my witness, Master Shakespeare, you are not arrested. Nor shall you be, so that you do as you are bid. Now come. Soonest there, soonest gone."

"I am your servant," Shakespeare said, ever so glad he was not—or apparently was not—the other man's captive.

Morning twilight had begun to chase the dark from the eastern sky when they got down to the Thames. Even so early, half a dozen boatmen shouted at them, eager for a fare. "Whither would you go, my lord?" one of them asked after the fellow sent to fetch Shakespeare set a silver groat in his hand.

"Westminster," the big man answered.

"I'll hie you there right yarely, sir," the boatman said. He proved good as his word, using both sail and oars to fight his way west against the current. The wind did indeed blow briskly from the east, which helped speed the small boat to Westminster. They got there faster than Shakespeare would have cared to walk, especially when he still would have had trouble seeing where to put his feet.

His—guide?—took him through the maze of palaces and other state buildings. He heard Spanish in the lanes and hallways almost as often as

English; Westminster was the beating heart of the Spanish occupation of his country. The mere word made him queasy—it was often used of a man's lying with a woman. And, indeed, through his soldiers King Philip had thrown down Queen Elizabeth, thrown down all of England, and. . . .

"Bide here a moment," the Englishman with the deep voice said, and ducked into an office. He soon came back to the doorway and beckoned. "Come you in." Turning to the man behind the large, ornate desk, he spoke in Spanish: "Don Diego, I present to you *Señor* Shakespeare, the poet." Shakespeare had little Spanish, but followed him well enough to make sense of that. The Englishman gave his attention back to Shakespeare and returned to his native tongue: "Master Shakespeare, here is Don Diego Flores de Valdés."

Shakespeare made a leg to the Spaniard. "I am honored beyond my deserts, your Excellency," he said. In fact, he was more nearly appalled. Diego Flores commanded all of King Philip's soldiers in England. *What knows he?*

Instead of translating, as Shakespeare had expected, his guide politely inclined his head to the Spanish grandee and withdrew. Flores proved to speak good if accented English, saying, "Please seat yourself, *Señor* Chakespeare." He waved to a stool in front of the desk. Like most Spaniards, he made a hash of the *sh* sound at the start of Shakespeare's name and pronounced it as if it had three syllables.

"Thank you, my lord." Shakespeare perched warily on the stool. He would sooner have fled. Even knowing flight would doom him made it no less tempting. He took a deep breath and forced some player's counterfeit of calm on himself. "How may I serve you today?"

Don Diego Flores studied him before answering. The Spanish commandant was in his fifties, his beard going gray, his hooked nose sharper in his thin face than it might have seemed when he was young. When he said, "I am told you are the best poet in England," he sounded like a man not in the habit of believing what he was told.

"Again I say, your Excellency, you do me too much honor."

"Who surpasseth you?" Flores asked sharply, the Spanish lisp making his English sound old-fashioned. When Shakespeare did not reply, the officer laughed. "There. You see? Honor pricks you on, more than you think. This I understand. This I admire. If it be a sin to covet honor, I myself am the most offending soul alive." He jabbed a thumb at his own chest. "And so—for this were you summoned hither. Because you are the best."

"What would you of me? Whatever sort of poet I be, I am a poet of English. I know not the Spanish tongue."

"*Claro que sí*," Don Diego said, and then, seeing Shakespeare's puzzled expression, "But of course. You are desired *because* you write English so well." Shakespeare was sure he looked more puzzled than ever. Flores continued, "Have you not heard that King Philip, God love him, fails in regard to his health?"

Was that a trap? *Ought I to claim ignorance?* Shakespeare wondered. After some thought, he rejected the idea: the King of Spain's decline was too widely known to make such knowledge dangerous. Cautiously, the poet said, "Ay, your Excellency, I have heard somewhat of't."

"*Muy bien*. Very good." The Spaniard again translated for himself, though this time Shakespeare followed him perfectly well. Crossing himself, Flores went on, "Soon the good Lord will summon to his bosom the great King."

"May King Philip live and reign for many years." Shakespeare saw no way to say anything else, not to Philip's commandant in England.

"May it be so, *sí*, but Philip is a mortal man, being in that like any other." Flores sounded impatient; perhaps he knew more of the state of Philip's health than was common gossip in London. "To make for him a memorial, a monument: it is for this I summoned you hither."

"My lord?" Shakespeare still felt at sea. "As I told you, I am a poet, a player, not a stonecutter."

The Spanish grandee snorted. One unruly eyebrow rose for a moment. He forced it down, but still looked exasperated; plainly, Shakespeare struck him as something of a dullard. That suited Shakespeare well enough; he wished he struck Flores as a mumbling, drooling simpleton. The officer gathered himself. "May the memorial, the monument, you make prove immortal as cut stone. I would have from you, *señor*, a drama on the subject of his Most Catholic Majesty's magnificence, to be presented by your company of actors when word of the King's mortality comes to this northern land: a show of his greatness for to awe the English people, to make known to them they were conquered by the greatest and most Christian prince who ever drew breath, and to awe them thereby. Can you do this thing? I promise you, you shall be furnished with a great plenty of histories and chronicles wherefrom to draw your scenes and characters. What say you?"

Do I laugh in his face, he'll hold me lunatic—and stray not far from truth. How can I do't? Another thought immediately followed that one: *how can I say him nay?* Shakespeare did his best: "May't please your Excellency, I find myself much engaged in press of business, and—"

Don Diego Flores de Valdés waved that aside with a dry chuckle. "For his Most Catholic Majesty, himself the best, none save the best will serve. We bind not the mouths of the kine who tread the grain. Your fee is an hundred pound. I pay it now, and desire you to set to work at once, none of us knowing what God's plan for King Philip may be." He took from a drawer a fat leather sack and tossed it to Shakespeare. Chuckling again, he added, "And what say you now of this *business* of yours?"

Dizzily, Shakespeare caught the sack. Gold clinked sweetly. Nothing else could be so heavy in so small a space, for Flores would scarcely try to trick him with lead. *An I live, I am rich. But how* can *I live, with Burghley and the Spaniard both desiring plays of me?* He had no answer to that. "I am your servant," he murmured once more.

"*Sí, es verdad.*" Don Diego didn't bother translating that. He pointed to the door. "You may go. I look for the play in good time."

Shakespeare rose. He left—almost staggered from—the commandant's chamber. The big Englishman with the deep voice waited outside to take charge of him. As they walked down the hall, Shakespeare saw Thomas Phelippes writing in a nearby room. Did Phelippes have anything to do with this? If so, did that make it better or worse? Again, Shakespeare had no answer.

IV

"SHAKESPEARE WILL WRITE A PLAY ON THE LIFE OF HIS MOST Catholic Majesty?" Lope de Vega dug a finger in his ear, as if to make sure he'd heard correctly. "Shakespeare?"

Captain Baltasar Guzmán nodded. "Yes, that is correct. You seem surprised, Senior Lieutenant."

"No, your Excellency. I seem astonished. With the Archbishop of Canterbury and, it appears to me, everyone else in the world suspecting him of treason, why give him such a plum? He is, without a doubt, a fine writer—"

"And you are, without a doubt, naive." Guzmán smiled. Lope made himself smile back, in lieu of picking up his stool and braining his arrogant little superior with it. That supercilious smile still on his face, Captain Guzmán continued, "If Shakespeare is well paid, he may be less inclined to treason. This has been known to happen before. If he writes a play praising King Philip, he may be too busy to get into mischief." He ticked off points on his fingers as he made them.

"But what sort of play will he write?" Lope asked. "If he *is* a traitor—I don't believe it, mind you, but *if* he is—won't he slander the King instead of praising him?"

"Not with the Master of the Revels looking over his shoulder every moment," Guzmán replied. "If the Master finds even a speck of slander in the play, it will not go on the stage—and *Señor* Shakespeare will answer a great many pointed questions from the English Inquisition, from Queen Isabella and King Albert's intelligencers, and from Don Diego Flores de Valdés. Shakespeare may be a poet, but I do not think him a fool. He will know this, and give us what we require."

Lope didn't care for the way Captain Guzmán eyed him. *You are a poet, and I do think you a fool*, the nobleman might have said. But what he *had* said made more than a little sense. "It could be," de Vega admitted reluctantly.

"Generous of you to agree. I am sure Don Diego will be relieved," Guzmán said. Lope stiffened. He was more used to giving out sarcasm than to taking it. Guzmán pointed at him. "And one more thing will help keep us safe against any danger from *Señor* Shakespeare."

"What's that, your Excellency?"

"You, Senior Lieutenant."

"Your Excellency?"

"You," Baltasar Guzmán repeated. "Shakespeare is writing about King Philip of Spain. You are a Spaniard. You are also mad for the English theatre. What could be more natural than that you tell the Englishman what he needs to know of his Most Catholic Majesty, and that you stay with his troupe to make sure all goes well? He will be grateful for it, don't you think?"

"What I think," Lope said, "is that you may be committing a sin under the eyes of God by making me enjoy myself so much."

Captain Guzmán laughed. "I will mention it to the priest the next time I confess. I think my penance will be light."

"I hope you're right. . . . You *order* me to go to the Theatre, sir?" de Vega asked. His superior nodded. Lope wondered how much liberty he'd just received. "This will be the whole of my duty till the play goes before an audience?"

Guzmán nodded again. The pleasure that shot through Lope was so intense, he thought he would have to add it to *his* next confession. But then the nobleman said, "This is for the time being. It may change later. And if any emergency or uprising should occur—"

"God forbid it!"

"God forbid it, indeed. But if it should, you will help meet it as I think best."

"Of course, your Excellency. This goes without saying. I am, first of all, a servant of his Most Catholic Majesty, as is every Spanish man in this dark, miserable land."

"*Muy bien*. I did want to make sure we had everything clear." Something flickered in Baltasar Guzmán's eyes. Amusement? Malice? Perhaps a bit of both: "And with you, Senior Lieutenant, I was not sure *anything* went without saying. *Buenos días*."

"*Buenos días*," Lope echoed. He rose, bowed himself almost double, and left the captain's chamber without showing he'd felt, or even noticed, the gibe. It was either that or draw his rapier and have at Guzmán. He didn't want to fight. For one thing, the man *was* his superior, and entitled to such jests. For another, although de Vega did not despise his own skill with a sword, Captain Guzmán was something of a prodigy with a blade in his hand. Set against the requirements of honor, that shouldn't have mattered. The world being as it was, it did.

When Lope got back to his own chamber, he found Diego snoring away. He'd expected nothing less. He didn't bother shaking his servant. He booted him instead, taking out some of the anger he couldn't spend on Captain Guzmán.

Shaking Diego was often a waste of time anyway. Kicking him worked better. "*¡Madre de Dios!*" he exclaimed, and sat bolt upright. He blinked at Lope, his eyes tracked with red veins.

"Get up, you dormouse, before I seethe you in honey," de Vega snarled. "You can't sleep away the whole day."

Diego groaned. "Not more playacting," he said. In face, under Lope's merciless direction, he had performed well as Turín, the servant in *La dama boba*. And why not? He *was* a servant. All he had to do was play himself, remember his lines—and stay awake.

But Lope shook his head. "No, not more playacting for you." Ignoring Diego's sigh of relief, de Vega went on, "But *I* may be doing more of it—and in English, no less."

"Why has this got anything to do with me?" Diego asked around a yawn.

"I can read your mind, you rascal." Lope glared at him. "You're thinking, *My master will be off acting. I can lie here and sleep till the day of Resurrection*. You had better think again, wretch, or you'll sleep the sleep of a dead man. I'm going to need you more than ever."

"For what?"

"Perhaps for more acting," Lope said, and his lackey groaned again.

He took no notice of that. "Perhaps to carry messages for me. And perhaps for who knows what? You are my servant, Diego. You can work for me and do as I say, or you can find out how you like things on the Scottish border."

"*Madre de Dios*," Diego said once more, sadly this time. "Being a servant is a hard life. Who would say otherwise? I have to obey another man's orders, my time is not my own—"

"Oh, what a pity," de Vega broke in. "You cannot sleep every blessed hour of every blessed day. Every so often, you have to stand up and earn your bread instead of having it handed to you already dipped in olive oil."

"And where have you seen olive oil in England, *señor*, save in what we bring here from Spain for ourselves?" Diego said. "The English, they hate it. If that doesn't prove they're savages, what does it prove?"

"It proves you're trying to change the subject," Lope answered. "That won't work, though. That won't work, and you, by God, *will*."

"Life is hard for a servant with a cruel master." Diego sighed. "Life is hard for any servant, but especially for one so unlucky."

"If I were a cruel master, you would already be up on the Scottish border, or sent to Ireland, or else tied to the whipping post on account of your laziness," Lope said. "Maybe that would wake you up. Nothing else seems to."

"I do what I have to do, *señor*," Diego said with dignity.

"You do half of what you have to do, and none of what a good servant ought to do," de Vega retorted. "Maybe you should fall in love. You'd stay awake for your lady, and you just might stay awake for me, too."

"Fall in love with an Englishwoman? Not me, *señor*." Diego shook his head so vigorously, his jowls wobbled back and forth. He didn't seem to have slept through any meals. With a sly smile, he added, "Look what Englishwomen have given *you*—nothing but trouble. And I don't need a woman to give me trouble, not when I've got a master."

For a moment, Lope sympathized with his servant. His own superior, Captain Guzmán, had given him a good deal of trouble, too. But Guzmán had also just given him the freedom of the English theatre. That made up for all the trouble he'd ever had from the cocky little nobleman, and then some. And, no matter what fat, lumpish Diego said, women had their uses, too.

Richard Burbage stared at Shakespeare. "Tell it me again," the big, burly player said. "The dons are fain to have you make a play on the life of Philip?"

"Even so," Shakespeare said unhappily. The two stood alone on the outthrust stage of the Theatre. No apple-munching, beer-swilling, wench-pinching groundlings gaped at them from the open area around it; no richer folk peered from the galleries. It was still morning—rehearsal time. The afternoon's play would be *Prince of Denmark*. Burbage would play the Prince, Shakespeare his father's ghost. He'd just emerged through the trap door from the damp, chilly darkness under the stage. He'd written the lines they were practicing, but Burbage remembered them more readily than he did. On the stage, nothing fazed Burbage.

He threw back his head and laughed now, both hands on his comfortable belly. A couple of the tireman's assistants and an early-arriving vendor turned their heads his way, hoping they might share the jest. He waved to them, as if to say it was none of their affair. Had Shakespeare done that, they would have ignored him. Burbage they took seriously, and went back to whatever they'd been doing. Shakespeare sighed. Not by accident was Burbage a leading man.

Mirth still shining in his eyes, Burbage spoke for Shakespeare's ear alone: "Well, my duck, one thing it shows beyond doubt's shadow."

"What's that?" the poet asked.

"They suspect not your other commission."

"But how am I to do both?" Shakespeare demanded in an impassioned whisper. "Marry, how? 'Tis the most unkindest cut of all, Dick. Two plays at once? That will drive me mad, and madder till I see which be fated to journey from pen and paper to this." His wave encompassed the painted glory of the Theatre.

"A pretty gesture," Burbage remarked. "Do you use it when appearing, thus." He crouched as if coming up through the trap door, then stood with a broader, more extravagant version of Shakespeare's wave. " 'Twill help to draw the auditory into the business of the play."

"I'll do't," Shakespeare said, but he refused to let the other man distract him. "I've not yet sounded the whole of the company on the other. After this, how can I? They'll take me for the Spaniards' dog, and think I purpose luring 'em to treason."

"Another, haply, but not you, Will." Burbage set a hand on his shoulder. "You're an honest man, none honester, which everybody knows."

"And for which I do thank you." Shakespeare's laugh rang wild enough to make curious eyes swing his way again. He wished he'd been able to hold it in, but felt as if he would burst if he tried. "But honest! Were I honest to all here embroiled, I'd die the death i'the next instant."

"By no means." Burbage shook his head and looked somber. "In sooth, you'd die the death, but as slow as those who had you could in their ingeniousness make it."

"The devil damn thee black, thou moon-calf scroyle!" Shakespeare said, which only made Richard Burbage laugh. Still furious, Shakespeare went on, "Will Kemp'd use me so. From you, I hoped for better."

"Write your play on Philip," the actor told him. "Write it as well as ever you may, for who knows what God list? An we give't, we give't. An we put forth in its place some different spectacle—why, that too's God's will, and there's an end to it."

He would play the one as gladly as the other, reckoning the company would profit from either, Shakespeare realized. That made him no happier than he had been. If Burbage didn't care whether he strode the boards as Philip of Spain or in toga and crested helm as Gaius Suetonius Paulinus, did he truly care who ruled England? Did he truly care about anything but his own role and how the playgoers would see him? That was a question with any actor: with one who enjoyed—no, reveled in—such general acclaim as Richard Burbage, a question all the more pointed.

News of the play on King Philip's life raced through the company like wildfire. *Who will stop the vent of hearing when loud rumor speaks?* Shakespeare thought with sour amusement. *He, from the orient to the drooping west, doth unfold the acts commenced on this ball of earth, stuffing the ears with false reports.* He wished this report were false.

Will Kemp sidled up to him, still carrying the skull he'd use while playing the gravedigger come the afternoon performance. "You'll give me some words wherewith to make 'em laugh, is't not so?" he said, working the jawbone wired to the skull so that it seemed to do the talking.

"Be still, old bones," Shakespeare said.

Kemp tossed the skull in the air and caught it upside down. That only made its empty-eyed leer more appalling. "Philip's such a pompous, praying, prating pig, any play which hath him in't will need somewhat of leavening, lest it prove too heavy for digestion." The clown's voice became a high, wheedling whine.

"Here is the first I've heard you care a fig for the words I do give you," Shakespeare said tartly. "It were better that those who play own clowns speak no more than is set down for them."

Kemp's flexible face twisted into an expression so preposterous, even Shakespeare couldn't help smiling. "But Master William, my dove, my pet, my chick, my poppet," the clown cooed, "the pith of't it is, as I've said aforetimes, the groundlings laugh louder for my words than for yours."

"I pith on you and the groundlings both." Shakespeare stood with his legs spraddled wide, as if easing himself. Will Kemp gaped at him. *Forestalled, by God!* Shakespeare thought. *You were about to make your own pissy quibble, and looked not for the like from me.* He added, "The Devil take your laughs when they flaw the shape of *my* play, as *I've* said before. Hear you me now?"

"I hear." Kemp looked angry, angry and ugly. He started to say something more, then spun on his heel instead—for a big, bulky man, he moved, when he chose, with astounding grace—and stalked away.

Another caring more for himself than aught else. Shakespeare sighed. It was either sigh or weep from despair. *Someone will sell us to the Spaniards. Sure as Pilate's men nailed Jesu to the rood, someone will think first of thirty pieces of silver and not of all of England. Someone—but who?*

He wouldn't be burned alive, not for treason, or most of him wouldn't. They would haul him to Tower Hill on a hurdle, and hang him till he was almost dead. Then they'd cut him down and draw him as if he were a sheep in a shambles. They'd throw his guts into the fire while he watched, if he was unlucky enough to keep life in him yet. That done, they would quarter him and display his head and severed limbs on London Bridge and elsewhere around the city to dissuade others from such thoughts and deeds.

He shuddered. That was English law; Elizabeth had used Catholics who plotted against her thus. For all he knew, the Spaniards had worse punishments for traitors.

Somebody tapped him on the shoulder. He jumped and almost screamed. "I humbly do beseech you of your pardon, Master Shakespeare," Jack Hungerford said. "I meant not to startle you."

"My thoughts were . . . elsewhere," Shakespeare said shakily, and the tireman nodded. Shakespeare gathered himself. "What would you?"

"Why, I'd ready you for your turn on stage, of course," Hungerford replied, his eyes plainly asking, *How far off were your wits?* "The hour draws nigh, you know."

"I'll come with you." Shakespeare followed him as he'd lately followed too many men from whom he sooner would have fled.

Back in the tiring room, Hungerford was all brisk efficiency. He powdered Shakespeare's face and hands with ground chalk, then smeared black grease under his eyes for a skull-like effect. "Here, see yourself," he said, and pressed a glass into Shakespeare's hand.

Shakespeare studied the streaky image the mirror gave back. "Am I more haggard than I was before?" he murmured.

Hungerford, perhaps fortunately, paid him no attention. The tireman was rummaging through the company's robes to find a smoke-gray one shot through with silver thread. "You'll have a care with this down under stage," he said severely. " 'Tis the sole habiliment we have fit for a royal spook. Smutch it, and the cleaning costs us dear."

"I'll mind me of't."

"Good. Good. You'd better." Like any tireman worth his salt, Jack Hungerford cared more for his clothes and other properties than for the players who wore them. He thrust a polished pewter crown at Shakespeare. "See how't glisters like silver? There's not a ghost in all the world can match the Prince's father for finery."

"I've no doubt you're right, Master Hungerford." Shakespeare set the crown on his head. It was too small. He'd been playing the ghost ever since he wrote the tragedy, and had yet to persuade the tireman to get a crown that fit him.

Hungerford handed him a bowl full of shredded, crumpled paper. "Do you remember to set this alight just afore the trap door opens. 'Twill make a fine smoke wherewith to amaze the groundlings."

"I shall remember," Shakespeare promised gravely. "Do you recall in turn, I have played the role before. Do you further recall, I am he who devised it."

The tireman only sniffed, as a mother might when her son insisted he was a grown man. However much he insisted, she would never believe it, not in her heart. Hungerford never believed players knew anything. The more they said they did, the less he believed it, too.

A rising buzz came from out front: the day's audience, hurrying into the Theatre. When Shakespeare stood to go to his place under the stage and await his cue to rise through the trap door, Jack Hungerford grabbed the bowl full of paper scraps and set it in his hand before he could reach for it. "See you? You would have forgotten it," Hungerford said, triumph in his voice.

What point to quarreling with him? Shakespeare had bigger worries, swarms of them. "If you'd have it so, so it is for you," he said wearily. The tireman stirred, about to speak again. Shakespeare spoke first: "By my halidom, Master Jack, I'll not forget me the candle to light it with."

Hungerford nodded. By his expression, he couldn't decide whether Shakespeare had merely called him by his Christian name or had called him *a* Jack, a saucy, paltry, silly fellow. Since Shakespeare had intended that he wonder, the poet was well enough pleased.

He did make a point of remembering the candle. Hungerford would never have let him live it down had he forgotten after their skirmish. He also made a point of carrying it carefully, so he didn't have to come back and start it burning again. *Not out, brief candle*, he thought. *Light this fool the way through dusty gloom.*

He had to walk doubled over; had the stage been high enough to let him straighten up, it would have been too high to let the standing groundlings see the action on it. He peered out at the crowd through chinks and knotholes. He couldn't see much—the men and women in front blocked his view of those farther back. His ears told him more than his eyes could. It sounded like a full house, or something close, and it sounded like an enthusiastic one.

"It'll like thee well, Lucy," said a man standing close enough to Shakespeare for his voice to be distinct among the multitude. "The Prince of Denmark, he feigns he's mad, so—"

"Go to, Hal!" Lucy broke in. "I've not seen it afore, and I shan't thank thee for spoiling the devisings."

God bless you, Lucy. You're a woman of sense, Shakespeare thought. He knew too many playwrights who were too fond of boasting of their machinations. He thought them fond in the other sense of the word, for their plays seemed insipid to him when he knew ahead of time everything that happened.

Footsteps on the boards above his head. Words heard dimly through thick wooden planks: the sentinels Bernardo and Francisco, talking of the night. Shakespeare hurried over to the little platform under the trap door. He lit the papers. They caught at once, and began filling the space under the stage with smoke. It tickled his nose and his throat. He fought against a cough.

Horatio and Marcellus came on. Francisco left, his boots thumping. Shakespeare cocked his head to one side, listening for his cue. His chalky fingers closed on the trap-door latch. Bernardo raised his voice to make sure the waiting ghost heard: "... Where now it burns, Marcellus and myself, the bell then beating one—"

Shakespeare loosed the latch. Down swung the trap door. He'd made sure the hinges were well oiled, so they didn't squeal. Up he popped through the door, with a fine cloud of smoke around him. A woman shrieked, which made two more cry out in sympathy. If one screamed, others always followed. And he was good enough to make that first one scream.

He had no lines here, or in his next couple of appearances. He had but to stand, looking ominous and menacing, till his cue to stalk off, and then go below once more. One of the tireman's helpers crawled out to bring him another bowl full of bits of paper and a fresh candle. "You nigh gasted them out of their hose, Master Shakespeare," he whispered.

"Good," Shakespeare whispered back. "Get thee gone." The tireman's helper went back the way he'd come. Shakespeare crouched in the smoke under the stage, fuming a little himself. *I'd best know how to frighten them with the ghost*, he thought. *If not I, then who?* He had failed once or twice: he'd been bad, or the audience had been bad, or who could say what had gone wrong? He didn't dwell on the failures. Every player had them, in every role. But he'd made the most of the part far more often. *And so I shall again today.*

He hadn't long to brood. The ghost appeared again in the first scene, and again vanished without a word. Then he appeared once more in the fourth scene of the first act. He was once more silent, but he beckoned to Burbage as the astonished Prince of Denmark.

The fifth scene was his. He had to vanish once more at the end of the fourth, then come back up on stage through a trap door closer to the tiring room. And he had his lines, urging the Prince to action against his murderous uncle. Shakespeare spoke them in a rumbling, echoing voice that might indeed have come from beyond the grave. Gasps and a couple of muffled squeals told him his words and looks were striking home. He remembered to use the gesture Burbage had liked during the rehearsal. The other player beamed. Shakespeare wasn't sure it really added anything, but it pleased Burbage and it didn't hurt.

"Adieu, adieu, adieu!" Shakespeare said. "Remember me." He stretched the words out into something close to a wail, then sank through the trap door. By that time, the space under the stage was so full of smoke, it wasn't far from the sulphurous and tormenting flames to which the ghost said he must render himself up. He had a few lines from below later in the scene, and then an appearance in the third act, where the Prince could see him but his mother could not. After that, eyes stinging, he retreated to the tiring room. "Have a care with the robe, Master Will, do," Jack Hungerford said. "Here, sit you down. I'll get it off you." Once the robe was safe, he added, "Well played. I've rarely seen you better in the part."

"For which I thank you." Shakespeare rubbed his streaming eyes. " 'Swounds, give me a bowl of water, that I may wash away the smoke." He coughed. Now he could, without marring the play.

"You'll take off the chalk with water, but not the black," the tireman warned. "I have a cake of soap for that."

"Give it me, but plain water first."

Shakespeare was drying his face on a grimy towel when Burbage took advantage of a scene where he wasn't on stage to go back and clasp his hand. Pointing to Shakespeare, he started to laugh. "With your paint half off and all besmeared, your aspect is more fearful now than ever before the groundlings."

"I believe't." Shakespeare turned to the tireman. "Where's that soap, Master Hungerford?"

He washed again, then dried himself once more. "Better," Burbage said. "And the specter was as fine as you've ever given him." He imitated the gesture he'd urged Shakespeare to use. "Saw you how the audience clung to your every word thereafter, you having drawn them into the action thus?"

Shakespeare had seen no such thing, but he didn't feel like arguing. Things *had* gone well, no matter why. That would do. "They did seem pleased," he said.

"As they had reason to be. And now I needs must dash—I'm before 'em again in a moment." Burbage clapped Shakespeare on the shoulder, then hurried back toward the stage.

In his shirt and hose, Shakespeare watched the rest of *The Prince of Denmark* from the wings. In his present mood, a scene just past pleased him most: the one where the Prince admonished the players to speak trippingly and warned the clowns against making up their own lines. He stood for every poet ever born.

After the play ended, Shakespeare came out in his own person to take his bows. He used the gesture he'd made while playing opposite the Prince to show the audience who he was. And Richard Burbage, always generous, waved to him and called out to the crowd, "Behold the man whose play you saw!" That got him more applause. He bowed deeply.

The groundlings streamed out of the Theatre. By their buzz, they liked what they'd seen. Shakespeare retreated to the tiring room to don shoes and doublet and hat and talk things over with the company and with the players and poets and other folk who got past the glower of the tireman's burly helpers.

In came Christopher Marlowe, a pipe of tobacco in his mouth. As soon as Shakespeare caught the first whiff of smoke, he started to cough. "Marry, Kit, put it by, I prithee," he said.

"I will not, by God," Marlowe said, and took another puff. His eye swung to the beardless youth who'd played Ophelia, and who was now getting back into the clothes proper to his sex. "All they who love not tobacco and boys are fools. Why, holy communion would have been much better being administered in a tobacco pipe."

He reveled in scandal and blasphemy. Knowing as much, Shakespeare didn't react with the horror his fellow poet tried to rouse. Instead, he said, "Put it by, or I'll break it, and that gladly. Having spent the whole of the first act beneath the stage, I'm smoked and to spare, smoked as a Warwickshire sausage."

"Ah. Then you have reason for asking. I'll do't." And Marlowe did, knocking the pipe against the sole of his shoe and grinding out the coals with his foot. He gave Shakespeare a mocking bow. "Your servant, sir."

"Gramercy." Shakespeare returned the bow as if he hadn't noticed the mockery. Nothing could be better calculated to annoy Marlowe.

Or so he thought, especially when Marlowe gave him a shark's smile and said, "Damn you again, Will."

"What, for speaking you soft? An I huff and fume, will't like you better?"

"No, no, no." Marlowe made as if to push him away. "I know the difference 'twixt small and great. *De minibus non curat lex*. No, damn you for your *Prince of Denmark*."

This time, Shakespeare bowed in earnest. "Praise from the master's praise indeed."

"In this play, you are my master. And, since I fancy not being mastered, I aim t'overcome you. There are Grecian pots, 'tis said, with figures limned in contortions wild, and with the painter's brag writ above 'em: 'As Thus-and-So, my rival, never did.' After first seeing *The Prince of Denmark* last year, I set to work on *Yseult and Tristan*, afore which I shall not write, 'As Shakespeare never did,' but, when you watch it, you may take the thought as there."

"And then my turn will come round again, to see how I may outmatch you." Shakespeare's early tragedies owed a good deal to Marlowe, who'd led the theatre when Shakespeare came to London from his provincial home. Since then, Marlowe had chased him more often than the reverse. "We do spur each other on."

"We do," Marlowe agreed. "But you have in your flanks for now different spurs, of one sort . . . and another." He gave Shakespeare a sly look. "You're to make the Spaniards a *King Philip*?"

"I am." Shakespeare wasn't surprised Marlowe had heard about that. He didn't need to keep it secret, as he did the other piece. Of course, Marlowe knew about that, or something about that, too. Shakespeare wished he didn't. The other poet did not know how to keep his mouth shut.

Marlowe proved as much now, saying, "But will they see it? Or will the players strut the stage in other parts?"

Shakespeare had been pondering the same question. He didn't care to discuss it with anyone else, especially in the crowded tiring room, and most especially. . . . "Have a care," he hissed. "The Spaniard comes. Would you have had *him* hear you prattle of boys and tobacco and communion?"

"Danger is my meat and drink," Marlowe answered blithely, and Shakespeare feared that was true. Making a leg like a courtier, the other poet gave Lope de Vega his most charming smile. Even Shakespeare, for whom it was not intended, felt its force. "Master Lope!" Marlowe exclaimed. "Always a pleasure, and an honor."

"No, no—the pleasure is mine." De Vega returned the bow. He looked dapper and dangerous, the rapier on his hip seeming a part of him.

"I hear your comedy on the foolish woman was a great success," Marlowe said. Shakespeare had heard nothing of the sort. The less he heard of the Spaniards' doings, the happier he was. Marlowe went on, " 'Tis pity I have not Spanish enough to follow comfortably, else I had come to see how you wrought."

Lope de Vega bowed again. "You are too kind."

"By no means, sir." Yes, when Marlowe chose, he could charm the birds from the trees—*as can any serpent*, Shakespeare thought uneasily.

The Spaniard turned to him. "You will tell me at once, Master

Shakespeare: is the Prince of Denmark mad, or doth he but feign his affliction?"

Marlowe's eyes gleamed. "I have asked myself that very question. So would any man of sense, on seeing the play. But here we have a man of better sense, for he asks not himself but the poet!"

"He is but mad north-northwest," Shakespeare answered. "When the wind is southerly he knows a hawk from a handsaw."

"Fie on you!" de Vega said, as Marlowe burst out laughing. Lope went on, "You give back the Prince's words, not your own."

"But, good my sir, if the Prince's words be not my own, whose then are they?" Shakespeare said, his voice as innocent as he could make it. "Certes, I purpose the question being asked. And I purpose each hearer to answer in himself, for himself."

"Men seek God and, seeking, find Him—so saith the Grecian poet," Marlowe observed. "Who'd have thought the like held for madness?"

He and Shakespeare could, if they chose, hash it out over pint after pint of bitter beer. If Lope de Vega reckoned himself insulted, or trifled with, that was a more serious matter. But the Spaniard seemed willing to let it pass. He changed the subject: "You are to write a play on the life of his Most Catholic Majesty, I hear."

"I have been given that privilege, yes," Shakespeare said, *privilege* striking him as a better word than *cross*.

"You are fortunate in your subject, his Majesty in his poet," de Vega said—he made no mean courtier himself. Marlowe's glance was half rueful, half scornful. Lope continued, "It will please me very much to help you in your enterprise however I may."

"Truly, sir, you are too kind." The last thing Shakespeare wanted was Lope's help. "But there's no need for—"

"No, no." Lope waved his protest aside. "I insist." He grinned disarmingly. "For, by helping you, I help myself to coming to the Theatre whenever I please. Should you desire a veritable *hombre de España* to play a Spaniard, nothing would like me better."

Shakespeare wanted to shriek. He couldn't tell de Vega everything he wanted to, or even a fraction of it. But . . . "*Tacite*, Will," Marlowe said quickly.

In Latin, that meant *be quiet*. In English, it would have been good advice. Even in Latin, it was good advice. But was it also something more? Was it an allusion to Tacitus and to the *Annals*? How much did Marlowe know? How much did he want to show that he knew? And how much did Lope know, and how much was Marlowe liable to reveal to him for no more reason than that he could not take the good advice he so casually gave?

One of Lieutenant de Vega's eyebrows rose. In slow Latin of his own, he asked, "And why should Magister Guglielmus keep silent, I pray you?"

Damn you, Kit, Shakespeare thought. But Marlowe, a university man as fluent in Latin as in English, kept right on in the ancient tongue: "Why? To keep from offering you the role of Philip himself, of course. I doubt his company would stand for it, and I am certain Master Burbage's fury at being balked of the hero's role would know no bounds." He talked himself out of trouble almost as readily as he talked himself into it.

Richard Burbage had little Latin, but he did have the player's ability to hear his name mentioned at a remarkable distance. He came up to Marlowe and asked, "What said you of me, sir?" By the way he leaned forward and set his right hand on his belt near his sword, he would make Marlowe regret it if the answer were not to his liking.

But Marlowe spoke in English as he had in Latin: "I said you would mislike it, did Lieutenant de Vega here take the part of King Philip in the play Will is to write. He hath graciously offered to attempt some role in the drama, but that, meseems, were a part too great."

Just for a heartbeat, Burbage's eyes flashed to Shakespeare. The poet gave back a bland, blank face. He knew he couldn't trust the Spaniard, and didn't know he could trust Christopher Marlowe. If Marlowe had hoped to learn more than he already knew from the actor, he got little, for Burbage laughed, slapped him on the back, and said, "Why, Kit, no man can have a part too great—thus say the ladies, any road."

Shakespeare's laugh was relieved, Marlowe's somewhat forced—he had scant interest in or experience of what the ladies said in such matters. Lope de Vega scratched his head. " 'Tis a jest," he said. "I know't must be, but I apprehend it not." After Shakespeare explained it, de Vega laughed, too, and bowed to Burbage. "You have a wit of your own, sir, and not just with another's words in your mouth."

Will Kemp reckons otherwise, Shakespeare thought. Burbage bowed back to the Spaniard. "You are too kind, sir," he purred, meaning nothing else but, *I'm more clever than either of these two, and if I but wrote. . . .* He had a player's vanity, too, in full measure. It sometimes irked Shakespeare. Today he gladly forgave it. He would have forgiven anything that put the Spaniard off the scent.

But how, dear God, am I to write Lord Burghley's play with de Vega ever sniffing about? And even if Thou shouldst work a miracle, for that I may write it, how can we rehearse it? How can we offer it forth? He waited hopefully. As he'd feared, though, God gave no answers.

Lope de Vega couldn't have screamed louder or more painfully as a betrayed lover. He knew that for a fact; he'd screamed such screams before. This, however . . . "But, sir, you promised me!" he cried.

"I am sorry, Lieutenant," said Captain Guzmán, who sounded not sorry in the least. "I warned that, in an emergency, I would shift your duty. Here we have an emergency, and so I shall shift you."

"A likely story." Lope was convinced his superior intended to drive him mad. Guzmán knew how to make his intentions real, too. "What kind of emergency?"

"A soothsayer, prophesying against Spain and against King Philip," Guzmán answered.

"Oh," Lope said in crestfallen tones. Unfortunately, that *was* an emergency. Soothsayers and witches and what the English called cunning men caused no end of trouble. But then he had a brighter, more hopeful thought. "Could not the holy inquisitors deal with this false prophet? Surely such a rogue breaks God's law before he breaks man's."

Baltasar Guzmán shook his head. "They call it treason first and blasphemy only afterwards. They have washed their hands of the fellow."

"As Pilate did with our Lord," de Vega said bitterly.

"Senior Lieutenant . . ." Guzmán drummed his fingers on the desk. "Senior Lieutenant, I bear you no ill will. You should thank God and the Virgin and the saints that I bear you no ill will. Were it otherwise, the Inquisition would hear of that remark, and then, in short order, you would hear from the Inquisition. You have your pen, and some freedom in how you use it. You would be wise to guard your tongue."

He was right. That hurt worse than anything else. "I thank you, your Excellency," Lope mumbled, hating to have to thank the man at whom he was furious. He sighed. "Well, if there's no help for it, I'd best get the business over with as fast as I can. Who is this soothsayer, and where can I find him?"

"He is called John . . . Walsh." Captain Guzmán made heavy going of the English surname. "He dwells in"—the officer checked his notes—"in the ward called Billingsgate, in Pudding Lane. He is by trade a butcher of hogs, but he is to be found more often in a tavern than anywhere else."

"May I find him in a tavern!" Lope exclaimed. "I know Pudding Lane too well, and know its stinks. They make so much offal there, it goes in dung boats down to the Thames."

"Wherever you find him, seize him and clap him in gaol. We'll try him and put him to death and be rid of him once for all," Guzmán said. As de Vega turned to go, his superior held up a hand. "Wait. Don't hunt this, ah, Walsh yourself. Take a squad of soldiers. Better, take two. When you catch him, the Englishmen he has fooled are liable to try a rescue. You will want swords and pikes and guns at your back."

"Very well, sir." De Vega wasn't sure whether it was very well or not. Alone, he might slip in and get away with John Walsh with no one else the wiser. With a couple of squads at his back, he had no hope of that. But Captain Guzmán had a point. If he went after Walsh by himself and got into trouble, he wouldn't come out of Billingsgate Ward again. How had Shakespeare put it in *Alcibiades*? *The better part of valor is discretion*—that was the line that had stuck in Lope's memory.

He had no trouble getting soldiers to come with him. When he told the men eating in the refectory what his mission was, they clamored to come along. "By St. James, sir," one of them said, crossing himself, "the sooner we get rid of troublemakers like that, the better. They stir the Englishmen up against us, and that gives us no end of grief."

"Let's go, then," Lope said. Some of the Spaniards paused to gulp down wine or beer or stuff a last bite or two into their mouths, but for no more than that. They buckled on swords, picked up spears and arquebuses and back-and-breasts, set high-crowned morions on their heads, and followed de Vega south and east from the barracks towards noisome Pudding Lane.

London had been occupied long enough and grown peaceful enough to make a couple of dozen Spaniards tramping through the streets—obviously on some business, not merely patrolling—something less than ordinary. " 'Ware! 'Ware!" The cry rang out again and again. *So much for surprise*, Lope thought.

From farther away, he heard another cry: "Clubs!" That was the shout London apprentices raised when they went into a brawl. Before long, a pack of them—some armed with clubs, others carrying daggers or stones—came up the street towards the men he led.

"Give way," he shouted in English. "Give way, or you will be sorry for it!" He nodded to his own men. They were better armed than the apprentices, and armored to boot. They also looked eager to take on the youngsters who'd come up against them. The 'prentices stopped, wavered . . . broke.

One of the soldiers laughed. "They haven't got the *cojones* to stand up to real men," he said. "We beat them when we first got ashore, and we can beat them again if we have to."

"That's right," another soldier said. But then he added, "I'd sooner not fight, so long as we can hold 'em down without it." That perfectly summed up Lope's view of things.

He had wondered if his nose could guide him to Pudding Lane. But London was a city of such multifarious stinks, he had to ask his way. He had to ask his way twice, in fact; the first Englishman who gave him directions told him a lie and got him lost. *No, they don't all love us*, he thought.

But he made a better choice with the second man he asked. The fellow was sleek and prosperous, with fur trim on his doublet. He made a leg at Lope, and fawned on him like a dog hoping to be patted. "Ay, good my lord, certes; 'tis no small honor to enjoy the privilege of directing you thither." He pointed south. "Do you go to the church of St. George in Botolph Lane, and then one street the further, and you have it. God grant you catch whatever villain you seek, too."

"God grant it indeed." Lope crossed himself, and was not surprised to see the Englishman follow his lead. Folk who had clung to the Roman faith before the Armada came were likeliest to uphold the new Queen and King—and the Spaniards who kept them on their throne.

This man said, "We have seen too much of wars and strife. Let there be peace, of whatever kind."

"Amen," Lope replied. Privately, he thought that a craven's counsel. But it worked to keep the kingdom quiet. He would have had all the English so craven.

After more bows and a ceremonious leavetaking, Lope translated for his men what the sleek fellow had said. "Let's find the church, let's find the street, let's find the son of a whore we're after, and then, by God, let's find something to drink," one of them said. Several others nodded approval.

So did Lope. "We may find this Walsh and something to drink together," he said, "for I hear he prophesies in taverns."

The soldier who'd spoken before guffawed. "And after he's drunk enough, he's one of these piss-prophets," he said, which got a laugh from everyone else. Plenty of people made a living divining the future—or saying they did—by examining their clients' urine.

Someone emptied a chamber pot from a second-story window. No way to be sure if the stinking contents were aimed at the Spaniards. A couple of men—including the fellow who'd made the joke—got splashed, but most of the stuff just went into the mud of the street, which already held more than its fair share of ordure and piss. "Eh, Sancho, now *you're* a piss-prophet," one of the other troopers said. Sancho's reply was almost as pungent as the air.

Pudding Lane was only a couple of blocks long, but made up in stench what it lacked in length. De Vega marveled that he hadn't found it by scent. Along with all the usual London miasmas, he smelled pig shit, pig piss, rotting swine's flesh, pig *fear*. "Any man from this street must be a false prophet," he said, "for not even God Himself could stand getting close enough to him to tell him anything."

He started asking after John Walsh. "I don't ken the man," one hog butcher said. "Never heard of him," said a second. "An he be who I think he is, he died o' the French pox summer afore last," a third said. "A went home to Wales, a did, whence a came," a fourth offered. "Seek him in Southwark. He dwelleth there these days, with a punk from a pickhatch," a fifth declared.

Patiently, Lope kept asking. Sooner or later, he was bound to come on someone who either favored Isabella and Albert or simply craved peace and quiet. And he did. A lean man in a pigskin apron looked up from his work and said, "Belike you'll find him in the Blue Fox, half a block toward the Tower in East Cheap."

Again, Lope translated for his men. "A good thing we have you with us, *señor*," irrepressible Sancho said. "If we had to look for interpreters, everything would take three times as long, and like as not they'd tell us more lies than truth."

De Vega wasn't sure the lean man hadn't told a lie. But the tavern, to his relief, did prove easy to find. A signboard with the silhouette of a running fox, bright blue, hung above the door. "You men stay here in the street," Lope said. "I'll go in alone. If God is kind, I'll hear the man speaking treason from his own lips. Then I'll signal for you. "If not"—he shrugged—"again, it's God's will."

"Honor to your courage, Lieutenant," a soldier said.

"This for courage." Lope snapped his fingers. "I want to deal with this fellow as quickly as may be, for I have business of my own to attend to." Some of the men winked and sniggered and made lewd jokes he only half heard. Thanks to his reputation, they thought he meant business with a woman, or with more than one. *But is not the Muse a woman, too?* he thought.

He sat down at a table near the door in the Blue Fox. "Ale," he said when a barmaid came up to him: it was a word he could pronounce without revealing himself as a foreigner. He set a penny on the table. The woman snatched it up and came back with a mug of nasty, sour stuff. He wished he'd taken a chance and asked for wine.

But he didn't have to drink much. He nursed the mug and looked around. He also wished someone had described John Walsh to him. The place was full of Englishmen, most of them—by their talk and by the smell—pig butchers. Was Walsh here? Could he ask without giving himself away? If that fellow in the pigskin apron had steered him away from the wanted man and not toward him . . . *I'll make him sorry if he did. I'll make him worse than sorry.*

"Hear me, friends," a squat, homely, pockmarked man said, and the folk in the tavern *did* hear him: something close to silence fell. Lope pretended to drink ale as the pockmarked man—who also had on a pigskin apron over his jerkin and hose—clambered up onto a table and went on, "You know God hath it in His mind for us to be free o' the Spaniard, for doth He not say, 'When you therefore shall see the abomination of the desolation, spoken of by Daniel the prophet, stand in the holy place, (whoso readeth, let him understand)'? And understand we not all too well who is the aforesaid abomination of the desolation? And stand not his minions on the holy soil of England?"

"That's right, John!" someone called.

"Tell us more!" someone else added.

"Right gladly will I," said the pig butcher, who had to be John Walsh. "Again, in the selfsame book of Matthew, saith not the Lord, 'Then they shall deliver you up to be afflicted, and shall kill you: and ye shall be hated of all nations, for my name's sake. And then shall many be offended, and shall betray one another, and shall hate one another'? Saith He not that very thing? And are we not afflicted, yea, sore afflicted, and slain? And betray we not one another, and hate we not likewise one another? But hark ye to what He saith next. Hark ye, now: 'And because iniquity shall abound, the love of many shall wax cold. But he that shall endure unto the end, the same shall be saved.' "

He switched from Matthew to Revelations, but Lope had heard enough. Setting down his mug, he ducked out of the Blue Fox and beckoned to the soldiers. With them behind him, he stormed back into the tavern and shouted out a verse from Matthew that John Walsh had skipped: " 'And many false prophets shall arise, and shall deceive many.' " Then he switched to Spanish, shouting, "Arrest that man there on the table. Santiago and forward!"

"Santiago!" the soldiers roared. They rushed toward the preaching pig butcher.

"Limb of Satan!" an Englishman cried. He hurled his mug at Lope, who ducked. The mug shattered on the morion of the man behind him. Another flying mug hit a Spaniard in the face. He fell with a groan, his nose smashed and bloody.

A moment later, a Spanish sword bit into the pig butcher who'd thrown the mug that hurt the soldier. The Englishman shrieked. More blood spurted, improbably red. "Let it begin here, as St. John the Divine saith it shall begin at the end of days!" John Walsh bellowed. "The star called Wormwood and the smiting of the sun! Ay, let it begin here!"

"Wormwood!" the Englishmen yelled.

Lope wondered if they knew what the word meant. Not likely, he judged, but it made a fine rallying cry even so. As for him, he shouted, "We *must* take the false preacher now, or London goes up in riot!" It had happened before, though not for four or five years. If it happened again, the blame would land on him. Where would they send him then? The Scottish border? The Welsh mountains? Ireland, which was supposed to be worse than either? Was any place worse than Ireland? If any was, they'd send him *there*.

An arquebus bellowed, deafeningly loud in the close tavern. The lead ball buried itself in the wall. After that, the firearm was good for nothing but a clumsy club. In a tavern brawl, bludgeons and knives and swords counted for more than guns. De Vega wished for a firearm that shot more than one ball, or at least for one that could be reloaded quickly. Wishing didn't help.

The Spaniards' armor did. So did the extra distance at which they could do harm, thanks to their swords. But then an Englishman, an enormous fellow, picked up a bench and swung it like a club. The weapon was clumsy but potent. The Englishman felled two soldiers in quick succession.

Another swing almost caved in Lope's skull. But he ducked, stepped close, and stabbed the big man in the stomach with his rapier. The bench fell from the man's hands as he wailed and clutched at himself. "Come on!" Lope shouted. Only a small knot of stubborn defenders still protected John Walsh.

"Let's away out the back door!" one of them said. De Vega cursed in sonorous Spanish. He hadn't known the Blue Fox *had* a back door. He hurled himself at the Englishmen, doing his best to forestall their escape.

A couple of them tried to hustle Walsh toward the back of the tavern. They might have pulled him to safety, but he didn't seem to want to go. "Nay, nay!" he cried, struggling in their grasp as if they were arresting him. "Let it begin here! It must begin *here*!"

Sancho tackled him. When he went down, half a dozen Spaniards leaped on him, while the rest drove back or knocked down the Englishmen still on their feet. "Is he still alive?" Lope asked.

"Yes, Senior Lieutenant. He'll live to hang," one of his troopers answered.

"After this, I think hanging's too good for him," Lope said. "But tie him up and gag him. Gag him well, by God, or the filth he shouts out will bring the English down on us before we can get him to safety."

Even as things were, stones flew when they emerged from the Blue Fox. But another arquebusier brought his match to the touch-hole of his weapon. It roared and belched forth a great cloud of pungent smoke. And the ball, as much by luck as anything else, knocked an Englishman kicking. The others drew back, naive enough to believe the Spaniards likely to hit twice in a row. Knowing better than they what arquebuses could do, Lope silently thanked them for their caution.

Back at the Spanish barracks, Captain Guzmán asked, "You have the prisoner?"

"Yes, your Excellency," Lope replied.

Guzmán ignored his draggled state and the wounds his men had taken. He'd given the right answer. "*Muy bien*, Lieutenant," Guzmán said. "You may now return to the Theatre." Weariness fell from Lope. Guzmán had given the right answer, too.

SAM KING STEPPED ON WILLIAM SHAKESPEARE'S FOOT. "Ow!" Shakespeare yelped; the young man still wore muddy boots. A little more calmly, the poet added, " 'Ware wheat, Master King; 'ware wheat."

"I pray pardon, sir," King said. "I'm yet unused to the confines of this room." He spoke with a broad Midlands accent. Shakespeare had sounded much the same when he first came to London, but, wanting to take the stage, had had to learn in a hurry to sound like a Londoner born.

"By God, you're used to the confines of my toe, and to flatten it to flatter your fancy," Shakespeare grumbled. But then he sighed. "I own there's no help for't. And had the Widow Kendall taken in another lodger male in place of this Cicely Sellis, he'd trample me in your place."

"Ay, belike," Sam King said. " 'Tis monstrous strange Mistress Cicely should hire a whole room to herself of the old hag. 'Tis monstrous dear, too." His belly rumbled. "Marry, but I'm hungry," he muttered, more to himself than to Shakespeare. Whatever he did in the city—some of this and a little of that, Shakespeare gathered—it got him little money. His face had a pinched, pale look, and his clothes hung loosely on him.

The take at the Theatre had been good. As Christmas neared, people wanted to be gay. Shakespeare had gold not only from Lord Burghley but from the Spaniards as well. He took out three pennies and handed them to Sam King. "Here. Get yourself to an ordinary and eat your fill tonight."

To his amazement, King began to blubber. "God bless you, sir. Oh, God bless you," he said. "I tread on you, and then you give me good for evil, as our Lord says a man ought to do." His scrawny fingers closed over the coins. "I'll pay you back, sir. Marry, I will."

"An't please you. An you can without pinching," Shakespeare said. "An it be otherwise . . ." He shrugged. Threepence meant less to him than to Sam King. The skinny young man blew his nose on the fingers of the hand that wasn't holding the money, wiped them on his shabby doublet, and hurried out of the lodging house.

Shakespeare got out his writing tools and took them to the ordinary he favored. He was relieved not to find his fellow lodger there; King would have insisted on chattering at him when he wanted to work. *Love's Labour's Won* was almost done. He needed to finish it as fast as he could, too. For one thing, the company's patience was wearing thin. For another, he didn't know how long he had till Philip of Spain died. He would need to have both his special commissions ready by then, whichever one actually saw the light of day.

Kate the serving woman came up to him. "God give you good even, Master Will," she said. "The threepenny is barley porridge with boiled beef." He nodded. She went on, "There's lambswool, if you'd liefer have it than the common brewing."

"I would, and I thank you for't," Shakespeare answered. On a chilly December evening, warm spiced beer would go down well.

Maybe the lambswool helped his thoughts flow freely. Whatever the cause, he sat and wrote till he was the last man left in the ordinary. Only when his candle flame began to leap and gutter as the candle neared extinction did he reluctantly pick up his papers and quills and ink and go back to the lodging house.

"It's long past curfew, Master Shakespeare," Jane Kendall said severely when he came in. "I was afeard for you."

"Here I am." Shakespeare didn't want to talk to her. He threw a pine log on the hearth. Before long, it flared up hot and bright. The Widow Kendall sent him a reproachful stare. He never noticed it. He sat down at the table in front of the fire to write a little more while the log gave such fine light. His landlady threw her hands in the air and stalked off to bed.

He hardly noticed her go. It was one of those magical evenings where nothing stood between his mind and the sheet of paper in front of him. He'd been writing for some time—how long by the clock, he couldn't have said, but twenty-five or thirty lines' worth, with scarcely a blotted word—before realizing he wasn't alone in the room. The new lodger, Cicely Sellis, stood in the doorway watching him work.

"Give you good den," she said when he looked up. "I misliked troubling you, your pen scratching along so fast."

"I do thank you for the courtesy," Shakespeare answered. "There are those—too many of 'em, too—will break into a writing man's thoughts for no more reason than to see him stop and scuff the ground, wondering what he meant next to say."

"Some folk, able themselves to shape naught of beauty, are fain to mar another's work, for that they may not find themselves outdone. An you'd back to't, make as though I am not here. You'll offend me not." Cicely Sellis was five or ten years older than Shakespeare. She'd probably been a striking woman till smallpox scarred her face; beneath the flawed skin, her bones were very fine. She wore no ring. Shakespeare didn't know whether she was spinster or widow.

"Again, my thanks," he said. When he stretched, something crunched in his back. It felt good. He twisted, hoping he could get more relief. He noticed his hand was cramped, and wondered how long he'd

been writing all told. "I can pause here. I have the way now, a
not wander from it when I resume."

"Right glad I am to hear you say so." A gray tabby wandered in
Cicely Sellis. It stropped itself against her ankles. She bent and scratch
it behind the ears. It began to buzz. It wasn't a big cat, but purred very
loudly. "There, Mommet, there," she murmured. When she looked up again, she asked, "You'll soon have finished the play, Master Shakespeare?"

"God willing, yes," he answered.

"I hope to see't," she told him. "I've seen some others of yours, and they liked me well. Can I get free, I'll pay my penny again."

"No poet can hope for higher praise," he said, which won a smile from her. He went on, "Have you a hard master, then, one who keeps you at it every minute?"

She nodded and pointed to her chest. "I do, sir, the hardest: mine own self." She stroked the cat again. It purred even louder. Its eyes were green. So were hers. She studied him. "If you would have . . . questions answered, haply I could help you."

"Ah." He'd wondered what she did. No wonder she'd wanted a room all to herself. "You are a cunning woman, then?" He wouldn't say *witch*, even if they amounted to the same thing.

And Cicely Sellis, sensibly, wouldn't answer straight out. "Marry, Master Shakespeare, in this world of men a woman needs must be cunning, mustn't she, if she's to make her way? Now I hear something, now I say something, and the world turns round." She nodded almost defiantly, as if to say, *Make of that what you will.*

Shakespeare didn't know what to make of it. In London as elsewhere in England, elsewhere all through Christendom, witches, or people claiming to be witches, were a fact of life. They did at least as much good for the sick as fancy physicians, as far as he could tell. Did they take their power from Satan? People said they did. Now here before him stood one of the breed. He could ask her himself, if he had the nerve.

He didn't.

"I am . . . content with my lot," he said. If she were truly a witch, she would see he was lying.

He couldn't tell whether she did or not. She gave him half a curtsy. Her eyes glinted, as the cat Mommet's might have done. "No small thing have you said there, nor no common thing, neither," she replied at last. "The richest man in the world, be he never so healthy, be he wed to a young and beautiful wife who loveth him past all reason, hath he contentment? Not likely! He will hunger for more gold, or for more strength of body, or for some other wench besides the one he hath, or for all those things together. Is't not so, Master Shakespeare?"

"Before God, Mistress Sellis, I think you speak sooth," Shakespeare answered.

She stroked Mommet again. He was an uncommonly good-natured cat; as soon as she touched him, his purr boomed out, filling the room. She said, "I have once or twice before been styled soothsayer. I do not say I am such, mind, but I have been so styled."

Shakespeare nodded. "I believe it. If it be so, belike you make a good one." He intended no flattery, but meant every word. What she'd said about a rich man's restless desire for *more* showed she could see a long way into the human heart. That had to be as important for a soothsayer as for a poet crafting plays.

She studied him again. He had rarely known such a measuring glance from a woman—or, indeed, from a man. Marlowe's gaze came close, but it always held an undercurrent of mockery absent from her expression. Her eyes *did* shine like a cat's. He wondered what trick of witchcraft made them do that. Of nights, a cat's eyes, or a dog's, gave back torchlight. A man's eyes, or a woman's, did not. But Cicely Sellis' did.

Mommet suddenly stopped purring. His fur puffed out till he looked twice his proper size. He hissed like a snake. A freezing draught blew under the door, making the hair on Shakespeare's arms prickle up, too, and sending a swarm of bright sparks up the chimney as the flames flared.

In a deep, slow voice not quite her own, Cicely Sellis said, "Beware the man who brings good news, and he who knows less than he seems."

"What?" Shakespeare said.

The one word might have broken the spell, if spell there was. The cat's fur smoothed down on his back. He sprawled on his side, licked his belly and privates, and began to purr once more. The fire eased. And the cunning woman, her eyes merely human eyes again, frowned a little and asked, "Said you somewhat to me?"

"I did." Shakespeare went on to repeat, as best he could, what she'd told him.

Her frown deepened. "*I* said that?" she asked.

"On my oath, Mistress Sellis, you did." Shakespeare crossed himself to show he meant it.

Witches were supposed to fear the sign of the cross. Cicely Sellis showed no such fear. She only shrugged her shoulders and laughed a nervous-sounding laugh. "I will believe you, sir, for that you have no cause to lie to me thus. But as for the words . . ." She shook her head. "I recollect 'em not."

"No?" Shakespeare pressed it a little. Cicely Sellis shook her head again and pressed a hand to one temple, as if she knew pain there. Being a player himself, Shakespeare knew acting. As best he could judge, the cunning woman was sincere in her denial. Bemused, he tugged at his little chin beard. " 'Tis passing strange, that."

"So it is." Mistress Sellis rubbed the side of her head once more. She yawned. "Your pardon, but I'm fordone. Mommet, come." The cat followed her into the room she'd hired from Widow Kendall as obediently as if it were a dog.

Was it a cat? Or was it the cunning woman's—the witch's—familiar spirit? Shakespeare had trouble imagining a familiar spirit, a demon surely reeking of brimstone, purring with such content as it lay on the floor. *But then, what know you of demons?* the poet asked himself. *As little as may be, and wish it were less.*

He tried to write a bit more. That bothered him less than it would have the day before. He yawned, too. He could go to bed with a clear conscience now. He knew where *Love's Labour's Won* was going, and knew he *would* finish it in a day or two. Then on to *King Philip*, and to . . . the other play.

His bedroom was dark when he went in. Jack Street's snores made the chamber hideous. Shakespeare knew he himself would have no trouble sleeping despite the racket; he'd had time to get used to it. How—indeed, whether—Sam King could manage was a different question.

Shakespeare didn't bother with a candle when he stowed his writing tools in the chest by his bed. He'd dealt with the lock so often in darkness, he might almost have been a blind craftsman whose fingers saw as well as most men's eyes. The click of the key in the lock made Street the snoring glazier mumble and turn over, though how he heard that click through his own thunderstorm was beyond Shakespeare. The poet sighed—quietly—and yawned again.

As he slipped the bottle of ink back into the chest, his fingers brushed a new and hence unfamiliar bulk: the translation of the *Annals* he'd picked up in front of St. Paul's. " 'Sdeath," he whispered: a curse that was at the same time at least half a prayer. The translation itself was innocent. But if anyone thought to search for it, his death was likely whether it were found or not. That would mean Lord Burghley's plot was betrayed.

He shut the chest, locked it, and pulled off his boots. The wooden bed frame and its leather straps creaked as he lay down and burrowed under the covers. Despite yet another yawn, sleep would not come. His mind spun faster than the spinning hand of a clock. *How can Burghley's plan hope to escape betrayal? There's surely far more to't than one poor poet and a play that may never been seen. Can he do so much with so many under the Spaniards' very noses without their suspecting? 'Tis false we English breed no traitors. Would 'twere true, but these past nine years have proved otherwise.*

What *did* Burghley purpose? Shakespeare shook his head. *Ignorance, here, is bliss. What I know not, no Spaniard can rip from me.* He wished he didn't know it was tied to word of Philip's death. But the English nobleman had had to tell him that. He needed some notion of how long he had to write the play and to train the actors of his company to perform it.

That thought made him shake his head. He still didn't know whether all of Lord Westmorland's Men would appear in a play that, if Lord Burghley's rising failed, could only be judged treason. If he sounded a player and the man refused, what could he do? Could he do anything? Would not the very act of doing something make a disaffected player more likely to go to the Spaniards, or to the lickspittle English who followed Isabella and Albert?

Questions, questions. *When questions come, they come not single spies, but in battalions.* All the questions were out in the open. Answers skulked and hid and would not show themselves, either by light of day or in these miserable, useless, pointless nighttime reflections.

Shakespeare shook his head again. His bed let out another creak. Jack Street grunted, shifted, and, for a wonder, stopped snoring. In the third bed in the room, Sam King sighed softly. Had he been awake all this while, poor devil? Shakespeare wouldn't have been surprised. Street's cacophony took getting used to.

After some more squirming, Shakespeare felt sleep at last draw near. But then he thought of his curious meeting with Cicely Sellis, and rest retreated once more. She was a cunning woman indeed. Whoever called on her would get his money's worth, however much he paid. She was probably even cunning enough to keep from falling foul of the Church, which took *Thou shalt not suffer a witch to live* ever more seriously these days.

What had she meant when her voice changed there for a little while? Some sort of warning, without a doubt. But did it come from her alone, from God, or from Satan? Shakespeare ground his teeth. How could he know? Come to that, did Cicely Sellis herself know?

One more yawn, and sleep finally overmastered him. He woke in darkness the next morning. With the winter solstice at hand, the sun wouldn't rise till after eight of the clock, and would set before four in the afternoon. In the kitchen, porridge bubbled above the fire. Shakespeare filled a bowl with it. It was bland and uninteresting: barley and peas boiled to mush together, with hardly even any salt to add savor. He didn't care. It filled the empty place in his belly for a while.

Most of the lodgers were already gone before Shakespeare rose. Regardless of whether it was light or dark, they had their trades to follow. Cicely Sellis, by contrast, came into the kitchen just as the poet was finishing. The cunning woman nodded but said nothing. She too had her own trade to follow, but could follow it here at the lodging house. By the way Widow Kendall beamed at her, she was paying a pretty penny for that room of hers. *Enough to make the widow raise the scot for the rest of us?* Shakespeare wondered worriedly. He doubted he could stand even one more vexation on top of so many.

When he went out into the street, he found he would have no accurate notion of when the sun came up, anyhow. Cold, clammy fog clung everywhere. It likely wouldn't lift till noon, if then. Shakespeare sucked in a long, damp breath. When he exhaled, he added fog of his own to that which had drifted up to Bishopsgate from the Thames.

He should have gone straight to the Theatre. He might have found some quiet time to write before the rest of the company came in and began rehearsing for the day's play.

Instead, though, he wandered south and east, away from the suburbs beyond the wall and down towards the river. He didn't know—or rather, didn't care to admit to himself—where he was going till he got there. By the time he neared the lowland by the Thames, the fog hung a little above the ground.

But even the thickest fog would have had a hard time concealing the Tower of London. Its formidable gray stone wall and towers shouldered their way into the air. People said Julius Caesar had first raised the

Tower. Shakespeare didn't know whether that was true or not, though he'd used the conceit in a couple of plays. The Tower surely seemed strong and indomitable enough to have stood since Roman days.

However strong it seemed, it hadn't kept the Spaniards out of London. And now, somewhere in there, Queen Elizabeth sat and brooded and waited for—deliverance? *Can I help to give it her? Or give I but myself to death?*

V

After Christmas Mass, Lope de Vega and Baltasar Guzmán happened to come out of the church of St. Swithin together. Lope bowed to his superior. "*Feliz Navidad*, your Excellency," he said.

Guzmán, polite as a cat, returned the bow. "And a happy Christmas to you as well, Senior Lieutenant," he replied. "I have a duty for you."

De Vega wished he'd ignored courtesy. "On the holy day?" he asked, dismayed.

"Yes, on the holy day." Captain Guzmán nodded. "I am sorry, but it is necessary, and necessary that you do it today." He didn't sound sorry. He never sounded sorry. He was stubborn as a cat, too; he went on, "I want you to take yourself to the church of St. Ethelberge"—another English name he massacred—"and ask the priest there if this poet friend of yours, this Shakespeare, has come to partake of our Lord's body and blood on the anniversary of His birth."

"Ah." However much Lope wished otherwise, Captain Guzmán was right here, as he had been with going after John Walsh—this *was* a necessary duty. "I shall attend to it directly. And if he has not?"

"If he has not, make note of it, but do no more now," Guzmán replied. "Then we watch him closely ten days from now. If he celebrates

Christmas by the old calendar, the forbidden calendar, we shall know him for a Protestant heretic."

"Yes, sir." Lope sighed. "Heretic or not, we surely know him for a splendid poet."

"And if his splendid poetry serves Satan and the foes of Spain, isn't he all the more dangerous for being splendid?" Guzmán said.

And he was right about that, too. Again, Lope wished otherwise. Again, he sighed. But, because Captain Guzmán was right, de Vega asked, "How do I find this church of St. Ethelberge?" He had almost as much trouble with the name as his superior had done, and added, "Where do the English find such people to canonize? Swithin here, Ethelberge there, and I hear there is also a St. Erkenwald in this kingdom. Truly I wonder if Rome has ever heard of these so-called saints."

"I have plenty of worries, but not that one," Baltasar Guzmán said. "If the Inquisition and the Society of Jesus found these saints were fraudulent, the churches dedicated to their memories would not stay open."

He's right yet again, Lope thought, surprised and a little resentful. *Three times in a row, all of a Christmas morning. He'd better be careful. If he keeps that up, I may have to start taking him seriously. He wouldn't like that, and I wouldn't, either.* Since Guzmán hadn't answered him the first time, he tried again: "How do I find St. Ethelberge's church, Captain?"

"It's Shakespeare's parish church, *sí*? Shakespeare lives in Bishopsgate, *sí*? Go to Bishopsgate. You know the way there, *sí*?" Guzmán waited for Lope to respond. He had to nod, for he did know the way to and through that district: it led out of London proper to the Theatre. "All right, then," the captain told him. "Go to Bishopsgate. If you find the church yourself, fine. If you don't, ask someone. Who wouldn't tell a man how to get to a church on Christmas morning?"

He was, of course, right yet again. "I go," Lope said, and hurried off toward Bishopsgate as much to escape Captain Guzmán and his alarmingly sharp wits as to find out whether Shakespeare had been to Mass. Even though the day was gloomy, London's houses and public buildings made a brave show, being decorated with wreaths and strands of holly and ivy, now and then wound up with broom. Many of the ornaments had candles burning in them, too. In the first couple of years after the coming of the Armada, such signs of the season had been rare. Elizabeth and her heretic advisors discouraged them, as they'd discouraged so many observances from the ritual year. But, with the return of Catholicism, the customs that had flourished before Henry VIII broke with Rome were also coming back to life.

Many doors stood open, the rich odors of cookery wafting out warring with those of garbage and sewage. From Advent, the fourth Sunday before the Nativity, to Christmas Eve, people restricted their diets. On Christmas Eve itself, meat, cheese, and eggs were all forbidden. But Christmas . . . Christmas was a day of release, and also of sharing. Only skinflints closed their doors against visitors on Christmas Day.

A man in what looked like a beggar's rags with a roast goose leg in one hand and a mug of wine in the other came up the street toward Lope. By the way he wobbled as he walked, he'd already downed several mugs. But he gave Lope an extravagant bow all the same. "God bless you on the day, sir," he said.

"And you, sir," de Vega replied, returning the bow as if to an equal. On Christmas, as on Easter, were not all men equal in Christ?

Lope did have to ask after St. Ethelberge's church. But people indeed proved eager to help him find it. He got there just when a Mass was ending. And he got his answer without having to ask the priest, for with his own eyes he saw Shakespeare coming out of the church in a slashed doublet of black and crimson as fancy as anything Christopher Marlowe might wear.

Lope thought about waving and calling out a greeting. He thought about it for a heartbeat, and then thought better of it. He ducked around a corner instead, before Shakespeare spotted him. What excuse could he offer for being in Bishopsgate on Christmas morning, save that he was spying on the English poet? None, and he knew it.

He got back to the barracks in the center of town without asking anyone for directions. That left him proud of himself; he was strutting as he made his way to Captain Guzmán's office. And he'd been right, and Guzmán, for once, wrong. That added to the strut. He looked forward to rubbing his superior's nose in it.

Whatever he looked for, he didn't get it. When he opened the door, Guzmán wasn't there. His servant, Enrique, sat behind his desk, frowning in concentration over a quarto edition of one of Marlowe's plays. He read English better than he spoke it, though still none too well.

He didn't notice the door opening. Lope had to cough. "Oh!" Enrique said in surprise, blinking behind his spectacles. "Good day, Senior Lieutenant."

"Good day," Lope replied politely. "Where's your principal?"

"He was bidden to a feast, sir," Guzmán's servant replied. "He left me behind here to take your report. Did the priest at this church with the name no sane man could pronounce see *Señor* Shakespeare at Mass today?"

"What do you do if I tell you no?" de Vega asked, trying not to show how angry he was. Guzmán could send him off to Bishopsgate on Christmas morning, but did the noble stay around to hear what he'd found? Not likely! He went off to have a good time. *And if I'd been here, maybe someone would have invited me to this feast, too.*

"I bring his Excellency the news, of course," Enrique said. "After that, I suppose he sends out an order for Shakespeare's arrest. Do I need to go to him?"

"No." Lope shook his head, then jabbed his chest with his thumb. "I myself saw Shakespeare leaving the church of St. Ethelberge"—he could pronounce it (better than most Spaniards, anyway), and didn't miss a chance to show off—"not an hour ago, so there's no need to disturb Captain Guzmán at his revels."

"I'm glad," Enrique said. De Vega wondered how he meant that. Glad he didn't have to go looking for Guzmán? But then the servant went on, "From everything I can tell, the Englishman is too fine a poet for me to want him to burn in hell for opposing the true and holy Catholic faith."

"*Tienes razón*, Enrique," Lope said. "I had the same thought myself." *And if Enrique agrees with me, he must be right.*

"Do you have any other business with my master, Lieutenant?" the servant asked.

Yes, but not the sort you mean—this shabby treatment he's shown me comes close to touching my honor, Lope thought. But he wouldn't tell that to Guzmán's lackey. He would either take it up with the officer himself or, more likely, decide it wasn't a deliberate insult and stop worrying about it. All he said to Enrique was, "A happy Christmas to you."

"And to you, *señor*." As Lope turned to go, Enrique picked up the play once more. He read aloud:

> " '*O lente, lente currite noctis equi:*
> The stars move still, time runs, the clock will strike,
> The devil will come, and Faustus must be damned.
> O, I'll leap up to my God! Who pulls me down?'

This is very fine poetry, I think."

"And I," de Vega agreed, "even if he borrowed the slowly running horses of the night from Ovid."

"Well, yes, of course," said Enrique, who, despite being a servant, somewhere had acquired a formidable education. "But he uses the line in a way that makes it his own. He doesn't just trot it out to show how learned he is."

"A point," Lope said. "Marlowe is a very clever man—and if you don't believe me, ask him."

Guzmán's servant grinned. "Meaning no offense to you, *señor*, but conceit is a vice not unknown amongst poets."

"I have no idea what you're talking about, Enrique," de Vega replied, deadpan. They both laughed. Lope closed the door behind him and headed for his own quarters.

He expected to discover Diego there, snoring up a storm. Christmas was a holy day, too holy for almost all work (not that Diego felt like working on the most ordinary day of the year, either). But the servant's bed was empty. Lope crossed himself. "Truly this is a day of miracles," he murmured.

In his own little inner room, he found paper and pen and ink. He opened the shutters, to take such advantage of England's fleeting December daylight as he could, and began to write. Maybe Christmas was too holy for that, too. De Vega had no intention of asking a priest's opinion about it.

A RAGGED MAN ON A STREET CORNER THRUST A BOWL OF SPICED wine at a pretty woman walking by. "Wassail!" he called.

She looked him over, smiled, and nodded at him. "Drinkhail!" she replied. He handed her the bowl and kissed her on the cheek. She drank, then gave him back the bowl.

"A happy New Year to you, sweetheart!" the ragged man called after her as she went on her way. He sang in a surprisingly sweet, surprisingly true baritone:

"Wassail, wassail, as white as my name,
Wassail, wassail, in snow, frost, and hail,
Wassail, wassail, that much doth avail,
Wassail, wassail, that never will fail."

William Shakespeare tossed the fellow a penny. "A happy New Year to you as well, sirrah."

The ragged man doffed his cap. "God bless you on the day, sir!" He held the bowl out to Shakespeare. "Wassail!"

"Drinkhail!" Shakespeare replied, and drank. Returning the bowl, he added, "I'd as lief go without the kiss." Some Grecian, he couldn't remember who, had said the like to Alexander, and paid for it. Marlowe would know the name.

With a chuckle, the ragged man said, "And I'd as lief not give it you. But by my troth, sir, full many a fair lady have I bussed, and thanks to the wassail bowl I owe." He lifted the cap from his head again. "Give you joy of the coming year."

"And you." Shakespeare walked past him. A couple of blocks farther on, another man used a wassail bowl to gather coins and kisses. Shakespeare gave him a penny, too. He got in return a different song, one he hadn't heard before, and did his best to remember it. Bits of it might show up in a play years from now.

All along the crowded street, men and women wished one another happy New Year. They'd done that even back before the coming of the Armada, for the Roman tradition of beginning the year in wintertime had lingered even though, before the Spaniards came, it had formally started on March 25. As with the calendar, Isabella and Albert had changed that to conform to Spanish practice. People called 1589 the Short Year, for it had begun on March 25 and ended on December 31.

Snow crunched under Shakespeare's shoes. Soot and dirt streaked it. Back in Stratford, snow stayed white some little while after it fell. Not here. Stratford was a little market town; he would have been surprised had it held two thousand souls. London had at least a hundred times as many, and more than a hundred times as many fires belching smoke into the sky to smirch the snow sometimes even before it fell.

A snowball whizzed past his head from behind. He whirled. The urchin who'd thrown it stuck out his tongue and scurried away. With a shrug, Shakespeare went on walking. He'd thrown snowballs when he was a boy, too. *And my aim was better*, he thought, though that might have been the man's view of the boy he'd been.

He strode past a cutler's shop, then stopped, turned, and went back. The Widow Kendall had broken the wooden handle on her best carving knife not so long before, and had complained about it ever since. She kept talking about taking the knife to a tinker for a new handle, but she hadn't done it. Like as not, she never would get around to doing it, but would grumble about what a fine knife it had been for the rest of her days. A replacement, now, a replacement would make her a fine New Year's present.

"Good morrow, sir, and a joyous New Year to you," the cutler said when Shakespeare stepped inside. "What seek you? An it have an edge, you'll find it here." Shakespeare explained what he wanted, and why. The cutler nodded. "I have the very thing." He offered Shakespeare a knife of about the same size as the one Jane Kendall had used.

"Certes, 'tis a knife." Shakespeare tried the edge with his thumb. "It now seems sharp enough. But will't stay so?"

"The hardest knife ill-used doth lose his edge," the cutler replied, "but it hath a better blade than most, and will serve for all ordinary work. And surely she for whom you buy't hath a whetstone?"

"Surely." Shakespeare had no idea whether Jane Kendall owned a whetstone. He supposed she must; how could she keep a kitchen in good order without one? Setting the knife down on the counter, he asked the next important question: "What's your price?" When the cutler told him, he flinched. "So much? Half that were robbery, let alone the whole of't. 'Tis for a tallowchandler's widow, not silver clad in parcel gilt for the kitchen of a duke."

They haggled amiably enough. Not for all his poet's eloquence could Shakespeare beat the cutler down very far. At last, still muttering under his breath, he paid. The cutler did give him a leather sheath for the knife. "The better your widow cares for't, the better 'twill serve her. Dirt and wet breed rust as filth breeds maggots."

"I understand." Shakespeare didn't intend to lecture his landlady on housewifery. What the Widow Kendall would say to him if he showed such cheek did not bear thinking about.

He took the knife back to his lodgings. On the way there, he slipped a halfpenny into the sheath. Giving the Widow Kendall the knife without the propitiatory coin would have been inviting her to cut herself with it.

"Oh, God bless you, Master Will!" she exclaimed when he handed her the knife. She gave him a muscular hug and stood on tiptoe to kiss him on the cheek. That was another kiss he could have done without; her breath stank with eating toasted cheese. He did his best to smile as she said, "I've thought me of getting a new one since that handle broke, but. . . ." She shrugged.

But you'd sooner have done without, or gone on with the old marred one, than have fared forth yourself to a tinker's or a cutler's, he thought. "May you have good use of't," he said.

"I'm sure I shall," she said. "Come take a mug of ale, an't please you."

That mug was the only New Year's gift he had from her. Since he'd expected nothing more, he wasn't disappointed. But Christopher Marlowe came by the house later that day and gave him a copy of Tacitus' *Annals*—in the original Latin. "I dare hope you may find it . . . inspiring," the other poet murmured.

As was Marlowe's habit, he'd spent lavishly. The book was bound in maroon leather and stamped with gold. Shakespeare wanted to hit him over the head with it; with any luck, it would smash in his skull. How much did Marlowe know? How much did he want Shakespeare to think he knew? How badly did he want to drive Shakespeare to distraction? *That, more than the other two together*, Shakespeare judged.

Showing Marlowe he'd drawn blood only encouraged him to try to draw more. With a smile, Shakespeare answered, "I'm sure I shall. The treason trials under Tiberius, perchance?" Ever so slightly, he stressed the word *treason*.

Marlowe bared his teeth in something that looked like a smile. "Treason? What word is that? And in what tongue? Tartar? I know it not."

"Perdie, Kit, may that be so," Shakespeare said. "May the day come when that Tartar word's clean forgot in England."

Laughing, Marlowe patted him on the cheek, as an indulgent father might pat a son. "Our lines will fail or ever that word's routed from our . . ." He drew back, sudden concern on his face. "Will, what's amiss?"

"You will find a better time to speak of failing lines than when my only son's but a little more than a year in's grave," Shakespeare said tightly. His fists bunched. He took a step towards the other poet, whom he saw for a moment through a veil of unshed tears.

Marlowe backed away. "Pardon my witlessness, I pray you," he said.

"I will—one day," Shakespeare answered, angry still. Marlowe left the lodging house moments later. Shakespeare wasn't sorry to see him go, not only because of what he'd said but also because he wouldn't linger to make more gibes about Tacitus and treason that might stick in someone's mind.

Though it was snowing hard on Sunday, Shakespeare made a point of going to Mass at the church of St. Ethelberge the Virgin. It was, by

Pope Gregory's calendar, the fourth of January—by England's old reckoning, December twenty-fifth. He wanted to be sure he was seen at Catholic services that day. If he were not, he might be suspected of observing Christmas on the day the Spaniards—and the English Inquisition—deemed untimely. Since he truly deserved suspicion, he had all the more reason not to want to see it fall on him. The pews in the little church were more crowded than usual. Maybe—probably—he wasn't the only soul there making a point of being seen.

He went to St. Ethelberge's again two days later, for the feast of Epiphany, the twelfth and last day of Christmas. A gilded brass Star of Bethlehem hung from the rood loft. Some of the parishioners put on a short drama about the recognition of the Christ Child by the Three Kings. Shakespeare found the performances frightful and the dialogue worse, but the audience here wasn't inclined to be critical. In the Theatre, the groundlings would have mewed and hissed such players off the stage, and pelted them with fruit or worse till they fled.

After Twelfth Night passed, the mundane world returned. When Shakespeare went off to the Theatre the next day, he carried with him the finished manuscript of *Love's Labour's Won*. He flourished it in triumph when he saw Richard Burbage. "Here, Dick: behold the fatted calf."

Burbage just jerked a thumb back toward the tiring room. "I care not a fig to see't, not until Master Martin hath somewhat smoothed it."

With a sigh, Shakespeare went. Geoffrey Martin, the company's prompter and playbook-keeper, would indeed dress the fatted calf he carried. He had a habit of writing elaborate, impractical stage directions. And, like any author in the throes of enthusiasm, he sometimes made mistakes, changing a character's name between appearances or giving a line or two to someone who happened not to be on stage at the moment. Martin's job was to catch such things, to have scribes prepare parts for all the principal actors in a play, and to murmur their lines to them if they faltered during a performance.

Martin also worked closely with Sir Edmund Tilney, the Master of the Revels, who made sure nothing blasphemous or treasonous appeared on stage. If Lord Burghley's plan was to go forward, Martin had to be part of the plot.

The prompter was about forty. He'd probably been handsome once, but nasty scars from a fire stretched across his forehead, one cheek, and the back of his left hand. The work he had—precise, important, but out of the public's eye—suited him well.

"Good morrow to you, Master Shakespeare," he said, looking up from a playbook. "Here at last, is it? We've waited longer than we might have, to see what flowed from your pen."

"I know, Master Martin," Shakespeare said humbly. "I'm sorry for't." Facing the prompter made him feel as if he were back in school again, the only difference being that Geoffrey Martin wielded a pen of his own, not a switch.

He read faster and more accurately than anyone else Shakespeare knew. That pen of his drank from the ink pot on the table in front of him, then darted at the manuscript of *Love's Labour's Won* like a striking asp. "When *will* you learn to put stage directions in a form players can actually use?" he asked, more in sorrow than in anger: he said the same thing every time Shakespeare handed him a manuscript.

"Your pardon, Master Martin," Shakespeare said. "I do essay precision, but—"

"You succeed too well," the prompter told him, also not for the first time. "With directions such as these, you break the action like a man disjointing a roast fowl. Simplicity, sir—simplicity's what wins the race."

Shakespeare wasn't convinced Martin was right. Like any playwright, he wanted things just so, with all the actors moving at his direction as Copernicus and his followers said planets moved around the sun. But the prompter's word carried more weight in such matters than his. As Martin went from one page to the next, Shakespeare did presume to ask, "What think you?"

"Aside from these wretched stage directions, very pleasant, very gay," Geoffrey Martin answered. "Without a doubt, the company will buy the play of you. And then you'll put all your work towards the new *King Philip*, is't not so?"

"As much of it as I may, yes," Shakespeare answered. The prompter's question gave him the opening he needed: "Tell me, Master Martin, what think you of—?"

But before he could finish the question, Martin lifted a hand. "Hold," he said, and such was the authority in his voice that Shakespeare fell silent. "Here in your second act, you have entering three lords and three ladies."

"I do," Shakespeare agreed, looking down at what he'd written—the second act seemed a long way off these days.

"See you here, though. Only two of these ladies speak: the one Rosaline, the other Katharine. What point to the third one, the one you style Maria?"

"Why, for to balance the third lord, of course," Shakespeare answered.

Geoffrey Martin shook his head. "It sufficeth not. Give her somewhat to do, or else take her out."

"Oh, very well," Shakespeare said testily. "Lend me your pen, then." He scratched out a name and substituted another. "Now hath she this passage, once Katharine's."

"Good enough." Martin read on. After a bit, he looked up and said, "I am much taken with your Signor Adriano di Armato, your fantastical Venetian. Some poets I need not name might have sought instead to make of him a Spaniard, the which the Master of the Revels would never countenance."

Shakespeare's first thought had been to make him a Spaniard, to get the extra laughs mocking the invaders would bring. But he too had concluded Sir Edmund would never let him get away with it. Again, though, he had the chance to ask the question he wanted, or one leading towards it: "What think you, Master Martin, of having to take such care to keep from rousing the Spaniards' ire?"

"Working with the Master would be simpler without such worries, no doubt of't," the prompter replied. "But you'll not deny, I trust, that heresy's strong grip'd yet constrain us had they not come hither. I have now the hope of heaven. Things being different, hellfire'd surely hold me after I cast my mortal slough."

"Ay, belike," Shakespeare said, none too happily. Without a doubt, Geoffrey Martin had given him an honest answer, but he hadn't said what Shakespeare wanted to hear.

"Why? Believe you otherwise?" Martin asked—he'd heard how half-hearted Shakespeare's answer sounded, which the poet hadn't wanted at all.

"By my troth, no," Shakespeare said, this time using his experience on the stage to sound as he thought Geoffrey Martin would want him to.

"I should hope not, sir," the prompter said. "King Philip, God keep him, is a great man, a very great man. He hath from ourselves saved us, and in our own despite. Of whom else might one say the like, save only our Lord Himself?"

"Even so," Shakespeare said, and got away from Martin as fast as he could. The players he'd sounded had all been willing, even eager, to help try to expel the Spaniards from England. The tireman had been noncommittal. The prompter, plainly, took the Spaniards' part. And if Geoffrey Martin suspected treason, he knew important ears into which to whisper—or shout—his suspicions.

"Why the long face, Will?" Burbage called when Shakespeare wandered out onto the stage again. "Mislikes he the mouse your mountain at last delivered?"

"Nay, the jests seemed to please him well enough," Shakespeare answered. "But he hath . . . misgivings . . . in aid of . . . certain other matters."

Someone clapped him on the shoulder. He jumped; he hadn't heard anybody come up behind him. Will Kemp's elastic features leered at him. Cackling with mad glee, the clown said, "What better time than the new year for a drawing and quartering? Or would you liefer rout out winter's chill with a burning? I'll stake you would."

"Go to!" Shakespeare exclaimed. "Get hence!"

"And wherefore should I?" Kemp replied. "I know as much as doth Dick here." Before Shakespeare could deny that, the clown continued, "I know enough to hang us all, than the which what could be more?"

Put so, he had a point. Burbage said, "The object is not to let others know enough to hang us all—*others* now including a certain gentleman (marry, a very certain gentleman he is, too) who all too easily can confound us."

"Knew you not that Geoff Martin hath his nose in the Pope of Rome's arsehole?" Kemp said with another mocking smile.

" 'Steeth, Will—soft, soft!" Shakespeare hissed, the ice outside having nothing to do with the chill that ran through him. "He need but cock his head hither and he'll hear you."

"He's right, man," Burbage said. "D'you *want* your neck stretched or your bowels cut out or the flesh roasted from your bones? Talk too free and you'll win your heart's desire."

"O ye of little faith!" Kemp jeered. "Dear Geoff's prompter and book-keeper. He hath before him a new play—so new, belike the ink's still damp. What'll he do? Plunge his beak into its liver, like the vulture with Prometheus. A cannon could sound beside him without his hearing't."

Burbage looked thoughtful. "He may have reason," he said to Shakespeare.

"He may be right," Shakespeare said. "Right or wrong, reason hath he none. Where's the reason in a man who will hazard his life for nothing but to hear his own chatter? God deliver me from being subject to the breath of every fool, whose sense no more can feel but his own fancies."

"Doth thy other mouth call me?" Will Kemp retorted. He strode away, then stopped, bent, and spoke loudly with his other mouth.

"Whoreson beetle-headed, flap-eared knave," Shakespeare burst out—but quietly. He remembered all too well that, if he angered Kemp, the clown could betray him, too.

"A bacon-fed knave, very voluble," Burbage agreed, "but when have you known a clown who was otherwise?" He too spoke in a low voice. After a moment, he went on, "And what, think you, may we do about Martin?"

"In sooth, I know not," Shakespeare said miserably. "Would we could just sack him, but the company'd rise in revolt—and with reason (that word again!), did we try it without good cause."

Burbage nodded. "True. Every word of't true."

"But this business cannot go forward without him, nor with him in opposition," Shakespeare said.

"Look you to your part of't," Burbage told him. "Write the words that needs must be writ. Think on that, for none else can do't. As for the other—haply you misread Martin's mind and purpose."

"That I did not," Shakespeare declared.

"Well, as may be," Burbage said with a shrug. "But I say this further: we are embarked here on no small enterprise, is't not so?" After waiting for Shakespeare to nod, he went on, "We may be sure, then, we are not alone embarked. We need not, unaided, solve all conundrums attached hereto."

"It could be," Shakespeare said after some thought. "Ay, it could be. But, an we solve them not, who shall?"

"That is hidden from mine eyes, and so should it be, for what I know not, no inquisitor can tear from me," Burbage said. Shakespeare nodded again, a little more heartily; he'd had the same thought. Smiling, Burbage continued, "But to say it is hidden from mine eyes is not to say it hath no existence. Others, knowing little of the parts we play, will be charged with shifting such burthens as an o'erstubborn prompter. Is *that* not so?"

"It is," Shakespeare said. "Or rather, it must be. But would I knew it for a truth, not for an article of faith."

"As what priest or preacher hath not said?" Burbage answered with a laugh. "Write the words, Will. When the time comes, I'll say 'em. And what follows from thence . . . 'tis in God's hands, not ours."

He was right. He was bound to be right—which went some way towards setting Shakespeare's mind at ease, but not so far as he would have liked. It did let him get through the day at the Theatre without making a fool of himself, which he might not have managed had Burbage not calmed him.

A couple of evenings later, as the poet was making his way down Shoreditch High Street towards Bishopsgate after a performance, a man stepped out of the evening shadows and said, "You're Master Shakespeare, are you not?"

"I am," Shakespeare said cautiously. "And who, sir, are you?"

He used that *sir* from caution; had he felt more cheerful about the world and the people in it, he would have said *sirrah*. The fellow who'd asked his name looked like a mechanical, a laborer, in leather jerkin and laddered hose. When he smiled, he showed a couple of missing teeth. "Oh, you need not know my name, sir," he said.

"Then we have no business, one with the other," Shakespeare answered, doing his best to sound polite and firm at the same time. "Give you good den." He started on.

"Hold!" the stranger said. As he set a hand on the hilt of his belt knife to emphasize the word, Shakespeare stopped. In grumbling tones, the fellow added, "Nick said you were a tickle 'un. There's a name for you, by God and St. George! You ken Nick Skeres?"

Skeres had led him to Sir William Cecil. "I do," Shakespeare said reluctantly.

"Well, good on you, then." The stranger gave him another less than reassuring smile. "Nick sent me to your honor. You've someone in your company more friendlier to the dons than an honest Englishman ought to be?"

From whom had Skeres heard about Geoffrey Martin? Burbage? Will Kemp? Someone else altogether? Or had this bruiser any true connection to Skeres at all? With such dignity as he could muster, Shakespeare said, "I treat not with a man who hath no name."

"Damn you!" the fellow said. But he didn't draw that knife. Instead, exasperated, he flung a name—"Ingram!"—at the poet.

Christian name? Surname? Shakespeare couldn't guess. But the man had given him some of what he wanted. Shakespeare answered him in turn: "Yes, there is such a one, Master Ingram."

"His name's Martin, eh? Like the bird?" Ingram asked. With odd hesitation, Shakespeare nodded. So did the other man. "All right, friend." He touched the brim of his villainous cap. "God give you good even," he said, and vanished once more into the deepening shadows. The poet stared after him, scratching his head.

"SURELY, *SEÑOR* SHAKESPEARE, YOU KNOW THAT HIS HOLINESS POPE Sixtus promised King Philip a million ducats when the first Spanish soldier set foot on English soil, and that he very handsomely paid all he had promised," Lope de Vega said. "A million gold ducats, mind you."

"Yes, I understand," Shakespeare replied. "A kingly sum, in sooth."

They sat with their heads together in the tiring room at the Theatre. De Vega puffed on a pipe of tobacco. The smoke rising from it fought with that from torches, lamps, and braziers. "I am glad you follow, sir," he said. "This needs must appear in the play on his Most Catholic Majesty's life."

Shakespeare had been scribbling notes in a character Lope could not have deciphered had his life depended on it. Now he looked up sharply. "Wherefore?" he asked. "It doth little to advance the action, the more so as Pope and King never met to seal this bargain, it being made by underlings."

"But it shows how beloved of his Holiness was the King," Lope replied.

"By the King's own deeds shall I show that," Shakespeare said, "deeds worth the showing on a stage. Here, he doth—or rather, his men do—naught but chaffer like tradesmen at the market over the sum to be paid. Were this *your* play, Master de Vega, would you such a scene include?"

After some thought, Lope spread his hands. "I yield me," he said. He sucked at the clay pipe, hoping the smoke would calm him. Working with Shakespeare was proving harder than he'd expected. The Englishman knew what was required of him: a play celebrating and memorializing Philip II's life and victories. But he had his own ideas of what belonged in such a play and how the pieces should fit together.

Having won his point, he could be gracious. "My thanks, sir," he said. "Sith the play'll bear my name, I want it to be a match for the best of my other work."

"For your pride's sake," Lope said.

"For my honor's sake," Shakespeare said.

Lope sprang from his stool and bowed low, sweeping off his hat so that the plume brushed the floor. "Say no more, sir. Your fellow poets and players would think less of you, did you write below your best. This I understand to the bottom of my soul, and I, in my turn, honor you for it. I am your servant. Command me."

"Sit, sit," Shakespeare urged him. "I own I stand in need of your counsel on the incidents of your King's life and on how to show 'em, the which is made more harder by his seldom leaving Madrid, those in his command working for him all through the Spanish Empire."

"Even so." Lope returned to his seat. He eyed the English poet with considerable respect. "You have more experience bringing history to the stage than I."

Shakespeare's smile somehow didn't quite reach his eyes. "When I put words into the mouths of Romans, I may do't without fear the Master of the Revels will think my ghosts and shadows speak of matters political."

Lope nodded. "Certes. This is one of the uses of the distant past." He leaned forward. "Here, though, not so distant is the past of which we speak. How thought you to portray the King's conquest of the heretic Dutchmen?"

"Why, through his kinsman, the Duke of Parma."

"Excellent," Lope said. "Most excellent. Parma being dead, no unsightly jealousies will to him accrue."

They kept at it till the prompter summoned Shakespeare to sort out something or other in the new play he'd offered the company. A harried look on his face, the English poet returned a couple of minutes later to say, "Your pardon, Master de Vega, but this bids fair to eat up some little while. He hath set upon my pride a blot, catching me with my characters doing now one thing, now another quite different. Having marred it, I now needs must mend it."

"*Qué lástima*," Lope said, and then, in English, "What a pity." He got to his feet. "I am wanted elsewhere anon. Shall we take up again on the morrow?"

" 'Twere better the day following," Shakespeare answered.

Lope nodded. "Until the day. *Hasta luego, señor.*" Shakespeare dipped his head, then hurried off. De Vega left the Theatre. He'd come on horseback today. One of the tireman's helpers had kept an eye on the beast to make sure it would still be there when he came out. Lope gave the Englishman a halfpenny for his trouble. By the fellow's frown, he'd hoped for more, but every man's hopes miscarried now and again.

Riding through the tenements that huddled outside the city wall, Lope felt something of a conquering *caballero*. He'd seldom had that feeling afoot. Now, though, he looked down on the English. *From literally looking down on them, I do so metaphorically as well*, he thought. *A man's mind is a strange thing.*

The English knew him for a conqueror, too. That made his passage harder, not easier. They got in his way, and feigned deafness when he shouted at them. They flung curses and catcalls from every other window. They flung other things, too: stones to make his horse shy and rear, lumps of filth to foul the beast and him. He never saw his tormentors. The ones not safe inside buildings melted into the crowds on Shoreditch High Street whenever he whirled in the saddle to try to get a glimpse of them.

By the time he got back down to Bishopsgate, he was in a perfect transport of temper. One of the Irish gallowglasses at the gate, seeing his fury, asked, "Would your honor have joy of us breaking some heads for you, now?"

"No. Let it go. You cannot hope to punish the guilty," Lope said, once he'd made sense of the heavily armed foot soldier's brogue.

With a laugh, the Irishman said, "And what difference might that make? 'Sdeath, sir, not a groat's worth. A broken head'll make you shy of tormenting a gentleman afterwards, be you guilty or no."

But Lope repeated, "Let it go." The gallowglasses and kerns brought over from the western island looked for excuses to fall upon the English. Considering what the English had done in Ireland over the years, they had reason for wanting revenge. But the outrage their atrocities spawned made them almost as much liability as asset for the Spaniards and for Isabella and Albert.

Lope rode into London. He still drew catcalls and curses. Inside the wall, though, Spaniards were more common, as were Englishmen who favored the Spanish cause. A man who flung, say, a ball of dung ran some real risk of being seen and noted. Catcalls Lope took in stride.

When he got back to the barracks, the stable boys clucked at the horse's sorry state. "And what of me?" Lope said indignantly. "Am I a plant in a pot?"

"It could be so, *señor*," one of them answered. "And if it is, you're a well manured plant, by God and St. James." He held his nose. His friends laughed. Had the misfortune befallen someone else, Lope might have laughed, too. Since it was his own, laughter only enraged him. He stormed off to his chamber.

There he found his servant, sleeping the sleep of the innocent and just. "Diego!" he shouted. Diego's snores changed timbre, but not rhythm. "*Diego!*" Lope screamed. The servant muttered something vaguely placating and rolled from his back to his belly. Lope shook him like a man trying to shake fleas out of a doublet.

Diego's eyes opened. "Oh, *buenos días, señor*," he said. "Is it an earthquake?"

"If there were an earthquake, it would swallow you as the whale swallowed Jonah," Lope said furiously. "And do you know what? Do you know what, you son of a debauched sloth?"

His servant didn't want to answer, but saw he had no choice. "What, *señor*?" he quavered.

"If there were an earthquake, it would swallow you as the whale swallowed Jonah, *and you wouldn't even know it!*" Lope bellowed. "Scotland—"

That got Diego's attention, where nothing up till then really had. "Not Scotland, *señor*, I beg you," he broke in. "The Scots are even worse than the Irish, from all I hear. May the holy Mother of God turn her back on me if I lie. They cook blood in a sheep's stomach and call it supper, and some say it is the blood of men."

"Scotland, I was going to say, is too good for you," de Vega snarled. He had the satisfaction of watching Diego quail, a satisfaction marred when his servant yawned in the midst of cringing. "By God, Diego, if you fall asleep now I'll murder you in your bed. Do you think I'm lying? Do you want to find out if I'm lying?"

"No, *señor*. All I want to do is . . ." Diego stopped, looking even more miserable than he had. He'd undoubtedly been about to say, *All I want to do is go back to sleep*. He wasn't very bright, but he could see that that would land him in even more trouble than he'd already found. A querulous whine crept into his voice as he went on, "I thought you'd stay at that damned Theatre a lot longer than you did."

"And so?" Lope said. "And so? Because I'm not here, does that mean you get to lie there like a salt cod? Why weren't you blacking my boots? Why weren't you mending my shirts? Why weren't you keeping your ears open for anything that might be to my advantage, the way Captain Guzmán's Enrique does?" *Why does that vain little thrip of a Baltasar Guzmán get a prince among servants, while I'm stuck with a donkey, and a dead donkey at that?*

Diego said something inflammatory and scandalous about exactly how intimate Enrique and Captain Guzmán were. "How would you know that?" Lope jeered. "When have you been awake to see them?"

"It's true, *señor*," Diego answered. "Everybody says so."

Lecturing his servant on what "everybody said" was worth struck de Vega as a waste of breath. But his pause was thoughtful for more reasons than that. If Guzmán really did prove a *maricón*, a sodomite, he might lose his position. He would, in fact, if he brought scandal to himself or to the Spanish occupiers as a group. And who would benefit if Baltasar Guzmán fell? *I would*, Lope thought. *People can call me a great many things, but a sodomite? Never!*

Diego's narrow little eyes glittered nastily. "Are you thinking what I'm thinking?"

"No," Lope said, not without well-concealed regret. "I am thinking that maybe you would do better asleep after all. When you're awake, your mind goes from the chamber pot to the sewage ditch. For I happen to know Captain Guzmán had a mistress till they quarreled a few months ago."

"And why would they quarrel?" Diego asked. "If he'd sooner—"

"*¡Basta!*" Lope said. "And not just enough but too much. Get up. Get out of here. Do what you're supposed to do. Then, once you've done that—which will include cleaning the clothes I have on, for the English threw filth at me and my horse today—once you've done that, I say, you'll have earned your rest, and you'll enjoy it more."

His servant looked highly dubious. De Vega supposed he had some reason. The only way he could enjoy his rest more would be to make love without waking up. Diego also thought about making some remark on the state of Lope's clothes. Again, he was wise to think twice. Grumbling under his breath, he did at last get out of bed.

Lope pulled off his boots, shed his stinking netherstocks and hose, and got out of his befouled doublet. He changed quickly; the room was cold. And then he went off to make the day's report to Captain Guzmán. "Damn you, Diego," he muttered under his breath as he went. No matter what everybody said about Guzmán—if everybody said anything about him—Lope still had to deal with him. That was hard enough already, and would be harder still if de Vega watched his superior out of the corner of his eye, looking for signs he might be a sodomite.

Before he got to Guzmán's office, he ran into Enrique. Or had Enrique contrived to run into him? Eyes wide with excitement behind the lenses of his spectacles, Captain Guzmán's servant said, "Tell me at once, Senior Lieutenant—what is it like, shaping a play with *Señor* Shakespeare?"

"I don't shape here," Lope said, remembering he might have to watch Enrique out of the corner of his eye, too. "I only have some lumber to sell. Shakespeare is the carpenter. He cuts and carves and nails things together. He'll do it very well, too, I think."

"He has a mind of his own?" Enrique asked.

"*¡Por Dios, sí!*" Lope exclaimed, and the clever young servant laughed. "You can think it's funny," de Vega told him. "You don't have to work with the Englishman."

Enrique sighed. "Oh, but I wish I did!"

"Is your master in?" Lope asked.

"Yes, I think so," Enrique said. "He was at a . . . friend's house last night, but he said before he left that he'd try to return in good time."

He said *amiga*, not *amigo*: the "friend" was of the feminine persuasion. *So much for what everybody says*, Lope thought. "Have you seen her?" he asked. "Is she pretty?"

"I should hope so, *señor*!" Enrique said enthusiastically. "A facc like an angel's, and tits out to here." He held a hand an improbable distance in front of his chest.

So much indeed for what everybody says, de Vega thought. When he walked into Baltasar Guzmán's office, the young captain looked like a cat that had just fallen into a bowl of cream. And when Guzmán asked, "What's the latest, Senior Lieutenant?" he didn't sound as if he'd bite Lope's head off if he didn't like the answer. He must have had a night to remember.

I wish I were in love again. I probably will be soon, but I'm not now, and I miss it. Sighing, de Vega summarized his session with Shakespeare. He also summarized the English attitude toward lone Spaniards on horseback: "Only my good luck they chose to throw more dung than stones. I might not have made it back if they'd gone the other way."

Captain Guzmán said, "I'm glad you're safe, de Vega. You're a valuable man." While Lope was still gaping, wondering if he'd heard straight, his superior added, "And I'm glad things are going so well with the English poet. Keep up the good work."

Lope left his office in something of a daze. Maybe Guzmán's *amiga* really did have the face of an angel and tits out to *there.* Lope couldn't imagine what else would have made the sardonic nobleman seem so much like a human being.

"Where's Master Martin?" Shakespeare asked in the tiring room at the Theatre. "He was to have the different several parts from *Love's Labour's Won* ready to go to the scribes, that they might make for the players fair copies."

"Good luck to 'em," Will Kemp said. "There's not a rooster living could read your hen scratchings."

The clown exaggerated, but not by a great deal—not enough, at any rate, to make Shakespeare snap back at him. Richard Burbage looked around. "Ay, where is he?" Burbage said, as if Kemp hadn't spoken. "Geoff's steady as the tides, trusty as a hound—"

"Ah, Dick," Kemp murmured. "You shew again why you're so much better with another man's words in your mouth."

He'd made that crack before. It must have stung even so, for Burbage glared at him. A couple of players laughed, but they quickly fell silent. Not only was Burbage a large, powerful man, but he and his family owned the Theatre. Insulting him to his face took nerve—*or a fool's foolishness,* Shakespeare thought.

"Pray God he hath not absconded," Jack Hungerford said.

That drew a loud, raucous guffaw from Will Kemp. "Pray God indeed!" the clown said. "He's to the broggers with all our papers, for the which, they'll assuredly pay him not a farthing under sixpence ha'penny—he's rich for life, belike."

He got a bigger laugh there than he had when he mocked Burbage. Shakespeare didn't find the crack funny. "Loose papers may not signify to thee, that hast not had pirates print 'em without thy let and without thy profit," he growled. "As ever, thou think'st naught for any of the company but thyself. Thou'rt not only fool, but ass and dog as well."

"A dog, is it?" Kemp said. "Thy mother's of my generation; what's she, if I be a dog?"

Shakespeare sprang for him. They each landed a couple of punches before the others of the company pulled them apart. Smarting from a blow on the cheek, Shakespeare snarled, "A dog thou art, and for the sake of bitchery." He didn't know that Kemp sought whores more than any other man, but flung the insult anyhow, too furious to care about truth.

Before the clown could reply in like vein, someone with a loud, booming voice called out from the doorway to the tiring room: "Here, now! Here now, by God! What's the meaning of this? What's the meaning of't, by God?"

"Constable Strawberry!" Burbage said. "Good day, sir."

"Good day," Walter Strawberry said. He was a jowly, middle-aged man who looked like a bulldog and had little more wit.

"I hope you are well?" Burbage said. The Theatre belonging to his family, he dealt with the constable. "I have not seen you long; how goes the world?"

"It wears, sir, as it grows," the constable replied.

"Ay, that's well known." Burbage's tone grew sharper: "Why come you here?" He quietly paid the constable and his helpers to stay away from the Theatre except when the players needed aid.

"First tell you me, what's this garboil here in aid of? What's it about, eh?" He pointed to the men holding Shakespeare and the others with a grip on Kemp.

"Words, words, words," Shakespeare answered, twisting free. "Good words are better than bad strokes, and the strokes Will and I gave each other were poor as any ever given. We are, meseems, friends again." He looked toward the clown.

Kemp had also got loose. "Most friendship is feigning, most loving mere folly," he said. Shakespeare stiffened. With a nasty smile, Kemp added, "But not ours." He came over to Shakespeare and planted a large, wet, smacking kiss on his cheek, whispering, "Scurvy, dotard, thin-faced knave," as he did so.

His acting wouldn't have convinced many, but it sufficed for Constable Strawberry. "Good, good," he boomed. "High spirits, animal spirits, eh?"

"Why come you here?" Richard Burbage repeated, as Shakespeare and Kemp, both cued by *animal spirits*, mouthed, *Ass*, at each other.

"Why come I here?" the constable echoed, as if he himself might have forgotten. He coughed portentously, then went on, "Know you a certain wight named Geoffrey Martin?"

"We do," Burbage answered.

Will Kemp said, "A more certain wight never was born, by God." Strawberry ignored that, which probably meant he didn't understand it.

"Why come you here?" Burbage asked for the third time. "Hath aught amiss befallen him?"

"Amiss? Amiss?" Walter Strawberry said. "You might say so. You just might—an you reckon murther aught amiss, you might."

"Murther?" The dreadful word came from half the company, Shakespeare among them. Horror and astonishment filled most voices. Shakespeare's held horror alone. He realized he was not surprised, and wished to heaven he were.

"Murther, yes, murther most foul," Constable Strawberry said. "Master Martin, a were found besides an ordinary, stabbed above an eye—the dexterous one, it were—the said wound causing his deceasing to be. Murther, the which were to be demonstarted."

"Who'd do such a heinous deed?" Burbage said. Again, Shakespeare knew, or thought he knew, all too well. Ingram had looked the sort to be handy with a knife.

"Master Burbage, sir, I know that not. This while, I know that not," the constable said gravely. "I put it to you—ay, to all of ye—what manner of enemies had he, of foes, of rivals, of opposants, and other suchlike folk who wished him not well? Never set I mine eyne upon the man till overlooking his dead corpse, so haply you will have known him better than I."

Behind Shakespeare, someone murmured, "*Vere legitur, lex asinus est.*"

"What's that?" Strawberry said sharply. "What's that? If you know somewhat of the case, speak out! An you know not, keep a grave silence, like to Master Martin's keeping the silence of the grave. If you be lukewarm of knowing, spew nothing out of your mouths."

"Truly, you are a revelation to us," Will Kemp said.

"Doth any man here know who might have been the prime motion of the said Master Geoffrey Martin's untimely coming to dust?" the constable asked.

Shakespeare felt Richard Burbage's eye on him. Misery roweled him. *I meant it not to come to this*, tolled in his mind again and again, like a great iron bell. *Before God, I meant it not.* But come to this it had, whether he'd meant it or not. He couldn't even be surprised. Had he not embarked on treason, or what Isabella and Albert and their Spanish props would reckon treason, no one would have slain poor Geoff Martin. *And treason and murther ever keep together, as two yoke-devils sworn to either's purpose.*

Walter Strawberry looked from one player to another, searching the faces of men and boys, making them search their consciences. Shakespeare had never known the tiring room so silent.

He did not break the silence. Neither did Burbage.

"Well," the constable said at last. "Well and well and well, and yet, not so well. A man is murthered. His blood crieth out for revengeance. I had fondly hoped you might make the way more simpler—"

"Fondly, quotha," someone said in a penetrating whisper.

Strawberry stared, but did not spy the miscreant. He coughed and repeated himself: "I fondly hoped you might make the way more simpler, but an't be no, 'tis no. Whosoever the wretch that strook him down may be, I purpose discovering him. And what I purpose, I aim at. Give you good morrow." He turned on his heel and ponderously strode away.

That clotted silence held the tiring room for another minute or two, till the players were sure the constable was out of earshot. Then almost everyone started talking at once. Almost everyone: Shakespeare held aloof, listening without speaking. One wild guess followed another: footpads? an outraged husband? a creditor? a debtor?

"Methinks our prize poet done it," Kemp put in, "for that Master Geoffrey was ever changing his precious verses."

That roused Shakespeare to speech: "Did I slay on such account, you had been years dead, and more deserving of't than our poor prompter."

"Ah, but I make you better," the clown said smugly.

"Enough!" Richard Burbage's roar filled the room, startling everyone into momentary silence once more. He pointed first at Kemp, then at Shakespeare. "Too much, by God! Give over, else you quarrel with me."

Shakespeare nodded. After a moment, so did Will Kemp. Shakespeare wondered how long the truce would last. From what he knew of the clown, not long. And, of course, Burbage could throw wood on the fire, too. *And so can you*, Shakespeare reminded himself.

More quietly, Burbage went on, "We need a new man to perform the office of playbook-keeper and prompter as soon as may be, for we shall make proper ninnies of ourselves without him. Know ye of a man able to do't and at liberty?"

Nobody said anything. At last, Jack Hungerford spoke up: "I'll nose about. Players, now, players come and go, but we who tread not the boards incline more towards finding one place and holding it."

"We'll find someone," Burbage said with the air of a man trying to sound confident. "But meanwhile, we all must needs watch our fellows' backs. Any one of us may of a day be dull. If a player have forgot his part and be out, let him not go even to a full disgrace. Whisper to him—give him the words he wants. All will go forward, and all for the best."

Hungerford said, "Till we have our new man, it were better to give plays we have done before many a time and oft, that by familiarity we feel as little as may be the lack."

Burbage nodded to the tireman. "Well said." He eyed Hungerford in a speculative way. "Until this exigency be past, could you, Jack, undertake some of what Master Martin did, your helpers taking your place with costumes and the like?"

Hungerford looked unhappy. "I'd be scarce a 'prentice in's trade, as my helpers are scarce more than 'prentices in mine. 'Twould make us weaker all around than we are."

"Weaker in the whole of the fabric, yes, but without the rent this garment our company would otherwise suffer," Burbage said. "And only for a brief space of time, till we find the man can take poor Geoffrey's place."

Burbage usually thundered like Jove, browbeating, pushing the company along the path he wanted by force of will. Here, though, he roared as gently as any sucking dove, cajoling the tireman into doing what he wanted. In truth, Jack Hungerford needed little cajoling. "I'll do't," he said, "but only for a little while, mind."

"Gramercy," Burbage said, and made a leg. The tireman chuckled in embarrassed pleasure.

"Gramercy," Shakespeare echoed, moving his lips without sound. Had Hungerford stayed stubborn in his refusal, Burbage's eye likely would have fallen on *him* next. Who would do better for a makeshift prompter than the man who'd penned many of the plays in the first place and might reasonably be expected, therefore, to know everyone's lines?

And I have not the time in which to do't, he thought desperately. Two plays to write, not a word set down on either . . . and he still had to act, too. He wanted to cry. He wanted to scream. He wanted to lock himself in a room with nothing but his books and do nothing but set words on paper. He could have none of what he wanted.

They got through the afternoon's performance without disgracing themselves. As Shakespeare left the Theatre afterwards, Richard Burbage came up beside him. His shoulders sagged in a silent sigh, but he wasn't really surprised. Burbage said, "Sad for poor Martin's family. He had a new babe, I believe, o' the lady he wed after his first wife perished in the fire that marked him."

"Most piteous sad indeed." Shakespeare trudged down Shoreditch High Street towards filthy, crowded London: towards his home.

Burbage matched him stride for stride. After a while, he said, "Will . . ."

Shakespeare didn't answer. He just kept walking.

"Will . . ."

"What is't?" Shakespeare snapped. "Are you sure you want to know?" This time, Burbage was the one who didn't say anything. He only waited. After a moment, Shakespeare realized what he was waiting for. "God be my judge, Dick, I devised his death not."

"I thought naught other. There's none o' the killing blood in you—else, as you say, Will Kemp were long since sped." But Burbage's smile quickly faded from his fleshy lips. "That you devised it not, I believe with all my heart. That it grieved you, I believe also. That it amazed you, as it amazed us . . ." He shook his head. "No."

"Why say you so?" Shakespeare asked.

"For that you spake of Martin his Popery as hurtful to a . . . a certain enterprise," Burbage answered. "Was't the second Henry who cried out, 'Who will rid me of this turbulent priest?'—and behold! there's Becket dead."

Shakespeare laughed uneasily. That shot struck much too close to the center of the target. Trying to lead Burbage away from the truth he'd found, the poet said, " 'Tis treason or folly or both together to set alongside a king's my name."

Burbage, however, was not so easily distracted. "An I hire me another Popish prompter, will he too lie dead in a ditch the day after?"

"I know not," Shakespeare said.

"What think you?" the player persisted.

"I think . . . I think a great ship is setting sail. I am thereon, haply, one small sail. If the wind blow foul, 'twill tear me to ribbons—and they'll haul me down in a trice, and raise in my place another . . . and the ship'll sail on as before. Are you answered, Dick?"

"I am answered," Burbage said heavily. "And I'll inquire of those with whom I speak how they stand with Rome."

"Softly! Softly!" Shakespeare warned. "If they wonder why you put such questions, 'twere better never to have asked at all."

"You take me for a fool," Burbage said. "He's the other wight."

"Heh," Shakespeare said. "Another one who's fain to jape on's own."

"We're not on the boards now, Will."

"Think you not?" Shakespeare shook his head. "Till this . . . enterprise go forward, if it go forward, we are players everywhere, players always. Forget it at your peril."

Burbage chewed on that for a few paces. By the sour face he pulled, he did not like the taste. He pointed ahead. "There's Bishopsgate." He hurried on alone, flinging words back over his shoulder: "If you have the right of't, best not to be seen with you."

That hurt. It would have hurt worse had Shakespeare not been convinced he *was* right—which made Burbage right to avoid his company. The player passed through the gate and disappeared. Shakespeare followed more slowly. He felt he ought to ring a bell like a leper, to warn folk of his presence. His touch was liable to prove as deadly as any leper's. That he knew too well.

And then, when he was only a couple of houses from the one where he lodged, something else occurred to him. Geoffrey Martin had proved an annoyance to those who'd framed this plot. He'd proved an annoyance, and they'd brushed him aside as casually as if he were a flea on a doublet. *And if* I *prove an annoyance?* Shakespeare shivered. *But Lord Burghley styled me his strong right arm.* The poet shivered again. Plenty of people in the street that chilly afternoon were shivering, so he went unnoticed. *If I prove an annoyance, they'll brush me aside as yarely as poor Geoff Martin.*

Captain Baltasar Guzmán held up a sheet of paper to Lope de Vega. "We are ordered to take special notice, Senior Lieutenant, of any who profane Lent this year by eating of foods forbidden these forty days."

"We are ordered to do all sorts of foolish things," Lope answered. "This is more foolish than most. The English, from all I've seen in my time here, break the rules as often as they keep them." He exaggerated, but not by an enormous amount. A surprising amount of meat got eaten here in the weeks before Easter.

Guzmán waved the paper. "But this," he said portentously, "is a special year."

"How is this year special?" de Vega asked, as he knew he was supposed to do. "I know his Holiness has declared that 1600 will be a year of jubilee, but 1598?" He shrugged. "To me, it seems a year among years."

"Not so." His superior waved the paper again. Lope was getting tired of seeing it without being able to read it. Guzmán went on, "Ash Wednesday, this year, is the fourth of February, and Easter the twenty-second of March."

"They're early," Lope remarked. "Is that enough to make it special?"

"As a matter of fact, yes," Guzmán answered. "It is, it says here, as early as Easter can come." He waved that damned paper one more time. "This is, of course, the twenty-second of March by the calendar Pope Gregory ordained fifteen years ago."

"Yes, ten days earlier by the old calendar the heretics still love," Lope agreed. "But Easter isn't like Christmas—we don't have one day and they another."

"Ah, but this year, we do," Captain Guzmán said. "By their calendar, what we call the paschal full moon falls before the vernal equinox. They will count the Sunday after the *next* full moon as Easter—April the twenty-sixth by our reckoning, the sixteenth by theirs. Now do you understand?"

After a moment, de Vega nodded. "I think so. If their Easter is later, their Lent will begin later, too, and—"

"And they will find it no sin to eat meat during the first part of our Lent," Guzmán broke in. "They either have to keep the fast an extra month to make themselves both safe and what they call holy, or—"

Lope interrupted in turn: "Or break the law of God and the fast. I see it now, your Excellency. You're right—this is a special year." He wouldn't have wanted to keep the Lenten fast for more than two months, and he doubted whether many stubbornly Protestant Englishmen would, either.

Baltasar Guzmán nodded. "We can smoke out a lot of heretics who've hidden from us since the Armada landed. The sooner we get rid of the last of them, the sooner we'll have peace in the kingdom."

"Peace." Lope sighed. "It seems like one of those mirages that fool travelers lost in the desert. You follow the mirage, and what looks like water recedes before you. If we had peace here, maybe one day I could go home to Spain. I wonder if I would recognize Madrid. After so long here, I'd probably think it was beastly hot."

"One thing is certain, though," Captain Guzmán said. "As long as there are still Protestants in England, we'll have no peace. This kingdom has to follow the holy Catholic faith. All the world, one day, will follow the holy Catholic faith. Then, truly, peace will come." He crossed himself. His eyes glowed with a Crusader's vision.

"Yes." De Vega crossed himself, too. But then, incautiously, he said, "We've fought the Portuguese and the French, and they're Catholic, too—after a fashion."

Guzmán waved that aside. "When all the world is Catholic, there *will* be peace," he declared, as if challenging Lope to argue with him. Lope didn't. He might not have been so passionately certain of that as Guzmán was, but he believed it, too.

"Is there anything else, your Excellency?" he asked.

To his surprise and disappointment, Guzmán nodded. "Yes. What do you make of the murder of, ah, Geoffrey Martin?" He made heavy going of the dead man's Christian name.

"A robber, I suppose," Lope answered with a shrug. "I hear his purse was empty when the constables found his body."

"Robbery, perhaps, but what else?" his superior persisted. "He was a good Catholic, and now he's dead. We might have learned a great deal from him."

"Had someone approached him?" Lope asked. "If anyone had, I never knew it."

"Nor I," Guzmán said. "But that does not necessarily signify. He could have been talking to the English Inquisition with us none the wiser. The inquisitors always hold their cards close to their chests—sometimes too close to play them, I think, but they are not anxious for my opinion."

"Losing the prompter is a blow to the company," Lope said. "They will have to replace him as soon as they can."

"And with whom they replace him may be interesting." Captain Guzmán eyed de Vega. "If Shakespeare is as much an innocent as you think, he certainly has odd things happen around him."

"And if you think Shakespeare a footpad, your Excellency, you prove you do not know the man at all," de Vega replied.

"That is not what I said, Senior Lieutenant," Guzmán said, a distinct chill in his voice. "Please think about what I *did* say. You are dismissed." To show how very dismissed he was, his superior bent his head to his paperwork with him still in the office.

Seething, Lope gave Guzmán a salute whose perfection was an act of mockery. "Good day, your Excellency," he snarled sweetly. His about-face might almost have been a dance. He neither slammed Guzmán's door on walking out nor shut it silently, as Enrique had. Instead, he left it open. The captain's exasperated sigh and the scrape of his chair on the wood floor as he pushed it back so he could get up and close the door himself were music to de Vega's ears.

He knew nothing but thanks at escaping the barracks—thanks and cold, for snowflakes fluttered on the northwesterly breeze. *It's January. It could be snowing in Madrid, too*, he told himself. It was true. He knew it was true. It didn't help. When he thought of Madrid, he thought of a place where the vine and the olive flourished. He tried to imagine grapes and olives growing in London, and laughed at himself. Not even a poet's imagination stretched so far.

In the street outside the barracks, a Spanish soldier and a skinny Englishwoman were striking a bargain. He gave her a coin. She led him away. Before long, he would get relief. Lope didn't know whether to envy or pity him for being satisfied so easily.

"I'd sooner be a monk than buy a nasty counterfeit for love," he muttered. That didn't mean he enjoyed living like a monk. He had, though, ever since his two mistresses were so inconsiderate as to run into each other outside the Southwark bear garden. *Goodbye, Nell. Farewell, Martha. High time I found someone new.*

He wouldn't do it by the barracks. He knew that. The Spanish soldiers stationed there drew trulls as a lodestone drew iron. De Vega didn't want women of easy virtue. He wanted women who would fall in love with him, and whom he would love . . . for a while.

He wandered down towards the Thames, past the church of St. Lawrence Poultney in Candlewick Street. Not far from the church, a woman with a wicker basket called, "Whelks and mussels! Cockles and clams! Fresh today. Whelks and mussels . . . !"

Maybe they were fresh today, maybe they weren't. In this weather, even shellfish stayed good for a while—one of its few virtues Lope could think of. He eyed the woman selling them. She was a few years younger than he, wrapped in a wool cloak she would have thrown out two years before if she could have afforded to replace it. The worried look on her face told how hard life could be.

"Whelks or mussels, sir?" she said, feeling his eye on her. "Clams? Cockles? Good for dinner, good for supper, good for soup, good for stew." She all but sang the desperate little jingle.

"Cockles, I think," Lope answered, "though I should be pleased to buy anything from so lovely a creature."

Her weary sigh sent fog swirling from her mouth. "I sell that not," she said, voice hard and flat.

"God forbid I meant any such thing!" Lope exclaimed, though he had, at least to test her. He swept off his hat, bowed, and told her his name, then gave her his most open, friendly smile and asked hers.

"I oughtn't to tell it you," she said.

"And why not?" He affected indignation. "What shall I do with it? Make witchcraft against you? They'd burn me, none less than the which I'd deserve. Nay, sweet lady, I want it only for to write it on the door-posts of mine heart. My heart?" He couldn't remember which was right.

The girl with the basket of shellfish didn't enlighten him. A tiny smile did lift the corners of her mouth for a moment, though. She said, "There's a deal of foolery in you, is't not so?"

"I know not whereof you speak," Lope said, donning a comically droll expression.

That smile was like a shy wild thing he had to lure from hiding. He felt rewarded when he saw it. "I'm Lucy Watkins, sir," she said.

"My lady!" Lope bowed again. She wasn't his lady. Maybe she never would be. But he intended to make trial of that.

VI

Smoke from the fireplace, smoke from the flames under a roasting capon, and smoke from half a dozen pipes of tobacco filled the Boar's Head in East Cheap. Shakespeare's eyes stung and watered. "What's the utility of tobacco?" he asked the player beside him, who'd been drinking sack with singleminded dedication for some little while now. "What pleasure takes one from the smoking of it, besides the pleasure of setting fire to one's purse?" The stuff was, among other things, devilishly expensive.

The player blinked at him in owlish solemnity. "Why, to pass current, of course," he answered. After a soft belch, he buried his nose in the mug of sack once more.

"It suffices not," Shakespeare murmured.

"Pay him no heed," Christopher Marlowe said from across the table. Marlowe had a pipe. He paused to draw in smoke, then blew a perfect smoke ring. Shakespeare goggled. He'd never seen that before. It almost answered his question by itself. Laughing at his flabbergasted expression, Marlowe went on, "He is sensible in nothing but blows, and so is an ass."

"Is that so?" the player said. "Well, sirrah, you can kiss mine arse."

Marlowe rose from his stool in one smooth motion. "Right gladly will I." He came around the table, kissed the fellow on the mouth, and returned to his place. The drunken player gaped and then, too late, cursed and wiped his mouth on the sleeve of his doublet. Loud, raucous laughter filled the Boar's Head. Under it, Marlowe nodded to Shakespeare. "You were saying, Will?"

"What good's tobacco?" Shakespeare asked.

"What good is't?" Now Marlowe was the one who stared. "Why, let Aristotle and all your philosophers say what they will, there is nothing to be compared with tobacco. Have you tried it, at the least?"

"I have, four or five years gone by. I paid my shilling for the damned little clay pipe, and two shillings more for the noxious weed to charge it with, and I smoked and I smoked till I might have been a chimneytop. And . . ."

"And?" Marlowe echoed.

"And I cast up the good threepenny supper I'd had not long before—as featly as you please, mind, missing my shoes altogether—and sithence have had naught to do with tobacco, nor wanted to."

"Liked you the leek when first you ate of it? Or the bitter taste of beer?"

"Better than that horrid plant from unknown clime." Shakespeare shuddered at the memory of how his guts had knotted.

"By my troth, I was seeking for a fool when I found you," Marlowe said. "You have not so much brain as ear-wax; in sooth, there will be little learning die then that day you are hanged." He leered at Shakespeare. "And who knows which day that will be, eh, my chuck?"

"Go to," Shakespeare snarled. Marlowe *would* not keep his mouth shut. "More of your conversation would infect my brain. You draw out the thread of your verbosity finer than the style of your argument, you scambling, outfacing, fashion-mongering peevish lown."

"Well shot, Will," Thomas Dekker called. The young poet whooped and clapped his hands. Lord Westmorland's Men had put on his first play only a few weeks before. He lifted up his mug of wine in salute. "Reload and give him another barrel!" He drained the mug and slammed it down.

Shakespeare caught a barmaid's eye and pointed to Dekker. When she filled the youngster's mug again, Shakespeare paid her. Dekker was chronically short of funds; till Shakespeare's company bought his comedy, he'd been one step from debtor's prison—and now, rumor had it, was again.

Marlowe clucked reproachfully. "Buying a claque? I reckoned it beneath you. The Devil will not have you damned, lest the oil that's in you should set hell on fire." He emptied his mug, and gave the barmaid a halfpenny to refresh it. "I pay mine own way," he declared, drinking again.

"I am sure, Kit, though you know what temperance should be, you know not what it is," Shakespeare answered sweetly.

"Me? Me?" Marlowe's indignation was convincing. Whether it was also genuine, Shakespeare had no idea. "What of you, eh? I am too well acquainted with your manner of wrenching the true cause the false way."

As Shakespeare had with Dekker, so Marlowe also had a partisan: a boy actor of about fourteen, as pretty as one of the girls he played. He laughed and banged his fist down on the tabletop. Marlowe bought him more of whatever he was drinking—beer, Shakespeare saw when the serving woman poured his mug full again. He'd already had quite a lot; hectic color glowed on his cheeks, as if he were coming down with a fever.

Marlowe blew another smoke ring, then passed the pipe to the boy, who managed a couple of unskillful puffs before coughing piteously and turning even redder than he was. Marlowe took back the pipe. He kissed the stem where the boy's lips had touched it, then put it in his own mouth again.

Watching intently was a tall, thin, pale man who wore wore a rich doublet of slashed silk. His tongue played over his red lips as he watched Marlowe and the boy. "Who's that?" Shakespeare asked Dekker. He pointed. "I have seen him aforetimes, but recall not his name."

"Why, 'tis Anthony Bacon," the other poet replied. "He hath a . . . liking for beardless boys." He laughed and drank again. Shakespeare nodded. Not only had he seen Bacon, he'd visited the house Anthony shared with his younger brother, Francis, to see Sir William Cecil. He suddenly wondered what Anthony knew of the plot. Wonder or not, he had no intention of trying to find out.

Marlowe and Shakespeare weren't the only poets and players and other theatre folk dueling with words in the Boar's Head. Will Kemp had got George Rowley, an actor notorious for his slow thinking, splutteringly furious at him. As Rowley cast about for some devastating comeback—and looked more and more unhappy as none occurred to him—Kemp gave him a mocking bow and sang out, "Look, he's winding up the watch of his wit; by and by it will strike."

"I'll strike you, you—you—you . . . *fool*!" Rowley shouted amidst general laughter, which only got louder at his sorry reply.

"Is his head worth a hat? Or his chin worth a beard?" Kemp demanded of the crowd, and got back shouts of, "No!" that pierced the smoke and came echoing back from the stout oak beams of the roof. George Rowley surged up from his bench and did try to strike him then, but other actors held them apart.

Marlowe smiled across the table at Shakespeare. "Ah, the Boar's Head," he said fondly. "What things we have seen, done at the Boar's Head! Heard words that have been so nimble, so full of subtle flame—"

Shakespeare broke in, "As if that everyone from whence they came . . ." He paused in thought, then carried on: "Had meant to put his whole wit in a jest, and had resolved to live a fool the rest of his dull life."

"Not bad, Will," Marlowe said. "No, not bad, and all the better for the internal rhyme. . . . Purposed you that from when you began to speak?"

"An I say yes, you'll call me liar; an I say no, you'll call me lucky clotpoll," Shakespeare answered. The other poet grinned back at him, altogether unabashed. Shakespeare turned thoughtful. "Think you the like hath value in shaping dialogue?"

Marlowe leaned forward. "A thought of merit! It might lead mere leaden prose towards the suppleness of blank verse."

They batted the idea back and forth, nearly oblivious to the racket around them, till the pretty boy beside Marlowe, indignant at being ignored, got up to go. Shakespeare wondered if Marlowe would notice even that. Anthony Bacon did, he saw. Despite the lure of versification, the lure of the boy proved stronger for Marlowe. He spoke soothingly. When that failed to have the desired effect, he charged his pipe with tobacco, lit it with a splinter kindled from a nearby candle, and offered it to the boy. The youngster took another puff, made a horrible face, and coughed as if in the final stages of some dreadful tisick. Shakespeare's sympathies were with him.

Regardless of Shakespeare's sympathies, the boy and Marlowe left the Boar's Head together. Marlowe's arm was around the boy's waist; the youngster's head nestled against his shoulder. Bacon watched them hungrily. Anyone looking at them would have guessed they were sweethearts. And so, Shakespeare supposed, they were. But Marlowe could not hide—indeed, took pride in not hiding—his appetites. The English Inquisition might burn him for sodomy. Secular authorities, if they caught him, would merely hang him.

Maybe the talk with Marlowe was what he needed to get his wits going, though. That night, at the ordinary, he began work on the play Lord Burghley had asked of him. He wished he were as wealthy as one of the Bacons, or as Burghley himself. Committing treason was bad enough. Committing it in public . . .

He put a hand over his papers whenever Kate the serving woman came near. She found it funny instead of taking offense. "I'll not steal your words," she said. "Since when could I, having no letters of mine own?"

She'd said before she needed to make a mark instead of signing her name. Shakespeare relaxed—a very little. Whenever anyone but Kate walked past the table where he wrote, he kept on covering up the manuscript. That, of course, drew more attention to it than it would have got had he kept on writing. A plump burgess looked down at the sheet in front of him, shook his head, and said, "You need have no fear, sir. Nor God nor the Devil could make out your character."

Geoffrey Martin had voiced similar complaints. But poor Martin had been the company's book-keeper; he naturally had a low opinion of the hand of a mere poet. To hear someone with less exacting standards scorn Shakespeare's script was oddly reassuring.

After a while, Shakespeare was the only customer left in the ordinary. His quill scratched across the paper so fast, the ink on one line scarcely had time to dry before his hand smudged it while writing the next. He started when Kate said, "Curfew's nigh, Master Will."

"So soon?" he said, amazed.

"Soon?" She shook her head. "You've sat there writing sith you finished supper, none of you but your right hand moving. Look—two whole leaves filled. Never saw I you write so fast."

Little by little, Shakespeare came forward in time a millennium and a half, from bold, outraged Britons and swaggering Romans to London in the year of our Lord 1598. "I wrote two leaves? By God, I did." He whistled in wonder. He couldn't remember the last time he'd done so much of a night, either. Not even when he was finishing *Love's Labour's Won* had his pen flown like this.

"Is't something new, then?" she asked.

"Yes." He nodded. He could safely say that much. And he could safely let her see the manuscript, as she'd reminded him earlier in the evening, for she couldn't read it. And . . . all of a sudden, he didn't feel like thinking about the play any more. "Might I bide a little longer?" he asked. Kate nodded. She didn't seem much surprised.

Later, when they lay side by side on the narrow little bed in her cramped little chamber, she set her palm on the left side of his chest, perhaps to feel his heartbeat slow towards normal from its pounding peak of a few minutes before. Shakespeare set his own hand on hers. "What's to become of us, Will?" she asked.

He sighed. He'd run into altogether too many questions lately for which he had no good answers. Here was another. Having no good answers, he responded with a question of his own: "What *can* become of us? I've a wife and two daughters in Stratford. I've never hid 'em from thee."

Kate nodded. "Yes, thou'rt honest, in thine own fashion." That neither sounded nor felt like praise. But here they lay together in her bed, warm and naked and sated. If *that* wasn't praise of the highest sort a woman could give a man, what was it?

"I do love thee," he said. Kate snuggled against him. He leaned over and kissed her cheek, hoping he was telling the truth. He sighed again. "Did I have a choice . . ."

But before Shakespeare was born, Henry VIII had wanted a choice, too. When the Pope wouldn't give him one, he'd pulled England away from Rome. Now, of course, the invading Spaniards had forcibly brought her back to the Catholic Church. But even if Elizabeth still reigned, even if England were still Protestant, divorce was for sovereigns and nobles and those rich enough to pay for a private act of Parliament, not for the likes of a struggling poet and player who lived in a Bishopsgate lodging house, had a sour wife far away, and sometimes slept with the serving woman at the ordinary around the corner.

"Didst thou have a choice . . ." Kate echoed.

Before God, I know not what I'd do, Shakespeare thought. If he hadn't got Anne with child, he doubted he would have wed her. Years and years too late to worry about that now, though. *What therefore God hath joined together, let not man put asunder*. He'd heard that text in sermons more times than he could count since the Armada put Isabella and Albert on the English throne. Priests harped on it, to show that Protestants who countenanced divorce were heretics and sinners.

"Didst thou have a choice . . ." Kate repeated, a little more sharply this time.

Would she have me lie to her? Shakespeare wondered. He was just then and would keep on lying to practically everyone he knew. Why should a serving woman be different from anyone else? *Because I do—*

because I might—love her. Not a perfect answer, but the best he could do.

"Did I have a choice, my chuck . . ." Shakespeare sighed and shrugged, expecting her to throw him out of that narrow bed for not crying out that he would cleave to her come what might.

She startled him by laughing, and startled him again by kissing him on the cheek. "Perhaps thou art truly honest, Will. Most men'd lie for the sake of their sweetheart's feelings."

"I'll give thee what I can, Kate, and cherish all thou givest me. And now I had best be gone." Shakespeare got out of bed and began to dress.

"God keep thee, Will," she said, a yawn blurring her words. "Hurry to thy lodging. Surely curfew's past."

"God keep thee," he said, and opened the door to her room. He went out, closing the door behind him.

LOPE DE VEGA CAME UP TO THE PRIEST. THE ENGLISHMAN MARKED his forehead with the ashes of the "palm" (usually, in this northern clime, willow or box or yew) branches used the previous Palm Sunday. In Latin, the priest said, "Remember, thou art dust, and to dust thou shalt return."

Crossing himself, Lope murmured, "Amen," and made his way out of St. Swithin's church. Most of the people he saw on the streets, English and Spaniards alike, already had their foreheads marked with the sign of repentance that opened the Lenten season. Anyone who didn't, especially in a year when Catholics and heretics celebrated Easter more than a month apart, would get some hard looks from those whose duty was to examine such things.

Though it was still the first week of February, the day was springlike: mild, almost warm, the sky a hazy blue with fluffy white clouds drifting slowly across it from west to east. The sun shone brightly. A few more such days and flowers would begin to open, seeds to bring forth new plants, leaves to bud on trees.

Once, Lope had seen this weather hold long enough for nature to be fooled—which made the following blizzard all the crueler by comparison. He didn't expect this stretch to last so long. Usually, they were like a deceitful girl who promised much more than she intended to give. Knowing as much, he didn't feel himself cheated, as he had when he'd first come to England.

"I am sure you are brokenhearted that Lord Westmorland's Men have got a dispensation to let them perform through Lent," Captain Baltasar Guzmán said outside the church.

"Oh, of course, your Excellency," de Vega replied. He was damned if he'd let this little pipsqueak, still wet behind the ears, outdo him in irony. He touched his forehead, as if to say the ashes there symbolized his mourning. But then he went on, "Most of the acting companies gain these dispensations. They would have a hard time staying in business if they didn't." Acting companies were by the nature of things shoestring operations (Lord Westmorland's Men a bit less than most); they could ill afford losing more than a tenth of their revenue by shutting down between Ash Wednesday and Easter.

"Well, go on up to the Theatre, then," Guzmán said. "See if anyone is bold enough to flaunt his heresy to the world at large. Whoever he is, he will pay."

"Yes, sir," Lope said. "Sir, is there any further word of his Most Catholic Majesty? Shakespeare has asked after him. Not unreasonably, he wants some notion of how much time he has to compose the drama Don Diego Flores de Valdés set him."

"I have news, yes, but none of it good," Captain Guzmán replied. "The gout has attacked his neck, which makes both eating and sleeping very difficult for him. And the sores on his hands and feet show no sign of healing. If anything, they begin to ulcerate and spread. Also, his dropsy is no better—if anything, is worse."

Tears stung Lope's eyes. He touched the ashes on his forehead again. "The priest in the church spoke truly: to dust we shall return. But this is bitter, a man who was—who *is*—so great, having an end so hard and slow. Better if he simply went to sleep one night and never woke up."

"God will do as He pleases, Senior Lieutenant, not as you please. Would you set your judgment against His?"

"No, sir—not that it would do any good if I did, for He can act and all I can do is talk."

Guzmán relaxed. "So long as you understand that. With a man who makes plays . . . Forgive me, but I wondered if you arrogated some of the Lord's powers to yourself, since you make your characters and move them about as if you were the Almighty for them."

Lope looked at him in astonishment. "I have had those blasphemous thoughts, yes, sir. My confessor has given me heavy penance on account of them. How could you guess?"

"It seemed logical," Guzmán said. "You have a world inside your head, an imaginary world filled with imaginary people. Who could blame you for believing, now and again, that that imaginary world is real? You make it seem real to others in your plays—why not to yourself as well?"

"Do you know, your Excellency, I am going to have to pay serious attention to you, whether I want to or not," de Vega said slowly.

Baltasar Guzmán set a hand on his shoulder. "Now, now, Senior Lieutenant. You had better be careful what you say, or you'll embarrass both of us. Being your superior, *I* should do the embarrassing. Let me try: how is your latest lady friend?"

Lope wasn't embarrassed. He flashed Guzmán a grin. "She's very well, thank you," he said, and heaved a sigh. "I do believe she is the sweetest creature I ever met."

"And I do believe you've said that about every woman for whom you ever conceived an affection, which must be half the women in England, at the very least." Captain Guzmán grinned, too, a nasty, crooked grin. "How am I doing?"

"Pretty well, thanks," Lope answered. "You make me glad I'm going to the Theatre." He wasn't sorry to hurry away from St. Swithin's, for Captain Guzmán's shot had hit in the white center of the target. Lope *did* passionately believe, at least for a while, that each new girl was *the* one upon whom God had most generously bestowed His gifts. What point to loving someone, after all, if she weren't special? Lucy Watkins, now . . .

As he made his way through the teeming streets of London, he thought of her shy little smile, of her soft voice, of the pale little wisps of hair that came loose no matter how tightly plaited the rest was . . . and of the taste of her lips, of her uncommonly sweet smell, of the charms he hadn't sampled yet but soon hoped to.

A constable and a tavern-keeper stood arguing outside the latter's door. The constable wagged his finger in the other fellow's face. "Marry, there is another indictment upon thee," he said severely, "for suffering flesh to be eaten in thy house, contrary to the law; for the which I think thou wilt howl."

"All victuallers do so," the tavern-keeper protested. "What's a joint of mutton or two in a whole Lent?"

"In a whole Lent?" the constable said. "A whole Lent, with Ash Wednesday scarce begun? Thou'lt go to the dock for this, beshrew me if thou dost not. Every soul is of a mind to crush out Protestantism like it was a black-beetle in amongst the sallat greens. Bad business, heresy, terrible bad."

"Protestantism? Heresy? Art daft, George Trimble? What's that to do with a bit o' mutton?—for the which thou'st shown no small liking, Lents gone by."

"Liar!" the constable exclaimed, in tones that couldn't mean anything but, *In the name of God, keep your mouth shut!* He went on, "Besides, Lents gone by have naught to do with now. It's all the calendar, it is, that has to do with heresy."

"How?" the tavern-keeper demanded.

"Why, for that it does, that's how," George Trimble said. Lope sighed and went on his way. He could have explained what the problem was, but he didn't think either of the quarreling Englishmen would have cared to listen to him.

By now, the men who took money at the Theatre recognized Lope and waved him through as if he were one of the sharers among Lord Westmorland's Men. He wished he were. The life of a Spanish lieutenant was as nothing next to that which Burbage or Shakespeare or Will Kemp lived. De Vega was sure of it.

Kemp threw back his head and howled like a wolf when Lope walked into the Theatre. De Vega gave back a courtier's bow, which at least disconcerted the clown for a moment. Kemp, he noticed, wore no ashes on his forehead. What did that mean? Did it mean anything? With Kemp, you could never be sure.

Swords clashed as a couple of actors rehearsed a fight scene. One glance told de Vega neither of them had ever used a blade in earnest. Burbage, he'd seen, had some notion of what he was about. These fellows? The Spaniard shook his head. They were even worse than Shakespeare, who'd never pretended to be a warrior.

Burbage, now, boomed out the Scottish King's lines:

> " 'Canst thou not minister to a mind diseased,
> Pluck from the memory a rooted sorrow,
> Raze out the written troubles of the brain,
> And with some sweet oblivious antidote
> Cleanse the stuffed bosom of that perilous stuff
> Which weighs upon the heart?' "

" 'Therein the patient must minister to himself,' " replied the hireling playing the doctor.

Burbage frowned. Lope had seen the Scottish play a couple of times, and admired it. He knew, or thought he knew, what the actor was supposed to say next. And, sure enough, someone hissed from the tiring room: " 'Throw physic to the dogs.' "

" 'Throw physic to the dogs; I'll none of it,' " Burbage finished, and went on in his own voice: "My thanks, Master Vincent. The line would not come to me."

"No need to praise my doing only that for which you took me into your company," replied Thomas Vincent, the new prompter and playbook-keeper. He came out to nod to Burbage. "You should reprove me if I keep silence." He was about Lope's age, lean, and seemed bright. Lope had learned he went to Mass every Sunday. Before the Armada came, he'd been as zealous in attending Protestant Sunday services.

A trimmer, de Vega thought scornfully. *Whichever way the wind blows, that's the way he'll go*. But a lot of men, likely a majority, were like that. It made things easier for those who would rule them. *Shakespeare's like that, too*, Lope reminded himself. *He was no Catholic when Elizabeth ruled this land*. Which was one more reason to reckon him an unlikely traitor. He'd made his compromises with the way things were. The ones you had to worry about were those who refused to change, no matter what refusing cost them.

Geoffrey Martin, Lope thought. He'd paid no special attention to the prompter while Martin lived. Now that Martin was dead, it was too late. *Sir Edmund Tilney—or, if not the Master of the Revels, someone in his office—could tell me more about him*.

"Seek you Master Will?" Richard Burbage called.

"An you do, you've found him." But that was Will Kemp, not Shakespeare. The clown went from making a leg at Lope to collapsing in a heap before him: one of the better pratfalls he'd seen.

De Vega shook his head. "Many thanks, but nay. I have that for which I came." He bowed to Burbage (who looked surprised at his saying no) and to Kemp, resisting the impulse to try to match the fool's loose-jointed toppling sprawl. Then he hurried out of the Theatre.

Captain Guzmán didn't think of this. Maybe I'll learn something important. Even if I don't, I'll look busy. If I have my own ideas and follow them up, how can Guzmán complain about me? He can't—and if I'm busy on another play of my own, well, by God, he'll have a hard time complaining about that, too.

"HAVE YOU A MOMENT, MASTER HUNGERFORD?" SHAKESPEARE hated asking the question, and the ones that would follow. He hated it even more than he had when he'd spoken with Geoffrey Martin. When Martin gave the wrong answers, the inconvenient answers, Shakespeare hadn't known what would happen next. Now he did. If blood flowed, it would drip from his hands.

But the tireman only nodded. "Certes, Master Will. What would you?" He flicked a speck of lint from a velvet robe.

"What costumes have we for a Roman play?" Shakespeare asked.

"A *Roman* play?" The tireman frowned. "Meseems we could mount one at need." In most dramas, no matter when or where they were set, players wore clothes of current fashion. Audiences expected nothing else. But Roman plays were different. People had a notion that the Romans had dressed differently. And so actors strode the boards in knee-length white tunics and in gilded helms with nodding crests mounted (often insecurely) above them. Despite his answer, Hungerford's frown didn't go away. "Why ask you that, though? I know for a certainty we offer no Roman plays any time soon, nor Grecian ones, neither."

Shakespeare nodded nervously. "You speak sooth. But I am writing a Roman play, one that may be shown soon after it's done."

"Ah?" Hungerford quirked a gingery eyebrow; they'd held their color better than his hair or his beard. "This alongside your *King Philip*?"

"Yes," Shakespeare said: one syllable covering a lot of ground.

"You've much to do, then, and scant time wherein to do't," Hungerford said. Shakespeare nodded; that was a manifest truth. The tireman asked, "And what title hath this latest?"

"*Boudicca*," Shakespeare answered, and waited to see what would come of that. If Jack Hungerford knew Latin and remembered his Roman history, the title would be plenty to alarm him—and to hang Shakespeare, if he mentioned it to the wrong people.

But the name was only a nonsense word to Hungerford; Shakespeare saw as much in his eyes. "Scarce sounds Roman at all," the tireman said.

"It is, though," Shakespeare said, and summarized the plot in a few sentences.

Even before he finished, Hungerford held up a hand. "Are you daft, Master Shakespeare? Never would Sir Edmund let that be seen. No more would the dons. Our lives'd answer for the tenth part of't—no, for the hundredth."

"I know't," Shakespeare said. *Marry, how I know't!* "And yet I purpose going forward even so. What say you?"

Jack Hungerford didn't say anything for some little while. He stroked his chin, studying the poet. "You sought to sound me once before on this matter, eh?"

"I did," Shakespeare agreed.

The tireman shook his head. "No, sir. You did not. You fought shy of't then."

"And if I did?" Shakespeare threw that back as a challenge. "You hold my life in the hollow of your hand. Close it and I perish."

"I wonder," Hungerford murmured. "Tell me, an you will: did you discover yourself to Geoff Martin?" Shakespeare said not a word. He hoped his face gave no answer, either. Hungerford grunted softly. "If I say you nay, will Constable Strawberry, that good and honest man, sniff after my slayer like a dog too old to take a scent after a bone that never was there?"

"I devised not poor Geoff's death, nor compassed it," Shakespeare said.

"The which is not what I asked," the tireman observed. Shakespeare only waited. Jack Hungerford grunted again. "I'm with you," he said. "I have not so much life left, and mislike living on my knees what remains."

"Praise God!" Shakespeare exclaimed. "I know not how we could have gone on without you."

"With a new tireman, belike, as we have a new prompter," Hungerford said. "Will you tell me I'm mistook?" Shakespeare wished he could and knew he couldn't. Hungerford nodded to himself. "A Roman play, is't? But tell me what you require, Master Will, and you shall have't presently."

"My thanks." *My thanks if you cozen me not, if you fly not to the Spaniards soon as I turn my back.*

"Which of the boys thought you to play the part wherefrom the piece takes its name?" Hungerford asked.

"Why, Tom, of course," Shakespeare answered. "No woman, I'll swear, could better a woman personate."

But the tireman shook his head. "He will not serve."

"What? 'Swounds, why not?"

"Item: his elder brother is a priest. Item: his uncle is a sergeant amongst Queen Isabella's guards." Jack Hungerford ticked off points on his fingers as he made them. "Item: his father gave the rood screen at their parish church, such adornments having been ordained once more on our being returned to Romish ways. Item: the lad himself more than once in my hearing hath said he's fain on becoming a man to follow his brother into the priesthood." He glanced over at Shakespeare. "Shall I go on?"

"By my troth, no. Would you had not gone so long!" Shakespeare made an unhappy hissing noise. "Why knew I so little of the lad his leanings?"

"Why? I'll tell you why, Master Will." Hungerford chuckled. "To you, he's but a boy playing parts writ or by you or by some other poet. You think on him more than you think on a fancy robe some player wears, ay, but not much more. Did you think on him as a *boy*, now . . ." His voice trailed away, then picked up again: "I warrant you, I'd need to instruct Master Kit in none o' this."

"Belike that's so. Indeed, I'm sure Kit hath made it a point to learn all worth knowing of the boy, from top to bottom."

"Just so. Your bent being otherwise, you—" The tireman broke off. The look he sent Shakespeare was somewhere between reproachful and horrified. "You said that of a purpose."

"I?" Shakespeare looked as innocent as he could. His own worries helped keep glee from his face as he went on, "If the part be for another, as meseems it needs must, what of him? How keep we him in ignorance of this our design?"

"Haply his voice will break, or his beard sprout. He's rising fifteen," Hungerford said. "Some troubles themselves resolve."

"Haply." Shakespeare made the word into a curse. " 'Haply' suffices not. You spoke of Geoff Martin. Are you fain to have his fate befall a boy, for no cause but that he's of Romish faith? He will die the death, I tell you, unless he be eased from this company ere we give our *Boudicca*." *If ever we give't*, he thought unhappily.

The tireman frowned, too. "Sits the wind in that corner?"

"Nowhere else," Shakespeare answered. "What's a mere boy, to those who'd dice for a kingdom?"

"An they think thus, should they win it?" Hungerford asked.

"Are their foes better?" Shakespeare returned. "Saw you the auto de fe this past autumn?"

"Nay, I saw't not, for which I give thanks to God. But I've seen others, and I take your point." Jack Hungerford bared his teeth in what was anything but a smile. "Would someone's hands were clean."

"Pilate's were. He washed 'em," Shakespeare said. Hungerford showed his teeth again. With a sigh, Shakespeare continued, "Would they'd tasked another with the deed, but, sith 'tis mine, how can I do't save with the best that's in me?"

Hungerford eyed him. "They might have chose worse. In many several ways, they might have."

"You do me o'ermuch honor," Shakespeare said. The tireman shook his head. Shakespeare refused to let himself be distracted: "What of Tom? We *must* separate him from ourselves."

"If he is to be driven hence, Dick Burbage is the man to do't," the tireman said.

"I'll speak to him," Shakespeare said at once. The more someone, anyone, else did, the less he would have to do himself, and the less guilty he would feel. He looked down at his hands. They already had Geoffrey Martin's blood on them. He didn't want Tom's there, too. He didn't even want the burden of pushing Tom from Lord Westmorland's Men. He already carried too many burdens.

Only when he went looking for Burbage did he stop and think about the burdens the other player carried. Tom was without a doubt the best boy actor the company had. Once he was gone, which of the others would take his roles? Which of the others *could* take his roles? How much damage would his leaving cause to performances? On the other hand, how much damage would his staying cause to him?

Burbage listened with more patience than Shakespeare would have expected—with more patience, in fact, than the poet thought he could have mustered himself. At last, he let out a long sigh. "What of the company will be left once you have your way with it?" he asked somberly.

"Would you liefer see Tom dead?" Shakespeare asked.

"I'd liefer see him playing," Burbage said.

"Tell me he is not of the Romish persuasion, and have your wish."

With another sigh, Burbage shook his head. "I cannot, for he is." He set his meaty hand on Shakespeare's shoulder. "But hear me, Will. Hear me well."

"I am your servant," Shakespeare said.

"Buzz, buzz!" Burbage said scornfully. "Go to, Will. I dance to your piping now, and well we both know't."

"Would it were *my* piping, my friend, for my feet too tread its measures."

"The which brings me back to what I'd tell you. Mark my words, now; mark 'em well. The purpose you undertake is dangerous, the friends you have uncertain, the time itself unsorted, and your whole plot too light, for the counterpoise of so great an opposition."

"Say you so?" Shakespeare asked. "Say you so?"

"Marry, I do."

Shakespeare wished he could fly into a great temper. *I say unto you, you are a shallow cowardly hind, and you lie,* he wanted to shout. *By the Lord our plot is as good a plot as ever was laid, our friends true and constant! A good plot, good friends, and full of expectation! A good plot, very good friends! What a frosty-spirited rogue are you!*

He wanted to say all that, and more besides. He wanted to, but could not. "What of't?" he said, and did not try to hide his own bitterness. "We go forward e'en so—forward, or to the Spaniards. There's your choice, and none other."

Burbage's eyes had the look of a fox's as the hounds closed in. "Damn you, Will."

"Anon," Shakespeare said, understanding Burbage's hunted expression all too well—he'd felt hunted himself for months. "But, for now, you'll see to Tom?"

"I'll do't," Burbage said. *Forward*, Shakespeare thought.

"NOW HERE IS AN INTERESTING BIT OF BUSINESS." CAPTAIN BALTASAR Guzmán held up a sheet of paper.

Lope de Vega hated it when his superior did that. It was always for effect; Guzmán never let him actually read the papers he displayed. And Lope was in a testy mood anyhow, for his visit to Sir Edmund Tilney had yielded exactly nothing useful about Geoffrey Martin and whoever had slain him. With such patience as he could muster, de Vega said, "Please tell me more, sir."

"Well, Senior Lieutenant, you will know better than I how the pretty boy actors in these English theatrical companies draw sodomites as a bowl of honey draws flies," Guzmán said.

"Oh, yes, sir," Lope agreed. "It is a scandal, a shame, and a disgrace."

Captain Guzmán waved the paper. "We now have leave to go after one of these wicked fellows, and an important one, too."

"Ah?" de Vega said. "Who?" If it turned out to be Christopher Marlowe, he would go after the English poet with a heavy heart. Marlowe didn't hide that he loved boys. Far from hiding it, in fact, he flaunted it. He was so blatant about his leanings, Lope sometimes wondered if part of him wanted to be caught and punished. Whatever that part wanted, the rest of him would not care to be humiliated and then executed.

But Guzmán said, "A certain Anthony Bacon. Do you know the name?"

"*Madre de Dios*, I should hope so!" Lope exclaimed. "The older brother of Francis, the nephew of Lord Burghley . . . How did you learn that such a man favored this dreadful vice?" *How is it that you can think of arresting such an important man, with such prominent connections, for sodomy?* was what he really meant. The rich and the powerful often got away with what would ruin someone ordinary. But not here?

Not here. Guzmán answered, "Oh, this Bacon's habits are not in doubt. Even as long ago as 1586, when he was an English spy in France, he debauched one of his young servants. He was lucky the French court was full of perverts"—his lip curled—"or he would have suffered more than he did."

"We aren't arresting him for what happened in France while Elizabeth was still Queen of England, are we?" Lope asked. Even for a charge as heinous as sodomy, that might go too far.

But Baltasar Guzmán shook his head. "By no means, Senior Lieutenant. He has taken up with one of the boy actors in a company, and there can be no doubt he's stuck it in as far as it would go."

Do you know, do you have the faintest idea, what's being said of you and Enrique? Lope wondered. He shook his head. Guzmán couldn't possibly. He couldn't speak with such disgusted relish about what Anthony Bacon had done if he'd done the like himself, or if he knew people thought he'd done the like. Lope had seen good acting in the Spanish theatre, and in the English, but nothing to compare to Guzmán's performance, if performance it were.

"A question, your Excellency?" de Vega asked. Captain Guzmán nodded. Lope went on, "How is it that this falls to us and not to the English Inquisition? Bacon has committed the sin of buggery, not treason against Isabella and Albert or rebellion against his Most Catholic Majesty."

"As it happens, Don Diego Flores de Valdés referred the matter to us," Guzmán replied. "It may yet come down to treason. Remember—not so long ago, your precious Shakespeare visited the house Anthony and Francis Bacon share. Why? We still don't know. We have no idea. But if we take Bacon and squeeze him till—"

"Squeeze him till the grease runs out of him," Lope broke in. Captain Guzmán looked blank. Lope explained: "*Bacon*, in English, means the same as *tocino* in Spanish."

"Does it?" Guzmán's smile was forced. "Shall we stick to the business at hand? If we take Bacon and squeeze him, we may finally find out why Shakespeare was there—and from that, who knows where we might go? If it were up to me, Burghley would have lost his head with the rest of Elizabeth's chief officers."

"King Philip ordered otherwise," de Vega said. His superior grimaced, but that was an argument no one could oppose.

Guzmán said, "We will go seize Bacon, then. We will seize him, and we will see how he fries." He waited for Lope to laugh. Lope dutifully did, even if he'd made the joke first.

Half an hour later, the two of them rode hotspur out of London towards Westminster at the head of a troop of Spanish cavalrymen. They had passed through Ludgate and were trotting west along Fleet Street when Lope suddenly whipped his head around. "What is it?" asked Baltasar Guzmán, who missed very little.

"I thought that fellow walking back towards London, the one who scrambled off the road to get out of our way, was Shakespeare," de Vega answered. "Is it worth our while to stop and find out?"

Guzmán considered, then shook his head. "No. Even if it was, he could have too many good reasons, reasons that have nothing to do with the Bacons' house, for being on this side of London. Walking in his own city is not evidence of anything, and neither is getting out of the way of cavalrymen."

"*Muy bien*," Lope said. "I would have used these arguments with you, but if you hadn't been persuaded. . . ." He shrugged. "You are the captain."

"Yes. I am." Guzmán bared his teeth in a hunter's grin. "And now I want a taste of Bacon—of *tocino*, eh?" Now he wouldn't leave the pun alone.

The troop of horsemen pounded up Drury Lane. Westminster seemed to Lope a different world from London: less crowded, with far bigger, far grander homes, homes that would have done credit to a Spanish nobleman. Only the abominable weather reminded him in which kingdom he dwelt.

Captain Guzmán reined in. He pointed to a particularly splendid half-timbered house. "That one," he said. "Senior Lieutenant de Vega, you will interpret for us."

"I am at your service, your Excellency." Lope dismounted.

So did Guzmán and the cavalrymen. A few of the latter held horses for the rest. The others drew swords and pistols and advanced on the estate behind the two officers. "I hope the heretics inside put up a fight and give us an excuse to sack the place," a trooper said hungrily. "God cover my arse with boils if you couldn't bring away a year's pay without half trying." A couple of other men growled greedy agreement.

"By God, if they give us any trouble, we *will* sack them," Captain Guzmán declared. "They're only Englishmen. They have no business standing in our way. They have no *right* to stand in our way." The cavalrymen nodded, staring avidly—wolfishly—at the house upon which they advanced.

Pale English faces stared out of them through the windows, whose small glass panes were held together by strips of lead. Before de Vega and Guzmán reached the door, it opened. A frightened-looking but well-dressed servant bowed to them. "What would ye, gentles?" he asked. "Why come ye hither with such a host at your backs?"

"We require the person of *Señor*—of Master—Anthony Bacon, he to be required to give answer to certain charges laid against him," Lope answered. He quickly translated for Captain Guzmán.

His superior nodded approval, then turned and rapped out an order to the cavalrymen: "Surround the place. Let no one leave."

As the troopers hurried to obey, the house servant said, "Bide here a moment, my masters. I'll return presently, with one who'll tell ye more than I can." He ducked into the house, but did not presume to close the door.

"Can they hide him in there?" Lope asked.

"Not from us." Guzmán spoke with great conviction. "And I'll tear the place down around their ears if I think that's what they're trying."

The servant was as good as his word, coming back almost at once. Behind him strode a man made several inches taller by a high-crowned, wide-brimmed hat. The newcomer's enormous, fancy ruff and velvet doublet proclaimed him a person of consequence. So did his manner;

though no bigger than Lope (apart from that hat), he contrived to look down his nose at him. When he spoke, it was in elegant Latin: "What do you desire?"

So much for my translating, de Vega thought. "I desire to know who you are, to begin with," Captain Guzmán replied, also in Latin.

"I? I am Francis Bacon," the Englishman replied. He was in his late thirties—not far from Lope's age—with a long face, handsome but for a rather tuberous nose; a pale complexion; dark beard and eyebrows, the latter formidably expressive; and the air of a man certain he was talking to his inferiors. It made de Vega want to bristle.

It put Baltasar Guzmán's back up, too. "You are the younger brother of Anthony Bacon?" he snapped.

"I have that honor, yes. Who are you, and why do you wish to know?"

Guzmán quivered with anger. "I am an officer of his Most Catholic Majesty, Philip II of Spain, and I have come to arrest your brother, sir, for the abominable crime of sodomy. So much for your honor. Now where is he? Speak, or be sorry for your silence."

Francis Bacon had nerve. He eyed Guzmán as if the captain were something noxious he'd found floating in a mud puddle. "You may be an officer of the King of Spain, but this is England. Show me your warrant, or else get hence. For the house of everyone is to him as his castle and fortress, as well for his defense against injury and violence as for his repose."

Guzmán's rapier cleared the scabbard with a *wheep!* Lope also drew his sword, backing his superior's play. The troopers with pistols behind them pointed their weapons at Bacon's face. "Damnation to you and damnation to your castle, sir," the dapper little noble ground out. "Here is my warrant. Obey it or die. The choice is yours."

For a moment, Lope thought Francis Bacon would let himself be killed on the spot. But then, very visibly, the Englishman crumpled. "I beseech your Lordships to be merciful to a broken reed," he said. "Ask. I will answer."

In Spanish, Captain Guzmán said to Lope, "You see? Fear of death makes cowards of them all."

"Yes, your Excellency," de Vega answered in the same language. Watching Bacon's face, he added, "Have a care, sir. I think he understands this tongue, whether he cares to speak it or not."

"Thank you. I will note it, I promise you." Guzmán returned to Latin as he gave his attention back to the Englishman: "So. You are the brother of the abominable sodomite, Anthony Bacon."

"I—" Francis Bacon bit his lip. "I am Anthony Bacon's brother, yes. I said so."

"Where is your brother?"

"He is not here."

The point of Guzmán's rapier leaped out and caressed Bacon's throat just above his ruff, just below his beard. "That is not what I asked, Englishman. One more time: *where is he?*"

"I—I—I do not know. You may take my life, but before God it is the truth. I do not know. Day before yesterday, he left this house. He did not say whither he was bound. I have not seen him since."

"Tipped off?" Lope wondered aloud.

"By whom?" Captain Guzmán demanded. "What Spaniard would do such a wicked, treacherous thing?"

"Perhaps another sodomite, a secret one," de Vega said.

Guzmán grimaced and grunted. "Yes, damn it, that could be. Or it could be that *Señor* Home-is-his-castle here is lying through his teeth. He'll be sorry if he is, but it could be. We'll find out, by God." He turned and called over his shoulder to the cavalrymen at his back: "Now we take the place apart." The troopers whooped with glee.

One of the first things they found, in the front hall, was, not Anthony Bacon himself, but a painting of him. He was even paler than his brother, with a longer, wispier, more pointed beard and with a long, thin, straight nose rather than a lumpy one. But for their noses, the resemblance between the two of them was striking.

Pointing to the portrait, Lope told the cavalrymen, "Here is the wretch we seek. Whoever finds him will have a reward." He jingled coins in his belt pouch. The troopers grinned and nudged one another. With a grin of his own, de Vega said, "Go on, my hounds. Hunt down this rabbit for us."

The Spaniards went through the Bacons' home with a methodical ferocity that said they would have done well as robbers—and that might have said some of them had more than a little practice at the trade. They examined every space that might possibly have held a man, from the cellars to the kitchens to the attic. They knocked holes in several walls: some Protestants' houses had "preacher holes" concealed with marvelous cunning. A couple of troopers went out onto the roof; Lope listened to their boots clumping above his head.

They did not find Anthony Bacon.

His brother Francis asked, "How much of my own will they leave me?" By the way the troopers' pouches got fatter and fatter as time went by, the question seemed reasonable.

But Captain Guzmán was not inclined to listen to reason. His hand dropped to the hilt of his rapier once more. "You will cease your whining," he said in a soft, deadly voice. "Otherwise, I shall start inquiring amongst the younger servants here about *your* habits."

If he had any evidence that Francis Bacon liked boys, too, he hadn't mentioned it to Lope. But if that was a shot in the dark, it proved an inspired one. The younger Bacon sucked in a horrified breath and went even whiter than the portrait of his brother.

With more clumping, the cavalrymen on the roof came down. The ones who'd gone through the house returned to the front hall. "No luck, your Excellencies," their sergeant said. "Not a slice of this Bacon did we find." Now *he* was making de Vega's joke.

Lope did his best to look on the bright side. "We'll run him down."

Baltasar Guzmán nodded. "We'll run him down, or we'll run him out of the kingdom. Let him play the bugger in France or Denmark. They deserve him. Let's go." He led Lope and the troop of cavalrymen out of the house. Francis Bacon stared after them, but said not another word.

As Lope mounted his horse and started riding back to London, he thought, *Nobody would dare call Guzmán a* maricón *now, not after the way he's hunted Anthony Bacon.* The troop had almost got back to the barracks before something else along those lines occurred to him. *No one would dare call Captain Guzmán a* maricón *now, but does that really prove he isn't one?* He worried at that the rest of the day, but found no answer to it.

THE EXPRESSION WILL KEMP AIMED AT SHAKESPEARE LAY HALFWAY between a leer and a glower. "Well, Master Poet, what have you done with Tom?"

"Naught," Shakespeare answered, blinking. "Is he not here?" He looked around the Theatre. He'd just got there, a little later than he might have. He saw no sign of the company's best boy actor.

Kemp went on leering. "An you've done naught, what wish you you'd done with him?"

"Naught!" Shakespeare said again, this time in some alarm. Tom was a comely—more than a comely—youth, and such liaisons happened often enough in the tight, altogether masculine world of the theatre. But what might be a jest at another time could turn deadly now. If the Spaniards or the English Inquisition started wondering if he were a sodomite, they might also start wondering if he were a traitor. What was buggery, after all, but treason against the King of Heaven?

But from the tiring room came a sharp command: "Go to, Kemp! Give over."

Had Richard Burbage spoke to the clown like that, a fight would have blown up on the spot. Not even Kemp, though, failed to respect Jack Hungerford. He asked the tireman, "Know you somewhat o' this matter, then?"

"Ay, somewhat, and more than somewhat, the which is somewhat more than you," Hungerford answered.

"What's toward, then, Master Hungerford?" Shakespeare asked. Maybe, if everyone stuck to facts, no one would throw any more insults around. *And maybe the horse will learn to sing*, Shakespeare thought—one more bit of Grecian not quite folly he had from Christopher Marlowe.

"My knowledge is not certain, mind," the tireman said. Shakespeare braced himself to squelch Will Kemp before the clown could offer sardonic agreement there, but Kemp, for a wonder, simply waited for Hungerford to go on. And go on he did: "Some will know and some will have guessed Tom hath been . . . an object of desire for those whose affections stand in that quarter."

That proved too much for Kemp to resist. "When their affections stand," he said, "they want to stick 'em up his—"

He didn't finish. Somebody—Shakespeare didn't see who—shied a pebble or a clod of dirt at him. He let out an irate squawk. Before he could do anything more, Shakespeare broke in to say, "Carry on, Master Hungerford, I pray you."

"Gramercy. So I shall. As I said, he's a Ganymede fit to tempt any who'd fain be Jove. But even as Jove cast down Saturn, so Tom's Jove himself's been o'erthrown. Anthony Bacon's fled London, a short jump ahead of the dons."

"Bacon?" Shakespeare said. "Lord Burghley's nephew?" He'd met Burghley in the house that belonged to Anthony Bacon and his younger brother.

Hungerford nodded. "The same, methinks."

"He *is* fled?"

The tireman nodded again. "Not caught yet, by all accounts. He being a man of parts, haply he may cross to the Continent still free."

"To the Continent? No, sir. No!" Kemp said. "Were he continent, he'd need not flee, now would he? And forsooth! a man of parts. I knew not till this moment sausage was a Bacon's troublous part."

Shakespeare groaned. Hungerford looked pained. Kemp preened. Shakespeare asked, "Tom was Bacon's ingle, then? I own I have seen Bacon here, though never to my certain knowledge overtopping the bounds of decency."

" 'To my certain knowledge,' " Kemp echoed in a mocking whine. "Why think you he came hither? For the plays?" He laughed that idea to scorn, adding, "Quotha, his brother could write the like, did he please to do't."

"A rasher Bacon never spake," Shakespeare said indignantly. Will Kemp opened his mouth for another gibe of his own, then did a better double take than most he used on stage, sending Shakespeare a reproachful stare. The poet looked back blandly.

Missing the byplay, Jack Hungerford said, "I fear me Tom'll not return to the boards. He's smirched, and would smirch us did we use him henceforward."

That had several possibilities. Kemp rose to none of them. Shakespeare eyed him in some surprise. *The wealth of his wit outdone by the wealth of his choices?* the poet wondered. No other explanation made sense.

Then, suddenly, Shakespeare raised a hand to his mouth to smother a laugh. What did Paul say in his epistle to the Romans? *All things work together for good to them that love God*, that was the verse. Now he couldn't have to worry about either asking Catholic Tom to play Boudicca or finding some good reason for not asking him. He hadn't just found a good reason—the Spaniards themselves had handed him one.

But the more he thought about it, the less inclined he was to laugh. Maybe the way that verse from Paul's epistle had worked out here was a sign God truly lay on his side, Lord Burghley's side, Elizabeth's side, England's side. Shakespeare hoped so with all his heart. Their side needed every scrap of help it could get.

Hungerford went on with his own train of thought: "He being smirched, I wonder who'll play his parts henceforward."

Will Kemp had avoided temptation once. Twice, no. He said, "Why, man, had this Bacon not played with his parts, we'd worry on other things." The tireman coughed. Shakespeare would have been more annoyed at the clown had the identical thought not popped into his mind the instant before Kemp said it.

The day's play was another offering of *Romeo and Juliet*; they keenly felt Tom's absence, and the groundlings let them hear about it. Caleb, who played Juliet in his place, made a hash of his lines several times and wouldn't have measured up to Tom even if he hadn't.

Richard Burbage was not pleased. He bearded Shakespeare in the tiring room after the performance. "I am told this was the Spaniards' doing," he said heavily.

"I am told the same," Shakespeare answered.

Burbage glowered at him. "Were I not so told, I'd blame you. Since this madness of yours commenced, the company is stirred, as with a spoon—a long spoon."

"One fit to sup with devils?" Shakespeare asked, and Burbage gave him a cold nod. That hurt. To try to hide how much it hurt, Shakespeare busied himself with the lacings of his doublet. When he thought he could speak without showing what he felt, he said, "This came not from me, hath naught to do with me, and I am called a devil for't? How would you use me were I guilty of somewhat, having spent all your wrath upon mine innocence?"

"You came to me. You said, Tom needs must avoid, else . . . thus and so advanceth not. What said I? I said, I'd liefer see him playing."

"You said also you'd tend to it regardless."

Burbage ignored that. "Well, he's gone now." His gesture suggested crumpling a scrap of waste paper and throwing it away. Then he drew himself up. "I lead this company. D'you deny it?"

"Not I, nor would I never," Shakespeare said at once.

He might as well have kept silent. Burbage went on as if he had, repeating, "I lead this company. The land we stand on, the house we play in—we Burbages lease the one and own the other. D'you deny *that*?"

"How could I?" Shakespeare asked reasonably. "All true, every word of't."

"All right, then. All right." Burbage's angry exhalation might have been the snort of a bull just before it lowered its head and charged. "Here's what I'd ask of you: if *I* in any way obstruct you, who takes *my* place, and what befalls me?"

Shakespeare wished he could pretend he didn't understand what his fellow player was talking about. He couldn't, not without making himself into a liar. Miserably, he said, "I know not."

"God damn you, then, Will!" Burbage's thunderous explosion made heads turn his way and Shakespeare's, all over the tiring room. Shakespeare wished he could sink through the floor as he'd sunk down through the trap door while playing the ghost in *Prince of Denmark*.

When the buzz of conversation picked up again and let him speak without having everyone in the crowded room hear what he said, he answered, "There is in this something you see not."

Burbage folded his arms across his broad chest. "That being?" By his tone, he believed he saw everything, and all too clearly.

But Shakespeare said, "An *I* prove a thing obstructive, I too am swept away for another, I know not whom. You reckon me agent, Dick. Would I were. Would I might persuade myself I were, for a man's always fain to think himself free. Agent I am none, though. I am but tool, tool to be cast aside quick as any other useless thing of wood or iron."

He waited, watching Burbage. The player was a man who delighted in being watched. He probably made up his mind well before he deigned to let Shakespeare know he'd made up his mind. He played deciding as if the Theatre were full, and every eye on him alone. "Mayhap," he said at last—a king granting mercy to a subject who probably did not deserve it. Shakespeare felt he ought to applaud.

Instead, he said, "I'm for Bishopsgate. I've endless work to spend on *King Philip*."

"And on . . ." Burbage was vain and bad-tempered, but not a fool. He would not name, or even come close to naming, *Boudicca*—not here, not where so many ears might hear.

"Yes." Shakespeare let it go at that. He set his hat on his head. Having his own share of a player's vanity, he tugged it down low on his forehead to hide his receding hairline. He'd squandered a few shillings on nostrums and elixirs purported to make hair grow back. One smelled like tar, another like roses, yet another like cat piss. None did any good; over the past year or so, he'd stopped wasting his money.

The Lenten threepenny supper at his ordinary was a stockfish porridge. Stockfish took hours of soaking to soften and to purge itself of the salt that preserved it. Even then, it was vile. It was also cheap, and doubtless helped pad the place's profit.

Because the ordinary was crowded, Shakespeare worked on *King*

Philip there. The more of the other play he wrote, the more he worried about strangers' eyes seeing it. When he went back to his lodging house, he intended to sit by the fire and see if he could change horses. Most of the other people who dwelt with the Widow Kendall would lie abed by then.

His landlady herself remained awake when he came in. "Give you good even," she said.

"And you, my lady." Shakespeare swept off his hat and gave her a bow Lieutenant de Vega might have admired. Jane Kendall smiled and simpered; she enjoyed being made much of.

But her smile disappeared when Shakespeare put a fresh chunk of wood on the fire. He'd known it would, and had hoped to sweeten her beforehand. No such luck. "Master Will!" she said, her voice sharp with annoyance. "With the winter so hard, have you any notion how dear wood's got?"

"In sooth, my lady, you'd have set it there yourself ere long," Shakespeare said, as soothingly as he could. "You'd be wood to spare wood, would you not?" He smiled, both to sweeten her further and because his wordplay pleased him.

It failed to please her, for she failed to notice it. "Daft, he calls me," she said to no one in particular—perhaps she was letting God know of his sins. "Bought he the wood he spares not? Marry, he did not. Cared he what it cost? Marry, not that, either. But called he me wood? Marry, he did. He'll drive me to frenzy thus, to frenzy and to bed." On that anticlimactic note, she left the parlor.

Shakespeare pushed a table and a stool up close to the fire. He took out the latest sheet of paper for *Boudicca*—no others—and set to work. A couple of minutes later, he yawned. Over the years, he'd got used to writing plays in odd moments snatched from other work and sleep.

Something brushed against his ankle. Before he could start, the cat said, "Meow."

"Good den, Mommet." Shakespeare scratched the gray tabby behind the ears and stroked its back. Mommet purred ecstatically. When Shakespeare stopped stroking the cat so he could write, it sat up on its hind legs and tapped his shin with a front paw, as if to say, *Why don't you go on?*

He glanced down at it, a trifle uneasily. *Would a common cat sit so?* he wondered. *Or hath this beast more wit than a common cat?* Still purring, the animal twisted into an improbable pose and began licking its private parts and anus. Shakespeare laughed. Would a familiar do anything so undignified?

Cicely Sellis appeared in the doorway. "God give you good even, Master Shakespeare," she said—she certainly had no trouble pronouncing the name of the Lord, as witches were said to do. "Have you seen—? Ah, there he is. Mommet!"

The cat went on licking itself as Shakespeare answered, "And you, Mistress Sellis?"

She snapped her fingers and cooed. Mommet kept ignoring her. With a small, rueful shrug, she smiled at Shakespeare. "He does as he would, not as I would."

"Care killed a cat, or so they say," the poet replied.

Laughing, the cunning woman said, "If he die of care, he'll live forever. But how is it with you? Did he disturb you from your work? Do I?"

"No, and no," Shakespeare said, the first *no* truthful, the second polite. "I am well enough. How is't with yourself?"

"Well enough, as you say," Cicely Sellis answered. "Truly, I have been pleased to make your acquaintance, for your name I hear on everyone's lips."

"You ken my creditors, then?" Shakespeare said. "Better they should come to you for their fortunes than to me."

"A thing I had not heard was that you were in debt." She paused, then sent him a severe look. "Oh. You quibble on 'fortune.' "

"Had I one, my lady, I should not quibble on't."

She snorted. That made the cat look up from grooming itself. She snapped her fingers again. The cat rose to its feet, stretched, purred—and rubbed up against Shakespeare once more. "Vile, fickle beast!" Cicely Sellis said in mock fury.

Shakespeare reached down and stroked the cat. It began to purr even louder. "Ay, there's treason in 'em, in their very blood," he said.

"How, then, differ they from men?" she asked.

That put him back on uncomfortable ground—all the more so, considering what he was writing. He stopped petting the gray tabby. It looked up at him and meowed. When he didn't start again, it walked over to its mistress. "And now you think I'll make much of you, eh?" she said as she picked it up. It purred. She laughed. "Belike you're right." She glanced over to Shakespeare. "Shall I bid you good night?"

"By no means," he answered, polite once more: polite and curious. "You'll think me vain, Mistress Sellis, but from whose lips hear you of me?"

Vanity had something to do with the question, but only so much; he wasn't Richard Burbage. But he might learn something useful, something that would help keep him alive. The more he knew, the better his chances. He was sure of that. He was also sure—unpleasantly sure—they weren't very good no matter how much he knew.

"From whose lips?" Cicely Sellis pursed her own before answering, "I'll not tell you that, not straight out. Many who come to me would liefer not be known to resort to a cunning woman. There *are* those who'd call me witch."

"I believe it," Shakespeare said. *What's in a name?* he wondered. The English Inquisition could, no doubt, give him a detailed answer.

"Well you might," she said. "But believe also no day goes by when I hear not some phrase of yours, repeated by one who likes the sound, likes the sense, and knows not, nor cares, whence it cometh. 'Who ever loved that loved not at first sight?' or—"

Shakespeare laughed. "Your pardon, I pray you, but that is not mine, and Kit Marlowe would wax wroth did I claim it."

"Oh." She laughed, too. "It's I who must cry pardon, for speaking of your words and speaking forth another's. What am I then but a curst unfaithful jade, like unto mine own cat? I speak sooth even so."

"You do me too much honor," Shakespeare said.

"I do you honor, certes, but too much? Give me leave to doubt it. Why, I should not be surprised to hear the dons admiring your plays."

He looked down at what he'd just written. Queen Boudicca, who had been flogged by the Roman occupiers of Britannia, and whose daughters had been violated, was urging the Iceni to revolt, saying,

> "But mercy and love are sins in Rome and hell.
> If Rome be earthly, why should any knee
> With bending adoration worship her?
> She's vicious; and, your partial selves confess,
> Aspires to the height of all impiety;
> Therefore 'tis fitter I should reverence
> The thatched houses where the Britons dwell
> In careless mirth; where the blest household gods
> See nought but chaste and simple purity.

'Tis not high power that makes a place divine,
Nor that men from gods derive their line;
But sacred thoughts, in holy bosoms stor'd,
Make people noble, and the place ador'd."

What would the dons say if they heard those lines? *What will the dons say when they hear those lines?* He laughed. He couldn't help himself. *Give* me *leave to doubt they will admire them.*

Cicely Sellis misunderstood the reason for his mirth, if mirth it was. She sounded angry as she said, "If you credit yourself not, who will credit you in your despite?"

"Not the dons, methinks," he answered.

"But have I not seen 'em 'mongst the groundlings?" she returned. "And have I not seen you yourself in converse earnest with 'em? Come they to the Theatre for that they may dispraise you?"

Damn you, Lieutenant de Vega, Shakespeare thought, not for the first time. Not only did the man threaten to discover his treason whenever he appeared, but now he'd just cost him an argument. Shakespeare's fury at the Spaniard was all the greater for being so completely irrational.

When he did not respond, the cunning woman smiled a smile that told him she knew she'd won. She said, "When the dons and their women come to see me, shall I ask 'em how they think on you?"

"The dons . . . come to see you, Mistress Sellis?" Shakespeare said slowly.

"In good sooth, they do," she answered. "Why should they not? Be they not men like other men? Have they not fears like other men? Sicknesses like other men? Fear not their doxies they are with child, or poxed, or both at once? Ay, they see me. Some o' the dons'd liefer go to the swarthy wandering Egyptians, whom in their own land they have also, but they see me."

"Very well. I believe't. An it please you, though, I would not have my name in your mouth, no, nor in the Spaniards' ears neither."

Shakespeare thought he spoke quietly, calmly. But Mommet's fur puffed up along his back. The cat's eyes, reflecting the firelight, flared like torches as it hissed and spat. By the way it stood between Shakespeare and its mistress, it might have been a watchdog defending its home.

"Easy, my poppet, my chick, easy." Cicely Sellis bent and stroked the cat. Little by little, its fur settled. Once it began to purr once more, she looked up at Shakespeare. "Fear not. It shall be as you desire."

"For which I thank you."

"I'll leave you to't, then," she said, scooping Mommet up into her arms. "Good night and good fortune."

She spoke as if she could bestow the latter. Shakespeare wished someone could. He would gladly take it wherever it came from.

VII

LOPE DE VEGA LOOKED UP FROM THE PAPER. "I PRAY YOU, FORGIVE me, Master Shakespeare," he said, "but your character is not easy for one unaccustomed to it."

"You are not the first to tell me so," the English poet answered, "and I thus conclude the stricture holds some truth."

They sat on the edge of the stage in the Theatre, legs dangling down towards the dirt where the groundlings would stand. Behind them, swords clashed as players practiced their moves for the afternoon's show. Looking over his shoulder, Lope could tell at a glance which of them had used a blade in earnest and which only strutted on the stage.

But that was not his worry. The nearly illegible words on the sheet in his left hand were. He pointed to one passage that had, once he'd deciphered it, particularly pleased him. "This is your heretic Queen Elizabeth, speaking to his Most Catholic Majesty's commander as she goes to the Tower?"

Shakespeare nodded. "Just so."

"It hath the ring of truth," Lope said, and began to read:

> " 'Stay, Spanish brethren! Gracious conqueror,
> Victorious Parma, rue the tears I shed,
> A mother's tears in passion for her land:
> And if thy Spain were ever dear to thee,
> O! think England to be as dear to me.
> Sufficeth not that I am brought hither
> To beautify thy triumphs and thy might,
> Captive to thee and to thy Spanish yoke,
> But must my folk be slaughter'd in the streets,
> For valiant doings in their country's cause?
> O! if to fight for lord and commonweal
> Were piety in thine, it is in these.' "

"Will it serve?" Shakespeare asked anxiously.

"Most excellent well," Lope replied at once. "It is, in sooth, a fine touch, her pleading for mercy thus. How came you to shape it so?"

"I bethought me of what she might tell King Philip himself, did he come to London, then made her speak to his general those same words," Shakespeare said.

"Ah." Sitting, Lope couldn't bow, but did take off his hat and incline his head to show how much the answer pleased him. "Most clever. And then the Duke of Parma's reply is perfect—perfect, I tell you." He read again:

> " 'At mine uncle's bidding, I spare your life,
> For mercy is above this sceptr'd sway:
> 'Tis mighty in the mightiest; it becomes
> The throned monarch better than his crown;
> It is enthroned in the hearts of kings,
> And blesseth him that gives and him that takes.' "

"If it please you, I am content," the Englishman murmured.

"Please me? You are too modest, sir!" Lope cried. While Shakespeare—modestly—shook his head, the Spaniard went on, "Would King Philip might read these wondrous words you write in his behalf. As I live, he'd praise 'em. Know you the Escorial, outside Madrid?"

"I have heard of't," Shakespeare said.

" 'Twill be his Most Catholic Majesty's monument forevermore," Lope said. "And your *King Philip*, meseems, will live as long."

"May he have many years," Shakespeare said in a low voice. "May this play remain for years unstaged."

Lope crossed himself. "Yes, may it be so, though I fear me the day will come sooner than that." He tapped the sheet of paper with a fingernail. "I shall take back to my superiors a report most excellent of this."

"Gramercy," the Englishman told him.

"No, no, no." De Vega wagged a hand back and forth. " 'Tis I should thank you, *señor*. Again, you prove yourself the poet Don Diego knew you to be."

Will Kemp sidled up to them. "What business have you put in for a clown?" he asked in a squeaky whine.

"It is a play on the death of a great king," Lope said coldly; he did not like Kemp.

"All the more reason for japes and jests," the clown said.

"You are mistaken," de Vega said, more coldly still.

To his surprise, Shakespeare stirred beside him. "No, Lieutenant, haply not," he said, and Lope felt betrayed. Shakespeare went on, "Sweeten the posset with some honey, and down it goes, and sinks deep. Without the same . . ." He shook his head.

"I have trouble believing this," Lope said.

"Then who's the fool?" Will Kemp said. He went on, " ' 'A was the first that ever bore arms.' " A sudden shift of voice for, " 'Why, he had none.' " Back to the original: " 'What? art a heathen? How dost thou understand the Scripture? The Scripture says, Adam digged; could he dig without arms? I'll put another question to thee. If thou answerest me not, confess thyself—' "

"Confess thyself a blockhead," Lope broke in. "What is this nonsense?"

Quietly, Shakespeare said, "It is from my *Prince of Denmark*, sir, the which you were kind enough to praise not long since."

Kemp bent and took Lope's head in both hands. The Spaniard tried to twist away, but could not; the clown was stronger than he looked. Solemnly—and, Lope realized after a moment, doing an excellent imitation of Richard Burbage—Kemp intoned, " 'Alas, poor Yorick. I knew him.' "—as if Lope's head were the skull of the dead clown in the play. " 'I knew him, Horatio; a fellow of infinite jest, of most excellent fancy. He hath borne me on his back a thousand times; and now, how abhorred in my imagination it is! Here hung those lips that I have kissed I know not how oft.' " He kissed Lope de Vega on the mouth and let him go.

Furious, Lope sprang to his feet. His rapier hissed free. "Whoreson knave! Thou diest!" he roared.

"Hold!" Shakespeare said. "Give over! He made his point with words."

Kemp seemed too stupid to care whether he lived or died. Pointing to Lope, he jeered, "He hath no words, and so needs must make his with the sword." With a mocking bow, he added, "Fear no more kisses. I'm not so salt a rogue that you shall make a Bacon of me."

"All the contagions of the south light on you!" Lope said. But he did not thrust at the hateful clown.

He regretted his restraint a moment later, for Kemp bowed once more, and answered, "Why, here you are."

"Go to, both of you!" Shakespeare said. "Give over! Master de Vega, this once I will pray pardon in the clown's name, for—"

"I want no pardon, not from the likes of him," Kemp broke in, which almost got him spitted yet again.

"Silence! One word more shall make me chide thee, if not hate thee," the English poet told him. Shakespeare turned back to Lope. "I *will* pray pardon in's name, sir, for how else but by clowning shall a clown answer?"

Breathing heavily, de Vega sheathed his blade. "For your sake, Master Shakespeare, I will put by my quarrel."

But it was not for Shakespeare's sake, or not altogether, that he took it no further. Shakespeare gave him an honorable excuse, yes, and he seized on it. But Will Kemp—*demons of hell torment him*, Lope thought—had been right, and had proved himself right, no matter how offensively he'd done it. Lope wouldn't admit that to the clown, but couldn't help admitting it to himself.

"I thank you," Shakespeare said.

"Not I." Kemp minced away, sticking out his backside at every step.

Through clenched teeth, Lope said, "Let the doors be shut upon him, that he may play the fool nowhere but in his own house."

"In sooth, he's wise enough to play the role," Shakespeare answered with a sigh, "and to do that well craves a kind of wit."

"He doth indeed show some sparks that are like wit—but not much like it," de Vega said. "And what passes for his wit likes me not much."

With another sigh, Shakespeare said, "Have you not betimes seen it with players, that differences 'twixt whom they play and who they are smudge even in their own minds?"

"I have." But Lope would not leave it alone. "If this be so with Kemp, send him to . . . How is the place whither you send distraught and lunatic people called?"

"To Bethlem, within Bishopsgate," Shakespeare replied at once.

"To Bethlem, *sí. Gracias,*" Lope said. "Let him live there when not upon the stage, and make a spectacle for the general even when he plays not." The English poet only spread his hands, as if to ask, *What can you do?* And, since Kemp's foibles truly weren't Shakespeare's fault, de Vega spread his hand, too, silently answering, *Nothing at all.* Aloud, he went on, "I shall take my superior, as I say, a good report of your progress, which will also, I doubt not, shortly reach Don Diego's ear."

"I am glad it pleases you," Shakespeare said. "And, I warrant you, once Master Kemp hath the lines wherewith to work his foolery, he'll make a proper man, as one shall see in a summer's day; a most lovely, gentleman-like man."

"God grant it be so." Lope knew he didn't sound convinced. He bowed. "I go."

When he got back to the Spanish barracks, Enrique wouldn't let him in to see Captain Guzmán till he'd recited and translated Shakespeare's lines for Elizabeth and the Duke of Parma. When he'd finished, Guzmán's servant kissed his bunched fingertips like a lovesick youth. "Again, Senior Lieutenant, I envy you your fluency in English. If only I spoke better, I would be with you at the Theatre every moment until my principal beat me with sticks to hold me to his service."

Lope believed him. "His Excellency would beat you to get you *not* to do something," he observed. "With Diego . . ." He didn't go on. Enrique was clever enough—more than clever enough—to draw his own pictures. "And now that I have sung for the privilege, be so kind as to take me to your principal."

"Of course. If you will do me the favor of accompanying me . . ."

Baltasar Guzmán listened attentively to Lope. When de Vega started to quote the English, though, his superior held up a hand. "Spare me that. I don't know enough of the language to follow. Give me the gist, *en español.*"

"Certainly, your Excellency," Lope said, and obeyed.

When he'd finished, Guzmán nodded. "This all sounds well enough, Lieutenant. I have one question, though." Lope nodded, too, looking as if he awaited nothing more eagerly. Captain Guzmán asked, "Can you be sure no treason lurks here, that an Englishman would hear but you do not? You have harped on Shakespeare's subtlety before."

The question was better, more serious, more important, than Lope had looked for. "I—" he began, and then shook his head. "No, sir, I cannot be sure of that. I am fluent in English, but not perfect. Still, the Master of the Revels will pass on the play before it appears. I may miss this or that. He will not."

"Yes. That is so." Captain Guzmán nodded and looked relieved. "And Sir Edmund is most reliable." He clicked his tongue between his teeth. "I have to make sure he stays reliable, eh?"

"*Quis custodiet ipsos custodes?*" de Vega remarked.

"Just so—who watches the watchmen?" Guzmán turned Latin into Spanish. He eyed Lope, who felt a sudden horrible fear the little nobleman might decide he ought to do that job. But Guzmán shook his head, reading de Vega's thought. "You'll stay where you are. You're doing well there, and I have no one else who could take your place. So your precious Shakespeare really is writing this play, eh?"

"He really is, your Excellency," Lope answered.

"Good. Very good," Captain Guzmán said. "One more English whore—pay him, and he does what you want."

SHAKESPEARE WAS TIRED OF CHEESE AND STOCKFISH AND EVEN OF fresh fish. What he wanted was a beefsteak, hot and sizzling and full of juice. When he grumbled to Kate in the ordinary, she leaned toward him and spoke in a low voice. "You can have what you crave, though not for the threepence of a common supper."

"Ah?" He looked around. Only a couple of other men sat in the ordinary, and they were quietly arguing over some business deal. Even so, he answered in a whisper of his own: "Your master hath fitted out a close room for such dealings?"

"So hath he done, upstairs. For a shilling . . ."

With a laugh, Shakespeare shook his head. "Stockfish it shall be." Did its being forbidden make a threepenny beefsteak suddenly quadruple in worth? Not to him. *And you were wise to take no chances on betraying yourself in a small way, lest you discover your larger treason*, he thought.

Kate said, "I've heard this is not truly Lent at all, the which'd make the eating of meat at this season no sin."

"I've heard the same," Shakespeare admitted. "But the priests say otherwise, and theirs is the word of weight." He was pleased she thought he refrained from fear of sin as well as because of cost. The more he had to hide, the less he wanted anyone thinking he had anything.

He'd almost finished his unsatisfying Lenten supper when someone who was not a regular strode into the ordinary and looked around. Shakespeare needed a moment to realize that, though he hadn't seen the fellow here before, he knew him even so. The newcomer recognized him at the same moment, and walked over towards his table. "Master Shakespeare, an I mistake not," he said.

"Indeed, Constable Strawberry," Shakespeare answered. "Give you good even."

"And you." The constable perched on a stool. He waved to Kate. "A cup of sherris-sack, and yarely."

As the serving woman brought it, Shakespeare thanked heaven he hadn't brought *Boudicca* to the ordinary—although, he reminded himself uneasily, Walter Strawberry could also have come to the house where he lodged. Fighting that unease, he said, "What would you?"

"I'm turning up clods, you might say," Strawberry replied gravely. He nodded, pleased with his own turn of phrase. "Aye, I'm turning up clods."

See yourself in a glass, and you'll turn up a great one. The thought flickered through Shakespeare's mind. He bit back the urge to fling it in Strawberry's face. Will Kemp wouldn't have hesitated, but Kemp had less to lose. Wearing his polite player's mask, Shakespeare asked, "And what have you turned up?"

"Somewhat of this, somewhat of that," Strawberry answered. "For ensample, that you and the expired prompter, to wit one Geoffrey Martin, were prompt to quarrel not long before the time of his untimely demise. Forgive me for speaking prose, but there you have it."

"I have worked with Master Martin since coming to London and joining Lord Westmorland's Men." Shakespeare did his best to sound annoyed and not frightened. "We always quarrel when first I give him a play. Learned you that in your questioning?"

Constable Strawberry solemnly nodded. "I did, sir. Indeed I did. And what's the whyfore behind it?"

"That he would change what I would were left unchanged," Shakespeare answered. "Every man who shapes a play will quarrel thus with a company's prompter. Learned you *that* in your questioning?"

"I did, sir," Strawberry repeated.

"Then why"—Shakespeare almost said *whyfore* himself—"come you here?"

"Fear not, Master Shakespeare. I draw nearer the occasion of my occasion, so I do." The constable took a scrap of paper from his wallet, peered down at it, and then put it back. "D'you ken a man named Frizer?"

"Frizer?" the poet echoed. Strawberry nodded. Shakespeare shook his head and shrugged. "No, sir. That name I wot not of."

"Ingram Frizer, he calls himself," Strawberry went on.

Ice ran through Shakespeare. He hoped his surprise and dismay didn't show. That loud-mouthed knifeman who'd asked if Geoff Martin was causing trouble . . . The poet made himself shrug again. "I am none the wiser, sir."

"Ah, well. I've said the same thing, the very same thing, many a time, so I have." The constable held up his mug and called to Kate: "Here, my dear, fetch me another, if you'd be so genderous."

"So can she scarce help being," Shakespeare remarked.

"Ah, in sooth? That likes me in a woman, genderosity, so it does. I thank you for learning me of it." Strawberry laid a finger by the side of his nose and winked. When the serving woman refilled his mug, he patted her backside.

She poured wine in his lap. He let out a startled squawk. "Oh, your pardon, I pray you," Kate said sweetly, and went back behind the counter.

Strawberry fumed. "Methought you said she was genderous of her person," he grumbled, dabbing at himself. "I saw no hint of that—marry, none." He sipped what was left of the wine, his expression still sour.

"A misunderstanding, belike," Shakespeare said.

"Ay, truly, for I understood the miss to be of her person . . ." The constable took another pull at the mug, set it down, and looked at Shakespeare as if just realizing he was there. "Ingram Frizer," he said again.

"I told you, sir, I know not the man."

"You told me. Oh, yes, you told me." Constable Strawberry nodded and then kept on nodding, as if he ran on clockwork. "But you ken a man who knows the aforespoken Frizer."

"Not to my knowledge," Shakespeare said.

"Ah, knowledge." Strawberry was still nodding, perhaps wisely. "I know all manner of things I have no knowledge of. But I say what I say, the which being so in dispect of the man."

"*What* man?" Shakespeare demanded, hoping a show of temper would mask his growing fear. "I pray you, tell me who it is quickly and speak apace. One more inch of delay is a South Sea of discovery. Take the cork out of your mouth that I may drink your tidings. Pour this concealed man out of your mouth as wine comes out of a bottle."

"As you like it, sir, I shall. His name is Nick Skeres. Will you tell me you ken him not? Eh? Will you?"

Shakespeare would have liked to, but dared not. Too many people had seen him with Skeres, and might give him the lie. "Yes, we've met," he admitted. "We are not friends, he and I, but we've met."

"Not friends, is it?" Walter Strawberry leaned forward, using his bulk to intimidate. "Be ye foes, then? Say you so?"

"No," Shakespeare answered. "I say we are not friends. I ken the man not well enough to call him friend—nor he me, I'd venture."

"I see." Strawberry gave no sign as to whether he believed what the poet told him. "Know you where this Nick Skeres' locution is to be located?"

"Where he dwells, mean you?"

"Said I not that very thing?"

"I dare say. Your pardon, Constable, but I know not. As I told you, we are but acquaintances, not friends."

He waited tensely for the next question Strawberry would send his way. The constable was not bright, but he was diligent. He might—he plainly did—need longer than a more clever man would have to find his answers, but he had a chance of finding them in the end. Not tonight, though. Finishing his wine, he got to his feet. "I thank you for passing the time of day with me, Master Shakespeare, I do. Haply 'twill prove in your regard much ado about nothing. I hope it may so. Give you good den." He lumbered out of the ordinary.

"Who was that man?" Kate asked after Strawberry closed the door behind him. "Tell me he is your friend, and you shall no more be mine."

"God save me, no!" Shakespeare exclaimed. "He is a constable from Shoreditch, inquiring after the death of poor Geoff Martin, of which I believe I have spoke somewhat."

"A constable? I might have known," Kate said darkly. "With the help of a surgeon he might yet recover, and prove himself an ass."

"At bottom, he is nothing else—but an officious ass, mind."

"I would have more to say of him than that . . . but let it go, let it go.

Put his hands on me, would he? Marry, I'd best bathe, to wash the taint away. A constable!" She muttered something else, which Shakespeare, perhaps fortunately, could not make out.

He had intended going back to his lodging and working on *Boudicca* there. He'd just sat down in front of the fire, though, when Cicely Sellis came out of her room with a swarthy fellow who lifted his hat to her, said, "*Muchas gracias*," and then vanished into the night.

As casually as he could, Shakespeare said, "That was a Spaniard." He hoped his words covered the pounding of his heart.

The cunning woman nodded. "He is . . . friend to a woman who hath oft come hither, and so thought to ask of me a question of his own."

"I hope he paid well," Shakespeare said.

Cicely Sellis nodded again, and smiled. "He did indeed. The dons are fools with their money, nothing less. Whether I gave him full . . . satisfaction I know not, though I dare hope."

"Ah." Shakespeare had been about to ask what the Spaniard had wanted, and had been afraid she wouldn't tell him. Now he thought he knew, especially as the fellow was well into his middle years. "He hath a difficulty in rising to the occasion?"

"E'en so." Amusement glinted in Cicely Sellis' eye.

"And have you a physic for the infirmity in's firmity?" Shakespeare coughed. "I do but inquire from curiosity, mind."

"Certes." That amused glint got brighter. "How shall I say't? Oftentimes, if a man believe I have this physic, why then I do."

Shakespeare found himself amused, too. "Strong reasons make strong actions, then?" he asked.

"Betimes they do, Master Shakespeare," the cunning woman said. "Ay, betimes they do. Our remedies oft in ourselves do lie."

"A truth. Without doubt, a truth. Would more knew it."

Now Cicely Sellis shook her head. "Nay, say not so. Were it other than a secret close kept, who would visit cunning women? Do you publish it, and I starve." She clasped her hands together in mock distress.

"No." Shakespeare laughed out loud as he too shook his head.

"How not? How could it be otherwise?"

"How? I'll tell you straight. What's the common curse of mankind? Folly and ignorance. To wisdom man's a fool that will not yield. I do now mind me of a saying, 'The fool doth think he is wise'—and you may as well forbid the sea for to obey the moon, as or by oath remove or counsel shake the fabric of man's folly. That is truth, or there be liars."

"You think not much of them God made."

"I think God made them—fools," Shakespeare said. "Or will you quarrel?"

"Not I," Cicely Sellis said. "Never let it be said I could do such an unchristian thing as that. And I'll leave you to your work now, good sir, lest you find reason to quarrel with me." She dropped him a curtsy that might have come from a noblewoman—not that he'd ever had a noblewoman drop him a curtsy—and drew back into her room. "God give you good even," she said, closing the door behind her.

"And you," Shakespeare answered, though he wasn't sure she heard. He perched on the stool in front of the table, then nervously got up and put more wood on the fire. The Widow Kendall would complain in the morning when she found it gone, but she wasn't here now, and Shakespeare needed the light. He also needed to take a deep breath and calm himself before setting pen to paper on *Boudicca. First Constable Strawberry, then that whoreson Spaniard . . . 'Swounds, an I die not of an apoplexy, 'twill be the hand of God on my shoulder, holding me safe from harm.*

It was, perhaps, not by accident that his mind and his pen turned to the revolt Britain, under the queen of the Iceni, raised against the Romans, and to the Romans' horrified response. *How would they feel, seeing a province they thought subdued rise and smite 'em?* he wondered.

His pen began to move. Poenius Postumus, a Roman officer, began to speak on the page:

"Nor can Rome task us with impossibilities,
Or bid us fight against a flood; we serve her,
That she may proudly say she hath good soldiers,
Not slaves to choke all hazards. Who but fools,
That make no difference betwixt certain dying
And dying well, would fling their fames and fortunes
Into this Britain-gulf, this quicksand-ruin,
That, sinking, swallows us! what noble hand
Can find a subject fit for blood there? or what sword
Room for his execution? what air to cool us,
But poison'd with their blasting breaths and curses,
Where we lie buried quick above the ground,
And are, with labouring sweat and breathless pain,
Kill'd like slaves, and cannot kill again?"

Shakespeare paused to read what he'd just written, and nodded in satisfaction. He started to add something to Poenius' speech, but his pen chose that moment to run dry. Muttering, hoping he wouldn't lose his inspiration, he inked it and resumed:

> "Set me to lead a handful of my men
> Against an hundred thousand barbarous slaves,
> That have march'd name by name with Rome's best doers?
> Serve 'em up some other meat; I'll bring no food
> To stop the jaws of all those hungry wolves;
> My regiment's mine own."

He nodded again. Yes, that would do nicely. Poenius would later kill himself for shame at not having joined Suetonius' victorious army. Meanwhile, his anguished despair would move the play forward—and make the groundlings cheer his British, female foe.

After the Romans first conquered Britain, Tacitus said, they'd flogged Boudicca and violated her daughters. Rumor said the Spaniards had raped England's Virgin Queen after capturing her. Shakespeare didn't know whether rumor was true, but he intended to use it in the play.

But not tonight, he thought, yawning. He began to rest his head on his arms, then jerked upright with alarm tingling through him. If he fell asleep in front of the hearth and someone else got a look at what he was writing . . . If that happened, he was a dead man, and Lord Burghley's plan dead with him. He made himself get up and put away the deadly dangerous manuscript before he went to bed. His last thought as slumber seized him was, *I may not make this business easier, but I will not make it harder.*

WHEN LOPE DE VEGA WALKED INTO HIS CHAMBER, HE EXPECTED TO find Diego asleep. He wouldn't even have been angry if he had; it couldn't have been far from midnight. The dice had rolled Lope's way, and he'd stayed in the game longer than he'd expected. Gambling during Lent was probably a sin. Whether it was or not, it was certainly profitable.

A lamp burned in the outer room where Diego dwelt. The servant wasn't even in bed, but sitting on a stool. Lope grinned at him. "If you sleep all day, will you stay awake all night? Why aren't you . . . ?"

He'd intended to say *snoring*, but his voice trailed away. He stared at Diego in astonished dismay. His servant stared back, more appalled still. Diego had just cut a bite from a big chunk of roast beef, and now stopped with that bite halfway to his mouth. The dim, flickering lamplight was more than enough to show how pale he went.

"*Madre de Dios*," Lope whispered. "Diego, you idiot, have you turned Protestant now?"

Diego's fleshy jowls wobbled as he shook his head. "Protestant? God save me, no, sir!"

"How is God supposed to save you if you eat meat during Lent? Don't you know we're hunting Englishmen who do the very same thing? Are you out of your mind?"

"No, sir. I'm just hungry," his servant answered. "Bread and cheese, bread and cheese . . . To the Devil with bread and cheese!"

"No, no, no." Now de Vega was the one who shook his head. "To the Devil with eating meat at this season of the year. Or, I should say, the idea of eating meat at this season of the year has come straight from Satan."

"No such thing, sir," Diego said indignantly. "No such thing. I got hungry, that's all. It's nothing else."

"Nothing, eh? Suppose I call Captain Guzmán? Suppose I call a priest? Suppose I call a priest from the Spanish Inquisition, or the English? Will they think it's nothing? Would you have turned the color of whey if you thought it was nothing?"

Diego shot him a resentful stare. "What are you doing here, anyway? When you didn't come back and you didn't come back, I thought you were off screwing your new Englishwoman. If you hadn't walked in when you weren't supposed to, you never would have seen me."

"And you still would have sinned," Lope said.

"And so what?" his servant replied. "God would have known, and maybe my confessor, but nobody else. I'm not doing any harm."

Lope pointed to the chunk of beef. "Get rid of that. Wrap a rag around it so nobody can see what it is and get rid of it. You didn't think anyone would catch you, but now somebody has. And do you know what that means? Do you, Diego?"

"What?" Diego asked apprehensively.

"It means you are mine," de Vega answered. "Mine, do you hear me? I hold your life in my hand, and if I choose to squeeze. . . ." He held out his right hand, palm up, and slowly folded it into a fist. He made the fist as tight as he could, to make sure Diego got the idea.

His servant shuddered. "You wouldn't do such a thing, *señor* . . . would you?"

That last frightened question, one Diego surely didn't want to ask but also one he couldn't hold back, told Lope just how worried he was. "Maybe I wouldn't," Lope said. "But, on the other hand, maybe I would, too. That depends on you, don't you think?"

"On me?" Diego didn't like the sound of that.

"On you," Lope said again. "Maybe you were just hungry this once, as you say. If you were, maybe we can forget about it. If you keep your nose clean from now on—if you stay *awake*, by God, and if you do all the things you're supposed to do—then nobody needs to know about it. But if you think you can go on being lazy and useless, well, even if I can't wake you up, I'd bet the inquisitors damned well can."

Diego looked sullen. "That's blackmail."

"Yes, it is, isn't it?" de Vega agreed cheerfully. "A shame I need to blackmail you into doing what you ought to be doing anyhow, but if that's what it takes, that's what I'll do. You *will* stay awake from now on, won't you?"

"*Sí, señor*," Diego said, sounding more sullen still.

He sounded sullen enough, in fact, to make Lope wonder whether he might prove dangerous. *Best to forestall that*, Lope judged. "Don't even think about poisoning me or knocking out my brains while I'm asleep," he warned. "I'm going to write down just what I've seen, and I'm going to seal the letter and give it to someone I trust. If anything happens to me, you know what will happen to you, don't you?"

"*Sí, señor*," his servant repeated, his voice gloomy.

Lope smiled. "Very good. Now, while I'm writing suppose you take that roast beef away. Then come back and go to bed. You won't mind doing *that*, will you?"

"No, sir." Diego heaved an enormous sigh. He wrapped the offending meat in a rag, as de Vega had suggested, and carried it out. Lope went into his own chamber, using the lamp in the anteroom to light the one inside. Because he worked on plays in odd moments, he always had paper and pens and ink handy. He sat down on the stool and started to write.

Diego came back very quietly. As if by magic, the pen vanished from de Vega's hand and his rapier replaced it. "You don't want to try anything foolish, do you, Diego?" he said softly.

"*No, señor.*" The servant didn't even bother pretending he hadn't been thinking about it. "I guess I don't. Good night."

"Good night," Lope said. "When I finish what I'm working on here, I'm going to take off my boots and leave them out there for you to black. I'll expect them to be ready when I get up in the morning. You'll do a good job, won't you?"

"I'll take care of them, yes." Diego sounded like a man utterly without hope. Lope used the rapier to wave him out of the room. Once his man was gone, Lope did finish the letter—*better safe* went through his mind. He sealed the letter then got out of his boots and put them in the anteroom. When he went back into his bedchamber, he barred the door from the inside. As soon as the letter was in someone else's hands, he'd be reasonably safe. Till then—*better safe*, he told himself again.

Out beyond the barred door, Diego cursed quietly. His blasphemies were music to Lope's ears. Then Diego picked up the boots; their heels thumped together. Lope hugged himself with glee as he got into bed. Not even the threat of the Scottish border had turned Diego into a tolerable servant. The threat of the Inquisition, though, seemed to have turned the trick.

And when Lope woke the next morning, he found Diego already up and waiting for him. "Here are your boots, *señor*," the servant said tonelessly. All the mud and scuff marks were gone from them; the leather gleamed with grease. Still with no expression in his voice, Diego went on, "What else do you require?"

"Do I hear rain outside?" Lope asked. Diego nodded. De Vega said, "Well, in that case, you can fetch me my good wool cloak, and get me a hat with an extra wide brim."

"Just as you say," Diego answered, and went to do it. He didn't grumble. He didn't even yawn. It was like a miracle. Lope had no idea how long it would last, but aimed to enjoy it while it did. Taking the letter he'd written with him, he went off to get his breakfast. Even the porridge the barracks kitchen served up tasted better than usual this morning.

With a bowl of barley mush and a cup of wine inside him, he went to see his superior. As usual, Captain Baltasar Guzmán's servant intercepted him before he got through the door. "You're looking cheerful this morning, Senior Lieutenant," Enrique remarked.

"I *feel* cheerful," de Vega replied.

"Shakespeare's play goes well?"

"Yes, I think so," Lope said. If Enrique wanted to think that was why he felt happy, the servant was welcome to do so. De Vega added, "As a matter of fact, I'm going up to the Theatre as soon as I see Captain Guzmán. Is his Excellency in?"

"*Un momento, por favor.*" Enrique ducked behind the door, as if to see whether Guzmán was there, though he had to know perfectly well. But he was smiling when he came out again. "He says he is delighted to see you. Go right in."

"*Gracias.*" De Vega walked past Enrique and made a leg at Captain Guzmán, who nodded in return from behind his desk. "I trust your Excellency is well?" Lope said.

"I'll do," Guzmán said dryly. As Enrique had, he went on, "You look pleased with yourself today, Senior Lieutenant."

"And so I am, sir." Lope handed him the letter he'd written. "Would you do me the courtesy of holding this unread unless some misfortune befalls me?"

Captain Guzmán raised an eyebrow as he took the sealed sheet of paper. "Just as you say, of course. May I ask whether it has to do with your theatrical connections or with your women?"

"With neither," de Vega answered, and had the satisfaction of watching that eyebrow jump in surprise again. But Guzmán stowed the letter in his desk without another word. Lope bowed. "Many thanks, your Excellency. And now, if you'll excuse me, I'm off for Shoreditch."

"How alarmingly diligent," Guzmán murmured. He might almost have been Lope himself, talking to Diego. That comparison, perhaps fortunately, didn't occur to Lope till he'd got a horse from the stables and ridden out through Bishopsgate. When it did, the rain—a steady downpour—muffled his bad language so that only the couple of Englishmen closest to him turned their heads his way.

Lope squelched through the mud around the Theatre. The space within the wooden O where the groundlings would stand was muddy, too. On stage, actors rehearsed under the protection of a painted canvas canopy—the heavens, they called it. "Where is Master Shakespeare?" Lope called in English to Richard Burbage. "I see him not."

The big player's broad shoulders went up and down in a shrug. "He should have come hither," Burbage answered. "He should have, but he did not do't. I know not where he is myself, Master de Vega, and wish to heaven 'twere otherwise."

"Keep dry, now," the Widow Kendall called out as William Shakespeare left her house to go to the Theatre. With rain drumming down, the advice struck him as useless, but was no doubt kindly meant. He nodded and hurried away.

His belly growled as he hurried through Bishopsgate. Lent wore on him. But he dared not break the fast, not in this year of all years. He was much more virtuous than he might have been, to make sure the Spaniards paid him no special notice.

"Master Shakespeare?"

The voice came out of the rain. Shakespeare jumped. "Who is it?" he asked sharply, peering through the dripping early-morning gloom.

"Here I am, your honor."

Shakespeare's heart sank. He'd heard that sly, whining voice before, seen that clever, ugly face. "What would you, Master Skeres?" he said. "Let it be brief, an you can. I must to the Theatre."

Nicholas Skeres shook his head. "I fear me not, or not yet. You needs must come with me, and straightaway."

"Wherefore?" Shakespeare demanded.

Skeres' smile showed his bad teeth. It also made Shakespeare want to drive them down his throat. "The wherefore of't's not for me to say," Skeres answered. "Still and all, them as sent me, they'd not be happy did I come back to 'em solus."

"And who did send you?"

"Them you'll meet when I fetch you thither." From everything Shakespeare had seen, Nick Skeres delighted in being uninformative. He also delighted in the power he held over Shakespeare. When he said, "Come," the snap of command filled his voice.

And Shakespeare had to go with him. He knew as much. He hated it, but he knew it. He did say, "They'll miss me, up in Shoreditch."

Nick Skeres shrugged. "Better that than they miss you whose man I am." He turned away towards the southwest. Heart sinking, Shakespeare followed, however much he wanted to go in the opposite direction.

A horse trying to haul a wagon full of barrels through the muck blocked a narrow street. The wagon had bogged down. The driver rained blows on the horse's back. With all its strength, the beast strained against the weight and the mud. Then, with a noise like a pistol shot, it broke a leg. Its scream was like that of a woman on the rack.

"Cut its throat," Skeres said with a laugh. "It's knacker's meat now."

So it is, Shakespeare thought grimly. *And you'd cut my throat as heartlessly, you bloody, bawdy villain, did I likewise break down in your employ*. Nick Skeres laughed again, as if to say he knew what was going through Shakespeare's mind—knew and didn't care. And that was all too likely true.

"We've not far to go," Skeres said after a while.

"What? Hereabouts?" Shakespeare pointed. "There's the London Stone, the which signifies the Spaniards' barracks cannot lie a stone's throw distant. Beard we the dons in their den?"

Skeres laughed again, which did nothing to reassure Shakespeare. "They think the same: that none'd be so fond as to plot under their very noses." Even as he spoke, a squad of unhappy-looking Spaniards tramped past on patrol. One man glanced towards the two Englishmen and kept walking. The rest paid them no attention at all.

"Madness," Shakespeare muttered. Nick Skeres grinned at the Spanish soldiers, who disappeared round a corner one after another. Reluctantly—most reluctantly—Shakespeare nodded. "Though this be madness, yet there is method in't."

"E'en so," Skeres said. "Here. Come you with me. This is the house we seek."

The building in question was large and well made. "Whose it it?" Shakespeare asked.

"It belongs to Sir John Hart, the alderman," Skeres answered. "But that's nor here nor there."

Instead of going to the door and knocking, as he had at the Bacons' house in Drury Lane a few months before, he led Shakespeare to a side gate that opened onto an enclosed garden: one surely splendid in spring and summer, but sad now, with scarcely any green to be seen. "Who'd meet us here?" Shakespeare said, pulling his hat down lower to keep his face dry.

"Why, the men who're fain to see you. Who else?" Nick Skeres replied. Shakespeare glared. The other man looked back, unperturbed and resolutely close-mouthed. He took Shakespeare towards a rose arbor that no doubt perfumed the air and gave welcome shade when the sun shone high and hot, but that seemed as badly out of season as the rest of the garden now. As Shakespeare drew closer to it, he saw through the rain that two men sat in that poor shelter—waiting for him?

" 'Sblood, Master Skeres, they'll take their deaths," he exclaimed.

Shrugging, Skeres answered, "An they fret not, why should you?" He sounded altogether indifferent. The milk of human kindness ran thin in him, if it ran at all.

When Shakespeare ducked his way into the arbor, both waiting men slowly got to their feet. "God give you good morrow," Sir William Cecil rumbled.

Shakespeare bowed low. "And you, your Grace," he said. "But . . . should you not go inside, where . . . where it's warm and dry?" *Where I may hope you'll die not on the instant*, was what he meant. Lord Burghley was paler and puffier than he had been the previous autumn; he wheezed with every breath he took, and shivered despite being swaddled in furs.

But he shook his head even so. "Who knows what ears lurk within? As the matter advanceth, so advanceth also the need to keep't secret. And here, in sooth, we speak under the rose." He chuckled rheumily. Despite the laugh and his bold words, though, his lips had a bluish cast that alarmed Shakespeare. He gathered strength and went on, "When last we met, I told you my son would take this matter forward. Allow me to present you to him now. Robert, here is Master Shakespeare, the poet."

"I am your servant, sir," Shakespeare murmured, bowing to the younger man as he had to the elder.

Robert Cecil gave back a bow of his own. He was about Shakespeare's age, with a long, thin, pale face made longer still by the pointed chin beard he wore and by his combing his seal-brown hair back from his forehead. He would not have been a tall man even had he stood straight; a crooked back robbed him of several more inches. But when he said, "I take no small pleasure at making your acquaintance, Master Shakespeare, being an admirer of your dramas," Shakespeare bowed again, knowing he'd got praise worth having. The younger Cecil's voice was higher and lighter than his father's, but no less full of sharp, even prickly, intelligence.

Sir William Cecil sank back to the bench from which he'd risen. To Shakespeare's relief, his color improved slightly when he sat down. Switching to Latin, he asked, "How fares your play upon the rebellion of Boudicca?"

"I hope to finish it before spring ends," Shakespeare replied in the same language. "I am certain sure, my lord, you will already know I am also ordered to write a play upon the life of King Philip."

"Yes, I do know that." Lord Burghley nodded. "I also know the Spaniards are paying you more than I gave you at our last meeting. Robert, be so good as to make amends for that."

"Certes, Father." Robert Cecil reached under his cloak. His hands were long and thin and pale, too—hands a musician might have wished he had. He gave Shakespeare a small but nicely heavy leather sack. "We cannot let ourselves be outbid."

"By God, sir—" Shakespeare began, alarmed back into English.

The younger Cecil waved him to silence. "Did we fear betrayal from you, we'd work with another. This is for our pride's sake, not suffering our foes to outdo us."

"Gramercy." Shakespeare bowed once more.

"Your thanks are welcome but not needed, for doing this likes us well," Robert Cecil said. His father nodded. Shakespeare did not answer. No doubt the younger Cecil meant what he said. But Shakespeare knew he might have met with Ingram Frizer and his knife had he displeased the two powerful Englishmen.

In aid of which . . . "Constable Strawberry knows Ingram Frizer's name," the poet warned.

"We know of Constable Strawberry," Lord Burghley said with another wet chuckle. "Fear not on that score."

Robert Cecil nodded. "If he have wit enough to keep himself warm, let him bear it for a difference between himself and his horse."

"His wits are not so blunt as, God help us, I would desire them," Shakespeare said.

"Comparisons are odorous," the younger Cecil observed, proving he had indeed marked Walter Strawberry's style, "but not Hercules could have knocked out his brains, for he had none."

"Belike," Shakespeare said, "yet some of what your wisdoms would not have discovered, that shallow fool hath brought to light."

"He'll find no more," Robert Cecil said. With that Shakespeare had to be content—or rather, less than content.

"Nick!" Sir William Cecil said sharply.

"Your Grace?" Nicholas Skeres replied.

"Go walk the garden, Nick," the old man told him. "Bring back report of its beauties in, oh, a quarter hour's time."

Shakespeare would have resented such a peremptory dismissal. Skeres took it in stride. He dipped his head in what was more than a nod but less than a bow. "Just as you say, my lord," he murmured, and withdrew from the arbor.

Both Cecils stared at Shakespeare, who suddenly felt very much alone. "What—what would ye?" he asked, and felt blood rush to his face in embarrassment at hearing his voice quaver.

Lord Burghley said, "Here's what, Master Shakespeare: I'd fain hear some of your verses. The play advanceth, ay, but my course on earth doth likewise. The horses of the night of which Marlowe writ will not run slow for me. Give me some foretaste, then, of the dish I ordered but shall not eat."

"My lord, may you glut yourself with it," Shakespeare said. Lord Burghley only shrugged and gestured for him to go on. After a moment's thought, he did: "You are to understand, this is Boudicca, urging her stalwarts to war against the Romans."

"Ah, very good." That was Robert Cecil, not his father. "Give it us."

"I shall, as best I recall it," Shakespeare replied. "Here, then:

'Had we a difference with a petty isle,
Or with our neighbours, good sirs, for our land-marks,
The taking in of some rebellious lord,
Or making a head against commotions,
After a day of blood, peace might be argued;
But where we grapple for the ground we live on,
The liberty we hold as dear as life,
The gods we worship and, next these, our honours,
And with these swords that know no end of battle,
These men, besides themselves, allow no neighbour,
Those minds that where the day is claim inheritance,
And where the sun makes ripe the fruits, their harvest,
And where they march, but measure out more ground
To add to Rome, and here i'the bowels on us;
It must not be. No, as they are our foes,
And those that must be so until we tire 'em,
Let's use the peace of honour, that's fair dealing,
But in the end our swords. That hardy Roman,
That hopes to graft himself into my stock,
Must first begin his kindred underground, and be allied in ashes.' "

He waited. The two Cecils looked at each other. Slowly, magisterially, Lord Burghley nodded. So did his son, who despite his briskness deferred to the old man's opinion. Shakespeare felt as if he'd just received the accolade. Robert Cecil said, " 'Twill serve. Beyond doubt, 'twill serve. Have you more?"

Shakespeare beamed. "By my troth, you know how to please a poet!" William Cecil laughed; Robert allowed himself a thin chuckle. Shakespeare continued, "This is Caratach, Boudicca's brother-in-law and the great warlord of the Iceni—"

"We know our Tacitus, Master Shakespeare," Robert Cecil broke in.

"Your pardon, I pray," Shakespeare said. "The groundlings, however, will not: thus I needs must make it plain."

"Indeed. You know your craft best, and so 'tis I must ask your pardon," the younger Cecil said. "Carry on."

"So I shall. This is Caratach, I say, speaking to Hengo, who is his young nephew, and Boudicca's."

"And who is *not* in the text of the *Annals*," William Cecil declared in a voice that brooked no contradiction.

"In sooth, your Grace, he is not," Shakespeare agreed, "but I need him for the play, and so summoned him to being."

The two Cecils put their heads together. Sir William Cecil said, "Again, Master Shakespeare, we take your point. The play's the thing. Let us hear it."

"Gladly. Here is Caratach:

> 'And, little sir, when your young bones grow stiffer,
> And when I see you able in a morning
> To beat a dozen boys, and then to breakfast,
> I'll tie you to a sword.'

And Hengo replies"—Shakespeare did his best to change his voice to a boyish treble—" 'And what then, uncle?' " In his usual tones, he spoke for Caratach once more: " 'Then you must kill, sir, the next valiant Roman that calls you knave.' " Treble for Hengo: " 'And must I kill but one?' " His own voice for Caratach: " 'An hundred, boy, I hope.' " He tried to make the treble fierce, for Hengo's reply was, " 'I hope, five hundred.' " Through Shakespeare, Caratach said, " 'That's a noble boy!' "

Lord Burghley raised a hand. Shakespeare obediently fell silent. The old man said, "I chose wisely, to summon you. You make a fine fletcher for the shaft I purpose loosing at the dons. I—" He broke off and began to cough. He had trouble stopping. His face turned red and then began to turn blue. His son leaned towards him, raw fear on his face. William Cecil waved Robert back. At last, he mastered the coughing fit. Slowly—too slowly—his normal color, or rather pallor, returned. He went on, "Belike I'll loose it from beyond the grave, but may it fly no less straight for that."

"Amen, your Grace," Shakespeare said.

Rain dripping from the brim of his hat, Nicholas Skeres returned to the rose arbor. Nodding to Lord Burghley and Robert Cecil in turn, he said, "I'll take him away now." By the way he spoke, Shakespeare might have been a butt of ale.

"Yes, do, Nick." Robert Cecil spoke the same way, which set Shakespeare's teeth on edge. But then the crookback added, "He hath our full favor. Let all your friends know as much."

"I'll do't, sir. You can depend on Nick Skeres." Shakespeare could imagine no one on whom he less wanted to depend. But nobody in this mad game cared a farthing for what he wanted. Skeres turned to him with a half mocking grin. "You may not know't, Master Shakespeare, but I reckon you the safest man in London these days."

"What mean you?" Shakespeare asked.

That grin got wider. "There's not a ferret, not a flick, not a foist, not a high lawyer in the city but knows your name and visage—and knows you're to be let alone. God help him who sets upon you in Lord Burghley's despite."

"And my son's," Sir William Cecil said. "He will outdo me, as any man should pray his son will do."

Shakespeare wondered about that on several counts. He'd known plenty of men, his own father among them, who wanted to see their sons as less than themselves, not greater. More than a few of that type, far from advancing their sons, did everything they could to hold them back. And Robert Cecil, though surely a man of formidable wit, lacked his father's indomitable will. Maybe his slight frame and twisted back accounted for that. Or maybe the younger man would have been the lesser even had he been born straight. In the end, who but God could know such things?

And what is a playwright but a man who seeks to make a god of himself and creatures of his characters? Shakespeare shoved the blasphemous thought aside, though surely it had crossed the mind of everyone who'd ever touched pen to paper in hopes of writing something worth going up on stage.

Enough, he told himself, and bowed to the two Cecils. "My lords, again I say gramercy for the favor you show me."

"We do but give you your deserts," Robert Cecil answered. Shakespeare wondered whether that had an edge to it or he himself was seeing shadows where nothing cast them. He feared he wasn't. If a word from the Cecils—a word delivered through Nick Skeres, and perhaps through Ingram Frizer as well—could ward him against cheats and thieves and pickpockets and highwaymen, what could a different word do? He pleased the Cecils now. If ever he didn't . . . *An I please them not, 'twill be a mayfly's life for me.*

Skeres stirred. "We'd best away."

"Go you, gentles." Robert Cecil's smile was strange, bloodless, almost fey. "As for my father and me, why, how can we get hence, when never were we here at all?"

A bit of a ballad lately popular in London ran through Shakespeare's mind:

> *With an host of furious fancies*
> *Whereof I am commander,*
> *With a burning spear, and a horse of air,*
> *To the wilderness I wander.*
> *By a knight of ghosts and shadows*
> *I summoned am to tourney*
> *Ten leagues beyond the wide world's end.*
> *Methinks it is no journey.*

As Nick Skeres led him out of Sir John Hart's garden, he slowly nodded. Yes, "Tom o' Bedlam" fit well. He'd just given the Cecils some small taste of the furious fancies whereof he was commander. And if they both weren't knights of ghosts and shadows, who deserved the name?

Skeres peered over the gate before opening it. "Safe as can be," he said, sounding as if he wanted to reassure himself as much as Shakespeare. "Now go your way, sir, and I'll go mine, and I'll see you again when next there's need. Give you good morrow." Off he went, at a skulking half trot. He quickly disappeared in the rain.

Shakespeare started off towards the Theatre. A squad of Spaniards coming back to their barracks tramped right past him, their boots splashing in unison. Since they wore armor that they would have to grease and polish to hold rust at bay, and that kept trying to pull them down into the mud, they were likely even more miserable than he. None of them looked at him.

He hurried up towards Bishopsgate. Not far from the house where he lodged, a tall, thin, ragged man with a stout staff in his hand and a sword on his hip stepped into the middle of the street, as if to block his path. Heart pounding, Shakespeare boldly strode towards the fellow—who stepped aside to let him pass. Had the ragged man been a high lawyer who recognized him and let him go? Had the man decided he looked like someone who might put up a fight, and let him go on account of that? Or had he not been a robber at all? Shakespeare realized he would never know. Life offered fewer certainties than the stage.

When Shakespeare got to the Theatre, one of Jack Hungerford's helpers pointed to him and let out a delighted whoop: "God be praised, he's here!"

"In sooth, God be praised!" Richard Burbage boomed from center stage—his usual haunt. "We'd begun to fear you'd gone poor Geoff Martin's way, and the great and wise Constable Strawberry would summon one of us for to identify your moral remainders." Like most players worth their hire, Burbage had a knack for mimicking anyone he chanced to meet. He made no worse hash of the language than the constable himself, though.

"Some of us were less afeard than others," Will Kemp said. Shakespeare wondered—as he was no doubt intended to wonder—how the clown meant that. Had he meant to say some people remained confident nothing had happened to Shakespeare? Or did he mean some people wouldn't have cared had something happened? Better not to know.

"I pray your pardon, friends," Shakespeare said. "I was summoned to see someone, and had no choice but compliance."

He hoped the company would take that to mean he'd been called before Don Diego Flores de Valdés. Kemp, as was his way, drew a different meaning from it. His hands shaped an hourglass in the air. Several players laughed. So did Shakespeare.

His laughter abruptly curdled when Burbage said, "Your spaniel of a Spaniard came sniffing after you earlier today, and made away in some haste on hearing you'd come not."

"Said he what he wished of me?" Shakespeare asked, cursing under his breath. Lope de Vega, of course, would have no trouble learning he *hadn't* gone to Don Diego. *I did well, not using the lie direct*, Shakespeare thought.

"He'd fain hear moe *King Philip*, else I'm a Dutchman," Burbage answered, at which Will Kemp began staggering around as if in the last stages of drunkenness and mumbling guttural nonsense that might have been Dutch. Shakespeare laughed again. He couldn't help it. When Kemp let himself go, no man who saw him could help laughing.

He lurched up to Burbage and made as if to piss on his shoes. Burbage sprang back as if he'd really done it—and, had Burbage held still a moment longer, he might have. When he let himself go, he let himself go altogether. He stumbled after Burbage, who said, "Give over, Will."

Kemp spouted more guttural pseudo-Dutch gibberish and gave him a big, wet kiss on the cheek. Burbage exclaimed in disgust. He shoved Kemp away. The clown looked at him out of eyes suddenly huge and round with grief. "Thou lovest me not!" he wailed, and tears began sliding down his cheeks.

"Madman," Burbage said, half in annoyance, half in affection. Now Kemp bowed like a don. Burbage returned it. Kemp skittered up to him—and kissed him again. "Madman!" Burbage cried again—this time, a full-throated roar of rage.

"Not I." The clown let out a mourning lover's sigh. "With pretty Tom gone, I seek beauty where I find it." He puckered up once more.

"You'll find my boot in your backside, sure as Tom found Bacon's yard in his," Burbage said. Kemp's sigh wordlessly claimed he wanted nothing more.

Shakespeare asked, "Know you where de Vega went on leaving this place? Will he descend on me with a company of pikemen at his back, fearing me murthered?"

Nobody answered. Shakespeare made as if to tear his hair.

That only got him a scornful snort from Kemp, who said, "Leave clowning to clowns, foolery to fools. You have not the art of't."

"Wherefore should that hinder me?" Shakespeare replied. "You leave not sense to sensible men."

The players laughed and clapped their hands. Will Kemp's glower, this time, was perfectly genuine. He enjoyed making others the butt of his japes. When he had to play the role, though, it suited him less well.

Before he and Shakespeare could start another round of insults,

Richard Burbage asked the poet, "Doth the work thus far done suit the principal?"

Was he speaking of Don Diego or of Lord Burghley, of *King Philip* or of *Boudicca*? Shakespeare wasn't sure. He wondered if Burbage were sure. Either way, though, he could safely nod. "So I am given to understand."

"Good, then. Beside that, naught else hath great import." Burbage set his hands on his hips and raised his voice till it filled the Theatre: "Now that Will's back amongst us, and back with good news, let's think on what we do this afternoon, eh? The wives of Windsor shall not be merry unless we make them so."

Kemp fell to with more spirit than he often showed at rehearsals—but then, of course, he played Sir John Falstaff, around whom the comedy revolved. Even though the play ended with Falstaff's humiliation, the part was too juicy to leave him room for complaint. Indeed, after the rehearsal ended, he came up to Shakespeare and said, "Would you'd writ more for the great larded tun." He put both hands on his belly. He was not a thin man, but would play Falstaff well padded.

"More? Of what sort?" Shakespeare asked. He knew Kemp spoke because he wanted the role, but was curious even so. The clown might give him an idea worth setting down on paper.

But Kemp said, "He is too straitened in a town of no account. Let him come to London! Let him meet with princes. No, by God—he deserveth to meet with kings!"

Shakespeare shook his head. "I fear me not. I got leave to write of the third Richard, he being villain black. But, did I bring other Kings of England into my plays, and in especial did I speak them fair, 'twould be reckoned treason, no less than the . . . other matter we pursue. Can you tell me I am mistook?"

Will Kemp scowled. "Damn me, but I cannot. Devil take the dons, then! A bargain, Master Shakespeare—do we cast them down, give me Falstaff and a king."

If he had a reason to throw off the Spaniards' yoke, he would be less likely to go to them in a fit of temper or simply a fit of folly. "A bargain," Shakespeare said solemnly. They clasped hands.

LOPE DE VEGA AND LUCY WATKINS STOOD AMONG THE OTHER groundlings at the Theatre. The boy playing Mistress Page said,

"Good husband, let us every one go home,
And laugh this sport o'er by a country fire;
Sir John and all."

Richard Burbage, who played Ford, replied,

"Let it be so. Sir John,
To Master Brook you shall hold your word;
For he to-night shall lie with Mistress Ford."

A flourish of horns announced the end of the play. The actors bowed. Despite the rain that had been coming down all day, the Theatre erupted in applause. Lope clapped his hands. Beside him, Lucy hopped up and down in the mud, squealing with delight. De Vega smiled. "I am glade it pleases thee," he said. He had to repeat himself to make her hear him through the din.

She nodded, her eyes shining. "Ay, it likes me well. My thanks for bringing me hither."

"*El gusto es mío,*" Lope replied. And the pleasure *was* his; through the way *The Merry Wives of Windsor* enchanted her, he enjoyed it as he couldn't have if he'd come alone. The whelk-seller didn't try to pick it to pieces to see how it worked. She just let it wash over her, taking it as it came. Lope couldn't do that by himself. With her, he could.

William Shakespeare came out on stage. "Behold the poet!" Will Kemp shouted. The applause got louder still. Shakespeare bowed. Lucy Watkins whooped and blew him kisses. She wasn't the only one in the crowd sending them to him or to one or another of the players. After another bow, Shakespeare withdrew. The rest of the company followed him, one or two at a time.

"Art fain to meet them?" Lope asked.

She stared at him. "*Could* I?" she said, as if expecting him to tell her no.

He bowed. " 'Twould be my pleasure," he said. "Pleasing thee is my pleasure." Lucy leaned forward to peck him on the cheek. A man who smelled of onions standing behind them whooped and rocked his hips forward and back. Lope ignored the churl. He took Lucy's hand and led her towards the wings, towards one of the doors that opened onto the backstage tiring room. A delight of falling in love, as he'd said, was that which he took in making her happy.

Some small part of him knew that one day before too long he would spy another face, another form, that pleased him as much as Lucy's, or more. He would fall in love with the woman who had them, too. Maybe he would lose his love for the whelk-seller, maybe he wouldn't. He had no trouble staying in love with two or three women at once—till they found out about it. *Then* he had trouble. He tried to forget what had happened after the bear-baiting in Southwark.

Lucy helped by distracting him. "Look! A man guards the way. Will he give us leave to go forward?"

"Fear not, my sweet," Lope answered grandly. The tireman's helper had just turned a prosperous-looking merchant away from the door. De Vega pushed past the disgruntled Englishman, an anxious Lucy on his arm. "Good day to you, Edward," he said.

"Ah, Master Lope." The tireman's helper stood aside. "Go in, sir. I know they'll be glad to see you."

The look on Lucy Watkins' face was worth twenty pounds to him. "They'll be glad to see thee?" she whispered in what couldn't have been anything but awe.

"Certes," Lope said, and patted her hand. "They are my friends." Her eyes got wider still. He wanted to take her in his arms and kiss her on the spot, but didn't for fear of embarrassing her. She wasn't, and didn't act like, a trull, a woman of the town; if she gave herself to him when they were alone together, she behaved like a lady when in public.

"God give you good morrow, Master Lope," Richard Burbage called when de Vega and Lucy came into the tiring room. Lope bowed in return. Lucy's curtsy came a heartbeat slower than it might have, but was graceful as a duchess'. As if she were a noblewoman, Burbage made a leg at her.

"They *are* thy friends," she said in wonder, pressing closer to Lope.

"I'd never lie to thee, sweetheart," he answered, and knew he was lying.

Will Kemp had got out of the padded costume he'd worn as Falstaff. The water he'd used to wash paint and powder from his face still dripped from his beard. He was puffing on a pipe of tobacco. "Here," he said with an inviting smile, holding it out to Lope. Smoke eddied from his mouth and nose as he spoke.

"*Gracias.*" Lope puffed, too, blew out his own stream of smoke, and handed the clay pipe to Lucy.

"I've not done this before," she said doubtfully. Kemp snorted. Lope shot him a warning glance. For a wonder, he heeded it. Lucy raised the pipe to her lips. She sucked in smoke—and then coughed and choked and almost dropped the pipe. She made a horrible face. "What vile stuff! How can anyone take pleasure in't?"

Lope retrieved the pipe and gave it back to Kemp. "We have no trouble," he said. The clown nodded. Lucy only looked more disgusted. Will Kemp laughed. For once, he and Lope agreed completely.

Before that agreement could shatter, as it was likely to do, de Vega led Lucy away from the clown and over to Shakespeare. She curtsied to the English poet. He bowed over her hand, saying, "I am pleased to make your acquaintance, my lady."

"And I yours, sir," she said. "The play today—'twas a marvel. I all but split my sides laughing. When Falstaff hid amongst the washing—" She giggled.

Shakespeare raised an eyebrow, ever so slightly. "That it like you delights me," he said. Without words, his face said something else to Lope, something like, *You didn't choose her for her wit, did you?*

"Her pleasure becomes mine," Lope murmured. Lucy, still gushing about *The Merry Wives of Windsor*, didn't notice. Shakespeare gave back a thoughtful nod, part understanding; part, Lope thought, something else. *Here is a quirk worth remembering for a play*, was likely going through the English poet's mind.

"Hark you now, Master Lope," Shakespeare said. "Here's Don Juan de Idiáquez, King Philip's secretary—whose role, I hope, you'll essay—speaking to his royal master:

> 'Is the sun dimm'd, that gnats do fly in it?
> The eagle suffers little birds to sing,
> And is not careful what they mean thereby,
> Knowing that with the shadow of his wings
> He can at pleasure stint their melody;
> Even so may you the circle of the world.' "

Lope tasted the lines, then slowly nodded. "An honor to play so great a man. An honor to have such splendid words to say." Shakespeare nodded thanks for the compliment.

Lucy Watkins' eyes widened. "Thou'lt tread upon the stage, with Master Shakespeare here writing thee a part?"

"Even so, my beloved," Lope answered. Some women, especially those of higher blood, would have looked down their noses at him for it. To one who sold shellfish, though, the glamour of the theatre seemed perfectly real. Lope knew how tawdry a place it could be. In Lucy's eyes, it shone—and so, through her, it shone again for him, too, at least for a little while.

When he and Lucy left the Theatre a little later, they found the closest lodging they could. He never quite figured out whose arms first went around whom. Lucy had been less lively in bed than some women he'd known. No more. Up till then, he hadn't learned all that went into igniting her. He laughed at the moment they spent themselves together, something he'd hardly ever done despite all his many partners. The theatre had more enchantments than even he'd thought.

VIII

ALONG WITH THE REST OF THE PARISHIONERS, SHAKESPEARE came to the church of St. Ethelberge early on Easter morning, before the bells rang out that would have summoned them to Mass. As he walked into the church, deacons went up and down the aisles lighting candles and torches till the building blazed with light.

A small stone sepulcher stood against the north wall of the church. More candles burned before it; it was covered by a cloth embroidered with scenes of the Passion and the Resurrection. On Good Friday, a priest had laid the Host and a crucifix within it. Since then, men prominent in the parish had taken turns watching over the sepulcher, receiving bread and ale and some small payment for their service.

Now the clergymen formed a procession that went up to the sepulcher. A priest swung a censer over it. The sweet smoke tickled Shakespeare's nostrils. Another priest ceremoniously lifted the sepulcher cloth, while a third took the pyx that held the Host and returned it to its usual position above the altar.

Then, solemnly, yet another priest raised the crucifix from the sepulcher and carried it in triumph all around the church. The bells in the steeple clamored out joy. The choir sang *Christus Resurgens*: "Christ, rising again from the dead, dieth no more. Death shall have no more dominion over Him. For in that He liveth, He liveth unto God. Now let the Jews declare how the soldiers who guarded the sepulcher lost the King when the stone was placed, wherefore they kept not the rock of righteousness. Let them either produce Him buried, or adore Him rising, saying with us, Alleluia, Alleluia."

The crucifix was reverently placed on an altar on the north side of the church. Worshipers crept towards it, some on their knees, others on their bellies. Tears of rejoicing streamed down their faces as they adored the risen Christ.

Tears stung Shakespeare's eyes, too. His father had spoken of such ceremonies when he was a young man, and again in Mary's reign. Till the coming of the Armada, Shakespeare had never seen them himself. Elizabeth had suppressed them along with so much other Catholic ritual. They did have a grandeur, a passion (fitting word for this season of the year), missing from the Protestant liturgy she'd imposed on England.

Matins began. *And my treason thrive, all this once more'll be cast down*, Shakespeare thought. That saddened part of him, the part that responded to the drama of Catholic ceremonial. But the rest . . . *Did we choose it of our own will, well and good. But the dons forced it down the throat, as a farmer'll force an onion up the arse of a sick ox. Let them keep it.*

Mass followed Matins. At the end of the ceremony, Shakespeare queued up to receive communion. "Have to take my rights," someone in front of him muttered. He nodded, though the words hadn't been aimed at him. Taking communion on Easter Sunday marked one as part of the adult community; being denied the Host on this holiest of days ostracized and disgraced a man or a woman. In some towns—even in some churches in London, Shakespeare had heard—folk delinquent with parish dues could be refused the sacred wafer.

He reached the head of the line. "*Hoc est enim Corpus Meum*," the priest murmured, as he had so many times before, and popped the Host into Shakespeare's mouth. Sinners, it was said, choked on the Host. To prevent embarrassing accidents, a parish clerk stood by the priest with a chalice of unconsecrated wine. He offered it to Shakespeare, who took a mouthful to wash down the unleavened morsel.

Often, when he left the church after Easter Mass, the green of new spring growth offered its own symbolic resurrection. Not this year. With

Easter so early—only a day after the equinox—winter's grip still held the land. Trees and bushes remained bare-branched; the muddy ground was brown, with only the sickly yellow-gray of last year's dead grass showing here and there.

To his own surprise, he didn't much care. Maybe the Mass had inspired him. Or maybe . . . He stopped, a sudden delighted smile illuminating his face. *Do I not work towards England's resurrection?*

However much the thought pleased him, it did nothing for the fellow behind him, who bumped into him when he unexpectedly halted. "Here, pick up your feet, you breathing stone," the man grumbled.

"I pray pardon," Shakespeare said, and got out of the way. Still unhappy, the man who'd bumped him went up the street. Shakespeare followed more slowly. The glory of that notion still blazed in him. It struck him as a perfect cap for the day Christ rose from the dead.

It struck him as a perfect cap, that is, till he got back to the house where he lodged. Jane Kendall had gone to the early Mass, too, and had got back before him. She was already throwing fresh wood on the hearth. This day, for once, she cared nothing for expense. "God bless you, Master Will!" she said. "Now we feast!"

"Let it be so, my lady," Shakespeare answered. "Never before this year have I known Lent to seem so long."

"Nor I," his landlady said. "I had not thought on it thus, but you have the right of't. I wonder why it might be so."

"Haply for that Lent began so early," Shakespeare said. " 'Twas but the middle part of February, mind you."

Widow Kendall nodded. "Yes, it could be. But now Lent too is passed away. Will you do me the honor of carving the leg of pork I took just now from the fire?"

"A rare privilege!" Shakespeare cried, and bowed over her hand as he'd seen Lope de Vega bow over that of his latest lady friend. Jane Kendall giggled and simpered, playing the coquette for all she was worth. Shakespeare's stomach rumbled. He'd gone without meat for a long time at a hard season of the year, which made it seem even longer. Spit flooded into his mouth at the thought of finally breaking the fast.

As he carved slice after slice from the leg of pork, a few odd bits—or perhaps more than a few—found their way into his mouth. His landlady looked on indulgently. No matter how indulgent she looked, he did try to be moderate, and evidently succeeded well enough. "Pleaseth you the flavor?" she asked.

He made sure he swallowed the morsel in his mouth before answering, "Ay." He had no trouble sounding enthusiastic. The Widow Kendall had been lavish with cloves and cinnamon and pepper, and the meat was so fresh, it hardly even needed the spices to taste good—an advantage of Easter's coming in a cool season of the year.

One by one, the other lodgers came back to the house. Shakespeare exchanged Easter greetings with Jack Street and Cicely Sellis and Sam King and the rest. When Jane Kendall wasn't looking, he tossed Mommet a bit of pork. The cat made the treat disappear, then stared up at him as if to say, *Well, where's the rest of't?*

Everyone ate pork and bread and boiled parsnips smothered in melted cheese and drank the Widow Kendall's fresh-brewed ale. Shakespeare wondered if he were the only one not only eating meat but making a point of eating it where others could see. Nobody, now, could claim he was continuing the Lenten fast and waiting for what the old calendar reckoned to be Easter.

Jack Street patted his belly. "Oh, that's monstrous fine," the glazier said. "Would I were so full every day."

Sam King nodded. He still remained without steady work, so a feast like this had to be an even bigger treat for him than for the other man. Grinning at Street, he said, "So it's the emptiness within you, then, that roars forth when you sleep?"

That made everyone laugh—everyone but the glazier, who asked, "What mean you?"

"Why, your snoring, man," King said. "What else?"

"What?" Jack Street shook his head. "I snore not."

Despite making every night hideous for his fellow lodgers—and, very likely, for their neighbors to either side as well—he meant it. The more the others tried to convince him he did indeed snore, the less willing he was to believe it. "Let's to the church once more," Sam King said, "and I'll take oath on the Gospel there."

Street shook his head again. "Nay, I'd not have you forsworn for the sake of a jape."

"Tell truth and shame the Devil, Master Street: you *do* snore of nights," Shakespeare said.

" 'Tis not the many oaths that make the truth, but the plain single vow that is vowed true—and I vow, I snore not." Jack Street was beginning to sound angry. He gulped down his mug of ale, then reached for the pitcher to pour it full again.

Shakespeare began to wish Sam King had kept his mouth shut. The silence that hovered round the feasters was distinctly uncomfortable. If Street didn't want to believe he snored, how could the rest of them persuade him? They couldn't, but they knew the truth too well to be content with his denials, no matter how vigorous. This quarrel was liable to fester and burst out again weeks from now.

Cicely Sellis drew out the chain she wore around her neck. It had a sparkling pendant at the end of it, one that had been hidden in the valley between her breasts. The pendant caught firelight and torchlight as she swung it in a small arc, back and forth, back and forth. "Be easy, Master Street," she said in a soft, soothing voice. "Be easy. No cause for wrath. Be easy."

"And why should I, when all mock and fleer at me?" the glazier said.

The cunning woman didn't answer directly. She kept swinging that pendant in the same slow, steady rhythm. Ever so slightly, she shook her head. "By no means, Master Street," she said, still quietly. "We are your friends here. We are all your friends here. No one seeks to do you harm."

"Methought otherwise," Street said, but less belligerently than he'd spoken before. His eyes followed the cheap glass pendant as it moved. His head began to go back and forth at the same rate. Shakespeare had trouble keeping his eyes off the pendant, too, but he managed. Jack Street didn't even try.

"No one seeks to do you harm," Cicely Sellis repeated.

Sam King made as if to speak. Shakespeare used his long legs to kick the young man under the table. Something out of the ordinary was going on here. He didn't know what, but he didn't want to see the spell broken. Not till that phrase crossed his mind did he wonder whether he'd been wise to kick King after all.

Cicely Sellis went on as she had before: "All's well, Master Street. Naught's amiss. No need for fury. Hear you me?"

"I hear." Street's voice came from far away, as if he heard with but half an ear. His eyes, his head, still followed the pendant's motion, though he didn't seem to know they were doing it. When he reached for his mug of ale, he did so without looking away from the sparkling glass.

"Good." The cunning woman let the shiny pendant go back and forth for another minute or so, then asked, "Hear you me?" once more as she kept on swinging it.

"I hear," Street said, even more distantly than before.

"Then hear also there's no cause for fuss, no reason to recall the warm words just past, no purpose to holding 'em in your memory."

"No cause for fuss," Jack Street echoed dreamily. "No reason to recall. No purpose to holding."

"E'en so." Cicely Sellis nodded. "Shall it be as I ask of you, then?"

"It shall be so." The glazier tried to nod, but the motion of the pendant still held him captive.

"Good. Let it be so, then, and fret no more on't." Cicely Sellis stopped swinging the bauble, and tucked it away again. When she spoke once more, her voice was loud and brisk: "Would you pass me the pitcher of ale, Master Street? I'm fain for another mug myself."

"Eh?" Street started, as if suddenly wakened. "Oh, certes, Mistress Sellis. Here you are." He gave her the pitcher. With a chuckle, he said, "Belike you'll hold it better than I, for what I drank mounted straight to my head. Methought I dozed at table. I have had a dream, past the wit of man to say what dream it was; man had as well snore as go about to expound this dream. Methought I was—there is no man can tell what. And methought I had—but man is but a sleepy fool, if he will offer to say what methought I had."

"I'd drink somewhat of ale myself, Mistress Sellis, when you have poured your fill," Shakespeare said. Nodding, the cunning woman passed him the pitcher. He filled his mug, too, then quickly emptied it. Jack Street gave no sign of remembering the argument over whether he snored. He talked, he laughed, he joked. How had Cicely Sellis managed that?

Sam King leaned forward to take the pitcher after Shakespeare finished with it. The young man's eyes were wide and staring as he poured golden ale into his mug. He mouthed something across the table at Shakespeare. The poet raised an eyebrow, not having got it. King mouthed the words again, more exaggeratedly than before: "She's a witch."

That was indeed the other name for a cunning woman. Even so, Shakespeare kicked King under the table again. Some names were better left unspoken. And King did keep quiet after that. But the fear never left his eyes.

After the feast, Shakespeare stooped to stroke Mommet. The cat arched its back and purred. "You please him," Cicely Sellis said.

"Haply he'll fetch me a mouse or rat, then, as token of's praise," Shakespeare answered. Mommet twisted to scratch behind one ear.

Shakespeare thought he saw a flea fly free, but couldn't be sure: a flea on a rammed-earth floor simply disappeared. Mommet went on scratching.

With a smile, the cunning woman said, "You ken cats well." Shakespeare was the only lodger who spoke to her—or, for that matter, even acknowledged she was alive and in the house. If she noticed, she gave no sign of it.

In a low voice, he said, "You made them afeard." In an even lower voice, he added, "You made *me* afeard."

"Wherefore, Master Shakespeare?"

"Wherefore?" Shakespeare still held his voice down, but couldn't hold the anger from it—anger and fear often being two sides of the same coin. "Why else but for your show of witchery?"

"Witchery?" Cicely Sellis started to laugh, but checked herself when she saw how serious he was. "Thank you I be in sooth a witch?"

"I know not," he answered. "By my halidom, I know not. But this I know: no one else dwelling here hath the least doubt." He shook his head. "No, I mistake me. You are yet clean in Jack Street's eyes, for he recalleth naught of what you worked on him."

That got through to her. Her mouth tightened. The lines that ran to either corner of it filled with shadow, making her suddenly seem five years older, maybe more. Slowly, she said, "I but sought to forestall a foolish quarrel."

"And so you did—but at what cost?" Shakespeare's eyes flicked towards Sam King, who seemed to have set to work getting drunk. "Would you have the English Inquisition put you to the question?"

Cicely Sellis' gaze followed the poet's. "He'd not blab," she said, but her voice held no conviction.

"God grant you be right," Shakespeare said, wondering if God would grant a witch any such thing. "But you put me in fear, and I am a man who earns his bread spinning fables. Nay more—I am a man who struts the stage, who hath played a ghost, who hath known somewhat of strangeness. And, as I say, you affrighted *me*. What, then, of *him*?" His voice dropped to a whisper: "And what too of the Widow Kendall?"

"I pay her, and well." The cunning woman didn't try to hide her scorn. But her eyes, almost as green as her cat's, went back to Sam King. "I'd liefer not seek a new lodging so soon again."

"Again? Came you here, then, of a sudden?" Shakespeare asked.

Reluctantly, Cicely Sellis nodded. Shakespeare ground his teeth till a twinge from a molar warned he'd better do no more of that. Did the English Inquisition already know her name? Were inquisitors already poised to swoop down on this house? If they seized the cunning woman, would they seize her and no one else? Or would they also lay hold of everyone who'd had anything to do with her, to seek evidence against her and to learn what sort of heresy her acquaintances might harbor? Shakespeare didn't know the answer to that, but thought he could make a good guess.

"I meant no harm," Cicely Sellis said, "nor have I never worked none."

"That you have purposed none—that I believe," Shakespeare answered. "What you have worked . . ." He shrugged. He hoped she was right. He hoped so, yes, but he didn't believe it, no matter how much he wished he could.

CAPTAIN BALTASAR GUZMÁN LOOKED DISGUSTED. "I HAVE JUST learned Anthony Bacon has taken refuge at the court of King Christian IV," he said.

Sure enough, that explained his sour expression. "Something is rotten in the state of Denmark, then," Lope de Vega answered, "if its King will give shelter to a proved sodomite. He shows himself to be no Christian, despite his name—only a God-cursed Lutheran heretic."

Captain Guzmán nodded. "Yes, and yes, and yes. Every word you say is true, Senior Lieutenant, but none of your truth does us the least bit of good. Denmark and Sweden persist in their heresy, as they persist in being beyond our reach."

"Yes, sir," Lope agreed. "A pity he escaped us. If you like, though, we can always go back and arrest his younger brother."

"Nothing is proved against Francis Bacon, and the family has connections enough that we cannot proceed against him without proof. That too is a pity." Guzmán sighed. After a moment, though, he brightened. "Forty years ago, after Mary died and the English relapsed into heresy, who would have imagined we would grow strong enough to come here and correct them? In a generation or two, Denmark's turn, and Sweden's, may yet come."

"God grant it be so." De Vega crossed himself. So did his superior. With a grin, Lope went on, "I confess, your Excellency, I won't be sorry to miss that Armada, though."

"No, nor I." But Guzmán's eyes glowed with what Lope recognized after a moment as crusading zeal. "But after Denmark and Sweden are brought back into the true and holy Catholic faith, what then? The Russians do not admit the supremacy of his Holiness the Pope."

"Before I came to England, I'm not sure I'd ever even heard of Russia," Lope said. "Now I've talked to a few men who've been there. They say the weather in Russia is as much worse than it is here as the weather here is worse than Spain's. If that's so, God has already punished the Russians for their heresy."

"It could be," Guzmán said. "But it could also be that the men you talked to are liars. I don't think any place could have weather *that* bad."

"You may be right, your Excellency." Lope snapped his fingers, remembering something. "With Anthony Bacon in Denmark, is there any word that Tom, the boy actor from Shakespeare's company at about the same time, is with him?"

"Let me see." Baltasar Guzmán ran his finger down the report he'd received. He got close to the bottom before stopping and looking up. "He is accompanied by a handsome youth, yes. No name given, but . . ."

"But we are well rid of two sodomites, and the Danes are welcome to them," Lope said.

"We are well rid of them, yes, but better they should have gone to the gallows or the fire than to Denmark." Captain Guzmán had no give in him.

And Lope could hardly disagree. "You're right, of course, your Excellency. With some luck, we'll catch the next ones we flush from cover before they can flee."

"Just so, Senior Lieutenant. Just exactly so." Guzmán set down the paper. "Now you know my news. What have you for me?"

"Shakespeare continues to make good progress on *King Philip*," de Vega answered. "I wish your English were more fluent, sir. I'd quote you line after line that will live forever. The man is good. He is so very good, I find him intimidating when I sit down to write, even though he works in a different language."

"As things are, spare me the quotations," Guzmán said. "If anything's more deadly than listening to verses you don't understand, I can't imagine what it is." He steepled his fingertips and looked over them at Lope. "You are writing again, then? In spite of the intimidation, I mean?"

"Yes, your Excellency."

"Part of me says I should congratulate you," Baltasar Guzmán observed. "Part of me, though, believes I'm not keeping you busy enough. With everything else you have to do, how do you find time to set pen to paper?"

Guzmán had a habit of asking dangerous questions. He also had a habit of asking them so they didn't sound dangerous unless his intended victim listened carefully. Otherwise, a man could easily launch into a disastrous reply without realizing what he'd done till too late. Here, Lope recognized the trap. He said, "I will answer that in two ways, your Excellency. First, a man who will write does not find time to do it. He *makes* time to do it, even if that means sleeping less or eating faster. And second, sir, lately I've had more help from Diego than I've been used to getting."

"Yes, Enrique mentioned something about that to me," Guzmán said. "I would have thought you needed a miracle to get Diego to do even half the work a proper servant should. How did you manage it?"

"Maybe I was lucky. Maybe Diego saw the light," Lope answered, not wanting to admit his blackmail. "Or maybe it's simply spring, and the sun is waking him as it does the frogs and the snakes and the dormice and all the other creatures that sleep through winter."

"A pretty phrase, and a pretty conceit," Captain Guzmán said with a laugh. "But Diego has been your servant a long time now, and he's always been just as sleepy and lazy in the summertime as he has with snow on the ground. What's the difference now?"

"Maybe he's finally seen the error of his ways," de Vega replied.

"It could be. The only way he was likely to see such a thing, though, it seems to me, was up the barrel of a pistol," Guzmán said. Lope didn't answer. His superior shrugged. "All right, if you want to keep a secret, you may keep a secret, I suppose. But do tell me, since you are writing, what are you writing about?"

By the way he leaned towards Lope, he was more interested than he wanted to let on. He'd always held his enthusiasm for Lope's plays under tight rein. Maybe, though, he really enjoyed them more than he showed. Lope said, "I'm calling this one *El mejor mozo de España*."

" 'The Best Boy in Spain'?" Captain Guzmán echoed. "What's it about, a waiter?"

"No, no, no, no, no." Lope shook his head. "The best boy in Spain is Ferdinand of Aragon, who married Isabella and made Spain one kingdom. I told you, your Excellency—Shakespeare's rubbing off on me. He's writing a play about history, and so am I."

"As long as you don't start writing one in English," Guzmán said.

"That, no." De Vega threw his hands in the air at the mere idea. "I would not care to work in a language where rhymes are so hard to come by and rhythms so irregular. Shakespeare is clever enough in English—just how splendid he would be if he wrote in Spanish frightens me."

"Well, he doesn't, so don't worry your head about it," Captain Guzmán said—easier advice for him to give than for Lope to take. But he went on, "I did very much enjoy your last play, the one about the lady who was a nitwit."

"For which I thank you, your Excellency," Lope said.

"If this next one is as good, it should have a bigger audience than Spanish soldiers stranded in England," his superior said. "Write another good play, Senior Lieutenant, and I will do what I can to get both of them published in Spain."

"*¡Señor!*" Lope exclaimed. Baltasar Guzmán, being both rich and well connected, could surely arrange publication as easily as he could snap his fingers. Lope's heart thudded in his chest. He'd dreamt of a chance like that, but knew dreams to be only dreams. To see that one might come true . . . "I am your servant, your Excellency! And I would be honored—you have no idea how honored I would be—were you to become my *patrón*." He realized he was babbling, but couldn't help it. *What would I do, for the chance to have my plays published? Almost anything.*

Guzmán smiled. Yes, he knew what power he wielded with such promises. "Write well, Senior Lieutenant. Write well, and make sure the Englishman writes well, too. I cannot tell you to neglect your other duties. I wish I could, but I cannot."

"I understand, sir." De Vega was quick to offer sympathy to a man who offered him the immortality of print. He knew Captain Guzmán was saying, *Do everything I tell you to do, and then do this on your own.* Normally, he would have howled about how unfair that was. But when his superior dangled the prospect of publication before him . . .

I am a fish, swimming in the stream. I know that tempting worm may have a hook in it. I know, but I have to bite it anyway, for oh, dear God, I am so very hungry.

SHAKESPEARE LOOKED AT WHAT HE'D WRITTEN. SLOWLY, HE NODDED. The ordinary was quiet. He had the place almost to himself, for most of the folk who'd eaten supper there had long since left for home. He had the ordinary so much to himself, in fact, that he'd dared work on *Boudicca* here, which he seldom did.

And now . . . Ceremoniously, he inked his pen one last time and, in large letters, wrote a last word at the bottom of the page. *Finis.*

" 'Sblood," he muttered in weary amazement. "Never thought I to finish't." Even now, he half expected the Spaniards or the English Inquisition to burst in and drag him away in irons.

But all that happened was that Kate asked, "What said you, Master Will?"

"Naught worth hearing, believe you me." Shakespeare folded his papers so no untoward eye might fall on them. "I did but now set down the ending for a tragedy o'er which I've labored long."

"Good for you, then," the serving woman answered. "What's it called, and when will your company perform it?"

"I know not," he told her.

"You know not what it's called?"

"Nay," Shakespeare said impatiently. Too late, he realized she was teasing, and made a face at her. "I know not when we'll give it." He avoided telling her the title. She wouldn't know what it meant—no one without Latin would—but she might remember it, and an inquisitor might be able to tear it out of her. Shakespeare hadn't steeped himself in conspiracy his whole life long, as men like Robert Cecil and Nick Skeres had done, but he could see the advantages to keeping to himself anything that might prove dangerous if anyone else knew it.

Kate, unfortunately, saw he was holding back. "You're telling me less than you might," she said, more in sorrow than in accusation.

"Telling you aught is more than I should," Shakespeare said, and then, "Telling you *that* is more than I should."

He paused, hoping she would take the point. She did. She was ignorant, but far from stupid. "I'll ask no more, then," she said. "Go on. Curfew draws nigh." She lowered her voice to add, "God keep thee."

"And thee," Shakespeare answered. He rose from the stool where he'd perched most of the evening, bowed over her hand and kissed it, and left the ordinary for his lodging.

The night was foggy and dank. The moon, not quite two weeks after what the Catholic Church called Easter Sunday, was nearly new. It wouldn't rise till just before sunrise, and wouldn't pierce the mist once it did. A stranger abroad in the London night would get hopelessly lost in moments. Shakespeare intended to go back to the Widow Kendall's house more by the way the street felt under the soles of his feet and by smell than by sight.

His intention collapsed about a dozen paces outside the ordinary. Somebody came hurrying up from the direction of his lodging house. The fog muffled sound, too, so Shakespeare heard only the last few footfalls before the fellow bumped into him. "Oof!" he said, and then, "Have a care, an't please you!"

"Will! Is that you?" The other man's voice came out of darkness impenetrable.

Shakespeare knew it all the same. He wished he didn't. "Kit?" he replied, apprehension making him squeak like a youth. "Why come you hither?"

"Oh, God be praised!" Christopher Marlowe exclaimed—a sure danger sign, for when all went well he was likelier to take the Lord's name in vain than to petition Him with prayer. "Help me, Will! Sweet Jesu, help you me! They bay at my heels, closer every minute."

Ice ran through Shakespeare. "Who dogs you? And for what?" *Is it peculiar to you alone, or hath ruin o'erwhelmed all?*

"Who?" Marlowe's voice fluttered like a candle flame in a breeze. "The dons, that's who!"

"Mother Mary!" Shakespeare said, an oath he never would have chosen had the Spaniards not landed on English soil. He realized that later; at the moment, panic tried to rise up and choke him, so that he almost turned and fled at random through the shrouded streets of London. Something, though, made him repeat, "Why seek they you?"

"You know I fancy boys," Marlowe began, and some of Shakespeare's panic fell from his shoulders like a discarded cloak.

"Belike half of London knows you fancy boys," Shakespeare answered; the other poet had never figured out the virtues inherent in simply keeping his mouth shut. But if the dons wanted him *because* he fancied boys . . .

They did. Marlowe said, "Anthony Bacon was but the first. They'd fain rid the realm of all sodomites and ingles, and so they'll put me on the gallows if I into their hands do fall. But how could I be otherwise? Nature that framed us of our elements, warring within our breasts for regiment, did shape me so."

Even on the brink of dreadful death, he struggled to justify himself.

That constance left Shakespeare half saddened, half amused—and altogether frightened. "What would you of me?" he asked.

"Why, to help me fly, of course," the other poet answered.

"And how, prithee, might I do that?" Shakespeare demanded. "Am I Daedalus, to give thee wings?" He didn't know himself whether he used *thee* with Marlowe for the sake of intimacy or insult. Exasperated, he went on, "E'en had I wings to give thee, belike thou'dst fly too near the sun, another Icarus, and plummet into the briny sea."

"Twit me, rate me, as thou wouldst, so that thou help me," Marlowe said. "For in sooth, dear Will"—he laughed a ragged laugh—"where's the harm in loving boys? Quoth Jove, dandling his favorite upon his knee,

> 'Come, gentle Ganymede and play with me;
> I love thee well, say Juno what she will.' "

Shakespeare burst out laughing. He couldn't help himself. Only Marlowe could be vain enough to recite the opening lines from one of his own plays in such an extremity. With pleasure more than a little malicious, Shakespeare used a high, thin, piping voice to give back Ganymede's reply from *Dido, Queen of Carthage*:

> " 'I would have a jewel for mine ear,
> And a fine brooch to put in my hat,
> And *then* I'll hug with you an hundred times.' "

Marlowe hissed like a man trying to bear a wound bravely. "And here, Will, I thought you never paid my verses proper heed. Would I had been wrong."

"Would you had . . ." Shakespeare shook his head. "No, never mind. 'Tis of no moment now. You must get hence, if they dog you for this. Want you money?"

"Nay. What I have sufficeth me," Marlowe answered.

"Then what think you I might do that you cannot for yourself?" Shakespeare asked. "Hie yourself down to the river. Take ship, if any ship there be that sails on the instant. If there be none such, take a boat away from London, and the first ship you may. So that you outspeed the hue and cry at your heels, all may yet be well, or well enough."

"Or well enough," Marlowe echoed gloomily. "But hark you, Will: 'well enough' is not. Even 'well' is scarce well enough."

Nothing ever satisfied him. Shakespeare had known that as long as he'd known the other poet. Marlowe had a jackdaw's curiosity, and a jackdaw's inability to hold a course when something—or someone—new and bright and shiny caught his eye. Shakespeare stepped forward and reached out in the fog. One groping hand grazed Marlowe's face. He dropped it to Marlowe's shoulder. "God speed you, Kit. Get safe away, and come home again when . . . when times are better."

Marlowe snorted. "I hope I must not wait so long as *that*." He hugged the breath out of Shakespeare, and kissed him half on the mouth, half on the cheek. "You give good counsel. I'll take it, an I may."

"I'll pray for you," Shakespeare said.

"Belike 'twill do me no lasting harm," Marlowe answered. Having got the last word, he hurried away. The fog muffled his footsteps, and soon swallowed them. Shakespeare sighed. He'd done what he could. If nothing else, he'd talked Marlowe out of his blind panic. That mattered. It might matter a great deal.

"It might," Shakespeare muttered, trying to convince himself.

He made his way through the thick, swirling mist to the Widow Kendall's house. His landlady sat in the parlor, poking up the fire. "I wondered if we'd lost you, Master Will," she said as he closed the door behind him. "Thick as clotted cream out there."

"So it is," Shakespeare agreed. Beads of fog dotted his face and trickled from his beard, as sweat would have on a hot day.

"Will you waste my wood, to give you light wherewith to write?" his landlady asked.

"An it serve my purpose, madam, I reckon it no waste," Shakespeare said with dignity.

"Nay, and why should you?" the Widow Kendall replied. " 'Tis not you buying the wood you burn."

"Not so," Shakespeare said. "I buy it with the rent you have of me each month." She sent him a stony stare. Not wanting her angry at him, he added, "Be that as it may, I need no wood tonight. I finished a play at my ordinary, by the fine, clear light of the candles therein."

"I am glad to hear it," Jane Kendall said, "both for the sake of my wood and for the sake of your rent. So long as you keep writing, so long as your company buys your plays, you'll pay me month by month, eh?"

"Just so," Shakespeare agreed. Where Marlowe was pure, self-centered will, the Widow Kendall was equally pure, self-centered greed.

"And what call you this one?" she asked. "Will't fetch you a fine, fat fee?"

"Very fine, God willing," he said. As he had with Kate, he fought shy of naming *Boudicca* for her.

"Good, good," she said, smiling. His money, or some of it, was destined to become her money. "Is this the play on the life of good King Philip, then? That surely deserveth more than a common fee, its subject also being more than common."

He shook his head. "No, that will be a history—a pageant, almost a masque. The play I just now finished is a tragedy." That much, he thought he could safely say.

"I'll tell you what's a tragedy, Master Shakespeare," the Widow Kendall said. "What I needs must pay for firewood—marry, 'tis the bleeding of mine own life's blood . . ."

She went on complaining till Shakespeare took advantage of a brief lull to slip away to his bedroom. Jack Street lay on his back, his mouth wide open, making the night hideous. *Me? I snore not*, the glazier had insisted. Shakespeare laughed quietly. Street might not be able to hear himself, but everyone else could.

After a moment, the poet's laughter faltered. So far as he could tell, Street recalled nothing of the argument they'd had at Easter. Whatever Cicely Sellis had done to him, its effect lingered. Maybe it wasn't witchcraft. Shakespeare had yet to find another name that fit half so well, though.

He put his papers and pens and ink in his chest, and made sure the lock clicked shut. Then he pulled off his shoes, shed his ruff, and lay down on the bed in doublet and hose. His eyes slid shut. Maybe he snored, too. If he did, he never knew it.

When he woke the next morning, Jack Street's bed was empty. Sam King was dressing for another day of pounding London's unforgiving streets looking for work. "God give you good morrow, Master Will," he said as Shakespeare sat up and rubbed his eyes.

"And a good morrow to you as well," Shakespeare answered around a yawn.

"I'm for a bowl of the widow's porridge, and then whatever I can find," King said. The porridge was liable to be the only food he got all day. He had to know as much, but didn't fuss about it.

Shakespeare couldn't help admiring that bleak courage. "Good fortune go before you," he said.

King laughed. "Good fortune hath ever gone before me: so far before me, I see it not. An I run fast enough, though, peradventure I'll catch it up." He bobbed his head in a shy nod, then hurried out to the Widow Kendall's kitchen for whatever bubbled in her pot this morning.

Shakespeare broke his fast on porridge, too. Having eaten, he went up to the Theatre for the day's rehearsal. He worried all the way there. If inquisitors came after Cicely Sellis, would they search everywhere in the house? If they opened his chest and saw the manuscript of *Boudicca*, he was doomed. And another question, one that had been in the back of his mind, now came forward: even with *Boudicca* finished, how could the company rehearse it without being betrayed? The players would have to rehearse. He could see that. When word of Philip's death reached England, they would—they might—give the play on the shortest of notice. They would have to be ready. But how? Yes, he saw the question clearly. The answer? He shook his head.

He was among the first of the company to get to the Theatre. Richard Burbage paced across the stage like a caged wolf—back and forth, back and forth. He nodded to Shakespeare as the poet came in through the groundlings' entrance. "God give you good day, Will," he boomed. "How wags your world?" Even with only a handful of people in the house, he pitched his voice so folk in the upper gallery—of whom there were at the moment none—could hear him with ease.

"I fare well enough," Shakespeare answered. "And you? Wherefore this prowling?"

"I am to be Alexander today," Burbage reminded him. "As he pursues Darius, he is said to be relentless." He waved a sheet of paper with his part and stage directions written out. "Seemed I to you relentless?"

"Always," Shakespeare said. Burbage pursued wealth and fame with a singlemindedness that left the poet half jealous, half appalled.

Laughing, Burbage said, "It is one of Kit's plays, mind. A relentless man of his is twice as relentless as any other poet's, as an angry man of his hath twice the choler and a frightened man twice the fear. With his mighty line, he is never one to leave the auditors wondering what sort of folk his phantoms be."

Shakespeare nodded. "Beyond doubt, you speak sooth. But come you down." He gestured. "I'd have a word with you."

"What's toward?" Burbage sat at the edge of the stage, then slid down into the groundlings' pit.

In a low voice, Shakespeare said, "Marlowe is fled. I pray he be fled. Anthony Bacon, belike, was but the first boy-lover the dons and the inquisitors sought. An Kit remain in England, I'd give not a groat for his life."

"A pox!" Burbage exclaimed, as loud as ever—loud enough to make half a dozen players and stagehands look toward him to see what had happened. He muttered to himself, then went on more quietly: "How know you this?"

"From Kit's own lips," Shakespeare answered. "He found me yesternight. I bade him get hence, quick as ever he could—else he'd not stay quick for long. God grant he hearkened to me."

"Ay, may it be so." Burbage made a horrible face. "May it be so indeed. But e'en Marlowe fled's a heavy blow strook against the theatre. For all his cravings sodomitical—and for all his fustian bombast, too—he's the one man I ken fit to measure himself alongside you."

"I thank you for your kindness, the which he would not do." Shakespeare sighed. "We are of an age, you know. But he came first to London, first to the theatre. I daresay he reckoned me but an upstart crow. And when my name came to signify more than his, it gnawed at him as the vulture at Prometheus his liver." He remembered how very full of spleen Marlowe had been when Thomas Phelippes passed over him for this plot.

"Never could he dissemble," Burbage said, "not for any cause." In an occupied kingdom, he might have been reading Marlowe's epitaph.

"I know." Shakespeare sighed again. "I sent him down to the Thames. I hope he found a ship there, one bound for foreign parts. If not a ship, a boatman who'd bear him out of London to some part whence he might get himself gone."

"Boatmen there aplenty, regardless of the hour." Richard Burbage seemed to be trying to convince himself as much as Shakespeare. After a moment, he added, "What knows Kit of . . . your enterprise now in train?"

"That such an enterprise *is* in train, the which is more than likes me," Shakespeare answered. It was also less than the truth, he realized, remembering the copy of the *Annals* Marlowe had given him. But he said no more to Burbage. What point to worrying the player? If the Spaniards or the English Inquisition caught Marlowe, he knew enough to put paid to everyone and everything. And what he knew he would tell; he had not the stuff of martyrs in him.

"They seek him but for sodomy." Yes, Burbage *was* trying to reassure himself. Sodomy by itself was a fearsome crime, a capital crime. Next to treason, though, it was the moon next to the sun.

"The enterprise"—Shakespeare liked that bloodless word—"goes on apace. Last night, or ever I saw Marlowe, I wrote *finis* to *Boudicca*."

"Good. That's good, Will." Burbage set a hand on his shoulder. "Now God keep *Boudicca* from writing *finis* to us all."

A SQUAD OF SPANISH SOLDIERS AT HIS BACK, LOPE DE VEGA STRODE along the northern bank of the Thames, not far from London Bridge. Not so long ago, he'd taken a boat across the river with Nell Lumley to see the bear-baiting in Southwark. He kicked a pebble into the river. He'd crossed the Thames with his mistress—with one of his mistresses—but he'd come back alone.

He straightened, fighting against remembered humiliation. Hadn't he been getting tired of Nell anyway? Now that he was in love with Lucy Watkins, what did the other Englishwoman matter?

One of the troopers with him pointed. "There's another boatman, *señor*."

"*Gracias*, Miguel. I see him, too," Lope answered. He shifted to English to call out to the fellow: "God give you good day."

"And to you, sir." The boatman swept off his ragged hat (which, in an earlier, a much earlier, life had probably belonged to a gentleman) and gave de Vega an awkward bow. "Can't carry you and all your friends, sir, I fear me." His gap-toothed smile showed that was meant for a jest.

Lope smiled back. Some wherrymen took their boats out into the Thames empty to keep from talking to him. He'd do what he could to keep this one happy. With a bow of his own—a bow he was careful not to make too smooth, lest it be seen as mockery—he said, "Might I ask you somewhat?"

"Say on, Master Don. I'll answer."

Better and better, de Vega thought. "Were you here on the river night before last?"

"That I was, your honor," the boatman replied. "Meseems I'm ever here. Times is hard. Needs must get what coin I can, eh?"

"Certes," Lope said. "Now, then—saw you a gentleman, an English gentleman, that evening? A man of my years, he would be, more or less, handsome, round-faced, with dark hair longer than mine own and a thin fringe of beard. He styles himself Christopher Marlowe, or sometimes Kit."

He looked for another pebble to kick, but didn't find one. He did not want to hunt Marlowe, not after spending so much time with him in tiring rooms and taverns. But if what he wanted and what his kingdom wanted came into conflict, how could he do anything but his duty?

The wherryman screwed up his face in badly acted thought. "I cannot rightly recollect, sir," he said at last.

"That surprises me not," Lope said sourly, and gave him a silver sixpence. He'd already spent several shillings, and got very little back for his money.

Nor did he this time. The boatman pocketed the coin and took off his hat again. "Gramercy, your honor. God bless you for showing a poor man kindness. I needs must say, though, I saw me no such man." He spread his oar-callused hand in apology.

A couple of Lope's troopers knew some English. One of them said, "We ought to give that bastard a set of lumps for playing games with us."

Maybe the boatman understood some Spanish. He pointed to the next fellow with a rowboat, saying, "Haply George there knows somewhat of him you seek."

"We shall see," Lope said in English. In Spanish, he added, "I wouldn't waste my time punishing this motherless lump of dung." If the boatman could follow that, too bad.

The trooper who'd suggested beating the fellow said, "This river smells like a motherless lump of dung." He wrinkled his nose.

Since he was right, Lope couldn't very well disagree with him. All he said was, "Come on. Let's see what George there has to say." *Let's see if I can waste another sixpence.*

Gulls soared above the Thames in shrieking swarms. One swooped down and came up with a length of gut as long as Lope's arm in its beak. Half a dozen others chased it, eager to steal the prize. De Vega's stomach did a slow lurch. A pursuing gull grabbed the gut and made away with it. The bird that had scooped it from the water screeched in anger and frustration.

Boats of all sizes went up and down the river. "Westward ho!"

shouted the wherrymen bound for Westminster or towns farther up the Thames. "Eastward ho!" shouted the men heading towards the North Sea. Westbound and eastbound boats had to dodge those going back and forth between London and Southwark. Sometimes they couldn't dodge, and fended one another off with oars and poles and impassioned curses.

"Consumption catch thee, thou gorbellied knave!" a boatman yelled.

"Jolt-head! Botchy core! Moon-calf! Louse of a lazar!" returned the fellow who'd fallen foul of him. Instead of trying to hold their boats apart, they started jabbing at each other with their poles. One of them went into the river with a splash.

"Not the worst sport to watch," a Spanish soldier said.

"*Sí*," Lope said, and then went back to English, calling, "You there, sirrah! Be you George?"

"Ay, 'tis the name my mother gave me," the wherryman answered. "What would you, *señor*?" He pronounced it more like the English word *senior*.

De Vega asked him about Marlowe. He waited for the vacant stare he'd seen so many times before. To his surprise, he didn't get it. Instead, George nodded. "I carried such a man, yes," he said. "What's he done? Some cozening law, an I mistake me not. A barrator, peradventure, or a figure caster. Summat shrewd."

"Whither took you him?" Lope asked, excitement rising in him. Marlowe wasn't (so far as Lope knew) an agent provocateur or an astrologer, but he was a clever man—though he might have been more clever not to let his cleverness show. "Tell me!"

Now George looked blank. De Vega paid him without hesitation. The boatman eyed the little silver coin, murmured, "God bless the Queen and the King," and made it disappear. He nodded to Lope. "As you say, sir, not yesternight, but that afore't. Ten of the clock, methinks, or a bit later. I'd fetched back a gentleman and his lady from the bear-baiting at Southwark. . . ." He pointed across the Thames, as if towards a foreign country.

"I know of the bear-baiting, and of crossing the river," Lope said tightly. He knew more of such things than he'd wanted to. Shaking his head didn't make the memories go away. "What then?"

"Why, then, sir, I bethought myself, should I hie me home, for that it was a foggy night and for that curfew would come anon, or should I stay yet a while to see what chance might give? Fortune brings in some boats that are not steered, they say. And my boat—the wight whereof I speak, you understand—"

"Yes, yes." Lope fought to hide his impatience. Did this ignorant wherryman think him unable to grasp a metaphor? "Say on, sirrah. Say on."

"I'll do't," George said. "This wight came along the river seeking a boat. 'Whither would you?' I asked him. I mind me the very words he said. He said, 'You could row me to hell, and to-night I'd thank you for't.' Then he made as if to shake his head, and laughed a laugh that left me sore afeard, for meseemed 'twas a madman's laugh, and could be none other. And he said, 'Why this is hell, nor am I out of it.' I thought him daft, but—I see you stir, your honor. Know you these words?"

"I do. I know them well. They are from a play, a play writ by the man I seek. That your man spake them proves him that very man. Were he mad or not, you took his penny?"

The boatman nodded. "I did, for a madman's penny spends as well as any other. He bade me take him to Deptford, to the Private Dock there, and so I did. A longer pull than some I make, for which reason I told him I'd have tuppence, in fact, not just the single penny, and he gave it me."

"To Deptford, say you?" That was a shrewd choice. It was close to London, but beyond the city's jurisdiction, lying in the county of Kent. Till the Armada came, it had been a leading English naval yard; even now, many merchant ships tied up at the Private Dock. Lope knew he would have to go through the motions of pursuit, but any chance of catching Marlowe was probably long gone.

"Ay, sir. Deptford. He was quiet as you please in the boat—even dozed somewhat. I thought I'd judged too quick. But he was ta'en strange again leaving the boat. He looked about him, and he said, 'Hell hath no limits, nor is circumscribed in one self place; for where we are is hell, and where hell is there must we ever be.' I had a priest bless the boat, sir, the very next day, to be safe." He crossed himself.

Had he been a Catholic while Elizabeth ruled England? Maybe, but Lope wouldn't have bet a ha'penny on it. He also made the sign of the cross. "I think you need not fear," he told the wherryman. "Once more, Marlowe but recited words he had earlier writ." He wasn't surprised Marlowe had quoted his own work. He would have been surprised—he would have been thunderstruck—had Marlowe quoted, say, Shakespeare. The man was too full of himself for that.

"Are you done with me, sir?" George asked.

"Nearly." Lope took out a sheet of paper and pen and ink. He wrote, in Spanish, a summary of what the boatman had said. "Have you your letters?" he asked. As he'd expected, George shook his head. Lope thrust paper and pen at him. "Make your mark below my writing, then."

"What say the words?" The boatman couldn't even tell English from Spanish. De Vega translated. George took the pen and made a sprawling X. De Vega and one of his soldiers who was literate witnessed the mark. George asked, "Why seek you this fellow?" Maybe, despite the sixpence, he regretted talking to a Spaniard.

Too late for your second thoughts now, Lope thought as he answered, "Because he is a sodomite."

"Oh." Whatever regrets the Englishman might have had disappeared. "God grant you catch him, then. A filthy business, buggery."

"Yes." De Vega nodded. He meant it, too. And yet, all the same, no small part of him did mourn the pursuit of Marlowe. True, the man violated not only the law of England and Spain but also that of God. But God had also granted him a truly splendid gift of words. Lope wondered why the Lord had chosen to give the same man the great urge to sin and the great gift. That, though, was God's business, not his.

While he spoke in English with the wherryman, the soldier who'd witnessed the man's statement told the other troopers what was going on. One of them asked, "Sir, do we go down the river to this Deptford place?"

"I think we do," Lope answered, not quite happily. "I hope the Englishmen there don't obstruct us."

"If they do, we give 'em a good kick in the *cojones*, and after that they won't any more," another soldier said. The rest laughed the wolfish laughs of men who looked forward to giving the English another good kick.

George's boat wouldn't hold Lope and all his men. They had to walk along the riverside till they found a wherryman who could take the lot of them to Deptford. De Vega paid him, and off they went. "Eastward ho!" the boatman cried at the top of his lungs.

Though Deptford lay just down the Thames from London, Lope was conscious of being in a different world when he got out of the boat. London brawled. Deptford ambled. And he and his troopers drew more surprised looks and more hard looks in five minutes in Deptford than they would have in a day in London. London was England's beating heart, and the Spaniards had to hold it to help Isabella and Albert hold the kingdom. That meant they were an everyday presence there. Not in Deptford; once they'd closed the naval shipyard there, they'd left the place to its own devices.

Lope hadn't been asking questions along the wharfs for very long before a sheriff came up to question *him.* The fellow wore a leather tunic over his doublet to keep it clean, a black felt hat with a twisted hatband, slops, hose dyed dark blue with woad, and sturdy shoes. The staff of office he carried could double as a formidable club. He introduced himself as Peter Norris.

After Lope explained whom he sought, and why, Norris shrugged and said, "I fear me you'll not lay hands on him, sir: he's surely fled. These past two days, we've had a carrack put to sea bound for Copenhagen, a galleon bound for Hamburg, and some smaller ship—I misremember of what sort—bound for Calais. An he had the silver for to buy his passage, he'd be aboard one or another of 'em."

"I fear me you have reason, Sheriff," Lope said. No, he wasn't altogether sorry, however much he tried to keep that to himself.

"It sorrows me he hath escaped you. A bugger's naught but gallows-fruit," Norris said. "And you have come from London on a bootless errand, which sorrows me as well."

He sounded as if he meant it. Lope wondered if he would have seemed so friendly had the chase been for a traitor rather than a sodomite. The Spaniard had his doubts, but didn't have to test them . . . this time. He said, "For your kindness, sir, may I stand you to a stoup of wine?"

Norris touched the brim of his hat. "Gramercy, Don Lope. Eleanor Bull's ordinary, close by in Deptford Strand, hath a fine Candia malmsey."

The ordinary proved a pleasant place in other ways as well. It had a garden behind it that would prove more enjoyable when the plants came into full leaf. The proprietress showed Sheriff Norris, Lope, and his soldiers into a room with a bed, a long table, and a bench next to the table. De Vega and the Englishmen sat side by side. The Spanish soldiers sprawled here, there, and everywhere.

As Norris had said, Eleanor Bull's malmsey was excellent. Sipping the sweet, strong wine, Lope asked, "Can you find for me the names of the ships wherein Marlowe might have fled?"

"Certes. I'll send 'em in a letter," Peter Norris said. Lope nodded. Maybe the sheriff would, maybe he wouldn't. Either way, de Vega had enough for a report that would satisfy his own superiors. Norris hesitated, then asked, "This Marlowe . . . Seek you the poet of that name?"

" 'Tis the very man, I fear me," Lope replied.

"Pity," Norris said. "By my halidom, sir, his art surpasseth even Will Shakespeare's."

"Think you so?" Lope said. "I believe you are mistook, and right gladly will I tell you why." He and Sheriff Norris spent the next couple of hours arguing about the theatre. He hadn't expected to be able to mix business and pleasure so, and was sorry when at last he did have to go back to London.

Shakespeare had never imagined that one day he might actually want to find Nicholas Skeres, but he did. Skeres had a way of appearing out of thin air, most often when he was least welcome, and throwing Shakespeare's days, if not his life, into confusion. Now Shakespeare found himself looking for the smooth-talking go-between whenever he went outside, looking for him and not seeing him.

Skeres found him one day when spring at last began to look as if it were more than a date in the almanac, a day when the sun shone warm and the air began to smell green, a day when redbreasts and linnets and chaffinches sang. He fell into stride beside Shakespeare as the poet made his way up towards Bishopsgate. "Give you good morrow, Master Will," he said.

"And you, Master Nick," Shakespeare told him. "I had hoped we might meet."

"Time is ripe." Skeres didn't explain how he knew it was, or why he thought so. Shakespeare almost asked him, but in the end held back. Skeres' answer would either be evasive or an outright lie. Smiling, the devious little man went on, "All's well with you, sir?"

"Well enough, and my thanks for asking." Shakespeare looked about. If Skeres could appear from nowhere, a Spanish spy might do the same. That being so, the poet named no names: "How fares your principal?"

"Not so well. He fails, and knows himself to fail." The corners of Nick Skeres' mouth turned down. "Despite his brave spirit, 'tis hard, sore hard—and as hard for his son, who shall inherit the family business when God's will be done." He too was careful of the words he spoke where anyone might hear.

"Sore hard indeed," Shakespeare said. He had seen for himself in the house close by the Spanish barracks that the shadow of death lay over Sir William Cecil. That formidable intellect, that indomitable will—now trapped in a body ever less able to meet the demands they made on it? Shakespeare shivered as if a black cat had darted across the street in front of him. *When my time comes, Lord, by Thy mercy let it come quickly*. Till meeting Lord Burghley, he'd never thought to make such a prayer. But dying by inches, knowing each inch lost was lost forever . . . He shook his head. He feared death less than dying.

And well you might, bethinking yourself of the death the Spaniards or the Inquisition would give you. All at once, he wanted to do as Marlowe had done, to take ship and flee out of England. *I would be safe in foreign parts, with no dons nor inquisitors to dog me.* Speaking with Nick Skeres brought home the danger he faced.

That danger would only get worse after William Cecil died, too. Crookbacked Robert was naturally a creature of the shadows, and had thrived for years in the enormous shadow his great father cast. Once that shadow vanished, could Robert Cecil carry on in full light of day? He would have to try, but it wouldn't be easy for him.

"What seek you of me?" Skeres asked.

"Know your masters that my commission for them is complete?" Shakespeare asked in return.

Nicholas Skeres nodded. "Yes. They know. 'Twas on that account they sent me to you. I ask again: what need you of them, or of me?"

"The names of certain men," Shakespeare said, and explained why.

"Ah." Skeres gave him another nod. "You may rely on them, and on me." He hurried away, and soon vanished into the crowd. Shakespeare went on towards Bishopsgate. He knew he could rely on the Cecils; they would do all they could for him. Relying on Nick Skeres? Shakespeare shook his head at the absurdity of the notion and kept on walking.

At the Theatre that day, Lord Westmorland's Men offered *The Cobbler's Holiday*, a comedy by Thomas Dekker. It was a pleasant enough piece of work, even if the plot showed a few holes. Most of the time, Shakespeare—a good cobbler of dramas himself—would have patched those holes, or found ways for Dekker to do it himself, before the play reached the stage. He hadn't had the chance here, not when he was busy with two of his own.

It might have gone off well enough even so. Such plays often did. Good jests (even more to the point, frequent jests) and spritely staging hid flaws that would have been obvious on reading the script.

Not this time. Among the groundlings were a dozen or more Oxford undergraduates, come to London on some business of their own and taking in a play before or after it. The university trained them to pick things to pieces. They jeered every flaw they found and, as undergraduates were wont to do, went from jeering flaws to jeering players. Even by the rough standards groundlings set, they were loud and obnoxious.

Richard Burbage, who played the cobbler, went on with his role as if the Oxonians did not exist. Will Kemp, ideally cast in the role of the title character's blundering, befuddled friend, had a thinner skin. Shakespeare tried to calm him when he retreated to the tiring room during a scene in which he didn't appear: "This too shall pass away."

"May the lot of them pass away," the clown growled, "and be buried unshriven."

"Tomorrow they'll be gone," Shakespeare said. "Never do they linger."

"Nay—only the stink of 'em," Kemp said. But Shakespeare thought he'd soothed the other man's temper before Kemp had to go out again.

And then one of the university wits noticed an inconsistency Dekker had left in the plot and shouted to Kemp: "No, fool, you said just now she'd gone to Canterbury! What a knavish fool thou art, and the blockhead cobbler, too!" His voice was loud and shrill. The whole Theatre must have heard him. Giggles and murmurs and gasps rose from every side.

Burbage started into his next speech. Will Kemp raised a hand. Burbage stopped, startled; the gesture wasn't one they'd rehearsed. Kemp glared out at the undergraduates. "Is it not better," he demanded, "to make a fool of the world as I have done, than to be fooled of the world as you scholars are?"

Their jeers brought the play to a standstill, as he must have known they would. "Wretched puling fool!" they shouted. "Thou rag! Thou dishclout! Spartan dog! Superstitious, idle-headed boor!"

Kemp beamed out at them, a smile on his round face. "Say on, say on!" he urged them. "Ay, say on, you starveling popinjays, you abject anatomies. Be merry my lads, for coming here you have happened upon the most excellent vocation in the world for money: they come north and south to bring it to our playhouse. And for honors, who is of more report than Dick Burbage and Will Kemp?"

He bowed low. A moment later, Burbage swept off his hat and did the same. The groundlings whooped and cheered them. A couple of the university wits kept trying to mock Kemp and the other players, but most fell silent. They lived a hungry life at Oxford. Had it been otherwise, they would have paid more than a penny each to see *The Cobbler's Holiday*.

Will Kemp bowed again. "Have we your leave, gentles, to proceed?"

"Ay!" the groundlings roared. The same shout came from the galleries.

"Gramercy," he said, and turned back to Burbage. "I will kill thee a hundred and fifty ways. Therefore tremble and depart." As effortlessly as he'd stepped out of character, he returned to it.

"God keep thee out of my sight," Burbage retorted, and the play went on. The Oxford undergraduates troubled it no more. Kemp had outfaced them. Shakespeare hadn't been sure anyone could, but the clown had brought it off.

Afterwards, in the tiring room, everyone made much of Kemp. He was unwontedly modest. As he cleaned greasepaint from his cheeks, he said, "Easy to be bold, bawling out from a crowd like a calf—a mooncalf—seeking his dam's teat. But they went mild as the milk they cried for on seeing me bold in my own person, solus, from the stage."

"Three cheers!" someone called, and they rang from the roof and walls. Will Kemp sprang to his feet and bowed, as he had after subduing the university wits. That set off fresh applause from the crowd around him.

The noise made Shakespeare's head ache. He soaped his face and splashed water on it from a basin. The sooner he could leave the Theatre today, the happier he would be. He wanted to work on *King Philip*. The sooner that piece was done, the sooner he could start thinking of his own ideas once more. They might bring less lucre than those proposed by English noble or Spanish don, but they were *his*.

His face was buried in a towel when someone spoke in a low voice: "A word with you, Master Shakespeare, an I may?"

He lowered the linen towel. There stood the company's new bookkeeper and prompter, the late Geoffrey Martin's replacement. Having compassed the one man's death, Shakespeare dared not ignore the other. "What would you, Master Vincent?" he asked.

"I'd speak with you of your latest, Master Shakespeare, whilst other business distracts the company." Thomas Vincent nodded towards the crowd of people still hanging on Will Kemp's every word, still sniggering at his every smirk. He had the sense not to name *Boudicca*; as usual after a performance, not all the folk in the tiring room belonged to Lord Westmorland's Men.

And, for aught I know, we have our own spying serpent amongst us, as Satan did even in Eden, Shakespeare thought. "I attend," he told Vincent.

"A scribe shall make your foul papers into parts the players shall use to learn their lines," the prompter said.

"Certes." Shakespeare nodded. "My character, I know, can be less than easy to make out."

Thomas Vincent nodded, too, relief on his face. "I would not offend, sir, not for the world, but . . . You knowing of the trouble, I may speak freely."

"By all means," Shakespeare said. Vincent was more polite about it than poor Geoff Martin had been. Had Shakespeare believed all the late prompter's slanders, he would never have presumed to take pen in hand.

Even if Vincent was polite, he pressed ahead: "And, were your hand never so excellent, your latest still causeth . . . ah, difficulties in choosing a scribe."

Every time a new pair of eyes saw *Boudicca*, the risk of betrayal grew. Vincent did his best to say that without actually saying it. Shakespeare didn't need it spelled out. He knew it all too well, as he had since Thomas Phelippes first drew him into the plot. If a scribe writing out fair copies for the players took them to the Spaniards . . . If that happened, everyone in Lord Westmorland's Men would die the death.

But the poet said, "Fear not." Hearing those words coming from his mouth almost made him laugh out loud. Only when he was sure he wouldn't did he go on, "Haply I may name you a name anon."

"May it be so," Vincent said, and Shakespeare had to remember not to cross himself to echo that sentiment.

IX

IT WAS THE MIDDLE OF A FINE, BRIGHT MORNING. WHEN LOPE DE Vega walked into his rooms in the Spanish barracks, he found his servant curled into a ball under the covers, fast asleep. De Vega sighed. Diego had been almost unnaturally good and obedient these past few weeks. More surprising than his backsliding was how long it had taken.

Lope shook him, not at all gently. "Wake up! By God and St. James, *you're* not the best boy in Spain." Diego muttered something that had no real words in it. Lope shook him again, even harder this time. "Wake up!" he repeated.

His servant yawned and rubbed his eyes. "Oh, hello, *señor*. I didn't—"

"Expect you," de Vega finished for him, his tone sour. "You're supposed to do your job whether I'm here or not, Diego."

"I know, I know," Diego said sulkily. He yawned again, though he did get out of bed before Lope started screaming at him. "I'm sorry. I'm very sorry. It's only that . . . I get tired."

He meant it. He was the picture of rumpled sincerity. That he could mean it made Lope marvel. "And the less you do, the more tired you get, too," Lope said. "If you did nothing at all, you would sleep all day long and all night long as well—and you would love every moment of it. Are you a man or an oyster?"

"I am a man who likes oysters," Diego replied with dignity. "Now that you've got me up, what is it that's so important for me to do?"

"*El mejor mozo de España,*" Lope told him. "You may not be the best boy in Spain, or even England, but you're damned well in *The Best Boy in Spain*, and it's time to rehearse. Come on. Get moving. Do you want Enrique to give you the horse laugh?"

"You think I care about that *maricón*?" Diego said. "Not likely. If his arsehole isn't wider than the Thames—"

"Enough of your filth!" Lope exclaimed. "You've said it before, but you've got no proof. None. Not a farthing's worth. Not a flyspeck's worth. So keep your mouth shut and don't make trouble. It'll turn out worse for you than for the people you're trying to hurt, and you can bet on that."

"Oh, yes. Oh, yes." Diego struck a pose more dramatic than any he was likely to take in *The Best Boy in Spain*. "When an ordinary fellow says anything about a nobleman's servant, he's always wrong. Even when he's right, he's wrong."

"When an ordinary fellow talks about a nobleman's servant, he'd better be right," Lope said. "And you aren't, or you can't prove you are. So you'd better shut up about that."

"All right, *señor*. I'll keep quiet." Diego still sounded surly. "But you'll see whether I'm right or not. In the end, you'll see. And when you do, I'm going to say, 'I told you so.' "

"Don't gloat till you have the chance," Lope said. "For that matter, remember your station in life. Whether you're right or you're wrong, you're still a servant. You're still *my* servant. So don't gloat too much even if you turn out to be right."

That sat none too well with Diego. Lope could see as much. But the servant put on a pair of shoes and accompanied him to the courtyard where his makeshift company was rehearsing *El mejor mozo de España*. Even in Spain, it would have made a spartan rehearsal ground. Here in England, where de Vega could compare it to the luxury of the Theatre and the other halls where plays were presented, it seemed more austere yet.

Austere? Lope laughed at himself. *What you really mean is cheap, makeshift, shabby*. He wondered what Shakespeare would think, seeing what he had to work with. Shakespeare was a gentle, courteous man. He would, without a doubt, give what praise he could. He would also, and equally without a doubt, be appalled.

As Lope had expected, Enrique was already there. He sat on the ground, his back against a brick wall, as he solemnly studied his parts. He was to play several small roles: a Moor, a page, and one of Ferdinand's friends. When he saw Lope, he sprang to his feet and bowed. "*Buenos días, señor.*" Polite as a cat, he also bowed to Diego, though not so deeply. "*Buenos días.*"

"A good day to you as well," Lope replied, and bowed back as superior to inferior. Diego, still grouchy, only nodded. Lope trod on his foot. Thus cued, he did bow. Lope didn't want Captain Guzmán's servant offended by anyone connected to him.

Enrique didn't seem offended. He seemed enthusiastic. He waved sheets of paper in the air. "This is an excellent play, *señor*, truly excellent. No one in Madrid will see anything better this year. I'm sure of that."

"You are too kind," Lope murmured. He was no more immune to flattery than anyone else—he was less immune to flattery than a lot of people. When he bowed again to show his pleasure, it was almost as equal to equal. Diego looked disgusted. De Vega debated stepping on his foot again.

Before he could, Enrique asked, "Tell me, *señor*, is it really true what the soldier over there says? A real woman, a real Spanish woman, is going to play Isabella? That will be wonderful—wonderful, I tell you. The wife of an officer who could afford to bring her here, he told me."

De Vega shot Diego a look that said, *Would he be so happy about a woman if he didn't care for them?* His servant's sneer replied, *All he cares about is the play. If she makes it better, that's what matters to him.* With a scowl, Lope turned back to Enrique. "A woman, yes. A Spaniard, of course—could an Englishwoman play our great Queen? The wife of an officer? No. Don Alejandro brought his mistress—her name's Catalina Ibañez—to London, not his wife. And a good thing, too, for the play. A nobleman's wife could never appear on stage. That would be scandalous. But his mistress? No trouble there."

"Ah. I see." Enrique nodded. "I did wonder. But it is Don Alejandro de Recalde's woman, then? Corporal Fernandez had that right?"

"Yes, he did," Lope said.

Diego guffawed. "If I had a choice between bringing my wife and my mistress to this miserable, freezing place, I'd bring the one who kept me warmer, too."

"Be careful, or you'll be sorry," Enrique whispered through lips that hardly moved. "Here she comes."

Don Alejandro's mistress knew how to make an entrance. She swept into the courtyard with a couple of serving women in her wake. They were both pretty, but seemed plain beside her. She was tiny but perfect. No, not quite perfect: she had a tiny mole by the corner of her mouth.

Be careful, or you'll be sorry. De Vega knew Enrique hadn't been talking to him, and hadn't meant *that* kind of care when he was talking to Diego. But the servant's words might have been meant for Lope. He couldn't take his eyes off Catalina Ibañez . . . and where his eyes went, he wanted his hands and his lips to follow.

He swept off his hat and bowed as low to her as if she really were Isabella of Castile, the first Queen of a united Spain. "*Buenos días, Doña* Catalina," he said. A noble's mistress didn't really deserve to be called *doña*; out of the corner of his eye, he saw status-conscious Enrique raise an eyebrow some tiny fraction of an inch.

Catalina Ibañez accept the title as nothing less than her due. "*Buenos días*," she replied with truly queenly condescension. Her black eyes snapped. "Is everyone ready? Is everything ready?" *Everyone and everything had better be*, her tone warned. When Lope didn't say no, she nodded grudging approval. "Let's get on with the rehearsal, then. I have plenty of other things to do once I'm finished here." She tossed her head.

Be careful, or you'll be sorry. Lope hadn't lived his life being careful. He found it wildly unlikely he'd start now. Yes, Catalina Ibañez was a nobleman's plaything. Yes, she was trouble in a beautiful wrapping. Yes, she had no more pity and no more regard for anyone else than a cat did. Lope knew all that. Every bit of it was obvious at first glance. None of it stopped him from falling in love. Nothing had ever stopped him from falling in love.

He hadn't fallen out of love with Lucy Watkins. He didn't fall out of love with one woman when he fell in love with another. No, his way was to pile one love on another, adding delight to delight . . . till the whole rickety structure came crashing down on top of him, as it had outside the bear-baiting arena down in Southwark.

He gazed at Catalina Ibañez—and found her looking back, those midnight eyes full of old, cold wisdom. She knew. Oh yes, she knew. He hadn't said a word yet, but she knew everything there was to know. He didn't think she could read or write, but some things, plainly, she'd been born knowing.

Be careful, or you'll be sorry. Lope sighed. He saw no way this could possibly end well. He intended to go on with it, go through with it, anyhow.

Later. Not yet. *El mejor mozo de España* came first. Even set beside his love affairs, the words, the rhymes, the verses in his head counted for more. What had Shakespeare said in *Prince of Denmark*? *The play's the thing*—that was the line. "Take your places, then, ladies and gentlemen," Lope said. "First act, first scene. We'll start from where Rodrigo the page enters with his guitar and speaks to Isabella."

Rodrigo was played by the strapping Spanish corporal named Joaquin Fernandez. He was tall as a tree, blond as an Englishman, handsome as an angel—and wooden as a block. He stumbled through his lines. Catalina Ibañez replied,

> "*Tres cosas parecen bien:*
> *el religioso rezando,*
> *el gallardo caballero*
> *ejercitando el acero,*
> *y la dama honesta silando.*"

She wasn't just pretty. She could act. Unlike poor Fernandez (whose good looks still worried Lope), when she spoke, you believed three things seemed good to her—a monk praying, a gallant knight going to war sword in hand, and an honest woman spinning.

That had to be acting. De Vega couldn't imagine Catalina Ibañez caring about monks or honest women spinning—gallant knights were liable to be a different story. But, listening to her, you *believed* she cared, and that was the mystery of acting. If the audience believed, nothing else mattered.

On they went. Joaquin Fernandez had at least learned his lines. He might get better—a little. Catalina sparkled without much help. Lope knew how hard that was. No matter who surrounded her, this play would work as long as she was in it. De Vega felt that in his bones.

I wish Shakespeare had Spanish enough to follow this, he thought as the scene ended. *I wish he could see the difference using actresses makes, too.* He shrugged. The Englishman would just have to bumble along in his own little arena with its own foolish conventions. If that meant his work never got the attention it deserved in the wider world, well, such was life.

"Bravo, Corporal Fernandez!" Lope said. Fernandez blinked. He wasn't used to getting praise from the playwright. Lope went on, "And brava, *Doña* Catalina, your Majesty! Truly Spain will come into its own with you on the throne."

"Thank you, Senior Lieutenant," Catalina Ibañez purred. She dropped him a curtsy. Their eyes locked. Oh, yes, she'd noticed him watching her. Or rather, she'd noticed the way he watched her—not just as an author and director watched an actress, which he had every right to do, but as a man watched a woman he desired. If she wanted him, too, then in some sense he had every right to do that as well—though Don Alejandro de Recalde, her keeper, would have a different opinion.

"All right," Lope said. "Let's go on." He might have been speaking to the assembled players. People shifted, getting ready for the next scene.

Or he might have been speaking to Catalina Ibañez alone, all the rest of them forgotten. By the way her red, full lips curved into the smallest of smiles, she thought he was. Her eyes met his again, just for a moment. *Yes, let's*, they said.

Kate poured beer into Shakespeare's mug. "I thank you," he said absently. He'd eaten more than half of his kidney pie before noticing how good it was—or, indeed, paying much attention to what it was. Most of him focused on *King Philip*. He'd stormed ahead the night before, and he couldn't wait to get to work tonight. The candle at his table was tall and thick and bright. It would surely burn till curfew, or maybe even a little longer.

The door to the ordinary opened. Shakespeare didn't look up in alarm, as he'd had to whenever it opened while he was working on *Boudicca*. He'd seldom dared write any of that play here, but even having it at the forefront of his thoughts left him nervous—left him, to be honest, terrified. If Spaniards or priests from the English Inquisition burst in now, he could show them this manuscript with a clear conscience.

But the man who came in was neither don nor inquisitor. He was pale, slight, pockmarked, bespectacled: a man who'd blend into any company in which he found himself. The poet hardly heeded him till he pulled up a stool and sat down, saying, "Give you good den, Master Shakespeare."

"Oh!" Shakespeare stared in surprise—and yes, alarm came flooding back. He tried to hide it behind a nod that was almost a seated bow. "God give you good even, Master Phelippes."

"I am your servant, sir," Thomas Phelippes said, a great thumping lie: the dusty little man was surely someone's servant, but not Shakespeare's. Did he rank above Nick Skeres or under him? Above, Shakespeare thought. Phelippes, after all, was the one who'd brought him into this business in the first place.

Kate came up to the table. "Good even, sir," she said to Phelippes. "The threepenny supper is kidney pie, an't please you."

"Monstrous fine, too," Shakespeare added, spooning up some more of his.

Phelippes shook his head. "I have eat, mistress," he said. "A stoup of Rhenish wine'd please me, though."

"I'll fetch it presently." Kate hurried away and, as she'd promised, returned with the wine at once. Phelippes set a penny on the table. She took it and withdrew.

"What would you?" Shakespeare asked. "Or is't, what would you of me?"

"Seek you a scribe?" Phelippes inquired in return. "So I am given to understand."

Shakespeare frowned. "I grow out of patience with others knowing my affairs ere I learn of them myself."

"I know all manner of strange things," the dusty little man answered, not without pride.

He would never be a hero on the battlefield, nor, Shakespeare judged, with the ladies, and so had to make do with what he knew. Twitting him about it would only make an enemy. "Ken you a scribe, then?" Shakespeare asked. "A scribe who can read what's set before him, write out a fair copy, and speak never a word of't thereafter?"

"I ken such a man, but not well," Phelippes said with a small smile.

"That will not serve," Shakespeare said. "If you cannot swear he be trusty—"

Phelippes held up a hand. That small smile grew bigger. "You mistake me, sir. I but repeat a Grecian's jest when asked by someone who knew him not if he knew himself. I am the man."

"Ah?" Shakespeare was not at all convinced Phelippes was trusty. After all, he worked at the right hand of Don Diego Flores de Valdés. And yet, plainly, Don Diego's was not the only right hand at which he worked. Wanting very much to ask him about that, Shakespeare knew he couldn't: he would get back either no answer or whatever lie seemed most useful to Phelippes. But he could say, "I'd fain see your character or ever I commend you to Master Vincent."

"Think you my claim by some great degree outdoth performance?" Thomas Phelippes sounded dryly amused. His mirth convinced Shakespeare he likely could do as he claimed. Even as Shakespeare started to say he needed no proof after all, the pockmarked little man cut him off: "Have you pen and paper here?"

"Ay." Shakespeare left them on the floor by his feet while he ate, to keep from spilling gravy on them. He bent now, picked them up, and set them on the table.

"Good. Give them me, I pray you," Phelippes said. "I shall see what I make of your hand, and you will see what you make of mine." He looked at some of what Shakespeare had written, then up at the poet himself. "This is Philip, sending forth the Armada?"

"It is," Shakespeare answered. "But for myself, you are the first to see't."

"A privilege indeed," Phelippes murmured, and then began to read:

> " 'Rough rigor looks outright, and still prevails:
> Let sword, let fire, let torments be their end.
> Severity upholds both realm and rule.
> What then for minds, which have revenging moods,
> And ne'er forget the cross they boldly bear?
> And as for England's desperate and disloyal plots
> Spaniards, remember, write it on your walls,
> That rebels, traitors and conspirators
> Shall feel the flames of ever-flaming fire
> Which are not quenched with a sea of tears.' "

Looking up again, he nodded. " 'Twill serve—'twill serve very well. And a pretty contrast you draw 'twixt his Most Catholic Majesty's just fury here and the mercy of her life he grants Elizabeth conquered."

"Gramercy," Shakespeare said automatically, and then, staring, "How know you of that?"

Phelippes clicked his tongue between his teeth. "Your business is to write, the which you do most excellent well. Mine, I told you, is to know. Think you . . ."—the pause was a name he did not say aloud—"would choose me, would use me, did I not know passing well?"

Had he named that name, would it have been Sir William Cecil's or that of Don Diego Flores de Valdés? Or might he have chosen one as readily as the other? Shakespeare wished the question hadn't occurred to him. Phelippes openly avowed being a tool. Might not any man take up a tool and cut with it?

Phelippes tore off the bottom part of the sheet of paper on which Shakespeare had been writing. Shakespeare stifled a sigh. The other man surely would not pay him for the paper. Phelippes inked a pen. He began to write. Shakespeare's own hand was quick and assured, if not a thing of beauty. But his eyes widened as he watched Phelippes. The bespectacled little man's talents weren't showy, but talents he unquestionably had. The goose quill raced over the paper at a speed that put Shakespeare's best to shame.

"Here." Phelippes handed him the scrap he'd torn off. "Will it serve, think you?"

He'd copied out the bit of King Philip's speech he'd read before. Shakespeare stared. He himself used the native English hand he'd learned in school back in Stratford; his writing had grown more fluid over the years because he did so much of it, but had never changed its essential nature. Phelippes' studied Italian script, by contrast, was so very perfect, an automaton might have turned it out. And he'd written in haste here, not at leisure.

"You know full well 'twill serve, ay, and more than serve," Shakespeare answered. "I yield you the palm, Master Phelippes, and own I have not seen so fine a character writ so swift in all my days. The writing masters who show their art before the general could not outdo you."

He'd meant it for praise, but Thomas Phelippes only sniffed and looked at him over the tops of his spectacles. "Those disguised cheaters and prating mountebanks," he said scornfully. "Thread-bare jugglers, the lot of them. They write to be writing. I write to be read, and need no great show towards that end."

He prides himself in his very obscurity, Shakespeare realized. *He'd liefer be a greyhen, unseen against the heather, than a strutting peacock flashing his feathers for all to admire.* That struck the poet as a perverse pride. Most Englishmen—and Spaniards, too—gloried in display, so much so as to make deliberate self-effacement seem unnatural.

But that was wide of the mark. "I shall give Master Vincent your name," Shakespeare said. Phelippes nodded complacently. The poet asked, "How shall he inquire after you?"

"Never mind," Phelippes said. "So that he hath my name, it sufficeth me. Come the time, we shall know each the other." He rose from his stool. "Farewell." With no more flourish than when he'd come in, he slipped out of the ordinary.

"What a strange little man," Kate said a few minutes later—she seemed to need so long to realize Phelippes had gone.

"Strange?" Shakespeare considered that. After a moment, he shook his head. "He is far stranger than simply strange."

The serving woman frowned. "Will you speak in riddles?"

"How not, speaking of one?" He didn't explain himself. He wasn't sure he could have explained himself, poet though he was. But he knew what he meant.

When he went to the Theatre the next day, he told Thomas Vincent of Phelippes. The prompter nodded, but asked, "Hath he the required discretion?"

"Of discretion he hath a surplusage," Shakespeare answered. "He wants some of the goodly qualities framing a man of parts, but discretion? Never."

"I rely on your judgment, as I needs must here," Vincent said. "An you be mistook—" He broke off, as if he didn't even want to think about that.

Neither did Shakespeare, but he said, "Therein, I am not."

"God grant it be so," Vincent said. "And when may I look for *King Philip*?"

He was as pushy as a prompter should be. "Anon," Shakespeare told him. "Anon."

"Anon, anon," Thomas Vincent echoed mockingly. "Are you then metamorphosed into a drawer at the Boar's Head, ever vowing to cure ails with ale and never bringing the which is promised?"

"You'll have't, and in good time," the poet said, letting a little irritation show. "King Philip breathes yet, mind you. We stray close to treason, treating of his mortality ere it be proved."

"Don Diego hath given you his commission," Vincent said. "That being so, treason enters not into the question."

"The question, say you?" Shakespeare shivered, though the day was mild enough. When he thought of the question, he thought of endless hogsheads of water funneled down his throat, of thumbscrews, of iron boots thrust into the fire, of all the fiendish ingenuity Spaniards and home-grown English inquisitors could bring to bear in interrogating some luckless wretch who'd fallen into their clutches.

And he had no trouble at all seeing himself as a luckless wretch.

"How may I find this Master . . . Phillips, said you?"

"Phelippes," Shakespeare corrected. "He told me he would make himself known to you in good time."

"He told you that, did he?" Vincent turned his head a little to one side and brought a hand up to his ear, as if imagining he were listening to a conversation at which he hadn't been present. "Quotha, 'I shall make myself known to him in good time.' " He sounded preposterously pompous. "And then you would have nodded and said, 'Let it be so, Master Phelippes.' " Suddenly he stabbed a forefinger at Shakespeare. "But if he fail to make himself known to me?"

"Then we are betrayed, and God have mercy on our souls," Shakespeare said. Thomas Vincent asked him no more questions.

He wished the same would have been true of the players. He'd had to sound them out, one by one, knowing a wrong word in the wrong ear would bring catastrophe down upon them all. He felt as if he were defusing the Hellburner of Antwerp each time he spoke to one of them. At his nod, Richard Burbage had eased a couple of devout Papists from the company—both of them hired men, fortunately, and not sharers whom the other sharers would have had to buy out. Some of those who remained, and who knew what was toward, seemed to think it certain no one not of their persuasion was left in the Theatre. They were careless enough with what they said to make Shakespeare flinch several times a day—or, when things were bad, several times an hour.

It would have been even worse had they seen their parts for *Boudicca* and begun throwing around lines from the play. That would come soon enough—all too soon, Shakespeare feared. Even now, a robustious periwig-pated fellow named Matthew Quinn got a laugh and a cheer by shouting out that all Jesuits should be flung into the sea.

"Only chance, only luck, Lieutenant de Vega came not this morning, else he had been here to catch that," Shakespeare said to Burbage in the tiring room after the company gave the day's play.

"I have spoke to Master Quinn," Burbage answered grimly. "The rascally sheep-biter avouches he shall not be so spendthrift of tongue henceforward."

Will Kemp came up to the two of them puffing on a pipe of tobacco.

Still nervous and irritable, Shakespeare spoke more petulantly than he might have: "How can you bear that stinking thing?"

"How?" Kemp, for a wonder, took no offense. "Why, naught simpler—it holds from my nostrils the reek of yon affectioned ass." He pointed with his chin towards Matt Quinn. "And they style *me* fool and clown." He rolled his eyes.

"They call you by the names you have earned," Burbage said. "The names Master Quinn hath earned for this day's business needs must be named by Satan himself, none other having the tongue to withstand the flames therefrom engendered."

"Better Quinn were *dis*gendered," Shakespeare said. "The fright he gave me, I'd not sorrow to see him lose both tongue and yard."

"You're a bloody kern today," Kemp said.

"Nay." Shakespeare shook his head. "I thirst for no blood, nor want none spilled—most especially not mine own."

"Master Quinn *will* attend henceforth," Burbage promised. "He stakes his life upon't."

"The game hath higher stakes than that," Shakespeare said, "for his I reckon worthless, but I crave mine own to keep."

"And they style *me* fool and clown," Will Kemp repeated. Shakespeare left—all but fled—the tiring room a moment later. He knew this plot was all too likely to miscarry, but wished Kemp hadn't reminded him of it quite like that.

"Ah, my love, I must go," Lope de Vega murmured regretfully.

Lucy Watkins clung to him. "Stay with me," she said. "Stay with me forever. Till I met thee, I knew not what love was."

"Thy lips are sweet," he said, and kissed her. But then he got out of the narrow bed and began to dress. "Still, I must away. Duty calls." Duty would consist of more rehearsals for *El mejor mozo de España*. Lope knew he would go back to his games with Catalina Ibañez. The more he saw of Don Alejandro de Recalde's mistress, the more games he wanted to play with her. That didn't mean he despised Lucy, but the thrill of the chase was gone.

Softly, Lucy began to weep. "Would thou gavest me all thy duty."

"I may not. What I may give thee, I do." *What I don't give to Catalina*, Lope thought. Lucy knew nothing of the other woman. Lope dabbed at her face with the coverlet. "Here, dry thine eyes. We'll meet again, and soon. And when we do meet, let it be with gladness."

"I always come to thee with gladness," the Englishwoman said. "But when thou goest . . ." She shook her head and snuffled. At last, though, she too sat up and reached for the clothes she'd so carelessly let fall to the floor a little while earlier.

By then, Lope was pulling on his boots. He'd had plenty of practice dressing in a hurry. He didn't urge Lucy to move faster. Better—more discreet—if they weren't seen coming down the stairs together from the rooms above this alehouse. He kissed her again. "Think of me whilst we are parted, that the time until we meet again might seem the shorter."

Even as he tasted her tears on his lips, she shook her head. "Always it is an age, an eternity. Never knew I time crawled so slow."

He had no answer for that, or none that would make her happy. That being so, he slipped out of the cramped little room without another word. Before long, Lucy would come forth, too. What else could she do, after all? The stairs were uneven and rickety. He stepped carefully on them, and used care of a different sort going out through the throng of Englishmen drinking below. He walked very erect, hand on the hilt of his rapier, as if eager for one of them to challenge him. Because he looked so ready, none did.

Behind him, one of them asked, "What doth the don here?"

"What doth he? Why, his doxy," a drawer answered, and masculine laughter rose from the crowd. De Vega ignored it. The server wasn't even wrong, or not very wrong, though Lucy Watkins was no whore. She'd fallen in love with Lope as he'd fallen in love with her. If she hadn't, he would have lost interest in her right away. Getting to a woman's secret place was easy. Getting to her heart was harder, and mattered more.

His own heart leaped when he began directing Catalina Ibañez, explaining to her just exactly how she as Isabella was falling in love with the soldier playing Ferdinand of Aragon. *And if you as yourself happen to fall in love with me as I think I'm falling in love with you . . .* Lope thought. He intended to give Catalina all the help he could along those lines.

No matter what he intended, though, he had to restrain himself for the time being. "Don Alejandro, darling!" Catalina Ibañez squealed when a handsome, tawny-bearded fellow strutted into the courtyard where Lope was putting his mostly ragtag company through its paces. "You *did* come to see me rehearse!"

"I told you I would," Don Alejandro de Recalde replied, bowing to her. "I keep my word." He nodded to Lope. "You are the playwright, *señor*?"

"At your service, your Excellency," Lope said, with a bow of his own. *At your mistress' service. Especially at your mistress' service.*

If the nobleman knew what was in de Vega's mind, he gave no sign of it. With another friendly nod, he said, "I've been listening to Catalina practicing her lines these past few days, and I have to tell you I'm impressed. I heard a good many dreary comedies in Madrid that couldn't come close to what you're doing here in this godforsaken wilderness."

Slightly dazed, Lope murmured, "You're far too kind, your Excellency." He scratched his head. He wasn't impervious to guilt. Here was this fellow praising his work, and he wanted to sleep with the man's mistress? He took another look at Catalina Ibañez, at her sparking eyes, the delicate arch of her nose, her red lips and white teeth, the sweetly curved figure her brocaded dress displayed. *Well, as a matter of fact, yes,* Lope thought. *The game is worth the candle.*

"Do I hear you write plays in English as well as Spanish?" Don Alejandro asked.

"No, sir, that is not so. I speak English, but I have never tried to write it," de Vega answered. "I am working with *Señor* Shakespeare, though, on his play about his Most Catholic Majesty. The Englishman has even written a small part for me into his *King Philip*. That may be what you heard."

"Yes, it could be," de Recalde agreed, still friendly and polite. "Would you do me the honor of letting me see what you have here so far?"

Lope didn't really want to do that. The production was still ragged, and no one knew it better than he. But he saw no way to refuse a nobleman's request: however polite it sounded, it was really more a nobleman's order. He did feel he could warn de Recalde: "It won't be the show you'd see in a few more days."

"Of course. Of course." Don Alejandro waved aside the objection. "But I do want to see how my sweetheart's lines fit in with everybody else's."

He gazed fondly at Catalina Ibañez. Lope would have sold his soul for the look she sent the nobleman in return. But then she turned one equally warm on him, as she said, "He's given me such lovely words to use."

"He certainly has," Don Alejandro agreed. Because of his wealth and good looks, was he too complacent to believe Catalina might be interested in a man who had little to offer but words? If he was that complacent, did he have reason to be so?

I hope not, Lope thought. Aloud, he said, "Take your places, everyone! We're going to start from the beginning for his Excellency. . . . *¡Madre de Dios!* Somebody kick Diego and wake him up."

Diego rose with a yelp. "What was that for?" he demanded indignantly. "I wasn't asleep. I was only resting my eyes."

Arguing with him was more trouble than it was worth. De Vega didn't try. He just said, "No time for rest now, lazybones. We're going to take it from the top for Don Alejandro, so he can see what we've been up to."

"Ah, *señor*, since when have you wanted anybody knowing what you're up to?" Diego murmured, his eyes sliding towards Catalina Ibañez. Lope coughed and spluttered. Diego might make a miserable excuse for a servant, but that didn't mean he didn't know the man he served so badly. Instead of looking at Catalina himself, Lope glanced toward Alejandro de Recalde. The nobleman, fortunately, hadn't paid any attention to Diego.

"Places! Places!" Lope shouted, submerging would-be lover so playwright and director could come forth. Being all those people at once, he sometimes felt very crowded inside. Were other people also so complex? When he thought of Diego, he had his doubts. When he thought of Christopher Marlowe . . . *I won't think of Marlowe,* he told himself. *He's gone, and I don't have to worry about seizing him any more. But oh, by God, how I'll miss his poetry.*

De Vega's own poetry poured forth from his amateur company. He screamed, cajoled, prompted, and kept looking at Don Alejandro. Catalina's keeper plainly enjoyed *El mejor mozo de España*. He laughed in all the right places, and clapped loud enough to seem a bigger audience than he was. He didn't applaud only his mistress, either, which proved him a gentleman.

When the play ended, Catalina Ibañez curtsied to him. Then, deliberately, as if she really were Queen Isabella, she curtsied to Lope, too. He bowed in return, also as if she were the Queen. Don Alejandro de Recalde laughed and cheered for them both. Catalina's eyes lit up. She smiled out at the nobleman—but somehow managed to include Lope in that smile, too.

She's trying to see how close to the wind she can sail, he realized, *playing games with me right under Don Alejandro's nose. He'll kill her—and likely me, too—if he notices. But if he doesn't—oh, if he doesn't . . .*

Lope slid closer to her. As softly as he could, he murmured, "When can I see you? Alone?"

Had she shown surprise then, surprise or offense, he would have been a dead man. But she, unlike most of her companions here, really was an actress; Lope had had that thought before. "Soon," she whispered back. "Very soon." Her expression never changed, not a bit.

She's going to betray Don Alejandro, Lope thought. *How long before she betrays me, too?* His eyes traveled the length of her again. For the life of him—and he knew it might *be* for the life of him—he couldn't make himself worry about that.

THOMAS VINCENT HELD SHEETS OF PAPER UNDER SHAKESPEARE'S nose. " 'Steeth, Master Vincent, mind what you do," Shakespeare said. "None should look on those who hath not strongest need."

"Be you not amongst that number?" the prompter returned. "Methought you'd fain see our scribe his work."

"I have seen his work," Shakespeare said. "Had I not, I had given you the name of another."

But he took a sheet from Vincent even so. Thomas Phelippes had had to work like a man possessed to copy out all the parts of *Boudicca* so quickly. However fast he'd written, though, his script hadn't suffered. It remained as clear as it had been when he'd demonstrated it in Shakespeare's ordinary.

"You could get no better," Shakespeare said, and Thomas Vincent nodded. The poet gave back the part. "Now then—make this disappear. Place it not where any sneaking spy nor prowling Spaniard might come upon't."

"I am not so fond as you hold me," the prompter said. "None shall see it but he whose part it is—and him I shall not suffer to take it from the Theatre."

"Marry, I hope you do not," Shakespeare said. "Yet will even that suffice us? For know you, we may also be done to death by slanderous tongues."

"I know't well, sir: too well, by Jesu," Vincent replied. "Here I am come unto a fear of death, a terrible and unavoided danger."

"Let only the fear thereof be unavoided, the thing itself passing over us like the Angel of Death o'er the children of Israel in Egypt. From this nettle, danger, may we pluck the flower, safety."

Before Thomas Vincent could answer, one of the tireman's helpers who stood at the entrance to the Theatre began to whistle the tune to a particular bawdy song. The players on the stage, who'd begun learning their parts for *Boudicca*, switched on the instant to rehearsing the piece they would put on that afternoon. The prompter said, "Mark you, now—in sooth, they do vanish." He vanished himself, disappearing into the tiring room.

Shakespeare wished he too could disappear. No such luck. Instead, he walked out to greet Lieutenant de Vega, of whose arrival that bawdy song had warned. "God give you good morrow," he called, and made a leg at the Spaniard.

"And you, sir." Lope swept off his hat and bowed in return. "You are well, I hope?"

"Passing well, I thank you." Shakespeare didn't mind exchanging courtesies with de Vega. As long as they talked in commonplaces, peril seemed far away. It wasn't; he knew that full well. But it seemed so, and even the semblance of tranquility was precious.

"How fares *King Philip*?" Lope asked.

"Passing well," Shakespeare repeated, adding, "or so I hope." The commission he had from Don Diego Flores de Valdés was far safer than the one Lord Burghley had given him. Part of him hoped Lord Westmorland's Men would offer their auditors *King Philip*, not *Boudicca*. That would pluck safety from the nettle of danger. It would be a craven's safety, but safety nonetheless. Let *Boudicca* once see the light of day, and . . .

Let Boudicca *once see the light of day, and God grant I get free of England, as Kit hath done*, Shakespeare thought. England had lain under the Spaniards' boots for almost ten years now. *Could* she rise up and cast them out? If she could, why hadn't she long since?

"How fares King Philip himself?" he inquired.

Lope de Vega frowned. "Not well, I fear me: not well at all. Late word from Spain hath it he waxeth dropsical, his belly and thighs now much distended whilst his other members waste away."

He crossed himself. Shakespeare did the same. He couldn't quite hide a shudder. He'd seen the horrid bloating of dropsy, seen it rob its victims of life an inch at a time. They'd had to press a board against one luckless player's belly to help him make water, as if they were squeezing the juice from grapes in a wine press. Next to that, the swift certainty of the gallows seemed a mercy. *But you'd have no swift end, not now. . . .*

"Best you finish the play, quick as you might," de Vega told him. "Soon enough—all too soon—the company will show it forth."

"It lacks but little," Shakespeare said.

"Glad I am to hear you say so," the Spaniard said. "As soon as all the parts be finished, let your prompter give them to the scribes, that they might make fair copies of them for the players to learn by heart."

"Certes, your honor. Just as you say, so shall it be." Now Shakespeare bowed. "You know well the customary usages of a theatre not your own."

He put more sarcasm into that than perhaps he should have. De Vega, fortunately, did not seem to notice. He answered, "They are not so different from those of Spain. Your prompter is new to his work, not so?"

"Indeed, his predecessor having . . . died." Guilt stabbed at Shakespeare. He did his best not to show it. De Vega here might one day talk to Constable Strawberry, and Strawberry, in his own plodding way, had already connected Shakespeare and Ingram Frizer, though he didn't quite know what connections he'd made.

But, for now, Lope de Vega's attention focused on *King Philip* and the problems involved in producing it. "An he have trouble finding scribes fit for the matter, I ken a man who'd suit it."

"Ah?" Shakespeare said: the most noncommittal noise he could make.

Lope nodded. "Ay, sir: an Englishman already in the employ of Don Diego, and thus acquainted with all you purpose here. I have seen his writing, and know him to have an excellent character, most legible. He is called Thomas . . . ah . . . Phelippes."

He pronounced the name in the Spanish manner, as if it had three syllables. That kept Shakespeare from recognizing it for a moment. When he did, he felt as if a thunderbolt had crashed to earth at his feet. Lope knew Phelippes well enough to know what sort of scribe he made? Did the Spanish officer have a fair copy of *Boudicca*? Had he got it before Thomas Vincent got his?

Whom may I trust? Shakespeare wondered dizzily. *Vincent? Phelippes? Nick Skeres? Lord Burghley? Anyone in all the world?* The deeper into the plot he sank, the closer he came to the moment when the company would offer one play or the other, the more certain he became that no one had any business ever trusting anyone else.

"What think you, *señor*?" Lope asked when Shakespeare didn't answer right away.

"Master Vincent, meseems, hath already scribes enough for the work," Shakespeare said, picking his words with the greatest of care. "You were wiser, though, to speak to him in this matter than to me. He is quite out of countenance with my character, reckoning it to show mine own bad character."

The Spanish officer chuckled at his feeble wordplay, not knowing how hard Shakespeare was working to distract him and to conceal his own alarm. "As you suggest, so shall I do," de Vega said. "Shall I find him in the tiring room?"

"I know not," Shakespeare replied, hoping Vincent had had the sense, and the time, to hide the fair copy—the fair copy Thomas Phelippes had written out!—of *Boudicca.*

"I'll seek him there," Lope said, and off he went before Shakespeare could try to delay him any more. No howls of fright or fury came from behind the stage, so Shakespeare dared hope the prompter had proved prompt enough in concealing the dangerous play.

Shakespeare had only a small part in the day's production, Marlowe's *Caligula*. The poet was fled, but his plays lived on. Shakespeare would have been glad with more to do; he might have worried less. As things were, he'd never been so glad to escape the Theatre once the show was done.

He hadn't gone far towards London before Richard Burbage fell into step with him. "Give you good even," the other player said, and then, "It went right well, methought."

He'd played the title role, and milked it for all it was worth. Still, Shakespeare nodded; as Marlowe had written it, the role was worth milking. "This was the frightfullest Roman of them all," Shakespeare said.

"In sooth, he is a choice bit of work," Burbage said. "And, in sooth, could we but show more of what he did, he'd seem frightfuller yet."

"It wonders me the Master of the Revels gave Kit leave to present e'en as much as the play offers," Shakespeare said.

"Come the day, *we'll* show more than Sir Edmund wots of," Burbage observed.

"Come the day," Shakespeare echoed. "And, by what the Spaniard saith, the day comes soon: Philip hath declined further." He walked along for a few paces, then added, "Or, come the day, we'll give the auditors *King Philip*, and all will weep for fallen glory."

Burbage was also silent for a little while. "Peradventure we will," he said at last. "But ere I sleep each night, I pray God they'll see the other." Here in Shoreditch High Street, he named no names. Who could tell which jade or ragamuffin might take some incautious word to the dons or the English Inquisition?

"Well, Dick, your prayer, at least, is to the purpose," Shakespeare said wearily. "When I petition the Lord, it is that He let this cup pass from me. I fear me, though, He hears me not." He threw his hands in the air. " 'Swounds, why fled I not this madness or ever it laid hold of me?"

"The heart hath its reasons, whereof reason knoweth naught," Burbage said.

Shakespeare stopped in surprise. "That is well said. Is't your own?" When Burbage nodded, Shakespeare set a hand on his shoulder. "When next Will Kemp assails you as being but the mouthpiece for other men, cast defiance in's teeth."

"So I would, and so I will," the other player answered. "But gramercy for your courtesy."

"Your servant, sir," Shakespeare said. "Would I were penning some trifling comedy of lovers loving will they, nill they; I'd engraft your line therein fast as ever I could." He sighed. "Shall I ever again labor over aught so sweet and simple?"

"But if all go well . . ." Burbage said.

"Perhaps," Shakespeare said, and said no more. He didn't want his hopes to rise too high. They would only have further to fall.

Burbage might have sensed as much. Instead of going on with the argument, he pointed ahead. "Bishopsgate draws nigh. Spring at last being arrived, it likes me having daylight left once we've strutted and fretted our two hours upon the stage."

"Why, it doth like me as well," Shakespeare said in surprise. He clapped a hand to his forehead. "By my troth, Dick, I've scarce noted proud-pied April, dressed in all his trim, putting a spirit of youth in everything. Goose quill and paper have compassed round my life."

"Belike, for it's April no moe," Burbage told him. "These are May's new-fangled shows, and far from the best of 'em."

"May?" Shakespeare cried. "Surely not! Surely they'd have decked the streets with greenery, as is the custom, and burnt bonfires, and run up maypoles for that they might dance round 'em."

"Surely they would have. Surely they did. Surely you never marked it." Richard Burbage eyed him with amused pity.

"Wait!" Shakespeare snapped his fingers. "I mind me we gave the groundlings *The Taming of the Shrew* on the day. There! D'you see? I had some knowledge of it after all." That felt very important to him just then.

Burbage's expression changed not a jot. "And so we did. But why know you of it? Only for that it came to pass within the Theatre's bourne. Otherwise . . ." He shook his head.

As usual, Irishmen with long, hungry faces and fiery eyes stood guard at Bishopsgate. The gallowglasses glowered at Shakespeare and Burbage: the two players were big enough and young enough to seem dangerous no matter how mildly they behaved. One of the guards said something in his own musical language, of which Shakespeare understood not a word. Another started to draw his sword. But their sergeant—distinguishable only because he was a few years older and a little more scarred—shook his head. He waved the Englishmen into London, saying, "Pass through. Quick now, mind."

"Lean raw-boned rascals," Burbage muttered, but he made sure the gallowglasses couldn't hear him.

"I do despise the bloody cannibals," Shakespeare agreed, also in a low voice. "May they prove roast meat for worms."

"God grant it!" Burbage said. "That the dons lord it over us is one thing—they earned the right, having beaten us in war. But these red-polled swashbucklers?" He shook his head. "Men who'd never dare rise against the Spaniards will run riot to cast out Irish wolves."

"Ay, belike." Shakespeare wondered if Sir William Cecil had thought of inflaming Londoners against the savages from the western island. *Likely he will have*, the poet thought. *He sees so much; would he have missed that?* Still, he resolved to speak of it to Lord Burghley when next he saw him, or to Nick Skeres or Thomas Phelippes if he didn't see the noble soon.

Phelippes? Shakespeare kicked a pebble into a puddle. Whom did the clever, dusty little man really serve? Sir William? Don Diego? Or only himself, first, last, and always? As soon as Shakespeare shaped the question, he saw what the answer had to be. But where, in the end, would

Phelippes judge his interest lay? And how much would that cost everyone on the other side?

Burbage clapped him on the back. "I'm to mine own house. God give you good even, Will."

"And you," Shakespeare said absently. His head full of plots, he had to remind himself to turn off Bishopsgate Street and make for his lodging. Then he'd be off to the ordinary, to write as long as he could, and then back to the lodging once more, this time to sleep. "God save me," he muttered. "May Day passed by, and I knew it not." He wondered what else he'd missed, and decided he didn't want to know.

"Come on, Diego," Lope de Vega said impatiently from horseback. "You have only a donkey to mount. The two of you must be close cousins."

"*Señor*, I would never mount my cousin. The Good Book forbids it—and besides, she's ugly," his servant answered. As Lope blinked at such unexpected wit, Diego swung up into the saddle. The ass brayed pitifully at his weight.

"You have your costume?" Lope demanded. Diego set a hand on a saddlebag. De Vega nodded. "Good. To Westminster, then. They say England's Isabella may come to watch the play, to see Castile's performed on stage. She could make your fortune, Diego." *She could make mine*, he thought.

Diego said, "A servant playing a servant won't make much of a mark. You should have cast me as Ferdinand."

They rode away from the Spanish barracks at the heart of London and west toward the court center. Lope had to rein in to keep his horse, a high-spirited mare, from leaving Diego's donkey behind. "Ferdinand!" Lope said. "What mad dream is that? You're not asleep now, not so I can tell."

"But am I not the perfect figure of a king?" Diego said.

Surveying his rotund servant, de Vega answered, "You are the perfect figure of two kings—at least." Diego sent him a venomous glare.

Lope paid no attention. On such a day, he was happy enough to be outdoors. As always, spring had, to a Spaniard's reckoning, come late to England, but it was here at last. The sun shone brightly. The only clouds in the sky were small white ones, drifting slowly from west to east on a mild breeze. It had rained a couple of days before—not hard, just enough to lay the dust without turning the road into a bog.

Everything was green. New grass grew exuberantly: more so than it ever did in drier, hotter Castile. Trees and bushes were in new leaf. The earliest spring flowers had begun to brighten the landscape. Birdsong filled the moist air. Robins and chaffinches, cuckoos and larks, waxwings and tits all made music. They left England sooner and came back later than they did in Spain. Each spring, when they returned, Lope discovered anew how much he'd missed them and how especially empty and barren the winter had seemed without them.

Diego smiled to hear those songs, too. "Mesh nets," he murmured. "Birdlime. By all the saints, there's nothing can match a big plate of songbirds, all nicely roasted on spits or maybe baked in a pie. I don't think much of English cookery, but they make some savory pies. Beefsteak and kidney's mighty tasty, too, and you can get that any season of the year."

"Yes, that is a good one," Lope agreed. "And the song of the cow is much less melodious than that of the linnet or greenfinch."

"The song of the cow, *señor*?" Diego asked. Before de Vega could answer, his servant shook his head. "No, don't tell me. I don't think I want to know. It must be something only poets can hear."

"Not at all, Diego." Lope smiled sweetly. "For example, whenever you open your mouth, everyone around you is treated to the song of the jackass."

"Oh, I am wounded," Diego moaned. He clutched at his heart. "I have taken a mortal thrust. Send for the physician. No, send for the priest to shrive me, for I am surely slain."

"You are surely a nuisance, is what you are," Lope said, but he couldn't help laughing.

No more than a mile or so separated Westminster from London, with the space between the two cities only a bit less crowded than either one of them. De Vega never had the sensation of truly being out in the country, as he would have while traveling between a couple of towns in Spain. Whenever he looked to the left, a forest of sails on the Thames reminded him how brash and busy this part of the world was.

"Fancy houses," Diego remarked as they rode into Westminster. "You can tell this is a place for rich people. All the poor men—all the honest men—are back in London."

Lope couldn't help laughing at that, either, but for a rather different reason. London drew the ambitious, the hungry, the desperate from all over England. A lot of them discovered that, no matter how ambitious and desperate they were, they stayed hungry. The hungrier they got, the less likely they were to stay honest. London had more thieves and robbers than any other three cities Lope could imagine.

Those fancy houses drew his eye, too—again, for a different reason. "This is Drury Lane," he said. "Lord Burghley lives here, who was Elizabeth's chief minister. Anthony Bacon lived here, too, till the accursed sodomite fled the kingdom."

"Sounds like a good street for a fire," Diego said. "Just by accident, of course." He winked.

"I don't know what you're talking about," Lope answered, deadpan. The two of them exchanged knowing looks.

The Thames bent towards the south. The road followed it. De Vega and Diego rode past a tilt-yard and several new tenements before coming to a large area on their left enclosed by a brick wall. Over the top of the wall loomed the upper stories of some impressive buildings. "What's that?" Diego asked, pointing to the enclosure.

"That? That is Scotland," Lope said.

Diego scornfully tossed his head. "You can't fool me, boss. You've been scaring me with Scotland for a while now. I know what it is—that kingdom up north of here, the one where the wild men live."

"Some of the wild men," Lope amended. "But that yard, that too *is* Scotland." He crossed himself to show he was telling the truth. "When the King of the wild men comes to visit England, he is housed there, and so it took its name." He wished the present King of Scotland would come to visit England. But, despite honeyed invitations, Protestant James VI was too canny to thrust his head into the Catholic lion's mouth. Lope continued, "And there beyond lies Whitehall, where the company shall perform."

"Oh, joy," Diego said.

Whitehall had formerly been a noble's residence. Henry VIII, having taken it for his own, had enlarged it, adding tennis courts, bowling alleys, and another tilt-yard, with a second-story gallery from which he and his companions might observe the sport. Elizabeth had also watched jousts from that gallery, but neither Isabella nor her consort Albert much favored them. A wooden stage, not much different from that of the Theatre, had gone up on the tilt-yard, in front of the gallery. The highest-ranking English and Spanish grandees would view *El mejor mozo de España* from the comfort of the gallery. The rest, prominent enough to be invited but not enough to keep company with the Queen and King, would impersonate the groundlings who packed the theatres out beyond London's walls. They didn't have to pay a penny for the privilege, though.

In the makeshift tiring room behind the stage, players donned costumes, put on makeup, and mumbled their lines, trying to hold them in their memory. When Lope came in, Catalina Ibañez rushed up to him. "Oh, *Señor* de Vega, God help me, I'm so nervous!" she cried. "I want to explode!"

He glanced around to make sure Don Alejandro was out in the audience and not hovering backstage here, then leaned forward and gave her a kiss that might have seemed careless. "Don't you worry about a thing, sweetheart. You'll be wonderful!" he told her, and sent up a quick, silent prayer that he'd prove right.

A lackey rushed into the tiring room. "The Queen and King have taken their places in the gallery," he said.

"Then we'd better perform for them, hadn't we?" Lope said. "Come on, my friends, show them what you can do." He looked around again, to make sure everyone was ready. "Diego, in the name of God, don't fall asleep now!"

"I wasn't falling asleep," Diego said. "I was only—"

"Resting my eyes," Lope finished for him. "You've used that one before. Don't use it again, unless you want to get to know the real Scotland, not the yard here." One last quick, worried look. Then he nodded to Catalina Ibañez and one of her maidservants, who would open the play as Isabella and Doña Juana, her lady-in-waiting.

Catalina crossed herself. Her maidservant giggled. They went out onto the stage. The audience, which had been mumbling and buzzing, gave them its ears. As soon as Catalina Ibañez got on stage, she was fine—better than fine. Lope breathed a sigh of relief.

Everything went as well as he'd hoped. Everything, in fact, went better than he'd dared hope. The actors remembered their lines. Even the most wooden ones delivered them with some feeling. Diego made a better servant on stage than he ever had for real. An hour and a half flew by as if in a dream. The applause for the players was thunderous.

From the tiring room, Lope heard Catalina Ibañez call, "And here is the man who gave us these golden words to say: Senior Lieutenant Lope Félix de Vega Carpio!"

More applause as Lope, who felt as if he were dreaming himself, came out onto the stage and bowed to the audience—especially to the central gallery, where Isabella and Albert of England sat. How had Catalina learned his full name? No time to wonder about that now; Queen Isabella was calling, "Well done, *Señor* de Vega. You are a very clever fellow." Lope bowed again. Isabella tossed him a small leather purse. He caught it out of the air. It was heavy, heavy enough to be stuffed with gold. He bowed once more, this time almost double. Dazedly, he followed the company offstage.

Back in the tiring room, he went over to Catalina Ibañez and said, "How can I thank you for calling me out there?"

Her eyes were as warm with promise as an early summer morning. "If you're as clever as Queen Isabella says, *Señor* de Vega, I'm sure you'll think of something," she purred. Only later did he wonder whether she was really looking at him or at the purse he'd just got.

Sam King came up to Shakespeare in the parlor of the lodgings they shared. A little shyly, he said, "I have somewhat for you, Master Will." He held out his hand and gave Shakespeare three pennies—two stamped with the visages of Isabella and Albert, the third an older coin of Elizabeth's.

"Gramercy," Shakespeare said in surprise. Up till now, King hadn't had enough money for himself, let alone to pay back anyone else. Shakespeare had almost forgotten the threepence he'd given the younger man for a supper, and certainly hadn't expected to see it again.

But, a touch of pride in his voice, King said, "I pay what I owe, I do."

"Right glad am I to hear't," Shakespeare answered. "You've found work, then?"

"You might say so." But King's nod seemed intended to convince himself at least as much as to convince Shakespeare. "Ay, sir, you might say so."

"And what manner of work is't, pray tell?"

No sooner were the words out of his mouth than Shakespeare wished he had them back. Had Sam King landed an apprenticeship with a carpenter or a bricklayer, he would have shouted the news to the skies, and would have deserved to. As things were . . . As things were, he turned red. "I am . . . stalled to the rogue," he replied at last.

"Are you?" Shakespeare tried to sound happy for the man who slept in the same room as he did. For someone on his own and hungry in

London, even being formally initiated as a beggar had to seem a step up. Carefully, the poet went on, "God grant men be generous to you."

He wondered how long they would stay generous. King was young and healthy, even if on the scrawny side. A beggar with one leg or a missing eye or some other injury or ailment that inspired pity might have a better chance at pennies and ha'pennies and farthings. But King smiled and said, "There are all manner of cheats to pry the bite from a gentry cove, or from your plain cuffin, too. I've a cleym, now, fit to make a man spew an he see it."

"Have you indeed?" Shakespeare wasn't surprised to hear that. He'd known other beggars who used false sores to get money from those who saw them.

"Ay, sir," Sam King said. "And the moe I learn the art, the better the living I shall have of it." Yes, he might almost have been speaking of carpentry or bricklaying.

"May it be so," Shakespeare said, as politely as he could. He wished the other man would go away. He gave beggars coins now and again, and did not care to think of them as frauds.

King, though, bubbled with enthusiasm for his new trade. "I take crowfoot, spearwort, and salt, and, bruising these together, I lay them upon the place of the body I wish to make sore," he said, grinning. "The skin by this means being fretted, I first clap a linen cloth, till it stick fast, which plucked off, the raw flesh hath ratsbane thrown upon it, to make it look ugly; and then cast over that a cloth, which is always bloody and filthy."

Shakespeare's stomach lurched, as it might have in a small boat on rough water. Fascinated in spite of himself, he asked, "But doth your flesh not from such rude usage take true hurt?"

"Nay, nay." Sam King shook his head. "I do't so often, that in the end I feel no pain, neither desire I to have it healed, but I will travel with my great cleym from market to market, being able by my maunding to get quite five shillings in a week, in money and in corn."

"No wonder you could repay me, then," Shakespeare remarked. Five shillings a week wouldn't make a man rich, but he wouldn't starve on such earnings, either.

"No wonder at all," King agreed happily. "I company with two or three other artificial palliards, and we sing out boldly, thus. . . ." His voice rose to a shrill, piercing whine: "Ah, the worship of God look out with your merciful eyne! One pitiful look upon sore, lame, grieved, impotent people, sore troubled with the grievous disease, and we have no rest day nor night by the canker and worm, that continually eateth the flesh from the bone! For the worship of God, one cross of your small silver, to buy us salve and ointment, to ease the poor wretched body, that never taketh rest; and God reward you for it in heaven!"

Jane Kendall hurried into the parlor. "Begone! We want no beggars here," she began, and then checked herself. "Oh, 'tis you, Master King. Methought you some other tricksy wretch seeking to beguile silver by cleyms and other frauds. I'll not have such doings in this house. I know better."

She didn't mind if King begged elsewhere. She simply didn't want her lodgers tricked out of money that might otherwise assure her of her rent. Having dwelt in her house some little while, Shakespeare was certain of that. He said, "Fear not. He did but learn me his law, the which is indeed most quaint and bene."

"We'll say no more about it, then." The Widow Kendall heaved a sigh. "This place is not what it was—by my halidom, it is not. That I should have lodging here, all at the same time, a beggar and a witch and a poet . . ." She shook her head.

Shakespeare resented being lumped together with Sam King and Cicely Sellis. A moment's reflection, though, told him they might resent being lumped together with him. He said, "So that we pay what you require on the appointed day, where's your worry, Mistress Kendall?"

"So that you do, all's well," she answered. "But with such trades . . . Sweet Jesu, who ever heard of a rich poet?"

She could imagine a rich beggar. She could imagine a cunning woman with money. A poet? No. Shakespeare was tempted to brag of the gold he'd got from Lord Burghley and Don Diego. He was tempted, for a good half a heartbeat. Then common sense prevailed. The best way to keep from being robbed or having his throat slit was not to let on he had anything worth stealing.

Mommet stalked into the parlor. The cat rubbed the side of its head against Shakespeare's ankle and began to purr. A little uncomfortably, Shakespeare stroked it. The cunning woman's cat—her familiar?—had seemed to like him from their first meeting. What would an inquisitor on the trail of witchcraft make of that? Nothing good, Shakespcare was sure.

Sam King said, "Mistress Kendall, may I take a mug of your fine ale?" At her nod, King hurried into the kitchen. When he came back with the mug, mischief lit his face. He squatted by Mommet and poured out a little puddle on the floor.

The Widow Kendall's voice rose in sharp indignation: "Here, now! What do you do? Would you waste it?"

"By no means." King crooned, "Here, puss, puss, puss," to the animal. "Come on your ways—open your mouth—here is that which will give language to you, cat. Open your mouth!"

Mommet sniffed at the ale slowly soaking into the rammed-earth floor. The cat's head bent. Ever so delicately, it lapped at the puddle. Then it looked up. It eyes caught the firelight from the hearth and glowed green.

"What game play you at?"

Sam King started violently and made the sign of the cross. Shakespeare jerked in surprise, too. But it wasn't the cat that had spoken. It was Cicely Sellis, standing in the doorway to her room, hands on hips, her face furious.

"What play you at?" she asked again. "Tell me straight out, else I'll make you sorry for your silence."

"N-N-N-Naught, Mistress Sellis," King stammered, his face going gray with fear. "I was but, ah, giving your cat, ah, somewhat to drink."

"You play the palliard," the cunning woman said. "Play not the fool, sirrah, or you'll find more in the way of foolery than ever was in your reckoning. Hear you me?"

"I—I do," King answered in a very small voice.

"See to't, then," Cicely Sellis snapped. She made a small, clucking sound. "Come you here, Mommet."

Cats didn't come when called. Shakespeare had known that since he was a little boy in Stratford. Cats did as they pleased, not as anyone else pleased. But Mommet trotted over to Cicely Sellis like a lapdog. The cat's contented buzz filled the parlor.

That frightened Sam King all over again. "God be my judge, mistress, I meant no harm," he whispered.

The look the cunning woman gave him said *she* would judge him, and that God would have nothing to do with it. "Some men there are that love not a gaping pig," she said, "some, that are mad if they behold a cat. As there is no firm reason to be rendered why he cannot abide a harmless necessary cat, so he were wiser to show mercy, and pity, than to sport with a poor dumb beast that knoweth naught of sport. Or think you otherwise?"

"No." King's lips shaped the word, but without sound. He vanished into the bedchamber he shared with Shakespeare. Jane Kendall disappeared almost as quickly.

That left Shakespeare all alone with Cicely Sellis—and with Mommet. He could have done without the honor, if that was what it was. As she stroked the cat's brindled coat, he asked, "Go you to the arena to see bears baited, or bulls, or to the cockfights?"

To his relief, she didn't take offense, and did take the point of the question. Shaking her head, she answered, "I go not to any such so-called sports. I cannot abide them. I am of one piece in mine affections and opinions, Master Shakespeare. Can you say the same?"

"Me, lady? Nay, nor would I essay it, for my wits are all in motley, now of one shade, now another. And which of us is better for't?" Shakespeare asked. Cicely Sellis thought, then shrugged, which struck him as basically honest.

X

A SHARP COUGH BROUGHT LOPE DE VEGA UP SHORT. HE LOOKED back towards Shakespeare, who advanced across the stage of the Theatre. "You attend not, Master de Vega," Shakespeare said severely. "That was your cue to say forth your lines, and it passed you by. I had not known you as such an unperfect actor on the stage, who with his fear is put besides his part."

"Nor am I such." Lope bowed apology. "You pardon, sir, I pray you. 'Twas not fear put me out."

"What then?" Shakespeare asked, still frowning. "Whate'er the reason, you must improve, else you'll appear not. Would you have the groundlings pelt you with marrows and beetroots and apples gone all wormy? Would you have them outshout the action, crying, 'O Jesu, he does it as like one of these harlotry players as ever I see'?" The Englishman's voice climbed to a mocking falsetto.

"No and no and no." Lope shook his head. That *harlotry* struck too close to the mark. "I fear me I find myself distracted—a matter having naught to do with yourself or with your most excellent *King Philip*."

He wondered how much more he would have to say. But Shakespeare, after cocking his head to one side, got to the nub of it in two words: "A woman?"

"Yes, a woman," Lope answered in some relief. "She hath made promises, made them and then kept them not. And yet she may. This being so, I am torn 'twixt hope and fury."

He hadn't thought Catalina Ibañez would play him for a fool. He hadn't thought she *could* play him for a fool. But Don Alejandro's mistress had been all warmth and seductiveness when she didn't have to deliver, and had either kept from seeing him alone or been frustratingly cool when she did. It drove Lope mad: too mad to realize it might have been intended to do just that.

Will Kemp laughed. The clown pitched his voice high, as Shakespeare had: "If thou thinkest I am too quickly won, I'll frown and be perverse and say thee nay. So thou wilt woo." He let it drop back to its usual register: "Sits the wind so?"

He'd summed it up more neatly than de Vega had on his own. "Yes, just so," Lope answered. "What am I to do?"

"You are to have your lines as Master Idiáquez by heart, even an she be heartless," Shakespeare told him. "Let not your honor as a man touch your honor as a player, or no player shall you be."

"I understand," Lope said contritely. "You have reason, *señor*. My private woe should not unsettle this your play."

"As for the wench, a boot in the bum may haply work wonders, as hath been known aforetimes," Kemp said. "And if you cannot cure her by the foot, belike you'll do't by the yard."

He leered. Shakespeare snorted. So did the rest of the Englishmen in earshot. Lope scratched his head. He spoke English well, but every so often something flew past him. He had the feeling this was one of those times.

"I do know my lines," he said, ignoring what he couldn't follow. "Hear me, if you will:

> 'This cardinal,
> Though from an humble stock, undoubtedly
> Was fashioned to much honour. From his cradle
> He was a scholar, and a ripe and good one:
> Exceeding wise, fair-spoken, and persuading;
> Lofty and sour to them that lov'd him not,
> But to those men that sought him sweet as summer.
> And, to add greater honours to his age
> Than man could give him, he died fearing God.' "

"In sooth, you have them," Shakespeare agreed. "It were better, though, to bring them forth when called for."

"And so I shall," Lope promised. "Before God, I shall."

"Before God, ay—we are ever before God," Will Kemp said. "But can you stand and deliver before the groundlings? There's the rub."

He couldn't mean he thought the groundlings a more important and more difficult audience than God . . . could he? No one could be that blasphemous. The English Inquisition would get its hooks into a man who dared say anything of the sort—would get them in and never let go again. An ordinary man, fetched before the inquisitors, would have no defense. But a player, Lope realized, just might. He could say he'd put the thought of his craft ahead of his soul for a moment. He probably wouldn't escape scot-free, but might avoid the worst.

"Let us try again," Shakespeare said. "The more we work afore ourselves alone, the better we shall seem when the Theatre's full."

"Or not, an God will it so," Kemp said. "The best-rehearsed company will now and again make a hash of things."

"I have myself seen the same, more often than I should wish," Lope agreed.

"Ay, certes. So have we all," Shakespeare said. "But a company less than well rehearsed will make a hash of things more than now and again. Thus I tell you, once more into the breach, dear friends, once more, or close the show up with our bungled lines. Disguise fair nature with hard-summoned art. When the trumpet's blast blows in your ears, then imitate the action of the Spaniard."

"I need not imitate," Lope pointed out.

Shakespeare made a leg at him. "Indeed not, Lieutenant. But as for you others, I'd see you stand like greyhounds in the slips, straining upon the start. Follow your spirit, and upon your cue cry, 'God for Philip! Sweet Spain and Saint James!' "

Richard Burbage had left the stage, probably for the jakes. Returning, he clapped his hands and said, "By God, Will, I've gone off to war with words less heartening ringing in my ears."

"Never mind war," Shakespeare said. "Let us instead piece together this *King Philip*. Take your places. We shall once more essay the scene."

This time, Lope remembered his lines. He sent them ringing out into the empty Theatre. As he spoke and gestured, he tried to imagine the place full of noisy, excited people, all straining forward to catch his every word—and all ready to pelt him with whatever they had handy if he came up dry, or simply if they didn't care for what he had to say. From everything he'd seen, English audiences had less mercy in them than their Spanish counterparts. When they scented weakness, they went straight for the kill.

Here, though, Shakespeare seemed satisfied. "Enough for now, methinks," he said. "God grant we have time aplenty for further work herewith. The day's play, however, we must give at two o' the clock. That wherein we should be good betimes needs must yield pride of place to that wherein we must be good anon. Master Lope, gramercy for your work this day."

"The pleasure is mine." De Vega touched a finger to the broad brim of his hat in salute. The phrase was an English translation of a Spanish commonplace, but he meant it. "You—all of you—show me every day I am here what a company of players should be."

" 'Steeth, Master Lope, I take it as an insult that anyone should style me an exemplar," Will Kemp growled. "Do you withdraw it, or will you give satisfaction?"

For a moment, de Vega thought he'd truly been challenged. Then he thought he might draw on the clown, to cure him of such insolence once for all. But, after a pause that couldn't have spanned two heartbeats, he drew himself up as if affronted. "I, give satisfaction, sirrah? Do you take me for a woman?"

The players laughed. Will Kemp's grin showed uneven teeth. "By my troth, no," he answered. "D'you take me for Kit Marlowe?"

More laughter arose, the baying laughter of men mocking one another's prowess. "I am wounded," de Vega said, and clapped both hands over his heart.

"Which only shows you know not where Kit'd wound you," Kemp said, and clapped both *his* hands over his backside. That coarse, baying laughter redoubled.

Lope joined it. He'd admired—still did admire—Marlowe the poet. It was as if Marlowe the sodomite were some different creature, divorced from the other. Life would have been simpler were that true. But they both made up different parts of the same man. De Vega wondered, not for the first time, how God could instill such great gifts and such a great sin into the same flesh and spirit. He sometimes thought God did such things to keep mortals from believing they understood Him and getting an exaggerated notion of their own cleverness.

Does Marlowe's fall, then, save other men from sins of their own? he wondered. *If that be so, does it not make Marlowe like our Lord?* Lope shook his head. There was one bit of speculation his confessor would never hear. If it should reach an inquisitor's ears . . . No, Lope didn't want to think about that.

As Lord Westmorland's Men began going through the play they'd put on when the Theatre opened, de Vega walked out, swung up onto his horse, and rode back to London. This time, no one in the crowded tenements outside the wall troubled him: not beyond the usual catcalls and curses from behind his back. Ignoring those was always easier; trying to track down the folk who loosed them led only to frustration and fury.

At Bishopsgate, the Irish guards also recognized him for a Spaniard. From them, he got respect instead of scorn. Their sergeant, an immense man, made a clumsy leg at him. The common soldiers murmured in what might have been Irish or might have been what they reckoned English. Either way, it was unintelligible to Lope. He tipped his hat and rode on.

Not far inside the gate, he was struck by the spectacle of a handsome woman coming out of an ordinary with a cat perched on her left shoulder as if it were a sailor's bird. He reined in. "Give you good day, my lady," he said, "and why, I pray you, sits the beast there?"

She gave him a measuring look. "Good day to you, sir," she answered. Lope realized then she was a few years older than he; he hadn't noticed at first glance, as he would have with most women. Her smile held a certain challenge. "As for Mommet here—well, *porqué no?*"

Of course she would know him for a Spaniard by his dress, his looks, his accent. He laughed. "Why not indeed? What an extraordinary beast, though, to stay where you choose to set it."

The cat—Mommet—sent him a slit-eyed green stare a good deal more dismissive than its mistress'. Its yawn displayed needle teeth and a pink tongue. The woman said, "What cat is not an extraordinary beast? Come to that, what man is not an extraordinary beast?"

Lope blinked. He was in love with Lucy Watkins. He was also in love with Catalina Ibañez, a love that tormented his soul—among other things—all the more because it remained as yet unconsummated. Even so, a woman who spoke in riddles could not help but intrigue him. Love of the body, yes. Love of the spirit—yes, that, too. But also love of the mind, especially for a man with a leaping, darting mind like Lope's, a love neither of his two present amours returned.

"Who are you?" he asked urgently.

He wondered if she would tell him. A modest woman wouldn't have. But then, a modest woman wouldn't have spoken to him in the street at all. "I'm called Cicely Sellis," she answered, with no hesitation he noted. "And you, sir, are . . . ?"

With another woman, or with a woman of another sort, he would have given his rank and the rolling grandeur of his full name. To this one, he said only, "I am known as Lope de Vega." He couldn't help bowing in the saddle and adding, "Very much at your service, Mistress Sellis."

Mommet yawned again, as if to say how little his service meant. Cicely Sellis dropped him a token curtsy, careful not to dislodge the cat. "You are Master Shakespeare's friend," she said.

He started to cross himself—it hadn't been a question, but a calm statement of fact. Arresting the gesture, he demanded, "How know you that?"

"No mystery." Amusement sparkled in her eyes. "His lodging-house and mine own are the same, and full many a time hath he spoke your name."

"Oh." Lope wanted to ask what Shakespeare had said about him. Regretfully, he decided that wouldn't be a good idea. With a nod, he urged his horse forward. "I hope to see you again, Mistress Sellis."

"May it be so," she said, and English spring truly came home to Lope.

JACK HUNGERFORD SHOWED SHAKESPEARE A ROW OF CHEAP, RUSTY helmets somewhat brightened by splashes of silver paint. "With feather plumes, Master Will, they serve passing well for Roman casques," the tireman said. "See you how the cheek pieces I've added help give 'em the seeming of antiquity?"

Shakespeare reached out and touched one of those cheek pieces. It was, as he'd expected, nothing but cut tin, hardly thicker than a leaf of paper. That didn't matter. It would look all right to the audience. What the players wore and what the groundlings saw—or imagined they saw—were two very different things. He knew that. No one who'd ever gone on up on stage could help knowing it. Still . . .

"Can we not make it plainer who these Romans are, whom they personate?" he inquired.

Hungerford frowned. "They are Romans, not so?" He scratched his head.

"Ay, certes, they are Romans." Shakespeare drummed the fingers of his right hand on his hose. The tireman, who dealt in things, cared nothing for symbols. "But bethink you, Master Jack. They are Romans, yes. They are invaders, come to Britain to conquer her, to change for their own her ancient and ancestral usages. In the doing, they have cast down a Queen. . . ." How many examples would he have to string together? How long before Jack Hungerford saw where he aimed? Would the tireman ever see it?

Scratching again, this time at the side of his chin, Hungerford spoke in thoughtful tones: "They fair put you in mind o' the dons, not so?"

"Even so, Master Jack! Even so!" Shakespeare wanted to kiss him. Hungerford had seen where he was going after all. "Can you devise somewhat wherewith they have at once the seeming of Romans and Spaniards both?"

"Well . . . I have me these morions here," Hungerford said doubtfully, pointing to a row of Spanish-style helmets below the "Roman" ones. "Haply I might make shift to give 'em a crest of feathers or horsehair, here along the comb, so. . . ." He ran his finger from the front of a morion to the back to show what he meant.

"Yes! Most excellent indeed!" Shakespeare exclaimed. "By my troth, Master Jack, the very thing. At times, now, the Roman soldiery will be seen armored. Can this also call to mind the dons' equipage?"

"Oh, yes. Naught simpler there." Now that the tireman had the bit between his teeth, he could run. "A good English back-and-breast is like unto that which the Spaniards wear. An eagle daubed on the breast thereof should show the armor is purposed to stand for a Roman's, an't please you."

"Indeed—it pleases me greatly." Shakespeare nodded. "Now, one thing more. What have we here of queenly regalia?"

"Queenly . . . ?" Even with bit between his teeth, Hungerford didn't change gaits quickly; he needed a moment to shift his thoughts from one path to another. But then he snapped his fingers. "Ah! I follow! For the lad who is to play . . ." He snapped his fingers again, this time in annoyance. "Beshrew me if I recall the name."

"Boudicca," Shakespeare said patiently. How many people these days knew of the Queen of the Iceni, defeated and dead more than fifteen hundred years? Only those who'd fought through the *Annals*. Maybe his tragedy would change that. Then again, maybe it would never take the stage. But he had to go on as if he thought it would.

"Boudicca," Hungerford echoed. "A heathen appellation, if ever such there be. Well, what would you in aid of the garb purposed for that part, Master Will?"

"That it resemble a certain other deposed Queen's, as close as may be," Shakespeare answered.

He would not say the name. He didn't know why not. This conversation was already so manifestly treasonous, the name couldn't make it worse. But no one ever said it in today's England without a shiver of fear, without wondering who might be listening. He wondered if any girl child born after the summer of 1588 bore it. He had his doubts. He knew he wouldn't have given it to a little girl, not in an England ruled by Isabella and Albert. Maybe some folk were braver than he. No: certainly some folk were braver than he. But were any that brave, or that reckless?

Again, the tireman needed a heartbeat or two to catch up with him. "A certain other . . . ?" Hungerford said, and then nodded. "Oh. Elizab . . ." He stopped. He would not say all of the name, either. His eyes widened. "I take your drift. Whatsoever we may lack, I can get for barter from other companies. They need not know our veritable intent, only that it is to garb a Queen."

"You may say Queen Mary, an't please you," Shakespeare said. "She hath some small part in *King Philip*."

"As she had some small part in King Philip his life," said Hungerford, who was old enough to remember when Mary and Philip had briefly shared the English throne. He nodded. "Ay, that will suit well enough, should any presume to make inquiry. Are you fain to have me give him a red wig and powder his face white, as was . . . her custom for some years?"

"However your wit may take you," Shakespeare answered. "The greater the semblance, though, the more likely the play to seize the auditors."

"Then I'll do't," Hungerford said.

"And one thing more, Master Jack," Shakespeare said earnestly. "Come what may, suffer not Lieutenant de Vega to learn aught of what's afoot, else all's ruined."

"You need not tell me that," the tireman replied. "D'you take more for a witling? A soft and dull-eyed fool?"

The poet shook his head. "By no means, sir. But the enterprise hath such weight and urgency, I'd liefer warn without need than need without giving warning. 'Swounds, I meant no offense, and cry your pardon for any I gave."

Hungerford smiled. "Rest easy. I am not one to hold anger to his inward self, cherishing the warmth like a man in January new-come to hearth and home. And you speak sooth: 'tis no game we play, unless you'd style thus dicing o'er the fate of kingdoms."

Shakespeare sighed with relief. He still had no guarantee *Boudicca* would come off well, or that it would do as Sir William Cecil hoped and help rouse England against the Spanish occupiers. He had no guarantee the play would even appear on stage. (That gave rise to a new worry. If *Boudicca* didn't appear, if *King Philip* did, how could he reclaim the written parts? Any of those, should a Spaniard see it, would be plenty to get him dragged to Tower Hill, hanged, cut down, drawn, quartered, and burnt. His danger didn't end if *Boudicca* failed to play. If anything, it got worse.) But if his tragedy of the British Queen did reach the stage, Jack Hungerford would do everything in his power to make it look the way it should. And the tireman took it seriously. He understood the stakes for which they were playing.

Haply I make a better poet than did Kit Marlowe, Shakespeare thought. *But in all else he were better suited than I, being an intriguer and intelligencer born.* "O my Father, if it be possible, let this cup pass from me."

He didn't realize he'd said that aloud till Hungerford completed the quotation for him: "Nevertheless, not as I will, but as Thou wilt."

Was this God's will? Shakespeare checked himself. That was the wrong question. Everything, surely, was God's will. But was it God's will that the uprising should go forward and succeed?

How can I know? Shakespeare sighed again, on a very different note. Almost groaning, he said, "O God! That one might read the book of fate and see the revolution of the times."

"What fates impose, that men must needs abide," Hungerford said.

Shakespeare's nod was half glum, half exalted. "We have thrown our gloves to death himself, that there's no maculation in our hearts. If it be otherwise, if the canker of treason dwell in someone's bosom, we are all undone."

"Hanging and wiving go by destiny," the tireman said, a homely saw that would have made Shakespeare happier had his own marriage been better.

He left the tiring room and went out on stage, where rehearsal for

Boudicca went on. Burbage, as Boudicca's brother-in-law Caratach, traded barbs with Will Kemp, who played Marcus, a Roman soldier now captured by the Iceni, and with Peter Baker, the boy playing Caratach's nephew, Hengo.

> "Fill 'em more wine; give 'em full bowls.—
> Which of you all now, in recompense of this good,
> Dare but give me a sound knock in the battle?"

Burbage boomed the words: Caratach was a fierce, blustering soldier.

> "Delicate captain,
> To do thee a sufficient recompense,
> I'll knock thy brains out,"

Kemp replied. Marcus' talk was far bolder than his performance. He mimed gobbling down food in front of him.

"By the gods, uncle, If his valour lie in's teeth, he's the most valiant," the boy playing Hengo jeered. He shook his fist at Will Kemp.

> "Thou dar'st as well be damn'd: thou knock his brains out,
> Thou skin of man!—Uncle, I will not hear this."

"Tie up your whelp," Kemp told Burbage, exactly as if he were a proud Roman in barbarous hands.

Peter Baker capered about in a well-acted transport of fury.

> "Thou kill my uncle! Would I
> Had but a sword for thy sake, thou dried dog!"

"What a mettle this little vermin carries," Will Kemp muttered.

"Kill mine uncle!" the boy screeched.

"He shall not, child," said Burbage, as Caratach.

> "He cannot; he's a rogue,
> An only eating rogue: kill my sweet uncle!
> Oh, that I were a man!"

Peter Baker cried.

Will Kemp smirked.

> "By this wine, which I
> Will drink to Captain Junius, who loves
> The Queen's most excellent Majesty's little daughter
> Most sweetly and most fearfully, I will do it."

"Uncle, I'll kill him with a great pin," the youngster playing Hengo squeaked.

"No more, boy," Richard Burbage began. Before he could go on and drink to Kemp's Marcus in turn, the tireman's helper started whistling the bawdy tune of which he was so fond. Instantly, Peter Baker ran off the stage. Burbage went from fierce Caratach to majestic Philip by leaning forward a little, letting his belly droop down, and dropping his voice half an octave. Will Kemp was as quick to turn, chameleonlike, into a cardinal hounding the Mahometans of southern Spain: the drunken, lecherous Roman he had been was forgotten in the wink of an eye.

By the time Lope de Vega walked into the Theatre, what had been a rehearsal for *Boudicca* had metamorphosed into a rehearsal for *King Philip*. "Good morrow, gentles," the Spaniard called as he walked towards the stage. He waved to Shakespeare. "Give you good morrow, Master Will. You go on without me, is it not so?"

"A good day to you, Lieutenant," Shakespeare answered. "All of us must take our parts."

"That is so." Lope nodded. "Tell me something, an't please you."

"If I do know it, you shall know it," Shakespeare said. It sounded like a promise. But it was one he had no intention of keeping if de Vega wanted to know anything he shouldn't.

All Lope said, though, was, "Whensoever I come hither of late, some fellow in yon topmost gallery whistles the selfsame song. What is't? The music thereof quite likes me. Be there accompanying words?"

Shakespeare coughed. Richard Burbage kicked at the boards of the stage. Will Kemp guffawed. Still, Shakespeare could answer safely, so he did: "An I mind me aright, the ditty's named 'A Man's Yard.' "

"Not a tailor's yard, nor a clothier's yard," Burbage added, perhaps helpfully. "Any man's yard."

"Ah?" Lope looked unenlightened. "Can you sing somewhat of't for me?"

That made Shakespeare cough again, cough and hesitate. Very little made Will Kemp hesitate. He sang out in a ringing baritone:

> " 'Rede me a riddle—what is this
> You hold in your hand when you piss?
> It is a kind of pleasing sting,
> A pricking and a pleasant thing.
> It is a stiff short fleshly pole,
> That fits to stop a maiden's hole;
> It is Venus' wanton staying wand
> That ne'er had feet, and yet can stand.' "

He would have gone on, but Lope, grinning, held up a hand. "*Basta*," he said. "Enough; that sufficeth me. And now, *por Dios*, I take your jape of a few days past. We have such songs also in Spanish." He too began to sing. Shakespeare followed a little of it; he knew Italian and French, which were cousins to Spanish, and had picked up some of the conquerors' tongue itself during their ten years in England. From what he got of it, it was indeed of the same sort as "A Man's Yard."

He held up his hand in turn. "This sport were better suited to the alehouse than the Theatre. What would you here, Lieutenant de Vega?"

"What would I?" Lope said "Why, only to see how you fare, my friend, and how your company fares." He sat at the edge of the stage, his feet dangling down towards the dirt floor where the groundlings would stand come the afternoon. Shakespeare fought back a sigh. He wished the Spaniard had come for some specific reason. In that case, he would settle whatever needed settling and then leave. This way, he might stay all day, which meant no one could work on *Boudicca* all day.

"Every day that comes comes to decay a day's work in him," Will Kemp said. " 'Tis sweating labor, to bear such idleness so near the heart."

Twitting a Spaniard could be dangerous. The dons were touchy of what they called their honor. What an Englishman would pass off with a smile might send a Spaniard into a killing rage. Or, equally, it might not. Lope inclined his head to the clown. "My body shall be idle whilst my wits race. Better thus than contrariwise, meseems."

"Call you me Contrariwise?" Kemp bowed in return. "At your service, sir."

"In sooth, you have ever been contrary to the wise," Burbage murmured.

The clown bowed to him, too. "*Et tu, Brute?*" he said, pronouncing the name of the noblest Roman as if it were the ordinary word *brute*. Burbage winced.

So did Shakespeare, but he couldn't resist piling quibble on quibble: "Let it not be bruited about that we are aught but contrariwise to idleness."

De Vega's gaze went from one of them to the next in turn. "You give a better show now than when the groundlings spend their pennies."

"I say two things to that," Will Kemp declared. "*Imprimis*, say I, piss on all those who spend their pennies here." Shakespeare and Burbage both groaned. Lope de Vega only looked puzzled again, as he had at the title of "A Man's Yard." Before anyone could explain the English phrase to him, Kemp went on, "And *secundus*, say I, 'tis no wonder we're better now. Come the play, *he* writes all the lines." He pointed at Shakespeare by thrusting his thumb out between his first two fingers, and added, "I care not a fig for him."

"Thou knew'st not what a fig meant, till thy mother taught it thee," Shakespeare retorted, giving back the gesture. "And would thou wert a figment now." Kemp flinched. Burbage clapped his hands. De Vega sat at the edge of the stage, smiling and waiting for the next exchange.

"BY THE VIRGIN AND ALL THE SAINTS, MY DEAR, I WISH YOU HAD been there and understood the English," Lope told Catalina Ibañez. "They might have been fighting with rapiers, save only that their words pierced again and again without slaying, however much they might make a man wish he were dead."

Catalina shrugged. Her low-cut, tight-fitting bodice made a shrug worth watching. "From everything I've seen, actors are always bitchy," she said.

"No." He shook his head. "You make it less than it is. Could I have written this down as it was spoken, and then rendered it into Spanish—"

"It would probably sound petty and foolish," she broke in. "Such things always do, when they're not fresh." She looked at him from under lowered lashes. "Besides, Senior Lieutenant, did you bring me here to babble about mad Englishmen?"

"Certainly not, my beautiful one," Lope answered. "Oh, no. Certainly not." They sat side by side on a taffeta coverlet in the leafy shade of a small grove of willows in the yard by Whitehall, the yard given over to the Kings of Scotland whenever they chose to visit. No visit from King James seemed imminent, however much the Spaniards would have liked to see him fall into their hands. But the English kept up the yard and the buildings inside even so. Lope lifted a bottle. "More wine?"

"Why not?" Catalina answered. As he poured, a bird began to sing. She frowned. "What's that? I don't recognize the song."

"A seed warbler, I think," he answered. The name, necessarily, came out in English. "The bird does not dwell in Spain. I never heard it before I came here, either."

Catalina Ibañez listened for a little while, then tossed back the wine and shivered. That, for once, had nothing to do with nasty English weather. Summer was here at last. It wasn't a patch on summer in Madrid, but it was tolerable, perhaps a bit better than tolerable. Catalina said, "Even the birds here are foreigners. No wonder I always feel so alone."

"Alone?" Lope set his hand on hers. "Oh, no, sweetheart. How can you say such a thing, when you have . . . Don Alejandro?"

She looked over to him in surprise. She must have expected him to ask, *How can you say such a thing, when you have me?* Her nod showed a certain admiration, as if he'd made an unusual, thought-provoking move in a game of chess. Since he'd mentioned her keeper, she had to answer. And she did, with a toss of the head that sent her curls flying in pretty disarray. "Don Alejandro doesn't understand me," she said—an old gambit, but always a good one. "He's rich, he's important, but he has no idea what a woman wants."

Lope was neither rich nor important, and doubted he ever would be. As for the other . . . Slowly, he raised Catalina's hand to his lips. "What could a woman want," he murmured, "but to be adored?"

That was an old line, too. It didn't work precisely as he'd hoped. "Don Alejandro is the stingiest man in the world," Catalina went on, "and he doesn't give me presents or take me dancing or even"—she seemed to be reminding herself—"out on nice little picnics like this."

"Well," Lope said, "that is a pity." All at once, he began to wonder whether taking her on this nice little picnic had been such a good idea. She was beautiful, yes, undoubtedly, but was she any less mercenary than a scarred German soldier who sold his sword to the highest bidder and walked away if his pay fell in arrears?

Catalina seemed to realize she might have shown a card or two too many. She swayed towards him with melting eyes and said, "I'm so glad to go out anywhere at all, so very glad." She leaned closer yet.

To kiss her was the work of a moment. Altogether without thought, Lope did. Had he thought, he might have wondered who was doing what with whom, and for which reasons. But he'd never been in the habit of thinking around women. He'd hardly even imagined the possibility till his chance meeting with the odd Englishwoman with the cat. And so he kissed Catalina Ibañez, and things went on from there.

She sighed, deep in her throat, and twisted to press herself against him. "Ah, *querido*," she murmured when their lips parted at last. "You don't know how long I've wanted to do that."

"And I," Lope said. "Oh, yes, by God, and I." He kissed her again. Her mouth tasted of wine, but sweeter still.

Except for the twittering birds, they were all alone. The willow branches hung down almost to the ground, shielding them from prying eyes. The grass under the taffeta coverlet was long and soft and resilient. Catalina slapped Lope's hands away a couple of times as he began to explore her, but it was only for show, and they both knew it. She giggled when he nibbled the side of her smooth white neck. The giggle turned to a soft, almost breathless sigh as he slid down so his tongue could tease a nipple.

She sighed again, not very much later, when he poised himself above her and thrust home, as if with the rapier. Her thighs clasped his flanks. Her arms squeezed him as if she never wanted to let him go. English summer, he discovered, was more than warm enough to work up a pleasant sweat, provided one found the right company.

"Oh, Lope!" Catalina gasped, just before his moment of joy. Then she let out a little mewling cry that oddly made him think of Mommet, Cicely Sellis' cat, even though he'd never heard Mommet make a sound. Her nails, sharp as little daggers, scored his back. He drove deep and spent himself.

Her mouth twisted in regret when he pulled out of her. But she quickly started putting herself to rights. De Vega got dressed, too. He reached out to pat her bare backside as she pulled up her drawers. "Even more than I imagined," he told her.

"Imagined?" She raised a hand to her face, as if to hide a blush, as if to say she couldn't imagine a man hungrily imagining making love to her.

"It was all I could do," he said. "It was. But no more." Had he been a few years younger, he would have laid her down on the taffeta coverlet and taken her again then and there. He sighed for lost youth. There would be other chances, though, and soon. And he would be seeing Lucy Watkins again before long. It wasn't as if he'd fallen out of love with her when he fell in love with Catalina Ibañez.

And what might that Englishwoman with the cat be like between the sheets? Lope hadn't thought about finding a lover older than himself since he was eighteen. For that one, he thought he would make an exception.

"We had better get you back," he said to Catalina, shaking his mind free of the women he wasn't with. He gave the woman he was with a quick kiss. "I don't believe I ever enjoyed a picnic more."

"I should hope not." She drew herself up with touchy pride. *Oh, yes—this one is all ice and fire,* Lope thought. *Never a dull moment with her around.* He put the cork back in the wine bottle. He'd brought along a loaf of bread and a pot of honey, too. Honey and bread remained untouched. He smiled as he bundled them into the coverlet. *I tasted better sweets than honey today.*

Hand in hand, he and Catalina walked through the ankle-high grass of the yard no King of Scotland was likely to visit any time soon, towards the gate by which they'd come in. They'd gone about halfway from the willow grove when the gate opened. A tall, broad-shouldered man walked into the yard and strode purposefully towards them.

"*¡Ay, madre de Dios!*" Catalina Ibañez yelped. She dropped Lope's hand as if it were on fire. Under her paint, her face went white as milk. "It's Don Alejandro!"

Lope let the coverlet fall to the grass. The wine bottle clanked against the honey pot. He hoped they didn't break, but that was the least of his worries right now. His right hand fell to the hilt of his rapier. He'd worn it as much for swank as on the off chance of trouble. Without it, he'd be a dead man now.

I may be a dead man anyhow. Don Alejandro went from purposeful walk to thudding trot. His rapier leaped free of its sheath. The long, slim, deadly blade glittered in the sun. "De Vega!" the nobleman bellowed. "Ten thousand demons from hell, de Vega, what are you doing with my woman?"

Had de Recalde come in a few minutes earlier, he would have seen for himself what Lope was doing. By Catalina's delighted response, the nobleman would have learned something, too. This seemed neither time nor place for that discussion. Lope drew his own sword. But he gave as mild an answer as he could: "Talking about the theatre."

"Liar! Dog! Son of a dog!" Don Alejandro shouted, and roared down on him like an avalanche. Steel clattered from steel. Sparks flew. Catalina screamed. "Shut up, you little *puta*!" Don Alejandro shouted. "You're next!"

His first long, abrupt thrust almost pierced Lope's heart; de Vega barely managed to beat the blow aside. He couldn't counter. Fast as a striking serpent, Don Alejandro thrust for his belly. Only a hasty backwards leap saved him from owning a second navel. And any puncture a couple of inches deep probably meant death, either from bleeding or, more slowly and painfully, from fever.

Don Alejandro de Recalde was a picture fencer, with a style as pure as any Lope had ever seen. He kept his blade in front of his body and poised to strike at every moment, and he was quick and strong. He might have stepped out of a swordmaster's school and straight into the King of Scotland's yard. For their first few exchanges, Lope wondered how he could possibly come through the fight alive. And then, as he managed a thrust at Don Alejandro's belly and the nobleman beat his blade aside with a perfect parry, he suddenly smiled a most unpleasant smile.

His next thrust wasn't at Don Alejandro's midriff—it was at his face. Catalina's keeper turned that one, too, but not so elegantly, and he jerked his head back in a way no fencing master would have approved. Lope's smile grew wider and nastier. "Don't do a lot of real righting, you say?" he panted.

"I say *nothing* to you, de Vega," de Recalde snarled, and bored in again. "Nothing!" *Clang! Clang! Clang!* went their swords, as if they were battling it out up on stage.

But swordplay in real fighting was different from what went on with the groundlings cheering down below. It was different from what the fencing masters taught, too. Lope thrust at Don Alejandro's face again. This time, his foe didn't jerk away fast enough. The point pierced his cheek. The nobleman howled in pain. Blood ran down the side of his jaw. Catalina Ibañez shrieked.

"They don't show you that in school, do they?" Lope jeered. He knew perfectly well they didn't. Nobody included blows to the face in fencing exercises. They were too dangerous. Swordmasters who slaughtered their students or scarred them for life weren't likely to get much new business.

Don Alejandro tried to answer him, but blood poured from his lips instead of words. De Recalde was game. He kept on doing his best to skewer Lope. His best was alarmingly good—but not quite good enough.

Lope thrust at his head again, this time pinking his left ear. More blood flew. Don Alejandro shook his head and kept fighting. Both he and Lope ignored Catalina's screams.

Once more, Lope thought. He gave this thrust all the arm extension he had. His point pierced his opponent's right eye, pierced the flimsy bone behind, and penetrated deep into de Recalde's brain. With a grunt that seemed more surprise than pain, Don Alejandro toppled to the grass like a kicked-over sack of clothes. His rapier fell from fingers that could hold it no more. His feet drummed briefly, then were still. A sudden stench said his bowels had let go. Catalina screamed one last time. She gulped to a stop, tears streaming down her face.

"Stupid bastard," Lope said wearily, tugging his sword free and plunging it into the ground to cleanse it. "You never really tried to kill anyone before, did you? Well, by God, you won't try again, that's certain sure."

He wished he'd never killed anyone himself. But he'd fought his way to London after the Armada's army came ashore; if he hadn't killed a few Englishmen, they would most assuredly have killed him. He wished their souls a kind judgment from God—as he did now for Don Alejandro de Recalde's—but they were dead and he was alive and that was how he wanted it to be.

He turned to Catalina Ibañez. "Come on," he told her. "We have to let the authorities know what happened here. You are my witness I slew in self-defense."

She nodded. "You are my hero, my champion." she said. "You killed for my sake, for . . . for me." Tears still wet on her cheeks, she gave him a glance full of animal heat. Lope had never had a woman look at him that way for that reason. He hoped to heaven he never would again.

THE NIGHT BEFORE, SHAKESPEARE HAD FALLEN ASLEEP TO JACK Street's snores. Now he woke to them. As he yawned and got out of bed, he wondered if he would ever be able to go to sleep without the glazier's racket after a couple of years of it. He'd got so very used to it, he had his doubts.

Sam King lay asleep in the third bed in their common bedchamber. Street's snoring had stopped bothering him, too. Shakespeare got out of his nightshirt and into doublet and hose. The early-morning sun leaking through closed shutters gave him plenty of light by which to dress. In summer, day swallowed half the night, not the other way round. He reveled in the daylight, and reveled in it more because he knew it would dwindle again as the seasons spun through their never-ending cycle.

A kettle of porridge bubbled over a low fire on the hearth. Shakespeare dipped out a bowlful to break his fast. He poured a mug of ale from a pitcher on the counter, then sat down to eat.

Cicely Sellis came out of her room a couple of minutes later, with Mommet walking around and between her feet. "Give you good day, Master Shakespeare," she said, and got herself breakfast, too. As she sat down on a stool across the table from the poet, the cat puddled himself on top of her shoes.

"Give you good morrow as well," Shakespeare answered. "I hope the world wags well for you?"

"Passing well," she said. "How fares your friend, the Spaniard de Vega?"

"These past few days, I've seen him not," Shakespeare said. Then he started violently. He had all he could do not to sign himself with the cross. "How knew you we have an acquaintance?" *What witch's trick told you so?* was what he meant. As with crossing himself, though, he lacked the nerve for that.

But Cicely Sellis laughed a merry laugh. "No bell, book, and candle: by God I give you my oath." She showed no fear about using the holy sign herself. She never had. Laughing still, she went on, "For one thing, you have in my hearing spake his name, though peradventure you recall it not. For another, not long since I met the man himself in Bishopsgate Street—I daresay Mommet on my shoulder drew his eye. A man of much charm and wit, and much an admirer of yours."

Shakespeare only half heard her, even less after she showed she hadn't used the black arts to learn of Lope de Vega. Normally, he would have savored praise, and savored Cicely Sellis' company, too. Now he scraped his bowl clean, gulped his ale, mumbled, "I must away," and all but fled the lodging house. She'd convinced him she hadn't used witchcraft this time. She hadn't come close to convincing him she was no witch.

Someone two houses down flung the contents of a very full

chamber pot from an upstairs window out into the street. Even though it didn't come close to splashing Shakespeare, the stench made him wrinkle his nose. That stench also took the edge off his pleasure in the fine day. He hurried up towards Bishopsgate, hoping he'd get no more unpleasant surprises.

People streamed into London from the tenements outside the walls, to look for work, to buy and sell, or to drink. Fewer folk went in the other direction. "Whither away so early, now?" an Irish gallowglass asked as Shakespeare headed out. He made as if to step forward and bar the poet's path.

"I'm for the Theatre," Shakespeare answered.

"Faith, are you indeed?" the Irishman said. "Riddle me why, then. I'm after knowing these plays run of afternoons."

"In sooth, they do," Shakespeare agreed. "But we needs must practice or ever we play, else were the show not worth the seeing."

The Irishman scratched at his red whiskers. He scratched hard, caught something, and squashed it between his two thumbnails. Seeing that made Shakespeare want to scratch, too. Maybe getting rid of the vermin cheered the gallowglass, for he waved Shakespeare forward. "Pass on."

"Gramercy. God give you good day." Not least from fear, Shakespeare was always polite around the savages from the western island.

Out beyond the wall, the tenements were as crowded and squalid as anything within, maybe worse. Shakespeare strutted up Shoreditch High Street towards the Theatre as fiercely as he could. Footpads had never set on him, and he hoped a show of belligerency from a good-sized man would keep making them choose other targets.

Only the night watchman was at the Theatre when Shakespeare got there. He sat on a stool, his back against the wall by the outer entrance, his hat down over his eyes to shield him from the sunlight. Soft snores rose from him. Shakespeare hoped he'd been more alert during the night.

He paused in front of the entrance and coughed. The watchman's snores changed rhythm. Shakespeare coughed again, louder this time. The other man yawned and stretched and raised his hat enough to see out from under the brim. "Oh, 'tis you, Master Will," he said around a yawn that showed bad teeth. "Good day, sir. Go on in, an't please you. You're first here today."

"How know you that?" Like Pilate asking, *What is truth?* Shakespeare didn't want an answer. He nodded and went into the Theatre. The watchman pulled his hat down again. He was ready for more sleep.

He turned out to be right; no one from the company had gone past him while he dozed. Shakespeare had the Theatre all to himself. He looked up to the wide ring of heaven. A kestrel flashed by overhead. The little hawk never had any doubts of what prey nature intended it to take, nor of how to go about the tasks nature had appointed it. For his part, Shakespeare had never imagined he might envy a bird's pure simplicities. He'd never imagined it, but it was so.

While he stood with his feet on the hard-packed earth (it smelled faintly of spilt beer; despite the sweepers, nutshells, bits of bread, a broken clay pipe, and other refuse still lay all around), he stretched out his arms full length and wistfully flapped them. He envied the kestrel its ability to fly out of trouble, too.

From behind him, someone said, "Lo! Here the gentle lark, weary of rest, from his moist cabinet mounts on high, and wakes the morning."

Shakespeare spun round. There stood Richard Burbage, a grin on his handsome, fleshy face. "I am no songbird," Shakespeare said. "But the crow doth sing as sweetly as the lark when neither is attended."

"No songbird? Haply not, not in your own person," Burbage said. "But verily you give others music, killing care and grief of heart. Orpheus with his lute made trees bow themselves when he did sing. So you as well, e'en if it be through the throats of others."

"You are gracious," Shakespeare said, "and I thank you for't."

"How d'you come here, the hour being so young?" Burbage asked. "I had looked to be alone yet some little while, as usually chances."

"How, Dick? I'll tell you how." Shakespeare spoke of how Cicely Sellis had asked him about Lieutenant de Vega. "She ghasted me out of doors betimes, nor am I shamed to own it."

"And yet 'twas no witchery that you should speak, or even that they should meet. Passing strange, that." Burbage snapped his fingers. "I mind me we need not fear dear Master Lope for some little while, at the least."

"Wherefore say you so?" Shakespeare asked. "If Dame Rumor run abroad, she hath not caught me up."

"I supped yesternight at an ordinary close by the dons' barracks. There was talk in Spanish amongst 'em, and in English back and forth 'twixt the tapman and the drawer, the which I might follow. De Vega hath slain a man, a noble Spaniard."

" 'Swounds!" Shakespeare said. "Shall he be hanged for't?"

Burbage shook his head. "Methinks not. 'Twas in some affray over a woman."

"With Master de Vega? You astound me," Shakespeare said. Burbage laughed. He too knew—he could hardly help knowing—Lope de Vega's passion for passionate conquests. Shakespeare went on, "Still and all, that could be murther, did he lie in wait for his rival or smite from behind."

"Why, so it could," Burbage admitted. "I had not thought on it, the Spaniard seeming a tolerable man of his hands, but haply you have the right of't. I know not, nor could I glean it from the talk I overheard. But he shan't come hither soon, an I mistake me not."

"May it be so," Shakespeare said. "A few days' time to rehearse our *Boudicca* in peace were a blessing."

"Ay. Naught compares to moving about the stage for the refining of bits of business, and breaking off in the midst of a scene jars hardly less than breaking off in the midst with a wench," Burbage said.

"A fit figure, in view of what's passed." Shakespeare inclined his head.

"I'm certain sure she had a fit figure," Burbage said. "The Spaniard hath an eye for 'em."

"Hold the tireman's helper on high," Shakespeare warned. "If Master Lope return of a sudden, we dare not be caught out."

"That I know, Will," Burbage said heavily. "By my troth, that I know."

LOPE DE VEGA STOOD AT STIFF ATTENTION BEFORE CAPTAIN BALTASAR Guzmán. "Before God, sir, it was self-defense, nothing else," he declared. A pen scratched across paper off to one side: Guzmán's servant, Enrique, writing down every word he said. "Don Alejandro came at me sword in hand. If I hadn't defended myself, some other officer would be taking his statement now."

Some other officer might *be taking his statement now*, Lope thought. *Or, then again, maybe not.* Had Don Alejandro de Recalde slain him, how much of an inquiry would there have been? He was only a lieutenant, after all, from a family not particularly eminent. As likely as not, they would have buried him, patted Don Alejandro on the back for his fine swordsmanship, and gone on about their business.

Baltasar Guzmán, now, said nothing at all. He sat behind his desk, staring up at de Vega. "You will have questioned my companion," Lope said stiffly. "*Señorita* Ibañez's account should match mine."

"And so it does," Guzmán admitted, "or you would be in a great deal more trouble than you are."

"Your Excellency, if *Señorita* Ibañez's account does match mine, I should be in no trouble at all."

"Unfortunately, Senior Lieutenant, it is not quite so simple. What were you doing with the woman when Don Alejandro discovered the two of you alone together?"

"We'd had a picnic, sir," Lope said stolidly. "We were leaving the yard for the Kings of Scotland when Don Alejandro burst in." *Scratch, scratch, scratch* went the quill in Enrique's clever right hand.

"A picnic?" One of Captain Guzmán's eyebrows leaped.

"Yes, your Excellency. A picnic. The soldiers who came after the fight took the coverlet we sat on, and the wine bottle we drank from, and the mugs, and the bread and honey we had there."

"One—or two—can do other things on a coverlet besides sitting."

"No doubt, sir. We were having a picnic," Lope said. *Scratch, scratch, scratch.*

"Will you see *Señorita* Ibañez again?" Guzmán asked.

"How can I know, your Excellency?" de Vega answered. "She is . . . an attractive woman, and her protector—her former protector—is now unfortunately deceased."

"Yes. Most unfortunately. I saw the corpse," Captain Guzmán said. "When you fight a man, you don't do things by halves, do you, Senior Lieutenant?"

"Sir, he came at me bellowing like a bull. If I hadn't fought to kill, he would have killed me," Lope replied. That was not only true, it was what he had to say to keep himself safe. Guzmán's respect, though, however reluctantly granted, warmed him, for his superior was a formidable man with a rapier in his hand. De Vega added, "He was good with a blade—very quick, very strong, very clean—but purely a school fighter."

"Ah." Captain Guzmán nodded. "So that's how it was, eh? No, you don't learn those strokes in school. You learn them when you put your life on the line—or else you don't, as Don Alejandro didn't."

"What will become of me, *señor*?" Lope asked.

"Well, *I* believe your story—or most of it, anyhow," Guzmán answered. "As far as I'm concerned, you remain on duty. But you must understand, when you kill a nobleman the matter doesn't end with your immediate superior."

"Yes, sir," Lope said resignedly.

"It could be worse, you know," Baltasar Guzmán told him. "You could have killed de Recalde back in Spain. Then you wouldn't have to worry about your superiors alone. You'd have everyone in his clan hot for your blood, and all his friends, too. He doesn't have many kinsmen here in England, and he wasn't here long enough to make a lot of friends."

"No doubt you're right, sir." The same thing had occurred to Lope. "Is there anything more, sir?"

"Not from me, as I told you. But I also tell you something else: if you fall head over heels in love with Catalina Ibañez in the next few weeks, tongues will wag. I don't suppose anyone will be able to prove a thing, but tongues *will* wag."

"Nothing I can do about that, your Excellency," Lope replied.

"You could try keeping away from her," Captain Guzmán said. Lope stood mute. Guzmán sighed. "No point to puncturing a man if you can't enjoy yourself afterwards: is that what you're thinking?"

"Your Excellency, do you question my honor?" Lope asked, very softly.

Had Guzmán said yes, things would have taken a different turn. But the captain impatiently shook his head. "No, no, no, by no means. The Ibañez is only a mistress, not a wife. How can anyone lose honor over a mistress? But even the touchiest man will see there is a difference between honor and gossip and scandal."

"Very well, *señor*. I thank you for the advice."

Guzmán sighed. "By which you mean you have no intention of taking it. Well, you've already proved you're not shy about carving a man so the undertakers can't pretty him up. That will make some people think twice. Go on, get back to work, but bear in mind you may be summoned by others besides me."

Sure enough, Lope was in his room working on a report of doings at the Theatre when Enrique knocked on his door. Captain Guzmán's servant said, "Begging your pardon, Senior Lieutenant, but my principal has just received an order from Don Diego Flores de Valdés at Westminster. You are to report to him at once for questioning in the matter of Don Alejandro."

"Thank you, Enrique." Lope sighed and rose from the stool where he'd perched. "I'll go, of course." What else could he do when summoned by the commandant of Spanish forces in England?

As he was heading out of the barracks, his own servant came up the corridor towards him. "*Señor*, there is an English constable outside, a man named Strawberry." He said it with care. "He would speak to you. So says a soldier who knows a little English."

"A constable?" De Vega shook his head. "I am called before Don Diego Flores de Valdés. I have no time for this no-account Englishman now. I would have no time for the Queen and King of England now. Go back and tell the fellow, whoever he is, that I am very sorry, but I will have to see him some other day."

"I speak no English!" Diego wailed.

"Well, get that soldier again, then," Lope said impatiently, hurrying off towards the stables. "You found out what the constable wanted. He can find out what you want."

When he rode off towards Westminster, he got a glimpse of his servant and a large, middle-aged Englishman standing nose to nose in the street, each shouting at the other, neither understanding a word the other said. Maybe the English-speaking soldier had gone away. Lope smiled. Diego needed such exercise to keep his blood flowing. As for the other man, that Strawberry . . . Well, who cared about an English constable, anyhow?

Once Lope got to Westminster, he had to find Don Diego Flores de Valdés' office, which he'd visited only once. He knew he was getting close when someone called out to him: a thin, weedy, pockmarked Englishman who wore spectacles. "Oh, *Señor* Phelippes," Lope said, glad to see a face he knew. "The commandant's chamber is along this corridor, is it not?"

"Yes, that's right," Phelippes answered. Where Lope had spoken English, he used his fluent Spanish, finishing, "Congratulations on the skill of your right hand." His own right hand, still clutching a quill, made cut-and-thrust motions.

"For which I thank you." De Vega did his best to keep laughter off his face. He had a hard time imagining a man less dangerous than Thomas Phelippes. Hurrying up the corridor, he found Don Diego also scribbling away at something. He waited till the Spanish commandant look up from his work, then saluted. "I report as ordered, your Excellency."

"So you do. Come in, Senior Lieutenant, come in." Don Diego

drummed his fingers on the desk. He pointed to a stool in front of it. "Sit, if you care to. So you've had more woman trouble, have you?"

"Well . . ." Lope saw no way out of that one. "Yes, your Excellency," he said reluctantly.

"You'll get talked about, killing a social superior," Don Diego remarked.

"No doubt. But I preferred that to letting him kill me."

"Yes, I can see how you might. Don Alejandro was not the brightest man I ever saw, but he was brave, and we'll miss him. We haven't enough Spaniards here as is; we can't afford to kill each other."

"Yes, your Excellency," Lope said. "Better you tell me that, though, than that you tell him."

"He wouldn't agree with you—but then, he's not here to ask, is he?" Don Diego drummed his fingers again. "By your account, by his mistress' account, it was a fair fight." Those fingers went up and down, up and down. "The Ibañez woman, I'm sure, is great fun in bed. But damn me, Senior Lieutenant, if she's worth a man in his grave. She'll be as faithless to you as she was to Don Alejandro, and sooner, for he had more money to spend on her than you do."

No matter how infatuated with her Lope was, that held the unpleasant ring of truth. "I'll take my chances, your Excellency," he replied, for want of anything better.

"So you will," the Spanish commandant agreed. "So you do." He scowled. "Go on, get out of here. You have to keep an eye on the Englishmen at the Theatre. The good Lord only knows what they're planning, but it's something. I need a hound to smell out treachery. For that, you'll do. And a man who knows how to handle a blade is always an asset, too. Through the eye! *¡Madre de Dios!*"

"Your Excellency, with a life on the line, one does what one must do," Lope said.

"Yes. And that is why I am sending you back to your duty at the Theatre," Don Diego said. His long face was made to show sorrow, and it did now. "We will need you, we will need the play, before long. Word just here from Spain is that it is doubtful his Most Catholic Majesty shall leave his bed again. His doctors dare not move him, even to change the linen on his mattress. The end approaches." He crossed himself.

So did Lope de Vega. "I shall do all I can to ensure that he has his monument here," Lope said. "You may rely on me, sir."

"I do, Senior Lieutenant," Don Diego Flores de Valdés told him.

"That is why you are returning. For I still fear treason from the Theatre. I want you there to stop it."

"I've seen no sign of it," Lope said. "But if it rears its ugly head, I'll tear it out, root and branch."

IN THE UPPER GALLERY OF THE THEATRE, THE TIREMAN'S HELPER who did duty as a lookout started whistling "A Man's Yard." At once, the players who had been Romans and Britons hacking away at one another shifted positions and became Spaniards and Englishmen hacking away at one another. "By God!" Richard Burbage snarled at Shakespeare. "Is he here again?" He glared at the poet as if it were his fault.

Shakespeare spread his hands. "I did not bid him come."

"Unbidden guests are often welcomest when they are gone," Burbage said. "But of late he is never gone. How can we rehearse *Boudicca* under the eyes of a don? He bleeds us of time like a leech of blood, save that a leech may heal, whilst he doth only harm."

"I cannot mend it—and say not the name, never no moe," Shakespeare added. "He hath the Latin to know whence it comes and what it portends." In strode Lope. He wasn't very tall, but swaggered like a giant. Shakespeare smiled and waved to him. "Welcome!" he lied. "Give you good day."

"And a good morrow to you," de Vega answered, advancing towards the stage. He surveyed the struggling players with a critical eye. "Many of these would die quickly, did they take the field in earnest."

"They are not soldiers. They but personate them," Shakespeare said.

"But their personation wants persuasion," Lope said. Shakespeare glanced towards Burbage. Ever so slightly, the player nodded. He'd been a soldier, and knew whereof Lope spoke.

"A soldier's eye may discern the flaws, but will the generality?" Shakespeare asked.

"Those of them have fought in war will know they see no war upon the stage," Lope told him.

"We shall do what we can." Shakespeare did his best to hide a sigh. He didn't think de Vega noticed. Burbage did, and smiled. Shakespeare asked the question uppermost in his, uppermost in everyone's, mind: "How fares his Most Catholic Majesty?"

"He fares not well at all." De Vega's handsome face looked old and worn, as if he were speaking of his own dying father. "As I have said before, he is bedridden. The least movement pains him to the marrow. His sores advance apace. When the surgeons cut them to loose the pus, it hath a vile stench. He is dropsical—more so by the day, they say. And yet his heart is strong. He fails, but fails by degrees."

All over the stage, players nodded. Most men had watched deaths like that, as well as the quicker, easier, more merciful kind. Signing himself with the cross, Shakespeare said, "God grant him ease from suffering."

"May it be so." Lope also crossed himself. "It likes me to watch the work here advance."

"I had liefer see *King Philip* go unproduced," Shakespeare said.

De Vega made a leg at him. "You are gracious, Master Shakespeare, to say so."

I am an ordinary ramping fool, with no more brain than a stone, Shakespeare thought. Lope de Vega had taken him to mean he wanted Philip II to live forever. That was how he'd meant to be taken. But the Spaniard could have taken his words another way, as meaning he wanted to see some other play go on in place of *King Philip*. And he did. But to let Lieutenant de Vega know that would have meant nothing but catastrophe.

Burbage had noticed the same thing. With a growl that might have come from the throat of a bear chained to the pole in the baiting pit, he said, "You *will* make show of your wit, eh?"

"Wherefore should he not?" Lope asked. "Would you ask a poet to hide his wit? Would you ask a woman to hide her beauty?"

"A poet's wit may lead him into danger," Shakespeare said. "And a woman's beauty may likewise lead her—and him that sees her—into danger. Or would you say otherwise?"

Burbage suddenly brightened. Shakespeare couldn't resist preening a little, proud of his own cleverness. If anything could make Lope turn away from untoward meanings, thinking of himself and his brush with death ought to do it. The Spaniard's hand fell to the hilt of his rapier. A few inches of the blade slid from the sheath as he struck a pose. "Danger knows full well that Lope is more dangerous than he."

His strutting would have seemed laughable had he not just killed a man. As things were, he'd earned the right to swagger. "Beauty itself doth of itself persuade the eyes of men without an orator," Shakespeare said. "Will you bring to the Theatre the beauty hath ensnared you, that we all may marvel and envy you for your conquest?"

"Alas, no, I fear me, for she speaks not your tongue," Lope replied.

Will Kemp chose that moment to come out of the tiring room. The clown gave Lope a courtier's bow exaggerated to absurdity. "Whether she speak or no, doth her tongue not please you?" he inquired.

Maybe the Spaniard wouldn't understand just what Kemp meant. So Shakespeare hoped. Lope's English, while good, wasn't perfect. But it was good enough, and he did. "How dare you have her tongue in your mouth?" he snarled, and made as if to draw the rapier again.

"Never did I that, nor she neither," Kemp said. But he seemed less afraid than Shakespeare would have been, having insulted a man who'd proved himself sword in hand. "Put up," he told de Vega. "Know you not, an you blood your blade in a fool, 'twill surely rust?"

The absurdity of that stopped the Spaniard where nothing else might have. "But what then becomes of the fool?" he asked.

Kemp let out a horrible scream, clutched his belly, and thrashed and writhed on the stage in well-feigned agony. As abruptly as he'd begun, he left off. "Thus, belike," he answered, getting to his feet once more.

Lope laughed and shook his head. "Truly God must love fools," he said. "How may I do less?"

"How should you find it hard, where most men find it easy?" Kemp returned. "But then, did you not find it hard—"

"Enough!" Shakespeare and Burbage spoke the same word at the same time. Kemp flew to disaster like a moth to flame.

After that afternoon's performance, Shakespeare left the Theatre as soon as he scrubbed off his makeup. Usually, he would have stayed in the tiring room to share gossip and gibes, or else repair to a tavern to hash over the play with players and friends. Not today, not least because Lope de Vega came back there. Sometimes, keeping company with the Spanish officer was too much for him to bear.

But leaving brought him scant relief. As he hurried out of the Theatre, Constable Walter Strawberry marched in, a grim expression on his face. Shakespeare wondered if Strawberry were after him for more questions, but the constable, after giving him a somber nod, kept on going. So did Shakespeare, in the other direction.

He hadn't got far when a medium-sized, homely man of about his own age sidled up alongside him and said, "A good day to you, Master Shakespeare." His voice suggested he knew all manner of interesting things, some of them perhaps even licit.

"Master Skeres." Shakespeare hoped he sounded less dismayed than he felt. "And to you a good day as well, sir. I've not had the pleasure of your company for some little while." *Nor wanted it, neither*, he thought. "What would you?"

"I'd tell you somewhat I'd liefer not have to speak, but e'en so somewhat you should know," Nick Skeres answered.

When he didn't go on, Shakespeare asked, "And that is?"

"Lord Burghley's on his deathbed," Skeres said bluntly. "He'll not rise from it again, save to go in's coffin."

For Shakespeare, the news was like a blow in the belly. "God give him peace," he said. "He and Philip die together, as he said they would when first we met."

"Ay." Skeres' chuckle showed uneven teeth. "His mind's still hale, and he jests of't yet."

"What of . . . the enterprise?" Shakespeare would say no more than that, not in the open in Shoreditch High Street. Later, he remembered he should have spoken with Nicholas Skeres about raising the English mob against Spain's hated Irish soldiers. At the moment, with Skeres' news, the thought never entered his mind.

The other man replied without hesitation: "It goes forward as before, under Lord Burghley his son. And mark me, 'twill go as well under Robert Cecil as ever it could under his sire. Crookback though he be, his wit and will run straight."

"May you prove a true prophet." But Shakespeare couldn't help worrying—worrying even more than he had before. Sir William Cecil had been a power in the land longer than he'd been alive. He'd been in eclipse since the coming of the Armada, yes, but Robert, his son, seemed always to have dwelt and dealt in the shadows. Could he come out into the light now, at greatest need? *He must essay it*, Shakespeare thought, and kicked at the dirt. The timing couldn't have been worse.

XI

When Lope de Vega visited the Theatre with Lucy Watkins, he didn't take her back to the tiring room after the performance. Will Kemp or another would-be wit was too likely to ask him why he hadn't brought his Spanish lady instead. He didn't want Lucy finding out about Catalina Ibañez. Bad things happened when one of his ladies learned of another: so he'd painfully discovered.

But here, it seemed, he was bound to have trouble. He and Lucy had just left the Theatre on their way back into London when she said, "Is it true you killed a man?"

Unease prickled through de Vega. He tried his best to misunderstand her, saying, "My love, I am a soldier. This chances in the soldier's trade."

She shook her head. "No. Of late. A Spanish gentleman, they say."

"A nobleman, but by my troth no gentleman," he said. Then he stopped and sighed. He'd told her what she needed to know, or most of it.

And she'd already heard, or heard of, the rest, too. "They say you fought him over a lady."

As he'd called Don Alejandro de Recalde no gentleman, so he

wanted to call Catalina Ibañez no lady. But that wouldn't help. He sighed again. "Yes, that is so."

Lucy nodded. "I was fain to hear it from your lips first. I owed you so much, before saying farewell."

"Say no such thing!" Lope exclaimed. "I love thee!"

"And the other lady?"

"And her," Lope agreed.

"You may not love more than one," Lucy said sadly.

"Wherefore may I not?" he asked. "I have had this stricture laid against me ere now, but never have I grasped it."

"That I credit. But if you love two"—she'd stopped using *thou*, a bad sign—"then two will love you, each to herself wanting all you have to give, as she hath given all she hath. Can you in equal measure return the love of two? Give me leave to doubt. Loving more than one, you love not wisely, but too well."

"How can one love too well? A fond notion, a notion not possible."

"Love two women at but a single time—say you love two women at but a single time—and you love too well," Lucy insisted.

"Do but let me show thee thou art mistook, that—" Lope began.

"How? Wouldst thou put us twain, this Spanish hussy and me, in but a single bed?" Now Lucy used *thou* again, but in insult, not intimacy. "Whether she'd go or no, I would not, nor I will not. Where I shall go is far from thee, now and forever." Her voice held tears. "So we loved, as love in twain had the essence but in one. We were two distincts, division none: number there in love was slain. So between us love did shine, that one lover saw her right flaming in her lover's sigh. Either was the other's mine. But for us, lovers, now sigh a prayer." She walked away.

Love, to Lope, was like a child that longed for everything it could come by. Telling that to Lucy seemed unlikely to change her mind. "We that are true lovers run into strange capers," he called after her. "Alas that love, gentle in his view, should be tyrannous and rough in proof."

"In proof? Thou canst give no proof of love, not loving another besides myself." Lucy kept walking. A few paces farther on, she stooped, picked up a stone, and flung it at Lope with unladylike dexterity. If he hadn't ducked, it would have hit him in the face. She bent down for another stone.

"Fie! Give over!" Lope exclaimed. "I'll trouble thee—you—no more."

Lucy let the stone fall. "Would thou'dst never asked my name. Would thou'dst never spoke me fair. Would thou'dst never found thy

Spanish popsy fair, for thou canst not have her and me together. Mary, pity women!" She rounded a corner and was gone.

"Fret not, friend," said an Englishman who'd listened with amusement to the quarrel. "Women are like fish: another'll come along soon enough, to nibble the end o' your pole." He laughed.

So did Lope, when he got the joke a moment later. He didn't go after Lucy; that, plainly, was a lost cause. Instead, he trudged back towards Bishopsgate. He still had Catalina Ibañez's fiery affections, but he found he didn't want them right now. He wanted Lucy, whom he'd just lost. Had he lost Catalina and kept Lucy, he had no doubt he would have pined for the Spanish woman's caresses instead. *I know what I am, by God*, he thought. *What to do about it? That's a different question.*

The Irish soldiers at the gate recognized Lope for a Spaniard. They swept off their hats and bowed to him as he went by. He nodded in return. Once inside Bishopsgate, he slowed down and looked around. If he was lucky . . .

And he was. Cicely Sellis came out of a ribbonmaker's shop, a couple of yards of green ribbon wrapped around the left sleeve of the mannish doublet she wore, her cat following at her heel like a dog. Lope made a leg. "Mistress Sellis. So good to see you. Give you good day."

She curtsied as if he were a duke, not a junior officer. "And good day to you, Master Lope. How wags your world?"

"I have known it better," he replied.

"Why, surely those set over you have agreed you fought Don Alejandro only for to save your own life," she said. "How could it be otherwise, with Mistress Ibañez telling a tale like unto yours?"

"The difficulty lies elsewhere," de Vega said, before blinking and wondering how she knew of that. He started to ask, but found he lacked the nerve. He started to cross himself, but found he also lacked the nerve for that. *Bruja*, he thought, and shivered in the warm—for England, at any rate—July sun.

"Where?" Cicely Sellis asked. She didn't let him answer, but showed more of what might have been witchery by softly singing,

"On a day, alack the day!
Love, whose month is ever May,
Spied a blossom passing fair
Playing in the wanton air:
Through the velvet leaves the wind,

All unseen, can passage find;
That the lover, sick to death,
Wished himself the heaven's breath.
Air, quoth he, thy cheeks may blow;
Air, would I might triumph so!
But alack! my hand is sworn
Ne'er to pluck from thee thy thorn;
Vow, alack! for youth unmeet,
Youth so apt to pick a sweet.
Do not call it sin in me,
That I am forsworn for thee;
Thou for whom e'en Jove would swear
Juno but an Ethiop were;
And deny himself for Jove,
Turning mortal for thy love."

This time, Lope did cross himself, and violently. "How knew you of my affections?" he demanded, his voice harsh. "Tell it me this instant, else others holier than I shall ask it of you."

Her cat bristled at him, but she remained smiling, unconcerned. "This needs not the cunning woman's arts, Master Lope. You came towards me all cast down. When late you fought Don Alejandro, you kept company with his mistress, but is it not so you had also another sweetheart? An I mistake me not, she hath given you her farewell."

Bruja, Lope thought again. But maybe not. What she said made good logical sense—as much as anything to do with women ever made good logical sense. Slowly, grudgingly, he said, "You are a cunning woman indeed."

Cicely Sellis curtsied again. "For the which I thank you. And you have my sympathy—the which, like all such, is worth its weight in gold—for her who was too blind to see your true worth."

He stared at her, open-mouthed. It wasn't for her looks, though she was fair enough, and would have been lovely at eighteen. But he had never known a woman who used words as a bravo used a rapier—and was as deadly with them as any bravo ever born. "Before God," he breathed, hardly knowing he spoke aloud, "I must know thee better."

"And will you turn your back on Mistress Ibañez, cleaving only to me?" she asked.

With any other woman, he would have babbled promises, knowing they were lies. With Cicely Sellis, that seemed less than wise. What would she do if she caught him out? What could she do? *Do you really want to find out?* Lope asked himself, and knew he didn't. He sighed and shook his head. "Nay, I doubt I shall," he answered. His smile was crooked. "I thank God I am as honest as any man living that is a young man, and no honester than I."

The cunning woman smiled, too. "Every man hath his fault, and honesty is yours?" she suggested.

Yes, she had a dangerous tongue. And if it was dangerous in one sense, what might it do in another? Lope made himself stop his lewd imaginings while he tried to figure out how to reply to that. At last, he said, "Doubt truth to be a liar, but never doubt I love."

"What? Me?" Now Cicely Sellis paused. After a moment, she wagged a finger at him. "Nay, you said that not. You are clever, sir—haply, too clever by half."

"I could love thee. I would love thee," de Vega said.

"But not me alone," she said. It wasn't a question. She waited to see if Lope would deny it. When he didn't, she smiled once more and shook her head. "I'd not give all of my love for the part of another's—would not nor will not. Gladly would I be your friend, and as gladly be no more."

"Shall I beg thee?" Lope made as if to go to one knee in the muddy street. Laughing, Cicely Sellis gestured that he should stay on his feet. "Shall I serenade thee?" He strummed an imaginary lute and began to sing in Spanish.

"Give over!" she said with another laugh. "Shall the tiger change his stripes? I think not. Were I myself a different jade, I'd say, come, woo me, woo me, for I am in a holiday humor, and like enough to consent. But, being all of mine own, I'll not be but part of someone else's liking."

She sounded annoyingly like Lucy Watkins. "I am your friend, then," Lope said, knowing he'd get no more this day. "Those you make friends, and give your heart to, keep their friendship under their own life's key."

"Betimes," the cunning woman said. "Betimes, but not so oft as we'd fain have't." She offered up what at first sounded like a prayer:

> "Grant I may never prove so fond,
> To trust man on his oath or bond;
> Or a keeper with my freedom,
> Or my friends, if I should need 'em. Amen."

"*Aii!*" he said, wincing. Few men saw the world so sardonically, and even fewer women.

"I must away." Cicely Sellis scooped up her cat—Mommet, that was the beast's name—and set it on her shoulder, where it had perched when Lope first met her. As she started up Bishopsgate—towards the gate itself, the direction opposite to his—she added, "God give you good . . . friends."

"And you, lady," he called after her. "And you." He wanted to turn around and follow her. Only the certainty that that, right now, would cost him even her tenuous friendship kept him walking on into London, his feet dragging reluctantly through the dirt at every step.

William Shakespeare watched from the side of the stage as Lieutenant de Vega, as Juan de Idiáquez, declaimed what amounted to his epitaph for Philip II:

" 'Fair Spain ne'er had a king until his time.
Virtue he had, deserving to command:
His brandish'd sword did blind men with his beams;
His arms spread wider than a dragon's wings;
His sparkling eyes, replete with wrathful fire,
More dazzled and drove back his enemies
Than mid-day sun bent against their faces.
What should I say? his deeds exceed all speech:
He ne'er lift up his hand but conquered.' "

To Shakespeare's astonishment, the Spaniard, after delivering his lines, covered his face with his hands and wept. "Here, what's toward?" Shakespeare called, hurrying towards him.

Lope de Vega looked up at him, tears streaming unashamed from his eyes. "The beauty of your words hath pierced me to the heart," he answered. "Their beauty, ay, and their truth. For truly great Philip dies, and much dies with him. Spain shall be fatherless henceforth."

"Truly, Spain shall be fatherless henceforth," Shakespeare murmured, turning the line to the iambic pentameter of blank verse. He said it over again, then nodded. "Gramercy, Lieutenant. I shall append that to the end of your speech." He made a leg at Lope. "And I congratulate you: your first line in English." Actually, de Vega had made only four feet of the line, but Shakespeare wasn't inclined to quibble there.

Several of the players clapped their hands. Lope grinned and bowed. But Matthew Quinn, who played a Roman soldier named Decius in *Boudicca*, told Shakespeare, "Think an hour more; then, if your confidence grow strong on you, you'll leave it in place."

Sudden silence slammed down inside the Theatre. Shakespeare hoped his own jaw didn't drop too far. The first line and a half were taken straight from the hired man's part, while the last five words were the sort of half-line of blank verse any player could make up in his sleep.

Blank verse sounded like natural speech. Sounding like natural speech was its reason for being. Lope didn't, wouldn't, couldn't know the words came from *Boudicca*. But everyone else did, and the Spaniard did notice the dismay on the stage. "Is somewhat amiss?" he asked.

"No, naught." Shakespeare hoped he sounded convincing. "Merely a dumb-show: ay, an ass-head; a stuffed man; a very dull fool—in sooth, a most imperceiverant thing."

"I do not follow," Lope said.

Quinn did, entirely too well. "You breeder of dire events!" he shouted, his fat face purpling. "You sneaking fellow! You still and dumb-discoursive devil that tempts most cunningly!" He didn't quite come out and scream that Shakespeare was a traitor, but he didn't miss by much, either.

"Long-tongued babbling gossip!" Shakespeare retorted. "Damnable box of envy!"

"Enough!" Richard Burbage cried. "Hold! Give over, you rabble of vile confederates, or answer to me." He folded one hand into a massive fist.

Shakespeare fell silent. He'd already said too much. So had Quinn—much too much. And so, for that matter, had Burbage. The hired man, periwig slightly askew, looked ready to say much more. But Burbage advanced on him, that fist drawn back and ready to fly. Quinn thought better of it.

Lope laughed. "You are a band of brothers, and fight like it," he said.

"E'en so." Shakespeare laughed, too, he hoped convincingly. "And now, meseems, we should ready ourselves for the day's play. We shall resume *King Philip* on the morrow, or the day after."

"Be it so, then." Lope's voice held regret. "Would we might work more now, but I understand you must set the play at hand before the play to come." He touched the brim of his hat. "This day's rehearsal done, I must away, having other duties. Give you good morrow, gentles." He hurried out of the Theatre.

As soon as he was gone, Shakespeare and Matt Quinn started screaming at each other again. "Hold!" Burbage shouted again. He pointed at the hired man. "You, sirrah, played the sparrow astrut afore the cat. That he *doth* not pounce means not that he *may* not pounce." His finger swung towards Shakespeare. "And *you*, sirrah, strook too hard, putting us in danger worse than any sprung of Master Quinn's folly. Had the Spaniard commenced to dig . . . But he did not, and all's well. We go forward, then, with such caution as we may find."

"Your pardon, I pray you," Shakespeare said. He turned to Matthew Quinn. More reluctantly, he also said, "*Your* pardon, I pray," to the hired player.

"Let it go," Quinn answered. "When we play is time enough for these lines you have writ me."

"Ay. Fire 'em too soon, and they fail of their purpose." Shakespeare wondered why Decius' part excited the other man: it was neither large nor important. But then, Matt Quinn had never enjoyed much luck in the theatre. Despite more than a little talent, he'd managed to offend someone or to take sick at just the wrong moment four or five different times, killing whatever chance he might have had of becoming something more than a man who could do small roles well enough but would never get a big one. Maybe he was glad of any part he could claim.

And maybe, too, he was nothing but a loudmouthed fool. Shakespeare had known plenty of those in his years in the theatre. He did wish Lord Westmorland's Men hadn't been burdened with this one at this vital moment. Had he dared, he would have asked Burbage to sack Quinn. Glancing over towards the hired man, he shook his head. No, he didn't dare. Quinn knew too much—knew much too much. If he were sacked, if he were disgruntled, wouldn't he go straight to the Spaniards and sing his song? Shakespeare found it all too likely.

The afternoon's play was Shakespeare's *If You Like It*, which the company had performed many times before. In fact, Shakespeare remembered, they'd put it on the day Marlowe had first dragged him into this conspiracy. Having done it so often, the players didn't need a lot of rehearsal to be fresh. Shakespeare went back to his lodging as soon as he could after it was over.

When he returned to the Theatre the next morning, players and stagehands stood in little knots with their heads together. "Here, what now?" Shakespeare called; that was no sight he cared to see.

Edward, the tireman's helper, said, "Matt Quinn was dyeing scarlet at the Bull Inn yesternight, and he—"

"At the Bull Inn?" Shakespeare interrupted. "In Bishopsgate? Not far from mine own lodgings?"

"The same," Edward said. "And in's cups he did go on more than considerable from *Boudicca*, ay, and about the same. Will Kemp heard him, every word, as did all too many not initiate in our mystery."

"If men were to be saved by merit, what hole in hell were hot enough for Quinn?" Shakespeare cried, clapping a hand to his forehead. "Truly he is damned, like an ill-roasted egg, all on one side." He started to say more, and more fiery, still, but checked himself. "Where's Kemp? I'd have this from's own lips." He looked around. "Come to that, where's the drunken roarer himself? I'd have the tale of's folly from *his* own lips."

"Master Kemp's in the tiring room," Edward replied. "As for Master Quinn, he hath not deigned to spread himself upon our stage this day."

"Is he drunk asleep?" Shakespeare cried. "Or in the bought, illicit pleasure of his bed? At game a-swearing, or about some act that hath no relish of salvation in it? Then trip him, that his heels may kick at heaven, and that his soul may be damned and black as hell, whereto it goes."

Edward spread his hands. "I know not, Master Shakespeare. I know only, he is not here. As to the why of't . . ." He shook his head.

"If he repent of his drunken antic and, thinking to save himself from the fruit thereof, if he flee to the dons . . ." Shakespeare's voice trailed away, as Edward's had a moment before.

Richard Burbage came out of the tiring room just in time to hear that. "Marry, God prevent it!" he exclaimed. "But now I *will* sack that whoreson knave, Will. Speak not against it. Speak not of caution. My mind's made up." Having played many kings, he could sound like one at need.

"I'll say not a word," Shakespeare answered. "Meseems, though, amongst our other cares that's small beer."

"Who'll take his role, an he come not?" Edward asked.

Burbage stabbed out a finger at the muscular young man. "Will *you* essay it? He hath but a handful of lines, nor need you no dancing shoes with nimble soles."

Edward gaped. Then an enormous grin stretched across his face. "I'll do't, sir! Learn me those lines, and I'll have 'em by heart quick as boiled asparagus. Do you but show me whence I am to go on, and whither to go off, and I'm your man. God bless you for the chance!"

"What fools these youngsters be!" Will Kemp exclaimed emerging from the tiring room behind Burbage. His shoulders shook with laughter. He glanced towards Shakespeare. "Were you ever so all afire to make an ass of yourself before the general?"

"I? Hotter than Edward dreams of being," Shakespeare answered. "And now and again an ass I made of me. So do we all."

Matthew Quinn did not come to the Theatre. Edward took his part, and managed . . . well enough. Thomas Vincent had to hiss some of his lines to him the second time he came on, but he brought them out loud enough and remembered to face the audience so they could be heard. If nervous sweat darkened the armpits of his tunic, well, it was a warm day. Other players were sweating, too.

After the play, everyone made much of the tireman's assistant. Shakespeare heard Quinn's name come up only once. When it did, someone—he couldn't see who—said, "He is to us a dead man." Heads in the tiring room solemnly went up and down.

From the Theatre, Shakespeare had come down almost to Bishopsgate when a man stepped out of an alley and into his way on Shoreditch High Street. The fellow was about his own age, a wide-shouldered brunet, clean-shaven, with his hair cropped short, as Puritans had worn theirs before the Inquisition set out to stifle Protestantism of all stripes. His doublet might have been fine when it was new, but it hadn't been new for years. Instead of hose, he wore a sailor's striped trousers.

When he didn't move aside, Shakespeare said, "Yes? You want somewhat of me?" He gathered himself. If what the stranger wanted was his money, he'd get a fight first.

And then the fellow smiled, and spoke, and suddenly was a stranger no more. "By my troth, Will," he said, "if *you* know me not, then who will?"

"Kit?" Shakespeare gaped. "But—but—you took ship in Deptford!"

Even Marlowe's smile looked different without the fringe of beard and the long hair that had framed his face. "Ay, I took ship in Deptford—and left the ghastly scow in Margate. Sithence I've changed my seeming and my style: call me Charles Munday, if you please."

"I'll call you an idiot, a fond monster, a mad mooncalf dotard," Shakespeare exclaimed. "You could be safe away, but no! You'll have none of safety! Should any man pierce your shorn locks . . ."

"Where could I live but London?" Marlowe asked. "This place hath *life*! All other towns are as dead beside it."

"This place hath your death, on the gibbet or worse," Shakespeare said. "Where will you live? How will you eat?"

"Where, I'll keep in my own privity—what you know not, no inquisitor may rip from you," Marlowe said, and Shakespeare was forcibly reminded of his own danger. The other poet went on, "As for how, no man with a quick pen need—quite—fear starving, and that I have. How fares *Boudicca*?"

Even in mortal danger, Marlowe *would* speak of things better left unthought, let alone unsaid. "I know that name not," Shakespeare answered stonily. "Till the day, I know it not. E'en after the day, haply shall I know it not."

"You may be wise," said Marlowe—who, Shakespeare realized, hadn't changed his initials with his name. "Or, like as not, you may be but a different sort of fool, showing forth a different sort of folly."

Thinking of all the rehearsals for *Boudicca* he'd watched, Shakespeare could only nod.

LOPE DE VEGA FOUGHT TO KEEP HIS FACE FROM SHOWING HOW bored and how annoyed he was. How many times had Captain Baltasar Guzmán summoned him to his office, only to wave a sheet of paper in his face and then not let him see what it was?

But, though Guzmán waved this sheet of paper like any other, he startled Lope by handing it to him and saying, "Here. This may possibly be of some interest to you, Senior Lieutenant."

"Ah?" Lope rapidly read through it. His eyes got wider and wider with each succeeding line. He didn't realize how far his jaw had fallen till he needed to speak again and had to pull it up again. "But this . . . this, your Excellency . . . this is from a printer. A printer in Madrid. In . . . in the capital." Realizing he was babbling, he fell silent again.

Captain Guzmán nodded. "Yes, a printer," he said. "I told you that, if *El mejor mozo de España* succeeded, I would send it and *La dama boba* back to Spain, to put them before the civilized world. *El mejor mozo de España* won praise from no less than the daughter of his Most Catholic Majesty. I keep my promises."

"This says . . ." De Vega made himself stop starting and stopping every few words. "This says the printer likes the plays—he admires them, he says—and that he would be delighted and honored to put them into print. Delighted and honored! God and the holy Virgin and all the saints bless you, your Excellency! I am going to be in print! In print, at last! I shall be remembered forever!"

So many plays died with their creators. Once he was there no more, who cared about, who remembered, the children of his imagination? They died with him. As worms ate him, oblivion swallowed him. But to leave behind work in print . . . A hundred years from this moment, or two hundred, or four hundred, someone could take a book of his plays off the shelf, leaf through it, and decide to put on *La dama boba*. And when the lady nitwit went up on stage, Lope would live again.

With a sardonic smile, Captain Guzmán returned him to the present: "While you are here and merely mortal, Senior Lieutenant, do you recall any mention of Sir William Cecil at the Theatre?"

"Of Lord Burghley? No, your Excellency," Lope answered. "I don't remember ever hearing his name there, though I have heard he's dying."

"He is nearly dead. He is older than Philip, and fails faster. I never did understand why his Most Catholic Majesty spared him after the conquest, but that was his will. Maybe he respected a worthy foe; Burghley towered above the other men, the little men, who advised Elizabeth. Every Spanish officer I know is sure he had one last damnable plot in him, but no one ever sniffed it out."

"Over in Westminster, Don Diego said much the same thing, sir," de Vega said. "But I have seen nothing in the Theatre to make me think Lord Westmorland's Men involved."

"Not the murder of Geoffrey Martin?" Guzmán asked.

"No, sir," Lope replied. "For all that the mad English constable in Shoreditch mumbles about someone knowing someone who knows someone else—I think that's what he mumbles, for he speaks in riddles (often, I believe, riddles to himself)—he has no proof, none whatever, Martin's murder was anything but an ordinary knifing in an ordinary robbery."

"It could be." Guzmán's voice was studiously noncommittal. "Yes, it could be. But, in that case, what of the murder of Matthew Quinn?"

"The murder of—?" That brought Lope up short. "But I saw this Quinn alive and rehearsing only a few days, a very few days, ago. He's dead? When? How?"

"As for when, by the smell and the other signs, only a few days ago—I presume after you saw him last." Guzmán had a wit so dry, Lope had taken longer than he should have to notice it was there at all. Now he went on, "As for how . . ." He drew a finger across his throat.

"Where did they find him?" de Vega asked.

"In an alley behind and down the street from a tavern called the Bull Inn, in Bishopsgate," Baltasar Guzmán replied. "It is not far from *Señor* Shakespeare's lodgings, whatever that may mean. The body was found without a purse, without a penny, so this may have been a simple robbery. It may—but, then again, it may not."

"Yes." Lope plucked at his neat little chin beard. "One murder in a company of actors—that means nothing. I wouldn't mind murdering one actor in that company myself. But two? Two murders from the same small group do make you wonder. Was Quinn doing anything out of the way in this tavern?"

Guzmán favored him with an approving glance. He didn't get that many from his superior, and basked in this one. The nobleman said, "Now that, Senior Lieutenant, that is a very interesting question. What I wish we had is an interesting answer. We have no answer at all. No one we can find who was in the tavern that night admits to remembering Quinn at all. No one."

"Not even the taverner?" Lope scowled. "Quinn liked to hear himself talk, and he wore an ill-fitting periwig. He would not be easy to forget."

"Someone had stolen the periwig, too, by the time the body was found," Captain Guzmán remarked. Lope made a small, disgusted noise. Guzmán nodded and continued, "No, not even the taverner. He says Quinn wasn't a regular and he never wastes much time with people who aren't regulars. People who are regulars swear he is telling the truth."

"Would they say the same if we questioned them—properly?" De Vega had no trouble contemplating torture, but didn't care to come right out and name it.

"Another interesting question. Maybe, for that one, we'll find an answer," Baltasar Guzmán replied. "Meanwhile, though, I want you to work with this Constable Strawberry, who has been trying to catch whoever killed Geoffrey Martin. Maybe he can help us here, if these two killings are connected."

"Yes, your Excellency," Lope said dutifully. But he couldn't help heaving a sigh. "I don't much like this Englishman, though, and I don't think he's very bright."

"As may be—he is the man on the spot, and he has been working on the matter since Martin died," Guzmán said. "Martin was a good Catholic man. His killing should not go unpunished."

"Was Quinn a good Catholic man?" Lope asked.

Looking unhappy, Captain Guzmán shook his head. "No, or no one thinks so. Before we came here, he was a Protestant. He went to Mass afterwards, but no one ever thought he was pious."

"No link there, then," Lope said. Guzmán sent him a warning look. He hastily added, "But I'll go find out if there are any others."

Feeling put upon, he rode up to Shoreditch. When he got there, one of the watchmen who assisted the constable told him Strawberry was out on rounds. The fellow had only a vague idea of where Strawberry might be found. *I could be at the Theatre*, Lope thought resentfully, *not chasing down this slow-witted Englishman who isn't likely to know much anyway*.

He finally came upon Walter Strawberry marching up a muddy street, swinging a truncheon by its leather thong. "Give you good day, Constable," he called, hurrying towards the other man.

"Why, Master de Vega, as I live and expire," Strawberry said, tipping his hat. "Greetings and palpitations to you, sir."

"Er—thank you," Lope said. Listening to the constable always reminded him English was a foreign language. "I have just learned of the death of the player, Matthew Quinn."

"He died the death, indeed. Murther. Murther most foul, and robbery of's periwig—another felony besides," Strawberry said. "Mind you, I am factitious of who the miscegenate was."

"Are you?" Lope said. Constable Strawberry solemnly nodded. De Vega asked, "Think you this slaying hath connection to that of Geoffrey Martin?"

"Connection? Connection?" the Englishman said. "Why, man, if some low cove had not connection with Geoff Martin, and now with Quinn, they'd not be slain. Will you tell me I'm wrong?" He stuck out his jaw in challenge.

"Meseems you have mistook me," Lope said. "Be there in your view connection betwixt Masters Martin and Quinn?"

"Give me leave to doubt it, sir. They were both honest men, or honest enough, and with such vice square against all conjunctions Biblical—"

De Vega muttered a quick *Pater noster*. He hoped God was listening.

Trying to get through to Walter Strawberry was like going to the dentist, save that Strawberry drew sense rather than teeth. "Let me try once more," Lope said with what he reckoned commendable calm. "Think you the same man did slay these twain?"

"Ay, belike," the constable said—at last, a definite answer.

Lope felt like cheering. "And who was this man?"

"Why, the murtherer, assuredly." Strawberry stared at him. "Who else might he be?"

Another *Pater noster* did not suffice de Vega. Neither did crossing himself. Through clenched teeth, he asked, "What calls he himself?—this man you reckon the murtherer, I mean."

"Know you of a wicked cove, hight Ingram Frizer?"

"No, sir. I ken him not." Lope shook his head.

"Well, him I believe to be the benefactor in question."

"I am sorry, sir," Lope said. "I am most terribly sorry. One of us hath of your tongue a grasp imperfect. Which that may be . . ." He threw his hands in the air. "I own I know not."

"I have spake English since I was a puling babe: it is the tongue of my captivity," Strawberry said. "You, then, needs must be inerrant."

"Would I were!" Lope exclaimed. "Tell me more of this man Frizer." Maybe he would learn something. He dared hope. Stranger things must have happened, though none occurred to him offhand.

"He hath a knife and a temper and a quick way with both," Constable Strawberry said, and de Vega understood every word. The Englishman went on, "You being intermittent with them of the Theatre, I feel it recumbent upon me to give you fair warning: this Ingram Frizer hath acquaintance with Nick Skeres." He paused expectantly.

"Again, I am sorry, but this name I know not," Lope said.

"Do you not? Do you not indeed, sir? Well, Master Skeres, though he'll not slit your weasand with a cuttle, still and all he is a most vile cozening rogue, a cheat such that Judas In's Chariot hath not seen the like. And"—another portentous pause—"*he* hath acquaintance with Master Shakespeare, the poetaster."

"Poetaster? Shakespeare? You show yourself no judge of poesy, Master Strawberry, an you place him so low. Can it be doubted he is amongst the finest poets of our time? I think not."

"Can it be doubted he knows Nick Skeres? *I* think not," Strawberry returned.

Again, Lope understood every word, at least individually. What he didn't understand was what, if anything, all those words meant taken together. He muttered something nasty under his breath, knowing he had no choice but to try to find out.

AFTER ANOTHER PERFORMANCE AS THE GHOST IN *PRINCE OF DENmark*, Shakespeare scrubbed chalk and black greasepaint from his face in the tiring room. Every so often, someone would come up and tell him how frightful he'd been. His thanks were distinctly abstracted. He kept looking around the room, wondering if Christopher Marlowe would dare appear. His fellow poet would make a ghost even less welcome than that of the unhappy prince's father.

Thus far, no sign of Marlowe. Shakespeare knew nothing but relief. Maybe Kit's folly had limits after all. Maybe. He dared hope.

"Well played, Master Shakespeare! Most well played!"

Shakespeare had a towel over his eyes at that moment, but he didn't need to see to be sure who spoke to him. "For which kindness I do thank you, Lieutenant de Vega," he replied.

"It is nothing, nothing at all," Lope said grandly.

When Shakespeare took the towel away from his face, he got a surprise after all, for there beside the Spaniard stood Cicely Sellis, Mommet perched on her shoulder. Hoping to hide his alarm, Shakespeare bowed to the cunning woman. "Give you good day as well, Mistress Sellis."

"And to you," she replied. "I have more than once before seen you give the ghost, but never, methinks, better than today."

"You are too generous by half," Shakespeare murmured. *I'd liefer give than give up the ghost*, he thought. *But have I the choice?* He turned to Lope de Vega and murmured again, this time only two words: "How now?"

How are you now come hither with Mistress Sellis and not with the Spanish jade who cost a nobleman's life? was what he meant. By the way Lope coughed a couple of times and turned red, he understood all the words Shakespeare hadn't said. But he answered smoothly, saying, "We two, being friends and having in common a friend, were together glad to see him play his famous role."

"Just so," Cicely Sellis said. Her cat yawned.

De Vega smiled. Shakespeare didn't care for the expression; Mommet might have worn it playing with a mouse. The Spaniard was going to take his revenge. And he did. "Know you a man called Ingram Frizer, Master Shakespeare?"

I might have guessed, flashed through Shakespeare's mind. No one in the company had spoken much of Matthew Quinn's death. No one had seemed much surprised to hear of it, either, not when Quinn's tongue had flapped so free. But two murders in one company had drawn the dons' notice as well as that of Constable Strawberry, and Shakespeare didn't suppose he should have been much surprised at that.

No more than a heartbeat slower than he should have, he shook his head and answered, "Frizer? No, Lieutenant, I ken no one of that name." Nobody could prove otherwise—he hoped. A question of his own seemed safe: "Why ask you me of him?"

Sure enough, de Vega replied, "He is suspect in the murther of the player, Quinn."

"May the hangman sell the rope by which he dances on the air, then," Shakespeare said. "But why, I pray you, think you he and I be known each to the other?"

"For that you are both known to one Nicholas Skeres," the Spanish officer said, his voice suddenly hard.

How much did he know? If he knew enough, he wouldn't have brought Cicely Sellis along while he asked questions—he would have brought a squad of soldiers and dragged Shakespeare away. Realizing that helped the poet quell his fear. Lope was only fishing for whatever he might find.

Shakespeare resolved to give him as little as he could: "I have met Nicholas Skeres, ay, but he is no friend of mine. Indeed, I misdoubt him not a little; as I live, he is like as not a queer-bird, his name writ down in the Black Book." He had no idea whether Skeres had actually gone to prison and had his name inscribed in the register, but he wouldn't have been surprised. And he didn't mind in the least slandering a man he truly disliked. Skeres, he was sure, could take care of himself.

Lope said, "This marches with that which you told unto Constable Strawberry."

Damn Constable Strawberry for a very superficial, ignorant, unweighing fellow, Shakespeare thought. "Is not the truth the truth?" he said aloud. "That truth should be silent I had almost forgot."

"I know not whether 'tis truth or another thing," de Vega answered. "I do know I will find where truth be hid, though it were hid indeed within the center. That a man saith twice the same thing proves not its truth, but only his constancy."

"Are we not friends here?" Cicely Sellis asked. "Use friends each the other so?"

To Shakespeare's surprise, Lope bowed to her and said, "You are as wise as you are lovely. Let it be as you would have't, of course."

She sketched a curtsy. She didn't bend low, to keep Mommet from either falling off or sinking in his claws. "Gramercy," she said. "In a false quarrel there is no true valor."

Lope nodded. "That is well said."

"Indeed it is," Shakespeare agreed. But he knew the Spaniard hadn't stopped digging—he'd only paused while in the cunning woman's company. Even that was a good deal more than Shakespeare had expected. He watched the way de Vega's eyes caressed her. *He'd fain be more than friend*, the poet realized. *What tangled skein have we here, and how will it unravel?* He tried to imagine Lope coming regularly to the Widow Kendall's lodging-house, walking into Cicely Sellis' room, closing the door behind him. . . .

Would Mommet watch? he wondered. *Could a man bed a witch, her puckrel attending her? Would it not unman him?* He eyed her himself. *Would I know these things for the don's sake, or for mine own?*

Haply for mine own.

Cicely Sellis' eyes, gray as the northern seas, met his own—met them and held them. Not for the first time, he had the feeling she knew every thought in his head. Considering what some of those thoughts were . . . He feared he blushed like a schoolboy.

If the cunning woman truly could divine his mind, she gave no sign of it. She leaned towards Lope and spoke to him in a voice too low for Shakespeare to make out. The Spaniard nodded, his smile indulgent—and more than a little hungry. A moment later, he was making his good-byes to Shakespeare and leading her out of the tiring room.

Richard Burbage came over to the poet. "The don hath *another* new woman?"

Shakespeare only shrugged. "I cannot say. That he *would* have her, though, I doubt not. She is the cunning woman, hight Cicely Sellis, of whom I may once or twice have spoke."

Burbage's eyes got wide. "The one dwelling in your lodging-house?"

"The same."

"I hope that damned witch, that damned sorceress, hath wrought this hellish mischief unawares," Burbage said, his deep voice somber.

"Of . . . ?" Shakespeare let the title of the play hang unspoken in the air.

"Of that, and of other things," the player answered.

"So I hope as well, but Cicely Sellis, methinks, is unaware of very little."

"Will she discover to the Spaniard that which she knows?" Burbage asked nervously.

"I . . . think not." Shakespeare wanted to shake his head and say such a thing was impossible, unimaginable. He wanted to, but knew too well he couldn't. He and Cicely Sellis had hardly spoken of things political. Few in occupied England said much about such things, except to those they knew would not betray them. Trusting the wrong man—or woman—was among the worst mistakes anyone could make.

"You think not?" Richard Burbage echoed, and Shakespeare nodded. Burbage persisted: "No more than that can you say?" Now the poet did shake his head. Burbage looked very unhappy indeed, for which Shakespeare could not blame him. He asked, "And will she too meet the smiler with the knife under the cloak?"

That made Shakespeare blink. He'd used Chaucer as a source for a couple of his plays, but hadn't known Burbage read *The Canterbury Tales*. Asking him about that, though, would wait for some other time. "Why to me put you this question?" he said, speaking in a near-whisper to make sure no one else in the tiring room heard. "I knew naught of poor Geoff's murther aforetimes, nor of Matt Quinn's, neither."

Burbage said nothing. His silence felt more devastating than any words could have. Shakespeare grimaced and turned away. He'd told the truth. As so often happened, it did him no good at all.

And, when he got back to his lodging-house, he found Jane Kendall in a swivet. "A Spaniard!" the widow hissed at him as soon as he walked through the door. "She came hither with a *Spaniard*!" She crossed herself. Being sincerely Catholic, she preferred Isabella and Albert on the throne to Elizabeth, but had no great love for the stern soldiers who'd set them there. Such contradictions were anything but rare these days.

"Rest you easy, Mistress Kendall," Shakespeare said; another upset was the last thing he needed. "The don is known to me: a sweet-faced man; a proper man."

"But he is a don," the Widow Kendall said. "Be he never so sweet-faced, he is a don, a busy meddling fiend." She paused, then made the sign of the cross again. "And I dare not even rate her for't, lest she do me a mischief with her foul witchery." Her voice fell to a barely audible whisper: "Is he her sweetheart?"

"I know not, not to a surety," Shakespeare answered. "He'd have it so, meseems, but oft yawns a gulf 'twixt what a man would and what a woman will."

Jane Kendall sniffed. "Saith she, I am a widow. And how many queans and callets and low harlots say the same?"

Shakespeare thought Cicely Sellis might be a great many things. A whore? Never. He didn't argue with the Widow Kendall, though. He'd long since seen there was no point to that. He simply headed for his bedchamber, saying, "I needs must take pen and paper, and then I'm for the ordinary and supper and, God grant it, some tolerable verses."

His landlady couldn't complain so loudly as was her custom, not when she feared the cunning woman and so also feared being overheard. That let him get out of the house and off to the ordinary. By the time he came back, Jane Kendall had gone to bed. So did he, not much later.

He was on his way up to the Theatre the next morning when Nicholas Skeres slid out of a side street and fell into step with him. "Aroint thee!" Shakespeare exclaimed. "I'd liefer see a black cat cross my path than thee. I am suspect for that we are acquainted, and known to be acquainted."

Skeres didn't get angry, which disappointed Shakespeare—he longed for a quarrel, even a fight. "I'll begone anon," the clever but ill-favored man said. "First, though, you must know at once: Lord Burghley is no more. He died yesternight, in's sleep."

"God save us," Shakespeare whispered. He'd expected the news since the last time he saw Nick Skeres. Hearing it jolted him even so.

"God save us indeed," Skeres answered now. "God and good St. George save England—God and St. George and you, Master Shakespeare."

"I am sure as need be this cloth hath more threads than mine own," Shakespeare said, and Nicholas Skeres did not contradict him. He went on, "God grant Robert Cecil hath hold of them all." Skeres nodded, then slipped away. Shakespeare trudged on towards the Theatre, alone with his thoughts.

LOPE DE VEGA AND CATALINA IBAÑEZ SAT IN A TAVERN IN WESTminster, drinking sweet Rhenish wine and glaring at each other across the table. "You never take me anywhere," Catalina complained. "I might as well be in a convent, for all the fun I have with you."

"That is not so," Lope said indignantly. "Did we not go to the bear-baiting only two nights ago? Was it not a fine spectacle?" Going back to Southwark gave him a twinge, but he'd done it for Catalina. Since she was, at the moment, his only lover, he'd feared no disaster. Nor had he suffered one. He'd had a good time, and thought she had, too.

Maybe she had, but she didn't show it now. "Bear-baiting!" She laced the words with scorn. "Where are the balls, where are the feasts, where are the masques Don Alejandro used to take me to? I ask you that—where are they? You'd better have a good answer for me, too." Her eyes flashed dangerously.

With such patience as he could muster, de Vega answered, "My dear, Don Alejandro was a nobleman, and a man newly come from Spain. Of course he got invited to these things. I am only a senior lieutenant. I wish I were in great demand. Unfortunately, though . . ."

"Oh, why did I ever take up with you?" Catalina seemed more likely to be asking God than Lope.

Lope answered nonetheless: "For love?"

"Love?" She waved away the very idea. "When Queen Isabella tossed you that purse after we put on *El mejor mozo de España*, I thought you were going places. But the only place you want to go is the English theatre."

"I wish you spoke the language," Lope said. "There's so much to see, so much to admire, so much to learn."

Catalina Ibañez yawned in his face. "So much to be bored by. I've been bored every single minute since we started seeing each other."

"*Every* minute?" Lope said. "I think not, my dear." If she'd faked her pleasure, she was a far better actress even than she'd shown on stage.

She didn't deign to respond to the sly dig. Instead, she said, "I never should have told anyone you killed poor Don Alejandro in a fair fight. If you don't start treating me better, I'll tell people what *really* happened, there in that yard."

"What *really* happened?" Lope didn't spring from his stool. He didn't raise his voice. He didn't so much as lean forward. Menace filled his words and manner even so. "What do you mean? Tell me most precisely."

Intent on herself, Catalina Ibañez didn't notice the menace, not at first. "Why, how you lay in wait for him and . . . and . . ." Her voice trailed away.

Too late. Too slow. Lope said, "You will not do that." He spoke as calmly as if he were telling her, *The sun will come up tomorrow.* "If you think you can blackmail me, my sweet, you had better think again. Do you remember what Don Alejandro's body looked like? That could be you."

"You wouldn't d . . ." But Catalina once more failed to finish her sentence. Lope might. What would stop him? He'd already done it to Don Alejandro de Recalde.

"Do you want to try me? Do you want to find out what I would or wouldn't do?" Lope asked. "Go right ahead, my love. You'll learn everything you ever wanted to know, I promise you that."

"You are a monster! An animal!" Catalina said shrilly.

De Vega inclined his head. "At your service, *señorita.* Always at your service."

"My service!" she said. "The best service you could give me would be never to see me again."

"If that's how you would have it, so shall it be." Lope got to his feet. He swept off his hat and bowed low. "Pity a man died over so small and passing a thing as your affection, but such is life. But even if we are quits, do bear in mind that I shall know if you go telling lies about me to those in authority. You may think you can ruin me. You may even be right. But I promise you, I will have my revenge. Do you doubt it?"

Catalina Ibañez looked as if she would have liked nothing better than to do exactly that. But all she said was, "N-n-n-no"—as frightened a stammer as he'd ever heard.

He had no idea whether to believe her. He refused to worry about it either way. If she did go to the authorities with her lies, they might or might not take her seriously. Whether they did or not, honor demanded that he avenge the slight. He would do it, too, at whatever cost to himself. She had to know that. She wasn't wise in the ways of book learning, but she was shrewd.

With another bow, Lope said, "Farewell, my former dear. I shall remember you in my dreams—and, if God is kind, nowhere else." He strode out of the wineshop. A quick glance over his shoulder showed him Catalina staring after him, her eyes enormous in a face gone pale and yellow as goat's-milk cheese.

He went out into the street just in time to see Sir William Cecil's funeral procession pass by, carrying deposed Elizabeth's great counselor from Westminster to his final resting place in St. Paul's cathedral in London. De Vega hadn't thought any Englishman, especially one of such dubious loyalty, could be buried with so much pomp. But, when he saw how many people lined the street for a last glimpse of Lord Burghley's earthly remains even here in Westminster, a stronghold of Isabella and Albert and the Spaniards, he realized the powers that be hadn't dared say no to this procession, for fear of riots or worse.

Four white horses draped in black velvet decorated with Sir William's coat of arms drew the bier through the streets. More velvet, this of a deep purple hue, covered the coffin that held Cecil's corpse. Above the coffin was an effigy of the dead English nobleman, his arms folded over this chest in the shape of the cross. A canopy of black velvet, again picked out with the Cecil coat of arms, shielded the effigy from the August sun.

In the wake of the bier walked Robert Cecil, Lord Burghley's son. The pale little man with his twisted back seemed out of place in that robust sun; the black velvet of mourning he wore only accented his pallor. Just for a moment, his eyes met Lope's. He nodded, as if to a friend, and kept on walking.

Behind him came several other prominent Englishmen, of his generation and his father's. Lope recognized Francis Bacon, who, being Lord Burghley's nephew, could hardly be blamed for mourning his passing. Some of the others, though, surprised de Vega. Sir William Cecil had had more friends than he'd believed among the men who ran the country for Queen Isabella and King Albert.

Many of those men, no doubt, would have been as glad to run England for Elizabeth the heretic. Lope's eyes flicked east, towards the Tower where she remained. In an odd way, killing Mary Queen of Scots might have saved Elizabeth's life. Not wanting to be a regicide himself, King Philip hadn't imitated her and had let her live.

Catalina Ibañez came out of the wineshop. Seeing Lope standing there watching the funeral procession move on towards London, she snarled something that would have made a grizzled muleteer blush, then stalked away. *I don't suppose I'll see her again*, de Vega thought with a sigh. *I don't need to waste any worries on her, though. She's bound to land on her feet or on her back or wherever will do her the most good. But even so . . .* He sighed again.

Beside him, someone spoke in English-accented Spanish: "There's a dangerous foe of Isabella and Albert dead."

Lope started. "Oh. *Buenos días, Señor* Phelippes. My head must have been in the clouds, for I noted you not when you came up. I am most sorry." He bowed in apology.

Thomas Phelippes politely returned the bow. "Nothing to worry about, Senior Lieutenant." He continued to speak Spanish, where Lope had replied mostly in English.

"Tell me," de Vega said, "what think you of Robert Cecil, Lord Burghley's son and heir?"

To answer that, Phelippes returned to English himself, as if he couldn't be scornful enough in Spanish: "Small curs are not regarded when they grin. He is as full of quarrel and offense as my young mistress' dog. An untaught puppy, by my troth: you shall see him heave up his leg, and make water against a gentlewoman's farthingale."

Lope laughed in delight at the unexpectedness of that. "Not the man his father was, then, by your reckoning?"

"Not half the man, sir, not in any particular," the Englishman answered. "Not in height nor in girth, not in years nor in wisdom, not in paunch nor in pizzle: a dear manikin, such a dish of skim milk as the world hath not seen the likes of since Nero's day."

"You ease my mind," Lope said. "I shall take your opinion to Captain Guzmán, who hath some concern o'er the son of such a father."

"Far from fearing such as Robert Cecil, your good captain may set all plain sail and dread naught," Thomas Phelippes said. "I have told Don Diego Flores de Valdés the same."

"By God, sir, this is good to hear," de Vega said. "I grieve only that his Most Catholic Majesty will not long outlive the foe he in's mercy spared."

"The Lord moves in mysterious ways, blessed be His name." Phelippes crossed himself. Lope did the same. The pockmarked, bespectacled little Englishman continued, "I had me the privilege of writing out the parts from Shakespeare's *King Philip*, making fair copy for the players' use. Though it were builded of brick and marble, a man might have a lesser monument."

"Mine own thought is much the same," de Vega agreed.

Phelippes bowed again. "May that production come not soon," he said. "And now, sir, your pardon, but I must away." He hurried off in the direction—Lope thought it was the direction—of the palace where he and Don Diego helped administer the Spanish occupation of England. Lope had intended to go back to London, but Lord Burghley's funeral procession would surely clog the Strand for some time to come. With Catalina Ibañez gone, he ducked back into the wineshop instead.

Whenever Shakespeare left his lodging-house or the Theatre these days, the first thing he did was anxiously peer in all directions. He didn't want to see Nick Skeres coming his way with more bad news. And he especially didn't want to see Ingram Frizer, who might come his way with death.

He was supping on boiled beef and marrow bones stewed with barley and parsnips and mushrooms when Thomas Phelippes walked into the ordinary. By then, he'd come into the place often enough that Kate called to him: "A cup of the Rhenish, sir, as you've drunk before?"

"If you'd be so kind, mistress," Phelippes replied. He pulled up a stool at Shakespeare's table and sat down, saying, "Give you good even."

Shakespeare had raised a bone to his lips. He sucked out the rich, delicate marrow with a small, almost involuntary, sound of pleasure. Then he set the bone back in the bowl; this was no low dive, nor was he a rustic or a ruffian, to throw his refuse on the floor. "God give you good den as well, Master Phelippes," he said grudgingly. Was the pockmarked little man a companion any safer than Skeres or Frizer? He had his doubts.

The serving woman brought Phelippes his wine. He set a penny on the table. She scooped it up. He eyed her as she walked off with it; candlelight glinted from the lenses of his spectacles. "A likely wench," he remarked.

"Think you so?" Shakespeare said, as neutrally as he could. He sprinkled some salt from the saltcellar into his stew. "What would you?" he asked in a low voice. "You came not, meseems, for to praise the lady's beauty, however praiseworthy she be."

Phelippes nodded. "There you speak sooth, sir." He pointed to the pewter spoon Shakespeare had brought to the ordinary. "Eat up, quick as you may. I'd have you come with me."

"What? Tonight? Now?" Shakespeare yelped. Thomas Phelippes nodded again. "Whither? Wherefore?" the poet demanded. "I'd purposed work of mine own this even. The one commission and the other both being done, as you will have seen"—he couldn't resist the gibe, for he remained unsure who Phelippes' true master was—"I dared hope I might pursue a notion no one set me."

"Be ever at enmity with cozening hope; he is a flatterer," Phelippes said. Shakespeare glared at him. Wasted effort: he gave no more heed than a snake to the frantic stares of a bird it swallowed. He went on, "Come away with me. Someone would fain take counsel with you."

"Someone?" Shakespeare echoed. Phelippes nodded once more. "Who?" the poet asked. The other man cocked his head to one side. The dancing candle flame filled his spectacle lenses with light and lent him for a moment an inhuman cast of feature. Shakespeare mouthed Robert Cecil's name. Phelippes gave him yet another nod. Knowing he couldn't refuse, Shakespeare did eat quickly. When he'd finished the meat and the parsnips, he took up his writing tools and got to his feet. "Lead on, Master Phelippes."

Seeing him head for the door instead of settling down to write, Kate called after him in surprise and alarm: "Is all well, Will?"

"Well enough, or so I hope," he answered. That wouldn't reassure her. He hoped it would unsettle Phelippes. If anything happened to him, the alarm would spread quickly. The other question was, did Phelippes—did Robert Cecil—care? Shakespeare had to believe they did. If they would kill him when he'd done them no harm, when he'd labored long and hard to aid their cause, how were they better than the dons?

Outside the ordinary, darkness hung thick, almost palpable. As August moved towards September, nights were getting longer again, and colder, too. When Shakespeare sighed, he could see the vapor of his own breath. Somewhere high overhead, an owl hooted. Tiny skitterings from close by the walls said rats and mice went about their business even so.

"Whither away?" Shakespeare asked again. In that smothering dark, he felt as much a skulker as the skittering vermin.

Instead of answering with words, Thomas Phelippes set off at a brisk pace. *Can I endure this arrogance? And from this fellow?* Sadly, Shakespeare knew he had no choice. He followed.

He wished he had Mommet's eyes. That would have kept him from stepping in several noxious piles and puddles. By Phelippes' low-voiced—and sometimes not so low-voiced—curses, he knew the other man had the same trouble. Somehow, that didn't console him.

Phelippes led him south and west. He didn't realize how far he'd come till he saw the great bulk of St. Paul's heaving itself up into the sky, blocking out the stars. Before long, Phelippes knocked at the door to a house that seemed neither rich nor poor. The knock had a curious rhythm to it: *a code*, Shakespeare thought. The door opened. "In—make haste!" someone said. Phelippes ducked inside.

Shakespeare followed once more. He wished he could turn and flee instead. If he did, though, he was grimly certain he would meet Ingram Frizer in the ruffian's professional capacity. Would Frizer smile as he drove the knife home? Shakespeare would not have bet against it.

Inside, light blazed from candles and torches and a leaping fire in the hearth, a fire better suited to winter than summer. Robert Cecil sat in a chair not far from the flames; perhaps his back pained him when he used a stool like most men. "Give you good evening, Master Shakespeare," he said, dipping his head in what was almost but not quite a seated bow.

"And to you, sir," Shakespeare replied. "My deepest condolement on your loss."

Lord Burghley's son waved him to a stool. As he perched there, nervous as a bird, the younger Cecil said, " 'Tis the kingdom should condole, not I. My father passed from us full of years, but England's savior died untimely. What he cannot now do, I needs must essay. How stand we in respect of your part therein?"

"You will know the play is writ," Shakespeare said, and Robert Cecil nodded. The poet went on, "You will also know Constable Strawberry sniffs after him who murthered both Geoff Martin and, now, Matthew Quinn."

Cecil nodded again. Thomas Phelippes said, "We merit our freedom not, an such a bedlam brainsick counterfeit module may make to totter the fabric of our designs."

"What Strawberry solus may not do, peradventure with confederates he may," Shakespeare said. "Belike you will know he concerts with Lieutenant de Vega."

Again, Phelippes was the one who spoke up: "And is not de Vega well and truly cozened? Does he not believe me friend to his enterprise? Can such a worthless post be feared?"

"Any man opposing us may be feared," said Shakespeare, who'd learned more about fear since the previous autumn than he ever wanted to know. He glanced towards Robert Cecil. Cecil kept his own counsel. He would have been a dangerous man in a game of cards; Shakespeare had no idea what he was thinking. He dared hope Cecil *was* thinking something, and reminded himself Lord Burghley had had a good opinion of his crookbacked son.

A servant brought in goblets of Sherris-sack and sugar to sweeten it. Everyone fell silent till the man bowed his way out of the room. Then, sipping the wine, Cecil asked, "And should I know aught else?"

Shakespeare started to shake his head, as Robert Cecil plainly expected him to do. But then he checked the motion. "Haply you should, your Honor."

One of Cecil's eyebrows rose, startlingly dark against the pallid skin of his forehead. His long, thin fingers tightened on the goblet's stem. But his voice showed nothing as he said, "Tell it me, then."

"As you know of Walter Strawberry, as you know he treats with the don, so, belike, you will know Kit Marlowe is returned to London."

That loosed a hawk amongst the pigeons. Robert Cecil started so violently, sugared sack slopped out of his goblet and onto the slashed black velvet of his doublet. "Why, thou infinite and endless liar!" Thomas Phelippes burst out.

"By my troth, sir, I am no such creature, and be damned to thine ignorant, oppressive arrogance for naming me one," Shakespeare answered angrily.

Before Phelippes could loose some hot retort of his own, Robert Cecil help up a hand. The gesture, though spare, was commanding; Phelippes fell silent at once. Shakespeare just had time to note that before the younger Cecil's gaze fell full on him. It was not a magisterial stare, such as Sir William had had. But its blazing intensity made it at least as arresting. Robert Cecil said, "Tell me at once—at once!—how you know this to be true."

"How, sir? Because I have seen him and spoke with him," Shakespeare said. "He hath cropped his hair close to his head and shaved his beard, so that a man might pass him in the street and know him not; but his voice is not so easily disguised."

"But he went to sea at Deptford," Thomas Phelippes said.

"In sooth: as I told him," Shakespeare replied. "And, quotha, he came ashore at Margate, for that he might hie back to London."

"Damnation take him," Phelippes said. "He were better gone. For he *will* make himself known. He can no more help spewing words than a malmsey-nose sot can help spewing wine."

"Do the Spaniards seize him, he dies the death," Robert Cecil said, "the which he must know."

"He doth know it indeed," Shakespeare said. "But he cannot avoid what plays out here, no more than can a jackdaw spying some trifling shiny thing serving to bait a snare."

Grimly, Cecil said, "A jackdaw snares but itself: until it be snared, and tamed, and taught, it hath no knowledge of human speech. Would the same were so of Marlowe."

"An the dons lay hold of him, how shall he save himself?" Phelippes asked.

The question hung in the air. Phelippes didn't answer it. Neither did Robert Cecil. Silence did the job for them. One possibility immediately occurred to Shakespeare—*by telling them all he knows*. That had been in his mind ever since he'd had the misfortune to discover his fellow poet hadn't had the sense to get out of England while he could.

Cecil looked his way again. "Gramercy, Master Shakespeare, for bringing this word to my notice. Doubt not I shall attend to't."

"By the which you mean, do your confederates find him, he likewise dies the death," Shakespeare said.

Now Cecil's gaze was perfectly opaque. Shakespeare realized he'd blundered, and might have blundered badly. It wasn't that he was wrong. It was, in fact, that he was right. Such things might better have stayed unspoken. Then the younger Cecil wouldn't either have to admit to planning Marlowe's untimely death or to tell a lie by denying it.

"Would he'd gone abroad," Thomas Phelippes murmured: as much of an answer as Shakespeare was likely to get.

"I shall ask once more, have you other news we should hear?" Cecil, this time, sounded as if he meant the question, not as if he were asking it for form's sake alone.

But Shakespeare shook his head. *When next I see Kit, I must tell him both sides'd fain know the color of's blood*, he thought. He didn't *know* he'd see Marlowe again, but found it all too likely. *Icarus flew nigh the sun, and perished thereby. Kit outdoth him in folly, first helping kindle the flame that now will burn him.*

Phelippes pointed towards the door. "We are in Paternoster Row, by St. Paul's," he said. "Knowing so much, can you wend your way homeward?"

"I can, an I be not robbed or murthered faring thither," Shakespeare answered. Nicholas Skeres had told him London's miscreants were ordered to leave him alone. He'd seen some signs it might be so. But he still remained far from sure Skeres' word was to be trusted. And, on a night as dark as this, even an honest footpad might make an honest mistake and fall on him.

The night wasn't so dark when he left the house as it had been when he got there: the third-quarter moon, looking like half a glowing gold angel or mark, had climbed up over the rooftops to the northeast. In fact, it made a pretty fair guide for Shakespeare as he hurried back towards Jane Kendall's lodging-house.

He was out after curfew. Twice he had to duck into shadowed doorways as a Spanish patrol—always several men together, as single Spaniards weren't safe on the streets past sunset—marched by. Once, somebody else out late didn't disappear fast enough. A Spaniard called out. The Englishman ran instead of coming forward. Shouting and cursing, the dons pounded after him. One of them fired a pistol. No scream followed, so Shakespeare supposed the ball missed. He waited till the soldiers had rounded a corner, then went on his own way.

He got home with no more trouble. He even got a little writing done. Sleep? He might have got a little that night. He wasn't sure.

XII

LOPE DE VEGA AND CICELY SELLIS STOOD JUST OUTSIDE THE DOOR to the cunning woman's room. As she set her hand on the latch, she said, "We are friends, mind you, Master de Vega, not lovers. I trust you'll recall as much when we go within, and seek not to paw me or do me other such discourtesies."

"God forbid it," Lope exclaimed, making the sign of the cross to show his sincerity. Then he let out a melodramatic sigh to show he wasn't so sincere as all that. She made a face at him. He winked and blew her a kiss, saying, "Teach not thy lips such scorn, for they were made for kissing, lady, not for such contempt. And my kissing is as full of sanctity as the touch of holy bread."

She rolled her eyes. "Love is merely a madness, and, I tell you, deserves as well a dark house and a whip as madmen do. Now—swear and swear true, or stay without my door."

"As you wish, so shall it be," Lope said solemnly. "This I swear." And if, once they were inside and alone together, she wished for something other than that he keep his distance, he would gladly oblige her. And if he could persuade her to wish for something other than that, why then, he would.

Something in Cicely Sellis' expression said she knew perfectly well what lay in his mind. That irked Lope; he didn't like women seeing through him. *She is a cunning woman, after all,* he reminded himself, and then, not for the first time, reminded himself of the other, shorter, name for a cunning woman: *witch.* Some things he might try with other women he would perhaps be wise to forget with this one.

"I shall take you at your word," she said, and opened the door. "Enter, an't please you."

He did, curious not least to see what a witch's room was like. It seemed ordinary enough: bed, stool, chest of drawers with basin and pitcher atop it, undoubtedly a chamber pot under the bed. The only thing even slightly strange was a box half full of raw, uncombed wool. That puzzled Lope till Mommet stuck his head out of the box and mewed.

"A clever nest," the Spaniard said.

"It suits him." Cicely Sellis waved to the stool. "Sit you down." She herself perched on the edge of the bed.

He would rather have sat beside her, but he couldn't very well do that, not when she'd been so definite. Mommet leaped from the box, paused to scratch behind an ear, and wandered over to sniff at his boots. He stroked the cat. It purred, then snapped. He jerked his hand away. Mommet went right on purring. "Faithless beast," he muttered.

"He is a cat," the cunning woman said. "From one moment to the next, he knows not what he'd have. Is he then so different from those who go on two legs?"

"Treason's in his blood," de Vega said.

"Is he then so different . . . ?" Cicely Sellis didn't repeat all of her last question, only enough to make it plain.

In doing so, she gave Lope an opening. "Know you of any such?" he asked, keeping his tone as light and casual as he could. "For surely you must hear all manner of fearful and curious things."

"The confessional hath its secrets," she said. "No less my trade. Who'd speak to a cunning woman, knowing his words were broadcast to the general? No less than a priest, I hear of adulteries and fornications and cozenings and, as you say, all manner of proof Adam's get be a sinful lot."

A cunning woman, of course, lacked the immunity of a priest hearing confession. Lope didn't mention that. She had to know it only too well. And, while she'd mentioned several kinds of things she heard about, she hadn't said a word about treason. If he pressed her on it, he would make her suspicious. Instead, he changed the subject, or seemed to: "How I envy you, lodging here cheek by jowl with Master Shakespeare. Hath he told you aforetime what his next play's to be?"

Cicely Sellis shook her head. "Nay, nor hath he spoke treason in my hearing, neither."

Lope's ears burned. He hadn't been so subtle there as he would have wished. If he acknowledged the hit, though, she would think him more interested in spying on her than interested in her. He *was* interested in spying on her, but that didn't mean he wasn't interested *in* her: on the contrary. "Right glad I am to know it, then," he said. "Ears so sweet as yours should hear no base, no gross, no disgusting thing."

She laughed. The cat sat up on its haunches like a begging dog, staring at her. "What should they hear, then?"

"Why, how beautiful thou art," he answered at once. "Thou dost teach the torches to burn bright—beauty too rich for use, for earth too dear."

That made her laugh again. "Said I not, we are friends? Say you so to all you hold in friendship?"

"I do not," Lope said. "But, whilst we *are* friends, I'd fain we were more. I own it. 'Twould curd my blood to say otherwise."

"You flatter me." Cicely Sellis drew out a sparkling glass trinket that hung on a chain around her neck. She let the pendant swing back and forth a couple of times; it drew Lope's eye as a lodestone draws iron. Then, smiling to herself, she tucked it back under her blouse, into the shadowed vale between her breasts. His gaze followed it till it disappeared. Seeing that made her smile wider. "You'd say the like to any woman you found comely."

That held some truth, but only some. "I have seen comely women aplenty," he said. "I have loved comely women aplenty. And, having done it, I find loving 'em for comeliness' sake alone doth stale." He thought of Catalina Ibañez, and wished he hadn't. "I'd sooner love one who might love me in return for reasons as several and various as mine for loving her."

"I tell you yet again, we are not lovers," she said.

"I tell thee yet again, would we were!" Lope exclaimed. Being balked only made him burn hotter.

"You flatter me," Cicely Sellis said once more.

"Nay, for flattery is lies, whilst I am full of truth," Lope said.

"When this man swears that he is made of truth, I near believe him, though I know he lies," the cunning woman said, as if to an audience only she could see. Then her attention unmistakably swung back to Lope. "Said you the like to Catalina Ibañez? Said you the like to Lucy Watkins? Said you the like to Nell Lumley? To Martha Brock? To Maude Fuller, or ever you dove out her window?"

De Vega gaped. "How know you of her?" He was sure Shakespeare didn't, which meant Cicely Sellis couldn't have heard about that from him.

"I have my ways," she said. He crossed himself, thinking, *Witch! She is a* bruja *after all.* Affecting not to notice, she went on, "Her sister is my washerwoman, and hath been known to gossip."

"Oh." Lope felt foolish. Cicely Sellis always had, or said she had, some natural means of gaining her knowledge. Maybe she wasn't a witch. Maybe, on the other hand, she just did a good job of covering her tracks. Who could know for certain? De Vega knew he didn't. Every time he thought he was sure, more confusion followed.

"Are you answered?" she asked.

"I am," he said, more or less truthfully. Rather more to the point, his ardor was cooled. He realized he would not lie with Cicely Sellis today. "Peradventure I had best get hence," he murmured, hoping against hope she would ask him to stay.

But she didn't. She only gave him a brisk nod. "That were best, methinks. I am ever glad to see you, Master de Vega, and to talk with you. You are a man of parts. Not all those parts, though, would I take into me."

Had a woman ever said anything bawdier in turning him down? Most women who let him into their beds never said anything bawdier. Jolted, he bowed, muttered, "God give you good day, then," and hurried out of her room.

He intended to hurry out of the lodging-house, too, but he almost ran over William Shakespeare on the way out. Both men exclaimed in surprise. Shakespeare said, "I had not looked to meet you here, Master Lope."

"Mistress Sellis is a friend, as you know," Lope said.

"Indeed," Shakespeare answered. The word seemed to hang in the air. What lay behind it? Jealousy? Had the English poet cast longing glances at Cicely Sellis, too? She'd given no sign of it. But what did that prove? He hadn't told her about his other lady friends, either—not that

that mattered, for she knew about them anyhow. An edge in his voice, Shakespeare asked, "And what passed betwixt you twain?"

Thinking to reassure him, de Vega answered, "We spoke of many things, yourself not least amongst 'em." If Shakespeare imagined the two of them talking, he wouldn't imagine them naked and entwined. They hadn't been, but imagination could prove more dangerous than fact, even in as normally unwarlike a man as Shakespeare.

But the Englishman remained pretty obviously unreassured. "How found my name its way into your mouths?" he asked, his voice harsh.

"Why, for your poesy—how else?" Lope said. "I told her how I envied her the chance to know your verses or ever anyone else may."

"That doth she not." Shakespeare's glower matched his tone. "None but mine own self hears even a line ere it go forth to Lord Westmorland's Men." He coughed, then spoke again with more self-control: "Thieves skulk everywhere, e'en as is. Is't not the same in Spain?"

"There you speak sooth," de Vega admitted, "and be damned to them." He made as if to step towards a stool in the parlor, to sit down and chat a while. Shakespeare shifted to put himself between Lope and the stool. Taking the hint, Lope left the lodging-house. *He is jealous of me, whether he'll admit it or not*, he thought sadly. *I hope it doesn't hurt our friendship*. But he didn't hope so enough to want to keep from seeing Cicely Sellis again.

THE GHOST IN *PRINCE OF DENMARK* WASN'T THE ONLY ONE SHAKESPEARE played. Crouched under the stage as the specter in Christopher Marlowe's *Cambyses King of Persia*, he peered out at the crowd through chinks and knotholes. Powdered chalk from his makeup and smoke that would rise with him through the trap door both tickled his nose; he hoped he wouldn't sneeze. The smoke made his eyes sting, too, but he couldn't rub them for fear of smearing the black greasepaint around them.

What *would* the groundlings do when—if—Lord Westmorland's Men put on *Boudicca*? He knew what Lord Burghley, Robert Cecil, and the other would-be rebels wanted the crowd to do on seeing a play about Britons oppressed by invaders from across the sea. Would the people give the plotters what they wanted? *An they give not, God give mercy to us all*, he thought gloomily.

He stiffened. There not ten feet away stood Lope de Vega, with Cicely Sellis beside him. She laughed at something the Spaniard said.

What were they talking about? Shakespeare turned his head and set his ear to the chink through which he'd been looking, but couldn't separate their talk from the rest of the noise. Finding Lope in his lodging-house had been a nasty surprise. If he'd still been working on *Boudicca* . . . He shuddered and shook, as if the sweating sickness had seized him.

Still shaking, he moved to another chink a few feet away. A moment later, he stiffened into immobility so thorough and profound, a glance from a cockatrice might have turned him to stone. There stood Marlowe. He remained clean-shaven and close-cropped, but he also remained himself. He wasn't very far from Lope; he wasn't very far at all. Would the don know him despite his altered seeming? If he shouted something like any groundling who'd poured down too much beer, would de Vega know his voice?

Shog off! Shakespeare thought at him, as urgently as he could. *Get hence! Aroint thee! Avaunt!* But Marlowe, of course, didn't move. He stood there as if no one had ever wanted to hang him for sodomizing boys. When a man with a tray of sausages pushed his way through the crowd, Marlowe bought from him and munched away like any tanner or stockfish-seller or dyer.

By then, Shakespeare wished he'd never started looking at the crowd in the first place. And so, when he spied Walter Strawberry a little to Marlowe's left, he didn't panic, as he might have otherwise. He'd already sunk down towards despair. The constable couldn't send him there, not when he'd got there on his own.

Performing in the play itself came as a great relief. While he trod the boards, he didn't have to—he couldn't—think about anything else. Hearing people gasp at his first appearance, hearing a woman up in the galleries let out half a shriek, assured him he still played a specter better than anyone else. He only wished he had more lines, the better to keep himself distracted.

Aye, I make me a passing fine ghost, he thought as he crouched under the stage again, awaiting his next scene. *Shall I make me a ghost in sooth ere this coil unravel to the fullest?* That seemed altogether too likely.

He came out on stage for his bows after *Cambyses King of Persia* ended, still in ghost makeup and turban. He saw de Vega applauding (and Cicely Sellis with him). He saw Marlowe applauding, too, which gave him an odd prick of pleasure. He even saw dour Walter Strawberry applauding. But the only thing that stuck in his mind was, *I go well acclaimed to my doom.*

Back in the tiring room, he accepted congratulations with half an ear. As it always did in a play with a ghost, the chore of getting off his unusually elaborate makeup gave him an excuse for not paying too much attention to people who came up to him. He could always soap and splash and scrub and say, "Gramercy," without really worrying about what they were trying to tell him. Today of all days, that suited him well. He wanted to escape from the Theatre—which was just how he thought of it—as fast as he could.

He said hello to Lope, and to the cunning woman on his arm. *Do they lie together?* he wondered. By the way they spoke and touched and looked at each other, he didn't think so, but they were both, in a way, players, and so likely better at dissembling than most. That made him wonder what else Lope might be concealing. Did the Spaniard know of *Boudicca*? Was he biding his time, waiting to scoop up all the plotters when the time was ripe?

There's a question I'd give much to ask. But Shakespeare had to dissemble, too. He had to dissemble, and to pray no one betrayed him before the day, whenever that day should come. And he had to pray the rising that would come on and after the day succeeded, for its failure likewise doomed him and all of Lord Westmorland's Men unless they could flee abroad ahead of Spanish—and English—vengeance.

He kept looking around the tiring room for Christopher Marlowe, especially after the company had given one of the other poet's plays. Kit had had the chance to flee abroad ahead of Spanish vengeance. He'd had it, and he hadn't taken it. *Zany*, Shakespeare thought. Marlowe did seem to have the sense to stay away from this chamber, where his disguise could not hope to hold up.

Shakespeare was about to slip out of the tiring room himself, out of the tiring room and out of the Theatre, when Walter Strawberry pushed his way towards him through the crowd. "Good day to you, Master Shakespeare," the constable boomed. "Good day."

"And the same to you, sir," Shakespeare answered.

"Your performance this day was ghastly, passing ghastly indeed," Strawberry said.

By his smile, that was evidently intended for praise. Shakespeare dipped his head in what he hoped would pass for modesty. "I thank you for your gracious kindness," he murmured. He didn't ask Strawberry what he wanted. If he didn't ask, maybe the constable would prove not to have wanted anything and leave him alone.

Forlorn hope. Strawberry planted his wide frame in front of Shakespeare and said, "Know you, in his last hours under this earth, Matt Quinn spake traitorously? It be so, a certain witness hath demurred to me."

"I knew this not, sir," Shakespeare lied, and did his best to spread confusion wherever he could: "But if he were a traitor, then belike he who slew him loved his country."

"Think you so, eh?" Constable Strawberry said. "Well, I have my suppositions on that. Ay, some suppositious coves yet run free, a murtherer's blood adrip from their fingers."

"Surely it were the blood of them that were murthered," Shakespeare said.

"The which is what I said, not so?"

"God forbid I should quarrel with your honor."

"God forbid it? God forbid it indeed! For I tell you, sir, them as quarrel with me have cause to beget it afterwards," the constable declared.

"I doubt not you speak sooth," Shakespeare said soberly.

"Mark it well, then," the constable said, "for the day of beckoning draws nigh."

"I shall keep your words ever within my mind." Shakespeare hesitated, then asked, "What sort of treason spake this Matthew Quinn?"

"Vile, unlawful treason: most vile. Know you another sort?"

"Might you make yourself more clear, more plain?"

"Why, sir, I aim to be as clear as the nose on my face, as plain as a peacock," Strawberry said. "And so I shall exculpate more upon this matter. The said Quinn did speak insultingly on the King of Spain, dislikening him to a common bawd."

"A bawd?" Shakespeare said, frowning.

Walter Strawberry nodded. "The very same, sir: a bawd which hath two debauched daughters. An this be not treason, what name shall you give it?"

Shakespeare didn't answer right away; he was trying to make the pieces fit together. And then, with sudden, frightening ease, he did. Whoever had given Strawberry the story must have misheard *bawd* for *Boudicca*, substituting a familiar word for the unfamiliar name. And the Queen of the Iceni had had two daughters the Romans had ravished. A good thing whatever witness the constable—and the Spaniards?—had found seemed to know nothing of Roman history, or he would have given a clearer picture of Matt Quinn's folly. From the report that had come back to the Theatre through Will Kemp, Quinn had said far more than Walter Strawberry knew.

"Be this not treason?" Strawberry repeated. "If it be not treason, what name would you give it? Would you call it plum pudding?"

"Treason indeed. I'd not deny it," Shakespeare said. "Haply his end came at the hand of some bold soul whose overflowing choler would not suffer him to hear good King Philip reviled so." Again, he did his best to lead the constable away from the true trail.

And, again, he did not get so far as he would have wanted. Constable Strawberry said, "This Ingram Frizer I have aforementioned is villain enough and to spare for murther and felonious absconding with his periwig both. By my halidom, I do believe him to be the perpetuator against Matthew Quinn."

Since Shakespeare believed the same thing, he had to tread with the greatest of care. He said, "Your honor will know better than I, for I have not met the gentleman you name."

"No gentry cove he, but a high lawyer and rakehell," Strawberry said. Once more, Shakespeare agreed. Once more, he dared not let Strawberry see as much. The constable went on, "Curious you twain should hold friends in common. Passing curious, I call it. How say you?"

"I say Nick Skeres is no friend of mine. I have said the same again and again. Will you not heed me, sir?" Shakespeare showed a little anger. Were he honest, he thought he would have done so. And it helped hide his fear.

Before Constable Strawberry could answer, another man came up to Shakespeare: an older man, jowly and leaning on a stick. Strawberry bowed to him. "Give you good day, Sir Edmund."

"And you, Constable," Sir Edmund Tilney answered. "Give me leave to speak to Master Shakespeare here, if you please."

"Certes, certes. Shall I gainsay the Master of the Revilements?" Walter Strawberry bowed again and withdrew.

Shakespeare too made a leg at Sir Edmund. "Good morrow, sir. What would you?"

The Master of the Revels looked around to make sure Strawberry was out of earshot before murmuring, "That man will trip to death on's own tongue."

"Nothing in his life'd become him like the leaving of it," Shakespeare said.

"He is an annoyance, but surely not so bad as that," Tilney said.

"His vexatiousness knows no bounds." With a sigh, Shakespeare added, "But it will be what it is, an I rail at it or no. I ask again, sir: how may I serve you?"

"In the matter o'er which I come hither, I am *your* servant, Master Shakespeare," the Master of the Revels replied. "I speak of your *King Philip*."

"Ah. Say on, sir. Whatsoe'er the play in your view wants, I shall supply. Direct me, that I may have the changes done in good time, his Most Catholic Majesty failing by the day." Shakespeare crossed himself.

So did Sir Edmund. His awkward motion told how full of years he'd been before the success of the Armada brought Catholicism and its rituals back to England. He said, "No need for change here, not by the standards of mine office. By the standards of dramaturgy . . . The purpose of playing was and is to hold, as 'twere, the glass up to nature. Methinks you have held it here most exceeding well."

"For the which you have my most sincerest thanks." Shakespeare meant every word of that. If all went as Robert Cecil hoped, *King Philip* would never be staged. Even so, the poet had worked as hard and as honestly on it as on *Boudicca*. He had no small pride in what he'd achieved. That the Master of the Revels—a man who'd likely seen the scripts for more plays than anyone else alive—should recognize its quality filled him with no small pride.

"You have earned your praises," Tilney said now. Shakespeare bowed. The Master returned the gesture. Then he asked, "Wherefore doth Master Strawberry make inquiry of you?"

"He is Sir Oracle, and, when he opes his lips, let no dog bark!" Shakespeare said sourly. Sir Edmund chuckled. But Shakespeare realized his answer would not do. Tilney could ask the constable himself. Better to lull him than to let Strawberry fan his suspicion to flame. The poet went on, "He seeks him who murthered Geoffrey Martin and Matt Quinn."

"He cannot believe you are the man?" Tilney said.

"No, sir, for which I thank God. But, quotha, the man he suspects and I both are known to the same man. From this I seem to lie under reflected suspicion, so to speak."

"Whom have you in common?" the Master of the Revels asked.

Shakespeare wished he would have picked a different question. "One Nicholas Skeres, sir," he said, again knowing Walter Strawberry could give the answer if he didn't.

"Nick Skeres?" Tilney said. Shakespeare nodded. " 'Sblood, I've known Nick Skeres these past ten years, near enough," Sir Edmund told him. "A friend of Marlowe's, Nick Skeres is. I'd not dice with him, I'll say that: he hath no small skill in the cheating law, and he'd not stick at sliding high men or low men or fullams into the game to gull a cousin. But a murtherer? I find that hard to credit, and I'd say as much to the constable's face."

"Gramercy, if you'd be so kind," Shakespeare said. He too thought Skeres would use dice with only high numbers or only low ones or weighted dice whenever he thought he could get away with it. "Master Strawberry's importunings do leave me distracted from seeing *King Philip* forward. Could you ease them . . ."

"I hope I may," the Master of the Revels said. "Zeal without sense is like a mast without stays—the man having the one without the other will soon fall into misfortune. Ay, Master Shakespeare, I'll bespeak Strawberry for you."

"For the which many thanks, sir. I'd be most disgraceful to you on account of't," Shakespeare said, deadpan.

Sir Edmund Tilney started to nod and turn away. Then he heard what Shakespeare had really said. After one of the better double takes the poet had seen, Sir Edmund guffawed. "You are a most dangerous vile wicked fellow," he said, "and you know your quarry as a cony-catcher knows his cony."

"Why, whatever can you mean?" Shakespeare said. This time, they both laughed. Tilney clapped him on the shoulder and went off to chat with Thomas Vincent. By the way the prompter smiled and nodded, Sir Edmund was also telling him Lord Westmorland's Men could legitimately perform *King Philip*.

Shakespeare peered into a looking-glass. He muttered under his breath—he'd missed some greasepaint below one eye, so he looked as if he had a shiner. He scrubbed at the makeup with a rough cloth, then examined himself again. This time, he nodded in satisfaction.

The sun hung low in the west when he left the Theatre. The equinox had come the day before. Soon, all too soon, days would dwindle down to the brief hours of late autumn and winter. A chill breeze that smelled of rain made him glad of his thick wool doublet.

He hadn't gone far towards London before he saw Marlowe perched on a boulder by the side of Shoreditch High Street. The other poet, plainly, was waiting for him. "Begone, you carrion crow, you croaker, you slovenly unhandsome corse," Shakespeare said.

"Your servant, sir." Marlowe descended from the rock and made a leg at him. "You *can* play the ghost: I deny it not. Henceforth, I'll hear in your voice dead Darius' words."

"I may play the ghost, but, do you not get hence, you'll have the role in good earnest," Shakespeare answered. "Robert Cecil knows you are returned to London. An his men find you, you are sped." He didn't tell Marlowe he was the one who'd given Cecil that news.

"Wherefore should he seek to jugulate me?" Marlowe asked.

"Play not the innocent with me, thou false virgin," Shakespeare said, wondering whether Marlowe were virgin anywhere upon his person. "You know o'ermuch of . . . this and that." He named no names, not with other people walking in Shoreditch High Street. "You know o'ermuch, and your tongue flaps like drying linen i'the wind. Cause aplenty to see you silent—is't not so?"

"Like drying linen i'the wind? Thou most lying slave!"

"Nay." Shakespeare shook his head. "By God, Kit, hear me: I tell you the truth." He clicked his tongue between his teeth in annoyance. He'd automatically come out with a line of blank verse, and not a very good one.

Marlowe noticed the same thing. "And ten low words oft creep in one dull line," he jeered—more blank verse, with a nasty barb.

"Mock an you would. Mock—but go. Stay and you die the death, if not from the likes of Ingram Frizer, then from the dons. What Cecil knows, belike they'll learn anon. Can you tell me I am mistook?"

They walked along, arguing. "I can tell you I'm fain to stay to see the hand played out," Marlowe said stubbornly.

"When first you learned the Spaniards dogged you, you nigh wet yourself for fear of 'em," Shakespeare said. "Then you were wise. This you show forth now, 'tis but a madman's courage. 'Steeth, did you not see you all but trod on de Vega's toes, there amongst the groundlings?"

"I saw him, ay, with yet another trull," Marlowe said, scorn in his voice. "What of it? He knew me not."

First the Widow Kendall had doubted Cicely Sellis' chastity. Now Marlowe did the same. Shakespeare hadn't argued with his landlady. He saw little point to correcting Kit, either. Instead, he tried once more to make the other poet see sense: "You are no player here. Being none, lie low, lest you bring yourself to the notice of them who'd lay you low. An you would—an you must—see how the hand plays out, but suffer it not to be played upon your person."

"The counsel of a craven," Marlowe said. "I looked for better from you, Will."

"You will throw your life away, you mad-headed ape. 'Tis pikestaff plain you care not a fig therefor: well, be it so. But in your lunacy will you throw old England away with it?"

"What's old England to me or I to old England, that I should weep for her?" Marlowe seemed genuinely curious.

"Say you so?" Shakespeare clapped a hand to his forehead. "You brought me to this game, marble-pated fiend, and now it likes you not? Fie on you!"

Marlowe laughed. "As though I were a Latin verb, you misconstrue me. For the game I care greatly; 'tis the game lured me back from Margate. I *will* see it played. An I may, I will play it. Ay, the game's the thing. But for England?" He snapped his fingers. "That for old England." With a nod, he ducked into the doorway of a tenement and disappeared.

Shakespeare started to go after him, then stopped, muttering a curse. What good would it do? None. Less than none, probably. Shakespeare didn't believe Marlowe despised his country, as he said he did. He was all pose, all outrageousness, all shock. But force him to it and he might decide he had to act on his pose. Better to leave him alone and hope he came to his senses on his own.

Better he had not left them, Shakespeare thought, but then, *Use every man after his desert, and who should 'scape whipping?* That cheery notion uppermost in his mind, he trudged on down towards Bishopsgate.

ENRIQUE STRETCHED OUT AN IMPLORING HAND TO LOPE DE VEGA. "Senior Lieutenant, you must let me know when you are to play Juan de Idiáquez on the English stage," Baltasar Guzmán's man said. "I will come to see you, though I still know less of the language than I should."

"I'll be glad to see you," de Vega said. "I fear it won't be long."

"I fear the same. Every ship from Spain brings worse word of his Most Catholic Majesty." Enrique crossed himself.

So did Lope. For all he knew, King Philip might already have died. Strange to think he would be in his grave back in Spain while here in England, till news of his death arrived, he still ruled. *A play could make something of those twists of time and knowledge*, Lope thought. He wondered how he might shape it.

"God protect the new King when his day comes," Enrique said.

Lope nodded. "Yes. God protect him indeed."

He and Enrique shared a glance. They both knew Philip III was not half, was not a quarter, of the man Philip II had been. Neither of them could say such a thing, but saying and knowing were far from the same. Lope feared for Spain in the reign of Philip II's son. He couldn't say that, either. He could pray. He'd done a lot of praying lately.

Or he could try to put his worries out of his mind. He bowed to Enrique almost as respectfully as he would have to Captain Guzmán, then said, "*Hasta luego*. I'm off to Bishopsgate."

Enrique smiled. "Good luck with your new lady friend, Senior Lieutenant."

What a pity she is only a friend, Lope thought, and then, *Well, if God is on my side, I may yet make her more.* To Enrique, he said only, "Thank you very much," and hurried out of the barracks in the heart of London.

But his little chat with Captain Guzmán's servant delayed him just enough so that, as he was coming out, he nearly bumped into Walter Strawberry, who was coming in. He couldn't escape the man, no matter how much he wanted to. With such grace as he could muster, he smiled and said, "Give you good day, Constable Strawberry."

"God give you good morrow as well, Lieutenant," Strawberry replied. "I have heard a thing passing strange, strange as any I have seen, the which, methought, I should bring to your honor's orifice."

"Say on," de Vega urged, hoping the Englishman would come to the point—if he had a point—and let him get on his way up to see Cicely Sellis.

In his own fashion, Walter Strawberry did: "Dame Tumor hath it, sir, that Christopher Marlowe, otherwise styling himself one Karl Tuesday, is returned to London and making himself unbeknownst hereabouts."

Lope stared. That *was* news—if true. "How know you this? Have you seen him?"

"As I told you, not with mine own ears," the constable answered. "But I have much attestation thereto, from certain of them that share his advice."

"His advice?" De Vega frowned, wondering what Strawberry was trying to say. Suddenly, a light dawned. "Mean you—?"

"I mean what I say, and not a word of it," Strawberry declared. "He hath the advice of Gomorrah, wherefrom is he also tumorously said to suffer from the malediction which hight gomorrhea, or peradventure from the French pox."

That held enough tangles to hide a swarm of foxes from the hounds, but Lope ruthlessly cut through them: "You have it from catamites and sodomites that Marlowe is returned to London?" He didn't know whether Marlowe was diseased, nor much care. That wasn't his worry, not now.

And Walter Strawberry nodded. "Said I not so?"

"One never knows," Lope murmured. He clapped the English constable on the shoulder. "You have done me a service to bring this word hither. Believe you me, sir, if Marlowe be in this city, we shall run him to earth. And now, I pray you, forgive, for I must away." He pushed past Strawberry and out into St. Swithin's Lane.

"But—" Strawberry called after him. He heard no more, for he was hurrying up the street, on his way to Bishopsgate at last. His rapier slapped against his thigh at every step.

His thoughts whirled. How could Marlowe have come back to London when he'd gone to sea? Why *would* he have come back? Knowing Marlowe fairly well, Lope made his own guess about that. Something was stirring, and the Englishman wanted to see it, whatever it was. Marlowe could no more stay away from trouble than bees from flowering clover. *What sort of trouble?* de Vega wondered. One thing immediately sprang to mind: treason.

This means more questions for Shakespeare, Lope thought unhappily. *If I find him at the lodging-house, I'll ask them now.*

But the old woman who ran the place shook her head when he asked if Shakespeare was there. "Surely you must know, sir, he is gone up to the Theatre, for to earn the bite wherewith his rent—*my* rent—to pay," she said nervously.

Lope thought about going up to Shoreditch straightaway, but decided it would keep. He had no proof Shakespeare knew anything of Marlowe's return. For that matter, he had no proof Marlowe *had* returned. De Vega hoped Walter Strawberry was wrong, both for Marlowe's sake and because that would mean less trouble lay ahead.

When he knocked on Cicely Sellis' door, she opened it at once. But when she saw him standing there, she started a little, or more than a little. "Oh. Master Lope. I looked for . . . another."

"For Christopher Marlowe?" de Vega rapped out, suddenly suspicious of everyone around him.

But the cunning woman shook her head. "I know him not," she said. If she was acting, she proved how fond and foolish England's ban on actresses was. "Why are you come here?"

"To speak with thee," Lope said, seizing the opportunity.

Her mouth narrowed in exasperation. "Come you in, then," she said, "but only for a moment, mind." Though she must have heard him use the intimate pronoun, she didn't follow suit.

As soon as Lope stepped inside, he realized she'd been waiting for a client. Astrological symbols were scrawled on the wall in charcoal, a circle inscribed on the rammed-earth floor. Tall candles burned to either side of the circle. Within it, Mommet scratched behind one ear to rout out a flea, then yawned at the Spaniard, showing needle teeth. It was de Vega's turn to say, "Oh," as light dawned, and then, "You'd tell a fortune." He dropped *thou* himself.

"Ay, and for a good price, too, of the which stand I in need," Cicely Sellis said. "Say what you would and then, I pray you, away. The bird comes anon."

And you don't want a Spaniard about to frighten him off, whoever he is, de Vega thought. *Well, fair enough*. Better trusting her intentions, he sighed dramatically and tried again: "I'd speak to thee of love."

Her smile showed more annoyance than amusement. "I tell you, sir, I've no time for't now. Speak me fair another day, an't please you, and who knows? Haply I will hear you."

"Haply?" he said, less than delighted at the hedge.

But Cicely Sellis nodded. "Haply," she repeated, her voice firm. "Would you have me promise more than I may give?"

"By my troth, I'd kiss *thee* with a most constant heart," Lope said.

She looked harassed. The cat, eerily reflecting her mood as it often did, bared its teeth again. After a moment, though, she said, "A bargain: one kiss, and then you go? If there be more between us, let it wait its proper occasion, which this is not."

"One kiss, then, lady, and I am hence," Lope promised. She nodded once more, and stepped forward. He took her in his arms. Having but the one chance, he made the most of it, clasping her to him so their bodies molded to each other. Her mouth was sweet and knowing against his.

The kiss went on and on. At last, though, it had to end. Lope's arms still around her, Cicely Sellis stroked his cheek. But she said only one word: "Farewell."

"*Aii*, thou'lt tear out my heart like the savage men of New Spain!" Lope cried. She only waited. He thought about the risks of breaking a bargain with a *bruja*—thought about them and found them formidable. Though his lips still glowed from the touch of hers, he bowed stiffly. "Farewell," he echoed, and, spinning on his heel, strode out of her room and out of the lodging-house.

Storming away, he almost ran into—almost ran over—another man heading for the Widow Kendall's house: a broad-shouldered fellow with a smooth face and with hair cut short. Lope took a step past the man, then froze, remembering what Walter Strawberry had told him. "Marlowe!" he said, and his sword seemed to leap from its sheath into his hand.

Christopher Marlowe whirled. He too wore a rapier. It flashed free. "The fig of Spain!" he shouted. His obscene gesture matched the words.

"Put up!" Lope said. "Put up and give over. You're caught. Even an you beat me, you're known to be in London. How can you hope to win free? Yield you now."

"I will not." Marlowe sighed and shook his head. "Base fortune, now I see, that in thy wheel there is a point, to which when men aspire they tumble headlong down." He seemed to speak more to himself than to de Vega. "That point I touched, and seeing there was no point to mount up higher, why should I grieve at my declining fall?" With no more warning than that, he thrust at Lope's heart.

Lope beat the blade aside. His hand had more to do with his answering stroke than did his brain, though perhaps he remembered his fight with Don Alejandro de Recalde. His point took Marlowe not in the right eye but above it. The English poet let out a shriek that faded almost at once to a rattling gurgle. He fell down in the street, dead as a stone.

A big, rough-looking blond man wearing a disreputable cap smiled at Lope, showing a couple of missing teeth. "Gramercy, your honor," he said, and touched the brim of that cap. "You just saved me a bit o' work, that you did." Before the Spaniard could ask him what he meant, he hurried away.

Another man said, "I shall fetch a constable hither." He too hurried off.

"Yes, do, and yarely," Lope called after him. "An you come on a Spanish patrol, fetch them likewise." He looked down at his rapier. The last couple of inches of the blade had blood on them, blood and Christopher

Marlowe's brains. He stabbed the sword into the ground to clean it, as he had after slaying Don Alejandro.

Lope was still waiting by Marlowe's body for the constable and for his own countrymen when bells began to chime, first at one church far away, then at another and another and another, till after no more than a minute or two the bronzen clangor filled all the streets of London. "What signifies that?" someone asked. Someone else shrugged. But Lope knew what it meant, what it had to mean, and ice and fire ran through him.

His Most Catholic Majesty, King Philip II of Spain, after so long dying, at last was dead. And Lope de Vega, standing there bare blade in hand, burst into tears like a little boy.

A DAPPER LITTLE GAMECOCK OF AN OFFICER RAPPED OUT A QUESTION in Spanish. Shakespeare looked to Lope de Vega, who translated it into English: "Captain Guzmán would know why Christopher Marlowe was bound for your lodging when we chanced each upon the other. I own, I too am fain to know the same."

"As am I," Shakespeare said. If his voice trembled, who could blame him? The dons had come for him at dawn, as he was about to leave the Widow Kendall's for the Theatre, and marched him here to their barracks instead. If they misliked the answers he gave them, he was assuredly a dead man—nor was he all that would die. He went on, "Methought Kit was fled abroad."

Had anybody who could recognize Marlowe seen him and Shakespeare together? If someone gave him the lie . . . He refused to dwell on that. If someone gave him the lie there, the Spaniards wouldn't merely question him. They would put him to the question, an altogether different and more painful business.

But all de Vega said was, "Plainly not."

You fool's zany, you stood close by him at Cambyses *and knew him not*, Shakespeare thought. Captain Guzmán flung more Spanish at him. Again, Lope de Vega did the honors: "He asks, how is't Constable Strawberry knew Marlowe was returned to London whilst you remained deep-sunk in ignorance?"

Damn Constable Strawberry. But Shakespeare knew he had to have a better answer than that. He said, "Belike the constable will have ears 'mongst the masculine whores of's bailiwick. Knowing Kit's pleasures, they'd learn he was in these parts or ever the generality heard it."

De Vega spoke in excited Spanish to his superior. Captain Guzmán's reply sounded anything but convinced. Lope spoke again, even more passionately. Guzmán answered with a shrug.

To Shakespeare, de Vega said, " 'Twas even so Strawberry got wind of't—thus he told me when I inquired of him."

"Well, then." Shakespeare dared risk indignation. "This being so, wherefore tax you me o'er that which I wist not of?"

After de Vega rendered that into his own language, Baltasar Guzmán growled something that sounded angry. "Thus saith my captain," Lope replied: "You standing on the edge of so many swamps of treason, how do your feet stay dry?"

"I am no traitor," Shakespeare said, as he had to. "Were I such a caitiff rogue, could I have writ *King Philip*?"

Once more, Lope translated his words into Spanish. Once more, he did not presume to answer himself, but waited for his superior to respond. Captain Guzmán spoke a curt sentence in Spanish. "That is what we seek to learn—if the worm of treason still begnaw your soul," was how de Vega put it in English.

" 'Still,' is't?" Shakespeare knew he was fighting for his life, and could concede his foes nothing. "My duty to your captain, Master Lope, and say this most precisely: by this word he assumes me treacherous, and proves himself no honest judge. He must forthwith retract it, as slanderous to my honor."

And how would Captain Guzmán respond to that? By letting him defend his honor with a sword? If so, he was a dead man. He had no skill at swordplay, whereas a Spanish officer was all too likely to be a deadly man of his hands. Lope de Vega had certainly shown himself to be such a man, at any rate.

But Guzmán nodded and then bowed low. He spoke in Spanish. "You have reason, quotha," Lope said. "Naught against you is proved, nor should he have spake as if it were. He cries your pardon therefor." Shakespeare bowed in return; he hadn't expected even so much. The Spaniard spoke again, this time harshly. "Naught against you is proved, saith he, but much suspected. We will have answers from you."

"I have given all I can," Shakespeare said, "and so shall I do. Ask what you would."

They pounded him with questions about Marlowe, about Nick Skeres, about Ingram Frizer, and about the late Sir William Cecil. They had most of the pieces to the puzzle, but did not know how—or even if—they fit together. Shakespeare told them as little as he could. He admitted having heard Marlowe and Nicholas Skeres knew each other. That wouldn't hurt Marlowe now, and Skeres remained safely out of the dons' hands.

When Shakespeare said he was thirsty, they gave him strong sack to drink. He wished he'd kept his mouth shut; the wine was liable to make him trip over his own tongue and fall to his doom. But he could not refuse it, not after he'd complained. He sipped carefully, never taking too much.

After some endless while, someone knocked on the door to Captain Guzmán's office. Guzmán snarled a Spanish curse. He pointed to the door. Lope de Vega opened it. In came a skinny, pockmarked Englishman wearing spectacles: Thomas Phelippes.

Shakespeare didn't know whether to rejoice or to despair. The Spaniards had not said a word about Phelippes, for good or ill. Did that mean the dusty little man had succeeded in covering his tracks? Or did it mean Phelippes was their man, a spy at the very heart of the plot?

Whatever he was, he spoke in Spanish far too quick and fluent to give Shakespeare any hope of following it. Before long, Baltasar Guzmán answered him sharply. Phelippes overrode the officer. Shakespeare caught the name of Don Diego Flores de Valdés, the Spanish commandant in England. He caught the name, yes, but nothing that went with it. Captain Guzmán spoke again. Once again, Thomas Phelippes talked him down. Guzmán looked as if he'd bitten into a lemon.

At last, Lope de Vega returned to English: "Don Diego being satisfied you are a true and trusty man, Master Shakespeare, you are at liberty to get hence, and to return to your enterprises theatrical. After *King Philip* be put before the general . . . then we may delve further into such questions as remain."

"Gramercy." Shakespeare could honestly show relief here. "And gramercy to you as well, Master Phelippes."

"Thank me not." Phelippes' voice came blizzard-cold. " 'Tis my principal's mercy upon you, not mine own. Don Diego hath a good and easy spirit. Mine is less yielding, and I do wonder at his wisdom, obey though I must. Get hence, as saith Master Lope, and thank God you have leave to go."

"By my halidom and hope of salvation, sir, I *do* thank Him." Shakespeare crossed himself. "For God shall be my hope, my stay, my guide and lantern to my feet." He crossed himself.

Phelippes and de Vega also made the sign of the cross. So did Captain Guzmán, when Phelippes translated Shakespeare's words. Then Guzmán made a brusque gesture: *get out*. The poet had never been so glad as to obey.

Outside the barracks, the day was dark and cloudy, with occasional cold, nasty spatters of drizzle. To Shakespeare, it seemed as glorious as the brightest, warmest, sunniest June. He'd never expected to see freedom again. A Spanish soldier—a fierce little man who wore his scars like badges of honor—coming into the building growled something at him, probably, *Get out of the way*. Shakespeare sprang to one side. The soldier tramped past him without a backwards glance.

Shakespeare hurried off towards the Theatre. "What is't o' clock?" he called to somebody coming the other way.

"Why, just struck one," the man answered.

Nodding his thanks, Shakespeare trotted on. The audience was filing into the wooden building in Shoreditch when he got there. One of the men at the cash box tried to take a penny from him. "Nay, 'tis Master Shakespeare," another man said. "Where were you, Master Shakespeare? You are much missed."

"Where? In durance vile," Shakespeare replied. "But I am free, and ready—more than ready—to give my lines with a good heart."

A cheer rose from the players when he rushed into the tiring room. Richard Burbage bowed as low as if he were a duke. Will Kemp sidled up to him and said, "We feared you'd ta'en sick o' the tisick that claimed Geoff Martin and Matt Quinn."

"Tisick?" the poet exclaimed. "You style it so?"

"Certes," Kemp said innocently. "A surfeit of iron in the gullet, was't not?"

"Away, away." That was Jack Hungerford. Even Kemp took the tireman seriously. He slouched off. Hungerford said, "Out of your clothes, Master Will, and into costume, for the apparel oft proclaims the man."

"Have I time for the change?" Shakespeare asked, for he would appear in the second scene of Thomas Dekker's comedy.

"You have, sir, an you use it 'stead of talking back," Hungerford said severely. Without another word, Shakespeare donned the silk and scarlet the tireman gave him.

Not the smallest miracle of the day, at least to him, was that he did remember his lines. He even got laughs for some of them. When he came back on stage to take his bows after the play was done, he felt as dizzy as if he'd spent too long dancing round a maypole: too much had happened too fast that day.

Afterwards, as he exchanged the gorgeous costume for his ordinary clothes, Burbage came up to him and said, "We did fear you'd found misfortune—or misfortune had found you. Why so late?"

"De Vega yesterday slew Marlowe outside my lodging-house," Shakespeare answered wearily. "A man need not see far into a millstone to wonder why Kit was come thither. The dons this morning gave me an escort of soldiery to their barracks, that they might enquire into what matters he carried in's mind."

"Marry!" Burbage muttered. His proud, fleshy face went pale. "And you said?"

"Why, that I knew not, the which is only truth." Whose ears besides Richard Burbage's were listening? Shakespeare let them hear nothing different from what he'd told de Vega and Guzmán. He added, "By my troth, I knew not that poor Marlowe was returned to London."

"Nor I," Burbage agreed. He too played for other ears—Shakespeare had told him Marlowe was back. Liars both, they smiled at each other.

When Shakespeare got back to his lodging-house after the performance, the Widow Kendall gave him an even warmer welcome than his fellow players had. "Oh, Master Will, I thought you sped!" she cried. "An the dons seize a man, but seldom returneth he."

"I am here. I am hale." Shakespeare bowed, as if to prove he'd undergone no crippling torture. " 'Twas but a misfortunate misunderstanding."

"Misunderstanding, forsooth!" Jane Kendall exclaimed. "A misunderstanding like to prove your death." She poked him with a pudgy forefinger. "And all centering on the accursed sodomite, that Marlowe, the which Mistress Sellis' Spaniard did slay in the street like a cur-dog this day just past."

Before Shakespeare could answer, the door to Cicely Sellis' room opened. Out came the cunning woman, with a plump, worried-looking Englishman. Mommet wove around her ankles. "Fear not, sir, and trust God," she told her client. "He will provide."

"May it be so, my lady," he said, as if she were a noblewoman. Bobbing a nod to Shakespeare and the Widow Kendall, he hurried out into the gathering gloom.

After he'd closed the door behind him, Cicely Sellis said, "Lieutenant de Vega is not my Spaniard, Mistress Kendall. And, though he'd fain make me his Englishwoman, I am not that, neither."

Jane Kendall signed herself. "By my halidom, Mistress Sellis, I—I meant no harm," she stammered. " 'Twas but a—a manner of speaking." She brightened. "Yes, that's it—a manner of speaking."

"Ay, belike." The cunning woman's words said she accepted that. Her tone said something else altogether. But then, as her cat went over to Shakespeare and rubbed against his leg, she gave him a smile full of what he thought to be unfeigned gladness. "Like Mistress Kendall, right pleased am I to see you here, to see you well, once more."

"I do own I am right pleased once more to come hither," Shakespeare answered. He wondered how Cicely Sellis could have known what he and their landlady were talking about. She had, after all, been behind a closed door. Were her ears as keen as that? Shakespeare supposed it was—just—possible. He stooped to scratch the corner of Mommet's jaw. The cat pushed its head into his hand and purred louder.

"Have a care," Cicely Sellis said. "The game is not played out." She sounded almost oracular, as she had that one time in the parlor when she didn't recall what she'd said after saying it.

"I am but a player and somewhat of a poet," Shakespeare said. "I'd not play at subtle games." He wondered if she'd remark on the difference between *would* and *will*. Instead, and to his relief, she only nodded.

He ducked into his bedchamber, got his writing tools and the new play—his own play!—he was working on, and went off to the ordinary for supper. "Will!" Kate cried when he came through the door. "Dear-beloved Will!" The serving woman threw herself into his arms and kissed him.

"Did I know it roused such affections in thee, I'd have the Spaniards seize me every day," Shakespeare said. That made a couple of men who were already eating chuckle. It made Kate pretend to box his ears.

After he'd supped, after he'd written, after the last of the other customers had left the ordinary, she took him up to her cramped little room. They both made love with something like desperation. "Oh, fond Will, what's to become of thee?" she said. "What's to become of us?"

Wanting to give her some soothing lie, he found he couldn't. "I know not," he said. After a moment, he added, "Ere long, though, I shall. We shall." *One way or another*, he thought, but did not say that. He caressed her instead.

"I fear for thee," she whispered.

"I fear for me," he answered. "But I needs must go on; this road hath no turning, the which I could not use e'en an it had."

"What mean'st thou?" Kate asked.

"I will not tell thee, lest I harm thee in the telling. Soon enough, thou'lt know." Shakespeare got up and quickly dressed. As he opened the door to go, he added another handful of words: "Come what may, remember me." He closed the door behind him.

When he got back to the lodging-house, he put a couple of chunks of wood on the fire to fight the night chill. The Widow Kendall had gone to bed, and couldn't scold him. From the room where Shakespeare would eventually sleep, Jack Street's snores reverberated. The poet waited till the fresh wood was burning brightly, then sat down in front of the fire and got to work.

He wasn't unduly surprised to hear a door open a few minutes later, or to see Cicely Sellis—and Mommet—come out into the parlor. "Give you good even," he said, nodding to the cunning woman.

"Good den to you," she answered, and sat on a stool while the cat prowled the room. "Do I disturb you?"

"By your being, now and again. By your being *here*"—Shakespeare gave her a wry smile and shook his head—"nay. I am enough bemoiled in toils and coils to . . ." His voice trailed away. He'd already said as much as he could say—probably too much.

Cicely Sellis gave him a grave nod, as if she knew exactly what he was talking about. Perhaps she did, for she said, "The matter of the dons, and of Master Marlowe cut down like a dog in the street." It did not sound like a question.

Shakespeare eyed her. How much had she heard from Lope de Vega? Whatever she'd heard, what did she think about it? He desperately needed to know, and dared not ask. Instead, he sat silent, waiting to hear what she said next.

Her shrug was small and sad. "You misdoubt me. So many on small acquaintance gladly entrust me with their all, yet you misdoubt me. Alack the heavy day."

"I may do only as I do," Shakespeare answered. "Did I say more—" Now he broke off sharply, shaking his head. That was too much, too.

"Peradventure you are wiser than the many," the cunning woman said. And yet, from her expression, she'd found out most of what she wanted to know. Shakespeare wondered how much his stumbles and sudden silences had told her. She went on, "Think what you will, I mean you no harm, nor England, neither." Before he could find any sort of answer to that, she clucked to Mommet. The cat came like a well-trained dog. With a murmured, "Good night," she went back into her room.

Shakespeare got very little work done after that.

When he walked into the Theatre the next morning, he found Lieutenant de Vega already there, in earnest conversation with Richard Burbage. Burbage was bowing and nodding. Seeing Shakespeare, de Vega bowed, too. "Be there proclamation made throughout the city," he said, "that Lord Westmorland's Men shall offer *King Philip* on Tuesday of the week following this now present, the thirteenth day of October, marking a month to the day of his Most Catholic Majesty's departure from this life for a better place." The Spaniard crossed himself; Shakespeare and Burbage made haste to imitate him. He went on, "So saith Don Diego Flores de Valdés, commander of our Spanish soldiers in England. Shall all be in readiness for the said performance?"

"Ay, Master Lope, so long as you show forth Juan de Idiáquez as he should be seen," Shakespeare answered.

"I already told you ay, Master de Vega," Burbage said heavily. "That being so, you need not seek the scribbler's assurances besides mine own."

As head of the company, he was, of course, quite right. All the same, the bold way he said it might have offended Shakespeare. Not today. His heart pounded. At last, the date was set. Without a word, he bowed to Burbage and to Lope de Vega.

For his life, Shakespeare could not have said which play Lord Westmorland's Men put on that afternoon, though he had a role in it. He came back to himself on his way home from the Theatre, when a little hunchbacked beggar, filthy and clad in rags, came up to him and whined, "Alms, gentle sir? God's mercy upon you for your grace to a poor, hungry man."

Instead of walking past him or sending him on his way with a curse, Shakespeare stopped and stared. Where he had not known the visage, he recognized the voice: there before him, ingeniously disguised, stood Robert Cecil. Lord Burghley's son grinned—grinned a little maniacally, in fact—at the look on Shakespeare's face. Gathering himself, the poet whispered, "What would you, sir?"

"Why a penny, of your kindness," Robert Cecil said, and Shakespeare *did* give him a coin. Under cover of capering with delight, Cecil went on, also in a low voice, "You shall not give *King Philip* come Tuesday next, but your *Boudicca*. If all follow well from that and other matters now in train, England her liberty shall regain. Till the day, be of good cheer and dread naught."

Off he went, begging from others in Shoreditch High Street. Shakespeare walked on towards the Widow Kendall's, and his dread grew with every step he took.

SEEING THE BRIGHT SUN THAT SHONE DOWN ON LONDON ON THE appointed day, Lope de Vega couldn't have been more delighted. When his servant came into his inner chamber, he beamed sunnily himself. "What a grand day, Diego! It might be spring, not autumn," he said. "The heavens do all they can to make *King Philip* well received."

"*Sí, señor.*" Diego sounded altogether indifferent. "That English constable, that Strawberry, is waiting outside. He wants to talk with you about something."

"Today? Now? Oh, for the love of God!" Lope felt like tearing his hair. "I have no time to deal with him. I need to go to the Theatre to rehearse. What can he want?"

Diego shrugged. "I don't know. I don't speak English."

"By all the saints, neither does he!" Lope calmed himself. "I can't escape him, I see. Bring him in. I'll deal with him as fast as I can."

Walter Strawberry's solid bulk seemed to fill the little chamber to overflowing. "God give you good morrow, sir," he rumbled.

"And to you as well, Constable," de Vega answered. "What's toward? Be quick, if you can; I must away to the Theatre anon."

"Ay, sir. Quick I am, and quick I'll be. And, being quick, I'll tell you somewhat or ever I die."

Whenever Lope listened to Strawberry, he felt himself going round in dizzying circles. Keeping a tight grip on his patience, he nodded. "Say on."

"Know you, sir, that Master Shakespeare hath ta'en to talking to buggers in the street?"

"Buggers?" De Vega scratched his head. "Surely you are mistook, Christopher Marlowe being dead."

The constable looked as bewildered as Lope felt. "Marlowe? Who said aught of Marlowe? I speak of buggers with palms for alms outstretched, amongst the which is a little dancing crookbacked wight who bears a passing verisimilitude unto Master Robert Cecil."

Cecil's was perhaps the only name that could have gained Lope's complete and immediate attention. "Say you so?" he murmured, leaning towards Strawberry. "Say you so indeed? Be you certain of this?"

"I am." Walter Strawberry nodded. "It hath been witnessed by witnesses thereto, and likewise by those who have seen the same. An it be not the same Robert Cecil, he hath a twin unrecked, though himself but the wreck of a man."

"Have you any other evidence past this which your witnesses, er, witnessed?" Lope asked. "Shakespeare denies all treasonous associations, and assuredly in the favor of Don Diego Flores de Valdés stands high. With reason, he having writ a splendid, yes, a most splendid, play on the life of his late Most Catholic Majesty, in which I shall have the honor of performing later this day. All this being so, you see, I am not fain to seize him without strongest proofs of's guilt."

"What I have, sir, I have given you," Constable Strawberry said. " 'Tis my bounding duty, and I have bounded hither for to do it."

"Damnation," de Vega muttered. Strawberry had brought him just enough to alarm him, but not enough to let him act, especially not after Shakespeare had wriggled free of trouble after Christopher Marlowe's return to London. Lope stroked his little chin beard as he thought. Suddenly, he pointed at the constable. "Have you searched his lodging? If he have done treason, he will have done't with his pen. Why else engage a poet, a maker of plays, in the enterprise? Have you, then?"

"Not having a warrant?" Strawberry seemed genuinely shocked. "No, sir, I have not. That were beyond my bounds altogether, and beyond the bounds of any honest Englishman."

"A plague take all bounds, you—you bounder!" Lope burst out. He stabbed a thumb at his own chest. "*I* am no Englishman, for which I thank God. If I desire to search, I may search. I may—and, by the Blessed Virgin, I shall." Secure in the power the occupiers held, he had no doubt of that whatever.

Neither did Constable Strawberry. "You will do as you shall do. I have not the right nor the writ." He turned to go. "Adieu; be vigitant, I beseech you."

Vigitant or not, Lope hurried up to Shakespeare's lodging-house. The hour was still early enough to leave him content with the world and the way it shaped. *What do I do if I find proof here?* he asked himself. The answer seemed clear enough. *I play in* King Philip, *then arrange for Shakespeare's arrest.* He sighed. Arresting the poet after he'd written such a play seemed a pity, but what choice was there? None de Vega could see.

He hoped Shakespeare was already off to the Theatre. He would have a fight on his hands if he tried to search while the Englishman was still there. He touched the hilt of his sword. He didn't want a reputation for killing playwrights, but he would take that reputation if he had to.

When he got to the lodging-house, he found Cicely Sellis in the parlor saying farewell to an early client. The man showered her with blessings as he left. The cunning woman dropped de Vega a curtsy. "God give you good day, Master Lope," she said. "Why are you come here at such an hour?"

"In search of treason against his Most Catholic Majesty, the King of Spain," Lope said harshly. Mommet had sprawled by the hearth. At Lope's tone, the cat sprang to its feet, its fur on end, its tail puffed out like a bottle brush. He ignored it, asking, "Is Master Shakespeare here, or is he gone up to the Theatre?"

"Why, he is more than an hour gone," Cicely Sellis answered. She cocked her head to one side and gave Lope a slow, half sad smile. Catalina Ibañez would have laid down her life to own a smile like that; it left the Spaniard weak in the knees. The cunning woman added, "And here I hoped thou wert come to see me."

"Truly?" Lope said. Cicely Sellis didn't even nod. Just by standing there, she let him know it was and could be nothing but the truth. His pulse thudded. Whatever he did now, no one would take anything of Shakespeare's from this place while he did it. He had the time. He was sure he had the time. He made a low leg at her. "My lady, I stand ever at thy service." And he *did* stand, too, or part of him did.

"Come, then," she said, and went back into her room, Mommet trotting at her heels. Lope followed, eager as a green boy his first time. He closed and barred the door behind him.

As at his last visit, fat candles lit the closed room almost as bright as day. Mommet curled up in a corner, yawned once, and went to sleep. Cicely Sellis sat down on the bed. When Lope would have joined her there, she smiled again and, saying, "Anon, anon," waved him once more to the stool in front of it.

More than a bit sulkily, he perched there. "Thou'dst not tease, I trust?" he said. The intimate pronoun was sweet in his mouth.

"Marry, no," she replied. "And yet never would a woman be ta'en for granted thus."

De Vega was no green boy. Much experience told him she spoke the truth. He dipped his head to her. "As thou'dst have it, so shall it be, though I needs must say in delay there lies no plenty."

"Prithee, bear with me," she said. "We that are lovers run into strange capers."

Before he could answer, she reached up and drew something out from under her dress: that sparkling glass pendant he'd seen once before, dangling on the end of its long chain. She swung it back and forth, back and forth. Lope thought it might have been a nervous habit, for she hardly seemed to know she was doing it. The pendant caught the candlelight and drew his eye to it as it swung. He looked away now and again, but his gaze kept coming back.

"Nay, a woman mislikes ever being hurried, ever being rushed, ever being told to give, and give forthwith." For all that her words might have shown annoyance, Cicely Sellis spoke in a soft, calm, smooth voice. "Is't not sweeter when freely offered, when tendered with full heart, with glad heart, with heart brimful of love, than when rudely seized ere the time be ripe, ere she be fully ready, ere she would do that which, in the fullness of time, she assuredly *will* do?"

"Assuredly," Lope echoed, his voice abstracted. He'd only half noted her words. His eyes kept following that sparkling pendant, back and forth, back and forth. After a little while, he wasn't sure he could have taken them away from it. But he didn't want to, so what difference did that make?

The cunning woman talked on, as smoothly and quietly as before. De Vega could not have told what she said; he noted her voice mostly as soothing background to the endless motion of the pendant. Back and forth, back and forth . . . Watching it, he felt almost as if he were falling asleep.

Before too very long, she asked, "Dear Lope, hearest thou me?"

"Ay." The sound of his own voice left him dully surprised; it might have come from far, far away.

"Hearken well, then, for I speak truth," she said. He nodded; in that moment, he could not possibly have doubted it. Even as he nodded, his eyes swung back and forth, back and. . . . She went on, "Master Shakespeare hath done no treason. Hearest thou me?"

"I hear. Master Shakespeare hath done no treason." When she said it, when he affirmed it, it might have been carved in stone inside his mind.

"He hath no papers treasonous here: hence, no need to search. Hearest thou me, dear Lope?"

"No papers treasonous. No need to search." When she said it, when *he* said it, it was *so*. Holy Scripture could have been no truer for him.

"Nor hast thou need to seek him this day in the Theatre, for all will be well there," the cunning woman murmured.

"Idiáquez . . ." Lope began. Idiáquez glimmered in the glitter of glass and was gone. "No need to seek. All will be well."

"All will be well," Cicely Sellis repeated. She led him through her catechism twice more. Then, as she stopped swinging the pendant and tucked it back into place, she said, "In token thou hast heard me well, when I bring my hands together thou'lt blow yon candle"—she pointed—"and then become again thine own accustomed self. Hearest thou me?"

"Ay, blow out that candle," Lope said. Cicely Sellis clapped her hands. He blinked and laughed, feeling as refreshed as if he'd just got out of bed after a good night's sleep. Then, laughing still, he sprang off the stool and blew out one of the candles by the head of the bed.

"Why didst thou so?" she asked.

"Its light shone in mine eyes," he answered. One quick step brought him to her. "And now, my sweet, my love, my life—" He took her in his arms.

She laughed, down deep in her throat. "Thine own accustomed self," she said, and it seemed to Lope for a heartbeat that he'd heard those words before. But then his lips came down on hers, and hers rose up to his, and he cared not a fig for anything he might have heard.

XIII

"WHERE'S DE VEGA?" "WHERE'S THE POXY SPANIARD?" "Where's the don?" Inside the Theatre, the questions tore at Shakespeare, again and again.

"I know not. Before God, I know not!" Trying to escape them, he fled from the stage back into the tiring room.

Richard Burbage pursued him, relentless as fate personified. "See you not, Will, we needs must *know*?" Burbage said. "Had he come hither, we'd have seized and bound him, knocked him over the head, and gone forward with good heart. But *where is he?* Will he burst in the instant we are begun, soldiers at his back, crying, 'Hold! What foul treason is this?' *Will* he, Will?"

"I know not," Shakespeare said again. Desperate for the escape he knew he could not have, he perched on a stool and hid his face in his hands. He pressed the fleshy bases of his thumbs against his closed eyes till swirling flashes and sparkles of color lit the blackness that he saw.

Better he should have covered his ears, for Burbage persisted: "Were we not wiser, were we not safer, to give *King Philip* and not . . . the other play?" Even now, he would not name it. "We still can, and right well you know it."

"Dick, I know naught—naught, hear you?" Shakespeare wanted to scream it. Instead it came out as not much more than a whisper. "There is no wisdom in me, only a most plentiful lack of wit. And I say further, e'en with Lope seized and bound, I should not have gone forward with good heart, for sure safety lurks nowhere in this tangled coil."

Burbage grunted as if taking a blow in the belly. Shakespeare wondered why. As far as he could tell, he'd spoken simple truth, the only truth he knew. Voice a pain-filled groan, the player asked, "What to do, then, Will? What are we to do?"

Reluctantly, Shakespeare lowered his hands and looked up at him. "An you must think on somewhat, think on this: when they hang you for a traitor, would you liefer hang as traitor to the King of Spain or 'gainst old England?"

"I'd liefer *not* hang," Burbage said.

Shakespeare laughed bitterly. "Too late, for already your complexion is most perfect gallows—as is mine own."

Burbage glared at him. "Damn you."

"Ay." Shakespeare nodded. "And so?"

"Come then, cullion." Burbage reached out and, with frightening effortless strength, hauled him off the stool and to his feet. The player let him go then, but he followed Burbage back onto the stage. "Hear me, friends," Burbage boomed, and his big voice filled the Theatre. From all over the building, heads turned his way. "Hear me," he said again. "We give *Boudicca*—and God help us every one."

He had better, Shakespeare thought.

Will Kemp gave Burbage a mocking bow. "Thou speakest well, as always. And how the hangman and the worms do love thee."

With a shrug, Burbage answered, "Be it so, then. Had I ordered *King Philip* shown this day, you might have said the same."

"Would you not sooner hang for an Englishman?" Shakespeare added, his spirits beginning to revive now that the die was cast.

By way of reply, Kemp tugged at his codpiece. " 'Tis better far to be well hung than well hanged."

"Go to!" Shakespeare exclaimed as the company erupted in bawdy laughter. After that, the players went about their business with better hearts. Shakespeare had no doubt they still knew fear—he certainly did himself—but they seemed more able to put it aside. In a quiet moment, he made a leg at Will Kemp. The clown grabbed his crotch again.

Groundlings began strolling into the open space surrounding the stage on three sides. Some of them waved to the players, others to friends they recognized or to vendors already selling sausages and wine and roasted chestnuts. Folk more richly dressed took their places on benches in the galleries. More vendors circulated there.

A gentleman in silk and velvet and lace, his snowy ruff enormous and elaborately pleated, passed through the growing crowd of groundlings to call to Richard Burbage: "How now? I'm told you sell no places at the side of the stage?"

Bowing, Burbage nodded. "I cry your pardon, sir, but you're told true. The spectacle we shall offer needs must be fully seen by all. Those places interfering with the view of the general, we dispense with 'em today. They shall again be sold come the morrow."

The gentleman still looked unhappy, but Burbage's answer left him nothing upon which to seize. He turned and went back towards the galleries. Burbage and Shakespeare exchanged a look. The player's answer had been polite, plausible, and false. The real reason the company was selling no seats on the stage was to keep aristocrats of Spanish sentiment from drawing their swords and attacking the actors when *Boudicca* went on in place of *King Philip*—which the signboards outside the Theatre still announced.

Shakespeare spied plenty of aristocrats in the galleries. Some few he knew to be of Spanish sentiment. About others, who could say? But even those Englishmen who served the dons most heartily might do it for the sake of their own advantage rather than conviction. If they saw the wind blowing in a new direction, might they not shift with it? *They might*, the poet thought. That had a corollary he wished he could ignore: they might not, too.

Burbage waved the last few players out on stage strutting before the groundlings or chatting with them back into the tiring room. Shakespeare could smell the sharp stink of fright rising from many of them. No doubt it rose from him as well. Burbage said, "Be of good cheers, lads. Speak the speech, I pray you, as you have learnt it; let it come trippingly off the tongue. And as you play, bear one thought ever in your minds: if all go well this day, we are made men forevermore. Not one of us will lack for aught the rest of the days of his life."

He wanted the company to see the wind blowing in a new direction, too. By the way the players nodded, they did. But then Will Kemp stirred. Shakespeare could guess what he was going to say—if all went not so well, the rest of the days of their lives would be few, and filled with pain. Shakespeare caught the clown's eye and shook his head. *Not now*, he mouthed. Kemp laughed and stuck out his tongue, but he kept quiet.

Somewhere in the distance, hardly audible through the buzz of the crowd in the Theatre, a church bell chimed the hour: two o'clock. Richard Burbage pointed to Shakespeare. "Will, you'll give the prologue?"

No! So much of Shakespeare wanted to scream it. But he couldn't, not now. He wondered what part of courage was no more than the urge not to look ridiculous in front of one's friends. No small part, if he was any judge. He licked dry lips and nodded. "I will."

"Go, then, and God go with you," Burbage said.

Something like quiet fell in the Theatre as Shakespeare slowly strode out towards the center of the stage. He had never felt so alone. He wished one of the trap doors through which ghosts appeared would open and swallow him up. But no. He was here. What could he do but go on?

He stood still for a moment, letting all eyes find him. Then, into that near-quiet, he said,

"His Most Catholic Majesty is dead;
Meet that we here gather to mark his end.
I come to praise Philip. His tomb's afar
But his strong hand lies on us even yet.
As I'm but a scribbler, this play's the thing
Wherewith to note the nature of the King.
Imagine this stage Britain, long ago;
Here comes Boudicca, to seek her vengeance
'Gainst the Romans, who harshly, cruelly whipp'd
The Queen of the Iceni and ravish'd
Both her young defenseless virgin daughters.
Beginning with this struggle, starting thence away
To what may be digested in a play.
Like or find fault; do as your pleasures are:
Now win or lose, 'tis but the chance of war."

Shakespeare withdrew to mostly puzzled silence punctuated by spatters of applause—no, his prologue didn't match what the signboards outside promised. As he withdrew, he saw three or four men, both from among the groundlings and in the galleries, rapidly starting thence away. No doubt they were off to Sir Edmund Tilney: of course the Master of the Revels had spies here to make sure the play presented matched the one advertised and approved.

But those spies wouldn't reach Sir Edmund, not this afternoon. Shakespeare devoutly hoped they wouldn't, anyhow. Jack Hungerford's helpers, the men who took the audience's money, and a double handful of ruffians hired for the day were charged with letting no one leave the Theatre till the play was done. By then, it would be too late.

For the dons, Shakespeare wondered, *or for us?* Before he could fret any more, out went a wordlessly chanting Druid, the boy actors playing Boudicca and her daughters, and Richard Burbage, sword on his hip, as Caratach. For better or worse, it was begun; no stopping now, not till the end.

"Ye mighty gods of Britain, hear our prayers;
Hear us, you great revengers; and this day
Take pity from our swords, doubt from our valours,"

said Joe Boardman, who played Boudicca. He wasn't quite so good as Tom would have been, but he wasn't a Catholic, either. Excitement added life to his voice as he went on,

"Double the sad remembrance of our wrongs
In every breast; the vengeance due to Rome
Make infinite and endless! On our pikes
This day pale Terror sits, horrors and ruins
On our executions; claps of thunder
Hang upon our arm'd carts; and 'fore our troops
Despair and Death; Shame past these attend 'em!
Rise from the earth, ye relics of the dead,
Whose noble deeds our holy Druids sing;
Oh, rise, ye valiant bones! let not base earth
Oppress your honours, whilst the pride of Rome
Treads on your stock, and wipes out all your stories!"

With a great waving of arms, the hired man playing the Druid responded,

"Thou great Taranis, whom we sacred priests,
Armed with dreadful thunder, place on high
Above the rest of the immortal gods,
Send thy consuming fire and deadly bolts,
And shoot 'em home; stick in each Roman heart
A fear fit for confusion; blast their spirits,
Dwell in 'em to destruction; through their phalanx
Strike, as thou strik'st a tree; shake their bodies,
Make their strengths totter, and topless fortunes
Unroot, and reel to ruin!"

Epona, Boudicca's elder daughter, took up the cry of condemnation against the Roman occupiers:

"O, thou god
Thou fear'd god, if ever to thy justice
Insulting wrongs and ravishments of women
(Women sprung from thee), their shame, the sufferings
Of those that daily fill'd thy sacrifice
With virgin incense, have access, hear me!
Now snatch thy thunder up, 'gainst these Romans,
Despisers of thy power, of us defacers,
Revenge thyself; take to thy killing anger,
To make thy great work full, thy justice done,
An utter rooting from this blessed isle
Of what Rome is or has been!"

The first murmurs rose from the crowd as people began to realize what sort of praise for King Philip this was likely to be. Boudicca's younger daughter, Bonvica, continued in the same vein, saying,

"See, Heaven,
O, see thy showers stol'n from thee; our dishonours—
O, sister, our dishonours!—can ye be gods,
And these sins smother'd?"

An attendant lit a fire on the altar before which the Druid stood. Boudicca said, "It takes: a good omen."

As Caratach, Richard Burbage took a step forward and drew his sword to pull everyone's eye to himself. His great voice would have done the same when he declared,

> "Hear how I salute our dear British gods.
> Divine Audate, thou who hold'st the reins
> Of furious battle and disordered war,
> And proudly roll'st thy swarty chariot wheels
> Over the heaps of wounds and carcasses
> Give us this day good hearts, good enemies,
> Good blows o' both sides, wounds that fear or flight
> Can claim no share in; steel us with angers
> And warlike struggles fit for thy viewing.
> A wound is nothing, be it ne'er so deep;
> Blood is the god of war's rich livery.
> So let Rome put on her best strength, and Britain,
> Thy little Britain, but great in fortune,
> Meet her as strong as she, as proud, as daring!
> This day the Roman gains no more ground here,
> But what his body lies in."

"Now I am confident," Boudicca said. They exited to the wailing of recorders.

But for that music, vast silence filled the Theatre as the players left the stage. Into that silence, someone from the upper gallery yelled, "Treason! Treason most foul! You—!" A scuffle broke out. With a wild cry, someone fell out of that gallery, to land with a thud amongst the groundlings. No one cried treason any more.

"Play on!" someone else shouted from that same gallery. "By God and St. George, play on!" A great burst of applause rang out. Awe prickled through Shakespeare. *They do remember they are Englishmen*, he thought.

On came the Romans for the second scene of the first act. When the audience took in their half Spanish helms and corselets, even the innocents and dullards who'd missed the point of the play up till then suddenly grasped it. And when one of those Romans said,

> "And with our sun-bright armour, as we march,
> We'll chase the stars from heaven, and dim their eyes
> That stand and muse at our admired arms,"

the hisses and catcalls that rose from all sides told just how admired Spanish arms were.

Back in the tiring room, Burbage said, "It doth take hold."

"Ay, belike." Shakespeare dared a cautious nod.

"It doth take hold *here*," Burbage amended. "What of the city beyond the Theatre?" Shakespeare could only shrug, hoping Robert Cecil and his confederates had planned that as well as this. Burbage had no chance to stay and question him further; he was on again in the next scene.

As it had in real life more than fifteen hundred years before, the great rebellion of the Iceni against tyrannical Roman rule built on the stage. A legionary officer cried on in despair,

"The hills are wooded with their partizans,
And all the valleys overgrown with darts,
As moors are with rank rushes; no ground left us
To charge upon, no room to strike. Say fortune
And our endeavours bring us into 'em,
They are so infinite, so ever-springing,
We shall be kill'd with killing; of desperate women,
Neither fear nor shame e'er found, the devil
Hath ranked 'mongst 'em multitudes; say men fail,
They'll poison us with their petticoats; say they fail,
They have priests enough to pray us to nothing.
Here destruction takes us, takes us beaten,
In wants and mutinies, ourselves but handfuls,
And to ourselves our own fears paint our doom—
A sudden and desperate execution:
How to save, is loss; wisdom, dangerous."

Swords, pikes, and halberds clashed against one another. Led by Burbage/Caratach, player-Britons chased player-Romans from the stage. How the crowd roared!

And Boudicca cried out, too, in exultation:

"The hardy Romans—O, ye gods, of Britain!—
Rust of arms, the blushing shame of soldiers!
These, men that conquer by inheritance?
The fortune-makers? these the Julians,

> That with the sun measure the end of nature,
> Making the world one Rome, one Caesar?
> How they flee! Caesar's soft soul dwells in 'em;
> Their bodies sweat sweet oils, love's allurements,
> Not lusty arms. Dare they send these 'gainst us,
> These Roman girls? Is Britain so wanton?
> Twice we've beat 'em, Caratach, scattered 'em;
> Made themes for songs of shame; and a woman,
> A woman beat 'em, coz, a weak woman,
> A woman beat these Romans!"

Before Richard Burbage could deliver Caratach's answering line, someone said, not too loudly, one word: "Elizabeth!" The name raced through the Theatre. Excitement raced with it, as if the mere mention of that name, for ten years all but forbidden, could remind everyone of what England had been before the Spaniards came—and what she might be again. Shakespeare nodded to himself. He'd hoped for that. To see what he'd hoped come true . . . What writer could ask for more?

And Burbage, as Caratach, let Elizabeth's name echo and reecho before saying,

> "So it seems.
> A man, a warrior, would shame to talk so."

Boudicca asked,

> "My valiant cousin, is it foul to say,
> What liberty and honour bid us do,
> And what the gods let us?"

"No, Boudicca." Caratach shook his head.

> "So what we say exceed not what we do.
> You call the Romans fearful, fleeing wights,
> And Roman girls, the lees of tainted pleasures:
> Doth this become a doer? are they such?"

"They are no more," Boudicca said. "Do you dote upon 'em?" Caratach shook his head again.

> "I love a foe; I was born a soldier;
> And he that in the head on's troop defies me,
> Bending my manly body with his sword,
> I make a mistress. Yellow-tress'd Hymen
> Ne'er tied a longing virgin with more joy,
> Than I am married to the man that wounds me:
> And are not all these Romans? Ten battles
> I suck'd these pale scars from, and all Roman;
> Ten years of cold nights and heavy marches
> (When frozen storms sang through my iron cuirass
> And made it doubtful whether that or I
> Were more stubborn metal) have I wrought through,
> And all to try these Romans."

Boudicca wouldn't listen to him, of course. There lay the tragedy: in her overreaching herself, in thinking she could drive the mighty Roman Empire from Britain's shores. *And do we likewise overreach ourselves with the Spaniards?* Shakespeare wondered. He shivered. *An we do, we die harder than ever the British Queen dreamt of dying.*

The play went on. The Romans, hard pressed by the Iceni, went through agonies of hunger. Will Kemp's Marcus did a clown's turn to make light of it. He said,

> "All my cohort
> Are now in love; ne'er think of meat, nor talk
> Of what provender is: hearty *heigh-hoes*
> Are sallets fit for soldiers. Live by meat!
> By larding up our bodies? 'Tis lewd, lazy,
> And shows us merely mortal. It drives us
> To fight, like camels, with bags at our noses."

He capered comically before resuming,

> "We've fall'n in love: we can whore well enough,
> That the world knows: fast us into famine,
> Yet we can crawl, like crabs, to our wenches.
> Fall in love now, as we see example,
> And follow it but with all our salt thoughts,
> There's much bread saved, and our hunger's ended."

Hands to his own large belly, he left the stage.

Shakespeare hurried up to him. "Well played!"

"How not?" Kemp said. "Belike, when I'm up on the gibbet, the hangman'll give me the selfsame praise. May you stand beside me to hear't."

"An you go to the gallows, am I like to be elsewhere?" Shakespeare asked.

"An *you* go to the gallows, I should like to be elsewhere," the clown replied.

Poenius, the officer who would not send his legionaries to help Suetonius, cried out in despair as the Britons advanced against his fellow Romans:

> "See that huge battle coming from the hills!
> Their gilt coats shine like dragons' scales, their march
> Like a tumbling storm; see them, and view 'em,
> And then see Rome no more. Say they fail, look,
> Look where the arm'd carts stand, a new army!
> Death rides in triumph, Drusus, destruction
> Whips his fiery horse, and round about him
> His many thousand ways to let out souls.
> Huge claps of thunder plow the ground before 'em;
> Till the end, I'll dream what mighty Rome was."

Still more combat crowded the stage. Now, instead of Iceni routing Romans, the Romans, reviving, routed in their turn the Britons. The groundlings—yes, and the galleries, too—wailed in dismay as Boudicca and her daughters and Caratach mured themselves up in a last fortress to stand remorseless, relentless Roman siege. Poenius fell on his sword for shame.

In the fort, Boudicca raged against the soldiers who had failed her, shrieking,

> "Shame! Wherefore flew ye, unlucky Britons?
> Will ye creep into your mothers' wombs again?
> Hares, fearful doves in your angers! Fail me?
> Leave your Queen desolate? Her hopeless girls
> To Roman rape and rage once more? Cowards!
> Shame treads upon your heels! All is lost! Hark,
> Hark how the cursed Romans ring our knells!"

From the balcony above the tiring room, which did duty for the battlements of the fort, Epona spoke to the Roman general, Suetonius:

> "Hear me, mark me well, and look upon me
> Directly in my face, my woman's face,
> Whose sole beauty is the hate it bears you;
> See if one fear, one shadow of terror,
> One paleness dare appear apart from rage,
> To lay hold on your mercy. No, you fool,
> Damned fool, we were not born for your triumph,
> To follow your gay sports, and fill your slaves
> With hoots and acclamations. You shall see—
> In spite of all your eagles' wings, we'll work
> A pitch above you; and from our height we'll stoop,
> Fearless of your bloody talons."

She cast herself down to death. When Shakespeare heard groans, when he heard women weep—yes, and some men, too—he knew that, regardless of what happened outside the Theatre, he'd done all he could in here.

Meanwhile, among the Romans who besieged the Britons' stronghold, Will Kemp's Marcus declared,

> "Love no more great ladies, is what I say;
> No going wrong then, for they hold no sport.
> All's in the rustling of their snatch'd-up silks;
> They're made but for handsome view, not handling,
> Their bodies of so weak and soft a temper
> A rough-pac'd bed'll shake 'em all to pieces;
> No, give me a thing I may crush."

He illustrated, with great lascivious gestures. The crowd, which had mourned the death of poor ravished Epona, now laughed lewdly at a soldier relishing more rape.

But, a moment later, the groundlings cheered when Caratach and a last host of Iceni sallied. Caratach cut down Marcus—and Richard Burbage likely enjoyed killing Kemp, if only in the play. After that victory, Caratach said,

"My hope got through fire, through stubborn breaches,
Through battles that were hard to win as heaven,
Through Death himself in all his horrid trims,
Is gone forever, ever, now, my friends.
I'll not be left to scornful tales and laughter."

He threw himself at the Romans surrounding Suetonius and died fighting.

Inside the fortress of the Iceni, hope died, too. As the Romans below besieged them, Boudicca and Bonvica stood on the battlement where Epona had killed herself. Bonvica asked, "Where must we go when we are dead?"

"Strange question!" Boudicca told her younger daughter.

"Why, to the blessed place, dear! Eversweetness
And happiness dwells there."

"Will you come to me?"

"Yes, my sweet girl," Boudicca answered.

"No Romans? I should be loath to meet them there."

"No ill men," Boudicca promised,

"'That live by violence and strong oppression,
Are there; 'tis for those the gods love, good men."

"Dearest mother, then let us make an end," Bonvica said. "Have you that dram from the kindly Druid?"

They drank poison together. Bonvica died at once. Boudicca, who'd let her daughter have the greater share to be sure of death, lasted till the Romans, led by Suetonius, burst into the fortress and up onto the battlement. "You fool," she told the general.

"You should have tied up death when you conquer'd;
You sweat for me in vain else: see him here!
He's mine, and my friend; laughs at your pities.
And I will be a prophet ere I die.
Look forward now, a thousand years and more.
A royal infant,—heaven shall move about her!—
Though in her cradle, yet doth promise
Upon this land a thousand thousand blessings,

Which time shall bring to ripeness. She shall be—
Though none now living will behold that goodness—
A pattern to all princes living with her,
And all that shall succeed: Sheba was never
More covetous of wisdom and fair virtue
Than this pure soul shall be: all princely graces
With all the virtues that attend the good,
Shall still be doubled on her; truth shall nurse her.
She shall be lov'd and fear'd. Her own shall bless her;
Her foes shake like a field of beaten corn.
In her days every man shall eat in safety;
Her honour and the greatness of her name
Shall grow, and make new nations. She shall flourish
In all the plains about her. Our children's children
Shall see this, and bless heaven."

"Thou speakest wonders," Suetonius said, awe in his voice.

"She will be your true and natural Queen,
Bred, born, and brought up amongst you. So will
You most naturally, like British men,
Defend her, fight for her, and not only
Guard her with danger of your lives, but also
Aid her with your hands and livings. You will
Fight for your country, your dearest country,
Wherein you shall be nourished. It will be
Your native soil, and therefore most sweet, for
What may be more belov'd than your country?"

Dying Boudicca managed a feeble nod, and sent her last words out to a breathlessly silent Theatre:

"E'en so; 'Tis true. Oh!—I feel the poison!
We Britons never did, nor never shall,
Lie at the proud foot of a conqueror,
But when we do first help to wound ourselves.
Come the three corners of the world in arms,
And we shall shock them. Naught shall make us rue,
If Britons to themselves do rest but true."

She fell back and lay dead.

Shakespeare strode forward, to the very front edge of the stage. Into more silence, punctuated only by sobs, he said,

"No epilogue here, unless you make it;
If you want your freedom, go and take it."

He stood there, waiting, for perhaps half a dozen heartbeats. This was even harder than when he'd spoken the prologue. If he'd failed here . . . Suddenly, without warning, silence shattered—not into applause, but into a great roar of rage at all that England had endured in the ten years since the Spaniards came and forced Isabella and Albert onto the English throne. Had Shakespeare been the foreign Queen or King, that roar would have made him tremble.

Being who he was, he stared out in wonder at the audience. Everything they'd held in for these ten long years now loosed itself at once. Crying, "Spaniards' dogs!" and other things, far worse, the groundlings turned on a handful of their own number known to like the invaders too well. Up in the galleries, several real fights broke out—more of the upper classes, those who could afford such places, favored the Spaniards and Isabella and Albert.

More struggling men, and a couple of shrilly shrieking women, too, fell or were flung down amongst the groundlings. Their hurtling bodies sent the folk below sprawling, and must have badly hurt some. The groundlings punched and pummeled and kicked—and, no doubt, robbed—the richer folk who'd, literally, fallen into their hands. They assumed anyone who was cast down loved the dons. Shakespeare wondered if they were right.

In the middle gallery, the fanciest in the Theatre, an aristocrat in a fine doublet of glowing white silk made his voice rise above the din: "To the Tower! To the Tower, to free the Queen!" He was a handsome man a few years younger than Shakespeare, with dark hair, a sandy beard scanty on the cheeks but long on the chin and cut square at the bottom, and red, red lips. "To the Tower, and I will lead you!" As if on cue, a sunbeam gleamed from the rapier he brandished.

"To the Tower! To the Tower! To free the Queen!" One man with firm purpose was plenty to fire all the others. When the aristocrat descended, the groundlings swarmed up to him and raised him on their shoulders.

"Who's yon gentry cove?" Shakespeare asked the players on the stage behind him. They'd come out to take their bows, but the crowd, full of a greater passion, had all but forgotten them.

"Why, know you not Sir Robert Devereux?" Richard Burbage sounded surprised. Shakespeare only shrugged. He'd never worried much about recognizing aristocrats by sight. He left that to Burbage, a socially more ambitious man—indeed, a climber if ever there was one.

And then Edward the tireman's assistant, now a budding actor who still wore his "Roman" helmet and corselet, raised his sword as Devereux had done. "To the Tower!" he cried. "To the Tower, to free the Queen!" He ran past Shakespeare, jumped down off the stage, and joined the roaring throng pouring out of the Theatre.

Eight or ten young players, some who'd portrayed Romans and others Iceni, followed him, allies now against the Spaniards. "To the Tower!" they shouted, one after another. The youth who'd played Epona threw down his wig and rushed after them, still in a woman's shift.

And then, to Shakespeare's amazement and dismay, Burbage and Will Kemp tramped forward together, both of them plainly intent on marching on the Tower of London, too. Shakespeare seized Burbage's arm. "Hold, Dick!" he said urgently. "Let not this wild madness infect *your* wit. Can a swarm of rude mechanicals pull down those gray stone walls? The soldiers on 'em'll work a fearful slaughter. Throw not your life away."

Before Burbage could answer, Will Kemp did: "The soldiery on the walls *may* work a fearful slaughter, ay, an they have the stomach for't. But think you 'twill be so? A plot that stretcheth to the Theatre surely shall not fall short of the Tower."

Shakespeare pondered that. Of course, William Cecil's plans—Robert Cecil's now—went far beyond this production of *Boudicca*. The poet had seen that from the beginning. He'd seen it, but he hadn't seen all of what it meant. Here Kemp certainly saw more than he had.

Burbage added, "Having come so far, Will, would you not watch what your words have wrought?"

"Thus spake Kit Marlowe of's return to London," Shakespeare said, "and much joy he had of't." But Burbage and Kemp both jumped down onto the hard-packed dirt where the groundlings stood. Once more, Shakespeare discovered the desire not to seem a coward to his friends could push him forward where fear of death would have held him back.

Cursing under his breath, damning himself for a suicide and a fool, he sprang down, too.

Another stage-Roman landed beside him and offered him a knife, saying, "I can well spare it, for I have me also this fine long sword."

"My thanks," Shakespeare said. What good the dagger would do against the arquebuses and cannon of the garrison in the Tower, he couldn't imagine. Having it somehow gave comfort even so.

Only one narrow doorway led into and out of the Theatre, the better to keep cheats from sneaking in without paying. The crowd took some little while to filter out through it. Shakespeare wondered whether the delay would stifle spirits. But no; shouts of, "To the Tower!" and, "To free the Queen!" and, "God bless good Queen Bess!" doubled and redoubled.

When at last Shakespeare escaped the building, he saw several thick columns of black smoke rising from different parts of London. Through the din and gabble around him, the distant crackle of arquebuses and pistols going off and the deeper, slower boom of cannon fire came to his ears. The city was already rising against the occupiers.

"Said I not so?" Will Kemp bawled in his ear.

"You did. And you had the right of it." Shakespeare gave credit where it was due, admitting what he could hardly deny.

Roaring down towards Bishopsgate, the crowd from the Theatre cried Elizabeth's name again and again, ever louder, ever more fiercely. They called down curses on the heads of Philip II, Philip III, and every Spaniard ever born. They cursed Isabella and Albert, too. And, every now and again, one of them would bawl out a line or two from *Boudicca*. Pride flowered in Shakespeare's breast. *I am father to this*, he thought: *not the sole father, but father nonetheless.*

They hadn't come far into the rickety clutter of tenements and shops and dives of Bishopsgate Ward Without the Wall when a constable—not Walter Strawberry, but a younger, thinner man with a red-blond beard—stepped into the middle of the street, held up a hand, and shouted, "Stand, there! Stand, I say! What means this unseemly brabble?"

They showed him. Someone at the head of the baying pack stooped, picked up a stone, and flung it. It caught the constable in the face. Shakespeare, taller than most, saw blood spurt as the constable's nose smashed to ruin. With a moan, the man clutched at himself and sank to his knees. The pack rolled over him, punching, kicking, stomping, stabbing.

By the time Shakespeare went past, the constable was hardly more than a red smear trampled into the stinking muck. The poet's stomach lurched. He stumbled on, fighting not to spew up his guts. *And I am father to that*, he told himself, wishing he could find a sweet, soothing lie instead: *not the sole father, but father nonetheless.*

People stared from windows and doorways. Even here, murder was seldom done so openly. Even here, curses were seldom cried so loud, or from so many throats at once. And if anything could draw shopkeepers and laborers, robbers and thieves, barmaids and trulls, open murder and loud curses seemed the proper lodestones. The crowd swelled, as if by magic.

Every step closer to Bishopsgate raised more alarm in Shakespeare. The Spaniards and wild Irishmen standing guard at the gate would not let themselves be taken unawares, as the luckless constable had done. (Had he a wife? Children? He'd come home to them no more.) If they had time, they would close the gates against this storm. Even if they didn't, they'd surely stand and fight.

Daylight was fading, the sun sinking down through smoke towards Westminster. More than enough light remained, though, to show that Bishopsgate stood open. Cheers rose from countless throats, cheers and a renewed cry: "To the Tower! On to the Tower!"

Blood splashed the gray stone walls of the gateway. One Spanish boot lay crumpled close by. Those were the only signs Shakespeare saw that soldiers had ever stood here. Were they dead? Fled? *Some dead, assuredly*, he thought, eyeing the bloodstains and that boot and wondering what had befallen the man who'd worn it.

"On to the Tower! To the Tower! To free Elizabeth! To free the Queen!" Those savage shouts grew louder as the crowd from the Theatre—and from the tenements beyond the walls—swarmed into London like a conquering army. *But how much like a conquering army?* Shakespeare wondered, and then wished he hadn't.

They weren't the only swarm loose in the city. More cries and curses rose: some single spies, some in battalions. Madness was loosed here. Maybe Robert Cecil had worked better than even he knew.

"A don! A don!" A new shout went up. So might hunters have cried, *A fox! A fox!* Shakespeare got a glimpse of the Spaniard, saw horrified amazement spread across his face, saw him turn and start to run, and saw an Englishman tackle him from behind as if in a Shrove Tuesday football match. The Spaniard went down with a wail. He never got up again.

If the Spaniards could have put a line of arquebusiers in front of the rampaging crowd from the Theatre and poured a couple of volleys into it, it would have melted away. Shakespeare was sure of that. A line of armored pikemen might have halted it, too. Even as things were, groundlings and folk from the tenements—some still yelling about freeing Elizabeth—broke away to plunder shops that tempted them.

But no line of ferocious, lean-faced, swarthy Spaniards appeared. Shouts and cries and the harsh snarl of gunfire suggested the dons were busy, desperately busy, elsewhere in London. When chance swept Shakespeare and Richard Burbage together for a moment, the player said, "Belike they'll make a stand at the Tower."

"Likely so," Shakespeare agreed unhappily. Those frowning walls had been made to hold back an army, and this . . . thing he was a part of was anything but.

Up Tower Hill, where he'd watched the auto de fe almost a year before. A great roar, a roar full of triumph, rose from the men in front of him as they passed the crest of the hill and swept on towards the Tower Ditch and the walls beyond. And when Shakespeare crested the hill himself, he looked ahead and he roared, too, in joy and amazement and suddenly flaring hope. Will Kemp had been right, right and more than right. All the gates to the Tower of London stood open.

After tenderly kissing Cicely Sellis goodbye, Lope de Vega stopped in a nearby ordinary for his dinner and a cup of wine with which to celebrate his conquest. The cup of wine became two, then three, and then four: a conquest like that deserved a good deal of celebrating. By the time he started off towards the Spanish barracks, the clock had already struck one. That didn't worry him. As far as he could remember, he had nowhere else he needed to be.

As far as he could remember . . . Others, though, might remember further. He'd just turned into St. Swithin's Lane when a startled shout came from up ahead: "Lieutenant de Vega! *Madre de Dios, señor*, what are you doing here at this hour?"

"Oh, hello, Enrique," Lope said. "I'm coming back to the barracks, of course. What else should I be doing now?"

He meant it for a joke. But Captain Guzmán's servant stared at him and answered, "What else should you be doing? *Señor*, aren't you going to play, shouldn't you be playing, Don Juan de Idiáquez in Shakespeare's *King Philip* less than half an hour from now? I was going up to the Theatre to see you. By God and all the saints, sir, I never expected to find you here."

"Don Juan de Idiáquez . . ." Lope gaped. He said the name as if he'd never heard it before in his life. Indeed, for a moment that seemed to be true. But then it was as if a veil were torn from in front of his eyes. Memory, real memory, came flooding back: memory of why he should have been at the Theatre, and memory of why he'd gone to Cicely Sellis' lodging-house—to *Shakespeare's* lodging-house!—in the first place.

He crossed himself, not once but again and again. At the same time, he cursed as foully as he knew how—magnificent, rolling, guttural obscenity that left Enrique's eyes wider than ever and his mouth hanging open. De Vega didn't care. He wanted a bath, though even that might not make him feel clean again. He wondered if anything would ever make him feel clean again.

"That *bruja*, that whore—she bewitched me, Enrique, she bewitched me and she swived me and she sent me on my way like a . . . like a . . . like an I don't know what. And that means, that has to mean—"

"I don't understand, *señor*," Enrique broke in. "I don't understand any of this."

"Do you understand treason? Do you understand black, vile, filthy treason? And treason coming soon—soon, by God!—or she never would have . . ." De Vega didn't waste time finishing. He whirled and started back up St. Swithin's Lane.

"Where are you going?" Enrique cried after him.

"First, to kill that *puta*," Lope snarled. "And then to the Theatre, to do all I can to stop whatever madness they're hatching there." Even in his rage, he realized he might not—probably would not—be able to manage that by himself. He stabbed out a finger towards Enrique. "As for you, go back to Captain Guzmán. Tell him to send a troop of men up to the Theatre as quick as he can. Tell him it's bad, very bad, as bad as can be. *Run*, damn you!"

Enrique fled as if ten million demons from hell bayed at his heels. Lope started up towards Bishopsgate at a fast, purposeful stride, halfway between a walk and a trot. Black fury filled him. He'd never imagined a woman could use him so. Mercenaries like Catalina Ibañez he understood. But what Cicely Sellis had done to him was ten, a hundred, a thousand times worse. Not only had she stolen a piece of him, she'd taken her pleasure with him afterwards to waste more of his time and to make sure he didn't get that piece back.

And I wouldn't have, either, if I hadn't run into Enrique, he thought savagely. *But I am myself again, and she'll pay. Oh, how she'll pay!* His hand closed hungrily on the hilt of his rapier.

He'd just turned onto Lombard Street and passed the church of St. Mary Woolnoth when he spied a Spanish patrol ahead of him. "You men!" he called, and gave them a peremptory wave. "Come with me!"

Their sergeant recognized him. "What do you want with us, Lieutenant de Vega? We have places we need to check, and we're running late."

Lope set his hands on his hips. "And I have a *bruja* to catch and treason to put down," he rapped out. "Which carries the greater weight?"

Gulping, the sergeant stiffened to attention. "I am your servant, *señor*!"

"You'd better be. Come on, and my God come with us!"

The bells of St. Mary Woolnoth rang out two o'clock. All across London, dozens, hundreds, of church bells chimed the hour. De Vega cursed. He should have been up at the Theatre. Lord Westmorland's Men should be presenting *King Philip*. Were they? If they weren't, what were they giving instead? He didn't know. He couldn't know. But he could guess, and all his guesses sent ice racing along his spine.

And then, all at once, he had more things to worry about than Lord Westmorland's Men. Someone on a rooftop flung a stone or a brick at the patrol. It clanged off a soldier's morion. The man staggered, but stayed on his feet. "You all right, Ignacio?" the sergeant asked.

"Yes, thanks be to God—I've got a hard head," the soldier replied. "But where's the cowardly son of a whore who threw that? I'll murder the bastard."

Before the sergeant could answer, a chamber pot sailed out of a second-story window—not just the stinking contents, but the pot, too. It shattered between two Spaniards, spattering the whole patrol with filth. And then, while they were still cursing that, a pistol banged. With a howl of pain, a soldier slumped to the ground, clutching his leg. Crimson blood streamed out between his fingers.

High and shrill and blazing with excitement, a voice cried out in English: "Death to the dons!"

And, as if that one voice were a burning fuse leading to a keg of powder, a whole great chorus took up the shout. "Death—Death—Death to the dons!" In a heartbeat, the cry echoed up and down the streets of London. "Death—Death—Death to the dons!"

Lope's mind went clear and cold as the ice he'd imagined he felt. Suddenly, the patrol that had seemed so reassuringly strong felt tiny and helpless as a baby. He nodded to the sergeant. "This is it. They are going to rise." His own voice held eerie certainty.

The sergeant tried to peer up at all the windows overlooking the street. Smoke still eddied in front of one. The shot had come from there, but what odds the pistoleer still lingered? Slim, slim. He didn't order his men after the assassin, as he would have without that daunting cry. Instead, nodding to Lope, he asked, "And what do we do now, *señor*?"

"We win or we die—it's that simple," de Vega answered. But it wasn't, quite. He looked around, too, as the sergeant had, trying to see every which way at once. Plainly, the patrol would never get to the Theatre, nor even to Bishopsgate. He wished that soldier hadn't been wounded. He couldn't bear to leave the fellow behind, but bringing him along would hamper them. "We'd better get back to the barracks," he said reluctantly. "We'll have numbers on our side there."

"Yes, sir." The sergeant sounded relieved. Now that he had orders, he knew what to do with them. "José, Manuel: bandage Pedro's leg and get him up with his arms over your shoulders."

Both soldiers knelt to do as he told them, but one said, "We can't do much fighting that way, Sergeant."

"We'll worry about that later. Quick, now!" To punctuate the underofficer's words, another stone thudded down into the street. It hit no one, but could have smashed a skull if it had. Seeing it, hearing it, made Lope acutely aware he wore a felt hat with a jaunty plume, not a high-combed morion.

Pedro howled again when they hauled him upright. And the sergeant proved cleverer than de Vega had suspected: one of the soldiers supporting the wounded man was lefthanded, so they both had their swords free even with his arms draped over them.

"Let's get moving," Lope said, and they started back the way they had come.

"Death—Death—Death to the dons!" The cry seemed to come from everywhere at once, from near and far. More stones and more reeking waste flew out of windows. A furious trooper fired his arquebus at one of their tormentors, but only a mocking laugh rewarded him. And then the patrol had to pause while he reloaded: an empty arquebus was nothing but an awkward club.

Lope hated every heartbeat of delay. How long before the Englishmen nerved themselves to fight in the streets, if they weren't already elsewhere in London? How long before weapons long hoarded in hope came out of hiding? Not long, he feared, and he didn't have enough men at his back.

Half a dozen Englishmen, a couple armed with swords, the rest with bludgeons, came out of St. Mary Woolnoth and formed a ragged line across Lombard Street. "What do we do, *señor*?" the sergeant muttered.

"We fight if we have to, but let me try something first," Lope answered in a low voice. Then, in English, he shouted, "Stand aside, in the name of the Queen!"

He hissed out a great sigh of relief when they *did* stand aside. One of them doffed his cap and made a clumsy leg at de Vega, saying, "We cry your pardon, sir, but we took ye for a pack of stinking Spaniards."

"God bless Elizabeth!" another Englishman added.

They all nodded. So did Lope. He led the patrol past them without another word. If he spoke too much, his accent would betray him. And betrayal enough was already loose in London this day. If they dared speak imprisoned Elizabeth's name, if they believed he, leading soldiers, also spoke of Elizabeth and not Isabella . . . If that was so, treason ran far deeper than even de Vega had dreamt.

Behind him, one of the Englishmen said, "Come. Let's to the Tower, and help to set her free." Their departing footsteps were quick and purposeful. They thought they could do it. Whether they proved right or wrong, their confidence chilled Lope.

"Sergeant!" he said sharply.

"*¿Sí, señor?*"

"Who garrisons the Tower of London? We, or the English?"

"Why, some of each, sir. We both want to make sure Elizabeth the heretic stays there till she dies, eh?" The sergeant hadn't understood any of what Lope or the street ruffians said in English. De Vega's dread only grew. In times like these, how far could any Spaniard trust an Englishman?

As he and the patrol turned down into St. Swithin's Lane, a sharp volley of gunfire came from the south, from the direction of the barracks. He wanted to order a charge. With the wounded soldier slowing everyone else and hampering two healthy men, he couldn't.

Englishmen swarmed up the street towards them. They were fleeing, not fighting. No cries of, "Death to the dons!" burst from their throats. They'd met death, and didn't like him. When one of them spied de Vega and his comrades, he cried, "Here's more o' the foul fiends! We are fordone!" But he and his friends pounded past before Lope and his little force could hope to halt them.

Bodies lay in the lane, some unmoving, some thrashing in pain. Spanish soldiers moved among them, methodically putting to the sword any who still lived. More Spaniards, pikemen and arquebusiers, formed a line of battle in front of the barracks. One of the soldiers with sword in hand looked up from his grim work and growled, "Who the devil are you?" as Lope led the patrol towards him.

"Senior Lieutenant de Vega," Lope answered.

The other Spaniard's face changed. "Oh! You're the fellow who knew this mess was coming. Pass on, *señor*—pass on. If we hadn't had a few minutes' warning of trouble, those damned Englishmen might've taken us unawares."

"De Vega! Is that you?" From one end of the line of battle, Captain Guzmán waved.

"Yes, your Excellency." Lope waved back.

"God be praised you're all right," Guzmán said. "When Enrique came running back here with your report, I feared we'd never see you again. I was about to go after you to the Theatre when we were attacked ourselves."

"Never mind the Theatre, or me." Even Lope, far from the least self-centered man ever born, knew some things were more important than he was. "The English are going to try to free Elizabeth from the Tower. If they do—"

Always the courtier, Guzmán bowed to him. "I am the senior officer present right now. I was going to hold the barracks against whatever they threw at us. Now you've given me something more urgent to do. *Muchas gracias.*" He shouted orders. More Spanish soldiers came tumbling out of the building and rushed up from the south: a few hundred all told, Lope judged. Guzmán said, "Form a column, boys. We have to get to the Tower, and it's liable to be warm work. Are you up to it?"

"Yes, *sir*!" the soldiers roared. By the way they sounded, no Englishman could stop them or even slow them down.

Baltasar Guzmán bowed again. "May we have the pleasure of your company, Senior Lieutenant de Vega?"

"Of course, your Excellency. But I have a wounded man here, and—"

"Leave him." Guzmán's voice was hard and flat. "We can't bring him, and we can't spare men to guard him. I'm sorry, but that's how it is. Will you tell me I'm wrong?"

He waited for Lope's reply. Lope had none, and he knew it. At his nod, José and Manuel eased Pedro to the ground. *What is he thinking?* Lope wondered. He shook his head. Better not to know.

Captain Guzmán raised his voice: "To the Tower, fast as we can go. For God and St. James, forward—*march!*"

"For God and St. James!" the soldiers shouted. Off they went, a ragged regiment against a city. To see them strut, the city was the outnumbered one.

Perhaps half a mile separated the barracks from the Tower of London. Moving as fast as they could, the soldiers might have got there in five minutes: they might have, had nobody between the one and the other had other ideas.

Guzmán marched the Spaniards towards the river to Upper Thames Street, which became Lower Thames Street east of London Bridge and which led straight to the Tower. That the street close by the Thames led straight to the Tower, though, quickly proved to have been obvious to others besides him. No sooner had his men turned into Thames Street and started east than bricks and stones flew down from rooftops and windows: not the handful of them that had greeted Lope's patrol in Lombard Street, but a regular fusillade. The missiles clattered from helmets and corselets. Men cursed or howled when stones struck home where they weren't armored. A soldier who got hit in the face crumpled without a sound. A moment later, another went down.

"What do we do, Captain?" a trooper cried.

"We go on," Guzmán answered grimly. "If we stop and kill Englishmen here, we have great sport, but we don't get where we need to go on time. *Forward!*" Lope admired the nobleman's discipline. Had he himself commanded the Spaniards, he knew he might have yielded to the sweet seduction of revenge against the cowards and skulkers who plagued them. Guzmán had better sense.

Just past the church of All Hallows the Less, a barricade blocked Thames Street: planks and carts and rubbish and rocks and dirt. The Englishmen behind it brandished a motley assortment of halberds and bills and pikes and swords. Two or three arquebus muzzles poked over the top, aimed straight at the oncoming Spanish soldiers. "Death to the dons!" the Englishmen shouted.

Captain Guzmán's lips drew back from his teeth in a savage smile. "Now we can come to close quarters with some of these motherless dogs," he said. "Give them a volley, boys, and then show them what a proper charge means."

The front rank of arquebusiers dropped to one knee. The second rank aimed their guns over the heads of the first. On the other side of the barrier, the Englishmen fired their few guns. Flames belched from the muzzles. A bullet cracked past Lope and smacked wetly into flesh behind him. A soldier shrieked. Puffs of thick gray smoke clouded the barricade.

Then Captain Guzmán yelled, "Fire!" The end of the world might have visited Upper Thames Street. The roar of twenty-five or thirty arquebuses was a palpable blow against the ears. More smoke billowed. Its brimstone stink and taste put Lope in mind of the hell to which he hoped the volley had sent a good many Englishmen. Screams from in back of the barricade said some of those bullets had struck home. Baltasar Guzmán gave another order. "Charge! St. James and at them!"

"*¡Santiago!*" the Spaniards cried. Swordsmen and pikemen swarmed past the arquebusiers towards the barrier blocking their way. They scrambled over it and tore openings in it with their hands. The English irregulars behind the barricade chopped and hacked at them, trying to hold them back. A pistol banged, then another. The irregulars yelled as loudly for St. George as Guzmán's men did for St. James.

As the Englishmen held them up at the barricade, more bricks and stones rained down on the Spaniards from the buildings on either side of Thames Street. The pikeman next to de Vega dropped his weapon and staggered back, his face a gory mask. But, even with the help of the barrier, the English couldn't stop Guzmán's men for long. Lope sprang up onto a cart and then leaped down on the far side of the barricade. A halberdier tried to hold him off. He rushed forward and ran the Englishman through. In the press, a polearm was too clumsy to do much good.

After the irregulars lost the barricade, the ones still on their feet tried to flee. The Spaniards cut and shot them down. "Forward!" Captain Guzmán shouted again, and forward his men went. The bulk of

London Bridge loomed to Lope's right. But, before he and his comrades got even as far as the bridge, another barricade loomed ahead. This one looked more solid than the one they'd just overwhelmed. And, from the east, Englishmen rushed to defend it. Sunlight glinted off armor over there. De Vega cursed. At least some English soldiers who had served Isabella and Albert were now on the other side, the side of rebellion.

Arquebuses and pistols bellowed: more than had defended the first barricade. A Spaniard near Lope who'd turned his head at just the wrong instant staggered back, half his jaw shot away. Blood fountained. His tongue flapped among shattered teeth. Horrid anguished gobbling noises poured from that ruin of a mouth.

"A volley!" Captain Guzmán commanded. But, in the disorder after the first fight and pursuit, the volley took longer to organize. Meanwhile, those English guns kept banging away at the Spanish soldiers in the street in front of them.

Indifferent to the enemy fire, the arquebusiers elbowed their way forward and into position, some kneeling, others standing. They might have been one man pulling the trigger. De Vega wondered if he would have any hearing left at the end of the day. Crying, "*¡Santiago!*" the Spaniards rushed at the second barricade.

The fight at the first barrier had been savage but brief. The English hadn't had enough men there to hold the position long. Things were different here. Real soldiers with corselets and helmets of their own were far harder to down than irregulars had been. They wielded pike and sword with the same professional skill as Lope and his countrymen. And the irregulars who battled alongside them seemed altogether indifferent to whether they lived or died. If one of them could tackle a Spaniard so another could stab him while he was down, he would die not only content but joyous.

As before, the English had set up the barricade between tall buildings. Stones and bricks and saucepans and stools—anything heavy and small enough to go out a window—rained down on the Spaniards. Pistoleers fired from upper-story windows, too.

Lope grabbed a morion someone had lost and jammed it onto his head. It was too big; it almost came down over his eyes. He didn't care. It was better than nothing. He pushed his way forward, trying to get to the barricade. A wounded Spaniard, clutching at the spurting stumps of two missing fingers, stumbled back past him, out of the fight. He slid forward into the place the other man had vacated, and found himself next to Captain Guzmán. "Ah, de Vega," Guzmán said, as if they held wine goblets rather than rapiers.

"Can we get to the Tower?" Lope asked.

"I hope so," Guzmán answered calmly.

"How many more barricades in front of us?" Lope went on. The captain only shrugged, as if to say it didn't matter. But it did, especially if every one of them was held this stubbornly. Lope persisted: "Should we try some different street to get there?"

"This is the shortest way," Guzmán said.

He was right, in terms of distance. In terms of time, in terms of effort and lives lost . . . "I beg pardon, your Excellency," Lope said, "but how much good will we do if we get there tomorrow with three men still standing?"

"I command here, and I must do as I think best," Captain Guzmán replied. "If I go down and you take charge, you will do what you will do, and the result will be as God wills. In the meantime, we have a job to tend to here in front of us, *sí*?"

Lope found no answer to that but pushing forward once more. A dead Spaniard lay just in front of the barricade. Lope scrambled up onto his corpse. A man behind him shoved him onto a dirt-filled barrel blocking the street. An Englishman thrust at him. He beat the spearhead aside with his blade. A pistol ball whined malevolently past his ear.

If I stay up here, I'll surely die, he thought. He couldn't go back, either. Shouting, "*¡Santiago!*" at the top of his lungs, he leaped down on the far side of the barricade. An Englishman partly broke his fall. He rammed his sword into the man's chest. It grated on ribs. The irregular let out a bubbling shriek and crumpled, blood pouring from his mouth and nose. Lope had a bad moment when he couldn't clear the blade, but then all at once it came free, crimson almost to the hilt. "*¡Santiago!*" he yelled again, and slashed wildly, trying to win himself a little room, trying most of all not to be killed in the next instant.

He wasn't the first Spaniard down on this side of the barricade. A couple of soldiers were down indeed, and wouldn't rise again till Judgment Day. But others, like him, cut and thrust and cursed and fought to clear space for their fellows to follow them. An arquebus—a Spanish arquebus—went off right behind him, from atop the barricade. That bullet almost killed him, too. Instead, it smashed the left shoulder of the Englishman with whom he was trading swordstrokes. As the man yowled in pain, Lope thrust him through the throat and stepped forward over his writhing body.

Here, though, more and more foes rushed into the fray, shouting, "Death to the dons!" and "Elizabeth!" and "God and St. George!" Most of them were unarmored. Many of them were unskilled. But their ferocity . . . Having sown the wind with ten years of harsh occupation, the Spaniards now all at once reaped the whirlwind. If the Englishmen could stop them from reaching the Tower only by piling up a new barricade of their own dead flesh, they seemed willing—even glad—to do it.

A stone, luckily a small one, clattered off Lope's snatched-up helmet. He stumbled, but kept his feet. To go down, here, was all too likely to die. He howled an oath when a knife slashed his left arm. His own backhand cut, as much instinct as anything else, laid open the face of the burly man who'd wounded him. Opening and closing his left hand several times, Lope found muscles and tendons still worked. He laughed. Much he could have done about it if they hadn't! He couldn't even bandage himself. He had to hope he wouldn't bleed too badly.

The Spaniards would gain a step, lose half of it, gain two, lose one, gain one, lose it again. Then a dozen or so arquebusiers got up onto the barricade together and poured a volley into the English—again, a ball just missed de Vega. As wounded enemies toppled, Spanish soldiers pushed past them.

A sergeant tugged at Lope's wounded arm. He shrieked. "Sorry, *señor*," the sergeant bawled in his ear. The fellow was also wounded; he'd had his morion knocked off, and sported a nasty cut on his scalp. Gore splashed his face and his back-and-breast. "What are your orders?"

"*My* orders?" Lope shouted back. "Where the devil's Captain Guzmán?"

"Down, sir—a thrust through the thigh," the underofficer answered. De Vega grimaced; a wound like that could easily kill. The sergeant went on, "What now, sir? We've got more of these fornicating Englishmen coming up behind us now, and more and more on the rooftops, too. What do we do? What *can* we do?" He sounded frightened for the whole Spanish force.

Till then, Lope had been too busy to be frightened for anyone but himself. He called quick curses down on Guzmán's head. If the captain hadn't taken them to the Tower the most obvious way . . . *It might not have mattered at all*, de Vega thought. He couldn't change routes now.

He couldn't split his force, either, not when it was beset from all sides. He saw only one thing he *could* do.

"Forward!" he said. "We have to go forward. Tell off a rear guard to hold back the Englishmen behind us. Come what may, we *must* reach the Tower." Captain Guzmán had been right about that.

Forward they went, half a bloody step at a time. Every soldier they lost was gone for good. Fresh Englishmen kept flooding into the fight.

Even through the din of his own battle, Lope heard a great racket of gunfire from ahead, from the direction of the Tower of London. He didn't know what it meant, not for certain, but he did know he misliked it mightily. Then an Englishman he never saw clouted him in the side of the head with a polearm—this one, unlike the fellow de Vega had killed, found room to swing his weapon even in the crowd. The world flared red, then black. Lope's rapier flew from his hand. He swayed, shuddered . . . fell.

RAVENS. THE GREAT BLACK BIRDS HAD ALWAYS ROOSTED ON, NESTED on, the Tower of London. Now, careless of the swarms of live Englishmen flooding into the Tower, the scavengers settled on the sprawled and twisted bodies on the battlements and in the courtyard. Most of the dead were Spaniards, but more than a few Englishmen lay among them. Every once in a while, the birds would flutter up again when someone pushed too close, but never for long. They hadn't enjoyed such a feast in years.

Shakespeare shivered to see the ravens. He'd been sure the carrion birds would peck out his eyes and tongue and other dainties after he was slain. And it might yet happen—he knew that, too. He had no idea how the uprising fared in the rest of London, in Westminster, elsewhere in England. Here by the Tower, though, all went well, so his fears receded for the moment.

"The Bell Tower!" people shouted. "She's in the Bell Tower!" They streamed towards it. No need to ask who *she* was. Hardly any need even to call out her name, not now. Were it not for her, this throng never would have come to the Tower.

Beside Shakespeare, a graybeard said, "She was in the Bell Tower aforetimes, too. Bloody Mary mewed her up there, forty years gone and more."

Bloody Mary. Amazement prickled through Shakespeare. Who, since the Armada landed, had dared use that name for Elizabeth's half sister? No one the poet had heard, not in all these years. Truly a new wind was blowing. *May it rise to a gale, a mighty tempest*, he thought.

Soldiers in armor—dented, battered, blood-splashed armor—stood guard at the base of the Bell Tower. Their spears and swords and arquebuses—and their formidable presence—kept people from rushing up into the Tower to the rooms where Elizabeth had passed the last ten years. Ruddy cheeks, blue eyes, beards of light brown and yellow and fiery red proclaimed them Englishmen. Shakespeare wondered if any Spaniards were left alive here. He hoped not.

"Back! Keep back!" an officer yelled. Half the plume had been hacked off his high helm, but his voice and his swagger radiated authority. The crowd didn't actually move back—impossible, with more folk flooding into the courtyard every minute. But it did stop trying to push forward. In those circumstances, that was miracle enough. A peephole in the door behind the officer opened. Someone spoke to him through it. He nodded. The peephole closed. The officer shouted again: "Hear ye! Hear ye me! Her Majesty'll bespeak you anon from yon window." He pointed upwards. "But bide in patience, and all will be well."

Her Majesty. Again, Shakespeare felt the world turning, changing, around him. Since 1588, Philip II's daughter Isabella had been Queen of England. Maybe Isabella still thought she was. But this swarm of Englishmen thought otherwise. *God grant we be right.*

"Elizabeth!" Sir Robert Devereux's voice boomed out, even more full of command, more full of itself, than the officer's. "Elizabeth! Elizabeth! Come forth, Elizabeth!"

At once, the crowd took up the chant: "Elizabeth! Elizabeth! Come forth, Elizabeth!" It echoed from the gray stone walls of the Tower. Shakespeare shouted with the rest. "Elizabeth! Elizabeth! Come forth, Elizabeth!" The rhythm thudded in him, as impossible to escape as his own heartbeat.

The shutters of that window swung open. The chanting stopped.

A sharp-faced, gray-haired woman in a simple wool shift looked out from the window at the suddenly silent throng below. Staring up at her, Shakespeare at first guessed her a serving woman who would in a moment escort Elizabeth forward. When he thought of the Queen of England, he thought of her as she'd been portrayed throughout her reign. To be Elizabeth, she should have worn a magnificent gown. She should have sparkled with jewels. Her face should have been white and smooth despite her years, her hair a red that likewise defied time. A glittering coronet should have topped her head.

But then she said, "I am here. My own dear people of England, you are come at last, and I . . . am . . . still . . . here." Implacable determination blazed from her every word, even though most of her teeth were black.

"God save the Queen!" Robert Devereux shouted, waving his rapier. Again, the crowd took up the cry.

Elizabeth raised her hand. Once more, silence fell. Into it, she said, "God *hath* preserved me unto this hour, for the which I shall give praise to Him all the remaining days of my life." Her voice seemed to strengthen from phrase to phrase. Shakespeare wondered how much she'd used it these past ten years. With whom had she spoken? Who would have dared speak to her?

She went on, "And I assure you, I do not desire to live even one day more to distrust my faithful and living people. Let tyrants and foul usurpers fear. I have always so behaved myself, even in my long time of hardship and sorrow, that, under God, I have placed my chiefest strength and safeguard in the loyal hearts and good will of my subjects. Thus I stand before you at this time, not for my recreation and disport, but being resolved in the midst and heat of this glorious uprising to live or die amongst you all, never being made separate from you again. . . ."

Her voice caught. Tears stung Shakespeare's eyes. What *had* the imprisoned Queen gone through, here in the Tower, here in the hands of her enemies? "Elizabeth!" the crowd shouted, over and over again. "Elizabeth! Elizabeth!" Shakespeare joined it, yelling till his throat was raw.

Elizabeth raised her hand once more. "Now we are begun anew," she said. "I shall gladly lay down, for my God and for my kingdom and for my people, my honor and my blood, even in the dust. I know I have the body of a weak and feeble woman, but I have the heart and stomach of a king, and of a king of England too. And I think foul scorn that Spain or any prince of Europe should have dared invade the borders of my realm, or that Isabella and Albert falsely style themselves sovereigns thereof. Rather than any more dishonor shall fall on me, I myself will take up arms—"

This time, the roar of the crowd stopped her: a savage wordless roaring bellow that said she could have led them barehanded against all the hosts of Spain, and they would have torn the dons to pieces for her.

Even Shakespeare, not the boldest of men, looked about for a Spaniard to assail, though he was not sorry to discover none.

"I am not so base minded that fear of any living creature or prince should make me afraid to do that were just," Elizabeth said when she could make herself heard again. "I am not of so low a lineage, nor carry so vile a wit. You may assure yourselves that, for my part, I doubt no whit but that all this tyrannical, proud, and brainsick invasion and occupation of my beloved England will yet prove the beginning, though not the end, of the ruin of that kingdom which, most treacherously, even in the midst of treating peace, began this wrongful war. Spain hath procured my greatest glory that meant my sorest wrack, and hath so dimmed that light of its sunshine, that who hath a will to obtain shame, let them keep its forces company. And contrariwise, who seeketh vengeance for great wrongs done, and requital for the burthens borne in our long captivity, let them go forward now, with me, and God defend the right!"

She stepped away from the window. For a moment, Shakespeare thought she cared nothing for the plaudits of the crowd. As a man of the theatre, he knew what a mistake that was. But then the door behind the English soldiers at the base of the Bell Tower opened. There stood Elizabeth, still in that simple, colorless shift.

How they all roared, there in the dying day that suddenly seemed a sunrise! Sir Robert Devereux dashed forward, past the armored guardsmen, to stand beside the Queen. Bowing low, he murmured something to her, something lost in the din to Shakespeare. Whatever it was, Elizabeth nodded. And then the poet saw, then everyone saw, what it meant. Devereux stooped, lifted her as lightly as if she were a toddling babe, and set her on his bull-broad shoulders. Cheers and shouts redoubled. Shakespeare had not dreamt they could.

From that unsteady perch, Elizabeth once more raised a hand. Slowly, quiet gained on chaos. The Queen said, "My loving people, I might take heed how I commit myself to armed multitudes. I might, but I shall not. I myself will be your general, judge, and rewarder of every one of your virtues in the field as we overthrow and utterly cast down the vile usurpation which hath oppressed this my kingdom these ten years past. I know already for your forwardness you deserve rewards and crowns; and I do assure you, in the words of a prince, they shall be paid you."

Another roar, this time coalescing into a fresh shout of, "Elizabeth!

Elizabeth! Elizabeth!" From Devereux's shoulders, she waved again. Little by little, a new cry replaced her name: "Death—Death—Death to the dons!" And the smile stretching itself across Elizabeth's face when she heard that would have chilled the blood of any Spaniard every born.

Shakespeare shouted with everybody else. As he shouted, rewards and crowns ran through his mind. He hadn't undertaken *Boudicca* in hope of reward. Looking back, he couldn't recall just why he *had* undertaken it, save from fear of being slain should he refuse. But he'd already been handsomely paid (and paid by the Spaniards, too, for the play that never was). If now Elizabeth herself should look on him with favor . . .

If now this uprising triumphed, which was as yet anything but assured. Sir Robert Devereux strode into the crowd, crying, "Forward now! Forward, for St. George and for good Queen Bess!"

People swarmed forward, not against the Spaniards but towards him and Elizabeth, to call out to her, to touch her, simply to see her at close quarters. Devereux pushed on, irresistible as if powered by a millrace, to take Elizabeth from the Tower where she'd languished so long and into her kingdom once more.

Someone bumped Shakespeare: Will Kemp. The clown made a leg—a cramped leg, in the crush—at him. "Give you good den, gallowsbait," he said cheerfully.

"Go to!" Shakespeare said. "Meseems we are well begun here."

"Well begun, ay. And belike, soon enough, we shall be well ended, too." Kemp jerked his head to one side, made his eyes bulge, and stuck out his tongue as if newly hanged.

With a shudder, Shakespeare said, "If the wind of your wit sit in that quarter, why stand you here and not with the Spaniards?"

"Why?" Kemp kissed him on the cheek. "Think you you're the only mother's son born a fool in England?" He slipped away, wriggling through the crowd like an eel, making for the Queen. Shakespeare didn't follow. He simply stood where he was. Too much had happened too fast.

As things chanced, Elizabeth passed within a couple of feet of him. Their eyes met for a moment. She had no idea who he was, of course. How could she, when he'd come to London only months before she was locked away? But she nodded to him as if they'd been close for years. Anyone might have done the same. But only a few, only the greatest players, could do it and make the people at whom they nodded feel they'd been close for years. Shakespeare was sadly aware he didn't quite have the gift. Richard Burbage did. So too, in his twisted way, did Will Kemp. And so did Elizabeth.

"Death to the dons!" Shakespeare shouted, and followed the little old woman who was his Queen out of the Tower, out into London.

XIV

When Lope de Vega first came to himself, he didn't think he was awake at all. He thought he had died, and found himself in some stygian pit of hell. Slowly, so slowly, he realized he lived and breathed, but he feared he was blind. Then he saw that the blackness all around lay in front of his eyes, not behind them. Such blackness had a name. He groped for it and, groping, found it. Night. This was night.

He groaned and tried to sit up. That was a mistake. Motion fanned the throbbing agony in his head. His guts churned. He heaved up whatever his stomach held. Only little by little did he also notice sharper pain from his left arm, as from a cut. Had he been wounded there? He couldn't remember, not at first.

At first, he had trouble remembering his name, let alone anything else. He had no idea why he lay in the middle of some London street—yes, this was London; that much he knew—covered in blood and, now, puke. He had no idea who the corpses under him and around him and sprawling across his legs were, either. But that they were corpses he did not doubt; no living man's flesh could be so cold.

More cautiously this time, he tried again to sit. The pain forced another moan from him, but he succeeded. Crossing himself, he wriggled away from the dead body on him. But he could not escape them all. They were too many, and he too weak to move far yet.

Why such slaughter? Who were these slain? The why he could not recall, not with bells of torment clanging in his head. The who? There not far away, face pale and still in the moonlight, lay the sergeant who'd told him Captain Guzmán was down. He remembered that. How Guzmán had come to fall, though, remained beyond him.

And not just Guzmán. "*Madre de Dios*," Lope whispered softly, and crossed himself again. The corpses piled around him were all Spaniards, scores of Spaniards. He shuddered. His guts knotted anew, though now he had nothing left in him to give back.

Even as the spasm wracked him, what had to be cold truth slid into his clouded wits. *They threw me here because they thought I was dead, too.* At the moment, he rather wished he were. But then he saw a body with a slit throat gaping wide like a second mouth, and another, and another. They'd made sure of a lot of men. They hadn't bothered with him. He breathed. His heart beat—his temples thudded each time his heart beat. His eyes fell on another cut throat. No, he didn't—quite—feel like dying yet.

They? The English. It had to be the English. They'd risen. They must have risen. But why still eluded him. Everything had been peaceful, as far as he could remember. He should have played Juan de Idiáquez in *King Philip* at the Theatre. Had he? He didn't think so.

Nothing was peaceful now. Along with the death stench of so many men, he smelled more smoke than he should have even in smoky London. The night was alive, hideously alive, with shouts and screams from far and near. Somewhere a block or two away, a pistol banged. The report made Lope's head want to explode.

King Philip . . . The Theatre . . . Shakespeare . . . Cicely Sellis . . . De Vega stiffened. The chain of associations took his thoughts down a road closed till then. "That *puta*!" he gasped. "That *bruja*!" She'd bewitched him, seduced him, made him forget all about the Theatre, so that he went back towards the barracks instead, went back towards the barracks and. . . . He cursed. He'd lost it, whatever it was.

He tried to stand. He needed three separate efforts before he could. Even then, he swayed like a scrawny sapling in a storm. A chorus of drunken English voices floated through the air: "Death—Death—Death to the dons!" The Englishmen howled out laughter and obscenities, then took it up afresh. "Death—Death—Death to the dons!" More gloating laughter.

Lope's legs almost went out from under him. He staggered over to a wall and leaned against it. He'd heard that chorus before. He'd been fighting his way towards the Tower of London. He remembered that, and barricades in the streets, and every damned Englishman in the world running toward him and his comrades with whatever weapon he chanced to have. And . . .

"And we must have lost," Lope said. Explaining things to himself seemed to help. "By God and St. James, we must have lost." They'd shouted *Santiago!* He remembered that, too. His throat was still raw with it. But God and St. James hadn't heeded them.

The Tower of London . . . Even with his wits scrambled, he knew who was kept there. He'd known that as long as he'd been in England. And, just in case he hadn't, those roaring, drunken Englishmen started a new chorus: "God bless good Queen Bess!"

Elizabeth free? If she was, she'd draw rebels as the North Pole drew a compass needle. England had never been much more than sullenly acquiescent to the Spanish occupation. Given time, it might have become quieter. But a rising now . . . A rising now could be very bad, and he knew it.

He laughed, a small, crackbrained laugh. *Crackbrained indeed*, he thought through his pulsing, pounding headache. This rising, plainly, was already about as bad as it could get.

Quiet footfalls—three or four Englishmen coming up the street. De Vega froze into immobility. The wall that half held him up was shadowed. They didn't see him. The thought of a live Spaniard never entered their minds, anyhow. They intended plundering the dead.

They shoved bodies this way and that. "We are come too late," one of them said sorrowfully. "Too many others here before us: we have but their leavings."

"You will steal, James, an egg out of a cloister," another replied; by the way he said it, he meant it as praise. "Think you not you'll find somewhat worth the having?"

"Haply so," James replied, "yet where's the ironmongery they had about 'em? Gone, lost as a town woman's maidenhead. We could have got good coin for casques and corselets and swords, but see you any of the like? I will rather trust a Fleming with my butter or an Irishman with my aqua-vitae bottle than those others to have spared the Spaniards' cutlery."

Soldiers and scavengers robbed the fallen after battle. They had since the beginning of time. Lope had done it himself here in England. But never had he heard it so calmly, so cold-bloodedly, hashed over.

"Here's a crucifix—might be gold," another robber said. Moonlight flashed from a knifeblade as he cut it free.

The one called James remained gloomy, saying, "Mind me, Henry: 'twill prove but brass when your glaziers gaze on't come daylight. Were't gold, it had been gone long since." But then he stooped and let out a soft grunt of pleasure. "Or peradventure I'm mistook, for here's a fine fat purse yet unslit, the which I cannot say of this wight's weasand."

Off to the west, a sharp volley of arquebus fire was followed a moment later by another, and then by the deep boom of a cannon. "Shall we cast down the dons and cast 'em out, think you?" the man called Henry asked.

"What boots it?" someone else replied. "Or the dogs tear the bear or the bear rend the dogs, the rats in the wainscoting thrive." They all laughed, and then, self-proclaimed rats, stole away.

Lope realized he had better leave, too. His comrades' bodies would draw more plunderers, and some might spy him. He could not have fought a mouse, let alone a rat. And he discovered he had nothing with which to fight. His rapier was gone. He hadn't even noticed till that moment. And, when his hand went to the sheath of his belt knife, sheath and knife had likewise vanished. Sure enough, plenty of robbers had already visited the Spaniards.

Where do I go? he wondered. *What do I do?*

More gunfire off to the west decided him. If there was still real fighting off in that direction, he would—he might—find his countrymen there. And if he found Englishmen before his countrymen, he would likely also find his death. He staggered up Thames Street, weaving from side to side like a sot. He made his way past two barricades, now mostly but not quite torn down, and past more bodies. He still remembered little of the fight, and nothing of the blow that had almost caved in his skull. He wondered if he ever would.

Little by little, his wits did seem to be coming back to life. Things like a raging thirst and the vile aftertaste of vomit in his mouth began to register, where before they'd been nothing but background to the thundering misery in his head. The river, he remembered, lay only a block away. He turned town an alley and made his way towards it at the best pace he could muster. He would have outsped any snail. A tortoise? Possibly not.

Across the Thames, a great fire—no, two—blazed in Southwark. The light hurt Lope's eyes, as it might have after too much wine. He looked down—looked down at himself for the first time since waking amongst the dead. His stomach lurched yet again. He was all over blood, from head to foot.

He needed several heartbeats to figure out it wasn't all his. It couldn't be. If it were, he'd have had none left inside him. How many others had bled on him while he lay senseless? Too many. Oh, far too many! He stumbled on towards the river. When at last he reached it, he sank to his knees, at least as much from weakness as from thirst, though he was very dry indeed. He cupped his hands and brought water to his mouth. It tasted of mud and—blood? He couldn't tell whether the blood was in the water or on his hands or on his face. He drank and drank, then splashed more water onto his cheeks and forehead. The cold hurt dreadfully for a moment, but then seemed to soothe.

He knew he should go looking for his countrymen again. He knew . . . but he was at the very end of his feeble strength. He lay by the Thames, panting like a dog, watching the fires on the far bank spread and spread.

"Death—Death—Death to the dons!" That hateful chant rose up once more, somewhere behind him. If the English found him here, they would give him the death he'd almost had before. He couldn't make himself care, or move.

Even in the midst of this madness, boats still made their way across the Thames, and up and down it. Shouts of, "Eastward ho!" and, "Westward ho!" and, " 'Ware, you crusty botch of nature!" rang out, as they might have at any hour of any day or night.

A large boat, one with at least a dozen men at the oars, came out of the west, making for London Bridge. In the stern sat a man and a woman. He slumped to one side; she sat very straight and stiff. As the boat passed by Lope, the rowers all pulling flat out to speed it down the river, she said something in Spanish. De Vega couldn't make out her words, but the tongue was unmistakable. She sounded furious. The man answered in the same language, but with a guttural accent, more likely German than English. The boat slid down the Thames, under the bridge, and away to the east.

They're free. They've escaped, Lope thought vaguely, though he had no idea who *they* were. He tried to get to his feet, tried and failed. Instead, he sank down into something perhaps a little closer to proper sleep than to the oblivion from which he'd emerged a little while before. As London boiled around him, he curled up on his side and snored.

SHAKESPEARE FELT DRUNK, THOUGH HE'D HAD NO MORE THAN A couple of mugs of ale hastily snatched up and even more hastily poured down. He'd been up all through the wild night, up and running and shouting and now and then throwing stones at Spaniards. Now he stood in Westminster, watching the sun rise bloody through the thick clouds of smoke above London and Southwark.

Cries of, "Death to the dons!" and, "Elizabeth!" and, "Good Queen Bess!" rang in his ears. Here and there, Spaniards still fought. Off in the distance, a shout of, "*¡Santiago!*" was followed by a ragged volley of gunfire and several screams.

Richard Burbage clapped Shakespeare on the back. Soot stained the player's face; sweat runneled pale tracks through it. *Belike mine own seeming is the same*, Shakespeare thought. Burbage's eyes were red-tracked, but glowed like lanterns. "Beshrew him if we've not broke 'em, Will!" he said.

"You may have the right of't," Shakespeare said in slow, weary wonder. "By God, you may." He yawned. "But where be Isabella and Albert? We've none of us set eyes on 'em here."

"I know that, and it likes me not," Burbage answered. "They may yet rally dons and traitors to their side, do we not presently bring 'em to heel." He yawned too, enormously.

Three Englishmen marched another, better dressed than they, up the street at sword's point. "I tell you, you do mistake me," their captive said. "I have ever loved Elizabeth, ever reckoned her my rightful sovereign, ever—"

"Ever an infinite and endless liar, an hourly promise-breaker, the owner of not one good quality," one of the men with a sword broke in. "Thou art a general offense, and every man should beat thee—and will have his chance. Get on!" He shoved the fellow forward.

"Now commenceth vengeance," Shakespeare remarked.

"Now commenceth cleansing," Burbage said. "For lo, the Augean stables were as sweet rainwater falling from heaven set beside the mire of iniquity that was our England these ten years gone by. Let the river of revenge flow free through it." He struck a pose, as if declaiming on the stage.

Shakespeare didn't argue with him. If Elizabeth triumphed, anyone who argued against rooting out every last man who might have helped the Spaniards and Isabella and Albert would endanger himself no less than someone arguing in favor of Elizabeth and her backers after she went to the Tower. How many injustices had the dons and their English henchmen worked then? *A mort of 'em*, the poet thought. And how many would the folk loyal to good Queen Bess work in return? He sighed. *No fewer*.

That mournful thought had hardly crossed his mind before another couple of men led another protesting prisoner past him and Burbage. "I tell you, gentles, I am no Spaniard's hound, but an honest Englishman," the fellow said, blinking nearsightedly back at his captors. He was thin and pockmarked, and carried a broken pair of spectacles in his left hand.

"Hold!" Shakespeare called to the rough-looking fellows who'd seized him. One of them held a pike, the other a pistol. Shakespeare was acutely aware of having no weapon but the dagger the player had given him at the end of *Boudicca*. But he went on, "I know Master Phelippes to be true and trusty."

Thomas Phelippes leaned towards him, peering, peering. "Is't you, Master Shakespeare? God bless you, sir! Without my precious spectacles, all past my nose is but a blur."

The man with the pistol swung it towards Shakespeare. The barrel suddenly seemed broad as a cannon's bore. "Go to, or own yourself likewise treacher, you detested parasitical thing," the ruffian snarled. "This accursed wretch was secretary to the Spaniards' commander—the which he denies not, nor scarce can he, being caught in's own den hard by the don's. And you style him a proper man? You pedlar's excrement, you stretch-mouthed rascal, how dare you?"

Showing anger to a man with a gun did not strike Shakespeare as wise. Picking his words with care, he answered, "I dare for that I know him to be one of Lord Burghley's—now one of Robert Cecil's—surest and most faithfullest intelligencers."

As he'd hoped, those were names to conjure with. The pistol wavered, ever so slightly. But the man holding it still sounded fierce as he demanded, "*How* know you this? And who are you, that you should know it? Answer quick, now! Waste no time devising lies."

"Heard you not Master Phelippes?—whose loyalty I also avouch," Richard Burbage boomed. "Here before you stands none other than the famous Will Shakespeare, whose grand *Boudicca* yesterday helped light the fire 'gainst the dons."

The man with the pike nudged the pistoleer. " 'Tis he, Wilf, by my troth—'tis. Have I not seen him full many a time astrut upon the stage? He'll know whereof he speaks. It were the gibbet for us, did we harm one of Crookback Bob's men."

Crookback Bob? Shakespeare couldn't imagine presuming to call Robert Cecil any such thing. To his vast relief, though, the man with the pistol—Wilf—lowered it. "Well, who's this cove with him, then?" he demanded.

Raw scorn filled the pikeman's voice: "What? Know you not Will Kemp when you see him?"

Burbage turned the color of a ripe apple. But Wilf's eyes almost bugged out of his head. "Will Kemp?" he whispered. "If the two o' *them* give this rogue their attestation, belike he is no rogue after all." He pushed Phelippes, not too hard, towards Shakespeare and Burbage. "Go with 'em, you, and praise God they knew you: else you were sped."

"Oh, I do praise Him," Phelippes said. "Rest assured, good sir, I do." He groped for Shakespeare's hand and squeezed it.

"Come," Wilf said to the pikeman. "Plenty of traitors undoubted yet to be smoked out." They hurried up the street.

Thomas Phelippes blinked towards Burbage, then bowed low. "And gramercy to you as well, Master Kemp," he said. "I would not seem ungrate—"

A grinding noise came from Burbage's throat. His voice a strange sort of strangled scream, he said, "I am not Will Kemp, nor fain to be he, neither." Plainly, he wanted to shout with all the force of his mighty frame. Just as plainly, he knew he must not, for fear of bringing the armed ruffians back at the run.

In a low voice, Shakespeare said, "Master Phelippes, I present you to my good friend and fellow player, Richard Burbage."

After clasping Burbage's hand, Phelippes said, "I cry your pardon, for I should have known you by your voice, be your face and form never so indistinct to mine eyne."

"Let it go, sir; let it go," Burbage said gruffly. "There's reason you mistook me, whereas that gross and miserable ignorance just gone. . . ." He shook his head. "By Jesu! That God should go before such villains!" He muttered more unpleasantries, these too low to make out.

"How fell you into the hands of such brabblesome coves?" Shakespeare asked Thomas Phelippes.

"How, sir? As you might think," Phelippes answered. "I came hither yesterday knowing the die was cast and purposing, if I might, to make it into a langret for Don Diego Flores de Valdés." Shakespeare bobbed his head, appreciating the figure; if one were to cast a die in such straits as these, a die not perfectly square would be the proper sort to cast. Phelippes let out a wry chuckle. "In the event, confusion proved well enough compounded even absent mine aid."

"What befell Don Diego?" Shakespeare asked. "A formidable wight, though he be a foe."

Phelippes nodded. "Formidable indeed. When report reached him the fighting waxed hot, he sprang to his feet, buckled on's sword, and fared forth to join it. 'A general's place is in the van,' quotha. I know not if he breathe yet."

"Haply he had been wiser to stay behind, so that the Spaniards might have some single hand fully apprised of all that chanced throughout London and its surround," Burbage said.

"Haply so," Phelippes agreed. "But the dons—and English soldiers, too, I'll not deny—call such a clerkly wisdom, and do otherwise dispraise it. When the blood's up in 'em, they would spill it from their foes, knowing they were reckoned white-livered cravens for hanging back. Fear of ill fame's worse cowardice yet, though they see that not."

"If Don Diego needs must away to the wars, might he not have left some other to be the head and central wit of the Spanish enterprise?" Shakespeare said.

"Why, so he did." Even without his spectacles, Thomas Phelippes managed a sly, sharp-toothed smile. The pockmarked little man bowed slightly. "Your servant, sir."

"Ho, ho!" Burbage thundered Jovian laughter. "And how many dons went astray on that account?"

"Perhaps a few." Phelippes' chuckle, meant to be self-deprecating, somehow seemed boastful instead. "Ay, perhaps a few."

"You are an army in one man," Shakespeare said, wondering how many other Englishmen had aided this rebellion more. Few. Very few. But would the chroniclers remember a man like Phelippes? Would anyone write a play about the way he'd helped the uprising? Shakespeare thought about that, then shook his head. Phelippes' role had been important, yes, but not dramatic in any ordinary sense of the word.

Burbage asked, "Know you where Isabella and Albert might be?"

Phelippes shook his head. "No, and would I did, for they might rally not only the dons but also Englishmen of stout Romish faith." He looked about, as if searching for the Queen and King, then laughed at himself. "They might stand beside me and I'd ken 'em not, so sorry are mine eyne without assisting lenses."

"What befell your spectacles?" Shakespeare asked.

Thomas Phelippes laughed again, this time in embarrassment. A blush brought blood to his sallow cheeks. "The most prodigious bit of bungling any man might manage, forsooth—the undone laces of mine own shoon tripped me up, whereupon I did measure my length upon the floor, and the spectacles, flying off. . . ." He sighed. "I felt a proper fool, but no help for't, not until God grant me the leisure to seek replacement for my loss."

"May that time come soon," Burbage said, "the which would signify our final victory o'er the Spaniards and all who'd oppress us."

Shakespeare's stomach growled. He'd been running on nerves and little else since the afternoon before, and was starting to feel the lack. "Simple hunger doth oppress me," he said. "I shall famish, a dog's death."

Burbage nodded, resting both hands on his protuberant belly. "Ay, e'en so," he said. "Bread and meat and wine—food fit for heroes. Or say rather, none can long the hero play without 'em."

"I pray you'll lead me to 'em, gentles, for I am not fit to find 'em on my own," Phelippes said.

"Let's seek nourishment, then," Shakespeare said, "and with good fortune we'll soon find ourselves in our aliment."

"Give over!" Burbage's groan had nothing to do with hunger. He rolled his eyes up to the heavens, muttering, "And they took *me* for clotpoll Kemp!" But no more than Shakespeare could he resist a quibble, for he wagged a finger at the poet and added, "Better fortune were to find our aliment in us."

They trudged through the streets of Westminster, past an Englishman pulling the boots off a dead Spaniard, past several dogs feeding at another corpse, past an Englishman hanged from the branch of an oak. A placard tied to the hanged man's body warned, LET THEM WHO SERVED SPAIN BEWARE. Thomas Phelippes was too shortsighted to see it, and Shakespeare didn't read it to him: that might too easily have been Phelippes dangling there.

Before long, they found an open tavern. Yesterday, the proprietor had probably bowed and scraped to Spaniards and to Englishmen in their pay. Now he served out beer and cheese and brown bread with a hearty, "God bless good Queen Bess!" The hanged man swung not far away. The taverner, plainly a flexible soul, did not care to join him.

And if, as may be, the dons cast us out again, 'twill be, "Buenos días, señores" *once more,* Shakespeare thought with distaste. But that distaste extended only to the man himself; his provender was monstrous fine.

Running feet in the street outside. A cry of, "Fled! They're fled! By God, they're truly fled!" A voice cracking with excitement—then several voices, as more took up the shout.

Shakespeare and Burbage leaped up from their seats. Mugs and chunks of bread still in hand, they raced out to hear more. Thomas Phelippes stumbled after them, almost tripping over a stool. "Wait!" Burbage said in a great voice, a voice that brooked no argument. "Who's fled?"

"Is it . . . Elizabeth?" Shakespeare quavered. His heart leapt into his mouth. If the Queen, having escaped the Tower, had to escape England as well . . . Fear rose up in him like a choking cloud. Were grim Spanish soldiers marching on London by the tens of thousands, ready and able to smash this uprising into the dust? *Can I get me to foreign parts ahead of 'em?*

But the man who'd brought the news shook his head. "Elizabeth? No, Lord love her, she's here. 'Tis Isabella and Albert who're fled like thieves in the night. We came upon a servant who packed 'em into a boat yesternight and watched 'em fare forth down the Thames, out of Westminster, out of London, to save their reeky gore. They're *fled*!"—another exultant whoop.

Burbage and Shakespeare stared at each other. Slowly, solemnly, they embraced. Shakespeare reached out and put an arm around Phelippes, too. Tears stung his eyes. "Thus far our fortune keeps an upward course," he said. "Now are we graced with wreaths of victory?"

"I have great hope in that," Burbage said.

"And I," Thomas Phelippes agreed.

"And I. And even I," Shakespeare whispered. "Perfect love, saith John, casteth out fear. Now I find me hope will serve as well, or peradventure better." He yawned till the hinges of his jaw creaked. "And now, with hope in my heart, I dare rest." To Burbage, he said, "If thou canst wake me by two o' the clock, I prithee, call me. Sleep hath seized me wholly."

But the player shook his big head. He yawned, too. "Not I, Will. Being likewise fordone, I'd liefer lay me down beside thee."

"Sleep, the both of you, and fear not," Phelippes said. "I'll stand watch, and wake you at the hour appointed: a tiny recompense for the service you have done me, I know, but a first building stone in the edifice of gratitude. Sleep dwell upon your eyes, my friends, peace in your breasts."

"Gramercy," Shakespeare said. Not far away was a lawn on whose yellowing grass several Englishmen already sprawled in slumber. Shakespeare and Burbage lay down among them. The poet twisted a couple of times. He reached up to brush away a blade of grass tickling his nose, then yawned once more and forgot the world.

LOPE DE VEGA STIRRED, MUTTERED, AND SAT UP. HIS HEAD STILL ached abominably, but he was closer to having his wits about him. Glancing up at the sun, he blinked in surprise. It was close to noon. He'd slept—or lain senseless—the clock around. He shook his head, and managed to do it without hurting himself too much more. This felt restorative, not merely . . . blank, like his previous round of unconsciousness.

An old woman coming along the riverbank towards him let out a startled cackle. "I thought you dead till you stirred," she said, her voice mushy and hard to understand because of missing front teeth.

"Not I," Lope answered. "What news?" He was glad he spoke English. If she realized he was a Spaniard, she might try to make sure he was dead—and, in his present feeble state, she might manage it, too.

"Well, you'll know Elizabeth's enlarged?" she asked. De Vega nodded. The old woman hadn't sounded certain he would know even that. Looking down at his blood-drenched clothes, Lope supposed she'd had her reasons. Seeing him with some working wits, though, she went on, "And belike you'll also know Isabella and Albert are fled, one jump in front of the headsman."

"No!" Lope said, but then, a moment later, softly, "Yes." That boat on the Thames the night before, when he was washing his face . . .

"I'll miss the dons not, an they be truly routed," the old Englishwoman said. "Vile, swaggering coxcombs, the lot of 'em."

"Yes," Lope said again, meaning anything but. The old woman nodded and went on her way. De Vega cocked his poor, battered head to one side, listening. He heard very little: no gunfire, no shouts of, *Death to the dons!* That had to mean London lay in English hands.

What do I do now? he wondered. He couldn't hire a wherry to take him out of the city, following Isabella and Albert's example. Maybe they'd fled to gather strength elsewhere and try to return. But maybe also—and more likely, he judged—they'd got away just ahead of a baying pack of Englishmen who would have killed them if they'd caught them. The old woman seemed likely to be right about that.

The first thing Lope did was drink again. He was thirsty as could be. He was hungry, too, but food would have to wait. He splashed more water on his head. The cold did a little, at least, to ease his pain.

Staying upright was easier than it had been during the night. Deciding where to go was harder, especially with his head still cloudy. He let his feet take him where they would. *They may be the smartest part of me now*, he thought.

They carried him in the direction of the barracks from which Spanish soldiers had dominated London for the past ten years. Before long, he stumbled past a pile of bodies like the one from which he'd emerged when he came back to his senses. He shuddered, crossed himself, and went on. No, his countrymen didn't dominate this city any more.

Just around the corner from that dreadful pile, he almost stumbled over the corpse of a gray-haired Englishman. The fellow had been knocked in the head. He hadn't bled much, and what blood had spilled ran away from his body instead of puddling under it. He wasn't far from Lope's size. A scavenger had already stolen his shoes and his belt pouch, but he still wore doublet and hose.

Lope stripped him—an awkward business, since he'd begun to stiffen—then got out of his own bloody clothes. The dead man's hose were a little too short, but the doublet fit well. Not only was the outfit far cleaner than what de Vega had worn, it also helped make him look more like an Englishman himself.

He wished he had a weapon of some sort, even if only an eating knife. Then he shrugged, which made his battered head hurt. There would be more bodies in the street, of that he was sure. Not all of them would have been thoroughly plundered, not yet.

He soon acquired a dagger a good deal more formidable than an eating knife. A few coins also jingled in his pouch—not so many as he'd had before he was robbed while lying senseless, but a few. The Englishman from whom he took them would never need to worry about money again.

Lope used a couple of pennies to buy a loaf and a cup of ale. The man who sold them to him gave him a hard look. "Your way of speaking's passing strange, friend," he remarked.

Are you a Spaniard? was what he meant. Lope answered, "It wonders me I can speak at all. Some caitiff rogue did rudely yerk me on the knob, wherefrom my wits yet wander."

"Ah." The tavernkeeper relaxed and nodded. "Ay, belike a filchman to the nab'll leave you crank for a spell. Well, give you good day, then."

"E'en so." De Vega drained the ale and walked on, tearing chunks from the loaf as he went. A club to the head could indeed make a man act like an epileptic for a while—as he knew only too well.

Half a block later, he turned up St. Swithin's Lane. As he walked past the London Stone and spied the Spanish barracks, hope suddenly soared in him: soldiers stood guard outside the entrance. But, when he drew nearer, that hope crashed to earth as quickly as it had taken flight. Those big, fair-haired, grinning troopers were Englishmen, not Spaniards. "God bless good Queen Bess!" a passerby called to one of them.

The man nodded. His grin got even wider. "Bless her indeed," he said. "You'll have seen, good sir, we've made a proper start at clearing the rats from their nest here."

With a wave and a grin of his own, the passerby kept on his way. He walked past Lope without recognizing him for what he was, as so many had already done. The English sentries likewise paid no attention to him. When he saw the corpses piled against the northern wall of the barracks, he discovered what the soldier had meant by *clearing the rats*. Most of the bodies there belonged to servants, for the Spanish soldiers who'd been in the barracks when the uprising broke out had gone off to try to hold the Tower of London—and, as Lope knew, had never got there. Their remains lay farther east.

But there was Pedro, the wounded soldier from the patrol Lope had led back here. And there lay Enrique, his clever head smashed in. He too had come back here at de Vega's orders. And . . . was that . . . ? Lope took a couple of steps towards the corpses to be sure. He had to fight his right hand down when it started to rise of its own accord—he couldn't cross himself here, not without giving himself away. But that *was* Diego, poor, fat, lazy Diego, who'd always been too indolent to threaten anyone or anything except his master's temper. The Englishmen hadn't cared. They'd murdered him along with the rest of his countrymen they'd caught.

"*Requiescat in pace*," Lope murmured. Tears stung his eyes. How anyone could have imagined sleepy Diego needed killing . . . Well, he would sleep forever now. "God have mercy on his soul." That was a murmur, too, a murmur in English, for safety's sake.

"See you one there who galled you in especial?" an Englishman asked. Lope had to nod. Again, any other response would have betrayed him. Hating himself, he went on. Behind him, the Englishman let out a gloating laugh. He admired the corpses Lope mourned.

Where be your gibes now? your gambols? your songs? your flashes of merriment, that were wont to set the table on a roar? Not one now, to mock your own grinning? quite chapfallen? Unbidden, the words from Shakespeare's *Prince of Denmark* rose in Lope's mind. He cursed under his breath. He'd been near here—oh, farther up St. Swithin's Lane, but only a stone's throw—when Enrique, smart as a whip Enrique now dead as Diego, made him realize Shakespeare was a traitor and Cicely Sellis. . . . When he thought of Cicely Sellis and what she'd done with him, to him, he wished the blow he'd taken had robbed him of even more of his memory. He recalled that all too well. Shame blazed in him, a self-devouring flame.

"But I can still have my vengeance," he whispered. He'd been on his way for vengeance the day before, when London erupted around him. He might even have got it, had he not chosen to bring the chance-met patrol with him. Who would have tried to stop one lone man? No one, most likely. Who would try to stop one lone man today? No one, or so he hoped.

Up St. Swithin's Lane again, then. Right into Lombard Street, as he'd done before. Past the church of St. Mary Woolnoth. He hadn't been far past it when church bells rang two o' clock and hell broke loose. He wasn't far past it today when they rang the same hour.

Along the street towards him came a long column of dejected men, their hands in the air: captive Spanish soldiers and officers. Their eyes, dark and dismal in long, sad faces, flicked over Lope. He recognized some of them. Some of them, no doubt, recognized him. No one said a word or gave a sign. The laughing, mocking English guards hustling them along took no notice of him.

As the last prisoners in the column tramped past, de Vega turned to look back at them. What would happen to them? He hoped they would be ransomed or exchanged, not killed out of hand. The Spaniards hadn't murdered captives after their victories in 1588. Could he dare hope Elizabeth's ragtag followers would remember?

He wouldn't know, not for a while, maybe not ever. "Step lively, you rump-fed ronyons!" an Englishman called. Few of the captured men would have understood him, but gestures and the occasional buffet steered them down St. Swithin's Lane.

Lope's business lay in the other direction. His right hand fell to the hilt of the dagger he'd found. He was too battered to step lively, but nobody required it of him. At the best pace he could manage, he made his way east along Lombard Street, towards Bishopsgate, towards his revenge.

SHAKESPEARE WOKE TO SOMEONE SHAKING HIM. HE YAWNED AND looked around, trying to remember where he was and what he was doing here. Beside him, Richard Burbage was sitting up, also yawning and trying to knuckle sleep from his eyes. Thomas Phelippes spoke anxiously: "Your pardon, gentles, for it still lacks somewhat of two o' the clock, but I must away, and thought you better roused than left to sleep past the hour you set me."

"You must away?" Shakespeare paused to yawn again. He wouldn't have minded sleeping longer, not at all. "Wherefore?"

Phelippes didn't answer. Nicholas Skeres, who stood next to him, did: "For that he is summoned presently to Robert Cecil's side."

"Ah." Shakespeare nodded. No, Phelippes couldn't very well refuse that summons to keep standing over a couple of players. "Would Master Cecil see me as well?"

Skeres shook his head. "In due course, belike, but not yet."

That stung. Shakespeare had just reminded himself that he and Burbage didn't stand so high in the scheme of things. Having scornful Nick Skeres remind him of the same thing—having Robert Cecil remind him of the same thing through Skeres—made him wish this Westminster lawn would cover him up.

Phelippes said, "Mind you, Master Shakespeare, this signifies no want of respect for you, or for all you have wrought for England. But I stand—stood, I had better say—high in the Spaniards' councils; haply what I know o' their secrets will aid in our casting 'em forth."

"You do soothe me, sir, and in most gracious wise," Shakespeare said.

"Tom speaks sooth," Skeres said. "My principal's men have been abroad seeking him since yesterday, but in the garboil we found him not. He saith we (I myself, as't chanced) should not have found him, neither—should not have found him living, rather—were it not for you twain. In the kingdom's name, gramercy." By his tone, by his manner, he had every right to speak for England. Shakespeare found that as absurd as anything that had happened these past two mad days.

From Phelippes' tone, he didn't. "Lead. Guide. I follow as best I may," he told Skeres. "By your mustard doublet shall I know you—that I make out plain, spectacles or no." The two of them hurried off together.

Burbage heaved himself to his feet. "I'm away, too, Will. I must learn if Winifred be hale and safe, and the children." His face clouded at the last word. He and his wife had lost two sons in the past three years, and of their surviving son and daughter the girl was sickly.

"I'm with you as far as your house, an you'd have my company," Shakespeare said. Burbage nodded and gave him a hand to help him up. Brushing dry grass from himself, the poet went on, "Then to my lodging, that the Widow Kendall may know I live yet, and shall pay her rent—and that I may sleep in mine own bed."

"Onward, then," Burbage said. As they started east from Westminster, the player shook his head and laughed ruefully. "I'd give much to know how this our uprising fares beyond London. Isabella and Albert be fled, ay—but whither? Will they return anon, an army at their backs? Or do they purpose taking ship for Holland or Spain, there to preserve themselves?"

"I know not. Would I did," Shakespeare answered. "The inaudible and noiseless foot of time shall tell the tale."

Bodies lay here and there along the Strand and Fleet Street. Carrion birds rose from them in skrawking clouds as Shakespeare and Burbage walked past, then settled again to renew their feast. Most of the bodies were already naked, garments stolen by human scavengers there ahead of the birds.

"Holla, what scene is this?" Burbage said, pointing at the long column of men emerging from Ludgate and trudging towards him and Shakespeare.

Shakespeare shaded his eyes to peer through the cloud of dust the men kicked up. "Why, Spanish prisoners, an I mistake me not," he said a moment later. "So many swarthy souls cannot be of English race."

"You have the right of it," Burbage agreed when the head of the column came a little closer. "Those guardsmen—see you?—they're surely Englishmen."

"E'en so," Shakespeare said. One of the guards at the head of the column, a huge fellow with butter-yellow hair and beard who bore an old-fashioned cut-and-thrust broadsword—no fancy rapier for him!—waved cheerfully at the two men from the Theatre. Shakespeare and Burbage returned the salute. They left the road and stood on the verge as the prisoners shambled past.

Shakespeare stared at the stream of sad, dark faces. "Seek you de Vega?" Burbage asked.

"I do," the poet answered. "I'd fain know what befell him. Why came he not to the Theatre yesterday?"

"Whatever the reason, I'll shed no tears o'er him," Burbage said. "And in especial I'll shed no tears o'er the said absence, nor o'er its long continuance. I trembled lest he burst in halfway through Act Three at the head of a company of dons, crying, 'Give over! All's up!' "

"I had me the selfsame thought." Shakespeare knew he would never remember that first production of *Boudicca* without remembering the raw fear that went with it, the fear he could smell in the tiring room. He kept peering at the Spaniards. "Here, though, I see him not . . . nor any other."

"Eh?" Burbage said. "What's that?" Shakespeare didn't answer. He'd been eyeing not only the captives but also their guards, wondering if he'd find Ingram Frizer among the latter. Having already encountered Nick Skeres, he found the prospect of meeting another of Robert Cecil's men not at all unlikely. And the chances for robbery—and perhaps for murder as well—shepherding a column of prisoners offered seemed right up Frizer's alley. But Shakespeare saw no more of him than of Lope de Vega.

He and Burbage came into London through Ludgate. Not far inside the gate, on the north side of Bowyer Row, stood a church dedicated to St. Martin. Two priests, still in their cassocks, had been hanged from the branches of a chestnut beside the church. I SERVED ROME, said a placard tied to one of them. The placard tied to the other lewdly suggested just how he'd served the Pope.

Burbage stared, unmoved, at the dangling bodies. "May all the inquisitors suffer the same fate," he said in a voice like iron.

"May it be so indeed." Shakespeare knew he sounded fiercely eager. Fostered by the dons, the English Inquisition had had ten years to force the faith of Rome down its countrymen's throats. "They played the tyrant over us; let all their misdeeds come down on their own heads to haunt 'em."

He and Burbage walked on for a few paces. Then the player said, "If Elizabeth triumph here—which God grant—how many Papist priests'll be left alive in a year's time?"

"But a few, and those all desperate lest the hounds take them," Shakespeare said. Burbage nodded, plainly liking the prospect. Shakespeare sighed. Part of him would miss the grandeur of Catholic ritual. He knew better than to say any such thing: he had not the stuff of martyrs in him. He'd likewise meekly accepted the Romish rite after Isabella and Albert drove Elizabeth from her throne.

Old men here, men of Lord Burghley's age, would have seen their kingdom's faith change—Shakespeare had to pause to count on his fingers—five different times, from Catholic to Protestant to Catholic to Protestant to Catholic and now back to Protestant again. How could a man have any real faith left after so many swings? Better not to say that, either. Better not even to think it.

More dead priests either swung or lay in front of every church Shakespeare and Burbage passed. After a while, the corpses lost their power to shock. *Custom hath made it in me a property of easiness*: Shakespeare's own words sounded inside his head. Then he and Burbage came to St. Paul's. What the rampaging English had done to the priests there . . . Any man who could have stayed easy after seeing that had to be dead of soul.

"Oh, sweet Jesu," Burbage mumbled. He turned his head away. Shakespeare did the same. Too late, too late. He would spend years trying to forget, and knew he would spend them in vain.

Burbage dwelt in Cordwainer Street Ward, east of the great church. His house stood not far from the Red Lion, a wooden beast that marked a courtyard whose shops sold broadcloths and other draperies. As he and Shakespeare came up to the front door, it flew open. His wife dashed out and threw herself into his arms.

"God be praised, thou'rt hale!" Winifred Burbage cried, politely adding, "and you as well, Master Shakespeare." She gave her attention back to her husband. "This past day a thousand deaths I've died, knowing what thou'dst essay, dreading for that you came not hither. . . ." She was a well-made woman in her late twenties, auburn-haired, blue-eyed, worry now robbing her of much of her beauty.

Burbage kissed her, then struck a pose. "I *am* hale, as thou seest. What of thyself, and of William and Isabel?"

"We are well." His wife seemed to be fighting to convince herself as well as him. "The broil commencing, we kept within doors. A don was slain yonder, in front of Master Goodpasture's." She pointed across the street. No sign of the body remained. Gathering herself, she went on, "But for that, all might have seemed to pass in some far country, but 'twas real, 'twas real." She shivered.

So did Shakespeare, who'd seen more than she of how very real it was. He set a hand on Burbage's arm. "I praise the Lord all's well with you, and now I must away."

"God keep you safe, Will," the player said. Winifred Burbage nodded. In times like these, that was no idle phrase, but a real and urgent wish.

Church bells chimed two as Shakespeare started away from Burbage's house. He shivered again. Had it been but a day since Lord Westmorland's Men gave *Boudicca* instead of *King Philip*? That seemed impossible, but had to be true. He'd never known twenty-four more crowded hours. On a normal day, the company would be offering another play even now. Not today. He hoped the Theatre still stood. If not, how would he make his living? Like any player, he worried about that despite the money he'd got from Lord Burghley and from the dons for his two plays.

A man swaggered up the street with a featherbed over his shoulder, a cage with several small, frantically chirping birds in one hand, and a pistol in the other. How many Englishmen had used the uprising as an excuse for rapine against their own folk? That had hardly crossed Shakespeare's mind before a woman several blocks away screamed. How many Englishmen were using the uprising as an excuse for rape, too? *They revel the night, rob, murder, and commit the oldest sins the newest kind of ways*, he thought sadly.

Here and there, fires still smoldered. Had the wind been stronger, much of London might have burned. He started to cross himself to thank God that hadn't happened, but arrested the gesture before it was well begun. Up till yesterday, not signing himself could have marked him as a Protestant heretic. Now, using the sign of the cross might make him out to be a stubborn Papist. Men of fixed habit, men who could not quickly and easily adapt to changing times, would surely die because others judged them to be of the wrong opinion. It had happened before, the last time ten years ago.

He turned up Bishopsgate Street and hurried north towards his lodging-house. Less than a day earlier, he'd roared south down the same street towards the Tower of London, shouting, "Death—Death—Death to the dons!" And death had come to a great many of them since, and to a great many Englishmen as well. Yes, death had had his day, and Shakespeare feared him not yet glutted.

Turning left off Bishopsgate Street, the poet made his way through the maze of side streets and stinking alleys to the Widow Kendall's house. When he passed the ordinary where he often supped, he murmured, "Oh, praise God," to see it unharmed. That likely meant Kate was all right. He almost stopped to let her know he was safe, but, yawning, kept on instead. Tonight would do. He desperately craved more sleep.

The front door to the Widow Kendall's house stood open. Shakespeare frowned. That was unusual. His landlady habitually kept it closed, fearing—with some reason—thievery. Then a shriek rang from within the house. Shakespeare broke into a run.

Jane Kendall screamed again as he dashed through the front door and into the parlor. Cicely Sellis held a stool in front of her as if she were a lion-tamer, doing her best to keep at bay a man who menaced her with a dagger that almost made a smallsword.

Altogether without thinking, Shakespeare tackled the man from behind. The fellow let out a startled grunt. The knife flew from his hand. The Widow Kendall let out another shriek. Shakespeare noticed it only absently. He bore the man to the ground as Cicely Sellis grabbed the dagger. His foe tried to twist and strike at him, but all his movements were slow and clumsy. Though anything but a fighting man, Shakespeare had no trouble subduing him.

And when he did . . . "De Vega!" he exclaimed.

A great swollen livid bruise covered the left half of Lope's forehead. Shakespeare marveled that anyone could take such a hurt without having his skull completely smashed. No wonder the Spaniard was slower and less formidable than he might have been.

Almost as an afterthought, Shakespeare remembered he too had a knife. He pulled it free and held it to Lope's throat. "Give over!" he panted. "Cease your struggles, else you perish on the instant."

De Vega tensed for a final heave, but then went limp instead. "I yield me," he said sullenly. When he stared up at Shakespeare, one pupil was bigger than the other.

"Wherefore came you hither?" the poet asked him. "And why your menace 'gainst Mistress Sellis?"

"Wherefore?" Lope echoed. "For to kill this *bruja*, this witch, this whore—"

"I am no man's whore," Cicely Sellis said. Shakespeare noted she did not deny the other.

"Heaven be praised you came when you did, Master Will," the Widow Kendall said. "Methought there'd be foul, bloody murther done in mine own parlor."

"Haply not, had you helped more and wailed less," the cunning woman told her, voice tart.

Jane Kendall glared. She looked as if she wanted to answer sharply but did not have the nerve. Shakespeare would have thought twice before angering Cicely Sellis, too.

He pulled his attention back to Lope de Vega. "Say on. What mean you?"

De Vega hesitated, then shrugged. "Well, why not? What boots it now? Having heard you were seen consorting with Robert Cecil in the street, I hastened hither yesterday, to learn if you purposed treason despite your fine verses on his Most Catholic Majesty."

Shakespeare shivered. So some spy had recognized Robert Cecil even with his beggar's disguise! By what flimsy threads the uprising had hung! But they hadn't broken, not quite. Shakespeare asked, "How hath this aught to do with Mistress Sellis?"

"Why, we chanced to meet in this very parlor," Lope answered, as if Shakespeare should already have known that. "We chanced to meet and, she asking why I was come, I spake the truth, thinking her honest—"

"And so I am," Cicely Sellis said. By the Widow Kendall's expression, her opinion differed, but she held her tongue.

"She bade me enter her chamber," Lope continued. Jane Kendall stirred yet again. Yet again, she dared do no more than stir. "She bade me enter her chamber," the Spaniard repeated, "and there she bewitched me. By some foul sorcery, she cast oblivion upon me, made me to forget why I'd come hither, made me to forget I was for the Theatre bound, there to play Don Juan de Idiáquez. . . ."

At that, the Widow Kendall did cross herself. Her lips moved in a silent paternoster. Cicely Sellis only shrugged. Mommet came out of her chamber and wove around her ankles. Bending to scratch behind the cat's ears, she said, " 'Twas but the same sleight I used to calm Master Street this Easter past." Mommet purred. He pushed his face against the cunning woman's hand.

"Ah," Shakespeare said: the most noncommittal noise he could make. He'd thought what she did to Jack Street then was witchcraft, and no mere sleight. His landlady's fear-filled eyes said she thought the same.

"And then," Lope went on, "and then . . ." He shot a furiously burning glare at the cunning woman. "And then she did lie with me in love, to maze me further and lead me astray from my purpose in coming hither. Nor did she fail of hers." Reproach filled his voice. *For himself or for her?* Shakespeare wondered. *Belike both.* His own gaze flicked from de Vega to Cicely Sellis and back again. He hadn't expected to be so jealous of the Spaniard.

Jealousy wasn't what Jane Kendall felt. "So thou *art* a doxy, then," she spat at Cicely Sellis. "Whore! Trull! Poxy callet!"

"Oh, be still, you stale, mouse-eaten cheese," the cunning woman replied. "Your virginity, your old virginity, is like one of those French withered pears: it looks ill, it eats dryly."

The Widow Kendall stared, popeyed with fury. Having had a husband, she surely was no virgin. And yet, after what she'd called the younger woman, the word seemed to stick to her, and in no flattering way.

Calmly, Cicely Sellis nodded to Shakespeare. "Ay, I lay with him. Both you and he had made it pikestaff plain somewhat of no small import was afoot, the which he must not let nor hinder. I lay with him, and thought of England."

"Of England?" Lope yelped. "I on her belly fell, she on her back, and she bethought her of *England*? Marry, what a liar thou art, Mistress Sellis! 'Twas not of England, but of thy—" He seemed to have lost the English word. Shakespeare did not supply it. De Vega, miffed and more than miffed, addressed his words to him: "I do assure you, Master Will, her caterwauls were like to those coming from the throat of this accursed beast, her witchy familiar." He jerked a thumb towards Mommet.

The cat arched its back and hissed. Cicely Sellis flushed. By that, Shakespeare judged she likely had thought of other things besides England when she bedded Lope, and taken more pleasure than she cared to admit now. But that didn't mean she *hadn't* thought of England. And if she'd kept the Spanish officer from going through the papers in Shakespeare's chest, she might have saved the uprising. Had the dons had even a few hours to make ready . . . Shakespeare didn't want to think about that.

He said, "One may do for love of country that which one would not else." De Vega howled. The Widow Kendall sniffed. The cunning woman nodded again. Was that relief on her face? Shakespeare couldn't be sure, not least because up till now she'd always been so much in control of herself that he didn't recall her wearing such an expression before.

"I still say—" Jane Kendall began.

"Wait, an't please you," Shakespeare said. His landlady blinked; he seldom presumed to interrupt her. He went on, "You were wise, Mistress Kendall, to say not that which may not be mended. For the times *do* change, will you or nill you, and it will go hard for those who change not with them."

The times *would* change, if the rebellion succeeded. He didn't know it would. But the Widow Kendall didn't know it wouldn't. And, as one who'd shown herself to be a devout Catholic these past ten years, she stood to lose perhaps a great deal if people she knew denounced her. She licked her lips. Shakespeare could see that realization growing in her. She must have seen—the dons had made sure all England saw—what happened to stubborn Protestants. With a new spin of the wheel, it would be the Papists' turn. She exhaled with what might have been anger, but said not another word.

Cicely Sellis nodded towards Lope. "What would you with him, Master Will?" she asked.

"I?" Shakespeare sounded startled, even to himself. He'd never held a man's life in his hands before. If he cut de Vega's throat here in the parlor, no one would think the less of him (save possibly Jane Kendall, on account of the mess it would make). If . . . He sighed and shook his head. "I have not the murtherer's blood in me," he said, as if someone had claimed he did. "He acted but from duty, and from loyalty to his own King. Let him be made prisoner, to be ransomed or exchanged or otherwise enlarged as fate allow."

"Gramercy," Lope said softly. "I am your servant." He managed a ragged chuckle. "And, but for yon witch, I should have made a *splendid* Don Juan de Idiáquez."

That jerked a laugh and a nod from Shakespeare. "Ay, belike," he said, and then, " 'Twould like me one day to see *King Philip* on the stage. An you bide yet in England, Master Lope, the part's yours."

De Vega gave him a crooked grin. "With our Lord, I say, let this cup pass from me."

Shakespeare had had that thought, too. "Come now," Shakespeare said, gesturing towards the door with his knife. "I will give you over into the charge of those whose duty is to take captives, for I know there be such men. Think not to flee, neither. You have yielded—and flight would prove the worse for you, we English holding London."

"Before God, I shall not flee." As Lope got to his feet, he put a hand to his bruised head. "Before God, I *cannot* flee far. But I would not, even if I could. I have seen your London wolves stand like greyhounds in the slips, straining at the start, and would not have them dog my heels."

"Let's away, then," Shakespeare said. "By my troth, I'll give you into the hands of none others but them that will hold you safe until you may once more be set at liberty." De Vega nodded. Even that small motion must have pained him, for he hissed and gingerly touched his head again. Shakespeare made a leg at Jane Kendall and Cicely Sellis. "Farewell, ladies."

His landlady dropped him an awkward curtsy by way of reply. Cicely Sellis dipped her head, murmuring, "I stand much in your debt, Master Will."

And how would I have that debt repaid? he wondered. *In the same coin she gave the Spaniard?* He shoved Lope. "Let's away," he said again, sounding rough as a soldier.

He didn't have to take de Vega far. They'd just come out into Bishopsgate Street when a fresh column of captives shambled down from the north. "Move along, you poor cuckoldy knaves; you louts; you remorseless, treacherous, lecherous, kindless villains," shouted the Englishman at their head. "Ay, move along, or 'twill be the worse for you, you blackguards, you virgin-violators, you inexcrable dogs." Most of the Spaniards couldn't have understood a word of the abuse he showered on them, but they did understand they had to keep moving.

Shakespeare waved to that loud Englishman, calling, "Bide a moment! I've another don here, for to add to your party."

"Well, bring him on, then, the damned murtherous fat-kidneyed rascal," the fellow replied.

Careless of whatever anguish it might have cost, Lope gave him a courtier's bow. "I am thy servant, thou proud disdainful haggard," he said.

It must have sounded like praise to the Englishman. "You're a sweet-tongued losel, eh?" he said. "Belike the lickerish ladies think the same?" De Vega nodded, which the man didn't seem to expect. He jerked a thumb towards the captives. "Get in amongst 'em. No trouble, or you'll be sorry for it."

"I am already sorry for it," Lope replied, but he took his place with the rest of the Spaniards. Away they went, down deeper into London.

As Shakespeare turned back towards his lodging-house, a brisk spatter of gunfire rang out not too far away: close enough, at any rate, for him to hear the cries of wounded men immediately afterwards. The fight for London hadn't quite finished. He couldn't tell whether the cries were in English or Spanish. Men in torment sounded much the same in either language.

The sun was sinking fast, though clouds and smoke—more of the former and less of the latter than he'd seen the day before. Most of the time, he would have gone to the Widow Kendall's and then to his ordinary for supper. He'd already been to the lodging-house. The excitement with de Vega had chased sleep from him—and there stood the ordinary, its door open and inviting.

When he walked in, Kate was setting candles on the tables and lighting them with a burning splinter. One man had already taken his place near the hearth. He was cutting up the beefsteak that sat on a wooden trencher in front of him. "Will!" Kate exclaimed, and dropped the candles she was holding. She ran to him, took him in her arms, squeezed the breath out of him, and kissed him. "Sweet Will! God be praised I see thee whole and hale!" She kissed him again.

"A right friendly dive, this," said the man with the beefsteak, a grin on his greasy face.

Shakespeare ignored him. Holding Kate, kissing her, he forgot about Cicely Sellis. No, that went too far. He didn't forget about her, but did put her in perspective. She was a temptation: a sweet one, but no more. Kate . . . Were he not tied to Anne back in Stratford, he would gladly have made her his wife.

He pushed that thought aside, as he had to. "As you see me," he said, "and passing glad to see thee." Now he kissed her. The fellow by the hearth whooped. Neither of them paid him the least attention.

At last the kiss ended, but they still clung to each other. Kate asked, "What wouldst thou, my darling?"

"Thou knowest full well what I would," Shakespeare answered. "What I will, what I can, what I may . . ." He shrugged. "Thou knowest likewise the difficulties, the impediments, the obstacles before me. I have not lied to thee." He took a certain forlorn pride in that. Kate nodded. He went on, "An I be able them to thrust aside, I'll do't in a heartbeat."

"May it be so. Oh, may it be so! With all in flux, who can say this or that shall not come to pass? If Elizabeth be free o' the Tower—"

"She is," Shakespeare said. "With mine own eyne I saw her leave it, borne on Sir Robert Devereux his shoulders."

"Well, then," Kate said, as if that proved something. Maybe, to her, it did. "Who could have dreamt such a thing, e'en a week gone by? So great a miracle being worked for England, why not a smaller one, for us twain alone?"

"Ay, why not?" Shakespeare agreed, and kissed her once more. That he remained alive and free to do it struck him as more than miracle enough right now.

WHEN ONE OF LOPE DE VEGA'S LOVERS CAUGHT HIM WITH ANOTHER outside the bear-baiting arena in Southwark, he'd thought the round wooden building, so like a theatre in construction, would remain forever the scene of his worst humiliation. Now here he was back at the arena, and humiliated again: the English were using it to house the Spanish prisoners they'd taken. He squatted glumly on the sand-strewn dirt floor where so many bears and hounds had died.

The beasts were gone, taken away to another pit. Their stenches lingered: the sharp stink of the dogs and the bears' ranker, muskier reek. With so many captives packed into the place, the commonplace smells of unwashed men and their wastes were crowding out the animal odors.

Gray clouds gathered overhead. If it rained, the arena floor would turn to mud. Lope knew he would have to find himself a place in one of the galleries. *I should have done that sooner*, he thought. But he hadn't had the energy. He'd been sunk in lethargy since taking the blow that almost broke his skull, and especially since failing to avenge himself on Cicely Sellis. After that failure, nothing seemed to matter.

Not far away, one of his countrymen asked another, "In the name of God, why does no one rescue us?"

"Those who win, rescue," the other Spaniard said. "If we are not rescued, it is because we do not win."

That made much more sense than Lope wished it did. The first Spaniard said, "But how can we lose to this English rabble? We beat them before—beat them with ease. Are they such giants now? Have we turned into dwarfs these past ten years?"

"Our army is scattered over the country now," the other man answered. "English soldiers were supposed to do much of the job for us, so a lot of our men could go back to the Netherlands and put down the rebels there."

"Oh, yes. Oh, yes!" the first captive said. "The English did a wonderful job of holding down the countryside—till they turned on us like so many rabid dogs."

Lope said, "And the Netherlands have risen in revolt again, too, or so the English say. Just when we thought we had them quiet at last . . ." He wanted to shake his head, but didn't. Even now, more than a week after he'd been struck down, such motion could bring on blinding headaches. After a moment, he continued, "And who knows what Philip III will do once word of this finally reaches him?"

Neither of the other men answered for a little while. At last, one of them murmured, "Ah, if only his father were still alive." His friend nodded. So did Lope, cautiously. Philip II would have had the determination to fight hard against an uprising like this. That, of course, was not the smallest reason the English had waited till he was dead to rebel. And everyone knew all too well that Philip III was not the man, not half the man, his father had been.

That night, cannon fire off to the east interrupted Lope's rest. He wondered what it meant, but no one inside the bear-baiting arena could see out. He'd just dozed off in spite of the distant booms when an enormous explosion, much larger than a mere cannon blast, jerked him upright and make him wonder if his head would burst as well. After that, the gunfire quickly diminished. An almost aching silence returned. Having nothing else he could do, he lay down and went back to sleep.

When the sun rose, the Englishmen who came in to feed their captives were jubilant. "Some of your galleons essayed sailing up the Thames," said the fellow who handed Lope a bowl of sour-smelling porridge, "but we sent 'em back, by God, tails 'twixt their legs."

"How, I pray you?" Lope asked. He shoveled the porridge into his mouth with his fingers, for he had not even a horn spoon to call his own.

"How? Fireships, the which we sent at 'em from just beyond London Bridge," the Englishman answered. "The current slid the blazing hulks against your fleet sailing upriver, the which had to go about right smartly and flee before 'em: else they too had been given o'er to the flames. As indeed the *San Juan* was—heard you not the great roar when the fire reached her magazine?"

"The *San Juan*?" Lope crossed himself, muttering an *Ave Maria*. He'd come to England in that ship.

"And the *San Mateo de Portugal* lies hard aground," the fellow added, "hard aground and captured. I doubt not e'en you cock-a-hoop dons'll think twice or ever you try the like again." He went on to feed someone else.

"What does he say?" a Spaniard asked Lope. "I heard in amongst his English the names of our ships."

De Vega translated. He added, "I don't know that he was telling the truth, mind."

"It seems likely," the other man said. "It seems only too likely. Would a lie have such detail?"

"A good one might," Lope answered, though he knew he was trying to convince himself at least as much as the man with whom he was talking.

Day followed day. No Spanish force fought its way into London. At least as much as anything else, that convinced Lope the Englishman had told him the truth. The longer he stayed in the bear-baiting arena, the plainer it grew that the English uprising was succeeding.

With the arena still full of prisoners, some of the Londoners' usual sport was taken away from them. Escorted by armed and armored guards, they began coming in to view the Spanish captives. Lope suspected it was a poor amusement next to what they were used to. *Maybe they'll set mastiffs on us instead of on the bears*, he thought. He took care never to say that aloud. When it first crossed his mind, it seemed a bitter joke. But the English might do it, if only it occurred to them.

Most of the men who came to see the Spaniards showed them a certain respect. Anyone who'd fought in war knew misfortune could befall even the finest soldiers. The women were worse. They jeered and mocked and generally made Lope think the guardsmen were protecting his countrymen and him from them rather than the reverse.

And then, one drizzly day, he saw a black-haired, black-eyed beauty on an English nobleman's arm. The nobleman stared at the Spaniards as if at so many animals in a cage. So did his companion, who laughed and murmured in his ear and rubbed against him and did everything but set her hand on his codpiece right there in front of everyone. And he only strutted and swaggered and slipped his arm around her waist, displaying to the world the new toy he'd found.

Slowly and deliberately, Lope turned away. He might have known

Catalina Ibañez would make the best of whatever happened in England. He could have told that nobleman a thing or two, but what point? Besides, sooner or later the fellow would find out for himself.

De Vega did hope Catalina didn't recognize him. By now, the beard was dark on his cheeks and jawline as well as his chin. To her eye, he should have been just one more glum and grimy prisoner among so many. Having her gloat over his misery would have been more than he could bear. He watched her out of the corner of his eye.

She gave no sign she knew him: a tiny victory, but all he'd get in here. She laughed again, a sound like tinkling bells, and stood on tiptoe to kiss her new protector on the cheek. Chuckling indulgently, he patted her backside. Lope prayed for a bear, or even for mastiffs. God must have been busy somewhere else, for Catalina and the Englishman strolled out of the arena together.

XV

As it had on that fateful afternoon six weeks earlier, absolute silence reigned in the Theatre. Into it, Joe Boardman once more spoke Boudicca's final lines:

> "We Britons never did, nor never shall,
> Lie at the proud foot of a conqueror,
> But when we do first help to wound ourselves.
> Come the three corners of the world in arms,
> And we shall shock them. Naught shall make us rue,
> If Britons to themselves do rest but true."

The Queen of the Iceni died again.

As he had then, Shakespeare strode forward past Boudicca's body. As he had then, he ended the play:

> "No epilogue here, unless you make it;
> If you want your freedom, go and take it."

And, as he had then, he stood there at the front of the stage and waited for whatever came next.

What came, this time, was applause, wave after wave of it, from groundlings and galleries alike. Shakespeare's eyes went to the velvet-upholstered chair that had been set up in the middle gallery. He bowed low to Queen Elizabeth.

She inclined her head by way of reply. She had once more the outward seeming of a Queen: her gown glimmering with pearls, her great ruff starched and snowy, pale powder banishing the years from her face, a coronet in place in her curly red wig. Yet to Shakespeare's mind she'd never been more queenly than when she spoke, all unadorned, from the window in the Tower.

Behind the poet, the players who'd acted in *Boudicca* came forward to take their bows. At the earlier performance, they hadn't got the plaudits they deserved. The play had aimed at firing the audience against the Spanish occupiers, and met its aim even better than Shakespeare dared hope. That meant the players, though, went all but forgotten.

Not now. The audience clapped and stamped their feet and shouted and roared. Lord Westmorland's Men bowed again and again, but the tumult would not die. Robert Cecil—now Sir Robert—who sat beside Elizabeth, leaned towards her and spoke behind his hand. Shakespeare saw her smile and nod. Then she rose to her feet and blew the company a kiss. Along with everyone else, Shakespeare bowed once more, lower than ever. The din in the Theatre redoubled.

At last, after what seemed forever, it began to ebb. A trumpeter behind Elizabeth's seat winded his horn. The sharp, clear notes drew everyone's attention. Elizabeth rose once more and said, "Lord Westmorland being a proved traitor and Romish heretic who hath fled with the dons, and the name of a former company of players having fallen into misfortunate disuse, it is my pleasure to ordain and declare that the players here before me assembled shall be known henceforward and forevermore as the Queen's Men, betokening my great favor which for most excellent reason they do enjoy."

That drew even more applause than the play had. Once again, Shakespeare bowed very low. So did all the members of the company behind him. When laughter mingled with the applause, Shakespeare looked over his shoulder. There was Will Kemp, turning his reverence to the Queen into a silly caper. Burbage looked horrified. When Shakespeare glanced up towards Elizabeth in the gallery, she was laughing. Maybe that said Kemp knew her humor better than Burbage did. Maybe—perhaps more likely—it said the clown couldn't help clowning, come what might.

The trumpeter blew another flourish. He had to blow it twice before the crowd heeded him and quieted. Elizabeth said, "Be it also known that I purpose rewarding the players of the Queen's Men with more than the name alone, the which is but wind and air, good for vaunting but little else. Your valor in giving this play when the foul occupiers of our land would vilest treason style it shall of a surety be not forgot. That I am Queen again over more than mine own chamber I am not least through your exertions, nor shall I never forget the same."

Cheers rang out again, some of them hungry: not so much envious as speculative. *They shall have favor and wealth. How can I dispossess 'em of those, taking them for mine own?* Shakespeare could all but hear the thoughts behind the plaudits. Had he been standing amongst the groundlings or even in the galleries, such thoughts might have run through his head, too. *Consumption of the purse is so often incurable, who'd not seek a remedy therefrom?*

One more trumpet flourish rang out. Trailed by Robert Cecil, the Queen descended from the middle gallery. Instead of leaving the Theatre, though, she made her way through the groundlings towards the stage. They parted before her like the Red Sea before Moses. In black velvet, the younger Cecil might have been her shadow behind her.

"How may I ascend?" she asked Shakespeare, who still stood farthest forward of the company.

He pointed back towards the right. "Thitherward lies the stair, your Majesty."

With a brusque nod, she used the stairway to come up onto the stage. Sir Robert remained at her heel. Fear gnawed Shakespeare. If anyone in the audience meant her ill, he had but to draw a pistol and. . . . But no one did. Elizabeth's confident, even arrogant stride said she was certain no one would. Perhaps that confidence helped ensure that no one would. Perhaps. Shakespeare remained nervous even so.

The Queen walked up beside him. She looked out over the audience for a moment, again seeming almost to defy anyone to strike at her. Then she said, "Know, Master Shakespeare, you are much in my mind and heart for writing this *Boudicca* in despite of the Spaniards, showing forth no common courage in the doing."

I was more afeared of Ingram Frizer's knife than of the dons, Shakespeare thought. Sometimes, though, not all the truth needed telling. Here, he could and did get by with a murmured, "Your Majesty, I am your servant."

Elizabeth nodded again. "Just so. And you served me right well, in a way none other might have matched." Shakespeare knew a stab of grief for Christopher Marlowe. But even Kit had said he was best suited for this business. Then the Queen added another sharp word, one that cast all thoughts of Marlowe from his mind: "Kneel."

"Your Maj—?" Shakespeare squeaked in surprise. Elizabeth's eyes flashed. Awkwardly, Shakespeare dropped to his right knee.

"Your sword, Sir Robert," Elizabeth said.

"Is ever at your service, your Majesty." Robert Cecil drew his rapier and handed it to the Queen.

By the way she held it, she knew how to use it. She brought the flat down on Shakespeare's shoulder, hard enough to make him sway. "Arise, Sir William!" she said.

Dizzily, Shakespeare did, to the cheers of his fellow players and of the crowd in the Theatre. Queen Elizabeth returned the rapier to Robert Cecil, who slid it back into its sheath. "Your—Your Majesty," Shakespeare stammered, "I find me altogether at a loss for words."

"This I do now forgive in you, for that you were at no loss whilst setting pen to page on this play, which did so much to aid in mine own enlargement and England's freedom from the tyrant's heel," Elizabeth replied. "The necessity of this action makes my speech the more heartfelt, hoping you will measure my good affection with the right balance of my actions in gratitude for yours, for the which I render you a million of thanks. Sweet is my inclination towards you, whereby I may demonstrate my care: of this we shall speak more anon." She swept off the stage, Sir Robert Cecil once more following close.

Out she went, through the groundlings. They cheered her as lustily as before, and turned back to shout, "Hurrah for Sir William!" Still dazed, Shakespeare bowed to them one last time before leaving the stage. *And had we given* King Philip, *and had the rebellion failed, Queen Isabella might have dubbed me knight this day*, he thought, *at which spectacle these selfsame folk would have cheered no less.*

And if they had given *King Philip*, and if Isabella had knighted him, would he be thinking Elizabeth might have done the same had the company presented *Boudicca*? He shook his head, not so much in denial as in reluctance to get caught up in the tangling web of what might have been. Going back to the tiring room was nothing but a relief.

He found no peace there. Players kept coming up to pay him their respects. So did the tireman, the bookkeeper, the tireman's helpers, and everybody else who managed to get into the crowded room. Some of them were really congratulating him. More, he judged, were congratulating his rank.

That thought must have occurred to Will Kemp, too. After bowing low—far too low to a knight (or to a duke, for that matter)—the clown said, "Ay, by my halidom, you're a right rank cove now," and held his nose.

"Go to!" Shakespeare said, laughing. " 'Tis the stench of your wit I'd fain rout from my nostrils."

"Had I more rank, I'd be less. Had God Himself less, He'd be more," Kemp said.

"Your quibbles fly like arrows at St. Sebastian." Shakespeare mimed being struck.

"Arrows by any other name would smell as sweet," Kemp retorted. Shakespeare flinched. However fond of puns he was himself, he'd never looked to see *Romeo and Juliet* so brutalized. Loftily, Kemp added, "The same holds not for me."

"Naught holds for you," Richard Burbage said, coming up beside him. "Nor honor nor sense nor decency."

"Ah, but so that you love me, Dick, all's well!" Kemp cried, and planted a wet, noisy kiss on Burbage's cheek.

"Avaunt!" Burbage pushed him away, hard. "Aroint thee, mooncalf!"

The clown sighed. "Alas, that love, so gentle in his view, should be so tyrannous and rough in proof." He puckered up again.

"Good Lord, what madness rules in brainsick men," Burbage said.

"I am not mad; I would to heaven I were," Kemp replied. "For then, 'tis like, I should forget myself." He capered bonelessly—and more than a little lewdly.

Burbage looked ready to thwack him in good earnest. "Give over, the both of you," Shakespeare said.

Will Kemp gave him another extravagant bow. "I'd sooner be a cock and disobey the day than myself and disobey a knight."

"Half cock, belike," Burbage said.

"I yield to your judgment, sweet Dick, for you of all men surely are all cock as well."

"Enough!" Shakespeare shouted, loud enough to cut through the din in the tiring room and make everyone stare at him. He didn't care. "Give over I said, and give over I meant," he went on. "The Queen hath said we are to be rewarded according to our deserts, and you'd quarrel one with another? 'Tis foolishness. 'Tis worse than foolishness: 'swounds, 'tis madness. Did we brabble so whilst in the mist of terrible and unavoided danger we readied *Boudicca* for the stage?"

Shaming them into stopping their sniping didn't work as he'd hoped. Burbage nodded. "Ay, by my troth, we did," he declared.

Kemp only shrugged. "Me, I know not. Ask of Matt Quinn."

Shakespeare threw his hands in the air. "Go on, then," he said. "Since it likes you so well, go on. You were pleased to play on cocks. Strap spurs on your heels, then, and and tear each other i'the pit." Will Kemp stirred. Shakespeare glared at him. *That* quibble never got made.

As the players left the Theatre, Burbage caught up with Shakespeare and said, "There be times. . . ." His big hands made a twisting motion, as if he were wringing a cock's neck.

"Easy," Shakespeare said. "Easy. He roils you of purpose."

"And I know it," Burbage replied. "Natheless, he doth roil me."

"Showing him which, you but urge him on to roil you further."

"If he prick me, do I not bleed? If he poison me, do I not die? Have I not dimensions, sense, affections, passions? If he wrong me, shall I not revenge? The villainy he teacheth me I will execute, and it shall go hard but I will better the instruction."

"He is a clown by very nature," Shakespeare said. "It will out, will he or no. And he hath a gift the auditors do cherish—as have you," he added hastily. "The company is better—the Queen's Men are better—for having both you twain."

"The Queen's Men." Burbage's glower softened. "There you have me, Will. A prize worth winning, and we have won it. And I needs must own he holp us in the winning." He was, when he remembered to be, a just man.

When Shakespeare walked into his lodging-house, he found Jane Kendall all fluttering with excitement. "Is it true, Master Shakespeare?" she trilled. "Is it true?"

"Is what true?" he asked, confused.

"Are you . . . Sir William?"

He nodded. "I am. But how knew you that?"

Before his landlady answered, she took him in her arms, stood on tiptoe, and kissed him on the cheek. With her blasting and scandalous breath, he would rather have had a kiss from Will Kemp's lips. He didn't say so. He would have had no chance anyhow, for she was off: "Why, I had it from Lily Perkins three doors down, who had it from her neighbor Joanna Ball, who had it from Peg Mercer, who had it from her husband Peter, who had it in his shop in Bishopsgate Street from a wight returned to London from the Theatre. Naught simpler."

"I see," Shakespeare said, and so, in a way, he did. Rumor ran so fast, before long it would likely start reporting things *before* they happened. *As well it did not with* Boudicca, he thought, *else the dons had found some way to thwart us.*

"Sir William," the Widow Kendall repeated, fluttering her eyelashes at him. "To have a knight dwelling in mine own house—dwelling so that he may pay his scot, I should say."

"Fear not, Mistress Kendall," Shakespeare said. "Whilst I be no rich man, still I am not poor, neither. Have I ever failed to pay what's owed you?"

"Never once—the proof of which being you dwell here yet," his landlady replied. Shakespeare hid a sigh. She loved him for his silver alone.

The door to Cicely Sellis' room opened. Out came the cunning woman, with a round-faced matron with a worried expression. Almost everyone who came to see her had a worried expression. Who that was not worried would come to see a cunning woman? Mommet bounded out and started sniffing Shakespeare's shoes, which to his nose must have told the tale of where the poet had been.

"Rest you easy. All will be well," Cicely Sellis told her client. "That which you dread shall remain dark—"

"God grant it be so!" the other woman burst out.

"It shall remain dark," Cicely Sellis said soothingly, "an you betray yourself not by reason of your own alarums internal."

"I would not," the woman said. "I *will* not. God's blessings upon you, Mistress Sellis." Out she went, seeming happier than she had a moment before.

Shakespeare wondered what she didn't want revealed. Had she collaborated with the Spaniards? Or had she simply taken a lover? He was unlikely to find out. If he were putting this scene in a play, though, what would he choose?

If he were putting this scene in a play, he would be hard pressed to find a boy actor who could reproduce the terror and loathing on Jane Kendall's face as she stared at the cunning woman. *Whore*, she mouthed silently. *Witch*. But she said not a word aloud. Cicely Sellis paid her rent on time, too.

She nodded now to Shakespeare. "God give you good even, Sir William."

The Widow Kendall jerked. That proved too much for her to bear. "How knew you of's knighthood, hussy?" she demanded. "These past two hours, were you not closeted away with bell, book, and candle?"

She had that wrong. Bell, book, and candle were parts of the ceremony of excommunication, not the tools of the witch who might deserve it. Shakespeare knew as much. By the glint of amusement in Cicely Sellis' eye, so did she. She didn't try to tell her landlady so. All she said was, "Did you not call Master Shakespeare Sir William just now? And did not Lily Perkins bring you word of the said knighthood, clucking like a hen the while? I am not deaf, Mistress Kendall—though betimes, in your disorderly house, I wish I were."

After a moment to take that in, Jane Kendall jerked again. Shakespeare looked down at Mommet to hide his smile. The cunning woman had got her revenge for the Widow Kendall's mouthed *whore.* When his face was sober again, he nodded to her and said, "Good den to you as well, Mistress Sellis."

"I do congratulate you, you having done so much the honor to deserve," Cicely Sellis said.

"My thanks," Shakespeare answered.

"May your fame grow, and your wealth with it, so that, like any rich and famous man, you may build your own grand house and need no longer live in any such place as this," the cunning woman told him.

Jane Kendall jerked once more. "Naught's amiss here!" she said shrilly. "An you find somewhat here mislikes you, Mistress Sellis, why seek *you* not other habitation?"

"For that I can afford no better," Cicely Sellis said. "The same holds not for Master Shakes—for Sir William."

"No better's to be found," Jane Kendall asserted. Cicely Sellis said nothing at all. Her silence seemed to Shakespeare the most devastating reply of all. And so it must have seemed to his landlady, too, for she yelped, "Why, 'tis true!" as if the cunning woman had called her a liar to her face.

And Cicely Sellis was right: he could afford finer than a one-third share of a Bishopsgate bedchamber. Whether he wanted to spend the money for better was a different question. He had in full measure the player's ingrained mistrust of good fortune and fear it would not last. How many men had he known who, briefly flush, spent what they had while they had it and then, misfortune striking, wished they hadn't been so prodigal? Too many, far too many.

He didn't care to come out with that openly. And so, instead, he smiled and said, "Why, how ever should I lay me down without Jack Street's nightingale strains, as from some pomegranate tree, to soothe mine ears and weigh my eyelids down?"

"Nightingale?" Cicely Sellis shook her head. "A jackass braying through a trump of iron might make such sounds were he well beaten whilst he blew, but assuredly no thing of feathers."

"He's not so bad as that." The Widow Kendall did her best to sound as if she were sincere.

"Indeed not: he's worse by far," Cicely Sellis said. "And Master Will—Sir William—lieth not behind stout doors which with distance do help the unseemly racket to abate, but in the selfsame chamber. That he be not deafened quite wonders me greatly."

The odd thing was, Shakespeare had meant what he said. However appalling he'd found the glazier's snores when Street first moved into the lodging-house, they were only background noise to him these days.

"Know you, Sir William, you are and shall ever be welcome here, so that you pay the rent when 'tis due." Not to save her soul could Jane Kendall have omitted that qualifying clause.

"I thank you," Shakespeare said dutifully. He might have been less dutiful had he not known she would have told Ingram Frizer the same as long as whatever men the ruffian killed in the parlor were not themselves tenants of hers.

With autumn dying and icy-fanged winter drawing nigh, night came early. Shakespeare made his way through darkness to his ordinary. "Sir William!" Kate exclaimed when he walked into the smoky warmth and light. She dropped him a pretty curtsy.

He started to ask how she knew, as he had back at the lodging-house. Then someone at a table by the fireplace waved to him. There sat Nick Skeres and Thomas Phelippes. "Will you sup with us, Sir William?" Skeres called. By the way he slurred his speech, he'd already drained the goblet in front of him a good many times.

Shakespeare took a stool and sat down beside Phelippes. The sallow, pockmarked little man's face was also flushed behind his new spectacles. At first, Shakespeare thought the firelight lent him color. Then Phelippes breathed wine into his face. "Is it a celebration?" the poet asked.

"Naught less, Sir William, by my troth," Phelippes said grandly, more warmth—more expression generally—in his voice than Shakespeare was used to hearing from him. Raising his goblet, he called out to Kate: "Somewhat to drink here, prithee! My throat's parched as the Afric desert!"

"Anon, sir, anon," she answered, as servers often did when they were in less of a hurry than their customers.

"What sort of celeb—?" Shakespeare stopped. He pointed first at Phelippes, then at Skeres. "Do I behold, by any chance, Sir Thomas and Sir Nicholas?"

"You do, Sir William." Nick Skeres—Sir Nicholas Skeres now—nodded and giggled.

"Bravely done, gentlemen." Shakespeare clasped hands with Phelippes and Skeres in turn. He'd suspected the one and feared the other, whose appearances, like those of a petrel, foretold storms ahead. But the storms had passed, and the fear and suspicion with them. They'd all been on the same side, and their side had won. That was plenty to make them a band of brothers, at least for tonight.

Kate set bowls of beef stew before Skeres and Phelippes. "My thanks, sweetheart," Skeres said, and leered at her. Shakespeare eyed his new "brother" as Abel must have eyed Cain.

But his jealousy passed when he saw Kate ignoring Skeres. Pointing to a bowl, he asked, "That's this even's threepenny supper?" She nodded. Shakespeare said, "I'll have the same, then, and sack for accompaniment."

"Another penny," she warned, as if he didn't know as much already.

"Be it so," he said.

"I'll bring it you presently, Will—Sir William." Kate hurried off.

"Is not our hostess of the tavern a most sweet wench?" Skeres watched her hips work as she went.

"She's an honest woman," Shakespeare replied with some asperity.

"She is a woman, therefore to be won." Nick Skeres ran his tongue wetly over fleshy lips. "She's beautiful and therefore to be wooed." A dull thump came from under the table. Skeres yelped and grabbed at his ankle. "Here, what occasioned that?" he said.

"Thou jolthead, seest thou not she's the poet's?" Phelippes hissed. Shakespeare didn't think he was supposed to catch that, but he did.

Skeres kept rubbing at the injured ankle, but his face cleared. "I cry your pardon, Sir William—I knew not," he said.

Shakespeare waved it aside. Kate brought him his goblet of sack, saying, "Supper in a moment." He nodded, watching Skeres. Skeres watched the serving woman. Shakespeare nodded again, this time to himself. He'd expected nothing else. He trusted Kate. Skeres? He didn't think anyone would ever be able to trust Sir Nicholas Skeres.

He raised his goblet. "Your good health, gentlemen," he said, "and God save the Queen!"

They all drank. "God hath saved her indeed," Phelippes said. "Likewise hath He saved this her kingdom, that all feared lost for ever to the dons and to the priests."

Kate set Shakespeare's bowl of stew before him. This time, Skeres' gaze didn't light on her bosom or her haunches. The newly minted knight lifted his glass of wine. "Here's to the Cecils, father and son," he said. "Without 'em—" He shook his head.

"*Sine quibus non*," Thomas Phelippes said. Shakespeare nodded. Without the Cecils, there would have been no uprising. He and Skeres and Phelippes drank.

"A pity Lord Burghley lived not to see his grand scheme flower," Shakespeare said. "He was Moses, who led his folk to the Promised Land, but to whom it was not given to enter therein."

"But he died well pleased in his son, the which was not given to Philip of Spain," Phelippes replied. A Philip still ruled Spain, of course, but not *the* Philip. Philip II would always be *the* Philip. "This I know full well, having seen the King's despatches to Don Diego Flores de Valdés. Philip III speaks no French. He prefers to stay indoors, playing the guitar. He hath not learned the use of arms, nor knows he naught of matters of state. So spake his father, the King."

"God grant it be so, that Elizabeth may the more readily outface him." Shakespeare finished his goblet of sack and waved for another. Kate brought it to him. The knife he used to skewer chunks of meat was the one he'd got from the Roman soldier at the Theatre.

"Having regained her throne, she *hath*, methinks, outfaced him," Thomas Phelippes said. "For how shall he again bring England under the yoke? Why, only by another Armada. Hath he the will? E'en with the will, hath he the means? By all I've seen, nay and nay."

That was so reasonable, so plausible, and so much what Shakespeare wanted to hear, he wouldn't have argued with it for the world. Nick Skeres saw something else: "Without the dons to back 'em, we'll revenge ourselves on the damned howling Irish wolves, too."

"Ay." Shakespeare nodded. He remembered—how could he forget?—the shivers Isabella and Albert's Irish mercenaries had always raised in him. "Let them have their deserts for bringing terror to honest Englishmen." What England had done in Ireland never entered his mind. He thought only of what England might soon do in Ireland once more.

Phelippes also nodded, wisely. "That lieth already in train," he said.

"Good." Shakespeare and Skeres spoke together. They might fall out on many things. Concerning Irishmen, they were of one mind.

Kate brought more sack several times. Shakespeare knew his head would pound come morning. Morning would be time enough to worry about it, though. Meanwhile . . . Meanwhile, Nick Skeres emptied his goblet one last time, got to his feet, and burst into song:

> "The master, the swabber, the boatswain, and I,
> The gunner and his mate
> Loved Moll, Meg, and Marian, and Margery,
> But none of us cared for Kate.
> For she had a tongue with a tang,
> Would cry to a sailor, go hang!
> She loved not the savor of tar nor of pitch,
> Yet a . . . poet might scratch her wherere she did itch,
> Then to sea, boys, and let her go hang!"

Several people in the ordinary laughed. A couple of men clapped their hands. Shakespeare spoke to Thomas Phelippes: "Get this swabber hence forthwith, ere he swab the floor." He clenched his fists. He'd had enough wine to be ready to brawl if Phelippes said no.

But Phelippes answered, "And so I shall, Sir William." He turned to Skeres. "Come along, good Sir Nicholas. You've taken on too much water; your wit sinks fast."

"Water?" Skeres shook his head. "No, by God. 'Twas finest Sherris-sack."

"All the worse—wine'll sink what floats on water." Phelippes steered him towards the door. He nodded once more to Shakespeare. "Give you good night, Sir William."

"And to you, Sir Thomas, so that you get him away," Shakespeare said. Skeres started singing again. Phelippes pushed him out the door and into the street.

Kate came over to Shakespeare. "That Sir Nicholas is truly a knight?" she asked.

"Methinks he is a knight indeed," Shakespeare answered. "I trust not his word alone, but Master Phelippes—Sir Thomas—I do credit. Whate'er Skeres might do, he'd not lie about such business."

The serving woman shook her head in bemusement. "A strange new world, that hath such people in't."

"Ay, belike." But after that careless agreement passed Shakespeare's lips, he realized Kate's remark held more truth than he'd first seen. Newly free after ten years under Spanish dominion, England could hardly help being a strange place. Those who'd served the dons were paying for it; those who'd suffered under them were raised high. Few had dared trust very far under Isabella and Albert, and a good many might not dare trust very far under Elizabeth, either.

Kate's thoughts stayed on the personal. "He had no call to sing of me so," she said, "nor of you, neither."

"He's a cunning cove, Nick Skeres, but not so cunning as not to think himself more cunning than he is," Shakespeare said.

He watched Kate work through that and smile when she got to the bottom of it. She went off to bring supper to a couple of men at another table. He waited patiently, sipping wine, till the last of the other customers went home. Then, Kate carrying a candle, they walked up the stairs to her room. As she began to undress by that dim, flickering light, she turned away from him, all at once shy. Her voice low and troubled, she said, "A player may love a serving woman, but shall a knight?"

In that cramped chamber, one step took him to her. He caught her in his arms. Under his hands, her flesh was soft and smooth and warm. He bent close to her ear to answer, "Assuredly he shall, an't please her that he do."

She twisted around towards him. Her kiss was fierce. "What thinkest thou?" she said.

His mouth trailed down the side of her neck to her bared breasts. He lingered there some little while. She murmured and pressed him to her. "Ah, sweet, there's beggary in the love that can be reckoned," he said. He couldn't have told which of them drew the other to her narrow bed.

Afterwards, though, she fought tears while he dressed. When he tried to soothe her, she shook her head. "Thou'rt grown a great man," she said. "Wilt not find a grand lady to match thee?"

"Why, so have I done," he replied, and kissed her once more.

"Go to!" She laughed, though the tears hadn't gone away. "Thou'rt the lyingest knave in Christendom, and I love thee for't." She got out of bed to put on her own warm woolen nightgown. "Now begone, and may thou soon come hither again, sweet Sir William."

"Alas that I go," he said, and took the candle stub to light his way downstairs.

He was almost back to his lodging-house before pausing to wonder how his wife would greet the news of his knighthood. When he did, he wished he hadn't. Anne's first worry, without a doubt, would be over how much money it was worth. He shrugged. What with one thing and another, she wouldn't need to fret about that. He had plenty to send back to Stratford. She and his daughters would not want. Past that . . . Past that, Anne wouldn't care, and neither did he.

His head did ache when he got up in the morning. A mug of the Widow Kendall's good ale with his breakfast porridge helped ease the pounding. The reticent sun of late autumn was just rising when he started for the door. Sir William he might be, but he had a play to put on at the Theatre.

Or so he thought, till the door opened when he was still a couple of strides from it. A tough-looking fellow with a rapier on his belt came in. "Sir William Shakespeare," he said. It wasn't a question.

Even so, Shakespeare wondered if he ought to admit who he was. After a couple of heartbeats' hesitation, he nodded, asking, "What would you?"

"You are ordered to come with me."

"Ordered, say you? By whom? Whither?"

"By her Majesty, the Queen; to Westminster," the man snapped. "Will you come, or do you presume to say her nay?"

"I come," Shakespeare said meekly. The Theatre would have to do without him for the morning.

He got another surprise when he went outside: a horse waited there to take him to Westminster, yet another armed man holding its head. The beast looked enormous. Shakespeare mounted so awkwardly, the bravo who'd gone in to get him let out a scornful snort. He didn't care. He hadn't ridden a horse since hurrying back to Stratford to say farewell to his son Hamnet, and he couldn't remember his last time on horseback before that. He nodded to the tough-looking man. "Lay on, good sir, and I'll essay to follow."

"Be it so, then," the man said, doubt in his voice.

He urged his horse forward with reins, voice, and the pressure of his knees against its sides. Shakespeare did the same. His mount, a good-natured and well-trained mare, obeyed him with so little fuss that, by the time he'd gone a couple of blocks, he felt as much centaur as man. The man who'd held the poet's horse brought up the rear on his own beast.

"Way! Make way!" the bravo in the lead bawled whenever they had to slow for foot traffic or other riders or wagons and carts. "Make way for the Queen's business!" Sometimes the offenders would move aside, sometimes they wouldn't. When they didn't, Shakespeare's escort bawled other, more pungent, things.

Outside the entrance to St. Paul's, the head and quartered members of a corpse were mounted on spears. They were all splashed with tar to slow rot and help hold scavengers at bay. Despite that, Shakespeare recognized the lean, even ascetic, features of Robert Parsons before he saw the placards announcing the demise of the Catholic Archbishop of Canterbury. SIC SEMPER TYRANNIS! one of those placards declared.

Was't for this you so long ate the bitter bread of exile? Shakespeare wondered. *Was't for this you at last came home?* Parsons might have answered ay; he had the strength and courage of his belief no less than his foes of theirs. *And much good he got from them*, Shakespeare thought. A rook, the bare base of its beak pale against black feathers, fluttered down and landed on top of the dead churchman's head. Tar or no tar, it pecked at Parsons' cheek.

More bodies and parts of bodies lined the road from London to Winchester. Rooks and carrion crows and jackdaws and sooty ravens fluttered up from them as riders went past, then returned to their interrupted feasting. Looking back over his shoulder at Shakespeare, his escort said, "May those birds wax as fat on the flesh of traitors as Frenchmen's geese crammed full with figs and nuts."

Shakespeare managed a nod he feared feeble. He rejoiced that England was free. But revenge, no matter how sweet at first, grew harsh to him. He saw the need; he would have been blind not to see the need. But he could not rejoice in it. Others, many others, felt otherwise.

As Isabella and Albert had before her—and, indeed, as she often had before them—Elizabeth stayed at Whitehall. Servitors who'd likely bowed and scraped before Philip II's daughter and her husband shot Shakespeare scornful glances for his plain doublet and hose. But their manner changed remarkably when they found out who he was.

Elizabeth's throne was off-center on the dais. Till a few weeks before, two thrones had stood there. At the Queen's right hand, on a lower chair, sat Sir Robert Cecil. Since he was small and crookbacked, he had to tilt his chin up to speak to his sovereign.

Making his lowest leg to Queen Elizabeth, Shakespeare murmured, "Your Majesty."

"You may stand straight, Sir William. God give you good day." As Elizabeth had been at the Theatre, she was armored against time with wig and paint and splendid gown. Only her bad teeth still shouted out how old she'd grown.

"I am your servant, your Majesty," Shakespeare said. "But command me and, if it be in my poor power, it shall be yours. By my troth, I . . ."

The Queen's eyes remained sharp enough to pierce like swords. Under that stern gaze, his words stumbled to a stop. He hardly dared breathe. Then Elizabeth smiled, and it was as if spring routed winter. "I called you here not to serve me, but that I might reward you according to my promise when I made you knight," she said. "That you shall not want, it pleaseth me that Sir Robert settle upon you the sum of . . ." She looked to Cecil.

"Three hundred fifty pound," he said.

"Gra—Gramercy," Shakespeare stammered, bowing deeply. Along with what he'd got from Sir Robert's father and from Don Diego for *Boudicca* and *King Philip*, he was suddenly a man of no small wealth. "I am ever in your debt."

"Not so, but rather the reverse," Elizabeth said. "How joyed I am that so good event hath followed so many troublesome endeavors, laborious cares, and heedful undertakings, you may guess, but I best can witness, and do protest that your success standeth equal to the most thereof. And so God ever bless you in all your actions. For myself, I can but acknowledge your diligence and dangerous adventure, and cherish and judge of you as your grateful sovereign. What you would have of me, ask, and I will spare no charge, but give with both hands. Honor here I love, for he who hateth honor hateth God above."

Shakespeare gaped. Did that, could that, mean what it seemed to? He could name whatever he wanted in all the world, and the Queen would give it to him? Before he could begin to speak, Sir Robert Cecil did, his voice dry as usual: "Sir William, I say this only—seek no more gold of her Majesty, for she hath it not to give, England yet being all moils and disorders."

"I understand." Shakespeare hadn't intended to ask for more gold. That would have been like asking for a fourth wish from a fairy who had given three: a good way to lose all he might have gained. He paused to gather his thoughts, then spoke directly to Elizabeth: "Your Majesty, when a lad in Stratford I made a marriage I do repent me of. Romish doctrines being once more o'erthrown"—he saw in his mind's eye the rook landing on Robert Parsons' tarred head outside St. Paul's—"you may order it dissevered, an it please you."

"Have you issue from the said union?" Elizabeth asked.

"Two living daughters, your Majesty, and a son now two years dead," he answered. *Hamnet, poor Hamnet.* "I would settle on the girls' mother a hundred pound of your generous bounty, that they may know no want all the days of their lives."

"A hundred fifty pound," Elizabeth said sharply. Shakespeare blinked. He hadn't expected that kind of dicker. But he nodded. So did the Queen. She turned to Sir Robert. "Let it be made known to clerks and clerics that this is my will, to which they are to offer no impediment."

"Just so, your Majesty," Cecil said.

The Queen gave her attention back to Shakespeare. "Here, then, is one thing settled. Be there more?"

Three wishes, he thought again, dizzily. "Your Majesty will know," he said, "that whilst I wrote *Boudicca* I wrote also another play, this latter one entitled *King Philip.*"

Elizabeth nodded. "I do know it. Say on, Sir William. You pique my curiosity. What would you in aid of this *King Philip*?"

Shakespeare took a deep breath. "King Philip the man is dead, for which all England may thank a God kind and just. By your gracious leave, your Majesty, I'd fain have *King Philip* live upon the stage."

"What?" Queen Elizabeth's eyebrows came down and together in a fierce frown. He'd startled her, and angered her, too. "This play you writ for the dons, for the invaders and despoilers and occupiers"—she plainly used the word in its half-obscene sense—"of our beloved homeland, praying—I do hope—it would ne'er be given, you'd now see performed? How have you the effrontery to presume this of me?"

Licking his lips, Shakespeare answered, "I ask it for but one reason: that in *King Philip* lieth some of my best work, the which I'd not have go for naught."

Would she understand? All he had to make his mark on the world were the words he set on paper. He marshaled no armies, no fleets. He issued no decrees. He didn't so much as make gloves, as his father had. Without words, he was nothing, not even wind and air.

Instead of answering directly, Elizabeth turned to Sir Robert. "You have read the play whereof he speaketh?"

Cecil nodded. "I have, your Majesty. Sir Thomas Phelippes, whilst in the employ of Don Diego, made shift to acquaint my father and me therewith."

"And what think you on it?" the Queen inquired.

"Your Majesty, my opinion marches with Sir William's: though Philip be dead, this play deserves to live. It is most artificial, and full of clever conceits."

The Queen's eyes narrowed in thought. "Philip did spare me where he might have slain," she said musingly, at least half to herself, "e'en if, as may well be, he reckoned the same no great mercy, I being mured up behind Tower walls. And I pledged my faith to you, Sir William, you should have that which your heart desireth, wherefore let it be as you say, and let *King Philip* be acted without my hindrance—indeed, with my good countenance. 'Tis noble to salute the foe, the same pricking against my honor not but conducing thereto."

"Again, your Majesty, many thanks," Shakespeare said. "By your gracious leave here, you show the world your nobleness of mind."

Judging from her self-satisfied smile, that touched Elizabeth's vanity. "Be there aught else you would have of me?" she asked him.

He nodded. "One thing more, an it please you, also touching somewhat upon *King Philip*."

"Go on," she said.

"A Spanish officer, a Lieutenant de Vega, was to play Juan de Idiáquez, the King's secretary. He being now a captive, I'd beg of you his freedom and return to his own land."

"De Vega . . . Methinks I have heard this name aforetimes." Elizabeth frowned, as if trying to remember where. A tiny shrug suggested she couldn't. "Why seek you this? Is he your particular friend?"

"My particular friend? Nay, I'd say not so, though we liked each the other as well as we might, each being loyal to his own country. But he is a poet and a maker of plays in the Spanish tongue. If poets come not to other poets' aid, who shall? No one, not in all the world."

"De Vega . . . *Lope* de Vega." Queen Elizabeth's gaze sharpened. "I have heard the name indeed: a maker of comedies, not so? The guards at the Tower did with much approbation speak of some play of his offered before the usurpers this summer gone by. Following Italian, I could betimes make out their Spanish."

"Your Majesty, I have found the same," Shakespeare said.

"You are certain he is captive and not slain?"

"I am, having ta'en him myself," Shakespeare said.

"Very well: let him go back to Spain and make comedies for the dons, provided he first take oath never again to bear arms against England. Absent that oath, captive he shall remain." Elizabeth turned to Robert Cecil. "See you to it, Sir Robert."

"Assuredly, your Majesty," Cecil said. "This de Vega is known to me: not the worst of men." Coming from him, that sounded like high praise. "A kind thought, Sir William, to set him at liberty."

"I thank your honor," Shakespeare said. "It were remiss of me also to say no word for Mistress Sellis, a widow dwelling at my lodging-house. Her quick wit"—*amongst other things*, the poet thought—"balked Lieutenant de Vega of learning we purposed presenting *Boudicca* in place of *King Philip*, and haply of thwarting us in the said enterprise."

"Let her be rewarded therefor," Elizabeth said. She asked Sir Robert Cecil, "Think you ten pound sufficeth?"

"Peradventure twenty were better," he said.

Elizabeth haggled like a housewife buying apples in springtime. "Fifteen," she declared. "Fifteen, and not a farthing more."

Sir Robert sighed. "Fifteen, then. Just as you say, your Majesty, so shall it be."

"Ay, that well befits a Queen." Elizabeth's face and voice hardened. "As who should know more clearly than I, having thrown away—upon my troth, cruelly thrown away!—in harshest confinement ten years of this life I shall have back never again, wherein not in the least respected was one single word from my lips." For a moment, she seemed to imagine herself still in the Tower of London, to have forgotten Robert Cecil and Shakespeare and her guardsmen and the very throne on which she sat. Then she gathered herself. "Be there aught else required for your contentment, Sir William?"

"Your Majesty, an I may not live content by light of your kind favor, I make me but a poor figment of a man," Shakespeare replied.

"A courtesy worthy of a courtier," the Queen said, which might have been praise or might have been something else altogether. "Very well, then. You may go."

"God bless your Majesty." Shakespeare bowed one last time.

"He doth bless me indeed," Elizabeth said. "For long and long I wondered, but . . . ay, He blesseth me greatly." Shakespeare turned away so he wouldn't see tears in his sovereign's eyes.

RAIN PATTERED DOWN ON LOPE DE VEGA. IT HADN'T SNOWED YET, for which he thanked God. Next to him, another Spanish soldier coughed and coughed and coughed. *Consumption*, Lope thought gloomily. He was just glad the black plague hadn't broken out among his miserable countrymen. No snow. No plague. Such were the things for which he had to be grateful these days.

And his headaches came less often. He supposed he should have been grateful for that, too, but he would have been more grateful to have no headaches at all. On the other hand, if he hadn't been thwacked senseless and left for dead, he probably would have died in the savage fighting that had claimed so many Spaniards. He—cautiously—shook his head. *Damned if I'll be grateful for almost having my head smashed like a melon dropped on the cobbles.*

An Englishman—an officer, by his basket-hilted rapier and plumed hat—strutted into the bear-baiting arena. Lope paid him no special attention. Plenty of Englishmen and -women still came to the arena to look over the Spanish prisoners as if they were the animals that had formerly dwelt here. Lope had seen Catalina Ibañez on her Englishman's arm only that once. One more small, very small, thing for which to be grateful.

Then the officer took out a scrap of paper and peered down at it, shielding it from the rain with his left hand. "Lope de Vega!" he bawled. "Where's Lieutenant Lope de Vega? Lope de Vega, stand forth!"

"I am here." De Vega got to his feet. "What would you, sir?"

"Come you with me, and straightaway," the Englishman replied.

"God's good fortune go with you, *señor*," the consumptive soldier said.

"*Gracias*," Lope said, and then, louder and in English, "I obey."

The officer led him out of the arena. Only a few feet from where Lope's two mistresses had discovered each other, the fellow said, "You are to be enlarged, Lieutenant, so that you give your holy oath nevermore to bear arms against England and presently to quit her soil. Be it your will to accept the said terms and swear your oath?"

"Before God, sir, you mean this? You seek not to make me your jest?" Lope asked, hardly daring to believe his ears.

"Before God, Lieutenant, no such wicked thing do I," the English officer replied. "The order for your freedom—provided you swear the oath—comes from Sir Robert Cecil, by direction of her Majesty, the Queen. I ask again: will you swear it?"

"Right gladly will I," de Vega said. "By God and the Virgin and all the saints, I vow that, if it be your pleasure to set me at liberty, I shall never again take up arms against this kingdom, and shall remove from it fast as ever I may. Doth it like you well enough, sir, or would you fain have me swear somewhat more?"

" 'Twas a round Romish oath, but I looked for none other from a Spaniard," the officer said. "I am satisfied indeed, Lieutenant, and declare you free. God go with you."

Lope bowed. "And with you, for your generous chivalry." He hesitated, then let out an embarrassed chuckle. "I pray your pardon for a grateful man's foolish question, but how am I to get me hence without a ha'penny to my name?—for my purse was slit or ever I was ta'en."

"Did you ask me this, I was told to give you these: two good gold angels, a pound in all." After returning the bow, the Englishman set the coins in Lope's hand. "Sir William saith, Godspeed and and safe journey homeward."

"Sir William?" Lope scratched his head. "I know none of that name and title but Lord Burghley, may he rest in peace." He made the sign of the cross.

The English officer started to do the same, then abruptly caught himself and scowled. *He forgot he is a Catholic no more*, de Vega thought with amusement he dared not show. The Englishman said, "Whether you ken him or no, Lieutenant, he doth know you. Which beareth the greater weight?"

"Oh, that he know me, assuredly. And I do thank you for conveying to me his kind gift." *For not stealing it*, he meant. The English officer had to think someone would check on him.

"You are welcome." The officer pointed north, towards the wharves of Southwark and, across the Thames, London. "There, belike, you'll find a ship to hie you to France or the Netherlands."

A man strode towards the bear-baiting arena: a tall fellow about Lope's own age, with neat chin whiskers and a high forehead made higher by a receding hairline. "There, belike, I'll find a friend." De Vega waved and raised his voice to call, "Will! Thought you to find me within? You're come too late, for they've set me free."

"God give you good day, Master Lope," Shakespeare answered. "And if you be new-enlarged, He hath given you a good day indeed. Will you dine with me?"

"I would, but I may not, for I am sworn to quit England instanter."

"Who'd grudge your going with a full belly?" Shakespeare said. "To an ordinary first; and thence, the docks."

Lope let himself be persuaded. After the prisoner's rations he'd endured, he couldn't resist the chance for a hearty meal. Half a roast capon, washed down with Rhenish wine, made a new man of him, though Shakespeare had to lend him a knife with which to eat. He stabbed the fowl's gizzard and popped it into his mouth. When he'd swallowed the chewy morsel, he said, "You do me a great kindness: the more so as I would have slain you when last we met."

"That was in another country," Shakespeare said—not quite literally true, as Isabella and Albert had fled the night before, but close enough. The English poet added, "And besides, the witch lives yet."

"A great sorrowful pity she doth live," Lope said.

"None take it amiss you served Spain as best you might," Shakespeare said. "Mistress Sellis did likewise for England."

"*Puta,*" Lope muttered, but let it go.

"At Broken Wharf in London lieth the *Oom Karl,*" Shakespeare remarked. "She takes on board woolen goods, bound for Ostend and sundry other Flanders ports. Might she serve your need?"

"Peradventure she might." De Vega sighed. "A swag-bellied Hollander ship, by her name, with a swag-bellied Hollander captain at the con. I'd liefer not put my faith in such, but"—another sigh—"betimes we do as needs must, not as likes us."

"There you speak sooth, as I well know," Shakespeare said.

"Ah?" Lope said. "Sits the wind so? Which reckon you the play under compulsion, that which holp to free your heretic Queen, or that which would have praised a Catholic King?"

To his surprise, Shakespeare answered, "Both. Nor knew I which would play, nor which be reckoned treason, until the very day."

"Truly?"

"Truly," the English poet said, and Lope could not help believing him.

"That is a marvel, I'll not deny," he said, and rose to his feet.

Shakespeare got up, too. "The *Oom Karl,* said you?" he asked. Shakespeare nodded. Lope had asked only for form's sake. He remembered the name of the ship. It might indeed serve him well. Ostend lay within the Spanish Netherlands. From there, he could easily find a ship bound for Spain and home.

Home! Even the word seemed strange. He'd spent almost a third of his life—and almost all his adult life—here in England. What would Madrid be like after ten years, under a new King? Would anyone there remember him? Would that printer Captain Guzmán knew have put his plays before the world? That might help ease his way back into the Spanish community of actors and poets. He dared hope.

"I'm for Broken Wharf, then," he said.

"Good fortune go with you." Shakespeare set a penny on the table between them. "Here: this for the wherryman, to take you o'er the Thames."

"My thanks." Lope scooped up the coin. "You English be generous to your foes, I own. This fine dinner and a penny from you, Master Will, and I have a pound in gold of some English knight to pay my way towards Spain."

"Do you indeed?" Shakespeare murmured. He gave de Vega an odd, almost sour smile. "Belike we think us well shut of you."

"Belike you should." Lope came around the table, stood on tiptoe, and kissed Shakespeare on the cheek. "God guard thee, friend."

"Spoke like a sprightful noble gentleman," Shakespeare said, and gave back the kiss. "If we do meet again, why, we shall smile; if not, why then this parting was well made."

"Just so." Lope left the ordinary without looking back. When he got to the river, he waved for a boatman.

Waving in reply, the fellow glided up. He touched the brim of his cap. "Whither would you, sir?"

"Broken Wharf, as close by the *Oom Karl* as you may," de Vega replied.

"Let's see your penny," the wherryman said. Lope gave him the coin—stamped, he saw, with Isabella and Albert's images. Well, they'd fled England before him. The wherryman touched his cap again. His grin showed a couple of missing teeth. "Broken Wharf it shall be, your honor, and right yarely, too."

He did put his back into the stroke, and his heart into the abuse he bawled at other boats on the river. He had to fight the current; Broken

"Fear not, my sweeting, for justice *is* done: they have not more than I," Shakespeare assured her, and her eyes went wide once more. He nodded. "By my halidom, Kate, 'tis true."

"Right glad was I to wed thee, taking thee for no richer than any other player who might here chance to sup," Kate said. "An't be otherwise . . . An't be otherwise, why, right glad am I."

"And I," Shakespeare said. He kissed her. The kiss took on a life of its own. They still clung to each other when the door opened and a customer came in.

The man swept off his hat and bowed in their direction as they sprang apart. "Your pardon, I pray ye. I meant not to disturb ye."

"You are welcome, sir," Kate said as the fellow sat down. "What would you have?"

"Some of what you gave your tall gentleman there'd like me well," he replied, "but belike he hath the whole of't. That failing, what's the threepenny supper this even?"

"Mutton stew."

"Is it indeed? Well, a bit o' mutton's always welcome." The man winked at Shakespeare. Kate squeaked indignantly. Shakespeare took an angry step forward. The customer raised a hand. "Nay, sir; nay, mistress I meant no harm by it. 'Twas but a jest. For mine own part, I am one that loves an inch of raw mutton, and I am well-provided with three bouncing wenches. I'd not quarrel over a foolish quibble."

Shakespeare didn't want to quarrel, either, but he also didn't want to look like a coward in front of Kate. He sent her a questioning glance. Only when she nodded did he give the other man a short, stiff bow. "Let it go, then."

"Many thanks, sir; many thanks. For your kindness, may I stand you to a mug of beer? And your lady as well, certes." The stranger lifted his hat again. "Cedric Hayes, at your service. I am glad you see, sir, that where a man may fight at need, 'tis not that he needs must fight." Hayes plucked a knife from his belt. With a motion so fast Shakespeare could hardly see it, he flung the blade. It stuck, quivering, in the planking of a window frame. An instant later, another knife thudded home just below it.

" 'Sblood!" Shakespeare said. "Any man who fought with you would soon repent of it, belike for aye."

"Ah, but you knew that not when you chose courtesy." Hayes rose, went over to the knives so he could pull them free, and sheathed them again. " 'Tis a mountebank's trick, I own, but mountebank I am, and so entitled to't."

"Might you show this art upon the stage, Master Hayes?" Shakespeare asked.

"Gladly would I show it wheresoever I be paid for the showing," the knife-thrower replied. "Who are you, sir, and what would you have me do?"

Shakespeare gave his name. Proudly, Kate corrected him: "*Sir* William Shakespeare."

"Ah." Cedric Hayes bowed. "Very much at your service, Sir William. I have seen somewhat of your work, and it liked me well. I ask again, what would you have me do?"

"In some of the company's plays—*Romeo and Juliet* and *Prince of Denmark* spring first to mind—your art might enliven that which is already writ. An you show yourself trusty, I shall write you larger parts in dramas yet to come."

"I am not like to a trusty squire who did run away," Hayes said. "Where I say I shall be, I shall; what I say I shall do, that likewise."

"Most excellent," Shakespeare said. "Know you the Theatre, beyond Bishopsgate?"

"Certes, sir. Many a time and oft have I stood 'mongst the groundlings to laugh at Will Kemp's fooling or hear Dick Burbage bombast out a blank verse."

Burbage wouldn't have been happy to hear Kemp named ahead of him. Shakespeare resolved never to mention that. He said, "Go you thither at ten o' the clock tomorrow. I shall be there, and Burbage as well. We'll put you through your paces, that we may know your different several gaits."

"Gramercy, Master Shakespeare—Sir William, I should say." Hayes raised his mug. "A fortunate meeting."

"Your good health," Shakespeare said, and he drank, too.

After Cedric Hayes finished his supper, he left the ordinary. Shakespeare got out pen and ink and paper and set to work. What a relief, to be able to write without having to fear the gallows or worse if the wrong person happened to glance over his shoulder at the wrong moment!

He didn't have to look up anxiously whenever someone new came into the ordinary, either. Being able to concentrate on his work meant he got more done. It also meant he did look up, in surprise, when a man loomed over him. "Oh," he said, setting down his pen and nodding to the newcomer. "Give you good even, Constable."

"God give you good Eden as well," Walter Strawberry replied gravely. "May you obtain to Paradise."

"My thanks," Shakespeare said. "Why come you hither?"

Before answering, Strawberry grabbed a stool from a nearby table and sat down across from the poet. "Why, sir? Why, for that I may hold converse with you. But converting's thirsty work, and so"—he raised his voice and waved to Kate—"a cup of wine, and sprackly, too!"

"Anon, sir, anon," she said, and went back to whatever she was doing.

When the wine didn't arrive at once, Constable Strawberry sent Shakespeare an aggrieved look. " 'Anon,' saith she, yet she comes not. Am I then anonymous, that she doth fail to know me?"

Shakespeare scratched his head. Was Strawberry garbling things as usual, or had he made that jest on purpose? Probably not, not by his expression. Shakespeare gave Kate a tiny nod. She rolled her eyes, but brought the constable what he'd asked for.

"I thank you," he said grudgingly. "I'd thank you more had you come sooner."

"There's the difference 'twixt our sexes," Kate agreed, her voice sweet.

"Eh? What mean you?" Strawberry demanded. Kate pretended not to hear him. Shakespeare stared down at the tabletop so the constable wouldn't see his face. Strawberry muttered to himself, then spoke aloud: "I thank God I am not a woman, to be touched with so many giddy offenses."

"Just so, sir," Shakespeare said. "Why are you come? I asked aforetimes, but you said not."

Strawberry frowned. Maybe he had trouble remembering why he'd come to the ordinary; Shakespeare wouldn't have been surprised. But then his heavy features brightened. "Methought you'd fain hear the report from mine own lips."

"Better the report from your lips, sir, than from a pistol," Shakespeare said gravely. "But of what report speak you?"

"Why, the one I am about to tell, of course," the constable replied.

"What is the point? The gist? The yolk? The meat?"

" 'Tis meet indeed I should tell you," Strawberry said.

"And as for the point, it lieth 'neath his hat," Kate muttered.

"What's that? What's that? Am I resulted? 'Swounds, no good result'll spring from that, I do declare."

"Spell out your meaning plain, then," Shakespeare urged.

"And so I shall, by bowels and constipants," Constable Strawberry said. "You have denied acquaintance with the felonious cove hight Ingram Frizer."

"I do deny it still," Shakespeare said. Yes, the two men he knew Frizer had killed had died at the order of Sir Robert Cecil or his father. Yes, Sir Robert sat at Elizabeth's right hand these days. But who could say how many others Frizer had slain? Who could say how many he'd robbed or beaten? Anyone who admitted knowing him was either a fool or a felonious rogue in his own right—Constable Strawberry, for once, hadn't misspoken in describing Frizer so.

As if the poet had avowed knowing Frizer rather than denying it, Strawberry said, "Belike you will rejoice to hear he is catched."

"If he be the high lawyer and murtherer you say, what honest man would not rejoice?" Shakespeare said. "May he have his just deserts."

"Nay, no marchpane, no sweetmeats, no confits for that wretch," the constable replied. "He lieth in gyves in the Clink, and lieth also, in's teeth, in declaiming he hath done naught amiss. An I mistake me not, there's plenty a miss he hath done could give him the lie, too."

"I know not. If truth be known, I care not, neither," Shakespeare said. "And in aid of misses, I care but for one." He smiled at Kate. She came over the stand behind him and set her hands on his shoulders.

"Ah? Sits the wind so?" Walter Strawberry asked. Shakespeare and Kate both nodded. He reached up and put his right hand on hers. Strawberry beamed. "Much happiness to you, then—and may you know no misfortune, Master Shakespeare."

Again, Shakespeare wondered whether he used his words cleverly or just blindly. Before he could decide, Kate said, "Style him as is proper, Master Constable: he is Sir William."

"You, sir, a knight?" Strawberry said.

"I am," Shakespeare admitted.

"Marry, I knew it not." Constable Strawberry looked from him to Kate and back again. "And marry you shall, meseems. Well-a-day! I do congregate you, and wish you all domestic infelicity."

Kate growled, down deep in her throat. Now Shakespeare forestalled her. Patting her hand, he said, "I thank you in the spirit with which you offer your kindly wishes."

"Spirits? Not a bit of 'em, Sir William—'tis wine before me." Strawberry got to his feet. "And now, having come, I must needs away. Good night, good night." He lumbered out of the ordinary.

The poet stared after him, confused one last time. Was that *Good night, good night* or *Good night, good knight* or perhaps even *Good knight, good night*? Shakespeare decided he didn't care. He stood up, too, and kissed his intended, and forgot all about Walter Strawberry.

Historical Note

For the Spanish Armada to have conquered England in 1588 would not have been easy. King Philip's great fleet would have needed several pieces of good fortune it did not get: a friendlier wind at Calais, perhaps, one that might have kept the English from launching their fireships against the Armada; and a falling-out between the Dutch and English that could have let the Duke of Parma put to sea from Dunkirk and join his army to the Duke of Medina Sidonia's fleet for the invasion of England. Getting Spanish soldiers across the Channel would have been the hard part. Had it been accomplished, the Spanish infantry, the best in the world at the time and commanded by a most able officer, very probably could have beaten Elizabeth's forces on land.

Had the Spaniards won, Philip did intend to invest his daughter Isabella with the English throne; through his descent from the house of Lancaster, she had a claim to it. He also did intend to marry her to one of her Austrian cousins; Albert is the one she wed in real history. In his plots leading up to the sailing of the Armada, Philip was willing to seek the death of most of Elizabeth's advisers, but wanted Lord Burghley spared. Thus I thought it legitimate to preserve him alive for purposes of this novel.

Nicholas Skeres and Ingram Frizer are two of the men who, in real history, killed Christopher Marlowe in what may (or may not) have been deliberate murder rather than a brawl over the bill at Eleanor Bull's ordinary at Deptford on May 30, 1593. Frizer was the one who actually inflicted the deadly wound. Skeres, by his record, preferred con games to out-and-out violence. The date above is Old Style; the difference between England's Julian calendar and the Gregorian (which in real history was not adopted in the English-speaking world until 1752) plays its role in the story here.

Edward Kelley, counterfeiter and alchemist, was an associate of John Dee's—and also, like Skeres and Frizer and Marlowe himself, belonged on the fringes of the murky world of Elizabethan espionage. So did Anthony Bacon, Francis' older brother, who was indeed involved in a scandal pertaining to what the Elizabethans called sodomy in France before the time of the Armada. Francis himself had similar tastes, though in real history they did not come to light till well into the seventeenth century.

Very little of what is supposed to be *Boudicca* and *King Philip* is my own work; I am not a true Elizabethan blank-verse beast, as George Bernard Shaw called Marlowe. Most of *Boudicca* is taken from John Fletcher's *Bonduca* (a variant on the name of the Queen of the Iceni, who is also widely, though incorrectly, known as Boadicea). Fletcher was Shakespeare's younger contemporary, and probably though not certainly his collaborator in *Henry VIII*, *The Two Noble Kinsmen*, and the lost *Cardenio*. A prolific dramatist, Fletcher collaborated most frequently with Francis Beaumont. My *Boudicca* does not follow his *Bonduca* in plot; he had his purposes, which are far removed from mine. I have taken his lines out of order and out of context, and have adapted them as I found necessary. He did not give Boudicca/Bonduca's younger daughter a name; I have supplied one. He called Judas the Roman soldier I have named Marcus—I do not believe Shakespeare would have been so unsubtle as to use that particular name. Other bits of the fictional drama here come from *Henry VIII* and Shakespeare's *King John*, from Marlowe's *Tamburlaine* (both the first and second parts), and from William Averell's *An Exhortacion to als English Subjects*, the last of which I confess to casting into blank verse.

A measure of the importance of drama in the Elizabethan world and its possible use in rebellions against the state is the presentation of Shakespeare's *Richard II* before the rebellion of the Earl of Essex (Sir

Robert Devereux)—Essex wanted to use the play to show the people of London that a sovereign might be overthrown. He failed, but that he made the attempt is significant.

What purports to be *King Philip* is made up of adapted bits and pieces of *Titus Andronicus* (it is fortunate that "Spain" and "Parma" scan the same as "Rome" and "Titus"), *The Merchant of Venice, Henry VIII*, and Thomas Hughes' *The Misfortunes of Arthur*.

Lope de Vega holds a position in Spanish literature not far removed from that of Shakespeare in English. He did in fact sail in the Armada, and was one of the lucky few to return safely to Spain. He had a lively time with women all through his life.

The alert reader will note cribs from Shakespeare scattered through the pages of *Ruled Britannia*. One of the pleasures of the research for this novel was reading all of Shakespeare's surviving work, and fitting in phrases and lines wherever they would go.

There really was a woman named Cicely Sellis charged with witchcraft, but she was not the same as the character in this book, and did not live in London. Captain Will Adams is also a historical figure. Constable Walter Strawberry is not, but his origins should be obvious.

Photo by B. Small

Harry Turtledove, the *New York Times* bestselling author of numerous alternate history novels, has a Ph.D. in Byzantine history. Nominated for the Nebula Award, he has won the Hugo, Sidewise, and John Esthen Cook Awards. He lives with his wife and children in California.